Anne Baker trained as a nurse at ~~Birkenhead~~ General Hospital, but after her marriage went to live first in Libya and then in Nigeria. She eventually returned to her native Birkenhead where she worked as a Health Visitor for over ten years before taking up writing. She now lives with her husband in Merseyside. Anne Baker's other Merseyside sagas are all available from Headline and have been highly praised:

'A stirring tale of romance and passion, poverty and ambition' *Liverpool Echo*

'Anne Baker imbues her heartwarming Merseyside novels with rich local characters' *Nuneaton Evening Telegraph*

'Highly observant writing style . . . a compelling book that you just don't want to put down' *Southport Visiter*

'A gentle tale with all the right ingredients for a heartwarming novel' *Huddersfield Daily Examiner*

'Truly compelling . . . rich in language and descriptive prose' *Newcastle Upon Tyne Evening Chronicle*

# LIVERPOOL LULLABY

# MERSEY MAIDS

## Anne Baker

headline

LIVERPOOL LULLABY first published in Great Britain in 1998
by HEADLINE BOOK PUBLISHING

MERSEY MAIDS first published in Great Britain in 1997
by HEADLINE BOOK PUBLISHING

First published in this omnibus edition in 2004
by HEADLINE BOOK PUBLISHING

10 9 8 7 6 5 4 3 2 1

ISBN 0 7553 2249 5

Typeset by Palimpsest Book Production Limited,
Polmont, Stirlingshire
Printed and bound in Great Britain by
Clays Ltd, St Ives plc

Papers and cover board used by Headline are natural,
recyclable products made from wood grown in sustainable
forests. The manufacturing processes conform to the
environmental regulations of the country of origin.

HEADLINE BOOK PUBLISHING
A division of Hodder Headline PLC
338 Euston Road
London NW1 3BH

www.headline.co.uk
www.hodderheadline.com

# A Liverpool Lullaby

# Book One

## 1909–1914

# CHAPTER ONE

*June 1909*

For Evie Hobson, Thursday morning started like any other, except that she couldn't help but notice the woman peering through the shop door at her. She seemed fearful, her nervous eyes following Evie up and down the counter. Evie saw her lips move and was sure she wanted to tell her something. She looked ill and pitifully weak, but then so did many of their customers.

Evie's father, Joseph Hobson, chemist and druggist, kept one of the busiest shops in Birkenhead. It occupied a premier position at the end of a small parade; it was bigger than its neighbours, square in shape with double doors set across one corner.

Evie sold a packet of hairpins from the front counter. There were two counters, and she was always conscious of her father working behind her on the back one that he called the drug run. His voice reached every corner, reverberating off the high cabinets that screened him from her view. On his side was a series of small mahogany drawers each with a Latin label. On hers were high shelves holding huge ointment jars.

'Painful piles?' Her father sounded irritable; his voice dropped slightly as a token to customer embarrassment but was still audible to everyone in the shop.

'Oak bark is what you need. Boil it in water for an hour. Then take your trousers off and sit over the steam until it cools. That should ease you. I'll give

3

you enough for three applications.'

Evie had heard it all before and no longer blushed. She was used to her father giving advice of an intimate nature. He was in one of his bad moods this morning. He'd had to give Johnny Simms, his senior apprentice, a day off, because last evening he'd dislocated his shoulder playing in a cricket match. As Johnny did much of the dispensing, this meant her father had more work to do.

Joseph prided himself on always being in control of his shop. He'd placed mirrors so he could see exactly what was going on in every corner. Evie knew they allowed him to watch her, his assistants and his customers. But likewise, in the mirror over the door she could see the back of the shop and him too when he came to speak to his customers.

'A packet of Pine Liptus throat lozenges, please.'

Evie moved down the counter to get them. From here she could see herself in one of the mirrors. She looked pale and the freckles across her nose seemed to stand out. Her dark hair was gathered up in a loose bun on top of her head. It looked insecure; several strands had broken free to hang down beside her chin. She tried to tuck them in. Her father was always telling her she looked untidy.

'A stick of shaving soap, please.'

The front counter had glass cases on top to display all manner of cosmetics and soaps. To reach the shaving soap, Evie had to ease herself past Miss Lister, the senior assistant, who had presided over the front counter for twenty years. She was in her late thirties but looked much older because she was so stout.

It was a dark morning, muggy and close, and thunder seemed to threaten. Her father's voice came again, crackling with ill temper.

'More of that sleeping draught I gave your baby? You

can't expect him to sleep night and day, you know. You mustn't give him too much.'

Joseph Hobson behaved as though he had the power of life and death over his customers. Evie reflected that he treated her and those who worked for him in the same way, and it made them all nervous. She heard the pages of the prescription book being flipped over to find the date of his original prescription. Joseph was meticulous in everything he did and expected the same standard from everybody working for him.

He reckoned he didn't get it from Bertie Pugh, the junior apprentice, and was always at his throat. Bertie was only nine months into his five years of training and was made to spend a good deal of his time dusting and polishing.

'The best way to find out where everything is kept,' Joseph was in the habit of telling him. Bertie also helped out at the front counter when they were busy. Today, with Johnny off nursing his injured shoulder, he was working on the back counter.

Bertie had a problem with acne. When he'd first started his apprenticeship, his face had been a mass of pustules and spots. Joseph had prescribed a lotion and informed him confidently that he'd soon have it cleared up. It had not improved one iota, though Bertie had appealed to him for further remedies and had applied them all conscientiously. Evie thought her father showed less patience with him as a result.

The succession of customers seemed never-ending. Evie sold two flypapers and then had a moment to look up. Her counter faced the window fronting on Argyle Street – it was filled with bedpans and feeding cups, crutches and splints. The woman she'd seen earlier was still there, watching her. Something about her drew Evie's sympathy.

She almost went out to speak to her, though Father forbade her to leave the counter without permission, but at that moment another customer was asking for rhubarb and ginger for his bowels.

The other shop window faced into the side street. It held four magnificent onion-shaped glass carboys filled with coloured water, the traditional symbol of the four elements of the alchemist adopted by all apothecaries: red for fire, green for earth, blue for water and yellow for air.

Evie caught a glimpse of the woman's pallid, waxy face between the coloured carboys and straightened up in surprise. Why was she hanging about? It was almost as though she had to find the courage to come in. She took a closer look. The woman was bent nearly double and had a matted black shawl pulled close about her head. It was only her manner that singled her out from their other customers. Evie could almost feel the intensity of her gaze. She decided she must speak to her, and on the spur of the moment she went to the door. The bell pinged as she opened it.

'Evie?' Her father's voice boomed through the shop, halting her in her tracks. 'Where do you think you're going?'

'Just to have a word . . .'

'Not now. There are customers waiting to be served.'

Evie glanced hastily outside, but the woman had disappeared. Obediently, she returned to the counter and sold a jar of Virol and a bottle of embrocation.

The shop seemed to fill with customers all at once; three came together to the counter in front of her. She was looking for lip salve for one when the doorbell clanged again and the woman lurched inside at last. She edged forward, holding Evie's gaze with feverish eyes, and seemed to be offering her a bag. Then, in the crush, one of the waiting customers stepped back against her, knocking her off balance and making her drop the bag and spill its contents. Bertie Pugh happened to be passing close enough to prevent her falling.

'You want to consult Mr Hobson, ma'am?' he asked as he collected up her possessions and put them back in her bag.

Evie thought she heard the woman say, 'No.' She was sure it was to her she wanted to speak.

'You need to sit down, ma'am,' Bertie was saying, and in truth she seemed to sag as he guided her to the wooden bench provided for customers who were waiting their turn to consult Joseph.

She'd been there only a few minutes when Joseph called: 'Next, please.' It was a refrain that punctuated the day. Now, with greater impatience, he shouted: 'Who's next?'

Evie looked up into the mirror. It was the woman's turn. She was making an attempt to stand but fell back on the bench. Joseph went towards her. When his voice came again, he sounded shocked, horrified even.

'Helen! It is you? What brings you here?'

Evie couldn't move. They were all attuned to her father's moods. His tension was immediately theirs. It was awe and fear that made them like this. Everything in the shop came to a standstill.

'I didn't think you'd ever come near here again.'

Evie couldn't take her eyes from the woman. She was very frail and her shabby black dress was spattered with mud up to the knees. Evie had thought her a stranger, and yet her father had called her by her given name and seemed to know her well. Every eye in the shop watched them. His voice was colder now.

'Why can't you leave me in peace? Do you want to ruin what I have left?' He was angry and at his most hurtful.

'It's Evie I want . . .'

'You leave her alone. I don't want you here. Didn't I tell you never to set foot in my shop again?'

Everybody saw the woman stare at him in horror and then slowly slump against him.

'Pugh,' he shouted, 'help me put this woman in the dental chair.' Joseph was aware that he should show concern for his customers, and occasionally he tried. 'She can recover there in peace.'

To Evie his concern sounded false, a front he had assumed for the benefit of listening customers. She was sure he didn't feel compassion. Not for anybody. Bertie had once whispered that he was a dry stick of a man and there wasn't an ounce of sympathy in him. She watched them half carry the woman between them, her chin on her chest, her head escaping now from the shawl, grey-haired and unkempt.

The dentist's room opened immediately off the shop. Many years ago, when he'd first come here, Joseph Hobson had pulled teeth too. Now he rented his room to a travelling dentist who came two days each week. Miss Lister took appointments for him.

Evie felt overwhelmed with curiosity. She'd never known a customer to be put in the dental room before. She was afraid the woman must be very ill.

'Sal volatile,' her father's voice boomed, and Bertie Pugh rushed to get it from the drug run. 'She's fainted.'

'Who is she?' Bertie whispered to Evie as he passed.

Evie wished she knew. Another customer was demanding her attention by rapping on the counter with a coin.

'I want something to cure the biddies. Can you get it for me? Or do I have to wait for your father?'

'Head lice, do you mean, Mrs Stott?' Her father was coming from the dentist's room with a face like thunder. 'Sassafras oil, Evie. Do you have a toothcomb?'

'Yes, you sold me one last time. Pick 'em up at school, they do.'

'Use vinegar and water to loosen the nits from the hair.'

'I do,' the woman said. 'You told me that last time.'

Bertie Pugh was coming out of the dentist's room. 'She's coming round,' he said.

'Leave her be. She can rest there for a while,' Joseph said crossly.

Joseph Hobson was below average height and slight in build. His head was thickly covered with steel-grey bristles. His brows were like miniature coils of barbed wire, drawn tightly together over a large nose. That, and the granite line of his chin, gave him a permanently angry expression.

Evie knew he thought himself a cut above his neighbours because he was an apothecary, a professional man who had his own business.

They were all kept busy for the rest of the morning. Evie sold hairnets and nail brushes and bottles of Matron Milly's Infallible Female Mixture. The rush only died down when there was a rumble or two of thunder, the heavens opened and rain started to come down in sheets. Evie went to the end of the drug run. Her father was writing in his prescription book and Bertie Pugh was washing out medicine bottles.

'Father, did that poor woman say she wanted to speak to me?'

'No! Why should she?'

'I thought I heard her.'

'You thought wrong.'

'Shall I see if she needs anything?' Nobody had been near the woman for an hour and a half.

'No,' he barked. 'You stay away from her.'

Evie hesitated, but her curiosity got the better of her. 'Who is she, Father?'

'Better if you keep your mind on your work.' The doorbell pinged again. 'Here's a customer for you to attend to.'

It didn't escape Evie's notice that he went to see the woman himself five minutes later. He was only in the room for seconds and looked a changed man when he came out. He was supporting himself against the door jamb.

'Mr Pugh?' His voice lacked its usual confidence. 'Go and fetch the policeman on crossing duty. By Central Station.'

Bertie Pugh stared at him as though he'd taken leave of his senses.

'Do what I say. A customer has died on our premises.'

'Died!' Bertie's eyes were out on sticks.

Evie felt the blood rush to her face. 'That woman's dead?'

'I've said so, haven't I?'

Her father seemed suddenly as bent as the woman had been. The habitual blue tinge to his chin was more pronounced.

'Get along with you, Mr Pugh. I want her out of here as soon as possible.'

Bertie shot out into the rain without his coat. Evie's hand covered her mouth as she remembered that Mr Tennant the dentist would be here this afternoon.

Another customer came in and her father attended to him as though nothing had happened. Evie felt in a turmoil. It was only when she saw that Miss Lister had cheeks the colour of paste and was clutching the edge of the counter for support that she collected herself and ran for the sal volatile for her.

A few moments later, Mr Pugh was bringing in the policeman.

'In here.' Her father hurried to join them in the dentist's room, his lips set in a thin straight line.

'Passed away on your premises, has she, Mr Hobson?' the policeman was asking. Raindrops were dripping from his cape.

'Yes.'

'Do you have any idea who she is?'

Joseph closed the door with a firm click and Evie could hear no more. Moments later, it opened again as Bertie Pugh came out.

'I know who she is.' She could see that Bertie was bursting to tell her. His face shone with the latest balm he'd been prescribed for his spots. 'She's a relative of yours.'

'Who then?' Evie asked. She knew of no such relative. By what name had her father called her?

'Your father said her name was Helen Katherine Hobson.'

'What?' She couldn't believe her ears. 'No. Can't be. That was my mother's name.'

'It's your mother?' Bertie's mouth opened in amazement.

'No, course not,' Evie said. 'She died when I was six years old.'

'Another relative with the same name?' he asked, frowning in concentration.

'No!' Evie had never heard of any.

The shop closed for an hour at twelve thirty. Usually they all went upstairs then, apart from Miss Lister, to eat the hot dinner that Matilda, their cook-general, prepared for them. Evie went up with Bertie.

'Shall I dish up?' Matilda wanted to know. 'Or had we better wait for your father to come to the table?' He was still closeted in the dentist's room.

Evie said: 'We'd better wait.'

Her mind was on fire. Her father had recognised the woman. 'It is you?' he'd asked. Could it be that her mother had not . . . ?

She swung on her heel and ran back downstairs. This was something she had to know now or she'd have nightmares. She flung open the door of the dentist's room. The policeman was just closing his notebook.

Her father's eyes met hers. 'Leave us, Evie, if you please. I don't want you upset.'

She was determined to stand her ground. 'I won't be upset.'

The policeman said: 'There'll have to be a post-mortem, sir. I'll arrange for her to go to the mortuary.'

'As soon as you can. I can't have her here. The dentist is due this afternoon. Two o'clock in this room.'

Evie demanded: 'Who is she?' She risked a glance. The shawl now covered the woman's face.

The policeman was moving towards the door. 'I'll be on my way then.'

'Thank you. As soon as you can then?'

'Yes, sir, I'll do my best.'

As soon as they were alone Joseph seemed to crumble. He leaned against the back of the chair and took out a large handkerchief to blow his hawk-nose.

'Who is she?' Evie persisted.

'Never you mind.' His face was drained of colour. His hand showed a slight tremor. He was more shaken by this than she'd first supposed.

'She's my mother, isn't she? Why did you tell me she was dead?'

She saw her father moisten his lips. Anger was boiling up inside her.

'Do you know what that did to me? I cried myself to

sleep for months. I missed her dreadfully.'

Joseph straightened up. 'And what about me? Do you think I didn't miss her? She ran off with another man. She didn't want either of us.'

'But you lied . . .'

'Better for you to think she'd died than that she was guilty of that. I didn't want to spoil your memories of her. She walked out and left you too, don't forget. She didn't care what happened to either of us.'

Evie was turned to stone. She felt sick.

'Remember it was me that brought you up. You'd have had precious little if you'd had to rely on her. I did my duty by you. I've kept a roof over your head all these years. I've fed you, clothed you and educated you.'

There was a lump in Evie's throat the size of an orange. Duty! Oh yes, everyone could rely on Father doing his duty. He'd shown her no love and precious little affection. Gently she lifted the shawl from the woman's face.

'Undernourished,' her father said.

The woman looked as though she'd been ill for a long time. There was nothing of her but skin and bone. Not undernourished, more wasted away. She looked pathetic.

'She ran away to have a better life, but she didn't get it.' There was contempt in Joseph's voice.

'Is that what she said? She was looking for a better life?'

'She told me she was in love with someone else. A flashy fellow. Looks as though he dumped her in the way she dumped us.' He sighed. 'We'll never know now.'

Evie could barely see the body. Her eyes kept misting over. She told herself it was an empty shell, not anybody now. It didn't seem like her mother. She could feel nothing for her except shivers. This was the first dead person she'd ever seen.

'Leave her be, Evie. We'd better go up and have our dinner.'

'Dinner!' Evie felt another wave of nausea. The lump in her throat was bigger than ever. 'I don't want . . .'

'You must. Put this out of your mind and come up and eat. How do you expect to work and stay healthy if you don't refuel your body? You'll feel better if you eat something. Believe me.'

'She was my mother! She wanted to speak to me, I know she did. I could see her looking at me. She wanted to explain . . . You shouldn't have lied, told me she was dead.'

He pulled at her arm. The shawl fell back over the dead face and Evie allowed herself to be led away. 'I grieved for her.'

'Better that than to expect her to come back. You were six years old, for goodness' sake. What else could I tell you?'

'All those lies about a road accident . . .' She'd never understand why he'd told her such a story. He'd said her mother had slipped when she'd got off at the back of one of those old two-horse omnibuses at Charing Cross, and fallen in front of a governess cart, frightening that horse. It had kicked her before she could get up.

It was such a cruel thing to say if it wasn't true. It had given Evie terrible nightmares. She had very definite memories of her mother. She remembered the care she'd taken when brushing her daughter's hair. The way she used to sit Evie on the table to fasten all those little buttons on the leather gaiters she used to wear in winter.

Her mother used to give out love. She remembered her voice as she sang; her laugh as she'd taught her nursery rhymes. The feel of her soft body as she cuddled her close. Her good-night kisses.

Her mother had played with her and read stories to her. She'd taken her to school every day. She remembered a soft blue dress and the petticoats that swished as she walked. She'd had soft brown hair piled high on her head. But she couldn't remember her face. Not the way she'd looked.

She'd been woken one night by her father's voice. It had been wild with anger but she'd never known why. Only that the anger was directed at her mother. Then the next day she'd been gone, and Father had told Evie about an accident in which her mother had been killed.

The sun had gone from her world. The change in her life was fundamental. There had been no more school. Father thought it better if he and Aunt Agatha saw to her education. Nobody played with her after that, nobody laughed or joked.

Matilda had been kind, but Evie had recognised a change even in her. She was afraid. If Father came near and found them talking, Matilda would hurry away to some suddenly remembered task. There was an atmosphere of oppression in the household after that.

# CHAPTER TWO

Evie found herself seated at the table with a plate of steaming red beef in front of her. Matilda always sat down with them for meals, as did Johnny Simms, who lodged with them. Bertie ate his dinners with them but his home was nearby and he lived out. The events of the morning cast a cloud. Nobody had much to say. Nobody ate much.

'Pull yourself together,' her father told her coldly. 'Come on, eat up.'

Evie had never felt this mutinous before. 'You're fond of telling everybody what they should do.'

'I know the human body. I know what's best for you.'

Evie put the food in her mouth and tried to swallow. Her mind raced with memories. Other things her father had said when she was six.

'Aunt Agatha will come and take care of us. We'll manage very well with her.'

Aunt Agatha was his older sister and very like him to look at. She had the same hawk-nose and darting grey eyes that missed nothing. The same wiry hair but with more grey in it, drawn back severely into a tight roll at the nape of her stringy neck. Agatha was a spinster with strict ideas about child-rearing. She shared with her brother an iron self-discipline, and together they did their best to instill that trait into Evie.

Agatha was efficient and thrifty in every aspect of home care and cookery. She could serve in the shop and act as dispenser. She wasn't qualified to prescribe as her brother was – he didn't believe women should be. He'd taught her just enough to make her useful to him on the back counter.

That was to be Evie's lot too. Joseph had been articled to an apothecary from the age of thirteen and saw no reason why Evie shouldn't learn to make herself useful in the shop in the way he'd had to. From the age of eight she was responsible for washing out all the medicine bottles returned by customers to collect the penny charged on them.

It was Aunt Agatha who decided that Evie's hair should always be drawn back into tight plaits. She chose the black boots that laced up over her ankles, similar to Agatha's own. She asked the local dressmaker to run up Evie's dresses, always from the same pattern and always in dark greys and browns. She ordered serviceable serge for winter and plain cotton for summer. Evie felt a frump and pleaded for lighter colours, but was not allowed them.

'They'll need washing twice as often,' she was told. 'What's the sense in making work?'

Joseph believed in an early bedtime. Evie was fourteen before she was allowed to stay up after eight o'clock at night. He also believed in early rising and liked to have breakfast over and see her opening her lesson books by half past seven. He gave her lessons in herbalism and Latin.

Aunt Agatha was in charge of her general education and saw to it that she was kept busy every minute of the day. Sewing and housekeeping skills were not neglected. On Sundays, she was taken to church and Sunday school, and taught the scriptures.

Agatha chose books of instruction for her to read, or stories written from a strong moral viewpoint. Reading for pleasure was not allowed until the evening meal had been eaten and cleared away.

Evie was not allowed to play with other children, and

on no account was she to encourage them to come to the shop. She was given to understand that the local children were not of her class. And anyway, Joseph Hobson believed in keeping himself to himself.

If she was ill, Father took her down to the pharmacy when it was closed. Evie remembered sitting on the bench provided for customers and being questioned about her stomach aches. Then he'd prescribe some remedy, and pound up the herbs with his mortar and pestle. For her, he'd make the powders, which she understood tasted horrible, into sugar-coated pills. That was the mark of her father's love.

Evie had also been taught the value of money by having to work for it. She'd been taking out the babies from the baker's shop next door every afternoon for the past five years; ever since she was thirteen and considered old enough. The older ones were in school now, but there was always a new baby needing her attention. This served as a means to get her out in the fresh air, learn responsibility for others and earn her own pocket money. All necessary lessons for a girl, in Joseph Hobson's view.

He told her that what she earned in this way was hers to keep. But it must be put into her money box, which was kept on the living-room mantelpiece. It stood on a small cash book, into which she was trained to enter all sums added or withdrawn, so that there was a running balance. Father checked on this regularly. Every Sunday, she must withdraw twopence, a penny for the church collection box at each service. She was told she needed prior approval to withdraw money for anything else.

She knew she disappointed both her father and her aunt. There were always red ink corrections scrawled across her lesson books. Her efforts in housework and shop work didn't please either. She saw Aunt Agatha as a jailor who never left her side. She felt caged.

She was fifteen, and had been told it was time to wear her plaits pinned up round her head, when George Appleby started to attend the same church. Evie felt an immediate change in her aunt, who seemed more cheerful and less constrained by duty. Joseph, on the other hand, seemed more morose. Evie only understood why when Aunt Agatha announced her intention of getting married. She found it hard to believe. Her aunt seemed too old.

Agatha said stiffly: 'Mr Appleby's asked me and I've said I would.'

Evie felt uplifted by the news; joy spread through her like a warm tide. There was nothing she wanted more, and it couldn't come soon enough for her. Mr Appleby was a missionary and a widower, whose first wife had succumbed to the unhealthy climate of central Africa.

'I don't think it's safe for you to go out there,' Joseph told his sister resentfully. 'The same fate could befall you.'

'I shall look after myself. Mr Appleby wants me to run the Sunday school and teach the native children their letters.'

Evie was delighted that the children of Africa rather than her would benefit from Agatha's discipline. The future suddenly seemed more rosy.

Before leaving, Aunt Agatha said: 'You'll have to look after the house for your father now, Evie. You're old enough and you've been well trained.' Her smile had been frosty. 'You'll manage well enough, I'm sure.'

Well trained or not, Evie was afraid she'd fall short of Agatha's standards.

'I'll not have that much time,' she'd faltered. 'Not to do everything you do.'

'Perhaps it's time you stopped taking next-door's

children out,' Father suggested, lifting his eyebrows of twisted wire-like hairs. 'That would give you another couple of hours every day and save your energy for more important things.'

That was the last thing Evie wanted. She never mentioned it again.

Her father didn't want Agatha to go. He was very tight-lipped about it. As soon as she had gone, he began to carp at Evie's efforts. She must be more thrifty. The housekeeping was costing more and she was gossiping with Matilda and allowing her to get lazy. From then on, Father directed the housekeeping.

With her aunt gone, Evie wanted to ditch the drab dresses she'd chosen for her. She thought the ten shillings a week her father allowed her for working in the shop very generous and wanted to spend some of it on new clothes. He told her off harshly.

'You mustn't waste, Evie. There's plenty of wear left in the clothes you have. Waste not, want not is what I say. You'll live to rue the day if you don't.'

This year, she'd been allowed to buy one new dress. It was light blue, but blue had not been her first choice. Father had thought red wool quite unsuitable and had forbidden it. Red was for hoydens and women of the street.

Evie hated her hairstyle. One night she sat in front of her dressing-table mirror looking at the plaits pinned round her head. She thought them frumpish and more suited to the middle-aged. On the spur of the moment she took her nail scissors to them and sheared six inches off each. She piled what remained of her hair into a loose bun in the style of Lillie Langtry, except that on her it didn't look quite so elegant.

Father was very cross and said she was cheapening herself. That her hair was untidy and looked a mess, and why did she want to make such a fool of herself? Bertie Pugh whispered that she was not to listen to him, it looked wonderful.

Her hair was too fine and silky to stay in position, and strands seemed always to escape and hang down by her face. Bertie assured her that didn't matter. Johnny and Miss Lister approved too.

By the time their dinner plates were being cleared away, Evie realised that her father was making a mighty effort to appear his normal self. He was the only one to have eaten a hearty meal. He even had a second helping of the beef. Evie did feel better with hot food inside her. Not good, but better than she had.

'Get yourself out to the park. Some fresh air will do you good,' he said briskly. This morning's events must not be allowed to change their routine. It was time for her to take next-door's baby out.

'She'll be gone to the mortuary by the time you come back, and we'll all be able to put it behind us.'

Evie noticed that he couldn't bring himself to call her mother by her name. She'd had the feeling that there was some mystery about her for some time. Matilda had said in an unguarded moment last year:

'How like your mother you are.'

'Am I? What was she like, Matty? I'd love to know more about her. Tell me what you remember.'

'No!' Matilda's voice had sounded strangled and she'd turned back to battering cod with uncharacteristic speed.

'Why not?' Evie had asked. 'Why does nobody want to talk about my mother? Father's just the same.'

'He's still grieving.' Matty had recovered her wits. 'It upsets him to talk about her.'

'It upsets me that nobody ever has,' Evie retorted. 'Not

you, or Aunt Agatha. You can't all be so locked in grief that you can't bear to remember her. Not after all these years. Doesn't anybody have happy memories of her?' It really had upset her that that was the case.

Now Evie put on her hat and coat and went slowly downstairs, knowing that she wouldn't be able to go out without seeing her mother once more. If she didn't see her now, there might never be another chance. Slowly she turned the knob on the door to the dentist's room. It was always closed up and airless.

It was hard to accept, even now, that this inert figure was the mother she'd thought had died eleven years ago. Father had been very wrong to lie about that. Evie was sure she'd have grieved less if she'd known the truth. And now to be told her mother had lived many more years! She wouldn't have believed it if she wasn't here in front of her eyes. There were knots in her gut. She was numb and sick with the horror of it.

She folded back the matted wool shawl. It was a face that ought to be as familiar to her as her own. Grey and waxy as it was, it had the same neat nose and even features that she had. She tried to imprint it on her mind. The outline became hazy as tears misted her eyes. Her mother had come back to see her before she died. Surely that meant she had loved her?

She looked round for the bag her mother had been carrying when she'd come into the shop. A grey canvas shopping bag, but it was not here now. If only Father had told her who the woman was when he first saw her, Evie would have been able to talk to her. Her mother wouldn't have had to die alone.

Blinking hard, Evie slowly covered the still form, closed the door softly and let herself out of the shop.

★   ★   ★

When Evie returned at four o'clock, there were two patients waiting for the dentist's attention.

'It's all right,' Bertie whispered. 'Everything's back to normal.'

Evie felt nothing would ever be normal again. 'My mother's gone then? The hearse came in time?'

'A hand cart. They didn't send the horse hearse for her. They don't if they're going to the mortuary.'

Evie couldn't get the vision of that out of her mind either. She had a terrible night. She'd been unable to think of anything but her mother since yesterday morning. She felt in a state of shock.

At breakfast, her father flared up when his bacon and egg was put in front of him.

'Matilda, you've overcooked it again. Just look at this egg, it's all dried up. Why can't you cook things as I like them?'

'I'm sorry.' His complaints made Matty nervous and apologetic. 'It's me feet. Giving me gyp they are. I can hardly walk this morning.'

Matilda had a round face, and her large pale cheeks were mottled with broken veins. She was well padded and could be motherly if Joseph were not about. It was to her that Evie had turned for comfort when she'd been a child. This morning her brown eyes showed distress.

'Can Evie do a bit of shopping for me? Get a few things for dinner?'

'Of course I can,' Evie told her, hoping to calm things down. She felt they were all walking on eggshells.

But Johnny Simms upset her father further by taking off his shirt and showing his shoulder, now black and blue with bruising.

'Still very painful, sir. Didn't sleep. I think another day to recover?'

'Damn it, Simms! You ask for time off to play that confounded game. You come home with your shoulder put out, begging for help. I put it back for you, I give you embrocation and a day off, and now you want still more.'

Evie knew Johnny wanted to use the time to study, because his final exams, his majors, were not so far off now. He was rarely to be seen without his copy of *Materia Medica* sticking out of the pocket of his white coat.

'And it's Friday,' Joseph exploded. 'One of our busier days.'

'Not as busy as Saturday, sir. If I rest now, I shall feel much better by then.'

Johnny was a good-looking young man, with smooth fair hair swept straight back from his forehead. They were all in awe of Joseph Hobson, but everyone knew Johnny was Joseph's favourite and could get away with more than the rest of them.

'All right, but I shall expect you to pull your weight next week.'

'Of course, sir.'

Evie watched Joseph's eyes go round the table. She knew Bertie Pugh had not pleased him yesterday. She had heard him shout several times: 'Look lively, lad. Why are you so dozy? Keep your wits about you.'

By nine o'clock, when the shop was opening, Evie couldn't even think straight, and it seemed Bertie couldn't either. Within fifteen minutes, she'd heard Father tell him off twice. Then he committed the cardinal sin. He made out a packet of powders to the wrong customer. The error was discovered only because that customer was expecting a bottle of cough mixture.

'You aren't capable, Mr Pugh,' Joseph exploded. 'Sometimes I wonder whether you should be allowed to continue in this profession. Get out of my sight. Go and help on the front counter.

'Evie? You can come and help me in the drug run today.'

Evie's heart sank. Although she felt permanently under surveillance in the shop, to work to Father's instruction in the back was much worse. As Father saw it, it was a privilege to make herself useful by writing to his dictation in the prescription book, to wrap up his powders and lotions.

'Couldn't I learn to be a real chemist like you, Father?' she'd once asked. 'I could help you much more then.'

'No,' he'd said.

'If Bertie Pugh can do it, I'm sure I could.'

'You're a woman. It isn't possible for you. A woman's role in life is to support her father or her husband.'

'I could help you more if . . .'

'You're being silly, Evie. Don't argue.'

Evie had had to accept that she'd be taught to fetch and carry for her father, and no more.

Ned Collins's step was jaunty as he walked into the centre of Birkenhead. He paused outside the Argyle Theatre to look at the billboards. Harry Lauder was top of the bill tonight. Ned bounded across the road, in front of a brewer's dray, to post a letter at the General Post Office opposite, and then back to stride on down Argyle Street towards Hobson's the Chemist. Evie Hobson had caught his eye some time ago and had filled his mind ever since. He thought her the prettiest girl he'd ever seen.

He went past the shop as often as he could, hoping to catch a glimpse of her. If possible, he found some reason to go inside. On his last day off, he'd asked Joseph Hobson to prescribe a cure for a hangover. His brother had been very grateful for it and he'd been able to stand around the shop for ten or more minutes. Evie had been serving most of that time, but she'd noticed him and asked if there was anything she could get him.

He was pleased because today he had two commissions to fulfil. He'd be able to speak to her. Perhaps get her to say something to him; something more than the transaction called for.

He could see Evie now in his mind's eye. A slight figure in a drab dress that reached to her ankles. That was covered with a starched white apron with straps crossing between her shoulder blades and tying in a big bow in the small of her back, trailing streamers down her skirt. She had dark silky hair and thick eyelashes that threw shadows on her cheeks and a delightful dimple that came when she smiled. Her eyes were big and soft and brown and could look happy, but were more often wary or anxious.

Ned knew that a lot depended on her father's temper. He was a terrible tyrant, but all the same, many in the community preferred to put their trust in Joseph Hobson when they were ill. The poor came in droves because he charged only for the remedies he made up for them, while Dr Jones, who practised round the corner, charged one shilling and sixpence for a consultation and then exacted another payment for the medicines he handed out.

His own mother thought Joseph Hobson's powders, pills and lotions more effective, as well as being cheaper. Customers put up with his shortness of manner and volatile temper because they respected his skills. He had the reputation of being a hard man who would do his best for them. He saw that as his duty.

From the doorstep the shop looked busy. All the better as far as Ned was concerned. He didn't mind waiting around inside, not one bit. His brothers laughed at him.

'You're aiming a bit high, aren't you? The apothecary's

daughter? What would she see in you?'

The bell clanged as he went in. Straight away he felt the atmosphere. Tension crackled in the air. Things were more fraught than usual. His heart lurched with disappointment when he saw that Evie was not in her usual place.

Then he heard her voice and knew she was helping her father on the back counter. Mr Hobson's face was heavy with irritation. Ned went forward until he could see her. Evie's eyes were frightened and had mauve shadows beneath them. He wanted to take her hand. No, he wanted to take her in his arms and comfort her.

Evie could see the shop filling up with customers. She was doing her best to please her father. He was pounding herbs to fine powder with his mortar and pestle. She felt all thumbs as she folded the doses into tiny papers with the exact precision her father required.

'Look lively, Evie,' he growled, as he pushed another prescription alongside one she hadn't finished. 'Be careful you don't get them mixed up.'

It was for pills this time, thank goodness, so she'd be able to catch up. It took Father longer to roll his powders into pills and coat them with sugar. Most customers were prepared to put up with the bitter taste of the powders because it was the cheapest way to buy the remedies.

Evie scurried back to the prescription book to fill it in. Cough mixture this time, for Mrs Gertrude Collins. Then she had to wrap the bottle in white paper with meticulous care, seal it top and bottom with hot wax and write the dose and the name of the customer on the pleat she'd folded down the front.

'Do put a move on, Evie, you're falling behind again,' Joseph complained as she moved past him.

He had his back towards her. After what had happened yesterday, the sight of his narrow shoulders covered by his white coat was enough to frighten her. She shrank at being reprimanded in front of customers and staff. But worse than any fear was the feeling of shame that she couldn't cope with the simplest of tasks. He'd always sapped her confidence. He showed no fatherly affection. No affection for anybody or anything. Everybody but Johnny Simms was scared of him.

She went to the end of the drug run and called: 'Mrs Collins? That will be sixpence, please.'

Neither of the two elderly ladies waiting on the bench looked up. Evie felt a momentary misgiving: had she got the name right? Her fingers were cold and she felt numb with agony.

She knew Mrs Collins by sight, a stout middle-aged woman. Everybody round here knew the large Collins family. It consisted mostly of boys, grown to manhood now. They all came in from time to time, generally in search of a cure for a thumping head. Father said they all drank like fishes, their mother included.

Evie didn't know how she let it happen, but somehow the newly filled bottle of cough cure slid through her fingers. She made a desperate grab to save it. The sound of shattering glass brought her father off his high stool.

'For goodness' sake, girl!' His hawk-nose was screwing up in outrage. 'How can you be so careless?'

Evie could feel her heart thudding against her ribs. She'd never done such a thing before.

'Look at the mess!' Dark-brown syrupy fluid was leaking out of the package. She tried to pick it up but the sodden paper parted and let the glass tinkle on to the floor. The next second it was crunching under her feet.

There was a fit of coughing from the bench and a

querulous voice rasped: 'Was that my physic she dropped?'

'No, Mrs Smith. It was mine, or rather my mother's. She asked me to get it for her.'

Evie registered that it was one of the Collins boys who answered. She thought he'd been studying the scented soaps in the glass case on the front counter.

'I'll make up another bottle,' Joseph told him shortly. 'I'm sorry you've been kept waiting.'

To Evie, he said: 'Better get this glass brushed up, before it causes more trouble.'

She ran for a floor cloth, a dustpan and a brush. The smell of cough mixture was filling her nostrils; it was so strong she could taste it on her tongue. The heavy fumes were warming her throat, spreading down to her lungs. She breathed in deeply, trying to still her thudding heart.

Down on the floor she could see herself in the mirror advertising Proctor's Pine Liptus Pastilles. There were brown splashes now along the hem of her dress. Her face looked drawn with worry and almost as white as her apron.

Ned Collins was standing too close. She could see cough mixture all over his boots. He was reading the advertisement.

' "Pastilles for dusty roads and a tendency to catarrh. For chest, throat and voice. A boon to singers, speakers and travellers." Are they good?'

She looked at him then. He had a pleasant smile. 'We sell a lot. One and threepence a box.'

'Evie?' her father called. He was pushing another bottle of medicine towards her, already wrapped. 'At seventeen, you should be capable of handling a bottle of medicine without dropping it. Try again.'

'Sorry, Father.'

She took it to the end of the counter. 'That will be sixpence, Mr Collins, thank you.'

'And a couple of corn plasters.' His eyes seemed to be searching for hers. 'They're for my mother, too.'

Evie went to the front counter and reached into one of the glass cases.

'Two?' She knew her voice sounded strangled.

'How much are they?'

She turned one over, looking for some clue. 'Four a penny, I think.' She couldn't see her father, but she knew he was listening.

'Two a penny,' Joseph corrected. He was always close enough to monitor everything she did and said. As she took out two corn plasters, two more fell to the floor.

'Evie! What's the matter with you today? You've got to be more careful.' Her father had come to see what she'd let fall and couldn't hide his exasperation.

'No harm done,' the customer said mildly. 'No need to go for the poor girl.'

That made Evie look squarely at Ned Collins. He was a handsome young man in his early twenties, with a thatch of curly brown hair. His eyes smiled into hers. They seemed full of sympathy, as though he wanted to share and lighten her misery. She warmed towards him.

'Stay out of this,' Joseph barked. 'It has nothing to do with you.'

Ned Collins crashed his coins down on the counter, scooped up the corn plasters and left without another word. He let the shop door bang behind him so that the bell set up a frenzied clangour.

'Scum of the earth, those Collinses,' her father said contemptuously. 'Irish tinkers.' Evie could feel herself shaking. She couldn't stand any more of this. She glanced at the clock.

'Had I better do that shopping for Matilda next? She wants me to get something for dinner.'

'For all the good you're doing here, you might as well. Get her list and let me see what she wants. Tell her we'll have liver and onions for dinner.' Liver was a favourite of his; the rest of them didn't care for it.

To pull the shop door shut behind her and get out was always a high spot in Evie's day. She gulped at the fresh air. Joseph always had to know exactly where she was going.

She walked slowly past the baker's next door, sniffing at the scent of freshly baked bread. Past the barber's shop with its red striped pole. It was steamy inside from the kettle kept simmering on the gas ring to provide hot water for shaving. She could smell the scented soap and bay rum wafting from the door as she passed. A man sitting waiting his turn looked up from the *Liverpool Advertiser* he was reading.

She called in at the grocer's and bought the half-pound of fig biscuits her father had added to Matilda's list. She wouldn't let herself look at the Meadow Creams, which she much preferred.

Bentley's, the butcher's, was the last shop in the row. With the lamb's liver in her bag, she went back to Darty's, the baker's. She wouldn't look at the display of cakes either, because she was never allowed to buy any of them. Her father's tastes were austere; he didn't approve of shop cake. He expected Matilda to make everything they ate. She made big cut-and-come-again plain cakes when she had time.

'Hello again.' Ned Collins was standing at this counter now, his eyes sparkling down at her, as though he was pleased to see her. Not sympathetic eyes after all; he had laughing eyes. He was in the middle of making his choice from the luscious delicacies set out in the window.

'Two buns with pink icing and two with white, please,

Polly. And I'll take a couple of jam tarts and four apple tarts, if you haven't burned them today.'

'We never burn them,' Polly Darty chuckled. She knew when she was being teased. She was a middle-aged matron with a plump figure showing how much she appreciated her husband's baking.

'And a lardy cake. My mother loves those.'

'How is she, Ned?'

Evie could feel her mouth beginning to water. The shop was filled with heavenly scents. She found it hard to believe that the Collins family her father so looked down upon could indulge themselves in this fashion.

'Give me one of your pork pies too. I'll eat that on the way home.' Ned's manner was relaxed. Everything about him suggested he enjoyed the pleasures of this world.

He said to Evie: 'Your dad lets you out, then?'

'I've just come for bread. The usual please, Mrs Darty. A white tin.'

Ned bit into his pork pie. He was making no attempt to leave the shop before she did. She wanted him to stay. She wanted to know him better. He was the first person who had ever tried to support her against her father.

'He was giving you a very hard time.' The friendly brown eyes were searching her face.

She couldn't openly admit that. Not so close to home. Father would half kill her if he knew! Polly Darty knew what he was like.

Evie managed: 'That's the way he is.'

'He's a hard man. Bloody-minded and foul-tempered, so they say. Don't they, Polly?'

'Perhaps not the easiest to get along with.' Polly was carefully noncommittal too, and wouldn't look at Evie now.

They all heard the baby cry for attention in the back of the shop.

'There's Herbie waking up,' Evie said.

'Wants his dinner. You'll be back to take him out at two?'

'Of course.'

Ned followed her out and seemed reluctant to leave her. He kept her talking on the doorstep of the pharmacy.

'Walk a little way with me. You don't want to rush back to your father, do you?'

'I have to. We're busy and Johnny Simms has the day off.'

He looked disappointed. 'But you'll be taking the Darty baby out at two?'

'Yes, to the park.'

'Good.' His eyes beamed down at her. 'I mean, you've got to have a bit of fun, haven't you? What's life for if it's all work?'

Evie couldn't have agreed more. She felt starved of fun. Starved of life itself. Through the glass in the shop door, she saw her father striding towards them, his face like thunder.

'Goodbye,' she said hastily. 'I've got to go.'

Once inside, she felt the medicinal fug close round her again. Her father was furious.

'You stay away from those Collinses, do you hear? They're a bad lot. I don't want you keeping such company. Putting his oar in where it's not wanted. He should mind his own business.'

Evie's heart was thumping wildly as she scurried upstairs with the shopping. A few minutes later she could hear Joseph pounding his mortar and pestle with ill-tempered zeal.

# CHAPTER THREE

As Evie unpacked the bag of shopping on the kitchen table, Matilda was peeling potatoes at the sink. She noticed for the first time that Matty's figure was not as well padded as it used to be. She had been a fixture in their household for as long as Evie could remember. Now she was looking older and not very well.

Evie did as much as she could to help with the housework, for she was afraid it was becoming too much for Matilda. She knew she worked long hours on her own; she'd rarely seen the older woman sit down. The nervous tremor of Matty's work-worn fingers was more marked today. When Father had turned on her, Evie had seen raw fear in her brown eyes.

It occurred to her now that Matilda must have known her mother well.

She said: 'A terrible thing, my mother coming back here to die.'

'Terrible. I can't get it out of my mind. I wanted to see her but your father wouldn't let me. Why did she come?'

'To see me. I think she wanted to tell me something.' Evie was getting used to the idea now. 'I feel so churned up . . .'

'It upset me too. I was right fond of your mother.'

Matilda wore her straight grey hair in a bun in the nape of her neck and covered most of it with a large, no-nonsense cotton cap. Like the shop assistants, she wore a large white starched apron. To show her lower station, Joseph insisted that instead of black she wear a print dress of striped cotton which came down to her ankles. Instead of boots, she wore incongruous red carpet slippers to ease her painful bunions.

Evie had tried to talk to her about her mother before but she'd never got much out of her. Matty had seemed on edge the moment Evie mentioned her name. Evie was in no doubt that Joseph had forbidden it.

'All these years . . .' Evie said. 'Did you think she was dead?'

The brown eyes were troubled. 'That's what your father said. He spoke of her as being in her grave, and you thought she'd gone to heaven. I suppose I came to believe . . . that perhaps she might have died.'

'That means you didn't.'

She saw Matilda swallow. 'You're a quick one. Determined too. You stand up to him better than she did. She didn't dare.'

'You knew she wasn't dead?'

'She told me she was leaving, you see. And I never heard of any funeral.'

Evie felt a surge of fear. She might dare, but that didn't mean she wasn't terrified of Father. Her heart began to hammer.

'She told you what was going on?'

The pounding from the drug run below ceased. They both paused to listen in case Joseph should be coming upstairs. Evie's voice dropped to a near whisper.

'It's all right . . .'

'He doesn't like me talking about her. Told me I mustn't. Not one word.'

'To me?'

'To anyone. He'd be furious if he knew about this. He threatened to sack me.'

'Please,' Evie pleaded. 'She told you she was leaving?'

'I knew she wanted to. There'd been an awful row.'

'Between Mother and Father?'

'She wanted to take you with her. She'd asked me to pack all your things.'

Evie's mouth felt dry. This was what Father was trying to keep from her. 'What happened?'

'She went to meet you as you came out of school. She was going to leave straight from there. But your father went too.

'She tried again the next day but he caught you both as you were going downstairs. Helen thought he'd be busy in the shop once it was open. That you'd both be out of the door before he could stop you.'

Evie caught her breath. Something stirred in the depths of her memory. She remembered clinging to Mother's coat. She was weeping and they were both hung about with bags and coats.

'Where was she taking me? Where did she go? You should have told me.'

'Look, lass, you were nobbut a child, and if your father said she was dead, it wasn't my place to say otherwise.'

'Matty!' Evie wanted to shake her. 'You've got to tell me everything now. Father stopped her taking me away with her. Then what happened?'

'She didn't know what to do, she was worried about you, distraught. She made me promise to look after you. See you was all right.'

'You did that, Matty. You were always kind. I used to come to you if I wanted a cuddle.'

'You came too often. Your father saw you and warned me off. He thought I was telling you things, but I wasn't. He said I must stop it anyway. I was spoiling you, softening you.'

Matty's voice dropped until Evie could hardly hear.

She held her hand in front of her mouth.

'Your mama gave me something to keep for you until you were old enough to understand. After what happened yesterday, I reckon that's now. Save my legs and run up to my room, Evie. There's a photograph of her in a frame.'

'Where? I've never seen it there. Never seen any photos of her.'

'Your father packed all her things away when she went. All those he could get his hands on.'

'Why? That's awful.'

Matilda was shaking her head. 'Not my place to question why. You'll find this one in the top drawer of my chest, at the back. I didn't want him to see it.'

Evie rushed up two flights of stairs to the attic where Matilda slept. The room was like a cell, plain and sparsely furnished. She had the framed picture in her hands in moments.

It made her gasp aloud. The eyes were so like her own. It was sepia and somewhat faded now, so it was hard to tell what her mother's colouring had been. She wore a high-necked Victorian blouse, all frills and furbelows. Evie feasted her eyes and was delighted to find a resemblance to herself. She took the photograph to her own bedroom and hid it in her bed before going back down to the shop to help her father.

'Where've you been until now? You know we're busy and you dawdle upstairs. You need to jump to it, young lady.' His wiry eyebrows were pulled down in a formidable frown.

At two o'clock, Evie steered the baby carriage out of the yard behind the bakery with one hand, and kept a firm hold on Herbie Darty's reins with the other. His plump arms reached up to the handle to push it too. At eighteen months, he was leaving babyhood behind.

This was her favourite time of day, when she could get away from her father and the shop for two whole hours. Yesterday's thunder had cleared and it was a cool summer's day. She lifted her face to the pale sun and tried to take pleasure from it. But today, she couldn't get her mother out of her mind.

She walked back along the parade of shops and looked both ways, wondering if Ned Collins would come. He'd said he would, but there was no sign of him. That disappointed her too.

Little Herbie was waddling on plump legs, already looking over-podgy from the buns he received to keep him quiet. Evie thought him a lovable child, full of energy and always happy. He cried only when he was hungry.

His father had to be up and in his bakehouse by four in the morning. By nine, he had the shop stocked with fresh bread and cakes and was ready to open. Evie had been told that he took a cup of tea and some fresh bread to Polly's bedside at seven, so that she could get dressed, get the children off to school and see to little Herbie.

They tended the shop between them during the morning, and after dinner at midday, Arthur Darty went to bed for a two-hour rest while his wife ran the shop on her own and Evie took the baby out for some fresh air.

Herbie was encouraged to take his nap before his dinner, and Evie's instructions were to keep him awake at all costs while he was out. He was to walk and run as much as possible and hopefully tire himself out, so that he could be put to bed and would sleep soon after having his tea.

There were not many places within walking distance that she could take him, and it depended upon the weather. For wet days, the best place was the big market hall. They could walk round there, up and down the aisles, and keep dry. She amused herself by pricing the goods on display: cotton and wool cloth, ready-made blouses, boots and shoes, hams and cheeses and pies, crockery, and fruit and vegetables. For better days, there was the recreation ground in Camden Street, but that could be commandeered by older boys playing rough games.

Evie loved to go up Grange Road, window-shopping in the fine shops, but it was a busy road and she dared not let her attention stray from Herbie there.

On warm days, Hamilton Square offered a bench for her to sit on and a bit of grass in the formal gardens, but much the nicest place for Herbie was Birkenhead Park, though it was also the furthest. There she could play games with him on the grass and he could run about freely. On such a fine day as today, it was the obvious place for her to go.

It took her about twenty minutes to push the perambulator there, but much longer if Herbie's stumpy legs were covering the distance too. She'd started up Conway Street when she heard feet thudding on the pavement behind her. She turned and found Ned Collins running after her.

'You went without me!' he accused, but his eyes danced with pleasure. He was puffed after his run. 'Didn't know whether you'd set out or not. Had to ask Polly Darty.'

'You asked her!'

Evie stopped, horrified. She knew exactly what her father would say. He'd see any boyfriend as a source of trouble, and he'd already warned her off the Collins family.

'It'll be all right. Told her not to mention it to your dad.'

Evie started to breathe again, hoping he was right.

'A bit strict, Polly said he was.' His brown eyes smiled down at her.

'Yes.'

Ned laughed. 'We're never going to reach the park at this rate. How do you stand this meandering?' He picked Herbie up and set him across his shoulders. The child chortled with delight. 'What a little roly-poly you are. You weigh a ton.'

After that, Evie had to skip along to keep pace with Ned's long stride. She told herself she wasn't going to worry about upsetting Father; she wasn't going to think about her mother either. She was going to enjoy Ned's company.

She kept stealing sideways glances at him. Trying to commit to memory the strong planes of his face, his curly brown hair blowing in the breeze and the spotted red kerchief round his neck.

They reached the park and went in through the grand entrance. Ned swung Herbie to the ground and let him walk between them, holding on to their hands. They were almost swinging him off his feet.

'The duck pond's the place,' Ned said.

'No,' she protested. 'I'm afraid he'll fall in, and he tried to paddle with his shoes on last month.'

There was a cricket match in progress. Ned paused to watch it for a moment. Herbie was crawling round. Evie unhooked his reins and sank to the grass beside him. He was safe enough just here.

Ned sat down beside her. There were so many things Evie wanted to know about him, but she didn't know how to ask. She'd never been alone with a man before. In the shop, her father was always within earshot.

She knew she was blurting it out: 'Don't you have to go to work?'

He smiled at her. 'I have got a job.'

'I know.'

'How?'

'All those cakes you bought.'

He laughed. 'I'm on the Isle of Man boats. Day off today.'

'Oh! A sailor . . .'

'Deck hand.'

Evie knew her father wouldn't approve of that either. He thought his position in life was considerably higher than that of a deck hand.

'Do you like it?'

'It's a job.'

'But the Isle of Man? I'd have thought you'd like to go further. You could see the world.' Evie could think of nothing she'd like better.

'No. Those who want to see the world are away for years. I did a three-year trip on a tramp steamer once. Nothing but work . . .'

'But you must have seen far-off places?'

'I saw a lot of docks. Whether it's New York or Cape Town, the docks don't look much different from those in this country. This way, I'm home regular, like. There and back in a day.'

His brown eyes were exploring hers. 'Do you want to get away from your dad? I would if he were mine. He's ferocious.'

She said nervously: 'He won't like me talking to you.'

'You're doing more than talking to me,' Ned laughed. 'You're here in the park with me. Keeping company.'

'You tagged on to me.'

'Course I tagged on to you. I liked the look of you. Besides, your dad was being horrible. Couldn't help feeling a bit . . . well, you know.'

'What?'

'I'd have liked to punch him on the nose.'

Evie couldn't hold it back any longer. 'I've always wanted a friend.'

'A boyfriend?'

'Any sort of a friend. Someone I could talk to.'

He took her hand in his. It felt comfortingly warm. 'Go on then,' he said. 'Talk to me. I'd like that.' She laughed but didn't know where to begin.

Ned was handsome. She liked the way he closed his eyes against the sun. She'd felt his support this morning when he'd stood up for her against her father. Ned was keeping an eye on Herbie now. He called out to him and obediently the child waddled back towards them.

She started to tell him how claustrophobic she found the pharmacy, how domineering her father was.

'He was in a terrible temper this morning. I still feel sick when I think about it.'

'Why?'

'Yesterday . . .'

It wasn't easy to talk about it. It sounded impossible, a nightmare. Evie swallowed hard. 'My father did a terrible thing. He told me my mother was killed when I was six years old. All these years I've believed she was dead.'

Ned's hand tightened on hers. Gently, then, he began drawing the whole story out of her.

'She died in the shop?' Even Ned shivered when she told him that.

'She was so near to speaking to me. Telling us where she'd been and what had happened to her. He said he hadn't heard from her from the day she left. She was terribly ill but he left her alone in the dentist's room, and I didn't even know who she was.'

Evie put her head down on the rough flannel of Ned's shirt. She felt his arm go round her shoulders and the tears start to her eyes.

'He forbade me think of her, but I can't stop.'

'Course you can't,' he comforted.

'He said she knew where I was and could have come back for me at any time. He said she didn't want anything to do with me.'

Ned's arm tightened across her shoulders, pulling her closer. 'That was cruel. A horrible thing to say.'

When Evie returned to the shop it was full of customers again. They were often busy in the late afternoon when people were leaving their work.

She took off her hat, tied on her apron and went behind the front counter, hoping her father would allow her to stay there. She sold a packet of Carter's Little Liver Pills and a jar of Eastern Foam Vanishing Cream.

Nothing seemed to have changed in the shop. Miss Lister and Bertie were trying to behave as if nothing out of the ordinary had happened. Her father's voice boomed out, full of impatience.

'What's that? Speak up, I can't hear you. Pain in your back?'

She knew from his brusque manner that he hadn't got over seeing her mother again. He wasn't usually this short with his customers, only with his staff. She felt better now she'd poured out her troubles to Ned. She felt comforted; it was a weight off her shoulders.

What bothered her now was that her father would notice how much higher her spirits were and guess the reason. She'd done what he'd forbidden and spent two hours with Ned Collins. That she'd dared to do it brought shivers of guilt. If Joseph found out, he'd be raving. He expected to control everything in her life, and it was the first time she'd ever disobeyed him.

She and her father usually went up to eat their tea at

five, leaving Johnny Simms in charge of the shop for half an hour. Today, Joseph sent Evie upstairs to find Johnny.

'Ask him to come down and relieve me,' he ordered. 'It won't hurt him to do that. He knows I can't trust Bertie Pugh to do it, not yet.'

Johnny's handsome eyes rolled up to the ceiling when she told him, but he put on his white coat and went straight down.

When she was alone with Father, sitting one each side of the table and eating their boiled eggs, he said:

'I've heard from the police. The post-mortem showed that your mother died of consumption. She was very far gone. Must have had it for years. There was nothing anyone could have done to help. The funeral's to be on Monday. I've told them I'll pay for that. Nobody need say my wife was a charge on the parish.'

'Will we go, Father?'

'I'll go because some might think it odd if I don't. There's no need for you.'

'I'd like to.' Evie moved egg round her mouth while her father thought it over.

'All right then. We'll both go. Though she hardly deserves it. She made her own bed, Evie. It's only right that she had to lie on it.'

Evie said nothing. It was safer to keep quiet.

'Your mother made bad friends. They led her astray. I don't want that to happen to you.'

She felt the hairs on the back of her neck stand up. It sounded as though he knew all about Ned. She must keep her friendship with him a secret whatever happened. Ned's brown eyes had laughed down at her when they'd parted this afternoon.

'I'll look out for you again when I have my next days

off,' he'd said. 'In about two weeks. Easy to spot you, pushing that big pram.'

Joseph went on: 'I've tried to bring you up properly. I don't want you to be tempted by the devil and come to the same sad end as your mother. I know I've been strict with you, but I've had to be.'

'I can't get it out of my mind,' she agonised. 'That my mother was living all these years and I didn't know.'

Joseph was clicking his tongue with impatience but she made herself ask:

'Do you have the bag she brought with her?'

'What bag?'

'A grey canvas shopping bag. I'd like to have it.'

His eyes were wide with outrage. 'She had nothing with her.'

'She did. It had books in it. She dropped them and Bertie picked them up. They might throw some light on where she's been all this time.' Evie sighed. 'If only I'd been able to speak to her, we might have found out about . . .'

'There's nothing to find out. Nothing that need concern you.'

She wasn't sure whether it was fear or nerves that was making Father so abrupt. 'I want no more of this nonsense. She's gone and that's the end of it.'

Evie's mind whirled. Clearly there was a lot to find out, but Father wanted to keep her in ignorance. It only served to whet her curiosity.

'Better if you forget all about your mother,' Joseph thundered. 'It's quite wrong to fill your mind with her affairs. She cut herself off from us years ago.'

Evie wanted to close her ears to such talk. 'I wish I could have told her how I felt. I wish there was some way I could find out where she's been . . .'

'Don't you try. Do you hear? I forbid it. She went back on her marriage vows, Evie. She didn't care what happened to me, or to you. I told her quite clearly that if she went she need never come back. I wouldn't have her. It's better that she's dead. Better for all of us. It finishes it now.'

Evie could feel the food sticking in her throat. She knew this would alter for ever how she thought of her father. She'd never felt close to him. Now an unbridgeable rift had opened up between them.

As Evie slid between her sheets that night, she found the framed photograph she'd hidden in her bedclothes. She pulled it out and studied her mother again by the light of her candle. She looked so pretty it was hard to equate her with the woman who had tried to talk to her in the shop and died so tragically soon afterwards in the dental chair.

Evie wondered how old her mother had been when the picture was taken. She turned the frame over, then opened the back to see if there was a date on the reverse of the picture. An envelope fell out on her eiderdown. She felt her heart turn over when she saw that it was addressed to Miss Evelina Hobson. A letter from her mother!

It slid through her nerveless fingers and fell to the floor. Evie swooped down after it. Within seconds she had the envelope open and began to read:

My darling Evie,
I feel torn in two by a trouble that is not of my making. Fate is making me choose between the two people I love best in all the world.
   I can either stay here with you and abandon the man I love, or go to him and turn my back on my beautiful little daughter. It seems I cannot have both

of you. Don't think because I choose to go that I love
you any the less. I hate leaving you but there are other
reasons that make it impossible for me to stay.

Try not to think ill of me. I do love you, dearest
Evie. I shall think of you daily and hope you are
growing up well and strong and happy.

Forgive me, please, and try to understand.

Evie felt the tears washing down her cheeks. She leapt
out of bed, pushed her feet into her slippers and pulled
on her dressing gown. Leaving her candle where it was,
she crept quietly out on to the landing. She thought her
father was still downstairs. She peeped over the banisters.
She could see the light showing under the living-room
door.

She crept up the attic stairs to Matilda's room as quietly
as she could. She wanted to show her the letter. She
wanted to find out more about what had happened to her
mother. Matilda was in bed, but she hadn't doused her
candle. She looked old and wizened with her nightcap
on.

'You found her note? She had only a minute to scribble
it.'

'Read it, Matty.'

'I can't see to read. Not by candlelight.'

'I'll read it to you.' Evie heard her voice shake as she
did so. When she came to the end, there was a silence.

Matilda said at last: 'Your mother tried several times to
take you with her. I heard your father shouting from the
landing, "She's my flesh and blood too. If you take her,
I'll follow you to the ends of the earth. You'll not take any
daughter of mine. I'll get her back, I won't rest until I
do." ' She sighed. 'He has looked after you, Evie, as your
mam knew he would.'

'But I don't understand what happened. Why did she want to leave home?'

Evie was aware at that moment of footsteps pounding up the attic stairs. She went cold with horror and just had time to push the letter into the pocket of her dressing gown. Matty's bedroom door crashed back on its hinges, making them both jump.

Joseph stood in the doorway, quivering with rage, still holding his candlestick before him though the flame had blown out in his angry rush upstairs.

'I won't have it, Evelina. I won't have you sneaking up here to gossip about things that are not your concern.'

Evie took a deep breath and said quietly, 'They are my concern. I need to know, Father. About what happened. Matty knew my mother. I hoped she might be able to . . .'

He turned on Matty and bellowed: 'What have you told her?'

'Nothing yet,' Evie said.

'Then she better hadn't. How many times have I to tell you, I won't have you going on about what is none of your business.

'It's the last time I'll tell you, Matty. You'll go if I have any more of it. Do you think I can't hear you? Whispering up here together.'

Johnny Simms's bedroom was on the same landing. He came to the door in his nightshirt.

'What's all the noise about? What's going on?'

'Get back to your room,' Joseph thundered. 'It's indecent wandering round like that. And this has nothing to do with you either.

'Come down to your own bed, Evie. Then we can all get some sleep.'

He made Evie go down before him. She could hear him groping in the semi-darkness.

'Discussing family matters with servants. Have you no sense? I wish your mother had never come back. She's caused nothing but trouble. A right hornet's nest of it.

'I think perhaps, after all, it would be a mistake for you to come to her funeral. What you need to do is to put her right out of your mind.'

'No, Father, please . . . I want to.' Evie knew she must say no more in case he forbade that. 'I'm sorry, Father. I won't do it again.'

She shot into her own room and closed the door behind her. She knew she must be more careful. Matilda had been frightened and upset. She mustn't bring Father's wrath down on her head again. Poor Matty, threatening to dismiss her like that! She was too old to start again with another family now. Evie decided she'd try to find out what she needed to know some other way.

# CHAPTER FOUR

For the funeral, Evie decided to wear her second-best grey coat. Aunt Agatha's influence had left her with plenty of clothes in sombre shades, and Father had said no new clothes must be bought.

Matilda, who had been refused permission to go, gave Evie a piece of black ribbon to sew on her sleeve as a mark of mourning. Joseph saw her doing it.

'Take that ridiculous band off,' he snapped. 'No need to draw attention to yourself.' Reluctantly, she did as she was told.

'Can I take some money from my money box?' she asked. 'To buy flowers.' She was afraid nobody else would.

'I've already spent enough on her funeral.' Her father's face was grim. 'No point in wasting good money.'

Bertie Pugh overheard that. 'I'll bring you some, Evie,' he told her. 'My mother won't mind if I pick a few for you from our garden.'

He'd arrived at the shop this morning with a great bunch of blue scabious and pink roses, and had even found some silver paper to wrap round their thorny stems. She carried them with her as she walked to church. Her father walked silently beside her, deep in his own thoughts.

The morning was dark and overcast; the church was gloomy inside. Evie thought it was empty, apart from the unadorned deal coffin on its stand, but then she heard the sound of hammering and found there were workmen repairing broken hinges on the door to the vestry.

She laid the flowers on top of the coffin before joining

Father in the pew. She knew Joseph had let it be known that he wanted no sightseers from the other shops along the parade.

'It's a private funeral,' he told everybody who asked. 'I want to keep it that way.' There were still only the two of them when the new curate came and conducted a brief service.

The rain that had threatened since dawn hurtled against the windows throughout. When the time came to go out to the grave for the interment, one of the workmen helped the curate trundle the stand with the coffin to the door. Evie felt the sting of tears as she followed with her father.

When they reached the porch the rain was drumming on the roof and bouncing off the flagstones outside. The waiting grave-diggers pressed back to shelter from the downpour.

'Perhaps we'll wait a moment,' the curate murmured nervously. Father was shuffling; Evie could feel his impatience. When, a few moments later, there was no sign of the downpour moderating, he said:

'We'll leave this to you, I think. We've done our duty. Yes, done our duty.' Evie was surprised and a little shocked to be pulled out into the rain and marched down the street.

'No point in standing by the grave to get soaked,' Father said as he towed her along. 'Besides, I need to get back to the shop. Don't like leaving young Simms in charge for too long. Not got his majors yet, after all.'

Evie was in her room when her tears came for the bleak and lonely burial.

Evie felt in limbo for a long time, but slowly the weeks began to pass. Johnny Simms's five-year apprenticeship came to an end. He passed his final exams and became a Licentiate of the Society of Apothecaries.

'There's no need for you to leave.' Joseph was in a good mood at breakfast the day Johnny received his results. 'My business is expanding.' He was smiling magnanimously round the table, as though about to bestow a great prize on Johnny.

'Plenty of work for two of us. I can offer you the job of assistant here. We've always got on well together, haven't we?'

Johnny's face went scarlet. 'I'm indebted, Mr Hobson. Most kind of you to say so.' Evie could feel his embarrassment, and it made her own toes curl up. She knew he couldn't wait to get away.

'But I've already had an offer and accepted it. A pharmacy in Liverpool.'

'You're going to leave? Just like that?' Joseph's attitude changed instantly. He looked incredulous.

'I thought you'd expect me to go. Apprenticeship completed . . .'

'You're very quick off the mark. I expected you to discuss your plans. Seek my advice.'

Evie met Johnny's gaze for a moment. He'd discussed his plans with everybody else. They were all envious that he was able to leave.

'Particularly when I've gone out of my way to help you learn. Allowed you the use of my books.'

Evie willed Johnny not to mention the times he'd been left to run the business on his own. Nor the number of nights he'd had to work until after ten.

'You have, sir. But I need to widen my experience now. Find out how another pharmacist . . .'

Joseph's cup crashed down on its saucer. As he leapt to his feet, his chair went back with such force it tipped over.

'You ungrateful boy! I don't know why I try so hard. After all I've done to help you make something of yourself.'

The dining-room door slammed shut and they heard his footsteps going up to his room.

'Thank goodness I'm going,' Johnny exclaimed, 'that's all I can say. Who'd want to stay and work for him if they had any choice?'

Matilda got up and started to collect the plates together. The colour had drained from her face.

'I can't stand all these upsets. I'd go myself if I wasn't so old. Nobody else would want me now. Not at my age.'

'Retire, Matilda?'

'I wish I could.'

'What would I do without you?' Evie wailed. 'Don't go, please.' When Johnny left there would be more pressure on her and Bertie to help in the drug run. She shivered at the thought.

'The man's half crazed,' Johnny said. 'Flying into a rage like that. Unreasonable behaviour, I call it. I'm going to pack my things and get out. He won't pay me if I work, not now I've said I'm leaving.'

Down in the shop, Evie whispered the news to Bertie Pugh. 'I dread the day you decide to go,' she told him.

'Can't help thinking I might be better going now,' he murmured.

Johnny's departure put Joseph in a terrible mood for a week. He advertised in the *Birkenhead News* for an assistant, and though he interviewed several pharmacists he ended up taking on another counter clerk instead.

It was exactly what Evie didn't want to happen. Bertha Lee was about thirty and unmarried. She'd worked in a chemist's shop before and soon got the hang of the work. As soon as she did, Evie had to work permanently in the drug run with her father.

Evie felt a nervous wreck. Father was always on her back

about some slip-up she'd made. She couldn't get her mother's fate out of her mind. The only thing that made life bearable was Ned. Over the following months, they met up on his days off when she took Herbie Darty to the park or round the market. There had also been a few evenings when it had been possible for them to see each other. Once she'd been baby-sitting the children next door when their parents went for a rare night out. She hadn't enjoyed that too much: she'd been on edge, afraid the older Darty children might hear them and come downstairs.

Little Herbie was late with his speech, but she was worried that sooner or later he'd convey to others that she was seeing Ned Collins regularly. Ned laughed at her.

'You're a real worry-guts. Polly Darty already knows. She can read the signs.'

Aunt Agatha had been keener on church-going than Joseph was: she'd attended both morning and evening services and taken Evie with her. While Father thought attending church once in a day was enough for himself, he continued to encourage Evie to go twice, as well as to Sunday school in the afternoon. On the rare Sunday when Ned was home, she met him instead. That they didn't have Herbie with them was a bonus.

She thought those Sundays utterly blissful. She could go out dressed in her best to meet Ned. But soon he wasn't satisfied; he wanted to see more of her.

'Tell your father you've been invited out to tea,' he urged. 'Then we can be together all afternoon and evening.'

Evie couldn't bring herself to do that. 'Nobody would invite me to tea on my own. Not without Father.'

'Somebody from Sunday school? Somebody he knows and approves of?'

She shook her head. 'It would make him suspicious. He'd wonder why they didn't seek his permission first and want to know all the ins and outs. Probably make a point of thanking them on my behalf next time he saw them.'

It meant she had to go home and eat her tea with Joseph and Matilda instead of staying with Ned, but even so they were blissful Sundays. Particularly the dark, cold evenings when they seemed to have the park to themselves. Ned could put his arms round her and kiss her, and there was nobody to see them do it.

She thought Ned was wonderful. It seemed a miracle when after a few weeks he said:

'You're very special, Evie. I've thought that for a long time.'

She smiled. 'From the moment I dropped your mother's cough mixture?'

'Long before then. Can't remember how many times I walked past your shop just to see you through the window. I used to beg my mother to let me go in and buy things for her.'

'You mean she didn't want that medicine?'

'Oh, yes. It did her good. But I encouraged her to keep taking it, so she'd empty the bottle and I could come for another.'

Evie stared at him in wonder.

'I'd try to talk to you, try to make you smile, just to see your dimple.'

'I don't remember you talking to me, I mean, not specially.'

'And you didn't often smile. How could you? Your father was always giving you the run-around. He bullies all of you. I'd hang back if Miss Lister was free to serve. Wait a bit until you were.'

She laughed.

'You're showing your dimple now. I've bought my shaving soap and razor blades from you for years. When you turned round to get them I'd see those apron strings tied in a big white bow in the small of your back.' He laughed with her. 'I wanted to pull them. Evie, I've been in love with you for ages.'

He gave her little gifts. She was thrilled with the silk stockings but she couldn't wear them in case her father should notice. She had lace handkerchiefs and a bottle of scent she dared not use either. She kept them hidden in her bedroom. She never spoke of him to anyone, not even Polly Darty. Ned didn't come near the parade of shops when she was likely to be about. As far as Evie was concerned, the fewer people who saw them together the better.

What she liked about him was that he seemed so happy; so contented with everything and everybody. He spoke of his family with affection and said: 'You must come home with me and meet them.'

One afternoon, he took her and Herbie to the Collinses' house, at the bottom of Jackson Street. It was within easy walking distance of the pharmacy but Evie had never been in that direction before. Father said that that area, caught between the gasworks and the railway lines, was a slum. He had lots of customers who lived there and he thought them a feckless lot. He said it was a dangerous and dirty place, and it was not safe for her to venture there.

Now, as Ned wheeled Herbie's carriage through the forbidden streets, she felt some trepidation. She always did when she disobeyed Father. It was the poorest part of town and the sight of heavy industry crowding close made it dreary. Ned's home was a two-up and two-down, and the front door stood open though it was a coolish day.

Evie tried not to look at the curtains, which were grey and torn.

His mother came out to meet them. She was short and stout and shapeless. Evie put out her hand, but she was gathered up in plump arms and kissed.

'Our Ned's so proud of you,' chortled Mrs Collins. 'Come on in.'

Evie was shocked to find how ramshackle their home was, and how poorly furnished. She tried not to notice the dust and the cobwebs. Aunt Agatha would have considered it in need of a good spring-clean. She would have said much the same of Gertie Collins: that a hot bath and some clean clothes would not go amiss. Gertie's hair may have been grey and lank with grease, but Evie felt the warmth of her welcome.

Gertie flung her bulk down on a sagging horsehair sofa and pulled Evie down beside her. Within seconds her hand was being cradled between two that were roughened by hard work. Evie saw it as a gesture of affection and support.

'Five lads I've got,' she had a hoarse, throaty chuckle, 'and Ned's the best of the lot. He'll make a good husband – not let you down.' That made Evie's heart beat faster. Ned had not mentioned marriage yet.

'I've gone through three husbands myself. A widow three times over. Would you believe such bad luck? Hope things are different for you, love.'

Ned made the tea, and with it Evie was offered cakes and biscuits of a standard considered luxurious and not to be indulged in at home. When later she told Ned this, he smiled.

'They're treats for us. Mam made an effort because she knew you were coming. She thinks you're posh, daughter of the apothecary.'

'She won't say anything to Father? When she comes to the shop?'

'I've warned her not to. And I've warned my brothers. They've promised to be careful. Not that they've been into the shop for ages. I've been getting what they want for them.'

Evie knew her father saw the Collinses as a rough lot. Even she thought Ned's brothers somewhat uncouth. Gertie made no secret of the fact they spent Saturday night at the local pub and usually brought a skinful home. But Ned was very different.

Evie knew that what she was doing was dangerous, that her father would be furious if he found out. Even more dangerous was the way she threw her arms round Ned and lifted her face to his. He was a passionate man who wanted more and more of her love and persuaded her to give it in the bushes in the park. But soon what they had wasn't enough for either of them. By Christmas, Ned was saying:

'I want to tell everybody you're my girl. I'm proud of you. I don't like this hole-in-the-corner business and I can't see enough of you. I want you to tell your father. Make it all above-board.'

'I can't!' Evie covered her face with her hands.

'But we can't make any progress unless you do. We can't change this.'

'You don't understand, he'll forbid me to see you. Then it'll be harder. He'll be watching me like a hawk.'

Ned laughed. 'He couldn't watch you more closely than he does already. Shall I come to the shop and tell him? Do it together, I mean.'

Evie's heart lurched at the thought, but she was also afraid that sooner or later somebody would see them together and tell Joseph. After all, Ned wanted to hold her arm as they walked down Conway Street. Sometimes he held her hand. To Evie, it felt like a time bomb ticking away. There were times when she felt sick with fear.

Spring came and the evenings grew lighter. There were more people about in the park when they went there on Sunday evenings. She knew that to be seen there alone with a man was a terrible risk. There were several thick shrubberies and Ned drew her deeper inside one or other of them, away from prying eyes. He also carried a macintosh to spread on the ground to protect their clothes. Evie grew more anxious. The risks she was taking seemed enormous.

'It's love I'm showing you,' he tried to explain. 'It's how I feel about you.'

'It's forbidden,' Evie breathed.

'It needn't be,' he insisted. 'Marry me, then it'll be the most normal thing in the world. Will you?'

Evie was in seventh heaven. Of course it was what she'd hoped for. Marriage followed courtship like night follows day, but for her, it seemed a huge and impossible step.

'Why not, Evie?' She could see Ned's love for her shining in his eyes. 'I love you and you say you love me.'

She smiled. 'You know I do.'

'All right then?'

She nodded, swept away by the thought of living openly with him, of being his wife. Nothing would give her greater pleasure. Ned's arms were crushing her against his strong, firm body. He was laughing with delight too.

'We'll do it. We'll get married as soon as we can.' Holding her close, he started making plans.

'We must look for rooms of our own. Won't be able to afford much to start with.'

Evie didn't care. Not even if the rooms were near his home.

He laughed again, excited at the prospect. 'But we'll manage. I've a bit put by. You won't be able to put off telling your father any longer.'

That came like a douche of cold water, but Evie knew Ned was right. She was seventeen, almost eighteen, but would still need her father's permission to marry. It was a sobering thought. She came down to earth with a bump.

'He won't allow it, I know he won't.'

'You'll have to ask him, Evie. Tell him about me. There's no way round that. Otherwise things have to stay as they are.'

She knew Ned had been growing restive because she'd been dragging her feet about this. For herself, she was being pulled both ways. Though she dreaded telling Father, she wanted to escape from the pharmacy, and even more, she wanted to marry Ned.

She made up her mind. 'I'll do it.'

'Do you want me to be there with you?'

She shook her head, afraid that the sight of Ned would infuriate Joseph before they had a chance to say anything.

'I'll have to choose the right moment. Wait until he's in a good mood.'

'Is he ever?'

'Well – he's not always in a bad one.' She knew she'd have to screw up her nerve to do it.

As she waited for the right moment, Evie went about her duties in the drug run feeling very much on edge. Both she and Bertie were improving with practice but it wasn't easy.

She rehearsed the words she would say to her father. She watched him, seeking some sign that he was in a better mood than usual.

The shop closed every night between seven and eight.

Last summer, it had often stayed open until ten, but Bertie wasn't considered competent to work alone. This meant that usually she had two hours alone with Father before bedtime.

After supper, Matilda always soaked her feet in a bowl of hot water, then climbed slowly and painfully up the steep stairs to her room in the attic. Evie sat on with her father, one each side of the empty grate in the austere sitting room directly over the shop. It was furnished with heavy Victorian furniture but there were no ornaments. Her father didn't care for ornamentation. She would watch him read, deep in his book, slowly turning the pages.

Every evening at supper, she'd will herself to do it that night, but the words remained unspoken. She couldn't find the courage.

Then came the day Evie had dreaded. She was walking back from the park with Ned. He was helping her push Herbie's baby carriage and his hand covered hers on the handle. He was laughing down at her, as he often did, when she caught sight of May Smart, wife of the barber who kept the shop further along the parade.

Evie pulled herself away but she knew it was too late. Mrs Smart had seen how things were between them. What made it worse was that she attended the same church – did the flowers there, in fact. Evie knew she'd have to tell her father now. He'd be even angrier if he heard it first from Mrs Smart.

'I'll come in with you now,' Ned said, squeezing her hand sympathetically. 'Get it over with.'

'No,' Evie quaked. 'Bertie will be there, and Miss Lister, and goodness knows how many customers. I couldn't, not in front of them. After supper is the best time. When I'm alone with him.'

'Promise?' He kissed her in the street then. If Mrs

# A LIVERPOOL LULLABY

Smart had seen that, it would surely have sent her straight round to the pharmacy. 'Promise you'll do it before my next days off?'

Evie had promised. But that evening her father had gone out after supper. She'd had to put it off the next day because he was in one of his moods. And all the time she dreaded seeing Mrs Smart come into the shop.

Time was going on, Ned's days off on Thursday and Friday were coming closer. She told herself she had to do it. She thought enviously of his lot, sailing backwards and forwards to the Isle of Man with no worries of his own.

By Wednesday, she felt she could delay no longer. But Bertha Lee had sent a message to say she was sick and had not turned up for work. That had made Joseph cross because Evie had had to take Bertha's place on the front counter. Then he had been made even more irritable when a customer said she couldn't afford the one and sixpence he wanted to charge for a prescription.

Even worse, just before they closed for dinner, Evie saw Mrs Smart come into the shop. She walked past to the drug run to consult her father. Evie didn't know where to put herself. She felt paralysed. Every second, she expected to hear him roar out her name.

A few minutes later, Mrs Smart was leaning against the front counter, smiling at her. 'I'll take a pot of cold cream, if you please.'

Evie's legs felt like lead. Had she by some miracle survived? When she turned back to the counter with it, Mrs Smart said:

'How fast you've grown up, Evie. It seems no time at all since you were a little girl; now I see you walking out with a young man.'

That took her breath away. Had Father heard? Certainly Miss Lister had. Evie's mouth was dry with panic. She

63

must do it today! It would be a disaster if Father heard about Ned through a third person.

She was shaking when she sat down at the dinner table. She realised he'd not heard Mrs Smart, when he prodded his piece of fried fish and said affably:

'Nice bit of cod, Matilda.'

Evie felt heartened. He was in a good mood. Bertie and Matilda got up from the table as soon as possible – they always did. Her father sat on over a second cup of tea as usual. This was the moment. Evie closed her eyes and took a deep breath.

'Father,' she said. 'There's something I want to tell you.'

She found his cold grey eyes searching her face. 'What?'

'I want to get married.'

His cup crashed down on his saucer. She could see he was astounded. He ran his fingers through the steel-grey bristles on his head.

'Who to?' It was a bark of rage.

'Ned Collins.'

'Don't be silly! You can't possibly marry him!' He was glaring at her. 'You haven't been seeing him? Meeting him behind my back?'

Evie swallowed. She couldn't deny that.

'You fool!' Her father's face was savage, the line of his chin hardened. 'You've got yourself involved with one of those awful Collins boys?'

'I want to marry Ned.'

'I've never heard of anything so ridiculous. Absolutely not. He's quite unsuitable and you're only seventeen. Plenty of time for you to think about marriage when you're older. Much better that you learn something about dispensing first. I need you to help me.'

Evie could feel her heart pounding. She was stiff with tension.

Joseph flared up anew. 'When has all this been going on? Not while you've been taking out that baby from next door?'

Evie couldn't answer. There was no need to. It was the only time she wasn't in the shop.

'What are you thinking of?'

'I love him.'

'Nonsense! You don't know what you're talking about. Love, indeed! You'll not take that child out again.' His grey eyes glowered at her.

'I trusted you. I should have had more sense. Picking up men in the park when you've got babies with you. I'm disgusted with you, Evie. You've let me down. Going behind my back like this.'

'Father, please listen . . .'

'You'll not do it again. I'm going straight round to tell Polly Darty she can find herself another baby-minder. I'll put a stop to you carrying on with Ned Collins. I ought to tan your hide for you.'

He leapt up from the table and stamped downstairs. She heard the pharmacy door being unlocked and the shop bell clanging furiously as he went out.

Evie couldn't move. Mrs Darty would be expecting her to pick up Herbie in five minutes. Not to take him out seemed a terrible privation, but even worse, she'd not be allowed to see Ned again.

Minutes later, her father came racing back upstairs. He'd worked himself up into an even greater rage.

'You're too young to be walking out with men. Alone too. I wouldn't trust a fellow like Ned Collins.'

He came closer. Evie couldn't look at his face. She'd never seen it so twisted with anger.

He grabbed at the collar of her dress, screwing up the material, tightening it until it half choked her.

'Father . . . stop . . .'

'I told you to stay away from the likes of him, and you didn't.' He twisted the collar tighter until she could no longer breathe. The room was turning black and beginning to spin round her. Just when she felt she was passing out, he gave her a quick push backwards. Coughing and gasping for breath, Evie fell against a chair.

'You're just like your mother! Heading down the primrose path. It leads to hell, Evie. You saw what she was like when she came back. D'you want to end up like her?'

Evie's eyes were stinging. She could feel the tears on her cheeks. She'd expected him to fly into a rage, but this was awful, worse than she'd feared. His anger was boiling over, and how was she to meet Ned now?

'You'll stay where I can keep an eye on you after this. Those Collins boys are wild. You must know their reputation. It isn't safe for you to be alone with men like that.'

She was shaking. Her father was coming close again. She gulped for air, trying to fill her lungs, trying to be prepared this time.

'He hasn't touched you, has he?' His face was within three inches of her own. Dark with suspicion. 'Has he?' he bellowed.

'No, Father,' she choked. 'No.'

She had to tell that lie. She was terrified. A moment ago she'd really thought he meant to finish her. Her head still swam, she could still see black spots before her eyes. What would he do to her if she admitted the truth?

Evie didn't know how she got through the rest of the day. She had great red weals on her neck, and her throat was too sore to speak. She didn't know why she'd gone to such lengths to tell Father in private, because the staff all knew before teatime. He kept coming to the front counter to have another go at her, making no secret of it. Miss Lister patted her shoulder, Matty gave her a hug and Bertie offered her a humbug to console her.

'We thought he was going to kill you,' he said.

All evening, her father had kept on at her. She'd been glad to go to bed to get away from him. But sleep was impossible. When she did doze off at last, she had a nightmare. She could feel his fingers on her throat, throttling her again.

He was in a worse mood by breakfast and she had a thumping headache. In the shop, she hardly dared speak to the staff, in case he thought she was discussing her difficulties with them, and her hoarse voice riled him further. She was frightened and she could see no way out.

Her only comfort was to think of Ned. He'd be home now and expecting to see her with Herbie at two o'clock. The morning seemed interminable. Dinner was eaten in stony silence, with Bertie shooting sympathetic glances in her direction.

Then, instead of going out to meet Ned, she had to go back down to the shop. She watched the hands of the clock creep on. By now, Ned would be waiting for her to turn into Conway Street. Another fifteen minutes dragged by and he'd know that she wasn't coming.

She served a middle-aged lady a thick pink hairnet to sleep in. Sold some soap to another, Vaseline to a third. This time of the afternoon was never busy. She could hear her father in the drug run, clearing his throat and turning the pages of his newspaper with quick, angry movements. There wasn't a lot for him to do either.

The doorbell pinged. Evie went cold when she looked up and found that Ned had come in.

'Are you all right, Evie?'

She was nodding, unable to find words. Conscious that everything they said could be heard by her father. Her heart was pounding as, in the mirror, she saw Joseph come to the end of the drug run.

'I thought it was you I could hear,' he said. 'Get out, I don't want you anywhere near my daughter.'

'Mr Hobson,' Ned took off his cap politely and drew himself up to his full five foot ten, 'I need to speak to you, please hear me out. I want . . .'

'I know what you want. I've already told Evie she's to have no truck with you. Going behind my back, that's what you've been doing. I'll not even think of letting her marry the likes of you.'

Evie could see the colour running up Ned's cheeks, the look of stunned shock spreading across his face. She'd tried to tell him this might happen, but he'd said there was no other way, she had to ask her father's permission.

Ned tried again: 'Mr Hobson, I'll take great care of Evie. I've got a job, I can afford to keep a wife. I love her, I promise . . .'

'Get out of my shop and stay away from my daughter. Do you hear? That's my last word.'

'Father, please . . .' she began.

Joseph Hobson advanced on Ned menacingly.

'All right, Mr Hobson, I'll go. I don't want to make any trouble.'

The look Ned gave Evie was anguished, but he managed a smile and a wink before he went.

# CHAPTER FIVE

Evie wished she hadn't opened her mouth. She should have kept her secret and the pleasure it brought. To lose Ned was to lose everything; she was left feeling sick with disappointment. She'd known what the likely outcome was and should never have let Ned persuade her otherwise. Now she felt like a prisoner. The only time Father wasn't at her side was when she went to Sunday school.

A week went by, the weals on her neck faded and her voice lost its hoarse note, but her nightmares continued and she felt shivers run down her spine each time Father turned on her in anger.

Then Bertha Lee sent word that she was not returning to work. She'd found another job.

'Good luck to her,' Bertie whispered. 'She's not bound to him like I am.'

Joseph was furious. There was no talking to him for days and they were short-handed in the shop. He said he might take another apprentice. She tried to look on the bright side. Another apprentice would mean she'd be back working on the front counter.

She missed Ned terribly but knew there would still be Sundays when they might be able to meet. It could take him a long time to arrange, because for the crew, a Sunday off was a popular option. Ned's turn didn't often come round, especially in summer, when a day out to the Isle of Man was within the pocket of many Merseysiders who could not afford a real holiday.

During the morning, Evie noticed a barefoot urchin

hanging back from the front counter when it was his turn to be served. She sold some razor blades to an elderly man and some Macassar hair oil to another. Her father's voice rose and fell behind her, exacting information from a customer suffering from aching varicose veins.

When Joseph turned back to the drug run to make up some ointment, the urchin crept up and said: 'Please, miss, can I have a halfpenny liquorice stick?'

His coin came across the counter with a note folded beneath it. Evie felt the blood rush to her cheeks as she read her name on it. She felt flustered with guilt and fear, and pushed it deep into her pocket before ringing up the till. The urchin was out of the shop in a flash.

Evie fingered the note all morning, knowing that it must be from Ned. It brought relief and happiness that he hadn't given up on her.

When dinnertime came, Joseph locked up the shop and led Evie and Bertie upstairs to the dining room. As a matter of habit he hung the keys on a keyboard at the top of the stairs.

Evie and Bertie had to pause for a moment behind him while he did this. They were close to the three framed photographs that hung alongside the keyboard. Joseph was pictured with his narrow chest bare, wearing tight leg-hugging breeches and looking incredibly young. In the first picture, he was holding up his Indian clubs. In the second, he was lifting heavy weights.

Joseph noticed Bertie studying the photographs and said: 'Exercise like that puts a man in control of his body, builds him up, allows him to do things he wouldn't otherwise be capable of doing.'

Evie understood that he kept these pastimes up. She heard him using the Indian clubs in his room sometimes, and she'd seen his weights there.

In the third picture, his face was clenched with determination and his bare fists were held up in a pugilistic stance.

'Were you a boxer, sir?' Bertie asked.

'In my youth.'

'What does it say?' In the gloom of the landing, Bertie was squinting at the lettering underneath. 'You won a title?'

'I won the regional lightweight title in 1881 and kept it for two years. Whatever I do, Mr Pugh, I aim to succeed at. I should have gone on, tried for a national title.'

'Rather a shame to give it up when you were winning.' There was a note of respect in Bertie's voice now. 'Why did you?'

'I was being pulled both ways. As a boxer I was punching to hurt, to cause cuts and bruises. It takes a certain attitude to go in the ring to win.'

'The killer instinct?'

Evie saw her father flinch. His grey eyes shone nervously. 'Perhaps. And in my work I was trying to heal human sicknesses and traumas.'

'You didn't want to inflict pain on others?'

'I was frightened of doing so. I was too good at boxing.'

As soon as dinner was over Evie ran upstairs to her bedroom, where she was safe from prying eyes. Her fingers were shaking as she opened the note.

My dearest Evie,

My next days off are Sunday and Monday the week after next. I'll see you in church at morning service. Give me a nod if you're still going alone to Sunday school. If so, I'll meet you in Conway Street at ten minutes to two.

Your father is a tyrant. Don't let him split us up. I couldn't bear it. I'm not giving up hope, you mustn't either. Run away from him, if that's the only way. I could rent a room for you, just say the word and I'll start looking. I'll look after you. I do love you. Always will.

Your ever-loving Ned.

The note gave Evie a feeling of warmth and support on one hand, but misgivings too. She loved Ned. All her instincts told her to trust him. What frightened her was that she would have to do what her mother had done.

The thought of being with Ned was heaven. To take a few of her things and walk out would not be impossible. She could leave Father a note saying she was sorry it had to be this way.

But the thought of doing it brought shivers of terror. What would Father do to her if something went wrong? If, after all, she didn't manage to get away? She decided to put off making any decision until she'd spoken to Ned again. She wanted to talk it through.

Evie was counting the days to that. At times it seemed Sunday would never come. When it did, it was a dark, overcast morning. She felt very much on edge as she walked to church with her father. She saw Ned immediately they went inside, his eager face telling her how pleased he was to see her again. He was not a member of the congregation and to see him there scared her. Father counted the Collinses as Irish, and everybody expected them to be Catholics.

Ned moved to another pew so that Joseph would not be sitting between them; so that she could look at him without turning too noticeably. She conveyed that she'd be able to meet him that afternoon. She could feel his eyes on her.

That brought little frissons of anxiety, she was so afraid Father might notice and demand to know what Ned was doing here. She was relieved when the service was over.

Then, as the vicar shook hands with his departing congregation at the door, causing a hold-up in the aisles, Father had time to talk to an acquaintance, a regular customer by the name of George Parry. Evie heard them discussing a book on church history and Mr Parry offered to lend it to Father.

'Will you be at evensong tonight?' he asked. 'I could bring it for you then.'

Evie froze in consternation.

Joseph hesitated. 'I don't usually come twice, but Evie always does. Perhaps you'd entrust it to her?'

Mr Parry's eyes met hers. 'Of course. I'll look out for you, Miss Hobson.'

Evie felt her spirits plummet. That meant she'd have to come to church. Her father would know if she didn't. Today of all days, when Ned was home. She turned to look for him. He was still near though the crowd was thinning. At the door, he mouthed the words 'Ten to two,' and walked away jauntily with his hands in his pockets.

By the time dinner was on the table, rain was coming down in torrents. The weather was so bad that Father actually suggested she might prefer to miss Sunday school.

'No sense in going out in this. And I'll come to church with you this evening. Collect that book Mr Parry promised me.'

That blighted Evie's expectations still further. It would deprive her of Ned's company on the walk there and back. Her stomach was churning with fear. She had to see him this afternoon.

She made herself say brightly: 'I'd like to go to Sunday school. This rain's too heavy to last.' Nothing must stop her going now. It would be her only chance to talk to Ned.

She put on her macintosh and borrowed Father's large umbrella. As she closed the pharmacy door and stepped out in the rain she was fizzing with anticipation. Ned was waiting for her. He held her arm tightly, hugging it to him.

'Where can I take you? We must get out of this rain or we'll be soaked.' His brown eyes were not laughing down at her as they usually did. He was in a sober and determined mood.

'A tram ride? That's it, a tram ride. Where would you like to go?'

'Anywhere.'

'You're shaking, Evie. I can feel you.'

'It's just the tension. Going behind Father's back. Coming to meet you and hiding it from him.'

His hand tightened on her arm. 'I brought trouble down on your head, didn't I? Asking you to tell him about me.'

'I thought he was going to kill me.' She told Ned how Joseph had twisted her collar until she'd nearly choked.

'I'm sorry. I knew he was strict. Harsh too, but I didn't think he'd treat you like that. Why?'

'He doesn't want me to leave home. Not ever. He has his plans for me – and everyone else in his little empire. None of us are allowed any choice.'

'It's power?'

'He wants to control us all, but particularly me.'

'You'll be a nervous wreck if you stay with him.'

'Sometimes I think I already am.'

'No. You haven't let him stop you so far. You've been doing what you want. You've still got the guts to get away from him.'

'I wish I was stronger. He's wearing me down.'

'He'd wear anyone down if they had to live and work with him.'

They got on the first tram that came along. It was going to the terminus at New Ferry. Ned sat close against her on the hard, narrow seat, holding her hand while the rain lashed against the windows.

'How am I going to get away?' Evie wanted to discuss all the possibilities sensibly. 'Father won't change his mind. He never does, once it's made up.'

'Do you want to wait?'

'What for?'

'Till you're twenty-one? I won't change my mind. Would you wait that long for me?'

'If I had to. But Father still wouldn't give his permission.'

'He wouldn't have to.'

'He won't accept you. Never will.' Evie tried to explain. 'I'd still have to run away from home.'

'I'll look after you if you do. I promise. We'll be married.'

'How?'

'We'll go to Gretna Green. I've heard it's possible.'

'We won't have that sort of money to spare, Ned.' She was trying to be practical. 'Not to go travelling round. All the way to Scotland.'

'Then we'll have to pretend you're already twenty-one. We'll get married somehow. Just walk out, Evie.'

'It's what my mother did,' she said with a shiver. 'I feel I'm following in her footsteps.'

When the tram reached the terminus, they stayed up on the top deck and then rode back to Woodside. The rain had eased a little but it was a cold, damp afternoon.

Ned took her arm and led her into Woodside Station, where they could stay under cover. They watched the London train arrive. Evie was keeping an eye on the station clock. Sunday school lasted only an hour. Add half an hour to walk both ways and perhaps another ten minutes could be spent chatting outside. She couldn't afford to be away from home much longer. The time was flying now she was with Ned.

'We won't be able to do this again tonight.' She told him that her father would be coming with her to church again, that it would be impossible. Ned walked her back towards Argyle Street but she was afraid to take him near the shop.

'Not a happy outing for you.' Ned was miserable when the time came to say goodbye. He kissed her cheek. It always made Evie uneasy that he kissed her so readily in the street. Anybody could be watching.

'Not happy for you either.'

'I'm always happy when I'm with you, you know that. I'll come to church tonight, just to see you.'

'No, Ned. We won't be able to say one word, and I'm afraid Father'll notice you and guess why you're there.'

'But I want to be with you. I love you. And I've no idea when I'll be able to get another Sunday off. Can't I see you tomorrow?'

Evie shook her head sadly.

'You still fetch your bread from Darty's?'

'Yes.'

'What time? I can be there.'

'I can't say. It depends on the shop, how busy we are.'

'Eleven o'clock?'

'I don't know. I'll try, but I won't be able to stay more than five minutes.'

'Even five minutes.' His soft brown eyes smiled down at her. 'It's better than nothing. I'll leave a message with Polly. About when I'll be home again. If you want to get in touch with me, she'll let me know.'

'Yes,' Evie agreed sadly. 'I'll have to go.'

Sitting at the tea table between Matilda and her father later that afternoon, Evie knew she'd settled nothing.

Either she had to stay here with Father, or she had to run away as her mother had done. The circumstances were different, of course, but she'd still be running away with the man she loved. Things could turn out as badly for her as they had done for her mother. She could slide down the primrose path to hell as Father had predicted. If she went, she could live to regret it. It made her flesh crawl with fear, but it was what she wanted to do.

She was going to have to pull herself together. Fight this panic and not let him dominate her. But all their church acquaintances and most of the customers would side with Father on this. It was very wrong for a girl like her to go against her father's wishes.

She managed to go for the bread at eleven the next morning and found that Ned had been waiting for her for some time. Polly was kind enough to push them into the living room behind the shop, where Herbie was asleep in his cot. They had ten minutes alone but for Evie Ned's kisses settled nothing.

Over the following days, there were times when Evie felt confident about going. She started to make preparations, sorting through her belongings to decide what to take with her. Then, at others, she thought of her mother's half-starved body and was terrified she'd suffer the same fate. The pros and cons went round in her mind until she felt quite unable to decide one way or the other.

Evie tried to keep her mind on Ned, but when she closed her eyes to sleep it was often her mother's ill and frightened face that came before her. She knew Father hadn't forgotten Helen either.

'You take after your mother,' he told Evie, his hawk-nose quivering with distaste.

Although Evie understood well enough that he wasn't

referring to her looks, she said: 'I've always known I must look like her. After all, I don't take after you.'

She was grateful not to have inherited his big nose. Hers was small and straight. Her nearly black hair, fair skin and dark-blue eyes didn't come from him either.

'Don't pretend you don't know what I mean! You've inherited her weak character. I should have expected trouble from you. Men were her undoing. She was easily led astray. You're already on that downward path. If you're not careful you'll end up the same way.'

Evie knew now that he was trying to keep something hidden from her, and that it must be important to him. She couldn't ask Matty again, for she'd already made enough trouble for her, and nobody in the shop had been here all those years ago.

Her father advertised that he had a place for another apprentice, and a tall, thin youth with glasses came by appointment to see him. Joseph told Evie that he thought Arthur Mitchell seemed keen, and that he'd be starting next week. That evening, he told Matilda to prepare a bedroom for the new apprentice.

Evie went to help her turn out the room Johnny Simms had used. Apart from that one and Matilda's, there were two other attic rooms up here, that were used to store household odds and ends. Evie had been wanting to have a good look through them for some time. To see if she could find her mother's belongings, particularly the grey canvas bag she'd seen her bring with her.

She helped Matilda make up the bed and sweep the floor. Then she went down to get some polish and a duster and saw that her father was reading in the living room. It seemed a good moment to make her search. She had a reason to be up on that floor.

The attic rooms were dusty and airless. She found

several boxes and an old cabin trunk full of clothes. She thought they might have belonged to her mother but she wasn't sure, and they didn't tell her what she wanted to know. Then she came across a wedding gown of white satin, packed carefully in a large box. Fingering the smooth cloth brought such a rush of emotion that she couldn't go on. She felt sure the dress must have been her mother's. Of the grey bag, there was no sign.

For the rest of the evening she could feel herself trembling inside. She was turning into a devious witch of a girl. Not a nice person at all. Going behind Father's back like this. But what else could she do, other than let him rule her life and dominate her totally?

The next day when she went for the bread and found the Darty bakery empty of customers, she asked Polly if she'd known her mother.

'No. Eleven years ago? I wasn't married then. It's only nine since we bought this business, but . . .' Polly's dark eyes darted towards the door.

'You do know something?' Evie said. 'Why did she suddenly leave home?'

'Only what Matty told me.'

'She talked to you? When? What did she say?' Evie leaned eagerly over the counter.

'She used to come in every day for the bread and a bit of a gossip. Well, who else did she have to talk to but a child? She'd stop for a natter at the butcher's and at the grocer's as well, and why not?

'Anyway, this day she happened to say you were still fretting for your mother, so I asked about her. I heard somebody else say there was something of a scandal at the time.'

'What d'you mean? What sort of a scandal?'

'Well, bigamy is what she said.' Polly put a hand in

front of her mouth to make sure the dreadful word went no further.

'My father? Committed bigamy? No!' Evie couldn't see him doing any such thing.

'No, your mother.'

Evie straightened up in disbelief. 'That's just gossip.'

'Well, I don't know. It's what Matty said. Then she really let her hair down and started going on about Agatha and all the other things that were happening at the time.

'It was a hot day and the shop door was propped open to let some air in. Your father was in with us before we saw him. He was dancing with rage, blue in the face with it. You know how he flares up.

' "I've caught you at it, Matilda. How many times have I got to tell you I won't have you spreading gossip about me? You deserve to be sacked for this. And you, Polly Darty, have a wagging tongue. Nosy parkers all of you."

'He glared round my shop. Jean from the barber's was here, and Connie from the paper shop.

' "I've enough trouble without you adding to it and spreading lies round the neighbourhood. I'll not have it, do you hear?

' "There's all sorts of rumours going round about me. I hear some of them, you know. That I've thrown my wife out, that she's run off with another man and all the takings from the business. All lies, as you very well know. You can all mind your own business, or I'll withdraw my trade."

'Well, Evie, you know how it is in trade. You must never insult a customer, never risk losing business. He put the fear of God into all of us, I can tell you. The women couldn't get out of my shop fast enough.'

'Polly, who would remember my mother? Connie and Jean, who were they?'

Polly was shaking her head. 'The butcher's has changed

hands and the paper shop too. It's a long time. The barber now, his father was running the shop then, but May Smart might be able to tell you more. She might have heard about it from her mother-in-law, though she won't be able to ask her now because she died last year.'

Evie was disappointed. The Smarts were on good terms with her father. He had his hair cut there; they met at church. She didn't think she'd dare ask Mrs Smart.

Polly rattled on: 'Matty always stood facing the shop door after that. She wasn't going to get caught again. Your dad told her she was to buy what was needed and come straight back. She wasn't to waste time gossiping. Matty said he timed her. She was scared of him, well, we all were. He can turn nasty in an instant.'

The first morning she felt sick, Evie put it down to the rich pork she'd eaten hot for lunch the day before and then again cold for supper. She said as much to her father, who prescribed Smith's tasteless dandelion anti-bilious pills. She'd heard him recommend them many times for queasy stomachs.

But when the following morning she awoke to the same feeling of nausea, and had in addition a feeling of heaviness in her breasts, she was overcome with terror. She'd heard the symptoms described to her father too many times to be in any doubt as to what they signified. She pulled the blankets over her head and stayed stiff with tension on her bed.

What wouldn't she give to have the dull future she'd foreseen. Nothing but work – it now seemed a luxury. Her fate was to be very much worse. She longed to lie still in bed and fight the nausea, but she dared not. Nor must she show any sign that might alert her father to her trouble.

She wished she'd not been so foolish as to ask him for the dandelion pills yesterday, though they had helped. She forced herself to sit at the breakfast table and eat bacon. Even look as though she was enjoying it.

With all the upset about her mother and the worry about asking Father's permission, she'd overlooked what should have happened. As soon as she went down to the shop, she consulted the calendar hanging in the drug run. Her dates had passed unnoticed. Evie felt a hot flush run up her cheeks. Father would kill her when he found out. What was she to do? She had palpitations every time she thought of it. She was sweating in panic, wanting to retch, but she dared not do other than act as she usually did. She helped herself to some more dandelion pills when nobody was looking.

This was another secret she had to keep from her father. She'd have to get in touch with Ned and then do what her mother had done. Now she had no choice.

That night in her bedroom, Evie wrote to Ned. She couldn't stop the anguish she felt from pouring out on the paper. She sealed it up carefully in an envelope and put it in her pocket. Next morning, when Matty asked her to run next door for a loaf, she hung around outside the baker's shop until there were no other customers, then gave her letter to Polly Darty.

'Will you hand this to Ned, please? Next time he comes in? It may not be for a while, he'll not have a day off until next week. You'll not forget?'

'He'll ask, Evie. I'll put it under the counter for him. He popped in last night on his way home. Bought some lardy cakes for his mother.'

Evie wished she'd brought the letter last night. She wanted him to know, wanted him to do something to help her. Goodness knows when he'd call in again. She felt desperate.

'Have you found somebody else to take Herbie out?'

'Yes, Gladys Pool wanted to do it. She seemed quite keen but she didn't turn up on Monday. Said she wasn't well. And she's never here on time. Can't rely on her in the way I could on you. I don't suppose your dad will relent?'

'Not a hope,' Evie sighed.

She went out into the sunlight. It seemed such a long time since she'd been out. She walked a few yards up the parade, wishing she could go further. From the placards outside the newsagent's, she saw that Birkenhead was arranging a big event in the park to celebrate the coronation of King George V and Queen Mary of Tek. There were to be massed children's choirs and a military brass band. Evie sighed again. She didn't feel in the mood for a celebration. And she had to go back to the shop or she'd be in more trouble.

As she folded paper round individual doses of her father's herbal cures, she tried to work out how she could take her belongings with her when she ran away.

Behind the shop was a cramped kitchen and a small store room. The staff lavatory was outside in the back yard. From the yard there was access to an entry, though the door was always kept locked for security reasons.

The store room was full of the winchesters, jars and wooden packing cases in which their stock arrived. Her father's herbs and poisons usually went straight into the drug run. Evie often worked here with Bertie, decanting the lotions from the winchesters into small phials and scooping ointment from the big jars to fill the one-ounce pots in which it was sold.

She found a few bars of scented soap remaining at the

bottom of a large wooden box. She made space for them in the display case on the front counter and pushed the box to the back of the room, well away from the other empties, which were stacked together. All their jars, boxes and crates were returned to the factories when empty, but Evie wanted to keep this one. She thought she could bring her things down a few at a time and pack them into it.

She dared not start too soon, in case they were discovered. Father took an active interest in every part of his business, including the store, even though Miss Lister was nominally in charge of that.

Evie decided to wait until she had some word from Ned. In the meantime, she sorted through her things in her room. There were no other preparations she could make.

Early the next morning, in the drug run, she was trying to hide her sickness and growing apprehension. Her father, opening the post, exclaimed with pleasure.

'I've been invited to the coronation celebrations in the park. As an official guest.'

'You're a prominent citizen, Mr Hobson,' a waiting customer told him. 'So you should be.'

'You're invited too, Evie.' Joseph passed the embossed card to her. She read that seats would be reserved for Mr Joseph P. Hobson and guest.

'I hear it's to be a big gala,' Bertie said. 'There'll be a tug-of-war for the men.'

'And a country-dancing display by schoolchildren,' Miss Lister added. 'You'll enjoy it.'

'I shall,' Evie said with as much enthusiasm as she could muster. The coronation was to be on 10 June, almost two weeks off. She hoped to be away before then.

# CHAPTER SIX

When Evie went to get the bread that day, Polly Darty beamed across the counter at her.

'Ned called in last night and I gave him your letter. He brought one back for you this morning.'

Evie flushed with relief. Ned understood she was in a hurry to get things settled. She pushed his letter into her pocket and swept out of the shop. She couldn't wait until dinnertime to read it. She walked to the end of the parade of shops, turned the corner and leaned against the wall. He'd had no envelope; instead, he'd stuck the page together with a dab of glue.

Dearest Evie,

I'm sorry I'm giving you more trouble. Truly sorry. We must get married now. We've got to talk about it. I'll be in the back entry behind your shop tonight between half nine and ten. Try to come out for five minutes to see me. If you can't, leave a note with Polly Darty about when the best time would be. I've got a day off next Thursday and then I'm having Coronation Day.

I'll look after you, Evie. Don't you worry yourself. Tell me if there's anything else you want me to do. I do love you.

Your loving Ned.

Evie was desperate to talk to him. She wondered if she'd be able to get out to the back entry without her father noticing. It all depended on whether he went down to work in the shop after it closed. Sometimes he did, to stock-take or make up his books.

She watched him all day. He and Bertie were not very busy. She hoped Joseph would be able to do all he needed in his books before closing time. The shop shut punctually at eight. They ate supper with Matilda. Father was still full of the invitation he'd received.

'I hear a special stand is to be erected for prominent people. The Mayor and Mayoress will be there, and all the managers from Laird's and Beaufort's. A good job you've got that blue dress after all. Perhaps you should get a new hat to go with it? I'll get a hansom to pick us up.'

'Or a car?' Evie suggested breathlessly. She couldn't imagine Father doing any such thing. He was far too austere in his habits. She helped clear the table, and while Matty was clattering dishes in the sink, she said:

'Ought we not to take Matilda with us, Father? She's hardly been out of the house for months. Her feet are too bad to walk far these days. But with a carriage to the door, she'd enjoy it.'

His voice was suddenly forbidding. 'It's not an occasion to which I'd want to take my servants, Evie. Anyway, she's not been invited.'

'Not to a seat in the stand, but she'd like to come to the park and see it all, I'm sure.'

'We won't be taking Matilda with us. Definitely not. In fact, I've been thinking lately that she's getting too old. Her cooking isn't what it was. Perhaps we should look for someone younger?'

Evie was shocked. 'But where could she go? She's lived with us for twenty years.'

'Twenty-four. She'd manage, they all do.'

Evie felt cold inside. He didn't care what happened to anybody. If he had no further use for their services, he was ready to cast them off.

'But she won't have saved much. Won't have been able to.'

'There are workhouses for those who don't save for their own needs.'

Evie shuddered. She was afraid Matty was already in dread of going to the workhouse. She could hear her filling a bowl with hot water to soak her feet before going upstairs to bed. She did it every night.

'Do you still prescribe something for her feet, Father?'

'It's arthritis and old age. Hot water alone eases the discomfort.'

'It's pain, not discomfort. Surely there's something more you can give her that would help?'

'A little camphorated oil rubbed into the joints, perhaps.'

'Can I get some for her, Father?'

She looked at the clock on the sideboard. It was ten minutes past nine. Too early, Ned would not be there yet.

'You're very concerned about Matilda all of a sudden. Camphorated oil will not turn the clock back. She's never going to walk like a forty-year-old again.' Joseph himself was just turned forty.

'I know that. But can I get some for her?'

'If you want to.' Father had lost interest. He moved to a more comfortable chair and opened his newspaper.

'I'll see if she'd like some. She's to rub it into the joints?'

'I've said so, haven't I?' Father was losing patience too.

Evie checked the clock, it was nearly quarter past. She went to the kitchen and talked to Matilda about camphorated oil.

'I've tried it,' she said. 'Your father gave me a bottle,

but nothing does me much good any more.'

'But it helps?' Evie wasn't going to give up. Not now she'd got Father's permission to go down to the shop.

'I suppose everything helps.'

Evie stood talking about the weather, what they would eat for dinner tomorrow, anything. The hands of the clock had never moved so slowly.

It was almost nine thirty. Father's eyes watched her as she crossed the landing from the kitchen. She knew he'd listened to all she'd said.

At the top of the stairs, Evie silently unhooked the keys she needed from the keyboard. Once down in the shop, she whipped a bottle of camphorated oil out of the glass case on the front counter, slipped it into her pocket and then went softly to the back door. She turned the key in the lock and crept up the yard. She'd brought the key to the yard door too.

The lock was stiff and she had trouble turning it. She hoped Father wouldn't look out of the window. It was still light enough for her to be seen. Ned was waiting in the entry, his face anxious. Evie was filled with relief to see him. She felt his arms come round her.

'Oh, Evie, I'm sorry.' He pulled her against him in a comforting hug. He was whispering, though there was no one within earshot. 'I blame myself. I should never have done it. You must let me be with you when you tell your father. I'll say it was all my fault.'

'He'll not let you say much of anything. You know what he's like. He'll throw you out of the shop as he did last time.'

She saw Ned stiffen. 'Better if I'm with you. I can't let you do this on your own.'

Evie shook her head. 'I can't tell him.' Hadn't Joseph twisted her collar until she'd nearly choked the day she'd first told him about Ned? He'd forbidden her to go near him and she'd continued to disobey. 'He'll half kill me. I'm afraid.'

She felt Ned pull her closer still. 'What will we do then?'

'I'll just walk out.'

'You'll come with me?'

'Yes.' She was going to do what her mother was said to have done. Run away with the man she loved. She found it hard to believe what Polly had told her, that her mother had committed bigamy. Surely not bigamy?

'We'll need to get married now.' Ned was lifting her chin so that she had to look at him. His eyes were gentle with love. 'You still need your father's permission for that. He'll give it when he knows about the baby. He'll be glad to.'

Evie knew he'd feel forced to now, but it would put him in a savage rage.

'Be it on your own head,' he'd say. 'What sort of a life do you think you'll have? You'd be a lot better off with me than you will with Ned Collins, I can guarantee that.'

'I can't tell him. I can't face him with it.'

'All right, love. Whatever you say. What do you have in mind?'

Evie quaked at her own daring. 'You said you'd rent a room for us.'

'When I got your letter last night I had a quick look round. There's two rooms in Henry Street. A front living room with front bedroom above. We'll have to share the kitchen and there's no real bathroom . . . Not like you're used to, I'm afraid.'

'It'll do for a start.' Evie tried to smile. At least Henry Street wasn't caught in that triangle of heavy industry where Ned lived now.

'I'll see about it tomorrow then. Fix it up. I'm thrilled

it's happening, Evie, you know that. I just wish it didn't have to be this hard for you.'

She told him about the wooden box in the store room and how she planned to fill it with things she wanted to bring with her.

'Is it big? Too big for me to carry?'

She nodded. 'You'll need something with wheels to move it.'

'Have you seen the cart we use to collect coke from the gasworks?'

'Yes, and it's just the thing, the box would fit across that. We could tie it on.'

'I can bring it round whenever you say the word.'

'I'll have to go back,' she worried. 'I don't want him to come down to the shop looking for me.'

'Coronation Day. It's my next day off. I'll fix up the rooms for then.'

'Father's been invited to the celebrations in the park. I'm to go with him. He's been given seats on the stand with the Mayor and Mayoress.'

'So the shop will be closed?'

'Yes, in the afternoon.'

'That's the best time, then,' Ned said quietly. 'I'll find you in the park.'

'There'll be a big crowd . . .'

'There won't be that many with seats on the stand. I'll find you. Just slip away and come to me.'

Evie was gripping his arm. 'There'll be speeches. Father won't be able to leave his seat once it starts. Not without making a show of himself.'

'We'll come straight back here, pick up your things and be away. It'll be a while before he realises you've gone for good.'

'Yes.' Evie felt excitement spiral through her. She was

very much on edge. 'But I can't stay any longer. Not now.'

Ned pulled her closer and kissed her. 'Till Coronation Day, then.'

She shot into the yard, closed and locked the door as quietly as she could and sped indoors, locking up behind her as she went. On the first floor she slid the keys back into their places. Father lifted his eyes from his book as she reached the living-room door. She knew he'd left it open to keep an eye on her. Her heart was hammering against her ribs. He must realise she'd been a long time.

To explain it, she held up the camphorated oil bottle she'd brought. 'Needed to fill more bottles.'

'I hope this isn't just an excuse to gossip with Matilda?'

Her knees felt weak with relief. 'No, Father. I won't be long.'

She ran up two more flights to the attic and knocked on Matty's door.

Matty was already in bed but had kept the candle alight. Evie insisted on removing her bed socks and rubbing the camphorated oil into her misshapen feet. Then she came down one flight and went to her own room.

Her heart still raced, she was too frightened to sleep. She tossed and turned well into the night. She hated being sly and going behind Father's back like this. She wasn't cunning by nature, and she wished she didn't have to do it. It filled her with guilt and made her feel like a criminal, but she could think of no other way. She couldn't stop herself shivering at the thought of what Father would do if he knew.

But he didn't know. He'd have come bounding after her if he'd noticed anything amiss. He might be watching her like a cat watches a mouse, but she'd made her arrangements with Ned.

*   *   *

Everybody was talking about the coronation. The papers had been full of the preparations in Westminster Abbey and descriptions of the gowns and robes that would be worn and the fashions that foreign royalty were wearing as they assembled in London.

Evie was counting the days until she could be with Ned. Each time she went down from her bedroom to the shop, she took something with her and hid it in the box in the store room. It was June, a year since she'd dropped his mother's cough mixture on the floor.

The new apprentice had started, and had taken Evie's place in the drug run. She preferred the front counter but she was counting the days she'd spend there. Only three more, then two, then one.

The day before Coronation Day, Polly Darty handed her another note from Ned, saying he'd taken rooms for them, and that he'd be waiting near the stand in the park.

Then the newsagent's placards were proclaiming that today was Coronation Day and had been declared a public holiday. Some shops didn't open at all and those that did were to close at midday.

Business was slow in the morning. Evie could feel the ball of excitement growing inside her. When she went to fetch the bread from Polly Darty just before dinner, she heard that every schoolchild in the land had received four shining halfpennies. They'd been told to keep and treasure them as a memento of this occasion for the rest of their lives.

Matty cooked roast beef and Yorkshire pudding, a dinner such as they usually had only on Sundays. Evie couldn't eat. Her nausea had gone by late morning but today there were butterflies in her stomach. She changed quickly into her blue dress, remade her bun and fastened her new straw hat on top. It was the prettiest hat she'd ever owned, fashionably large, with the crown covered in blue velvet flowers. As she went downstairs, she folded her best winter coat over her arm.

At the shop door she hesitated. 'Will I be warm enough without a coat?'

'You won't need it,' Joseph said impatiently. 'Come along, the hansom is waiting.'

It was what she'd been expecting. She ran back and tossed her coat over the banisters at the bottom of the stairs, then hurried out after him.

She was so used to seeing her father in his white coat that he seemed almost a stranger in his new silk top hat and morning coat. She looked across the bouncing haunches of the chestnut mare and knew that at any other time she'd have thought it a great treat to be riding in a carriage. Today she could think of nothing else but that soon she would be with Ned for good.

Evie knew every step of the way to the park, she'd walked it so many times with little Herbie. Today there was a procession of carriages going there. Crowds were trailing up the pavements on both sides of Conway Street, with barefoot children racing between more sedate members of the public.

Bunting stretched across all the main streets. Evie could hear it flapping in the blustery breeze. The sun sparkled down from a clear blue sky. As they approached the park, she could hear the military band playing. At the handsome gothic main gate, Father had to show his invitation before his hansom was allowed inside. They bowled along the main avenue towards the stand.

Evie was keeping a sharp look-out for Ned. She'd never seen the park so full of people, and was afraid that in the crush she'd never meet up with him. But she saw him with a wide smile on his face, waiting close to where guests were alighting from their carriages. He lifted his straw boater in greeting and his brown curls fluttered in the breeze.

She was filled with triumph. What she'd planned was going to be possible. All she had to do now was to give Father the slip. As though he could read her thoughts, his hand came out to hold her arm. He was leading her forward to meet the line of civic dignitaries waiting to receive them. Evie smiled politely and shook the hands offered to her, but she was filled with a feeling of urgency. She had to get away. Would it be better if she did it before they found their seats?

On his way up the steps of the stand, Father paused to exchange a few words with the vicar of their church. His wife, who ran the Sunday school, was with him. Filled with guilt, Evie murmured, 'Excuse me a moment,' and ran back down the steps.

Moments later, Ned took her hand and led her into the crush. His brown eyes were laughing down into hers. He was trying to hurry but they were walking against the crowd surging towards the stand. When they reached the main gate, they heard the band strike up 'Land of Hope and Glory' and knew the gala had started.

'You're going to miss all the fun,' he teased.

Everything worked out as Evie had planned. Ned collected his coke cart from the Dartys' yard, while Evie went through the shop and opened up the store room. She made one quick trip upstairs, to take her money box and cash book from the living-room mantelpiece. She was propping a note of explanation to Father in its place when Matty hobbled to the door.

'Goodness, you gave me a fright. I thought we must have burglars. What are you doing back so soon?'

'I'm leaving for good, Matty. Running away. Wish me luck,' she laughed.

'Glory be! What will your father say?'

'I'll never know.' She laughed again, gave Matilda a kiss on her cheek and ran downstairs, snatching up her best coat from the banisters as she passed.

She clung to Ned's arm as she walked away from her secure home. For better or worse she'd cut herself off. She'd set her feet on what Father called the primrose path to hell. The wheels on the coke cart squeaked at every turn. She felt triumphant, swept along with the excitement of the day, relieved it had gone without a hitch. Ned felt the same way, she knew. The only time he stopped smiling was to break into a laugh. Evie laughed with him.

When they reached the rooms he'd rented, she was pleased with them. They were better than he'd led her to believe, though the furniture was shabby and the crockery chipped. She was introduced to her landlord and his wife. They seemed a dour couple and she wasn't sure that she'd like them.

Ned opened the cupboards and showed her the food he'd bought in readiness. She recognised Darty's bread and cakes. It brought the first misgivings.

'I hope Father won't be able to find me. I've not gone far.'

'I haven't told Polly anything, just in case. But once we're married, he won't be able to take you back.'

'How can we get married without his permission?'

'I've got to marry you, Evie.' Ned wasn't laughing now but deeply serious. 'I've talked you into running away from home and got you into the family way. You want to marry me, don't you?'

There was such a look of hope on his face that Evie was blinking hard.

'Of course I do. I just don't see how.'

'It'll have to be the register office. I've already been along there. To ask about what's needed, I mean. There's a certificate your father has to sign, to give permission. But my mother has a friend who'll pretend to be your father. He's said he'll come with us when we make the arrangements and sign for you.'

'Forge Father's signature? But he's well known, because of the shop. Think of all his customers. What if . . .' Evie's mind boggled at the risk.

'Perhaps we should go to Liverpool and get married there. Or Wallasey, if you like.'

'Doesn't it have to be the town where we live?'

'I don't know. I didn't ask that. But I've an older brother who's married and has rooms in New Brighton, we could give his address. Probably safer to do that, do you think?'

'Will we be legally married?'

'Yes, I think so. Nobody can undo the knot once it's tied.'

'There's only one other way, and that's to wait until I'm of age.'

'That's nearly three years off.' Ned was aghast.

'We'll do it your way,' Evie said. 'We have to, don't we, for the sake of the baby?'

Ned had also bought sticks and coal and laid a fire in readiness in the grate. Now he lit it.

'It'll seem more like home when it blazes up,' he said.

'It isn't cold.'

'We need it to cook on here, Evie.' He showed her the trivet that stood on the hearth and could be swung over the flames to support a pan or a kettle. 'We'll start with a cup of tea.'

Evie thought it was like playing at house and rather fun.

* * *

Evie felt happier now she was away from her father. She'd made her choice and was sure it was the right one. Ned and his mother continued to buy from Darty's bakery, though Evie didn't dare. It was too close. Polly reported that Matilda sometimes came for the bread, though if her feet were very bad, Bertie Pugh or Miss Lister were sent. All of them had told Polly that Joseph had gone berserk when he realised what Evie had done. He'd said he wouldn't have her back if she came on bended knee.

It was what Evie had expected, but it made her feel guilty. Apart from that, she had a wonderful summer and felt as free as air. On the days Ned went to work, she played at being a housewife and cleaned their rooms and made a meal for when Ned came home.

But it took three hours to sail to the Isle of Man and three to return. The trip gave passengers two hours in Douglas. On top of that Ned had to be on the boat half an hour before it sailed, and there was the time it took him to walk to Woodside and take the ferry over to the Liverpool landing stage.

Evie had him home every night, but he seemed to spend precious little time with her apart from that. He had two days off every fortnight, and she thought they were heaven.

By the end of July, they'd managed to arrange their wedding. Evie wore her blue dress and flowered hat. Ned's family gathered for the event. Gertie Collins looked stouter than ever in a floral print she'd bought for the occasion.

Evie hung on to Ned's arm as they all took the ferry to Liverpool Pier Head and then caught another ferry to Wallasey. The marriage ceremony went without a hitch, just as Ned had assured her it would. She was glad to have a wedding ring on her finger.

'He had to see you right,' Gertie Collins assured her,

pulling her close in a hug. Her rolls of flesh yielded like a soft cushion. The rest of the family were equally free with their affection. All four brothers and the sister-in-law kissed her and welcomed her to the family. Evie felt she'd never been kissed so much.

They had to catch the bus to Ned's brother Alfie's house, where a good lunch had been laid out in readiness. But the Collins brothers could never pass a pub, and what better way was there to celebrate such a match?

Evie had never been in a pub before but she was persuaded into the lounge. She'd never tasted strong drink, either. Father took a glass of sherry before his Sunday dinner, and sometimes a glass of whisky to help him sleep at night, but he hadn't approved of alcohol for her.

Evie sipped the port and lemon that was put into her hand. The Collins men drank ale, and seemed to be settling in for a good session. But after one drink Ned stood up, and the women did the same.

'We're going to our Alfie's for something to eat,' Gertie told her other sons. Evie was led off towards the bus stop, and Alfie came running after them rather shame-faced.

His home was two cramped rooms, but there was a good spread of ham and pickles and a big variety of jellies and cakes set out on the table. Tea was made for those who wanted it, and there was ale for the others.

When Ned said it was time for them to go, much of the food that hadn't been eaten was parcelled up so they could take it with them. His brothers opened more ale.

'I'm not like them,' Ned told her, as they hung over the rail of the ferry boat and watched the murky water of the Mersey foam against the bow. 'Any more than you're like your father.'

Evie felt truly blessed to have Ned's love. She felt nurtured and valued for the first time in her life. There was a warmth about Ned. He was always thinking of some little luxury she might enjoy. He'd spend his last threepence on a bunch of violets for her.

His eyes caressed her across the table when they sat down to meals. His love made him get up to kiss her or gently stroke her cheek. He had a special smile for her.

But she didn't find it easy to settle to her new and very different life. She was living within a few minutes' walk of her father's shop and knew she'd have felt safer with more distance between them. She was also afraid that what she'd done had been very wrong. Her family set great store by doing their duty. She'd been brought up to listen to her conscience.

'Your father's a tyrant,' Ned tried to soothe her fears. 'You were scared of him. You needed to get away, you mustn't worry.'

His days off were idyllic now that they could spend the whole time together. On one of them, they called in on his mother. Gertie Collins always made a fuss of her visitors, and gave them a big welcome. They were sitting in her back room drinking tea when they heard a loud rat-a-tat on her front door.

'Who could that be?' Gertie put down her cup and went to see, leaving the door open. 'Can't be the rent man, I've paid him . . .'

Evie heard a man's voice, stiff with formality, say: 'Are you Mrs Gertrude Alice Collins?'

'Yes.' She sounded suddenly wary. Ned was on his feet, peeping up the hall.

He turned to mouth the words: 'It's a bobby.'

'The police?' Evie was aghast. Ned turned with a finger against his lips, but the look on his face alone would have silenced her.

The official voice boomed up the narrow hall. 'I'd like a word with you, can I come in?'

'What's it about?' Gertie was even more wary, scared even.

'You have a son, Edward Collins?'

There was a nervous pause. 'Yes.'

'He lives here with you?'

'No, no.'

'Then would you be good enough to give me his address?'

Evie held her breath. Her heart was drumming so loud she thought the policeman would be able to hear.

'He's away at sea,' Gertie said. 'What d'you want to know for? What's he supposed to have done?'

'It's in regard to a missing person. We've reason to believe he might know her whereabouts.'

Evie saw the colour drain from Ned's face.

'You'd better come in,' his mother said. 'This way.' She was taking the bobby into the parlour at the front, which was hardly used. Instantly, Ned was feeling for Evie's hand and drawing her cautiously out to the hall. The parlour door wasn't completely closed. Gertie was leaning against it.

'Away at sea, you say? How long has he been away?'

'I can't remember exactly. A year or so now it must be.'

'What's the name of his ship, Mrs Collins?'

Ned was drawing Evie out to the scullery, moving as quietly as possible. A moment later they were tiptoeing down the yard and out into the back entry. He was hurrying her then, faster, until they were running. They didn't stop until they were back in their own rooms, and even then Evie didn't feel safe.

'It's Father! He's got the police looking for me.'

'Mam won't say anything. You heard her. She said I was away at sea.'

'But they'll find us some other way.'

'Nobody knows our address.'

'All your family do.'

'They'll keep their mouths shut.'

'We've made everybody tell lies for us. I've done it myself. Done all sorts of devious things.'

'We had to get married,' Ned told her. 'We have to protect ourselves now.'

'I've got the collywobbles.'

'You worry a lot. I blame your father for that.'

When Evie stopped shaking she was able to tell Ned about the prescription book in which her father wrote down the names and addresses of every customer he prescribed for. That was the law. That was how he knew Gertie's address.

'Of course he wants you back,' Gertie said a few days later. 'What father wouldn't? He's doing his best, but he won't find you. I gave nothing away.'

Ned said in reassuring tones: 'Anyway, you're a married woman now. He can't force you to go back if you don't want to go.'

It took Evie a while to recover, and even longer to put her fears behind her, but apart from that, the weeks were beginning to drift past very pleasantly. As far as the weather went, it was not a good summer, but she thought it the happiest of her life.

When the summer season came to an end, the day-trippers, who this year had not flocked in their usual numbers to take the boat to the Isle of Man, ceased to go at all. There were autumn gales in the Irish Sea and the number of sailings was suddenly cut back to a winter timetable. Many of the crew lost their jobs, and Ned was

shocked to find he was amongst them. He hadn't been
expecting it. He'd been kept on all last winter, but then
last year, the weather had been better.

# CHAPTER SEVEN

'I'll soon find another job,' Ned said confidently. 'On the dredgers, or something like that.'

'Don't hurry.' Evie smiled. 'It'll be lovely to have you home all day. We can afford a week or two to ourselves, can't we?'

She was a thrifty housekeeper, having been trained by Aunt Agatha, and they had a little money in hand. She'd also managed to buy her own pots and pans and household linen, all of a better quality than had been provided by the landlord, and had accumulated most of the layette she'd need for the coming baby.

But Ned saw himself as the provider and had to start looking for work straight away. He spent his mornings tramping round the port offices and the shipping lines, and studying the jobs advertised in the *Birkenhead News* and the *Liverpool Echo*. As the weeks passed and he wasn't offered another job, he began to lose heart.

'There's only deep-sea jobs,' he worried, 'and that means being away for months, maybe years. I want a job where I can be home with you every night.'

Evie knew he wouldn't settle until he'd found another job. Money was suddenly much tighter and they couldn't spend it on doing things together. She could now appreciate how very poor the people living round her were. Most, and that included Ned's family, had no savings to fall back on.

Eventually, Ned said: 'I'll have to go deep-sea, Evie. I've got to earn some money and it's the only thing going.

It'll mean leaving you on your own. I hate doing that.'

Evie was nervous of the prospect. She wanted him with her. Her baby was due after Christmas. She couldn't see how she'd be able to manage on her own then. Ned put off the decision for another week or two, but eventually he signed on to a rusty freighter loaded with machine tools bound for Genoa. He chose it because it was due back in Liverpool before Christmas.

'Just in case I'm held up, I've asked my mother to do what she can. I mean, if it comes early and I'm not here.'

Evie had never seen Ned look so downhearted. She shuddered and hoped that wouldn't happen, but it worried her. This was their first real setback and she prayed that it didn't mean she was following her mother's downward spiral. All the same, she felt as though she was on the slippery slope.

Ned provided an allotment out of his pay which she collected every Friday from the shipping office, but he was not earning as much as he had done, and she decided she'd have to be even more thrifty.

She was lonely on her own and she didn't feel safe in the rooms Ned had chosen, because the landlord leered at her every time she went to the kitchen or the yard. She thought she could organise things better now that they didn't have to live close to Woodside to make it easy for Ned to travel to Liverpool every day. And most of all, she wanted to get further away from the pharmacy.

She decided she'd look for a whole house that she could rent. Within a few days she found what she was looking for near the old priory. Birkenhead Priory had been one of the first to be seized by Henry VIII, its treasures taken and the monks turned out. The first ferry across the Mersey had been started by the monks in the fourteenth century. Now the ancient slipway was used as a coal stage and was trapped between Clovers Graving Docks and Birkenhead Iron Works, where shipbuilding was carried on.

Evie looked at the ruins of the priory, where rank grass grew knee-high. The chapter house still had a roof on and had been restored at some time. She could make out the crypt and the great hall, but it was all so neglected and dismal.

Industry had blighted the whole area. There were small factories and warehouses, wood yards and coal stacks everywhere. The racket made by riveters and giant hammers in the shipyards went on all day. Mean streets of small houses crowded close, built to house the dock workers in the middle of the last century. Leicester Street was one of the better ones. On either side of it were dark, narrow courts. It was further away from the pharmacy, though Evie would have liked it more distant still. But it was something of a backwater, and Joseph would have no reason to come anywhere near.

She picked out a plain two-up and two-down terraced house with flat sash windows. The front door opened straight off the pavement into a narrow hall that went from back to front and from which the stairs went up. Evie knew she'd have to rent off some of the rooms, and this would make all the difference to her comfort and that of her tenant.

She still had the money that she'd brought with her. Ned had not wanted her to spend it on living expenses. He thought it was his responsibility to provide those. That was her money and she must spend it on herself or the baby. Evie had thought of it as their nest egg. Now she used it to buy good second-hand furniture and make the house as comfortable as she could. She bought some paint and smartened the rooms up. She made curtains for the windows and spring-cleaned and polished until the whole place shone.

Then she put a card in the window of a nearby newsagent, offering to rent two rooms in a respectable house to a single woman. She showed two ladies round and was delighted when one of them, a Miss Pringle, wanted to move in. She came with good references.

Ida Pringle was a spinster on the wrong side of fifty, employed as a lady typist in a nearby office. She was a stout woman with a rather plain, good-natured face and tiny shoe-button eyes. She dressed very smartly to go to work. Evie thought they'd get on reasonably well and was pleased that most of her own rent was met by what she was charging her tenant. She could manage now on what Ned sent her.

The time was passing. Evie was feeling more tired and growing ungainly. She made a Christmas pudding and a decorated cake, just as Matilda used to. All her preparations for the coming baby were complete and she was beginning to feel excited about it. Her main worry was that Ned would not be back in time.

She received letters from him, but the names of the small ports meant nothing until she found an old atlas in a second-hand book shop. After that she could follow his progress. When she went to the shipping office to collect her weekly money, she always asked the whereabouts of the *Redeemer*. When she heard it was heading back across the Bay of Biscay she was delighted.

Ned arrived home two days before Christmas, looking suntanned and healthy. He'd brought back several little gifts for her – an ivory fan bought in the Spanish port of Tarragona, a brooch from Palma, a leather purse from Morocco, a bottle of sweet wine from Malaga, dates from Tunis – and many pictures of the places he'd been.

Evie pored over the pictures. 'So many exotic places. You must have enjoyed seeing them.'

'I was thinking of you wherever I went,' he grinned. 'Couldn't think of anything else. All I wanted was to get back to you.'

They kept the fire roaring up the chimney in the back room and went out only to visit Ned's family and deliver the presents he'd brought for them.

Miss Pringle stayed out of their way as much as possible now Ned was home. Evie had the impression that she preferred him to be away. But Ida liked a laugh, and Ned could make her rolls of flesh shake with mirth when he joked.

The baby arrived on New Year's Eve, and Ned was there to fetch the midwife and boil the kettles of water she said were needed. Evie hugged her baby son in a surge of mother love, and decided that nothing in the world would ever part her from him. He was a strong baby with soft, thick brown hair like his father's. He slept well and fed well and was easy to manage. Together they chose the name Robert for him.

Ned was overwhelmed, and spent hours watching him while he slept in his cot. He nicknamed him Bobby. Evie felt that all the difficulties had been well worthwhile. She'd never felt so surrounded by love.

Within days Ned was worrying about getting another ship. He tried half-heartedly for a job in port, but when it wasn't forthcoming he signed on on an old ship that had brought sugar cane and rum from Barbados and was loading salt and manufactured goods for the return journey.

When he was leaving, he said to Miss Pringle: 'I'm glad you're here. It's better for Evie to have someone with her.'

'I don't like being alone either,' Ida told him. 'Evie's very good to me.'

Evie felt down when Ned went. She told herself fiercely that she had a lot to be thankful for. Little Bobby was a beautiful baby. All her love turned on him now; he was reason enough for everything she did. She also had a comfortable home and was free to live as she wanted to.

She took Bobby to see Ned's mother quite often, understanding that she'd want to shower her grandson with love too. Gertie would turn up on Evie's doorstep even more frequently, and Evie would put the kettle on so that they could share a cup of tea. She found her mother-in-law a comfort when Ned was away. Gertie was always reaching out to touch her, a hand on her arm or her shoulder to signal support. Evie thought about her father. They had never touched each other, never kissed, never shown affection like this.

Miss Pringle was captivated by Bobby too. Evie began cooking an evening meal for her. It was more economical and no more difficult to cook for two than it was for one, and she was glad of adult company at the end of the day.

Miss Pringle was jolly and optimistic by nature. She set great store by horoscopes and believed she could foretell the future for herself and her friends by reading their tea cups.

Many evenings, when she and Evie had finished their meal, she insisted they both swirl the dregs of their tea round the sides of their cups and upturn them on their saucers. She successfully foretold from Evie's tea leaves that Ned would be home before Easter.

He was home again for a month later that summer. This time Evie was determined to enjoy his company. She wouldn't let him worry about getting another ship, nor allow him to go back to sea after two weeks, as he felt he should.

But when he'd gone again and her evenings with Miss Pringle resumed, she realised that this would be the pattern of her life from now on. A husband she loved but rarely saw. When they were together, they had such joyous times. Like their honeymoon all over again.

Evie didn't know what she'd have done when Ned went away if she hadn't had Miss Pringle's company. It was having Ida in the house that kept her going.

Ned's ship hadn't even reached New York when Ida saw another baby's face in her tea cup. Evie hardly believed her, but a week or so later she realised it was true. She was going to have another baby.

'And Bobby only a few months old!'

Evie didn't know whether Miss Pringle was shocked at the speed with which she'd conceived again, or delighted that she'd managed to predict it. For her own part, she would have preferred to delay it a little, but she wanted more than one child. She knew Ned would welcome it too, that he wanted a big family.

This time Evie wasn't lucky enough to have Ned with her when her baby was born. She happened to be visiting her mother-in-law when she felt the first pains, and it was one of Ned's brothers who was sent running for the midwife.

Everything was normal and went well. Evie had a little girl she named Victoria. She managed well enough during the lying-in period. For a couple of weeks, Miss Pringle did much more about the house. She cooked the evening meal when she returned home from the office.

Gertie offered to look after Bobby for a week, and she brought him round to see Evie and the new baby every day. She always brought something with her for their midday meal, which they ate together. Evie began to appreciate Gertie. Ned had told her he'd grown up in a loving home. His mother might fall very short of Aunt Agatha's standards of housekeeping and cleanliness but she had Ned's way of wrapping everyone in her love.

By the time the baby was eight days old, Evie was feeling more her old self. Gertie came round wearing for the eighth time the same green skirt with a torn hem.

'Take it off and let me mend it,' Evie said. 'I'm just sitting here watching you work. It'll do me good to keep my fingers busy.'

'Your fingers are busy enough, lass,' Gertie said, but Evie insisted.

'It's too long. Caught my boot in the hem.' It came off, revealing several layers of petticoats, red flannel, striped navy and white twill, and what had once been white lawn.

'Then I'll shorten it.'

Evie also insisted on sponging off the mud from round the bottom, and she made Gertie put a flat iron in the fire to press the new hem.

'You've made it like new, love,' Gertie said with pleasure when she put it on again.

The following morning when she came in, Gertie was bursting with news: 'Guess where we've been this morning?'

She had a bag of shopping and she took out some iced buns and set them out on the table.

'Darty's?' Evie felt a shiver of fear. 'You didn't take Bobby there?'

'I did, and there's no need for you to worry.'

'But Father's just next door. He might have seen you.'

'Not him. Had his head down behind the back counter, and the shop was full of customers. Polly Darty was so pleased to see Bobby. She swung him up in her arms and took him into the bakery to show Arthur. 'Evie's little boy,' she said. 'Isn't he lovely?'

'When I said you'd got another, a baby girl this time, she said she knew you'd make a good mother. You were lovely with little Herbie.'

'How is he?' Evie choked.

'He's fine. And Polly sends her love.'

Evie stared into the fire for a long time. 'How's Father?'

'We don't go in his shop now, none of us do. I told you that.' They went to a chemist near the station now, though Gertie said his physic wasn't so good.

'Didn't Polly say anything?'

'Only that he's more bad-tempered than ever.'

'I wonder if he's managing all right.'

'That I can't tell you. I don't suppose Polly could either.'

'I wonder if Matilda's still there. I don't suppose Polly said?'

'Didn't mention her. You'll have to go round yourself if you want to know that sort of thing. It wouldn't hurt after all this time. It's so much water under the bridge now.'

'No.' Evie suppressed a shudder. 'You didn't tell Polly where we lived?'

'She didn't ask, love. But Polly won't say a word. Don't you worry.'

But Evie did worry. The Collins family were frequent customers at the bakery and had been friendly with the Dartys for a long time. Father was a customer too, and only next door. It was only too easy to see how a connection might be made.

Evie felt guilty because she'd walked out on Joseph in the same way her mother had, and she knew just how much that would upset him. She hadn't been the dutiful daughter he'd wanted. Gertie was still trying to ease her mind.

'Your dad ain't all that popular round there. Thinks

himself a cut above his neighbours, he does. Anyway, everything's changed now. You're a married woman with two lovely children. You can hold your head up with the rest of them. He's the one losing out. You don't need him.'

When Ned returned home, he was thrilled with his new daughter. He cuddled her in his arms and called her Queenie, and somehow the nickname stuck.

'Victoria's too big a name for a tiny scrap like this,' he laughed. 'You named her after the old queen, didn't you?'

He opened his arms to his growing family and seemed to have love enough for them all. He talked of adding to it in the future.

Ida Pringle pulled her flannelette nightdress over her head and climbed into her bed. Tonight, she'd try to get to sleep quickly. She blew out her candle and closed her eyes. Having a man in the house changed everything.

Evie and her husband were coming upstairs now. Creeping quietly, whispering softly like two doves. A little laugh, the creak of the bedsprings as they climbed in, a gentle murmur and then silence.

Ida had been so pleased with these rooms when she'd moved in. She had the two best rooms in the house, the largest bedroom in the front and the sitting room beneath it. They were comfortably furnished and nicely decorated, and she'd really taken to Evie, who was very sweet and welcoming.

There was a hot dinner ready every evening when Ida came home from work. She enjoyed playing with little Bobby, bouncing him on her ample lap until he squealed with laughter. She loved the long evenings by the fire, just her and Evie, gossiping and reading their cups. Ida counted Evie as a friend now that she'd lived in her house for over a year.

She wasn't so sure about Ned, though he seemed a nice enough fellow to talk to. Evie had married beneath her, that was obvious enough to anyone. Such silky hair that it was always escaping her bun to hang down beside her face in shining dark tendrils. Such a pretty girl to throw herself away on a husband like that.

The table was set for three in the evenings when he was home. He was always there between them, taking all Evie's attention. And after they'd eaten, he left Ida in no doubt that he expected her to go to her own lonely sitting room. She felt pushed out.

Oh, no! Ida listened, stiffening with distaste.

Ned didn't give anybody a chance to get to sleep. It was bad enough having him downstairs. He pawed Evie, always reaching out to touch her. She'd seen him kiss the nape of Evie's neck this evening. He made his needs so transparent.

Ida turned over in bed and pulled her blankets over her ears. She could still hear the rhythmic creak of the brass bedstead in the next bedroom. It was downright embarrassing to have to listen to such sounds through the wall. Great gusts and sighs and grunts too.

She'd felt sorry enough for Evie before he came home. There was something vulnerable about her. She really did have a lot to put up with. Every night, half an hour or less after they'd come up to bed, this started. He could make the marital bed rattle in earnest and it wasn't only at night. Sometimes she heard it in the morning too.

Still, he wouldn't be home for long. No doubt Evie was looking forward to his departure as much as Ida herself was. Really, men were disgusting creatures. There was only one thing they thought of.

Ida thanked God she'd managed to stay single. It had been touch and go when she was young, before she realised; before her sister Kitty was married and had such a terrible time. She hoped Ned Collins wouldn't be staying home for very long.

Evie's days were filled with child care now, and when Ned went away she was so busy she had less time to think of him.

Queenie was not such an easy baby as Bobby had been. She slept less and was difficult to feed. For the first time, Evie would have liked to have her father's expertise and experience. Many young mothers took their infants to his shop, he was used to weighing them. He prescribed for sleeping and teething problems, made ointments for the babies' bottoms and advised on more food or less food or different food so that they'd thrive.

If she had to pass his shop Evie always did it on the opposite side of the road, keeping a close watch on it as trams and carts and carriages swished between them. Sometimes she'd see Miss Lister serving on the front counter. Once she saw Bertie Pugh, but she never caught even a glimpse of Father, though she knew he was there.

The years were passing pleasantly enough, but she longed to see more of Ned. He was away so much of the time. She was finding it a struggle again to manage on the money he was able to set aside from his wages. It wasn't Ned's fault. She knew he kept very little for his own use. Their family was a growing responsibility and it was difficult to meet all their needs from one wage packet.

'I wish I'd learned to type like you,' she told Miss Pringle enviously. She knew that Ida earned more than Ned, and didn't have to travel the world to do it.

'Wouldn't help you now.' Miss Pringle screwed up her podgy face in thought. 'They don't employ married ladies as typists. Anyway, you have two babies. You have to stay home to take care of them.'

'Taking in washing is about the only way married women can earn a bit extra. There's at least two in this street that do it.'

'But you wouldn't want to, would you?'

'I've plenty of washing of my own,' Evie laughed. 'But it can be combined with looking after babies.'

'If you have bags of energy.'

'I do.' Evie counted herself lucky in that respect.

A month later, Miss Pringle came home bursting with news.

'Would you fancy an office cleaning job, Evie? That wouldn't be beneath you?'

Evie was dishing up stewed steak and dumplings.

'It's an early-morning job at the office where I work. Really early, I mean, five till half past seven. You could be home again before eight to get the children up for breakfast.'

Evie felt a surge of interest as she set the two plates on the table and pulled out her chair. 'But I'd have to leave the children . . .'

'They never need anything at that time of the morning, do they?' Ida's face shone with good intentions.

'No.' They never did. If Queenie was wakeful and crotchety it was always early in the night. Bobby slept like a top and was never any trouble.

'And I'm sleeping in the next room. If something out of the ordinary happens, I'll hear them and go in. They know me now and wouldn't be frightened.'

'Would you mind? I mean, it's awfully good of you.'

'If they wake up, I'll comfort them until you get back. You'll only be away for three hours or so, after all.'

'If you're willing . . .' Evie was hesitant. 'It's asking a lot.'

'No it's not. Shall I put your name forward? Do you want that?'

'Yes please.' Evie clasped her hands together. 'Oh, yes please. A job like that, the extra money would make all the difference.'

'Then I'll fix up for you to come in and have an interview. I've already had a word. I told the person who'd be your boss that you keep your house spotless. She's been having a spot of trouble with cleaners recently. There have been three in the last five months. I told her I thought you'd be reliable.'

'I will be,' Evie promised. She was trying to think. 'Henry Ball and Sons, you said the company was called? I've never understood, what exactly is their business?'

'I told you, they're West Africa merchants.'

'But what exactly is that?'

'Mr Ball has a fleet of ships that trade between Liverpool and West Africa. It's an old family business, been going for years.'

'Big business then?'

'Oh, yes.'

When they were having a cup of tea afterwards, Miss Pringle said: 'We must consult your tea leaves tonight, to see if you'll get the job.'

Evie sat back and smiled. She didn't really believe the tea leaves foretold anything, although Ida had been right once or twice. With the babies tucked up in bed, and a good fire burning in the grate, she saw it as a bit of fun.

'Come on,' Ida urged. 'Swill the last of your tea round the cup three times. Now upturn it on your saucer.'

Evie did as she was told and handed her cup over. 'Don't look for any more babies,' she said. 'We can't afford them. Dots are what I want, they signify gain by money, don't they?' She was learning the basic rules.

'There are dots. Well, just one or two.'

'That means a little more money?' Evie asked hopefully.

'Just a little. I can see a horse.'

'What does that mean?'

'A lover. There are dashes and clouds round him, which indicate he truly loves you, but there are difficulties he can't control keeping him away.'

'That must be Ned,' laughed Evie. 'No dots round him, I'm sure.'

'Oddly enough, there's a parasol too.' Miss Pringle's voice warmed with interest.

'What does that mean?'

'It's another sign for a lover. Your cup shows two.'

Evie laughed. 'I don't need another.'

'The dots are close to it. This one will have more money than Ned.'

'Just the money will do,' Evie sighed. 'What about the job?'

Miss Pringle said, 'It shows nothing. I don't know.'

Evie had seen the office of Henry Ball and Sons on Knox Street many times. It was just round the corner from her house. Nothing could be more convenient. It seemed an old-fashioned building, and somewhat run-down. She asked Gertie to look after the children for her when she went for the interview.

Feeling nervous, she went through the double doors into a vestibule. It had a floor of mosaic tiles and a mahogany counter. There was nobody about, but a notice near a brass bell told her to ring for service. Evie pressed her palm down on the spring plunger.

'Good morning.' A young clerk appeared immediately.

Evie said she'd come for a job interview, and the end of the counter was lifted to allow her in. The office seemed

117

an alien place. She counted eight men, each standing in front of a desk writing in a large ledger. Above each desk was a wire rack holding more ledgers. A young office boy was told to take her upstairs. The stone steps were steep and winding. Evie wondered if she would have to clean them too.

'This is the manager's secretary,' the boy said. 'He'll look after you.'

Evie had expected to see Miss Pringle. Instead, a gaunt, middle-aged man sat typing at a desk positioned in front of a door labelled 'Mr Byron Ball'.

'You found us all right then?' He offered her a chair. He wore a high, stiff collar, and Evie could see an angry red line where it was chafing his neck. 'He'll buzz when he's free to see you.' The man nodded towards the door. 'We're busy today. Have to get on.'

Every time he came to the end of a paragraph, he ran a finger inside his collar. Evie was interested in what he was doing. It seemed a very pleasant way of earning a living. She knew that more and more women were doing it now, Miss Pringle for one. It was not to be compared with taking in washing, or even shop work. After ten minutes she heard the buzzer. The secretary looked up.

'Just knock and go on in,' he told her.

Cautiously, she did so. Mr Ball had risen from the chair behind his desk and was on his way to meet her. He was well built, with powerful shoulders, and in his late thirties. He wore a formal chalk-striped suit with a stiff-collared shirt. His eyes seemed to question everything. He had a lot of straight brown hair.

'Come in, come in,' he urged, putting out his hand. His clasp was so firm it hurt a little. 'Have a seat. You've come about the vacancy we advertised?'

'Yes.' Evie tried to smile. She felt tense.

'What are your speeds?'

She was disconcerted. 'I work quite fast.'

'Quite fast?' His brow furrowed. 'Come on now, you'll need to be more exact than that.'

Evie wondered if she could claim to be very fast. 'Surely thoroughness is more important than speed,' she managed. 'I'm very thorough.'

Now he seemed at a loss. 'Miss Topping, isn't it? The lady typewriter?'

'No, no. I'm Mrs Collins, for the office cleaner's job.'

'Oh!' He was trying to control his smile. 'I'm afraid there's been a bit of a mix-up. You do look more like a lady typewriter.'

He laughed then, and his brown eyes met hers. There was nothing unkind about his gaze. It travelled from her face to her clothes. She was wearing her best winter coat with her straw hat, the one she'd bought for the coronation gala. It was still March, and the weather was chilly: a little early in the year for her hat.

'I only wish I could type.'

He laughed again. 'Miss Hooper looks after domestic matters. I leave that sort of thing to her. Somebody's got his lines crossed. Office cleaner, eh? You're very young for that. Our cleaning ladies are usually much older.' His eyes were assessing her again.

'The young have more energy,' she said.

He smiled again. 'Even very early in the morning?'

She told him about her two children and why those hours were the only ones that she could work. That Miss Pringle would listen for them while she was away.

'Our Miss Pringle?'

'Yes, she rents rooms from me. She said she'd speak for me. Recommend me.'

'Well, we'll give you a try. Have to. It would never do to

119

upset Miss Pringle. She's quite an institution here.'

He buzzed through to his secretary, who summoned Miss Hooper, a grey-haired lady nearing retirement age.

Miss Hooper frowned at Evie. 'I've been waiting for you. I thought you were late.'

'No, I was a little early. I'm a good timekeeper.'

'It seems the staff thought I should see her first,' Mr Ball put in, explaining the situation.

'I was surprised when you didn't come. Miss Pringle spoke very highly of you. She's sure you'll give satisfaction.'

'I'll do my best.'

'Since Mrs Collins comes so well recommended, I think we must give her a try,' Mr Ball put in. Evie warmed to him and tried to smile her thanks.

Miss Hooper was perspiring. 'You'd better come with me.'

'Goodbye.' Mr Ball was still smiling as she left.

When Miss Hooper got round to mentioning her wages, Evie thought them reasonably generous, and accepted gratefully. It was a job she was glad to have.

Her duties were explained to her and she was shown where the cleaning materials were kept. As Ida had told her, they were having problems with their cleaning and they needed someone to start straight away.

'Tomorrow morning, five o'clock,' Miss Hooper told her. 'There'll be someone with you for the first morning. To show you the ropes.'

Evie set her alarm clock for four thirty, blessing the forethought that had made her bring it with her. It had been a Christmas gift from her father and was a reliable one.

'Now you've no excuse to be late for breakfast,' Father had said, when she'd thanked him.

It seemed like the middle of the night when it went off. She silenced it as soon as she could, so as not to wake Miss Pringle or the children. She dressed quickly in the cold of pre-dawn, peeped into the back bedroom to reassure herself that her children were still asleep and set off.

The office was within easy walking distance, which was what had attracted Miss Pringle to her house in the first place. She was warm when she got there. It was not quite five o'clock and a middle-aged woman was unlocking the doors.

The woman started by lighting the gas mantles. 'So you're the new woman? You're just a slip of a girl. I hope you know what work is. You'll be on your own tomorrow.'

Evie found there was plenty to do. There were four grates which needed to be raked out and new fires laid, the tiled entrance hall to mop out and the brass knobs and knockers to polish. Then she had to swing something called a dummy, a great hinged polishing pad, over the wooden floors of the main office.

'You've got to move the desks every day and polish them regular. I do six each morning,' the woman advised. 'Different ones so they all get a turn.'

Then there were three smaller offices to clean, and countless waste-paper baskets to empty.

'Don't forget the lavvies out in the yard. There's a special mop kept out there and the ladies are very fussy about them.'

The time flew. When they were leaving, the sky was lighter in the east. Evie almost ran home to light her own fire and put on the pan of porridge to heat through. She was hungry and much in need of her breakfast.

Miss Pringle reported that the children had slept through and hadn't noticed her absence. All the same,

Evie felt it was wrong to leave them, and she played with them more than usual that morning. She loved them dearly.

Bobby was a bright-eyed miniature of his father. He was turned three now, and Ned was telling her it was time she dressed him in shorts. It was the fashion to clothe all infants, whether boys or girls, in skirts and pinafores. Queenie, a year younger, took after Ned too. They were both sturdy children with clear, healthy skin, brown eyes and brown curly hair.

After the children's dinner at midday, Evie put them down for a nap and took a rest herself. She went to bed an hour earlier than she used to, and found she could cope.

The money she earned made all the difference. She bought new shoes for both her children that week, and she looked forward to persuading Ned to stay home longer next time he came. To have him home for more than a week or two would be a wonderful treat for them all.

The years were passing. Evie thought she had everything she could possibly want and was content. Father had been wrong when he'd predicted she'd be in trouble if she married Ned. She thought of her mother often, and hoped life had been good for her during the years she'd been away from home.

Evie was so busy with her job and her family that when war fever gripped the nation it took her by surprise. Suddenly all the newspapers were full of the possibility of war. Everywhere she looked, there were posters saying 'England Needs You'.

Gertie Collins came round to see her in a terrible state. She said that her sons had taken leave of their senses. One had already signed up to join the army and another the navy, and the other two were talking of doing the same.

'I don't know what our Alfie's thinking of, a married man with three young sons. Where's the sense in him going?' She hoped his wife would be able to keep him at home.

'Afraid they'll miss the fun.' Gertie was scathing, but full of pride too that they wanted to fight for their country.

# Book Two

## 1914–1919

# CHAPTER EIGHT

That evening, as he was being driven home by his chauffeur, Byron Ball was thinking of Evie Collins. Such a pretty, well-spoken girl who'd seemed pathetically pleased to get the job of cleaning his offices. The only reason he could think of was that she'd made a disastrous marriage and had put herself in a position where she was in need of money. Yet she didn't give the impression of being unhappy with her lot.

Byron thought he knew all there was to know about disastrous marriages. And more than he wanted to about people who were dissatisfied with their circumstances. Being so dissatisfied with everything in his own life, he marvelled at Evie and saw her as a lesson to him.

It didn't help that nobody appreciated that he had difficulties. Since he was a lad, distant cousins, old aunts, other relatives and friends had all been saying to him:

'It's all right for you, Byron. You'll inherit the family business. Look what a success your father and grandfather made of it.

'Then there's Parkfield, the house you've always lived in, and goodness only knows what else they've managed to put by for you. A goodly pile, I'm sure. You're cushioned for life. You won't have to struggle to earn a crust like the rest of us.'

At one time, he too had thought himself very fortunate, but not any longer. Samuels swept the big open tourer through the gates of Parkfield and pulled up outside the front door. Grace, his twelve-year-old daughter, came hurtling round the side of the house to throw herself at him.

'Daddy, come and see Lulu, she's had four pups. They're absolutely beautiful. Just balls of fluff.'

Byron allowed himself to be led by the hand to what had once been the stables. It was Grace who looked after both Labradors, fed them and walked them. She was also keen on the cat and the tortoise, always bursting with enthusiasm for something new. He had countless things she'd made for him, leather bookmarks, boxes covered with shells, hand-stitched handkerchiefs and hand-knitted socks. He told himself he had Grace. Life hadn't dealt him a totally bad hand.

He had Norman too, but though he'd never admitted it to anyone, he didn't find him nearly so rewarding. He'd tried to interest his son in cricket, rowing and football, but he wasn't keen on outdoor sports, though Grace had taken them up with boundless energy. He'd introduced him to stamp-collecting and butterflies, and both had left Norman cold, though Grace had blown them up into a craze.

Byron had expected his son to be more like himself, but instead he'd clung to Veronica and the armchair near the fire. He felt there was no common ground between them on which he could make contact. Family life seemed a continual tug of war with Veronica, his wife of thirteen years, and Norman pulling on one end of the rope, and he and Grace on the other.

When they went indoors, Veronica met them in the hall, dressed up to the nines.

'What's the matter with you, Byron? I asked you to be home early and you're later than ever. You knew I wanted to go out, that I wanted Samuels and the car. I was worried you wouldn't have him here in time.'

'Aren't you having supper first?'

'I'm going to a dinner.' She belonged to a number of ladies' organisations. 'I told you last night.'

'Sorry.' He'd forgotten. 'He's here now. Run and tell him, Grace love.'

Veronica's face was lined, she had pale, bulging eyes and a permanently dissatisfied droop to her mouth. She was the most unrestful person he knew. She found it impossible to sit still, and she paced the hall now, waiting for the car to come round.

She bustled everywhere at great speed and was very involved with civic and church duties. She wanted status in the world and had come to the conclusion that Byron was not doing enough to provide it.

Byron poured himself a drink when she'd gone. He'd grown up in this rambling old house on Shrewsbury Road and had always loved it. He and Veronica had started married life in a small new house. He'd rented that, knowing that one day he'd inherit Parkfield and be able to move back. He'd looked forward to it as much as Veronica had.

But almost as soon as they moved in, Veronica had started complaining.

'You must do something about the draughts. It's freezing in here. Look at those gaps under the doors, and the windows don't fit properly. They rattle in the wind. It's quite an uncomfortable house, really.'

Byron had arranged for workmen to come in and have the doors rehung. Their foreman told him that the house was beginning to subside at the back. The floors had dropped, but to do anything about them would be a huge job. He bought draught excluders instead, which Veronica found ugly.

'We really do need central heating,' she went on. 'Everybody's having it put in.'

'The roof's more important,' Byron sighed. 'We lost another slate in the last gale.' The roof leaked like a sieve, but he kept putting that off because it seemed like throwing good money after bad.

'Carpets would help,' she went on. 'The house needs refurbishing from top to bottom. Your father neglected it.'

'He was old and ill and had lost interest.'

'For whatever reason, nothing's been done for the last twenty years.'

Parkfield also needed a large staff to run it. Fires had to be lit in every room. Byron was coming to the conclusion that he couldn't afford to run it. Anyway, they didn't need all this space. Nine bedrooms as well as servants' rooms.

Veronica's mouth began to develop a petulant droop, until nowadays it showed lines of permanent dissatisfaction. He knew she was disappointed. She'd wanted the status of living in a large house, of playing chatelaine. She was disenchanted with everything. Particularly with him.

Veronica had been an attractive girl thirteen years ago, tall, even a little taller than he was, and reed-slim. With her fair hair and coquettish ways, she'd swept him off his feet. She used to lift her pouting lips to be kissed, and her hands would be reaching out constantly to touch him. She wore low-necked dresses which displayed some of her heaving bosom. He'd been totally besotted with her. Their courtship had been rapid. With hindsight, Byron was afraid it had been too rapid.

As soon as she had his ring on her finger, she no longer seemed to welcome his attention. She very quickly told him that a nice man didn't bother his wife too often. She became pregnant with Grace far too quickly by her reckoning, and when she was expecting Norman two years later, she moved out of Byron's bedroom and had never returned. She complained that he was making too many demands on her, and thereafter Byron found himself paying for her favours.

She'd point out a pair of earrings or a string of pearls in a shop window, and if he bought them for her, he was allowed into her bedroom. He was getting there less and less often as the years passed. Veronica thought once a month quite enough, thank you.

She was five years older than he was. It had seemed nothing thirteen years ago, but she'd aged quickly. Her body was stringy, almost emaciated, and she didn't wear dresses with low necklines any more because her ribs could be counted right up to her collar bone.

Byron was making a point of getting to the office much earlier than he used to. He had his man Perkins wake him very early with tea and toast, then fill the hip bath in his dressing room while he ate it. He'd inherited Perkins from his father too, and wasn't comfortable with being waited on hand and foot, but it meant he could be out of the house in time to catch the first tram down to Chester Street. He walked to the office from there, leaving Samuels and his car to chauffeur the children to school and Veronica to her appointments with her hairdresser.

He told himself he was worried stiff about the possibility of a world war, about keeping the business afloat if war came. He needed to start work early in the day when his head was clear.

It took him months to admit that he was there before seven thirty in order to see Evie Collins. She certainly wasn't the average cleaning lady, despite her big blue apron. He thought her beautiful. She moved quickly and with such grace that she was a delight to watch. He couldn't drag his eyes away from her dark hair and fair skin.

Once he'd established the routine of coming in early, she had his fire drawing up and his office tidy and smelling of furniture polish before he got there.

'Good morning,' she'd say with the slow smile he found so attractive, and she'd go to the kitchen and bring him a cup of steaming tea because he'd once asked her to make one.

She'd busy herself then about his office, sweeping up the hearth, piling more coal on the fire, seeming to make reasons to stay with him while he drank his tea. She was so energetic. She said she had two children but he found it hard to believe because she looked so young.

Talking to Evie made a pleasant start to his day, and though he'd have liked to let his mind linger on her, he couldn't afford to.

'I've got worries, Evie,' he'd told her. 'Thousands of them.'

She'd turned from the hearth and her deep blue eyes had searched his face. 'The war? Everybody's worried it'll come.'

He gulped at the tea and tried to explain about the business. She was frowning, as though trying to understand.

'It's a big business, but it's in poor shape. I couldn't be in a worse position to ride out a war.'

For the last decade, he'd been trying to persuade his father to sell off some of the small ships they ran, while they still could. He'd tried to point out their business had been founded in the eighteenth century and everything had changed now that they were in the twentieth.

It wasn't as if there hadn't been steam vessels sailing regularly to the African Coast since the middle of the last century – and carrying more cargo than he could, quite apart from the mail and the passengers they took. How could Henry Ball and Sons, West Africa Merchants, compete against that?

'We do,' his father had insisted. 'And we make a profit. If we're able to do that, what's the point of selling up? It's an old-fashioned business, of course it is, our family have been running it for two hundred years. You ought to be proud of that, not want to close it down.'

Byron sighed. His father had run the business for forty years and had fought against relinquishing the reins until he was in his mid-eighties. New fleets of steamers were being built up by other firms and proving very profitable. Byron felt that they were being left behind and would soon be unable to compete for business.

He'd persuaded his father to buy the *Boadicea* just after Grace was born. She was a two-masted schooner-rigged vessel of eleven thousand tons, equipped with two engines. He'd hoped it would be the first step to a modern fleet. *Boadicea* had been built in 1890 in Plymouth, one of hundreds of ships of similar size and design being built at that time. She'd been tramping coal from Cardiff to Germany and returning with a cargo of grain.

They'd renamed her the *Grace Ball*. Unfortunately she hadn't proved noticeably more profitable than the small sailing ships.

On her first voyage to the Coast, they'd had trouble with the engines. Only the fact that she had sails too made it possible for her to return to Liverpool, where repairs could be carried out.

On the second voyage they'd loaded an additional cargo of coconuts and bananas in Las Palmas. Somehow rats had got in, and by the time they reached Liverpool they'd drained the milk from the coconuts and spoiled other cargo. A great deal had had to be dumped and the ship fumigated, resulting in a net loss for both voyages.

They'd kept the *Grace Ball* for a few years but she always had problems of one sort or another. His father had insisted on selling her in Athens. He thought her unlucky and there was no persuading him to buy more steamers. He'd closed his eyes to the fact that sailing ships were being used mainly in coastal trading and that the company profits were getting smaller year by year. It had been impossible to tell him that the world was changing and the business would have to change with it or die.

'We do it cheaper under sail,' the old man had insisted. 'The wind is free. Coal costs.'

'But the iron steamships are so much bigger and faster. They carry so much more cargo.'

'And need a larger crew, which also costs. There are still thousands of small vessels like ours. They're all making a profit for their owners or they wouldn't still be in use.'

And it wasn't just the ships. The warehouse had been in use since 1842 and the office had been built a year earlier. This part of town had changed out of all recognition in that time. It had gone downhill. Everything was too small and too old-fashioned.

Byron drained his tea cup and set it back on its saucer. 'But the biggest problem, Evie, is that the whole reason for this trade has gone. What my family shipped out to the Coast was used as currency.

'At one time, everyone who went out there had to buy their trade goods first and barter them for what they needed to survive. Missionaries had to trade glass beads and gin to lease land and buy building materials to erect their churches and schools. The Catholic Church was a good customer for more than a century. Now coins and notes are used there, just as in the civilised world.'

'But aren't you still shipping trade goods out there?' Evie asked.

Byron sighed. 'The natives still like Dane guns, enamel-ware and baubles of every sort. Things like that find a ready market in the ports along the Coast, so yes, I am.'

His father had died a year ago, and since then he'd managed to reduce their fleet of fifteen small sailing ships to twelve. Now, with war on the horizon, Byron wished he'd been less concerned with the prices he'd been offered and sold more of them.

When war was declared on August Bank Holiday Monday, it gave Byron a sinking feeling in his gut. He felt real fear. He said so to Evie.

Her smile was sad. He was watching for her dimple, but it didn't come.

'All the men I know are looking forward to it. They want to get away from their dull workaday lives. They expect war to bring thrills and adventure and fun.'

'And what do the women expect, Evie?'

'Heartbreak, I suppose. They're afraid of the fighting. Afraid they'll lose their loved ones.' He saw her shudder.

'Your husband?'

She nodded. 'He's a seaman, deep-sea. Always saying he hates to leave home, hates to leave me and the children. Yet war's no sooner declared than he's writing about joining the Royal Navy. If they'll have him.'

'You can try to persuade him otherwise. He hasn't signed on yet?'

'No, he's on a tramp due in from New York next week. But he'll not change his mind. He wants to fight for his country.'

Byron sighed. 'He might not be any safer on a cargo vessel. Not in war time.' That was his own worry. He had twelve cargo vessels plying the seas.

Evie's eyes fastened on his. 'I suppose my problems

seem very straightforward?' He could see she was frightened.

'More straightforward than mine, but more important too. People are more important. Perhaps I'm lucky, I don't think war will touch my family.' He had problems with Veronica he couldn't talk about, but plenty more he wanted to get off his chest. 'But it will bring difficulties to this business.' They seemed insurmountable.

'I don't think Germany will allow us to go on trading. Do you know what our ships bring in to Liverpool?'

'Palm oil, I'm told, and sometimes parrots.'

She could always make him smile.

'The crew bring parrots back to make a bit on the side. Parrots bring high prices here. The cargo is mainly palm oil. That's what keeps the great industrial machines of Britain turning, Evie. It's also needed to make soap and margarine. It's a valuable commodity in the war effort.'

He sighed again. 'I don't think my ships will be allowed to bring it in unhindered.'

'You could lose your ships, you mean? They could be sunk by the German navy?'

'Yes, I might lose my fleet as well as my cargoes.'

In the first week of the war, Byron went down to London to find out if compensation would be paid to ship-owners affected by enemy action. No one had been prepared to assure him that it would. He was told the Government had made no decisions as yet.

But he had to make his decisions. He talked them over with Evie the following morning.

'I can't leave my ships tied up in port, earning nothing. They have to trade if I'm to pay my crews.'

Evie sighed. She seemed as troubled by his problems as he was.

'Because they represent a goodly proportion of your company capital?'

That made him smile. 'You understand something of business matters then?'

Her smile widened. 'A little, but a very different business to yours.'

'I hope so. Mine's a dying company, Evie.'

'Surely not! It's big business. An office like this, and ships . . .'

'Dying all the same.'

Byron reflected that being in charge of a dying company was far more complicated than running one that was growing. And a lot less rewarding in personal as well as financial terms. The most important thing was to conserve the wealth the business had built up in its heyday. He was afraid there might not be much more.

The company had used shipping agents in New York and also New Orleans. He'd pondered and pondered, and decided that for the duration of the war, he'd try shipping the palm oil to America. The ships could go back to the Coast loaded with bicycles and Singer sewing machines. There was a ready market for those. He wished he knew how long the war would last.

But if he did that, there would be little for him to do here in Birkenhead. For one wild night, he'd been tempted to sail for the Coast and then on to America. Run his business from there for the duration.

There were several reasons why he couldn't do that. This office was one of them. He employed over thirty people here, most on good wages, a considerable sum each month. He had to find work for his staff or close this office down. The same went for his warehouse. Otherwise the wages would be money down the drain which would eventually bankrupt him.

'There must be something you can use all this for,' Evie said, her forehead creased in thought.

'Yes,' he agreed. A West Africa merchant was very much a general merchant. 'I have trading contacts in many commodities. Salt, for instance. That's always been lucrative.'

For over a hundred years, ships had been sailing from Liverpool to the Coast carrying the weight of their registered tonnage in salt. Henry Ball and Sons had wholesaled salt to other shipping companies.

'Perhaps cloth too.' That wasn't so certain. The African Coast liked such gaudy patterns, that couldn't be sold elsewhere. Plain khaki for the army now, perhaps . . .

'I shouldn't be keeping you, Evie,' he said suddenly. 'You'll want to get home to your children, not listen to my troubles.'

'I didn't realise,' she said, going to the door, 'how difficult things were for you. Your problems make mine seem needless worries.'

When she'd gone, Byron got up from his desk to stare out of the window. He could see over the graveyard of St Mary's and over the dry docks beyond to the river. There was always something of interest going on: tugs fussing about the big ships; smaller vessels scudding up and down the river under full sail. Most of the local coastal traffic was carried under sail. There was still a future for the sort of ships he owned. Not in his business, but others would want them. They had a market price.

He sighed. He'd done no work as yet. He was hungry, having come out without a proper breakfast. He usually made himself wait until he could have an early lunch. Today, he'd go out and have egg and bacon. He couldn't get Evie Collins out of his mind and he needed a full stomach to make his decisions.

\* \* \*

After only a few months, Evie knew that everybody was seeing the full horror that war brought. She found it terrifying. Two of Ned's brothers were killed in the trenches at Ypres with only a fortnight between them. She was spending more time with her mother-in-law, who had barely accepted Willy's death when the news reached her that Ben had died of his wounds.

'What a way for them to go.' Gertie was prostrated with grief. 'Such a struggle to bring them up, and for what? Battle fodder, that's all they were.'

And it wasn't just Ned's relatives. Evie kept hearing of neighbours and acquaintances who were losing their loved ones in the trenches. She was glad Ned had joined the navy. After all, Great Britain ruled the seas, everybody said so. Her navy was twice as strong as Germany's.

Food became scarce and almost unaffordable. Evie found it a struggle to get enough to feed her family and lodger. Now that Queenie was older, she didn't need a rest after her midday meal, so Evie couldn't have one either. She went to bed as early as she could and slept the sleep of the exhausted.

Once she'd settled into the routine of getting up early in the morning, she quite enjoyed it, particularly when the light summer mornings returned. It was a change to get out of her house. She worked alone and saw nobody but Mr Ball, who came in just as she was finishing. He always passed the time of day with her and she enjoyed that. She soon realised he was using her as a sounding board for his business worries.

'There's nothing I can do to help you,' she'd told him more than once.

'You listen, Evie. To talk my problems through makes me see them more clearly. I know then what's the best thing to do about them. So you do help.

'Wasn't I worried stiff at the beginning of the war? I was rerouteing all my ships to America, with an office full of clerks here and nothing for them to do.'

'You needn't have,' she said.

'No, they were all volunteering for the trenches like lemmings and handing in their notice. The staff melted away with the work.'

'It all turned out very well for you, Mr Ball.'

'I was lucky. And you helped. It was your idea that we should rent out some of our office space when we had no further use for it. And at the warehouse. Now we deal only in salt, we've rented storage there to other companies.'

Evie smiled. 'That's common sense. What I'd have done myself.'

'You pointed it out to me.'

'And you made sure I had just as much work by getting your tenants to pay me for their cleaning.'

'It was easy enough to make that part of the renting agreement. Better for me too. I know the whole office is looked after, and you tell me when things go wrong, like that burn on the floor. But once this war's over, they won't want to rent office space like this.'

'There you go, worrying again. You're always thinking so far ahead.'

'I have to. There'll be a lot of new offices built after the war and they'll all have central heating. No need for anyone to be setting fires in them then. I've had the roof botched here so many times.'

'Then you'll be able to rebuild this when it's over.'

'But when will that be? I hoped it would be over before now.'

'Doesn't everybody?'

Evie thought it a curious relationship. Mr Ball treated

her like an equal, going on about his business worries until she knew more about the company than Miss Pringle did, though she'd been promoted to being his personal secretary.

At home, Byron tried to avoid talking about his business to Veronica.

'What the company needs,' she was fond of telling him, 'is more dynamic management. You need to put your shoulder to the wheel and make it pay. If your father could do it, there's no reason why you can't.'

Veronica believed she knew what she was talking about. Her father had been a partner in the firm of accountants that had audited the books of Henry Ball and Sons for many years. She told Byron that it had been her ambition to follow in her father's footsteps and be an auditor too. She'd been articled to a firm of Liverpool accountants but had given up her training in its first months in order to marry him.

'We can't achieve profits like we did thirteen years ago.' Byron had done his best to explain why his business was dying.

The palm oil his father had shipped home had grown wild in the jungle. Nowadays, plantations had been planted and it was farmed. The companies owning the plantations controlled the market. Many used steam-powered vessels. The world had moved on. He couldn't compete, but he couldn't get Veronica to see that.

He'd given up trying now, since the awful suspicion that Veronica had married him for his income had become a virtual certainty. She'd grown impatient with him over the years. Increasingly demanding of money. Increasingly upset at seeing the profits of his business slide away.

He'd got into the habit of trying to head her off when

she started talking about the business, because she wouldn't listen. She argued back, nagging that he should do this or that to make more profit, trying to push him into something he didn't want to do.

That was the attraction of Evie Collins. She listened, and if she didn't have a helpful comment to make, she said nothing.

He now employed only one elderly clerk in the office and one tally clerk in the warehouse. Both were nearing retirement. Alfred, the office boy, was still with them, because he was too young for the forces. Apart from them, there was only Ida Pringle.

At the start of the war he'd employed fifteen accounts clerks. He'd been worried when they'd left practically *en masse*, worried enough to mention it to Veronica.

'I can come to the office and keep the account books for you. It'll save hiring another clerk and I shall be more reliable.'

'There's no need, Veronica,' he'd told her. 'You don't want to spend your time in the office. You've the house and the children to see to.'

'I don't intend to spend all day with you. I won't need to keep office hours like the hired staff. I think it'll be a good thing, I shall be able to put my finger on where you can make savings. It'll be good for me to take more interest in the business. The children don't need me so much now they are older, and the house ticks along. No, I need more to fill my day anyway.'

Byron was appalled. He was unable to stop her. She came when he least expected her, and nagged him to explain all manner of things with which he didn't want her to interfere.

He was relieved when the war took care of that. As the household staff left to take better-paid jobs in industry now that so many men were away fighting, Veronica found she couldn't spend so much time in the office.

She complained bitterly about the amount of work needed to keep the house running. She took the business accounts home with her to do there. Byron thought it the lesser of two evils. He thought she'd soon tire of it. She wasn't the sort to keep at it for long.

It was the first of June but a miserable morning. The rain was coming down in sheets as Evie went to the office at four thirty. She shivered, feeling depressed by the shortages war was bringing. It was 1916 and nobody could see an end to it. Ned had been away since January.

She felt desperately sorry for Gertie, for two more of her sons had been killed. Only Ned remained now. He'd been very shocked to hear about Alfie, and wrote that Evie must not think it would happen to him. The law of averages was against it.

Bobby had started school and loved it. But Evie had to be prompt getting home in order to get him up and ready. She was looking forward to the time when Queenie would go too, then her day would be easier.

She went about her cleaning with her mind on other things. The food she would have to find for her family before tonight. Whether Bobby was going down with a cold. He'd seemed snuffly last night.

She'd cleaned and tidied the whole office. There were no fires to set at this time of the year, but it was such a miserable morning she'd lit one in Byron's room. Now she put on more coal, and the room began to feel warmer.

A copy of *The Times* newspaper was delivered to the office every morning. Evie saw it as one of her duties to pick it up from the doormat by the front door and put it on Byron's desk. She usually gave the headlines a cursory glance, then the following morning, after he'd tossed it aside, she'd take it home and read it carefully. It was the only means she had of following the progress of the war. Some days, Miss Pringle brought it home with her at five o'clock.

This morning, the newspaper was wet when she picked it up. She took it to Byron's office and opened it out in front of the fire.

Her eye caught the headline 'Big Naval Battle in Jutland'. She was instantly transfixed. She dropped the paper when she saw clouds of steam being sucked out of it. Then picked it up and read on. Ned was serving on the *Indefatigable*. As soon as she saw the name of the ship, she could read no more. Couldn't even see the print through the haze of tears. She knew she was shaking.

She went to the kitchen like an automaton to make Byron's cup of tea, because it was that time of the morning. Easier to do what was routine and normal. She couldn't think of Ned being in a battle. She could see him now, suntanned and smiling. There was a lump in her throat. She was filled with an awful dread.

'Evie?' She turned from the kitchen window. 'What's happened?'

She snatched up the teapot and poured tea into the cup she'd set out in readiness. 'Your tea. Shall I take it to your office?'

'What's the matter? You look as though you've seen a ghost.'

She took a deep breath and tried to stop shivering. 'Your paper. There's been a big naval battle. The headlines . . . Ned . . .'

'His ship?'

'It's mentioned.'

Evie watched Byron take another cup and saucer

from the cupboard and pour more tea.

'Drink this. Come and sit down for a minute. You look as though you're going to faint. What does it say about the battle?'

'I don't know. Couldn't read any further.' She was in a blind panic now.

'Shall I read it to you?'

She was surprised to find herself sitting in the visitor's chair in front of his desk, with the cup of tea in front of her.

'Is that what you want?'

She couldn't stop her teeth chattering. 'I want to know what's happened to him. He's dead, isn't he?'

'I don't know,' Byron said, and began to read the article very slowly.

When he came to the name of Ned's ship, HMS *Indefatigable*, Evie drew in a sharp breath.

'I'm sorry,' Byron murmured. When she looked up, his eyes were deep pools of compassion.

'That's it then? Ned's been killed?' She felt numb.

'The ship's reported as being sunk.' His voice was soft. 'But it doesn't say all the crew were lost. There were other ships nearby. The *Invincible* for one, and the *Lion*. The first thing they'd do is pick up survivors. Your husband . . . he might be safe.'

She took a sip of tea but couldn't control the gasp of agony that was choking her.

'Evie?' Byron was on his feet close to her chair. 'I wish there was something I could do . . .'

She stood up and he put his arms round her in a hug. She rested her forehead against the fine worsted of his suit and let her tears flood out. She felt him holding her close against the warmth of his body. Then he made her sit down and finish her tea.

She asked: 'How can I find out? Whether Ned's been killed . . .'

'You'll be notified officially.'

'But when? I need to know now . . .' She felt agonised.

'I'll try and find out for you. I can't promise, but I'll try.'

'Yes.'

'I'll need to know his full name and rank.'

'Able Seaman Edward Albert Collins.'

'Go home, Evie. You'll be better there. I'll let you know if I have any news.'

As she went to the door, she could see he looked very concerned.

He said: 'Shall I take you home?'

'No, I'll be all right, it's only round the corner. Anyway, I have to take Bobby to school.'

Evie wanted to hope but she knew she mustn't. Something had died within her. She knew Ned was no more.

# CHAPTER NINE

When Evie had gone, Byron let out a long sigh. How could he not be moved by such obvious grief? He felt drawn to help her, take care of her during her time of trouble.

There must be some way of finding out direct, perhaps phone the Admiralty? But it was easier to ring Charles, his cousin, a Fleet Street reporter. Charles knew exactly how to get any sort of information. Might already know, for the paper published lists of those killed. He'd have to wait for an hour so so. Let Charles get to his desk. He hoped, for Evie's sake, that Edward Albert Collins had been lucky.

When Miss Pringle came to the office she already knew that Ned Collins's ship had gone down. Byron had letters to answer, and he tried to work, but he couldn't keep his mind on what he was doing, and it seemed that Miss Pringle couldn't either.

It was midday when Charles rang back to confirm the worst. Within twenty minutes of sighting the enemy fleet, the battleship *Indefatigable* had received a direct hit which had exploded its magazine and sent its fifty-foot-long picket boat flying hundreds of feet into the air. There had been no survivors from that vessel. Charles told Byron that the list of those who had perished would be published tomorrow morning within a black border. Ned Collins's name would be on it.

Byron sat for a while at his desk, wishing now that he hadn't tried to comfort Evie by telling her there was hope. He'd told her he'd let her know if he had any news; now he wished he hadn't done that either. It would go through him to see hope fade from her face. He thought he might just scribble a note and send Miss Pringle home with it. But in the end, he took his bowler and macintosh off the bentwood stand and went out.

The heavy rain of the morning had eased but it was drizzling and overcast. He'd checked Evie's address from his records. It wasn't far, only a few hundred yards. The house was one of a long row of small, flat-fronted houses. There were white net curtains at the window and the step had been recently holystoned. It looked cleaner and better cared for than its neighbours. Byron thought its smoke-grimed bricks and blue slate roof, wet and shiny in the rain, rather depressing.

Evie opened the door to him with a child in her arms; another was peering round her full skirts. She wore a simple dress of midnight blue. He'd never seen her without an apron before. Her face was white but she seemed more in control. There was the look of a madonna about her. She half smiled a welcome and stood back.

'Thank you for coming. Will you come in?'

His spirits dropped. He was going to dash all her hopes. He shook the raindrops off his bowler and followed her down the narrow hall to the back room.

'I'm afraid, Evie . . .' he began.

'I already know,' she said softly. 'This came mid-morning.' The official yellow envelope was on the table, the buff paper with the message half protruding.

'Excuse me a moment,' she said. 'I didn't take Bobby to school this morning, I think he's getting a cold, and now he's gone to sleep on my shoulder. I'll just put him down on his bed.'

When she'd gone, Byron edged the paper out of its yellow envelope, unfolded it and read: 'We regret to inform you that Able Seaman Edward Albert Collins went down with his ship . . . Please accept our sincere condolences.' He refolded the paper and pushed it back inside.

When he looked up, he saw that Evie's little daughter had been watching him from behind the rocking chair. He felt suddenly guilt-stricken. He'd been caught reading another's private correspondence.

'Hello,' he said, trying to bluff it out. 'What's your name?'

'Queenie.'

She was a beautiful child with big brown eyes that wouldn't leave his face and brown curly hair that hung to her waist. She wore a scarlet dress, covered by a fancy pinafore of broderie anglaise, and looked as well turned out as his own children.

'How old are you, Queenie?'

'Four.'

'I have a little girl, but she's a good bit older than you. Grace is twelve now.'

He felt very close to Grace, but he had to admit she wasn't as pretty as this child. Grace took after him; she'd grow up to be rather short and square.

He asked: 'Do you know who I am?'

She nodded seriously. 'Mr Ball.'

So she was intelligent too. He heard her mother's light footsteps on the stairs. When she came in, she sat down in the rocking chair and pulled the child up on her knee.

'Queenie's a lovely little girl,' he said.

'Her name's Victoria really. Ned started us all calling her Queenie.'

She was speaking more quickly than usual, and he saw now that she wasn't as much in command of herself as he'd first thought.

'And Bobby's name's not really Bobby,' the child told him, cuddling down against her mother. 'It's Robert.'

149

Byron thought the room surprisingly comfortable, and not unattractive. There was a fire in the kitchen range, making it cosy on this dark day.

He said: 'I'm dreadfully sorry, Evie. I wish I could have brought you better news.'

She was blinking hard. 'Awful to think he's never coming back to us.'

Byron could see love shining from her face as she spoke of her husband.

'All I've ever asked for was that we could be together. I ran away from home to be with him.'

'Did you?' He felt a stirring of interest. He'd known from the beginning that she should never have been a cleaner, that she didn't belong in this neighbourhood.

'My father didn't approve of Ned.'

'Not your class?'

'Not my father's class,' she corrected him. He realised she was using him as he'd often used her, as a sounding board for her worries. 'Class didn't matter, I knew it wouldn't. He loved me.'

'Don't you mind having to clean my office?'

'Not if it meant I could be with Ned. The trouble was, we had very little time together, and I always wanted more. He was always away. I did so want him to stay home with me. He felt he had to provide, you see. For us all.'

Byron saw the tears start to her eyes. She was struggling to control them.

'Whatever am I going to do now? I'll be the only breadwinner.'

He wanted to tell her he'd take care of everything. That he wanted very much to look after her and her family. That nothing would give him more pleasure. But he knew it wasn't the right time to say such things. Not while she was grieving like this.

'Go back to your family, Evie. They'll want to help you now.'

He could see her shaking her head sadly. 'I don't think so.' Queenie was curled up asleep on her lap now. 'At least we'll still have a roof over our heads, and I earn a little from you.'

'Not a lot. You all have to eat, and children cost more as they get older. I know, I've two of my own.'

'I'll manage somehow.'

'Evie, we talked a lot about my decisions. You helped me make them. Now the boot's on the other foot and I'd like to help you.'

'Make the right decisions, you mean?'

'In every way I can. I think your best plan is to go back to your own family. Perhaps they didn't approve of your husband, but you have beautiful children. They'll love them.'

He could see her shaking her head again. 'There's just my father.' Then, slowly, she began to tell him about her early life. 'He doesn't show his emotions, doesn't believe a man should. He didn't forgive my mother.'

Byron could hardly believe what she was telling him about her mother.

'If he couldn't forgive her, he won't forgive me,' she said. 'I can't go back.'

She told him about her Aunt Agatha. 'That's why I dress my children in pretty clothes. I want to see them look their best.' Her hand straightened out the scarlet skirt of Queenie's dress.

She spoke of the happiness Ned had brought her. Byron thought he'd been very lucky to have had her love. She'd brought warmth into his own life too.

For a year or more, he'd told himself she was too young for him, that his affection was that of a friend, but today had shown him how wrong he was. He'd felt sparks of jealousy as she spoke of her love for Ned. Such love as that had never come his way.

Byron couldn't stop himself walking past Joseph Hobson's shop. He'd meant only to look through the window but his curiosity was too much for him, and he had to find out what sort of a man Evie's father was. He went in and closed the door. The strong scent of the shop enveloped him: partly medicinal, partly disinfectant, yet with the scent of herbs and fancy soaps. This then was Evie's background.

He waited his turn amongst the really poor. He'd had a problem with his foot for several days and had put off doing anything about it. It was growing increasingly uncomfortable. He'd ask for some ointment to ease it.

He was watching Joseph Hobson as he worked methodically, slight and narrow-shouldered in his white coat. It was the turn of the woman in front of Byron. She was describing her cat's loss of fur and sore patches on his skin.

'Sounds like the mange,' Hobson said. The patient wasn't produced, but he pulverised herbs with his mortar and pestle to make a powder to dust over the cat.

'Yes?' Eyes of steel switched imperiously to Byron, who started telling him about his foot.

'I'd better see it,' Joseph ordered. He didn't wait for Byron to remove his shoe, but went back behind his counter to do something else. When he reappeared, his glance was cursory.

'Athlete's foot. I'll make up some ointment for you. It will cure it.' He looked a hard and angry man. A selfish man determined not to give an inch to others. Evie wasn't like that. She was all warmth.

Byron searched high and low through the shops to get some fruit and chocolate for Evie's children. He would have liked to buy her flowers but none seemed available. He wanted to give her comfort, but didn't know how. He still thought the best thing would be for her to take her children home and introduce them to her father. Surely he wouldn't refuse to help his only daughter and her children, not now her husband had died a hero's death, fighting for England. Not when Evie was going to need all the help she could get.

Byron deliberated whether he should go round to her house again, or give her the fruit and chocolate when she came to the office the next morning. But perhaps she wouldn't feel like coming in to work. He decided to go to see her. He couldn't get her out of his mind.

She looked surprised to see him again, but pleased with his gifts.

'It's very kind of you, Mr Ball. Thank you.'

'You don't have to come to work for the next day or two,' he said. 'You'll need time to yourself, to rest.'

'I'd rather work. Better if I keep busy. And as I said, I need the money.'

He wanted to say, I'll pay you a little more. Raise your wages. Make good the amount of your husband's allotment. He didn't, for he was afraid of offending her.

Instead, he began persuading her to go and see her father. Nagging her in the way Veronica nagged him. He was sure her father would want to help her. He didn't tell her he'd been anywhere near the pharmacy, and was surprised to find that the ointment had eased his foot already. The problem cleared up within a few days, just as Joseph Hobson had said it would.

Evie felt like a zombie in the first weeks after Ned's death.

Half the time she didn't believe he really was dead. After all, she hadn't actually seen his body, and he was away so much. She hardly knew what she was doing, but found she stuck to her usual routine even if she was in a near-trance.

She began thinking of her mother more often, as though Ned's death had awakened memories of an earlier loss. Her nightmares returned.

It had given Evie the fright of her life to see her mother in such a state.

'Only ninepence in her purse.' Father had laughed cruelly. 'She went hungry all right. I told her she would if she left. Serves her right.'

And he had predicted that Evie would suffer the same fate.

'You'll be on the same downward path. You've heard of the primrose path to hell?' He'd been full of contempt. The phrase had haunted her.

Now, without Ned, it seemed Joseph might be right. She was distraught. It scared her sick. She thought of the four pounds she had in her purse and wondered what she'd do when it was gone. She was thankful she'd made the effort to get Miss Pringle as a sub-tenant. Thankful too for her cleaning job. She knew she couldn't earn more, because she'd already done her best to add to her income. She needed Ned's help and support to bring their children up, and without his earnings, they wouldn't have enough to live on. It would be impossible for her to make ends meet.

'You mustn't worry your head about money,' Gertie Collins had comforted. 'Your dad's got plenty, hasn't he? He's well heeled. He'll not see you starve.'

'He might,' Evie said. She was afraid he would.

'I'd give my last penny to my kids,' Gertie said

indignantly. She remembered then that none of her boys was still alive, and a tear rolled down her cheek. With a little sob she added: 'Or to my grandkids. I couldn't see them starve.'

Evie put her arms round her. 'You're different, Gertie, very different.'

She was spending more time with Ned's mother, and tried to both give and take comfort. She knew Gertie couldn't help her with money. These days, she never had enough herself. When she'd had working sons living at home, there'd been money coming in. Now she had to rely on what she could earn, and Gertie never managed to keep any job very long.

She'd tried taking in washing but found that very hard, particularly when there were so many smuts from the railway yards nearby. She'd been a cleaner at the Argyle Theatre, and had odd nights as a barmaid at the Lighterman's Arms.

'I like that best,' she chuckled. 'More fun, like. But I'll never be more than a stopgap when someone's ill. A young girl behind the bar brings in trade, and I'm past doing that.'

At the moment, she had an early-morning office-cleaning job at the Westminster Bank.

'It's like getting up in the middle of the night,' she said sadly. 'And they're always finding fault with me work. Saying I'm not thorough enough. Cleaning's not my thing.'

Gertie also looked after a baby in the evenings while his mother worked as an usherette at the Queen's Hall. Evie knew she'd look after Queenie if she asked her. Now her sons were gone, Gertie loved to have her grandchildren round her. She often went to New Brighton to see Alfie's three little boys. Evie knew she'd have to pay her, though. Gertie couldn't afford to do it for nothing.

Queenie could be a bit of a handful, and in addition Bobby would need collecting from school at lunchtime and taking back. That meant a good walk from Gertie's house. Evie was afraid she'd be asking her to do too much. Gertie had been in a state before Ned's death; now she reckoned she'd paid the ultimate price for war. Five sons killed in combat. She hardly seemed to be coping now.

Her hair was in need of a wash and cut. Evie trimmed and set it for her, hoping it would make her feel better. She mended one of her dresses and took it home to wash. But it was the tip of the iceberg, and she wouldn't be able to do even that if she found more work. Gertie kept advising her to go back to her father.

'It's the only way, love. Take your pride in your hands and go. That's what I say. That's what our Ned would want you to do now.'

'My father's not the sort to . . .'

'Nonsense, Evie, you don't know what you're saying. Just look at your little Bobby. Doesn't your heart go out to him? Lovely children they are, both of them. His grandchildren. He's got plenty of money, his sort always has. He'll want to help you. Course he will. Who else would he want to give his money to?'

Evie needed a good deal of persuasion.

'Any father would want to help, especially when there are grandchildren,' Byron Ball told her. 'I know I would.'

But she'd seen the reception Joseph had given her mother when she'd come home. She was afraid Byron and Gertie were wrong, but the trouble was, she could think of no alternative. Not in the short term until Queenie went to school.

Evie felt a coward. She didn't want to ask her father for anything. The last time she had, he'd twisted her collar so hard she'd thought she'd choke, and that her end was coming.

She was scared of working close to him again. Of having to stand up to his domineering ways. She tried to tell herself things would be different now. She was older, she had her own home. And the thought of not being able to feed and clothe her children frightened her too. She'd have to go and see Father. She'd be a fool to leave any stone unturned.

Evie made up her mind to go the next Sunday. That gave her three days to bolster her courage.

By two o'clock on Sunday, she had the children ready in newly pressed clothes, with their hair washed and brushed. She'd primed them not to speak unless spoken to, and to be on their best behaviour. She felt proud of them as she walked down Argyle Street with a child swinging on each of her hands. Surely they couldn't fail to make a good impression?

She'd planned her visit for the time Father would be finishing his Sunday dinner, hoping to catch him feeling replete and content. Being Sunday, the shop was closed. For such occasions, there was a bell positioned high on the door frame, though it was rarely used. She reached up to it.

There was no response. She knew this part would have been easier if she'd come when the shop was open, but she couldn't talk to him in front of customers. She rang the bell harder. This time she heard his step on the stairs.

'All right, all right, I'm coming.' He sounded irritable. She heard him pull back the bolts. 'It is Sunday, am I to have no rest?'

The door opened six inches, and his cold grey eyes

stared into hers, astounded. She watched them go slowly from one child to the other.

'Hello, Father.'

'What do you want then?' His wiry eyebrows came down in a frown the way she remembered.

'I've come to see you. Brought my children to see you. This is Bobby and . . .'

'Two of them? Been breeding like rabbits, you and that Collins fellow. I hope he married you?'

'Yes, Father.' She hoped he wasn't going to probe too deeply into how she'd managed that.

'How many years is it now?'

'Six,' she faltered. 'Can we come in?'

'If you have to.' He stood back grudgingly. Evie's heart sank.

'How are you, Father?' He didn't look well. His hawk-nose was red at the tip and there was a bluish tinge to his chin.

'How am I? What do you care? Running away, leaving me in that park without so much as a word. I waited and waited . . . Worried stiff about you.'

'I'm sorry . . .'

'Sorry, is it?' The smell of the shop engulfed her, painfully familiar. But the sight of it was not. There were still two counters but they were back against the walls, along two sides of the square. The middle of the shop had been opened up.

'You've changed . . .'

'Modernised. Have to keep up to date.'

She was glad to see him making for the stairs. It might be easier to talk in the living room.

He asked: 'What's gone wrong, then? Something must have, to bring you back here.'

Evie swallowed hard. Nothing at all had changed

upstairs. The scent of Sunday's roast mutton hung heavily in the air. Her past seemed to be closing in on her.

'Ned's been killed.' Evie heard the quiver in her voice. 'He joined up at the beginning of the war, the navy. The Battle of Jutland, you read about that? He went down with his ship. Lost at sea.'

Joseph laughed cruelly. 'Really? I thought it more likely he'd be killed in a pub brawl.'

'He died a hero's death.'

'A hero – that scoundrel? Still, as things turned out, you needn't be ashamed.'

'We're proud of what he did, Father. He died for his country.'

'So that's what brings you back. You've fallen on hard times. The Collinses aren't the sort to take out insurance. Left you with nothing, has he, and two extra mouths to feed? I'm not surprised. I could foresee it happening, even if you couldn't. Though I'd have betted on the pub brawl, or that he'd go off with another lass.'

Evie could feel a ball of anger growing inside her. She swallowed it back. She had to try.

'I was hoping you'd let me come back to work on the front counter. Not a full day, I couldn't do that.'

His eyes were full of suspicion. 'Why? Won't anybody else employ you? Not worth your wages?'

'Bobby's in school, but there's Queenie to think of.' Evie squeezed her daughter's hand. 'She's a good little girl, not a lot of trouble. I thought perhaps Matilda wouldn't mind having her with her for a few hours each day while I was in the shop . . .'

'I mind, Evie,' he thundered. 'Matilda can't manage the work she has now. Look at this place. It's high time she cleaned it out.'

Queenie was twisting away, hiding her face in her

mother's skirts. Evie took a deep breath. If they were to have enough to eat, she had to get him to agree to this.

'It's just that I can't work anywhere else. Not until September. Queenie goes to school then. If you . . .'

'No! You'd be wanting to run off all the time to collect the other one from school anyway. I've been through all this before. Your mother was just the same.'

Evie closed her mind to the jibe about her mother. She felt she had to persist. 'I was hoping you'd help me, Father.'

'Help you? Why should I? You haven't given one thought to me all these years.'

'They are your grandchildren.' Gertie had thought that reason enough. Byron had thought Joseph would offer an allowance and refuse to let her work for it.

'So I'm family now, am I? It's a bit late to think of that. These children are your responsibility, not mine. No, you've made your bed and you can lie on it.'

Evie wished she hadn't come anywhere near him. His eyes were burning with venom.

'You left me, just like your mother did.'

She couldn't look at him. Her gaze went round the room, so achingly familiar.

'Yes, well, you've had your say about that.' Evie felt she'd failed. She turned away and saw Matty watching from the landing.

'Matty!' She rushed to her and kissed her cheek. A cheek that seemed to have aged much more than she would have expected in six years. 'Are you well?' Matty's round face sagged now, tired and careworn, but she was smiling at the children.

Evie introduced them, and Matty made much of them. Joseph ignored them, picking up his newspaper.

'While I'm here, Father, I'd like to collect some of my

160

things.' She'd left a heavy winter coat and a good pair of boots. She needed them now.

He glowered at her. 'You went. I didn't want any reminders.'

She said: 'Matty, keep an eye on my children for a moment.'

She whisked upstairs and flung open the door of her old bedroom. It pulled her up short to see that everything she'd ever owned had been cleared from the room. Every surface was bare. Every book and ornament gone. She opened her wardrobe. It was empty. The bed was draped in a grey cotton counterpane she'd never seen before. She went down to the living room more slowly. Matty had taken the children to the kitchen. Her father still glowered.

'I didn't know you'd be coming back asking for your old things. Why should I keep them for you? It is six long years.'

'I should have known you'd want everything cleared,' she said stiffly.

'I thought an apprentice might use it. Better room than those in the attic.'

Evie felt like crying. Coming back here had been a mistake. She'd known it would be. Why had she let Byron talk her into it? She turned on her heel and went to the kitchen.

'I shouldn't have come. How do you put up with him, Matty?'

'I have to.'

'You are all right?'

'I suppose so. You know how things are.'

Evie squeezed her hand sympathetically.

'Can we go home, Mummy?' Queenie tugged at her skirt.

'Yes, let's go.' She took them by the hand. The living-room door was still open. She'd been about to say goodbye to her father and tell him she wouldn't trouble him again, but a buff envelope propped up against a vase on the mantelshelf caught her eye.

'Is that a letter for me?' She went closer. It was addressed to Miss Evelina Mary Hobson.

Her father rattled his paper. 'Yes. Been here a week or two now. Didn't know what to do with it. Was thinking of putting it in the fire.'

Evie picked it up and pushed it in her pocket.

'Something to do with your Aunt Agatha, I expect.'

'What do you mean?'

'You haven't heard? She died out in the jungle. Just as I told her she would. Nobody believes what I tell them, but I'm always right.'

Evie was shocked. 'Died? When?'

'Must be a year or more now. She was another who wouldn't listen to sense. I don't know what's the matter with you women. You're all the same. Off with any man who crooks his finger at you.'

The passing years had softened Evie's feelings about Aunt Agatha. Perhaps she'd felt stifled by Father too. Evie wanted to know how she had died but Bobby was pulling on her sleeve. She asked: 'What's the matter, love?'

He whispered: 'Why doesn't he like us?'

Queenie was tugging her towards the door.

Evie said: 'We'd better go, Father.'

'Yes, you go. Everybody goes, then when things go wrong they expect me to welcome them back with open arms. I don't want you back. You'd only be off again the next time some fancy fellow looks twice at you.'

Evie went, wanting to escape as quickly as she could. She was angry. She should have known what to expect.

The children were upset too, asking questions she'd have preferred not to answer.

'How did you get on?' Miss Pringle wanted to know before she'd had time to take her hat off.

'Didn't get on at all. It was a disaster.' Ida's arms went round in her a comforting hug.

'Come and sit down, I'll put the kettle on for a cup of tea. What did he say?'

'He said no, why should he help me. It was my problem, not his.'

'There's still Gertie.'

Although Evie had decided not to ask Gertie, her mother-in-law had come round yesterday and offered to do what she could. That was Gertie's way. She'd said she'd look after Queenie if Evie could find work.

'She'd let Queenie run wild,' Evie said to Ida. Gertie couldn't control the little girl. Matty probably wouldn't be able to either, but at least in the shop Evie would have been close at hand.

The anger wouldn't leave her. Tears were stinging her eyes. She was no nearer finding a way to make ends meet.

'Oh, come on, Evie, you'll find something.'

'Whatever am I going to do without Ned? It's hopeless. I wish I could die too.'

Miss Pringle pursed her thick lips. Her tiny shoe-button eyes were sympathetic. 'Don't say such things. You've still got the children. You love them and they need you.

'You've had more from life than I've had, Evie. You still have your memories.'

Evie had put the children to bed when she remembered the letter. She went to her wardrobe and took it from the pocket of her best coat. It looked like a circular of some sort.

It was from a solicitor with an office in Hamilton Square. He invited her to call and see him, he said she'd hear something to her advantage.

Evie spent an hour speculating with Miss Pringle about what it could mean.

'Your aunt has left you something in her will.' Ida nodded wisely. 'What else can it be? Let's have more tea and I'll read your cup.'

Ida saw many dots, which she said meant that Evie was coming into money. Evie could see only miscellaneous tea leaves. She went to bed unable to think of anything else. Afraid she'd be disappointed. Afraid to hope Ida was right and that her problems might be over. But if so, she couldn't understand why Aunt Agatha hadn't left what she had to her missionary husband.

As soon as she'd put Bobby into school the next morning, she walked down to Hamilton Square with Queenie, full of hope. She found the right office. The clerk on the reception desk ushered her into an inner office to see one of the partners. He was plump and pompous and introduced himself as Mr Fenshaw.

'Ah, the estate of Mrs Agatha Evelyn Appleby. Yes, we have her will here.'

Evie discovered that it was over two years since Aunt Agatha had died, and her husband had died a few days before her in the same epidemic of blackwater fever.

'She's left you a small bequest. It amounts to . . . er, let me see. Yes, two hundred and five pounds. She says, so that you might enjoy some measure of independence.'

Evie felt relief flooding through her like a tide. It was followed by a wave of gratitude. Two hundred pounds was not a small amount to her, it was a small fortune. With that she'd be able to manage until Queenie went to school.

★　★　★

Evie went home feeling much better. Aunt Agatha was her saviour, the very last person she'd have expected to come to her aid. Perhaps, after all, Agatha had been fond of her but hadn't been able to show it.

The next morning Evie was full of vigour as she cleaned out the offices of Henry Ball and Sons. It gave her pleasure to tell Byron of her bequest and to ask his advice.

'Evie! That's marvellous.' He was pleased for her. She warmed to him. 'And how best to use it?

'If it's enough to buy the house you're renting, I'd do that. Then the rent Miss Pringle pays would be income you could use to live on.'

'I don't know whether it's for sale or how much it would cost. I'll have to ask the agent. Have to think about it too.'

'It would be better than putting the money in the bank and drawing on it to supplement your living expenses.'

'Yes.' That way the money could get used up and she'd have nothing to show for it. If she could buy the house, they'd always have a roof over their heads. And that seemed too good to be true.

# CHAPTER TEN

That morning, after Evie had gone home to her children, Byron sat on at his desk, staring into space. He'd made up his mind to help her himself and had been waiting for the right opportunity. Now he felt cheated that she'd received help from elsewhere.

He'd been telling himself he must give her time. Take things slowly. After all, she'd shown only too clearly how much she'd loved her husband.

He couldn't stop thinking of the moment he'd held her in his arms and felt her breasts press against him. It made him tingle now. She looked so young, so vulnerable, how could any man not want to help? He'd found himself watching her closely this morning. The way her dark lashes swept her cheek. He'd never seen her look so beautiful. She had eyes that would melt an iceberg. He couldn't believe her father had refused to help.

Byron couldn't get enough of Evie's company. He couldn't keep her longer in the mornings because she had to go home to get her child off to school. He knew he was coming to the office earlier and earlier. It was the only way he could spend more time with her.

Evie had laughed, and said she was coming to the office earlier too, so that she could get her work finished before he arrived. Now, on his suggestion, she made tea for them both. They sat down together to drink it and talked of their children.

'Best half-hour of my day,' Byron dared to tell her.

'Best of mine too,' she'd responded, and sent his hopes

sky high. It was all he could do to stop himself crossing the room and taking her in his arms again. But it would be wrong to do such a thing. It was still too early and might upset her.

That same evening, Byron went home to find himself in the middle of a domestic crisis. He couldn't bring himself to look across the supper table at Veronica's face. He'd never seen her so angry, her grey eyes flashing vitriol in his direction. She'd already unleashed her ire on the children. They were eating silently and keeping their heads down.

'What am I supposed to do now?' she demanded. 'There's a committee meeting tonight. How am I to get to that?'

Samuels, their chauffeur, had given notice last week, and today had been his last working day. He'd been asked to move out of his rooms by this evening.

'It's hard to get staff now,' Byron tried to soothe her. 'I'm sorry. With the war, there's plenty of jobs with shorter hours and better pay.' So far, he'd failed to find a replacement.

'But have you really tried?' Her anger flared up again. 'After all, it doesn't matter to you.'

Byron had tried hard. He always tried to placate Veronica. She'd virtually taken over Samuels and the car. She expected to have them waiting, ready to drive her wherever she wanted to go.

'I suppose I'll have to learn to drive myself.'

'You'd have found that easier last year,' Byron couldn't help pointing out. 'Samuels could have shown you how.'

'Damn Samuels,' she swore, clattering her knife and fork back on her plate.

Byron had offered to drive her down to the Town Hall

tonight, and before supper had gone to check that there was petrol in the car. He found the tank virtually empty. When he looked round for the cans in which the petrol was kept, he found they'd all gone.

There should have been at least half a dozen two-gallon steel cans. He had a ten-gallon drum, and only last month had managed to buy a forty-five-gallon drum and the equipment to siphon the petrol out. It was the only way to have a ready supply, since garages catering for the motorist were few and far between. And these days petrol was scarce, expensive and very hard to come by.

Byron had lost his temper. 'When did I last drive the car? Wednesday night. It was all here then.'

He turned to Veronica. 'Where's it gone? Has Samuels taken it?'

The car was kept in the old stables, and Samuels had occupied the rooms built over them that had once housed the groom.

'He moved his things out on a hand cart,' Veronica said.

'He made several journeys with it,' Grace added.

'Did he take my petrol cans?' Byron was filled with fury. He felt cheated. The car couldn't be used until he found more petrol.

'I don't know. The cart was piled high with his clothes and things.'

'It's not my fault.' Veronica was even more enraged. 'I'd need eyes in the back of my head to see what servants get up to these days.'

Byron sighed. 'I'm not blaming anybody.' He wanted to avoid the subject of servants. Veronica could go on about the lack of them for hours.

She said: 'Perhaps, if we got a pony and trap? Everybody's going back to horses these days. I'm sure I could manage, if it was a quiet animal.'

'Could we, Daddy?' Grace turned to her father excitedly.

Byron sighed again. 'Who's going to put the pony between the shafts for you, Veronica? I don't suppose you'd feel any more capable of that than of driving? Then the beast would need feeding, and his stable mucking out. Are you going to do that?'

'I will, Daddy,' Grace said. 'A pony would be such fun.'

He said dryly: 'It would be easier to walk down for the tram, as I do every morning.'

'So I'm reduced to taking the tram? Waiting at the stop with the servant girls?'

'You can always pick up a hansom or a motor taxi to come home.'

'Surely it's possible to get a cab to come here for me?'

'You can telephone for one,' Grace said. 'I know it can be done.'

'What's the number?'

Byron felt a surge of impatience. 'Lift the phone and ask the operator. She'll know.' He made himself relax. 'Shall I do it for you?'

'And that's how I'm to get the children to school?' Veronica wasn't going to give up easily.

'They can walk. It isn't far, especially for Norman.'

'On wet mornings?' Veronica asked belligerently. 'What then?'

'There's always boarding school,' Byron said. He knew he shouldn't keep arguing with her about boarding school, not in front of Norman. He was worried about his son. Norman was a mummy's boy. Too ready to cling to her. Too ready to sit back and let others do everything for him. He was like his mother to look at, tall and angular; rather gangling at the moment. Byron had told Veronica several times that he'd like Norman to go to boarding school.

'Why?' she'd demanded. 'You said you hated it when you were sent there.'

'I didn't enjoy it,' he admitted. 'But it taught me to look after myself. It'll make Norman more independent. Able to stand on his own feet.'

'He's only ten. I don't want to part with him yet. But Grace is old enough.'

Byron met Grace's uneasy gaze. 'It's different for girls. There's a good day-school here.'

'Daddy's little girl,' Veronica sneered. 'That means you don't want to part with her.'

'I don't,' Byron said, putting his hand on Grace's shoulder to reassure her. Grace was the apple of his eye. Quicker than Norman in every way. He often wondered how his children would cope with the business he'd leave them. He was afraid Norman wouldn't, but war was changing the expectations of women, Grace would manage. One thing was certain, the business he'd hand on would be very different from the business he'd inherited.

The war dragged on; Byron was pleased with the decisions he'd made. He'd wanted to keep his ships well away from any German naval vessels, so he'd been right to direct his fleet to American ports rather than continue bringing them to Liverpool. They were still making a profit for him. It was working out well.

Many small cargo ships were being sunk by the enemy. He didn't doubt that some of his would have been, had they been in European waters. He'd been wrong about compensation, though: substantial sums were being paid by the Government for vessels that were sunk. It didn't bring back the crews, though. Many lives were being lost at sea. Byron was glad his crews were not running that risk. He'd known many of them for years and counted some as friends.

The war was making it difficult to get coal, and therefore small sailing vessels like his were commanding higher prices around the world. Everything was scarce. He still thought it right for his firm to get out of shipping altogether. Once this war was over, he'd be able to charter space on other vessels, but now he could afford to bide his time. Prices of ships would go higher as everything grew scarcer. The only ships being built were fighting ships. Until things returned to normal, he'd still make money with his old-fashioned fleet. Even Veronica conceded that she'd been wrong to insist that he continue trading out of Liverpool.

The house was another matter. The big square building set in an acre of gardens looked imposing, but the roof was leaking badly. He couldn't count the number of times he'd sent men up to fix it. As soon as they stopped the water coming in at one place, it started somewhere else. He was coming round to the opinion that it would cost more to put Parkfield right than it would to build a new house.

'We can't live in it like this,' Veronica complained one night. 'It's a miserable place at the best of times, but now, in the middle of winter, it's colder inside than it is out.' She poked the fire savagely to make it blaze up. 'All these fireplaces and no coal to speak of. What are we coming to?'

'My feet are cold,' Norman complained from the depths of an armchair, where he was reading.

'Bring your chair closer to the fire,' his mother told him.

'Do hush,' Grace said, from the desk under the window where she was trying to do her homework. 'Why don't you put on double socks if you're that cold?'

'There's going to be a hard frost tonight.' Byron was none too warm himself. 'We could close half the place down.' There were four storeys. 'Why don't we shut off the top two floors?' He thought the furniture might be worth more than the building. He'd have to see that it was properly covered and cared for until after the war.

Veronica gave a mirthless laugh. 'What do you mean, shut off the top two floors? Nobody's been up there for months. You say your business is making money, but you quibble when it comes to spending a bit to make the place habitable.'

'It's too old,' Byron said. 'Too big. It needs an army of servants to run it. Just look at the garden. One man can't keep it tidy.'

Much as he loved the house, Byron was thinking seriously of pulling it down. It was no longer practical. He was toying with the idea of building a block of flats on its site. Or perhaps he'd apply for planning permission for four individual houses, and then sell the land for development.

'Surely,' Veronica was exasperated, 'it's more important to consider where we'll live? Business, business, that's all you ever think of.'

The next morning, Byron shivered as he climbed out of bed. It was still dark and the temperature in his bedroom seemed below freezing. He began to think seriously of renting a smaller house, now, right away. Something that was easier to keep warm. The ceiling in his bedroom was fifteen feet high; downstairs the ceilings were even higher, and that made the house almost impossible to heat.

The days when he'd had a manservant to bring him morning tea and run a hot bath had long since gone. These

days he made his own tea and toast and took a cup up to
Veronica. Down in the kitchen, the windows were opaque
with frost patterns. When he crossed the garden to the
garage, every branch of every tree was white with frost. It
looked beautiful, a winter's fairy tale. The air froze the
back of his throat as he breathed in. It came out in visible
clouds.

He was glad he'd managed to get more petrol and could
drive himself down to the office on mornings like this. He
inserted his starting handle and swung it hard. Again and
again the engine turned over, but wouldn't fire. He swore
under his breath. Unscrewed the radiator cap. He thought
the water in the radiator had frozen. Perhaps it would be
better to leave the car where it was. The road looked icy.

On the spur of the moment, he went back indoors.
He'd bought Grace a bicycle and he wanted to tell her
not to go to school on it this morning. He was afraid she
might skid on the ice.

When he looked in her bedroom she was still fast asleep
and breathing evenly. It seemed a shame to wake her
before it was necessary. Instead, he went to Veronica's
room and asked her to tell Grace when she woke up.

She scowled at him over her eiderdown. 'I can't stand
this weather.' The discontented droop to her mouth had
never been more noticeable.

The tram was late that morning. He carried on walking;
it was too cold to stand still. He was glad to get to the
office and feel the warmth of the fire Evie had built up for
him.

Her smile was warm and welcoming. 'Isn't it beautiful
outside today?'

Evie felt the war would never end, and she couldn't relax
until it was over. It had taken Ned's life along with millions

of others, and she didn't want it to take more. She was managing well enough, thanks to Aunt Agatha's legacy. She'd bought her house and knew now she'd always have a home for her children.

All the same, Ned's death had left a great empty hole in her life. There were times when her memory seemed to play tricks on her. She'd wake up in the middle of the night thinking he was still on a ship plying its trade around the Mediterranean and that he'd be home soon. The moment when she realised he was gone for ever always devastated her.

She tried to tell herself she was finding things easier now that both the children were in school, but she longed for Ned. She needed Ida's help and company here in the house, and she also needed Byron and his advice. The half-hour she spent with him every morning seemed to set her up for the day. She was very fond of them both, and between them they kept her going over the first difficult months.

As time went on, she knew that Byron was becoming more important to her. She found herself thinking about him, fantasising about what he was doing when she couldn't be with him. She found herself looking forward to her time with him, saving up the little happenings in her day to tell him. If his hand should touch hers as he took his tea cup from her, it left her tingling.

They talked about everything except how they felt about each other. She worried about that as she worried about most things, and made herself think of what they shared as friendship. After all, he was a married man.

Evie did her housework in the mornings. She had to take the children backwards and forwards to school, and that meant four journeys because they came home for their dinner, but the school was near. In the afternoons, she allowed herself the luxury of an hour's rest on her bed.

She was lying down, waves of sleep washing over her, when she heard the knock on her front door. She longed to ignore it and slide into sleep. The knocking came again. More insistent now.

Still sleep-fuddled, she threw off her eiderdown, pushed her feet into her slippers and ran downstairs, fastening the belt of her frock as she went. She was shocked to find Byron Ball on her doorstep, huddling into his greatcoat, his collar turned up around his pinched face. She'd never seen him look so dejected.

'Evie?' he croaked, his eyes awash with untold misery. She was instantly awake.

'Come in.' She had to take his hand and draw him into the hall in order to close the door and shut out the cold.

'You're frozen. Has something happened?' She knew it had. He'd been quite different when she'd seen him early this morning. 'Come to the fire.'

She took away the nursery guard and poked the fire till it blazed up, then drew up a chair for him. He hadn't moved.

'Byron?' She'd never called him that to his face in all the time she'd known him. She undid the buttons of his coat. Helped him off with it. Took it and his homburg out to the hall.

When she came back, he'd moved nearer the fire and was holding out his hands to the blaze.

'Shall I make you a cup of tea?'

It was what she always did for him. Then, on the hob, she saw the pan of broth she'd made for her children's midday meal because it was such a cold day. There was plenty left.

'Some ham broth? Have you eaten?'

He was shaking his head again.

'No wonder you feel so cold.' She swung the pan over the fire. Set out a bowl on the table and cut a slice of bread. When she turned back to him, his eyes were searching into hers.

'It's Grace,' he said. Evie knew all about Grace; he spoke of her often. 'She was knocked off her bike this morning on her way to school. A cart sliding downhill on the ice. Heavily laden and out of control. Pushing the two horses. One kicked her.'

Evie felt a stab of anguish. 'Is she – badly hurt?'

'She's dead, Evie. She was taken to the children's hospital. She died there an hour or so ago.'

'Oh my God!' She could see the tears welling in his eyes and threw her arms round him, trying to give comfort. With an agonised sob he pulled her closer and put his head down on her shoulder and wept.

'Why did it have to be my Grace? Why?'

Evie shook her head. She knew what it was to lose a loved one. 'I asked myself the same question when Ned died. He had the bad luck to be in the wrong place at the wrong time, and so did your Grace.'

He was shaking his head as he told her how he should have woken her this morning. How he should have insisted that she walk to school and not left a message with Veronica.

'Did she give her your message?' Evie asked.

He took out his handkerchief and wiped his face. 'She said she did, but that Grace went on her bike anyway.'

'You did your best. You delivered a warning,' Evie insisted. 'You couldn't have done more.'

She'd never seen Veronica Ball, and Byron didn't talk about her much. Never criticised her, but said enough to let Evie know that they were not on good terms. She'd asked Ida Pringle about her.

'She used to come to the office quite a lot at one time. Couldn't half throw her weight about. Always finding fault. Nobody liked her.'

Byron blew his nose hard. 'Veronica blames me; in fact, I blame myself.'

'You mustn't . . .' She wished there was some way she could ease his anguish.

'I bought the bike for Grace when Samuels left . . . It was a thirteenth birthday present. Second-hand, it had to be, there aren't any new ones being made, but it hadn't been used much. Almost full-sized, with strings over the back wheel to stop her skirts being caught in it, and a basket on the front to carry her school books. She was over the moon with it.'

'You can't blame yourself for giving it to her.'

'Veronica says I should take the children to school in the car, not let them go alone.'

'But Grace wanted to?'

He nodded miserably. 'She said there was hardly any traffic on the road. Even so, there was so much ice this morning . . .'

'You said you couldn't start your car this morning.'

He brightened. 'That's right, I couldn't.'

'Then you couldn't have taken her to school today. It was an accident. You've got to see it as that. You mustn't feel guilty.'

'Evie, I didn't want to drive her to school. Not any morning, however bad the weather. Do you know why?' His eyes searched into hers, and she shook her head.

'Because I want to get to the office early. If I drove the children to school, I'd be too late to see you.'

Evie felt her heart turn over. She'd seen it in his eyes and wondered. It was eighteen months since Ned had died, and there were times when she longed for a loving

companion to share her life. She'd known for some time
that she wanted it to be Byron, but she hadn't let herself
hope that he would want that too.

His eyes studied her feverishly. 'I love you, Evie. Surely
you must have seen . . . ?'

She couldn't speak, it was too momentous a discovery.

'So you see, I am to blame. Veronica's right.'

'No, Byron, it was an accident.' Evie's lips brushed his
cheek. 'A terrible accident. Are you to watch your children
every minute of the day? Could their mother not do more
if she thought it needed? Could . . .'

His lips found hers. He kissed her, but he wasn't giving
himself wholly to her. She understood that his mind was
on this tragic accident.

He moaned: 'What am I doing? I hardly know . . .'

She made him sit down and eat some broth. The colour
came back to his cheeks. She heard more of the terrible
details, of how Veronica hadn't got out of bed that
morning.

She felt moved by his distress and wished she knew
how to comfort him, but she couldn't let him stay long.
The moment came when she had to say: 'You'll have to
go now, Byron. It's time for me to walk up to the school.
I have to fetch my children home.'

'Can I come and see you again?' he asked as she fetched
his greatcoat. 'But no, I shouldn't. Forgive me, I'm hardly
myself today. It's asking too much, to come to your home.'

'I want you to,' she said gently. 'I want you to come
again.' She felt wrung out with his anguish, saddened at
another young life abruptly ended.

Evie had never found getting up in the morning so easy. It
was a delight to go to the office and get it ready for another
day's work. She found herself listening for Byron's step

on the stairs when the time drew close.

He'd come running up to kiss her as though it was his greatest pleasure in life. Almost every day, he'd ask if he might come to her house later on, when he knew she'd be alone.

She always put on her best clothes and redid her hair when her housework was finished so that she looked her best for him. Often, from her own little room over the front door, she'd lift her bedroom nets to watch for him coming and feel a shiver of pleasure when she saw him walking down the street.

In his homburg hat and heavy overcoat, Byron looked out of place in Leicester Street. He was not a handsome man in the way Ned had been, but he had an endearing habit of tossing his straight brown hair back from his forehead.

'I shouldn't come.' He smiled guiltily. 'I know it's wrong.'

Evie knew it too, but for once refused to listen to her conscience.

'I look forward to your visits,' she told him. 'I love having you here. All to myself.'

She wondered how she'd come to fall in love with him when he was the very opposite of Ned. He was so much older, more polished and more formal. There were twelve years between them, and he'd seemed too old at first, but now those years were falling away. There was intimacy in his smile and a yearning in his dark eyes that drew her close.

For the first time, Evie had a secret she kept from Gertie Collins and Ida Pringle. She was careful now never to mention Byron's name to either, but occasionally Ida would talk of him. She told Evie he was popular with his staff and had a reputation for treating everybody fairly.

He was a good man to work for, but her colleagues were somewhat in awe of him. It was yes, Mr Ball, and no, Mr Ball. He was the boss and he kept his distance.

That wasn't how Evie saw him at all. What she felt for Byron had crept up on her gradually, and she was very glad it had.

'I count myself lucky,' she told him. 'I thought when Ned died I'd never feel like this again.'

'Evie love, you've transformed my life. I find such peace here with you, but I'm putting you in a terrible position. I'm a married man.'

He'd held her in his arms as he told her about Veronica. How she was the sort of person who took; who thought only of herself. How she wanted money and possessions and status more than she wanted love.

'You're so different. You're the sort that gives, but I'm not sure I should let you.'

'It's what I want.'

'You're an honest widow and I'm going to ruin your reputation. I'll be seen coming here to your house. Your neighbours will count the hours I'm alone with you.'

'My next-door neighbour did ask.' Evie smiled. 'She wanted to know if you were my father.'

He laughed. 'Do I look that much older than you?'

'Not really. You look more sophisticated.'

He sighed. 'You do realise what you're getting into? I'm taking advantage of you.'

'No, you're not doing that. You're urging me to think carefully before I do anything.'

'I've so little to offer you. We met too late.'

Evie knew that the only way she could have his love was to become his mistress. She had plenty of time to think about it. She felt she was learning to be less nerve-racked about the decisions she had to make. She'd flouted

181

the rules of society before. She'd been only eighteen when she'd left home to be with Ned. Society didn't matter to her; what she'd done had been right for her then.

She'd been a widow now for two years and saw this as her second chance. She felt stronger now that she was twenty-six, and she was sure that Byron was right for her.

He took a late lunch break and came regularly to her house now, timing his visit for when she'd return from putting her children in afternoon school. It was another wet day, and she insisted in shaking the rain off his coat before she hung it on her hall stand.

'Even your face is wet.' His white handkerchief was showing in his breast pocket. She pulled it out to mop his face. He laughed and caught her in his arms. 'You take such good care of me.'

'I love you,' she whispered, and felt his arms tighten round her.

'You're sure, Evie? Quite sure?' She looked up into dark eyes that were shining with love. They held her gaze and she saw in them a need as great as her own.

'Certain.' She took a long, quivering breath. 'Absolutely certain.'

After six years of married life she felt well versed in the ways of men. She'd known that this moment would come. This morning, she'd put clean sheets on her bed and made her little room fresh and spotless. Now, as she took him up the narrow stairs, her heart was drumming in anticipation.

At the foot of her little white bed, he caught her to him. 'I feel very honoured,' he whispered before their mouths touched.

When the long years of the war finally came to an end in

November 1918, all England rejoiced. Byron felt he had much to be thankful for. It had played havoc with his business but he'd had time to make careful plans for when it was over. In the early months of peace, he started selling off his fleet of old-fashioned sailing vessels and was delighted with the high prices they achieved.

Trade between Liverpool and West Africa opened up again. Byron started sending out goods of the sort that had traditionally sold well out there: salt and cotton cloth, Dane guns and enamelware. If he hadn't a ship of his own to transport them, he chartered space on the mail boat that sailed every two weeks. Profits would never be what they had been, but it was the only business he knew.

He bought a building plot in the best part of Oxton, and Veronica started planning the new house. He would sell Parkfield when it was ready.

He also planned to put the office on the market. It was too old to keep patching up, and the whole focus of the town had changed. There was heavy industry all round him. It no longer suited his kind of business. Other companies in similar trades had moved elsewhere.

When Byron had heard in the second year of the war, that J. S. Connaught and Company was going into liquidation, he knew it was only through forethought and exceptional luck that his company had avoided the same fate.

The Connaught shipping line had had a much larger fleet of small sailing vessels than he'd had. Like his, they were old-fashioned. They'd also had a very fine office building in South Castle Street, the business centre of Liverpool. He'd had his eye on it for the last few years, waiting for the right time to buy.

He'd secured it a month before the end of the war at a knock-down price. He'd been lucky with his timing. He hoped that now the war was over, the site alone would be worth what he'd paid for it.

He'd talked to Evie many times about moving his office from Knox Street when the war was over. But now, quite suddenly, the moment was here, and he could see she was alarmed.

'The Connaught Building! It's too far for me to come in the mornings. I have to be home again before eight to get the children to school. And there's Ida Pringle to think of . . . She only took rooms with me because it was handy.'

'I'll bear your circumstances in mind, Evie. Of course I will.'

'But if you move . . . I mean, why central Liverpool?'

'I hope to get more business there.'

'Impossible for me. I can't . . .'

He took her hands in his. 'Listen a moment. It's just the place. The Connaught Line was a prestigious business when I was growing up. The building needs refurbishing from top to bottom, but when it's done, I'll be proud to own it.'

'It's big? Too big?'

'I'll only need a fraction of the space. I'm thinking of renting out the rest, floor by floor or even room by room.'

'But what about . . .'

'What about you?' He kissed her cheek. 'Would I forget about you? There's a flat on top. Three bedrooms and a much bigger living room than this. I'll put in a proper bathroom, central heating and electric light. You won't know yourself, everything you could wish for. What do you say?'

'You make it sound so easy . . .'

'It will be, Evie, I promise. There's nothing for you to worry about. I'll put in whatever you want.'

'It's not that. It's a big step. And Liverpool . . .'

'Right in the middle of the business centre.'

'The children will have to move schools.'

'Does that matter?'

'Perhaps not.'

'I'll help you find good ones. They won't lose out, I promise. I know you want to bring them up so they'll be able to earn a good living.'

He could see Evie turning it over in her mind. 'Say you will, love,' he urged.

She smiled. 'If you say it will be all right.'

He swept her into a bear hug. 'I promise. There'll be no outside privies there. Officially you'll be the caretaker, but I'll hire somebody to do the work. I don't want you to . . .'

'I want to work, Byron.' He could see she meant it.

'Then you won't have to do too much.'

'Just fancy – I won't have to leave the building to do it either.'

'I'll be just downstairs all day and can come up any time. You could even come down to see me.'

'What about this house?'

'Rent it out. If it were mine, that's what you'd tell me.'

He loved to see Evie smile like this. It spread across her face, lighting up her eyes and showing her dimple. 'It sounds just the thing.'

# CHAPTER ELEVEN

Evie loved to have Byron sit back in the armchair by her fire and hold forth on every subject under the sun. She told him she was afraid she might fall pregnant. For her it happened very easily.

'You're a terrible worrier,' he said, but he was sympathetic. 'It won't happen, I'm taking care of that.' He'd read books by Marie Stopes and thought he understood how to avoid it. He explained it at great length to Evie. She wanted to believe he was right. He was so much wiser in the ways of the world.

Evie was always uneasy if she went beyond her dates. It had happened once or twice. This time it had dragged on until she was several days overdue. She woke up one morning and the signs were unmistakable. She'd had two babies already; she knew she was pregnant again. It was eight months since she'd first led Byron up to her bedroom.

She felt catapulted into another crisis. She'd been through all this before with Ned. The first panic, the difficult decisions she'd have to make. And this time she couldn't run away to marry the father.

She had to dress hastily and rush out to the yard in the darkness of pre-dawn to be sick. She walked slowly to the office and went about her duties, waiting for Byron to come. She told herself he was a truly kind man and she could trust him. He came running upstairs as he always did to take her in his arms.

She whispered straight away: 'Byron, I think I'm having a baby.'

To break it more gently, she'd introduced doubt, though she felt none herself. His lips were against hers. He jerked back to look at her.

'My God! I'm sorry, I'm terribly sorry . . .' The colour had drained from his face. He looked scared, and that frightened her. She'd been trying to tell herself he'd be pleased. Not immediately, perhaps, but when he'd had time to get over the shock.

'I was so sure,' he said through tight lips. 'Those sheaths . . . It's my fault.'

She felt the tears start to her eyes. 'It takes two to do it.'

He smiled, pushed his brown hair back from his forehead. 'I'm sorry, love.'

'Don't be.' She felt a tear roll down her cheek.

'You're not?' His finger wiped it gently away.

Evie took a deep, shuddering breath. 'I'm nerve-racked. Frightened. It's not going to be easy. How do I tell my mother-in-law? And Miss Pringle?'

'Oh God, Miss Pringle.' His fingers stroked her face.

Evie tried to pull herself together. 'I'm a fatalist, I suppose. I half expected it to happen. I've been through this before. I'm trying not to be totally sorry. I like babies.'

'So do I, love, but there's a time and a place. We aren't married.'

'No,' she said quietly. She was assailed by terrible fears. Did he love her enough?'

'What am I thinking of?' Byron's lips came down gently on hers and his arms tightened round her again. 'Forgive me, Evie. I'll look after you. See you're all right. Of course I will.'

'You're pleased? Now you've got used to the idea?'

'I'm not used to it.' He was trying to smile. 'Not yet. I'm still in a state of shock. Give me time.'

* * *

January 1919 was cold and wet. The winter stretched ahead. The war might be over, but the shortages of everything were still with them.

Byron had worked on after the office closed that day, partly because he'd spent three hours with Evie at lunchtime and he had work he needed to finish.

It was dusk when he alighted from the tram and walked the last few yards home. He'd had no petrol for the car this month. He was thinking of his daughter, Grace. There were still days when he mourned for her. Thirteen years was a pitifully short life, and he'd had such high hopes for her.

Against the darkening sky, the black mass of Parkfield looked cold and uninviting. As he let himself in through the front door, he expected Veronica to greet him with more complaints about the house. The new one was like a dream, impossibly distant because there were no building materials available. The hall felt icy. He could see one of the curtains fluttering in the draught.

'There you are, Byron.' Veronica came dancing across the hall to kiss his cheek. It seemed a long time since she'd done that. 'You're late this evening, I was beginning to think something must have happened to you.' She was helping him off with his overcoat.

He tried not to recoil from such unusual behaviour. She smiled and said: 'Come and have a drink before dinner. There's just time.'

He was being led towards his father's old study. For the last few years they'd used that instead of the drawing room, which was over thirty feet square and impossible to heat from one fire. Even here, as well as the fire, Veronica had a paraffin heater, though it was giving out more fumes than warmth. She was still smiling at him, putting a tumbler of whisky and water into his hand, mixed just as he liked it.

'I've been into town today.' Her tone was oddly flirtatious. 'You know I've been looking for a fur coat? I really need it, and goodness knows how much longer this weather will last. There's nothing in the shops, of course. Well, they had a few cheap ones in coney. Nothing I liked.'

Byron knew what was coming now. Veronica wanted more money from him to buy a fur coat. He sat down, tried to switch off from her. She came and sat on the arm of his chair.

'I saw this chinchilla coat at Broads. Not new, but they said they could remodel it to fit me. It seems to be the only way to get decent furs now, don't you think?'

Byron sipped his whisky. 'I'd take the coney. It'll keep you warm and at least it'll be new.'

'Oh, but they said the chinchilla belonged to minor royalty. Supreme quality, there's a beautiful shine on the fur. It would be completely relined and nobody would know it wasn't new.'

'You do what you want.' Byron knew she would anyway.

'I want the chinchilla. I've made up my mind, but it will be quite expensive.'

'Anything you want is bound to be.'

'I was wondering if you'd help me buy it? I need another fifty.'

Byron sighed. It had taken Veronica a little longer than usual to get round to it. He opened his mouth to say no, that he gave her a very generous allowance and she must learn to manage on it. She didn't give him the chance.

'I'll just refill your glass.' She snatched it from his fingers. 'Then we must go and eat.'

They'd given up eating meals in the dining room except

in high summer. Nowadays they ate in the kitchen where the Aga was kept burning day and night. It was the only really warm room in the house. They had supper at seven o'clock sharp, so that Mrs Tilley, who came in daily, could get it on the table before going home. She was putting on her hat and coat in readiness now.

Byron felt the light and warmth envelop him. The savoury scent of steak and kidney pie cheered him. Mrs Tilley had a light hand with pastry. Norman was playing with his train set in the corner.

'Wash your hands and come and sit at the table, dear.' Veronica was pretending to be an entirely different person, light-hearted, loving even. Byron knew that if he gave her the money she wanted, he'd be offered a rare visit to her bedroom. Veronica was building up to it. Then, as soon as she had what she wanted, she'd be back to carping normality.

He couldn't help but watch her eating on the other side of the table, comparing her to Evie. Evie was the sort who gave freely; all she wanted was his love. From time to time he took her little gifts that Veronica would despise. A dozen eggs, a joint of beef. Some pears from the garden here. His reward was to see her face light up and her blue eyes sparkle as she thanked him.

He thought Evie truly beautiful, and he loved to sit beside her fire in her cosy little house. He felt heavy with guilt. It made matters worse because she'd said:

'I love you. Of course I want your child. Don't worry. It's not all bad. At least Bobby and Queenie are too young. I mean, they won't realise it's a half-brother or sister.'

He did worry. A child was a responsibility. Evie was a responsibility now. He had to do his best for them.

When they'd finished their meal, Norman filled the sink with water and dumped all the dirty dishes in it to await

Mrs Tilley's return in the morning. Veronica put away the food that remained.

Byron went back to his father's study to sit by the smoking fire, while Veronica oversaw Norman's homework and preparations for bed. She'd come to him, he knew, probably wearing what she considered to be her most glamorous négligé. She'd perch on the arm of his chair and eventually lead him up to her bedroom where, for once, she'd have lit the fire to take the chill off the room.

He poured himself another drink and made up his mind that this time he would not go along with Veronica's plans.

Two hours later, Norman came to say good night to him. He was a thin child, underweight for his age. Veronica devoted a good deal of time and energy to his homework but he didn't get good reports from school. Byron longed for Grace . . .

He'd got up to get himself another whisky when he heard Veronica's step in the hall. As he'd guessed, she was wearing a pink satin housecoat over a matching nightdress of pink lace.

'There you are, Byron,' she said, and ran her hand up his arm. 'Now then, would you like another whisky?'

'I'm helping myself as I usually do,' he said.

'I'm only trying to please you.' She gave a self-deprecating little laugh. 'You know that.'

'Too true,' he sighed.

'What would please you, Byron?' She was smiling, inviting him to suggest sex. How many times had he done that on cue? She teased, 'What can I give you?'

He took a deep breath. 'What I really want is a divorce.'

'Don't be silly . . .' Her smile was uneasy. It slid away, leaving a look of sour disbelief.

'I mean it.'

'No!' She was shocked. Her face was twisted and ugly.

'I'm a practising Catholic. I don't believe in divorce. You don't either.'

Byron tried to keep calm. 'I've changed my mind. You don't love me, Veronica. I doubt you ever did. You married me because you thought I'd be a good meal ticket. And you're disappointed even in that.'

Her eyes shone with horror. 'You married me for better or for worse. In the sight of God you promised to . . .'

'I know that . . . Haven't I been paying for it ever since?'

Byron knew that money had always been important to him. He'd spent years struggling to keep his business afloat; years working hard to stop the fortune his family had built up from leaking away. Now, suddenly, he was prepared to give it away. Evie was more important to him than money.

'I'll play fair with you,' he said slowly. 'I'll make over to you half of everything I have. You'll have your meal ticket and be able to buy as many fur coats as you want.' No use pretending it didn't hurt; he'd balked at doing this for a long time.

'No! A divorced woman! Are you going to turn me into that? Ruin my reputation? I won't be accepted anywhere. What sort of a life would I have then?'

'What sort of a life do we have now? Either of us? You can be the innocent party and divorce me. I'll arrange it. I'll give you grounds.'

Veronica straightened up. There was disgust in every line of her face.

'You've got another woman, haven't you? A fancy woman. A mistress.'

Byron winced but said evenly: 'There's somebody else, yes. Somebody I love.'

'Oh, don't tell me! You've got her pregnant. You want to make an honest woman of her.'

Byron swallowed. He didn't have to admit that that was the truth. His face told her everything.

'You want to make your bastard legitimate! Well, I'm not going to let you.'

She turned on him even more fiercely. 'I deserve better than this. I've borne two children for you, kept a good home for you, given you the best years of my life . . . I won't let you toss me aside.' She took another rasping breath. 'And what about Norman?'

'He'll want to stay with you. You're closer to him than I am. You shall have full custody.'

'But what about the business? You want to split everything in two. You'll leave your share to your fancy woman and her children. Norman will be the one to lose out. I'll not have that.'

'I'll treat him fairly.'

'You inherited it from your father. It's only fair Norman should have it in his turn.'

'Yes, well, if he's interested when he grows up.'

'It sounds as though you want to cut him out! You're going to . . .'

'No, Veronica. Norman can start working in the business just as I did, when he leaves school . . . If that's what he wants. If there's any sort of business left. It's difficult to see what the future holds there.'

'You want to throw us both over. Do us both down.'

'I won't do either of you down. Norman is still my son, I have no quarrel with him. What I want is my freedom. A divorce. I want to call an end to all this pretence.'

'Never! I'll never agree to it. Not on any terms. In the eyes of God I'm your wife and always will be. Your bastard will stay a bastard in my lifetime.'

Byron felt full of frustrations. He consulted a solicitor

about getting a divorce, but was told Veronica had given him no grounds for it. He was the guilty party, the one who'd committed adultery. If she was condoning that and didn't want a divorce, then there was nothing he could do about it.

He knew he had to change the direction of his business to meet present-day conditions, and was eager to make a start.

It was no longer necessary to be a ship-owner to trade with West Africa. Goods could be sent out quite cheaply on the mail boat, and it seemed to Byron that many small manufacturers were trying to gain a foothold in the market. He thought that with his experience and knowledge of import and export regulations, he could meet a growing need by acting for those who wished to sell abroad. He wanted to develop this if he could.

He now had plenty of capital, because he'd sold all his old-fashioned fleet. The last four had gone to a firm in Haiti and would carry cargo round the Caribbean.

He felt he'd done very well from them. Throughout the war, his sailing ships, mostly of less than a thousand tons, had sailed from Lagos to New York with cargoes of palm oil, rubber, parrots and monkeys and returned to the Coast with sewing machines, rum, tobacco and patent medicines. The round trip had taken six months and they'd been very much in demand when the war made steamers scarce. He'd lost none from enemy action. Several were now registered in Monrovia. All had made high prices, even the barque *Elma*, nearly forty years old.

With the capital, he'd bought shares in the businesses of others. It meant less work and worry, and provided him with income. He hoped business would boom for everybody as the country recovered from the effects of the war.

His plans for the new office were making only slow progress. He knew exactly what he wanted done to bring the building he'd bought in Liverpool up to date, but there were constant delays: getting the materials to do it was difficult. He wanted it finished so that Evie could move in.

He knew he'd put Evie in a vulnerable position and that it was in her nature to be nervous.

She said: 'I'm all right, Byron. I'm not going to worry about money or anything. I'm taking each day as it comes.'

'Are you worried about money?'

Byron could see she was, and it filled him with guilt and remorse. He eased his conscience by consulting his stockbroker and asking him to work out a balanced investment portfolio. Then he invested a good slice of his capital in Evie's name and gave her the share certificates. When she saw them, her blue eyes were wide with astonishment.

'Byron! It's a fortune! You've made all this over to me?'

'I don't want you to worry about money. It isn't important.'

'It is if you haven't enough for your needs. It was just the thought of another mouth to feed . . . In the years ahead, I mean. I wouldn't know what to do with money like this.'

'There's nothing you need to do. Leave it where it is,' he told her. 'I've opened a bank account for you. The income the capital earns will be paid in there. Enough for you to live on.'

'You don't have to . . .'

'I do. You're having my child. You must have financial security. Enough money to take care of yourself and your children.'

'But it's more than I'll ever need.'

'No, I want you to feel secure whatever happens. I don't want you to have to work.'

'If I hadn't been cleaning your office, we'd never have met. I don't think I want to stop just yet.'

'I do love you, Evie.'

She smiled and he saw her dimple come and go. 'I didn't think I'd ever have money like this. I don't know how to thank you . . .'

'You don't have to.'

'It's very generous . . .'

He smiled. 'I want you to think I'm generous, and I want to keep it away from Veronica.'

He felt a little guilty about that, but he made atonement by allowing Veronica to choose exactly the sort of house she wanted built on the site he'd bought. It wasn't going to be over-large. It had every modern convenience, so she'd be able to run it with just a cook-general and some daily help with the heavy cleaning. It was taking a long time to complete and it wasn't going to be to his taste, but he didn't mind that. He wasn't intending to live in it. Not now.

He sold the old house for its site and was sorry to see it being pulled down. It was the end to an era. It didn't please him at all when Veronica wanted to call the new house Parkfield too.

Evie had been filled with relief when he'd seen her in the office this morning.

'I made myself tell Gertie Collins yesterday. Time's going on and I didn't want her to notice. Not without my saying something first.' She was smiling, showing the dimples in her cheeks.

'Do you know what she said? I can hardly believe it. "I went through three husbands, Evie, but our Ned wasn't

197

fathered by any of them. That's why he was different. His father was a lovely man and Ned took after him. Married to someone else just like your fellow, he was. I'm not going to say it's wrong. I know things would have been different if our Ned was still alive." '

Evie had gulped. 'I was too full to say anything to her. I don't think Ned knew that about his father.'

This was one of the things Byron enjoyed about Evie. She was so happy when things worked out well for her. She never blamed him for making the problem in the first place.

He said: 'Are you going to tell Ida Pringle?'

'She keeps wanting to read my tea cup. She'll see it there sooner or later. Shall I tell her?'

'That's up to you, love.'

'It just that she knows both of us. It makes it that much harder.'

'I've told her I'm moving the office to Liverpool, but not that you'll have a flat in the building.'

'I'm going to have to say something soon. I don't want to upset her. She's upset enough about the new office. About having to travel further to work.'

He sipped at the tea she'd made for him. 'I'd rather you didn't offer her lodgings, Evie. We'd have no privacy if she lived with you. After all, if the flat was her home, she could pop up any time too.'

'She's been a good friend . . . We get on well.'

'With the new baby, you'll need all three of the bedrooms there. Bobby needs his own room now he's getting older. It'll mean big changes for us all.'

'Ida doesn't like changes. She's only got another year before she retires and she'd prefer things to stay as they are.'

'That's an idea!' Byron grinned at her. 'I could make it

worth her while to retire when we move. Wouldn't that be the best thing? What do you say?'

Evie had laughed up at him. 'She's looking forward to it. I don't think you'll have to twist her arm.'

'But you agree? It'll be safer for us. Nobody need notice me coming and going to your flat. You'll be happy with that?'

'Of course I'll be happy. If you talk to her about retirement, I'll tell her about us.'

Ida watched Evie frying the cod. It was filling the little kitchen with such heavenly scents. Evie was moving with quick, neat movements between the table and the stove. She was full of bounce and energy. It was impossible to believe she'd been up at half past four this morning.

'Are we ready?' Evie turned from the stove to check that they had what they needed on the table.

'Yes.' There were times when Ida couldn't take her eyes from Evie's face. Her fair skin had a slight sprinkling of freckles that gave her face a glow. Once, seeing such stunning looks would have given Ida a twinge of jealousy. Fate was so unfair. She was podgy and plain while Evie was really beautiful. But now she knew better. Evie's looks brought her the wrong sort of attention. Ida was afraid that men wouldn't leave her alone.

'Is the fish all right?' Evie was asking, and her blue eyes seemed to see what Ida was thinking.

'It's lovely. You're a good cook, Evie.'

Ida wondered for the umpteenth time whether she'd done the right thing by arranging for Evie to work at Henry Ball and Sons. There'd been rumours going round the office for some time. She'd ignored them. It could be sour grapes. Evie's looks could make other women jealous enough to say things that weren't true.

But it was whispered again that Evie Collins had caught the eye of the boss. That Byron Ball came in to the office every morning to see her. To be alone with her for half an hour.

At first, Ida had found that hard to believe. Mr Ball was a married man and a gentleman. He'd know he had no right to be looking at Evie Collins.

But on the way home from the office this evening, Ida had fallen in step with their next-door neighbour, a frail, elderly spinster, and offered to carry some of her shopping. The woman happened to say how close Evie and her father seemed, and how nice it was to see families like that. He was coming to the house to see Evie almost every day.

'Such a nice man. Don't see many as well dressed as him any more. Always wears a hamburg.'

Ida was truly shocked. Evie had told her all about her father, so she knew it couldn't be him.

Her mouth was suddenly dry. 'And a dark overcoat?'

'Yes, always says good morning if he sees me.'

It sounded like Mr Ball. For the first time Ida believed the rumours she'd heard. The truth must be worse if he was coming to the house nearly every day. Of course, he'd know she was safely in the office; he'd see her typing away at her desk before he set off.

And he was going out more than he used to. It was every day! And never at lunchtime, when Ida would be free to go home. At one time he used to tell her where he was going, but not any more. Ida felt quite shaky with the shock.

What was Evie thinking of? Getting embroiled with another man, even a gentleman like Mr Ball. Men were all the same. Only one thing they ever thought of.

But Evie could land herself in the most desperate trouble this way. Ida ought to warn her, but how? Evie hadn't confided in her. She wasn't supposed to know about this, and Mr Ball was her boss!

Ida made a pot of tea while Evie cleared the table, and afterwards suggested that she read her cup. When she looked at the scattering of tea leaves adhering to the sides, Ida wasn't sure what she was seeing, but she laid it on thick.

'I see crossed knives,' she said ominously. 'That means trouble.'

'What sort of trouble?' Evie wanted to know, not one whit worried. Ida wanted to say 'man trouble', but the words stuck in her gullet. She didn't want to fall out with Evie over this. She might be in need of her friends.

'There's another knife here at the very tip, blade upwards, that indicates scandal.'

Evie had been poking up the fire, but that brought her face jerking round.

'It won't be long coming,' Ida went on. 'It's near the brim, that means it's immediate. It's on the handle side too, which represents home.'

Evie was somewhat taken aback. Ida knew that that had registered. For good measure, she threw in another warning.

'There are leaves at the bottom of the cup and they generally mean ill fortune. Not a future to look forward to, I'm afraid.'

She could see the colour draining from Evie's cheeks. 'Thank goodness it's only the tea leaves saying these things,' she said in a strangled voice.

'I believe them. You said you did too. Didn't I tell you Queenie was on the way before you knew it yourself?'

Evie spent the next three days wondering just how much Miss Pringle knew. Byron said there was no way she could know anything. But the dire prophecies she'd made under the guise of reading Evie's cup had seemed like a warning. Evie wanted to tell her, to get it off her chest. It was going round in her mind, making her anxious. She felt she'd lost an opportunity not to have done it then. The prophecies had taken her by surprise. She hadn't been able to think fast enough.

A couple of days later, a Saturday, Ida came home from the office at lunchtime positively beaming.

'Such a weight off my mind, Evie, I can tell you. I was dreading that journey into Liverpool every day.' Her podgy face shone with relief.

'You're a bit later than usual.'

'Mr Ball wanted a word. I stayed talking.'

'I've made us some ham sandwiches. The children have gone to Gertie's.'

Ida sat down by Evie's fire as usual. 'Mr Ball's very generous. He's offered me the same pension I'd get if I worked for another year. He said I was the best secretary he'd ever had and he'd be sorry to lose my services, but he quite understood. All these changes, it was asking too much of me.'

Evie knew this was her chance. She was casting about for the words to tell her, but Ida went on.

'I'm afraid it's the end for you too, Evie. Liverpool's much too far away. Goodness knows why he has to change everything, but perhaps it's all for the best.' Evie didn't doubt Ida was pleased about that too. 'We'll both have much quieter lives.'

Evie poured them each a cup of tea. She had to get it out now. 'Mr Ball's been explaining his plans for me too. Guess what? He's asked me to be the caretaker of his new building.'

Miss Pringle gasped audibly. Evie rushed to tell her

more. 'It's much bigger than the old one and he's going to rent off most of the space.'

'But how can you get back in time to get the children to school?' Miss Pringle's eyes were mere slits above her plump cheeks.

'There's going to be a flat on top. I'm to have it rent-free. There's electric light and a proper bathroom . . .'

'You'll be living there?' There was no mistaking the horror in Ida's voice. 'Evie, I don't think you . . .'

'This is private information, Ida.' Evie swallowed hard. 'You mustn't say anything in the office. Mr Ball wouldn't want that. You see, he and I have an understanding.'

Miss Pringle's puffy eyelids lifted higher than Evie had ever seen them before. Her black button-like eyes were round with shock.

'You were right when you saw the horse and the parasol in my cup. Two . . . admirers. Ned and Byron Ball.'

Miss Pringle's Adam's apple was lost in folds of flesh, but Evie saw it move. Then Ida reached across the table and took both her hands in hers.

'Don't do it, Evie. You can't trust a man like that! There's only one thing they're after. Living there with just the children, you'd have no protection. He could do what he likes once the offices empty, and who's to know? Don't do it.'

'I've said I will . . .' Evie would have liked to chicken out. Leave the rest of her confession until later, but there was no stopping Ida.

'He'll use you, ruin you. Tell him you've changed your mind,' she urged earnestly. 'Before it's too late.'

Evie took a deep breath. 'It's already too late,' she said slowly. 'I'm expecting his baby.'

# CHAPTER TWELVE

Evie was unhappy about the way Ida had taken her news. Her manner cooled. She was prickly with ill humour.

'Byron Ball of all people! Having a child by him! Going to live under a roof that he owns. You'll be a kept woman! I'd be terrified. I don't know how you dare.'

Evie didn't want to admit to Ida that she had any misgivings.

'I did dare.' Now with a baby coming there could be no drawing back. Her only comfort was that this had happened before, with Ned, and had turned out fine. 'I have to trust Byron.'

'Trust him? You've sold your body. You might as well trust the devil.'

Ida's frostiness upset Evie and brought back all her old anxieties. She wasn't sleeping well; she had a nightmare, and felt her father's strangling fingers on her throat. She woke up choking. It revived all the unsettling memories of her mother. She wondered for the umpteenth time what had happened to Helen after she'd left the shop.

Evie poured all this out to Byron early on Monday morning.

He said rather sadly: 'I seem to be bringing you nothing but trouble. You can trust me, Evie, I promise. I shall try very hard to make you happy.'

She nodded and tried to smile. Ned had said much the same thing, in similar circumstances.

'I wish I wasn't such a bag of nerves.'

He took her hand between his. 'You aren't usually.

Bringing a baby into the world is a big responsibility. I'm just the same. When I have a new problem all my old ones return to overwhelm me.'

'Really? Gertie calls me a worry-guts.'

'We all worry. You'll feel better when things are more settled,' he said. 'Come out with me this morning. We'll go over to Liverpool. I want you to see my building, and especially the flat. I need to know if there's anything else you want done.'

Evie felt cheered. 'That would be a nice change.'

'Perhaps lunch?'

She shook her head. 'I can't. The children . . . Unless we leave it until tomorrow. I could ask Gertie if she'd mind seeing to them at dinnertime.'

'Tomorrow it is, then.'

Evie dressed carefully the next morning. She wanted to be as smart as possible. At ten o'clock Byron had his car outside her door. Evie hadn't had a day out for years and was determined to enjoy herself. She felt excited at the prospect.

Byron had talked endlessly about the building, but to actually see it, to go from floor to floor, looking in the rooms, and then to stand in the flat that would be her home, seemed to make everything much more certain.

Evie loved the flat. It was much bigger and smarter than her old house. The rooms would be heated with hot-water pipes and bulbous radiators. It had a proper bathroom, and hot water would come from the taps.

Lunch was long and extravagant. Evie had never been to such a smart hotel. In the afternoon, they looked at furniture and tried to decide what they'd need. Evie was going to rent her house out and intended to leave the furniture there.

'How about this?' Byron stopped at a double bed.

Evie felt the heat run up her cheeks. At the moment she was sleeping in a single bed because her room was so small. The double bed she'd shared with Ned was now used by the children. If it hadn't been for the fact that Byron came to her house, she'd have moved in with Queenie and put Bobby in the single room.

'Will you be able to stay with me? Every night?' It was something she had to ask.

'If you'll let me.'

'It's what I want.' Evie told herself she was silly to be anxious. A new life was opening up for her. She should be optimistic about it. But she couldn't be optimistic about Ida Pringle, for she was afraid she'd ruined their friendship for good.

Ida still felt shocked when she went to work on Monday morning.

'Good morning, Miss Pringle.' Byron's head had come up from his work and gone straight back down again. His pen scratched on the paper. It was what always happened.

Ida had spent the weekend angrily rehearsing what she was going to say to him. That she was disgusted with his behaviour. That he'd lured Evie away from her, ruined her life as well as Evie's.

'Good morning, Mr Ball,' was all she managed.

She flounced back to her desk. She couldn't get on with her work. Her mind was boiling with resentment. She'd given him respect up till now. She'd worked here for thirty years, for him and for his father before him. She'd liked Byron Ball. He came from a class above her. But that made it easier for him to get his way with someone like Evie. He'd taken advantage of her, a widow with two children to support.

Ida didn't understand how Byron had managed to do

it. To her his manner was always formal. He distanced himself from everybody. Never encouraged anybody to get close. Ida had believed she was the closest. She sat outside his door all day. She took his dictation and typed his letters, but never once had he ever mentioned any personal concerns to her. He never mentioned his wife and family, but like everybody else, she knew they existed.

The only time he'd ever mentioned Evie's name was when Ned's ship had been sunk. Then he'd told Ida how it was he knew, so she could go home and comfort Evie. It was what she'd expect a boss to do. He'd always seemed so honest and above board, yet he'd gone behind her back. Evie had gone behind her back too. That was what she didn't like. It left a nasty taste in her mouth.

Yes, she'd welcomed the chance to retire early, but that was when she'd thought her home life was happily settled and secure.

To find that Evie meant to leave her was very hurtful. She felt her whole life was collapsing. Things were moving too fast. Evie had explained that she could remain in the house, but she wasn't sure she wanted to be there all alone.

Evie had suggested she ask her sister to come and live with her, but the house wasn't in a good area and the whole reason for living there would be gone. She couldn't help this spiral of jealousy and resentment that the two people she spent her life with were abandoning her.

When the time came to move to the new flat, Evie asked Gertie to look after her children for the weekend. With all the packing and unpacking, she thought it better if she could give that her full attention. Byron was doing all he could to help.

'I'm afraid you're going to exhaust yourself,' he said.

Her baby was due in six weeks, and if she were truthful, she didn't have her usual energy.

Although Evie was officially going to be caretaker of the building, she found that Byron had hired a Mrs O'Casey to come in at five every morning to do the work. He'd asked her to clean through the flat in readiness, and she was waiting to help Evie unpack and get the place straight.

'There's Alice too,' he said, taking Evie into the kitchen, where a brisk thirty-year-old was unpacking boxes of food. 'She will come in daily to help you.'

'Help me?'

'With the housework.' Alice smiled.

'She cooks too,' Byron said.

'Plain cooking,' Alice said.

'What am I going to do?' Evie smiled. 'I thought I was coming here to do a job, not to be waited on hand and foot.'

'Not just yet. Not until after the baby's born. That's soon enough to decide how much you want to do.' The furniture she and Byron had chosen had already been delivered. They had two matching sofas covered in mustard-yellow fabric for the living room. Evie positioned one in front of the window to take advantage of the view over the rooftops to the docks and the river beyond. But she found that once she sat down, all she could see was the skyline opposite.

Outside, the trams clanked along the middle of the street. Motorcars, buses and horse-drawn vehicles of every description followed one another continuously in both directions. At the junction with Lord Street, traffic swirled round the statue of Queen Victoria.

It was never truly dark here. A yellow glow shone up from the streetlights and blue flashes sparked from the tram wires as the vehicles rattled past. Evie was never tired of peering down into the cavernous street below.

Although they were busy, and the flat seemed full of people and hardly private, Evie loved having Byron with her all the time. It seemed a luxury to have him to herself all night. A luxury to see him in slacks and pullover instead of his formal chalk-striped suits. She thought she could be truly happy here.

Gertie brought the children back in time for supper on Sunday evening. Alice had worked through the weekend, and had set out a cold meal on the table for them. She was on the point of going home.

'Is this where we're going to live?' Queenie stood in the middle of the living room, looking round with wide eyes. She had grimy knees and had spilled milk down the front of her dress. Bobby was none too clean either. He had his nose glued to the window, peering down into the street.

'Isn't it lovely?' Gertie's hoarse, throaty chuckle sounded round the flat. 'I'm dying to see it all.'

Evie showed them round. Gertie wanted to know all about the central heating, and was delighted to use the new bathroom before sitting down for a bite to eat. The children were tired and somewhat fractious, and they ate little.

Gertie got up to leave. She kissed Evie and the children and said: 'You've done her proud, Mr Ball. Evie's a lucky girl.'

When the door closed behind her, Evie said brightly to her children: 'Bathtime now. You can try out the new bath before going to bed. Come along.'

'Isn't Mr Ball going home?' Bobby asked, loudly enough for him to hear.

'No, dear.' Evie tried to keep her voice steady. She was

worried about how her children were going to take this. 'He's going to live with us now.'

'Instead of Miss Pringle? He's got rooms with us?' Evie started running the bath.

'Course not, silly,' Queenie said, sounding superior. 'He's the boss, isn't he? Mummy's boss. Have we got rooms with him?'

Evie knew she was floundering. 'It's not like that at all. He's your new daddy.'

'We don't want a new one.' Queenie stared at her defiantly. 'Do we, Bobby?'

'Take your shoes and socks off.'

'Not Mr Ball,' Bobby said. 'Not him. We love the daddy we've got.'

Evie went back to Byron with a heavy heart. The pleasure she'd found in her new home had evaporated.

'They'll accept me in time.' Byron pulled her down beside him on the new sofa. 'It can't be easy for them, this is a big change.'

'They remember Ned. Perhaps I've talked about him too much.' She'd kept the three photographs she had of him displayed in frames about their old home so they'd know what he looked like. She'd brought them here and put them in their rooms. She hadn't wanted them to forget Ned, but perhaps it was making it harder for them to accept Byron.

'Mum?' At the sound of Bobby's childish treble, Evie pulled free of Byron's arms and straightened up. He'd come to the living-room door in his striped pyjamas and was staring at them. His curly hair was rumpled, and he looked the image of Ned.

'Bobby! It's past your bedtime. You must go to sleep.'

'You forgot to read us a story.'

'Bobby, your mother's tired tonight. Go back to bed, there's a good boy.'

'We always have a story.' Queenie had come behind her brother. 'You know we always have a story.'

Evie tried to get up. She felt heavy and ungainly. Byron helped her to her feet.

'I'll read you a story,' he said. 'Have you got your books?'

'We want Mummy,' Queenie told him. 'We want Mummy to read to us, not you.'

Evie loved the feeling of having people all round her. The building buzzed with life during office hours. Byron was to run his business from two rooms on the ground floor. He planned to rent out the rest of the building. It took a little time, but gradually other businesses took up tenancies.

The Bulwark Insurance Company took the whole of the second floor, and a firm of solicitors the third. A notice by the front door offered separate rooms for rent at five shillings a week. All of the tenants wanted the caretaker to clean for them. Another cleaner had to be taken on to help Mrs O'Casey, and Evie found she had little to do except order the cleaning materials and see to the laundry.

She felt she'd gone up in the world. That she had money for everything she wanted now. One thing she did feel strongly about was that Bobby and Queenie should have the education and training to earn a decent living when they were grown up. Ned had never had that. It meant a great deal that his children should have a better start in life.

Byron had entered them in fee-paying schools. The best in the neighbourhood. Both had settled down well and their first reports were good.

They seemed to enjoy their new home. They both loved

riding in the lift. Eight-year-old Bobby raced it as it sped up to the ninth floor with Queenie inside. Evie had to ban them from playing in it. They found a new game. There were two flights of stairs, one up each side of the building. They started together in the front lobby, racing up to the flat each using a different staircase. Evie had to stop that too during office hours. She was afraid they'd disturb the workers.

On weekdays, Byron spent a good deal of his time with her in the flat. She could reach him in his office when she wanted to. She knew he was pleased with the arrangement.

'Fewer prying eyes here,' he said. 'And Veronica doesn't come so often now she has to cross the river.'

Evie felt safer. She was further from Father's shop. Nobody knew her here and she liked that. The only thing that bothered her was that the children didn't seem to be taking to Byron. She'd been at pains to keep them apart back in Birkenhead. Perhaps it was too much to expect that they would instantly meld into a family.

'We must give them time,' Byron said. 'Not rush things. It might be better if I'm not always here when they are. They need time alone with you. We can arrange that for them, can't we?'

They did. Evie got the children up in the mornings and saw them off to school, while Byron stayed out of their way. And again, when the children came home from school in the afternoon, he made himself scarce. He did most of his work in the evenings, so that Evie and the children could have time to themselves.

Gertie Collins was coming over on the ferry on Saturday mornings to take the children home with her. She loved having them to herself.

This meant that Byron and Evie could spend the afternoon alone in the flat. They went out to a theatre or to dinner in the evening, and had a lovely lazy Sunday.

'We can't ask Gertie to go on doing this for ever,' Evie said guiltily.

When Gertie brought the children home, Byron would go downstairs and work for an hour or two until they were in bed.

Bobby loved going over on the ferry with Grannie and staying in her house. There were no rules at Grannie's like having to wash your hands before meals. No set mealtimes either. When he was hungry he was told to help himself to whatever food he could find in the kitchen. Or Gran would give him a few pennies to get chips for them all from the chip shop.

'I love it when she takes us shopping,' Queenie sighed blissfully.

'Specially to that cake shop.'

'Darty's. They're friends of Grannie's.'

Bobby loved peering into the window where the cakes were all set out.

'Go on,' Gran would urge. 'Which one do you want then?' And he'd be torn between a cream bun and a jam tart, or possibly an Eccles cake. Queenie always knew what she wanted.

'Such a pretty little girl.' Mrs Darty would look at her with admiring eyes. 'She's beautiful. Takes after your Ned more than Evie. Going to turn a few heads when she's older.'

Then her quick dark eyes would dart to Bobby. 'Handsome little fellow you are too.'

It was just the same this Saturday. Gran and Mrs Darty talked for ages, punctuated by Gran's hoarse, throaty chuckle. Other customers came in and were served, and still they chatted on.

'How's Evie liking it over there?'

'Is he good to her?'

'Poor girl, getting caught like that with another little one.'

Bobby liked to sniff the lovely smell of baking and to pick out the ten cakes he'd choose if he was invited to take that many. Today, Queenie nudged him, pointing out the fly-catcher hanging over the sticky buns.

'Count the dead flies there. I make it a hundred.'

'You can't count to a hundred yet,' Gran had laughed. 'Isn't she a card?'

Bobby wrinkled his nose at the flies sticking to the tape.

'There's an awful lot. Is there room for any more? They look horrible, all those dead flies together.'

'Come on, you two.' Mrs Darty was taking a halfpenny from the till. 'Go and buy me a new one. Next door but one that way, the grocer.' She pointed. 'He sells them.'

Queenie grabbed the halfpenny first and was out giggling on the pavement in seconds.

'This way,' she said, pulling Bobby towards the chemist's shop next door. 'Let's go in here.'

Bobby clung to her. 'Gran'll be cross,' he whispered, peeping back round the cake-shop door. He could see her and Mrs Darty were talking again.

'You know what she's like about this place.' Queenie was at the chemist's door. 'Always craning her neck. Staring at him inside.'

'What are you looking at?' Bobby had asked her once. Gran had been quite strange about it and hadn't wanted to say. Queenie had kept on at her until she'd told them the man who owned it was their grandfather.

'Don't tell your mother I've told you,' she'd said, looking all round as though afraid of being seen on the doorstep. 'It's a secret.'

'It isn't,' Bobby had said. 'We know that. Mam took us inside once. We went upstairs. He wasn't nice to us, was he, Queenie?'

'Can't remember,' she'd said then.

Now she pulled at his coat. 'They sell fly-catchers in here. Let's go in. Why shouldn't we know what he's like if he's our grandfather?'

'Funny to think Mam lived here once.'

'And worked here. There's only ladies serving.'

'There's a man on the other counter.'

'That's not him.'

The door pinged loudly as a customer came out. Another was behind them waiting to go in. Bobby took his sister's hand and a moment later they were inside. It smelled very strange, and the man who'd come in behind them was urging him forward faster than Bobby wanted to go. Queenie felt like an anchor on his arm.

'Come on,' he urged, his heart pounding.

The next instant she shot forward until she could see inside the strange little room with all the shelves. She came back giggling. 'He's in there.'

Bobby saw a swirl of white, and an angry voice barked: 'What are you children up to? This is not a playground.'

He jumped as a large hand clamped on his arm, and looked up to find a ferocious face glowering down at him.

His voice quivered: 'We've been sent to buy a fly-catcher, sir.'

'The other counter for that.' The man's eyes burned with irritation. Bobby felt the grip on his arm slacken as he was turned round and given a little push.

'Remember, next time you come in, no horseplay. Miss Lister? Serve this lad with a fly-catcher. Let's get them out of here.'

Bobby had to nudge Queenie twice to get her to put

the halfpenny on the counter. She looked terrified. They were both glad to get outside and had to take deep breaths in front of the cake-shop window to make themselves feel normal again.

'I'm not having him as a grandfather,' Queenie hissed. 'He's nasty.'

'Didn't I tell you he would be?'

Back in the cake shop, Bobby's heart slowed its thumping. He closed his eyes and sniffed the heavenly smell of newly baked bread. Mrs Darty changed her fly-catcher and Gran went on talking.

When they were finally ready to depart, Polly Darty gave them each a custard tart to eat on the way home. The creamy egg custard in crisp pastry was delicious.

As soon as she'd finished hers, Queenie asked: 'Are we going to have a new brother or sister? Is that what you were telling Mrs Darty?'

'Oh, my! No, I said no such thing. Talking about somebody else, I was. Somebody we know and you don't.'

But later, when they were sitting on the mat in front of the fire and Gran had gone next door to try and borrow some tea, Queenie turned her big brown eyes on her brother.

'Bobby, we are going to have a new brother or sister. I know it.'

'Gran said no, you'd got it wrong.'

'I don't care what she said. It wasn't what she said to Mrs Darty.'

'But when will this happen?'

'I don't know that, do I?'

'I don't think you know anything.'

Queenie tossed her long brown curls over her shoulder. 'Didn't you hear Mrs Darty say: "Good Lord! What is the poor girl thinking of?" '

Bobby shook his head, he hadn't. He'd felt sort of shaken up. He hadn't been listening.

'You'd know more if you didn't day-dream so much.'

Byron went down to his office and let his eyes linger on the gilt wording printed on the half-glass in his door:

Henry Ball and Sons
Importers and Exporters to All Four Corners of the World.

Actually, most of his business was still with West Africa, but he had built up a little trade to America and hoped to expand to other regions.

He was very pleased with his decision to buy this building. There was a demand for rented office space, and it was now fully let. He'd kept only this one large, prestigious office on the ground floor for his own business. Once it had been used by a director of the Connaught Line. He'd partitioned off one end to make a private cubbyhole for himself. The larger part had been furnished with five desks.

One was occupied by Myrtle Parker, his new secretary. He'd chosen a middle-aged woman again, who was rather frumpish in appearance. She had a large mole on her chin with three long hairs curling from it. Byron found it took a conscious effort not to look at it.

He'd brought the three clerks with him from his Birkenhead office. Two had worked for him for years and were now nearing retirement. The other, Harry Penn, the junior accounts clerk, was aged nineteen and had finger-nails bitten down to the quick. Byron could see him gnawing away at them as he worked.

He said good morning to them as he went through to

unlock his desk. He took out a file and tried to get down to work. He'd been feeling on edge these last weeks as Evie's time drew closer.

She'd tried to reassure him, told him the baby wouldn't be early, she always went her full time. But now the waiting time was over, and her baby was due this very day. She was not overly large or ungainly, her cheeks were rosy and her eyes bright. He thought she looked the picture of health and more beautiful than ever. He'd asked her half a dozen times how she felt before he'd finished breakfast.

He was trying to keep his mind on other things, but today it was hard. He heard the outer door burst open, and looked up to see Veronica coming in. She'd come before when he'd first moved in, but he hadn't seen her for weeks. He could have done without a visit from her today of all days. His spirits sank further when he saw she had Norman in tow. She threw open the glass door of his cubbyhole without bothering to knock.

'Hello, Byron. I'm glad to see you're still in the land of the living.' Her big bulging eyes flashed resentment.

Frowning, he got slowly to his feet. 'What d'you mean?'

'You haven't been near for weeks. Why don't you come home?'

'I thought I'd made it clear that I wouldn't.'

Norman was crowding in. Byron went to close the door behind him but wasn't quite fast enough.

'You made it clear you had a fancy woman.'

Byron saw Harry Penn stir with interest at that. He lowered his voice.

'Do you have to let the whole office know our business? I said I wanted a divorce . . .'

'And I said you wouldn't get it. You're still a husband and father. You still have responsibilities to me and Norman, and I'm not going to let you forget it.'

'I haven't forgotten.' The whole point of keeping this business alive, of trying to tailor it to present-day needs and build it up was to provide for Norman.

He turned to his son. 'There's a job waiting for you here, when you need it. I'll teach you how to run this business, and when you've mastered it, I'll retire.'

Byron felt that was only fair. After all, he'd received a business from his own father. He could meet the needs of his new family from the rents of the Connaught Building and his investments. He didn't want to go on working until he was eighty, like his father had done.

'I can't say fairer than that, can I?'

'No, Dad, thank . . .'

'What you say and what you do when the time comes could be very different,' Veronica interrupted. 'I don't trust you. I don't like the way you've cut yourself off. You've shown no interest in the new house. You never come home now.'

'I didn't think you'd want me . . .'

'Surely you want to see Norman?'

'Yes, of course.' Byron looked uneasily at his son. He should show more concern for him. 'I've been busy these last few weeks, with the move and things. It's further away . . .'

'You can come for regular weekends. You need to, to keep in touch with Norman. And the new neighbours are asking about you. I want you to show your face, show some interest.'

'Not next weekend,' Byron said hurriedly, thinking of Evie. 'But I will come soon.'

'Right. Now the new house is finished, I'll have more time to come here.'

'There's no need,' Byron protested. 'I'm managing very well on my own.'

Veronica went to a file cabinet and pulled on a locked drawer.

'Where are the keys? I've always helped with your business accounts. I'd like to go on doing it, to keep an eye on Norman's inheritance.'

'Not in there.'

Veronica moved to another cabinet, that opened to her touch. 'What do you keep in that one?'

'Nothing that concerns you or Norman. I have interests other than this business.'

He watched the sour lines on her face deepen. 'You're splitting up your business. Hiding your assets. Keeping things away from me and Norman.'

Byron flushed with indignation. He was doing exactly that, but how could she expect otherwise?

'I've treated you fairly, Veronica. I've made the new house over to you and I'm paying you a generous allowance to live on. I've said I'm making provision for Norman. How I provide for myself as well has nothing to do with you.'

'It has! You've saddled yourself with two families to support. If you can't afford it, Norman and I will be the ones to go short. How can I have any confidence . . .'

Byron was on his feet. 'Veronica! I've told you what my intentions are. I don't care whether you have confidence or not. It would be better if you went home and let me get on with my work.'

'I've done a lot for the business in the past. I want to go on helping with your accounts.'

'In other words, you want a reason to see the books on a regular basis. Make sure the business will still be worth inheriting.'

There was suspicion on Veronica's face. 'How can I trust you?'

'You'll have to.'

Veronica had come to his old office for much the same reason. He'd expected to see her here. That was why he'd provided a spare desk in the front office. He led her out to it now. He didn't think she'd come often; she wasn't the sort to persevere.

'Here?' She looked sourly at Harry Penn, who was chewing his nails again. Then round at the other clerks, who were pretending to be too engrossed in their work to listen to this exchange.

'You won't want me working on company figures here. They need to be kept confidential. I need somewhere more private.'

'There isn't anywhere.'

'Perhaps if you moved this desk to your office?'

'There isn't room, surely you can see that?' He'd arranged it this way. He wanted to discourage her visits.

'I'm glad I've come.' She was showing anger now. 'I need to keep a closer eye on things.' Two chairs were pulled up to the desk. Files were being opened on it.

Their presence riled Byron. He was unable to work himself and unwilling to leave his office to them. Veronica was back and forth to him with questions, mostly about things that needn't concern her. He wished she hadn't chosen today to make such a nuisance of herself.

# Book Three

## 1919–1930

# CHAPTER THIRTEEN

It was a beautiful Friday in early September. Evie felt heavy and lethargic from the time she got up. At mid-morning she went out and walked down to the Pier Head. She stood against the railings in the spring sunshine and watched the seagulls swooping behind a small freighter as it chugged downriver.

She thought about her mother and wondered if she'd ever had another child. Perhaps, somewhere, she had a half-brother or sister? But her mother was a ghost she couldn't lay. She knew very little about her. All this was in her own mind.

Evie told herself she had financial security, she needn't fear that she was still treading in her mother's footsteps. She'd never be poor, nor would her children want for anything, thanks to Byron's generosity. She walked slowly back to the Connaught Building and peeped through the glass door into Byron's office on her way upstairs.

'I don't want you to come in,' he'd explained. 'Well, not often.'

'Not in my present condition?'

'More discreet if not at all, Evie. We don't want talk. Won't do either of us any good. I have to think of your reputation. Use the telephone to contact me.'

Evie saw several heads bent over their desks. But there were more people here than usual. Her attention was suddenly riveted on one in particular.

A woman with greying hair that showed the cut of a good hairdresser. She wore an expensive-looking costume in dignified black wool. Evie knew who she was although she hadn't seen her before. Mrs Ball was said to come to the office occasionally. Not every week, sometimes not for months at a time, but she came when she felt like it. Byron said she thought of herself as the company accountant. Ida Pringle had told her she had a high opinion of herself.

Evie shivered as she studied her through the glass of the door. This was the woman who was keeping her and Byron apart. Making what should be open and acknowledged a hole-in-the-corner affair.

She was taller and heavier than Byron, older too. Evie saw her look across the office and call for something. She had bulging, exopthalmic eyes and a deep, manly voice. Evie thought she looked sour, a bitter woman with deep lines of discontent marring her face.

She had to put her hand against the wall to steady herself. If she thought of Veronica Ball in those terms, how would the other woman see her? The woman who had stolen her husband. Ruined her life. A woman, much younger and more attractive, who had lured Byron away. A wicked, amoral woman, brazen and shameless, on the point of giving birth to his child. The room seemed to spin on a wave of guilt. Evie was afraid many would think she was all of those things.

She didn't notice him until he moved, a young lad of fourteen or so. Evie's heart turned over. She knew he must be Norman, Byron's son. She searched his face, looking for a likeness. It wasn't there. He wasn't as handsome as Bobby, not even as confident, though he was six years older. He was kicking the toe of his shoe against the desk, and she could tell he was bored. Hadn't she seen Queenie do that many times? A mother's boy, Byron had called him. She watched him pluck at Veronica's sleeve for attention.

Evie knew Veronica had brought Norman to his father's office to claim what she thought of as his rightful inheritance. How could she blame her? She felt a sudden dragging in her abdomen. She went up in the lift feeling light-headed and shaken.

She found that Gertie had called in to see her. 'I came over to get myself some new shoes and thought I'd pop in to see if the baby had come. Not on the way yet?'

'I've got the feeling it won't be long.' Evie collapsed on the sofa. 'Stay and have something to eat with us.'

Alice had boiled a joint of ham for lunch and made parsley sauce. Evie lifted the very latest in-house telephone to tell Byron it was ready.

'I can't come up.' His voice sounded taut with stress. 'Veronica's come. Better if I stay away from you while she's here. Are you all right?'

She told him she was, but she couldn't eat much and she felt the first pains as the meal was finishing. She drank tea with Gertie and admired her new shoes. By two o'clock she was sure labour had begun, and rang down to let Byron know. He came rushing up to see her and rang for the midwife.

'Veronica's still here. I feel I need to keep an eye on what she's doing.' He seemed on edge, couldn't stand still.

'I'll stay with Evie for a while,' Gertie said. 'Nothing's going to happen just yet.' She'd already filled several kettles and pans to get the boiling water that would be needed.

Byron came up again an hour later. 'I told Veronica she must go,' he told them. 'That she must have seen all she wanted to by now. I had to get rid of her.'

Evie watched him change out of his suit, put on a comfortable pullover. His face was set and anxious. There was no formality about him now.

When it was time for Bobby and Queenie to come home

from school, Gertie went to meet them. Byron gave her money and asked her to give them tea at the Kardomah café and then take them to the pictures.

For Evie, the pains seemed never-ending, though the midwife kept telling her she was making good progress. She was conscious of Byron's support, of his whispered endearments, of his hand holding hers, though the midwife had made him pull his chair to the head of the bed, out of her way.

When she said it was time for Byron to leave them, that the birth was imminent, Evie hung on to his hand and protested.

'I want him here,' she panted, feeling another pain building. 'I want him to stay.'

The gas and air mask went over her face again. The rubbery smell was horrible.

'Come on now, another big push,' she was told briskly. The pain was filling her mind and body, until she could think of nothing else. 'Keep pushing. We'll do it this time.' The room seemed to spin round her.

'A little girl.' She heard Byron's voice, thick with relief. 'She's lovely.'

She knew her baby was born at eight thirty that night, because the midwife timed it. 'She weighs in at seven pounds two ounces.'

A few minutes later a bundle was put into Evie's arms, and she found her new daughter gazing up at her with round blue eyes. They were locked together in minute examination of each other. Then Byron was there with tears in his eyes, trying to put his arms round both her and the new infant. Evie saw it as a moment of happiness and triumph.

When Gertie brought Bobby and Queenie in to see her in their nightclothes, Byron was still with her.

'Thank goodness that's safely over.' He was smiling. 'What shall we call the baby?'

Evie's older children were staring at him resentfully.

'What about Daisy?' Byron suggested. 'It's sweet and flowery. Do you like the name?'

Bobby said nothing.

'I like Poppy better,' Queenie said. 'Can I hold it?'

'Hold her,' Byron corrected gently. He made Queenie sit down and laid the child momentarily in her arms.

Byron felt sky-high on an emotional roller-coaster. He hadn't intended to stay and see his daughter born, but it was an experience he wouldn't have missed for worlds. He hadn't expected to feel like this. Evie had been wonderful, making so little fuss.

He'd held his newly born daughter in his arms, feeling absolutely thrilled. She looked as he remembered Grace looking at birth. He felt he was being given a second chance. He was ready to burst with love for mother and child.

When the midwife had made Evie comfortable for the night, he stayed with her, holding her hand.

'She's gorgeous. We'll be all right now, Evie. We're a family, an ordinary family.'

Evie was tired but trying to smile. 'I wish we were more ordinary.'

'We'll have a good life. You'll see.'

Gertie was staying the night in Queenie's room. At the midwife's suggestion, she'd made a temporary bed for Byron alongside Bobby's. When they'd all gone to bed and settled down, Byron crept into Evie's bed and snuggled down beside her, holding her close. He felt far too excited to sleep.

★ ★ ★

Now that the baby was born, Byron knew it would bring big changes, a new routine for them all. He hardly left Evie during the weeks of her lying-in. He wanted to be with her and the baby.

Evie said she wasn't concerned about their not being married, but he knew she was. It was her love for him that made her say otherwise. She worried about the effect the situation would have on Bobby and Queenie.

'I'm a bad example to them,' she said sadly.

'Of course you're not!'

Evie shook her head. 'Perhaps it's my own conscience. Perhaps I'm being silly.'

'They're too young to understand, love.'

'Perhaps. I keep telling myself I'm not going to be embarrassed, but I am.' She patted his hand. 'It's all right, I know it's something you can't change.'

Byron's arms went round her. 'I'm sorry, love. I take too much for granted.'

'Sometimes I feel like a loose woman.'

'You're not! Don't think like that. I love you, Evie. I wish things could be different for us.'

Once Evie was up and about again, Byron felt he should start spending a few hours in the flat when Bobby and Queenie were there. He wanted them to get used to seeing him with their mother.

Tonight was the first time he'd tried it, and he was well pleased up to now. They'd all eaten early in the evening and the children had cleared the dishes away to the kitchen so that they could use the table for their homework.

Evie had fed the baby. He'd pretended an interest in his newspaper, but he loved to watch her do that. Now she was nursing Daisy with a look of utter contentment on her face.

Bobby was poring over his geography books. 'Mam, I don't understand what it says here. What it's asking me to do.'

Evie got to her feet and put the baby in Byron's arms. 'Go to your daddy for a moment,' she said.

He tightened his hold on the infant. Daisy's eyes were wide open, staring up into his. Seeming to search his face. He felt such a wave of adoration. Bobby's voice cut across it.

'Is he Daisy's daddy?'

Byron knew that his head jerked up. Bobby's innocent gaze seemed somehow accusing.

'Yes,' Evie answered. Byron saw her tense up, afraid of what was coming.

'But not mine and Queenie's?'

She recovered and said: 'He is, Bobby, I keep telling you. Your first daddy was killed in the war and can't be with you any more. He'd want Byron to look after us all. He'd want you to have a new daddy.'

Byron beamed at her. Trying to tell her she'd said exactly the right thing. He felt it was all out in the open now. That he'd officially joined the family.

Byron went with Evie to register Daisy's birth. He wanted her to have his surname.

Evie had hesitated. 'If you feel strongly about it . . .'

He knew from her manner that she'd have preferred Daisy to be Collins like the other two.

'It'll split the family,' she tried to explain. 'Make Bobby and Queenie feel different. Make them pull in a different direction. They are already.'

But Daisy was Byron's daughter. He wanted her to have his name. He did feel strongly about it.

'You're besotted with Daisy,' she'd smiled.

'Aren't we all?'

'I certainly am. I'm enjoying her, she's lovely.'

That brought him some comfort. Bobby and Queenie were making it quite clear that they were not of like mind. It was troubling Evie.

'You mustn't worry,' he'd said. 'Time should sort that out.'

Evie was frowning. 'I wish I'd stopped to think about Bobby and Queenie. About what effect this would have on them.'

Byron felt full of love for her. He couldn't take his eyes from her troubled face. This was wrenching him in two. They were sitting on the yellow sofa, staring out into the night sky and the glow of lights reflecting up.

She said: 'Did you know that in the old days, women who committed adultery were forced to wear a red letter A on their breast so that everybody would know?'

'Evie, you haven't committed adultery. You're a widow.' He knew it was on her mind that he definitely had.

'I've had a child out of wedlock, and that's a sin. But I don't regret it. How could I regret having Daisy?'

She was trying to smile at him. 'History isn't clear about the fate of adulterous men, but poor Daisy would have been branded in that way.'

Byron could see a pulse beating in her throat. She looked at him squarely for a moment and her eyes were wet with tears. Then her dark lashes swept down against her cheeks and nothing he said would make her look up again.

He took her in his arms. 'Oh, Evie love. The war changed everybody's thinking. People don't worry so much about things like that now.'

As the New Year brought the start of a new decade, Evie

tried to put such thoughts out of her mind and get on with her new life.

She didn't like Byron leaving her at the weekends to see Norman. He seemed to sense that and didn't go more than once a month. She'd found out the hard way that a flat like this wasn't the best place for growing children. Having Daisy pegged her to it, yet the other two were wanting to get out and do things. They didn't like being confined and were always trying to escape to play elsewhere in the building. She hated to think what they could be getting up to. She forbade them to go out into the street. Queenie wasn't seven yet; Evie didn't really trust her out of her sight.

She didn't find Byron's absence easy to cope with. He worked Saturday morning and went over to see Norman after lunch. The first time, he didn't return until Sunday night, after she'd put the children in bed. She missed him. Now that she'd got used to having Alice do most of the cooking and cleaning, she missed her too. She had a day off on Sunday.

The building emptied in minutes at lunchtime on Saturday. There was less traffic in the streets. As it was in the business centre of Liverpool, the place seemed to die. Evie felt as if she and her children were the only people left in the world. When she said something of this to Byron, he stayed with her until Sunday morning and then went over to see his son just for the day.

That was better, but she much preferred the Sundays when Byron stayed with her and the children. Usually then he took them all for a run in his car in the afternoon. The children loved going to the beach at Formby. Even Bobby was pleased to go on trips like that.

The next Sunday Byron was away turned out to be a fine

summer's day. The flat was hot, with the sun flooding in. Bobby lay back on the yellow sofa and half closed his eyes. The sun dazzled and sparked off the new silver tea service on the sideboard.

He asked: 'Where did that come from?'

'It was a present,' Mam said, looking up from the baby.

'From Mr Ball?'

'Yes.' She smiled at him in the sad way that she had. 'Bobby, dear, couldn't you call him Dad?'

'He isn't my dad.' Bobby flushed with resentment. 'It's silly to call him that if he isn't.'

'He'd like it if you did. So would I.'

He said nothing.

Evie broke the silence: 'Queenie does.'

'Queenie only does it because . . .'

Queenie had been sitting in the opposite corner of the sofa. Now she dived across his legs, fixing him with her big brown eyes, stopping him from saying any more. Queenie called him Dad to get round him. She was after a new doll she'd seen in Lewis's window.

'If you really can't, Bobby . . .'

'Well, he isn't my dad.'

'Perhaps you could call him Uncle then? Uncle Byron. To call him Mr Ball is . . .'

Bobby slid lower on the sofa, putting his hands over his ears. He didn't want to call him anything. Mr Ball was always here. Pushing in where he wasn't wanted.

Outside the sun hardly reached into the deep canyon of South Castle Street.

'I wish something would happen,' Queenie said. 'It's awful quiet.'

'Like the grave,' Bobby agreed. They were so used to hearing the banging of doors and the whirr of the lifts and the sounds of lots of people below.

'Why couldn't we go to Gran's?' Queenie let her book slide to the floor. Bobby knew she was bored.

'You can't go every weekend,' Mam said. 'It makes a lot of work for her.'

'She likes having us.' Queenie pouted. 'She says we're no trouble. We want to go, don't we, Bobby? There's lots to do there.'

'Well, this week you can't.' Mam sounded a little short as she lifted the baby from one breast and turned it so it could feed from the other.

'You never have time for us any more,' Queenie complained. 'You're always busy with that baby. Feeding it or bathing it or playing with it or trying to get it to sleep.'

'You must call her Daisy, darling. "Her", not "it".' Bobby heard Mam say that about fifteen times a day.

'I wish it had never come,' Queenie had said to him when they were on their own. 'It never stops crying. It's a pain.'

'Mam likes it.'

'Yes, better than she does you and me.' Queenie had been angry. 'I wouldn't mind, but it's ugly.'

Bobby had to agree. The new baby had a shock of straight brown hair that stuck upwards. He'd even heard Gran say it would never be as pretty as Queenie.

'We'll go and see Miss Pringle this afternoon.' Mam looked up and gave them a wan smile. 'She's asked us to go for tea. You'll like that just as much, won't you?'

'No,' Queenie said mutinously. 'We like Gran's.'

Bobby met his mother's gaze. He knew she was upset. He tried to explain: 'Gran lets us stay up late and play out . . .' Queenie's foot jammed painfully into his tummy, making him gasp, but Mam didn't seem to notice.

It seemed an age before they were ready to go. Bobby

changed his shirt and washed his face without being told. Queenie got cross and impatient because it took Mam such a long time to get herself and the baby ready to go anywhere.

The perambulator, a new one, had to be packed with napkins and the baby dressed up in a woolly jacket and bonnet. It cried all the way down to the Pier Head, although there was a lovely breeze smelling of rope and tar and the sun sparkled on the water.

Queenie skipped along, happy now they were out. From the boat the Birkenhead bank looked leafy and green. It was an uphill walk to their old home. Soon they were walking through streets that were familiar.

Miss Pringle was smiling when she let them in. She seemed in a good mood. She kissed Queenie. Bobby remembered her being very cross before they'd moved to the flat. Quite tetchy with him. She'd kept complaining he was making a noise though he'd crept around like a mouse. Mam said Miss Pringle didn't want them to go. There was another old lady with her today, who was shaking Mam's hand.

'My sister, who's come to live with me,' Miss Pringle told them. The sister was fat too, with the same sort of rubbery face that Miss Pringle had, and the beginnings of a moustache. Miss Pringle pulled Queenie up on her knee, just as she used to in the old days. Like everybody else, she was very fond of Queenie.

Bobby thought it strange to be here in the front room again. The glass-fronted china cabinet was tightly packed with cups and saucers and glasses, but Miss Pringle had always kept a few more interesting things there. He liked the little clown made of deep red and blue glass with a white walking stick and black boots. There was a Buddha too, but Queenie liked the corn dolly best. Miss Pringle sometimes took them out so they could play with them.

Ida told her sister to open the cupboard now, and Bobby felt the cold glass of the clown against his hand. Once, Miss Pringle had kept a sugar pig in her cupboard too. They'd been allowed to play with that as well. Both he and Queenie were very fond of sugar pigs. They always had them in their stockings at Christmas. Sometimes they were white and sometimes pink. Miss Pringle's was rather grey.

'Why don't you eat it?' Queenie had asked her one day when she had it on her palm. 'They are for eating.'

'When you get to my age, you won't like all that sugar.'

'Can I have it then?' Queenie had asked eagerly. 'I love them.'

'I don't think you'd better have this one,' Miss Pringle had laughed. 'I've kept it for the last twenty years. A keepsake. My little niece gave it to me for my birthday. It wouldn't be nice to eat now.'

'I think I'd still like it. So would Bobby. I'd give him a bite.'

'No, it might make you sick. It won't be fit to eat after all this time.' She'd whipped it off Queenie's palm and put it back in her cupboard. 'We'll keep it as an ornament, shall we?'

It took weeks for Miss Pringle to notice it was gone. Then, one day, she came rushing to the back room where Bobby had been curled up in the rocking chair. Queenie had been playing on the rug at his feet. She jumped up straight away.

'Look at my farmyard,' she invited. 'I've got two new cows.'

'You didn't take my pig to play with, did you, Queenie?'

'Oh no, Miss Pringle,' she'd said, tossing her curls.

Ida had turned on Bobby then, catching both his hands

in hers and making him stand up. She'd asked sternly: 'Did you take my sugar pig, Bobby?'

He'd shaken his head while his cheeks had run with heat.

'You must own up if you did.' Her button eyes had held his in a long-drawn-out stare. He could see she believed he had.

He'd shaken his head again, feeling weak with guilt. Not because he had taken it, but because he'd eaten part of it. It had been so hard, Queenie had been unable to bite through it. He'd tried too but had failed to do more than put teeth marks on it. They'd had to take the coal hammer to it. There'd been trouble from Mam because they'd wrapped the pig in a clean tea towel and that ended up covered with dirty marks and coal dust.

Miss Pringle had been wrong about it making them sick. It hadn't, and the lumps had lasted longer in their mouths. Queenie reckoned that pig had tasted better than any other. Once the dusty taste had gone.

When all they had left was the string tail, she'd said: 'Mustn't get caught with this.'

Bobby had thrown it over the nursery guard on to the fire and shaken the towel there too. The sugar and coal dust had caused the flames to gust up the chimney. That had frightened them both. Bobby knew it was more than his life was worth to tell tales on Queenie.

Today the table was set for tea in the back room which used to be their living room. Miss Pringle often made pink blancmange and raspberry jelly for Sunday tea when they lived here.

'For the children,' she used to say. She'd made it for them again today. Afterwards, she started reading the tea cups.

'Lots of dots and dashes in your cup now,' she told Evie.

'That's the rent you pay me,' Evie laughed.

'Read my cup for me,' Queenie pleaded. 'Please.'

Miss Pringle made her go through the ritual of swilling the dregs round her cup and emptying them into her saucer.

'You're going to have a very happy life,' she told her. 'You'll be rich like your mother and marry young.'

'What about me?' Bobby offered his own tea cup. 'Will I be rich?'

'I don't see the dots and dashes for riches, not for you, Bobby.'

'I'll be a soldier though, won't I?' That was his ambition. To wear the red jacket and golden helmet of a guardsman.

'I don't see that for you either,' Miss Pringle said.

Bobby couldn't help pulling a face. He thought she was refusing to tell him what he wanted to hear. She didn't like him as much as she did Queenie.

Bobby liked living on top of the Connaught Building. He only had to mention the name at school and everybody knew the place. Most of the boys lived out in the suburbs, and came in on the trams. They thought the town centre rather a rough place to live until he mentioned the Connaught.

'You can see why,' Queenie told him when they were heading out to school one morning. 'Just look.'

There were three boys just ahead of them, wearing jerseys with their elbows out. Two had neither shoes nor socks.

'The pavement must feel icy to bare feet.' Bobby shivered and snuggled into his uniform gabardine.

Mam didn't like them playing out in the street here. She said the traffic and the horses were dangerous. Queenie said she wouldn't want to play out with those slummies and there was plenty to do inside.

The Connaught Building had white marble steps leading up to a massive front door. This led into a rather grand foyer with lots of polished mahogany. There were noticeboards on every floor giving the names of the companies who rented offices there.

All the offices were locked at night but that didn't deter Bobby and Queenie. There was a master key so the cleaners could get in. They soon discovered there was a kitchen on each floor, and most had a biscuit tin. Queenie was not above raiding them.

There was a commercial school on the third floor. It rented three rooms; one had a typewriter on every desk. They both had a go on them and then had to secrete the paper they'd used in the basement.

'I shall come here to learn properly when I'm old enough,' Queenie said.

On the teacher's desk was a gramophone with just one record. Queenie wound it up and set it to play. It was 'Alexander's Ragtime Band'. She sang with it. 'Come on and hear. Come on and hear.'

Often if they crept past the door during school hours they could hear the music belting out and the ten typewriters clattering in unison. Queenie hung round there quite a lot, chatting to the pupils.

Bobby was fascinated by a private detective who rented a single room on the fifth floor. 'Specialist in Matrimonial Cases', it said on his door. Sometimes he'd ask Bobby to go out to buy cigarettes for him. When he came back he'd reward him with a striped humbug.

# CHAPTER FOURTEEN

Bobby had bought a stamp album with his pocket money and was keen to build up a collection. He was down in the basement, looking through a waste-paper bin for discarded stamps, when another boy came in. He was about three years older, tall and skinny, with a home haircut.

'You're wasting your time. I've taken all the good ones.'

'Who are you?' Bobby wanted to know.

'Wilf Hutchins. I'm the office boy at Bulwark Insurance.' The second-hand suit he wore had been made for a man with wider shoulders. 'It's my job to open the post, and stamps are one of my perks.'

'You can't want them all?'

'Course I do. All the good ones, anyway. I can swap them or sell them.'

'Well, that's only Bulwark's. I live here, it's one of my perks to have them from the other offices.'

'Lots of people collect stamps and they get their hands on them before you can. I've asked round already, see. Those they don't want, they keep for me. The high-cost ones.'

Bobby felt piqued. 'Well, I should be able to have the stamps from Henry Ball and Company. My mother works for them.'

'Oh yes.' Wilf had canny brown eyes. 'She's Mr Ball's fancy woman, isn't she?'

'What d'you mean?' Bobby knew from his tone that fancy woman was a derogatory term.

'You know. His bit on the side. His lover.'

'How d'you know?' Bobby was indignant.

'Everybody knows here. You should hear the old spinsters in our office rattling on; sounding holier than thou about it.'

Bobby had been made aware, by Mam's obvious tension, that she was ashamed of something, but he couldn't have said what it was until Wilf spelt it out. He leapt to her defence.

'Well, they're all wrong and so are you. Mr Ball is her boss. She's the head caretaker here.'

'All right, all right.' Wilf held up a hand. He had a grin that stretched from ear to ear, showing perfect teeth. 'Don't get worked up about it. I'll bring you some stamps tomorrow, all right?'

Bobby went up in the lift fulminating about what Wilf had told him. He'd known something was wrong for Mam. He'd sensed it.

The flat seemed quiet, then he heard his mother's voice from her bedroom. The baby's cot was in there. He went to the door. She was changing the baby's napkin.

Bobby gulped and said furiously: 'They're saying things about you and Mr Ball downstairs. Nasty things. I told them it was all lies.'

That Bobby was upset was like a knife through Evie's heart. She could see him blinking hard, trying to hide his tears.

'What are they saying?'

'Calling you a fancy woman. A bit on the side. Why do you let that man come here? I hate him. I'm never going to call him Dad, nor Uncle Byron or anything.'

In a rush of guilt she put an arm round his shoulders. Pulled him down to sit beside her on the bed. What sort of an example was she setting her children?

It was all very well for Byron to say that everything was fine and they were just like an ordinary family. How could they be ordinary when this sort of thing happened?

'Oh, Bobby love,' she said. 'Don't worry about what you hear.'

'It's you I worry about, Mam. It's you they're talking about.'

Evie knew there was gossip about her and Byron. She'd been heading for the lift one day after taking Daisy for a walk when she saw Alice laughing with a clerk further down the corridor. She distinctly heard her say Byron's name. They were both so mortally embarrassed to see Evie that she was left in no doubt that some of the gossip was about her.

When she'd mentioned it to Byron, he'd said: 'Alice is well placed to know what's going on. She sees me here with you most of the day. People are bound to be curious. They know I own this building.'

'I don't like her talking about us,' Evie said. 'She'll have to go.'

'She knows the job isn't permanent, I told her it was only for a few weeks. It'll mean more work for you.'

'But more privacy. Anyway, I need more to do. I'll be happy to do the cooking.'

'The office cleaners can do the heavy cleaning. They can come up early in the morning while I'm opening up the office. And the laundry can be sent out.'

But by then their circumstances were common knowledge. Evie felt full of remorse. When she'd agreed to come here she hadn't foreseen this. She'd known before coming that she'd lost Ida Pringle's friendship. They still met and talked of their concerns, but there was a rift between them now. Ida had stepped back; she hadn't wanted their close companionship to continue.

Evie knew she'd been prepared to lose Ida. What she hadn't been prepared for was the pain the situation was causing Bobby. Or the enmity he felt for Byron.

The following day, Wilf Hutchins caught Bobby in the lobby. Bobby hadn't wanted to talk to him.

'I've brought my stamp collection to show you.'

Bobby was tempted, he wanted to see that.

'Come up to the office. It's all right, the boss is out.'

Bobby went. He liked going into the offices. A type-writer clacked away. From a drawer in the table on which he opened the post, Wilf brought out two full albums of stamps. Bobby looked through them, fascinated. Wilf brought out a fat envelope stuffed with swaps.

'For you,' he said. 'To get your collection started.'

Bobby couldn't resist Wilf's wide, cheerful grin and friendly overtures. He asked him countless questions about stamps and about his duties as office boy. He learned that Wilf's ambition was to be an insurance collector, because then he'd be given the use of a bicycle with the company name on it. He'd be able to get out of the office and go round the policy holders, collecting their premiums in weekly instalments.

After that, Bobby made a habit of calling in to the offices of the Bulwark Insurance Company to see Wilf. When he'd read his weekly copy of the *Magnet*, he gave it to Wilf in exchange for more stamps. It wasn't long before he was inviting Wilf up to the flat.

Byron pondered the sad mess he was making of everything. The years were passing. Daisy was four years old and he felt no closer to Bobby. If anything, things were getting worse.

Byron did little during normal working hours, choosing to spend that time upstairs with Evie and Daisy while the older children were at school. And here he was still at his desk long after the office had emptied. He worked late into the evening to give Evie time to get Bobby and Queenie to bed. As they grew older, of necessity, they went to bed later and he put off going up to the flat while they were still up. It rankled, and he was finding it harder not to bear malice.

It seemed a charade after all this time, but he knew Evie loved them all and it tore her in two to see them failing to get on.

Byron felt he'd done everything he could to get on better terms with Bobby. He'd tried taking him on outings, just the two of them, so they'd be on a one-to-one basis. He tried a football match, horse racing, dinghy racing on the river, cricket, men's things. He had no more success with Bobby than he had with his own son, Norman. After a few outings, Bobby had said he preferred to stay at home. Things seemed to go from bad to worse. It was making Evie unhappy. Casting a damper over them all.

He'd very much wanted Daisy to call him Daddy, but it had added to their difficulties. Made Bobby more determined not to accept him into the family. He knew Bobby resented him living in the flat. His silences and sidelong glances told him that. Byron felt that things would have been different if he and Evie were married. Bobby thought, although he couldn't put it into words, that Byron was compromising his mother. Well, he was. He was taking advantage of her generous nature.

Evie thought Queenie resented him too, but he wasn't sure. She was friendlier towards him. If only there were just Evie and little Daisy, all would be fine. The sad fact was, Byron told himself, he didn't feel comfortable anywhere these days.

On his visits to Norman, Veronica glowered at him with bitter intensity. He was left in no doubt that she hated him. He was going less often. It seemed pointless going at all, but if he let too many months go by without a visit, she complained. She wanted Norman to grow up knowing his father. She made him feel guilty.

Byron and Evie had had to work things out as best they could. At the flat he tried to keep out of Bobby's way as much as possible. One or two weekends each month, Gertie still took the older children home with her. He and Evie looked forward to that. It was the only time they seemed to have a normal life. Evie and Daisy were his family.

Then they'd get a baby-sitter and go out on a Saturday night. He felt guilty again because Evie seemed to have so little entertainment in her life.

The intercom rang at last. Evie's voice said: 'The children are in bed, Byron. Supper's almost ready.'

Bobby often dropped into the Bulwark Insurance office to see Wilf Hutchins. He asked him up to the flat but Wilf rarely came. He thought of Wilf as a grown man because he earned a wage. He'd discovered he was three years older than himself.

'How old were you when you started work then?'

'Thirteen.' Wilf was fifteen now.

'That's awfully young.' Nobody left Bobby's school until they were sixteen, and many went on to eighteen.

'I was sick of school anyway.' Wilf shrugged.

He kept a packet of Woodbines and a box of matches in his pocket and seemed to be lighting up whenever Bobby saw him. He'd have a few puffs and put it out, pushing what was left back into the packet for later. Even when only the butt remained, Wilf didn't throw it away.

'Why not?' Bobby wanted to know.

'I collect fag ends. Go round the desks I do, before we close. Empty all the ashtrays.'

'What for?'

He showed Bobby how to break them down and roll the tobacco bits in a fresh cigarette paper. 'I make new ones. It's cheaper this way. Want to try one?'

Bobby felt much older than his twelve years as he lit up, but he wasn't sure that he liked the acrid taste in his mouth.

'It's good to get them from the office. They're all nice and clean like. Lots of men walk the gutters looking for fag ends to reroll.'

Bobby wasn't sure he believed that. Mr Ball smoked cigarettes in their flat every day. The butts were often to be seen in the fancy ashtrays, proof that he was there while Bobby and Queenie were at school. Bobby had seen Mam dispose of them in the waste bin.

Wilf's fist prodded into his stomach in a friendly fashion. 'If you're asked what sort you smoke, you can say "Other People's".'

After four puffs, Bobby thought he'd had as much as he could take. Wilf showed him how to nip off the end before pushing it into the top pocket of his school blazer.

'It'll do you again, see.'

Bobby thought that with practice, he'd soon get the hang of it.

One Saturday morning, Bobby was on his way out of the building when he met Wilf on the stairs.

'You've got to come and see my bike.' Wilf was now sixteen and had been promoted to collector. 'It's kept in the basement.' Bobby watched him pedal off on the bike he'd been allocated and was very envious. Especially as he was allowed to ride it home and use it at weekends.

Soon, by special arrangement, he met Wilf in a quiet back street nearby and learned to ride the bike himself. Bobby could think of nothing more wonderful than having a bike of his own.

When his thirteenth birthday was due, Mam asked him what he'd like as a present. He didn't hesitate, although Mr Ball was having tea with them. Queenie said it was Mr Ball who provided most of the expensive things for them, and if only he played his cards right, he'd be given more. Bobby preferred to do without rather than be beholden to Mr Ball. But a bike was a different matter.

'I'd love a bike.' He couldn't stop that coming out.

Mr Ball looked very earnest. 'Your mother and I have talked about a bicycle . . .'

'I could go to school on it, Mam.'

'Your mother would like you to wait until you're older.'

'Thirteen's quite old. Wilf Hutchins started work . . .'

'The roads are busy round here.' Mam was frowning. 'Many more cars about since the war ended. More lorries too. It's not safe, Bobby.'

He hadn't expected that. Hope died within him. 'I'd be very careful.'

'Perhaps when you're older.'

'There must be something else you'd like,' Mr Ball was asking.

There were a thousand things he'd like, but not nearly so much as a bike.

Mr Ball's eyes were questioning. 'A train set?'

He nodded.

'Perhaps next year, Bobby, we could think of a bike.'

\* \* \*

When the train set came, Bobby had to admit it was magnificent, a Hornby Double O. He set it up in his bedroom and brought Wilf Hutchins up to see it. Wilf said he was very impressed, he'd never had a hope of anything so fine. Never seen one as good, except in a shop.

All the same, Bobby envied Wilf his Bulwark bike. On Friday afternoons, Wilf had to work in the office getting his weekly accounts up to date. He told Bobby that if he wanted to, he could take the bike out and ride it. Just so long as he had it back by five o'clock, which was going-home time.

Bobby rushed home from school that Friday, because he wanted to make the most of the three-quarters of an hour he'd have to ride the bike. He was looking forward to the school holidays, when he'd be able to have it all Friday afternoon.

The bike was propped up in the basement passage. He slung his school satchel and his cap in the cupboard where the buckets and mops were kept and wheeled the bike out through a side door.

It was a very heavy bike, and rather too big for him. He had first learned to ride it by putting one leg through under the cross bar, but now he could get his leg over and sit on the seat, if first he adjusted it to its lowest point.

It felt good to be astride the bike with the wind blowing through his hair. It was all downhill to the Pier Head and he could get up a decent speed. In front of him, he could see a horse-drawn beer waggon heading towards some dock road pub. He pulled out to overtake it, whizzing along now.

Traffic was fairly heavy, but Bobby was sure it was perfectly safe. Down on the Pier Head, which was usually thronged with passengers changing from the ferries to the buses and trams, was a lock-up kiosk selling sweets

*Anne Baker*

and newspapers. He had a halfpenny and wanted to get some treacle toffee. He waited for a break in the oncoming traffic and then sent the bike swooping across the great open expanse of cobbles. He did it properly, first looking behind him then putting out an arm to signal his intention.

The sudden jolt came without warning. There was a screech and a smell of burning rubber. His bike seemed to stop dead and he felt himself catapulting over the handlebars. Wilf had warned him to watch out for the tram lines: 'Be sure to cross them at right angles.'

Bobby knew what he'd done. He'd been riding in the same direction as the lines. His front wheel had locked in one of them. The crash knocked the breath out of his body. From the corner of his eye he saw the massive motor wheel come within inches. He heard the bike crumple under it like silver paper, then a searing pain shot through his left ankle and everything seemed to swim round him and go black.

When Evie heard the ring of her front doorbell she ran to answer it, half expecting to find that Gertie had come over to see her. She knew the man who stood there by sight. He looked anxious.

'Dixon,' he said awkwardly. 'Manager of the Bulwark Insurance Company, second floor.'

'Of course. Yes?'

'I'm sorry to have to tell you, Mrs Collins, but your son's been involved in an accident.'

'What?' She felt for the door post. She'd always had this fear; the roads were so busy here. 'What's happened?'

'He was riding one of our bicycles.'

'Is he . . . badly hurt?'

'I don't know. He's been taken to the children's hospital in Myrtle Street.'

Evie felt panic tighten her throat. She gasped: 'But how did he come to have one of your bikes?'

'I'm sending Wilfred Hutchins up to explain that. It's against company rules to lend it to anyone.'

Evie felt half paralysed with shock. As soon as Mr Dixon went, she rang down to Byron. Her mind was filled with the memory of Grace being killed in a bicycle accident.

'Please come up,' she said, and collapsed back on the sofa, hugging Daisy to her for comfort. It was after five o'clock and she'd been wondering where Bobby had got to. He was never this late. Queenie had been home from school this last half-hour.

By the time Byron arrived, Wilf Hutchins was standing awkwardly just inside the door, explaining how the situation had come about.

'He wanted to borrow the bike. I told him he could.'

'You shouldn't have . . .' Evie was all on edge. She kept glancing at Byron, knowing how he'd feel because of Grace. 'It was dangerous.'

Byron had gone white, and his voice was devoid of expression. He said to Wilf: 'What's done is done. Nothing can change it now. You'd better go home.'

'Sir, Mr Dixon says I'll get the sack for this.' Wilf's face screwed up with worry. 'Please . . .'

'Not now.' Byron's tone was not unkind. 'We've other things to think about.'

Evie blamed herself. She expected Byron to blame her too. In spite of Grace's accident he'd recommended that Bobby should have a bike for his birthday and be taught to ride it safely. He'd said: 'Grace was safe enough in normal conditions. It was just the ice.'

'I'll ring for a taxi, Evie,' he said now. 'You'll want to go and see Bobby.'

Evie wanted Byron to come with her. She wanted his

arm to hold on to, but she couldn't ask for it. He was somebody else's husband. Perhaps he wouldn't want to be seen supporting her in public.

It was Byron who rang the hospital and found out that Bobby was being admitted. That he had multiple fractures of his left ankle and would need surgery. It was he who steered Evie to Bobby's room and suggested she take his pyjamas and dressing gown.

'I don't suppose Bobby will want to see me.' He smiled sympathetically. 'I'll stay here and look after the children. Get them a meal.'

Queenie was glaring at him defiantly. 'I want to go with Mam.'

Byron paused. 'All right then, but you must be a good girl. Try and help her. I'll stay here with Daisy.'

Evie went up to the ward with Queenie's hand in hers. They found Bobby asleep.

'We had to give him something for the pain,' Sister explained.

He looked worse than Evie had expected. His hands and face were grazed and his cheeks were the colour of paste. She stood staring down at him, hating to think that her son's perfect body had been mutilated like this.

'His ankle is the serious injury,' Sister told her. 'An open wound with compound fractures, I'm afraid. He'll be put on the list to go down to theatre tomorrow.'

By the time they got home, Byron had given Daisy her supper and put her to bed. He'd set the table and had a meal prepared for them.

Queenie was subdued. She ate swiftly and seemed glad to go to bed. When Evie came back from tucking her in, Byron put a glass of brandy in her hand and pulled her down beside him on the sofa. She sipped the drink then put her head down on his shoulder and wept for Bobby.

His arm went round her shoulder in a comforting hug. 'He'll get better, love. The sister said he'd walk on it again, didn't she?'

'Yes, but he may be left with a limp.'

Evie couldn't stop her tears. Now they were as much for herself and Byron as they were for Bobby. She very much wanted to have this kind man as her husband.

Bobby was in hospital for three weeks and came home with his leg in plaster. Byron discounted the rent on the Bulwark Insurance Company's office by the amount required to replace the bicycle, on the understanding that that would be the end of the matter.

Wilf Hutchins came up to the flat to see Bobby the day he came out of hospital. The younger boy was lying on the sofa, looking out over the rooftops.

'Sorry about the bike,' he said. 'A car squashed it. Did you get into trouble?'

'Nearly got the sack for lending it to you.' Wilf's cheerful grin lit up his face. He dropped his voice because Evie could be heard clattering dishes in the kitchen.

'He's not a bad sort, is Mr Ball. He put in a good word for me. Made everything all right with the boss. He's all right.'

Bobby didn't agree. He felt full of resentment. Mr Ball wasn't treating his mother properly.

Daisy had started at Queenie's school three weeks ago and Evie feared that she hadn't yet settled in. She'd taken Daisy there for the first few days and the little girl had cried when the time came to leave her. The teacher had suggested that perhaps Queenie should bring her instead. Since then, Queenie had said there'd been no problem.

This morning, Daisy hadn't wanted to get up. 'Don't want to go to school, Mam,' she'd moaned.

'You have to go, darling,' Evie had insisted, and helped her dress.

At breakfast, the child had said again: 'Don't feel well, Mam.'

'In what way, love?' She'd put a hand on Daisy's forehead. It felt normal.

'Don't know.'

'A headache? Tummy ache?'

Daisy shook her head in misery. 'Don't want to go to school.'

Evie was afraid that this was because she didn't like her teacher. Daisy had already told her several times that she didn't.

'I think you should go.' Evie felt she had to be firm. 'You can't stay at home unless you're really sick.'

There was no comfort from Queenie. 'Hurry up and eat your breakfast or we'll miss the tram.'

Daisy pushed her half-finished plate away from her.

'Don't you want that bacon?' Bobby's fork was poised above it.

Daisy shook her head, and he whisked her bacon to his own plate. Evie felt a niggle of doubt then, and wondered if she'd made a mistake.

Queenie felt she was towing Daisy to the tram stop. 'Come on,' she urged. 'Let's get a move on.'

Once upstairs on the tram, amongst her own friends, Queenie pushed her sister against the window and ignored her, until Daisy dug her in the ribs and said: 'I feel funny. Sort of queer.'

'Sick, you mean? Queasy?'

Daisy nodded miserably.

'If you'd said that before, Mam would've let you stay home.'

'I feel worse now.'

'You ate too much banana custard last night.' Queenie wasn't sympathetic. 'More than your fair share. You'll be all right. Think of something else.'

Once she'd delivered her sister to her classroom, Queenie's mind was on her own affairs. She was not too pleased to be fetched from her art lesson in the middle of painting a cat. She thought it would be the best cat in the class. Instead, she was told that her sister had been sick and must be seen safely home.

'Fancy throwing up on the floor like that,' she told Daisy as they crossed the school yard. 'In front of everybody.'

'I couldn't help it.' Daisy was close to tears. 'I put up my hand to tell Miss Murgatroyd, but she took no notice. She was telling us about China.'

Queenie giggled. 'Bet that brought the lesson to a halt. You're all right now?'

'No, I've got pains in my tummy. I feel awful.'

Queenie took her hand and helped her on to the tram. 'I won't speak to you if you throw up again here. You'll make the conductor mad and he'll put us off.'

She saw Daisy close her eyes and sink back on the seat. As the tram jolted forward, she sat up straight again.

'It churns me up. My inside's all wobbly. It's swaying too much,' she moaned.

'I'll be glad to get you home,' Queenie said as they went up in the lift. She had to use her own front-door key to let them into their flat.

'Mam?' Daisy called, as they went into the living room.

'She won't be here.' Queenie was impatient. 'She'd have answered the bell if she was. She's gone out shopping or something. You'll be all right now you're home. I'll go back.'

'Will she be long?'

'How should I know?'

'Don't leave me, I still feel awful.'

Queenie watched Daisy climb on to the sofa and curl up at one end.

'Shall I get you the rug?' It was something Mam always did when they didn't feel well. She'd cover them with a tartan rug and tell them to go to sleep. Queenie did that, and decided that if Daisy nodded off, she'd go back to school. She plumped up a cushion and settled in the opposite corner to wait. The sky was dark over the rooftops opposite. It looked like rain.

She heard the lift whirr several times. Each time she thought it might be bringing her mother up, but each time it remained on a lower floor. Then, suddenly, she heard her outside on the landing, talking to somebody. A key turned in the lock and two people came in, laughing.

Queenie knew immediately that it was Mr Ball who was with her. She peeped over the back of the sofa. He had his back to her, Queenie could see that he was kissing Mam on the lips, as heartily as if he hadn't seen her for months. And Mother was opening her arms to him, welcoming his attentions. Queenie felt unable to move and was only half aware of Daisy pulling herself up to see over the top of the sofa too.

Mr Ball was helping Mam off with her coat. He tossed it over the back of their sofa without so much as a following glance. Queenie felt the fur collar tickle her cheek.

'Evie, love.' He was starting to undo the buttons on Mam's crimson wool dress, and she was letting him do it. Queenie could see her fingers fondling the hair at the nape of his neck, and she was pressing herself tightly against him. It was Daisy who broke the spell. She made a choking noise and pulled herself higher.

'Mamma, I'm sick. I've been sent home from school.'

Queenie sat up too, and saw her mother and Mr Ball shoot apart and spin round to stare at them. She thought they looked numb with shock.

'What's the matter, pet?' Mam's voice sounded strange. Her fair skin had flushed scarlet, right up her neck and into her cheeks.

'She threw up on the classroom floor.'

'Couldn't help it, Mam.'

'They made me bring her home,' Queenie told them. 'The other girls were holding their noses and pretending to puke too.'

Daisy wasn't far from tears again. 'Not after Miss Murgatroyd got some sawdust to cover it.'

Mam was holding out her arms to Daisy then. 'How d'you feel now?' She felt the little girl's head to see if she was hot. 'Are you better?'

'No, my tummy hurts.'

Mr Ball hovered, looking embarrassed. 'I'd better go. Shall I send for the doctor?'

'I don't know . . .' Mam was worried now.

'Better had, to be on the safe side.'

Mam was still shaking her head.

'I'll be downstairs, Evie. Let me know if you want one.'

He went then, shutting their front door quietly behind him.

Feeling tense, Evie fumbled to do up the buttons on her dress. She could scarcely breathe. Queenie was thirteen now, growing up, understanding more of the ways of the world. It must have been clear to her what her mother and Byron felt for each other. He'd had his hands inside her dress. Even married couples would keep that sort of love from their children's eyes. She braced herself for the awkward questions she was afraid would come.

Daisy mumbled: 'What was Daddy doing to you?'

That took Evie's breath away.

'Making love,' Queenie answered for her, her voice cold with condemnation.

Evie felt her cheeks burning. Oh God! How much had they seen?

Queenie went on: 'You make such a show of yourselves. Everybody talks about you. How do you think I feel? You're my mother! Why can't you get married like everybody else?'

Daisy piped up: 'Aren't you married to Daddy?'

Evie felt the word was being squeezed out of her: 'No.'

Queenie added: 'They're living in sin.'

'They ask me at school why Queenie's name is Collins and mine is Ball when we're sisters. Is Daddy going to marry you?'

'No!' Evie was aghast at the questions but felt powerless to deflect them.

'But he likes you. He kisses you a lot. I'm sure he wants to.'

'Wouldn't that be great?' Queenie mocked. 'He's rich and he's the boss here.'

'Don't say such things!'

Evie could see that Daisy still didn't understand. 'Don't you want to be married?'

'We can't always have what we want. It's not always possible.' Evie knew she was floundering.

'But he's Daisy's father. You want him to be our father too, you said so. I know you want to marry him.'

'Yes, well . . .'

'Bobby says you're already married.'

'Bobby? Is he here too?'

'No, he's been saying that for a long time. But I've told him he's wrong.'

Oh God! Her children talking like this! She'd had her head in the sand. It didn't bear thinking about. She couldn't leave it at that.

'Why has Bobby been saying that?'

'Because he wants it. Goes round telling everybody.'

Evie straightened up in consternation.

'I told him he's a fool. But he said, if you're not already married you soon will be.'

'Well, we won't.'

'Why not?'

'You know why not, Queenie! If you've heard so much talk, you must know. Byron's already married to someone else.' It sounded like a cry from her heart.

'It's supposed to be a secret, then, that you aren't married? I said to Bobby that that must be it.'

Daisy made a choking sound. 'I think I'm going to be sick again.'

Evie was glad to rush her to the bathroom and bring the conversation to an end. She should have explained the situation to her children. To have Queenie work it out for herself and then wring such an admission out of her!

And Bobby, poor Bobby, trying to make out that she and Byron were married. He'd been trying to shield her, and that pulled at her heart.

She wished she'd been more open with them. But she hadn't been able to because the whole world looked down on women who lived in sin, and it wasn't the way she wanted her children to think of her. And it debased what she and Byron felt for each other. Their relationship had been going on now for more than six years. That was as long as she'd been married to Ned. Byron had been unfailingly kind and generous. She owed him a lot, but she hadn't been able to explain that to her children.

Queenie passed the door as Evie was washing Daisy's face. 'I'm going back to school.'

Evie heard the front door slam behind her.

When she told Byron that Daisy had been sick again, he sent for the doctor. When he arrived, a couple of hours later, Daisy had fallen asleep.

Later, when Byron came up to see how she was getting on, he said: 'Evie, you look exhausted! Is Daisy . . . ?'

She shook her head. 'The doctor thinks it's just a bilious attack. Something she's eaten. He thinks she'll be all right tomorrow. It's Queenie I'm worried about.'

'I was mightily embarrassed that she caught us like that.'

'She said some hurtful things.' Evie shuddered. 'That everybody in this building knows about us; knows about Veronica too; that they gossip about us because we're living in sin.'

He put his arms round her. 'We've known that for a long time,' he said softly. 'You're not still upset about it?'

'I'm upset at the way it's affecting Queenie. She knows exactly what we are to each other. So does Bobby. They don't like us living like this.'

'Queenie can be a little minx.' Evie knew he'd always had a soft spot for her. 'We should have expected this, tried to explain to her.'

'And Bobby.' She told him what Queenie had said about Bobby. She felt his arms tighten round her.

'I'm sorry, Evie. I haven't been thinking either. I'm causing a lot of trouble for you.'

'I'm not setting a good example to my daughters, am I?'

Byron pulled her even closer. 'I'm taking advantage of you.'

'I always knew it had to be this way,' Evie said sadly. He loved her and not Veronica, and that had to be enough.

He lifted her chin and smiled down at her. 'Now they both know, Evie, there need be no further embarrassments.'

Byron went down to his office and shut himself away from everybody. He knew he wouldn't be able to work while his mind was swimming with self-reproach like this.

He hated to see Evie upset. He blamed himself. He'd let her down. He told himself he was a weak-kneed fool. He'd pandered to Veronica's wishes and Evie had suffered.

He tossed a file on to his desk, opened it and lifted a pen. His staff were close by. He'd had a glass door fitted to his cubbyhole so he could watch them, but it also allowed them to look in. He didn't want them to see him in this state.

He'd always thought of himself as a person who gave, but he'd taken too much from Evie. He should have taken a stronger line with her children. Let them know he was to be regarded as their father, that he had a position in their family. Instead he'd stood back and left everything to do with their care and discipline to Evie. He hadn't done enough to help her. He asked himself angrily what he could do about it now. He needed to calm down and make plans. He was good at planning ahead.

From now on he was going to look upon Evie's family as his own. He wasn't going to make himself scarce when Queenie and Bobby were about. That had been a mistake. He would throw his weight about more.

He would go once more to Parkfield. His visits were not improving his relationship with Norman. He'd pack what clothes and possessions he kept there and tell Veronica he wouldn't set foot over the doorstep again. He should have done that years ago.

In future, he would think more of Evie's needs. She was the one he loved.

# CHAPTER FIFTEEN

Evie felt that things improved after that. Byron was always about the flat and making an effort to be part of the family. He was determined that they would all enjoy life more. At weekends he took them on outings, and they had a holiday in London that pleased the older two.

The mid-1920s were bringing many changes. Women were given the vote. Byron said that class barriers were coming down and Edwardian propriety was gone. Evie felt a fashionable new woman when she shortened her skirts and had her hair bobbed.

Bobby was keen to build one of the new crystal sets. He and Wilf Hutchins started, but progress was much faster when Byron started to help. The three of them spent hours poring over instructions and catalogues of parts, and the whole family was thrilled when they could share earphones and hear 2LO calling from Savoy Hill. Byron enjoyed it so much, he bought more parts so they could do it over again, and Bobby could have a set in his bedroom.

Byron was opening a bottle of wine to go with the ham sandwiches Evie had made earlier. 'We're happy now, aren't we?'

'It's been a very happy day,' she agreed, flopping down on the sofa. She'd been to Daisy's bedroom to kiss her good night. The child was already asleep.

Today had been her seventh birthday, and to celebrate, Byron had taken all the family to the Royal Court Theatre to see *Peter Pan*. Evie thought fondly of her younger daughter. She was never going to be beautiful like Queenie. She had Byron's rather square figure and straight dark hair, but she had his gentle, easy-going manner too.

'Not just this evening.' Byron smiled. 'I mean generally. You are happy, Evie?'

She nodded. 'Contented.'

'Let's drink to our contentment then,' and he put a glass in her hand.

Evie dropped her voice. 'Things have been better since you built the crystal sets. You and Bobby . . .'

'We're on better terms? On the surface, perhaps, but deep down nothing's changed.'

'Not with Queenie either.'

'It's understandable,' he said gently. 'I came between you and them. It'll be all right when they're grown up. The teenage years are hard for all parents.'

'Where are the years going to? Teenagers already!'

Bobby and Queenie came noisily from the kitchen with the steaming mugs of cocoa they'd made for themselves. Evie thought they were all on a high after the excitement of the theatre.

Byron started to talk of something else. 'I told you I was taking Norman into the business? He's written to me. He wants to start in September.'

Evie said: 'I was beginning to think he'd changed his mind.'

'So was I. He decided to train as an accountant first. That'll be his mother's influence. She'd want him to do that.'

'A good idea, surely?' Evie said. 'For a career in business.'

'I'm glad, because he's old enough now to manage on his own when he's had a bit of experience.'

Evie smiled. 'And if he can't, it'll give him something

to fall back on.' She knew that business confidence was falling in the country. 'Your firm's all right?'

'Still expanding. Bucking the trend. I shall be handing it over to Norman in good shape.'

'That must please him.'

'He doesn't know. I haven't said a word about handing it over. Not to him or to Veronica. They think he's coming to work for me and I'll leave it to him in my will.'

'That's mean,' Queenie told him, biting into a sandwich. 'Why keep it to yourself?'

Evie jumped to his defence. 'Byron's never mean. He wants to see how Norman will turn out before he commits himself.'

Byron laughed. 'Kind of you to say that, Evie, but Queenie's probably right. His mother's always demanding her rights and Norman's. I didn't want to give her the satisfaction of knowing he'll get the company sooner than she expected.'

'But you have made up your mind?' Queenie wanted to know. 'You are going to give it to him?'

'Yes, within a couple of years at the most. I don't need to spend every day at that desk down there. I'm getting tired of it. I want more time to myself. I've plans . . . But I also have this obligation to do for Norman what my father did for me.'

'In other words, you'll make Norman rich?' Queenie took another sandwich.

'No, I'll make the business over to him. He might manage to make himself richer than he'd otherwise be. If he learns to run it properly.'

Queenie didn't take her beautiful eyes from him. 'And you're rich enough not to have to work any more?'

'Not rich.' Byron smiled as he refilled Evie's wine glass. 'But a wise man knows when he has enough.'

'I don't know why you're expected to give him anything,' Bobby said hotly. 'If he's an accountant, he can
earn a good living for himself. He mightn't want your
help. What if he wants to stand on his own feet?'

'He won't,' Byron said. 'Who in their right mind would
turn it down?'

Evie was finding her children's teenage years hard to cope
with. She no longer knew how to handle Queenie. She'd
always been a beautiful child and she was blossoming as
she grew older. She looked older than she was; by the age
of fifteen she looked adult, and Evie was afraid she was
embracing the pleasures of the adult world wholeheartedly.
She had Ned's large brown eyes and lustrous curly hair,
but Evie feared she didn't have his generous, loving nature.

Queenie seemed to have a will of iron. She was
determined to have her way with everything. Evie was
afraid she wanted to control what others did in the way
that Joseph Hobson, her grandfather, had.

Evie had thought herself daring when she was young,
but Queenie's daring left her breathless. All young people
seemed to smoke these days. Queenie even smoked in
public. She and Bobby talked of larks and japes.

'They're the bright young things of today,' Byron told
Evie.

Evie was half sorry she'd bought the wind-up gramophone for Christmas. Queenie had it blaring out endlessly
in the living room, practising the steps of the Charleston
and the Black Bottom. Evie had also heard it playing in
the basement during the school holidays and found
Queenie attracting office boys and junior clerks down
there. She'd had to put a stop to that.

Almost simultaneously, Queenie and Bobby seemed to

get fed up with school. There was vague talk about leaving. It wasn't what Evie had planned for them and it upset her. It was Bobby who made up his mind first.

'I'm seventeen,' he said. 'It's time I went to work.'

'There's no hurry. Better if you learn all you can first.'

'There's no end to learning, Mam. Wilf started work at thirteen.'

'You're not Wilf,' Evie told him. 'I want you to have every chance.'

'Mam!'

Ned hadn't had a decent chance. She felt so strongly that his son must. Bobby was becoming more and more like his father as he grew up. He still walked with a slight limp after that accident on the bike. It was more marked when he was tired.

'All right, we'll see if Byron can find a good opening for you.'

'No!' Bobby's ferocity shocked her. His brown eyes, usually so gentle, were angry. She found it hurtful that Bobby couldn't get on with Byron. She loved them both very much.

She had to protest. 'I didn't mean in his business, love. He knows every company in the Connaught Building, he's got a lot of pull. He's already said he'll be willing to help.'

'No, Mother.' Bobby's chin was determined. 'I'll find my own job.'

'But darling, you don't understand. If Byron puts in a word for you, your prospects will be better. I want you to have a reasonable start in life.'

'I don't want him to do anything for me.'

'He'll want to . . .'

'I don't want to be beholden to him. I'll do it myself.'

That took Evie's breath away. She'd known Bobby's antagonism for Byron ran deep, but she hadn't realised he'd turn down help from him. She'd thought things were improving now.

She took a deep breath: 'What are you going to do?'

'I'm going to apply to the banks. Wilf thinks a bank clerk would be the thing to be. It can be a career. In time, if I'm good enough and pass exams and things, I could rise to be manager.'

'It could be worse,' Byron said, when she told him. 'At least he isn't going to run away to join a circus. It might work out all right.'

Evie had to be content with that. Bobby found an opening he thought would suit him. He left school in July and started the following week at the Liverpool Savings Bank in Bold Street.

'You're a fool,' Queenie railed at him. 'Why don't you let Dad help you? A hand up now and you'd earn much more.'

Evie had wanted to say that too but had kept silent. Not that it made any difference. Bobby wouldn't listen to anybody.

'I want to leave school too,' Queenie announced the day after she had broken up for the summer holidays. She and Bobby had been mulling over the possibility of leaving for months. She'd persuaded him to come out with it first; after all, he was the elder. He'd taken the brunt of Mam's displeasure and got his own way. She felt it had cleared the way for her.

Now it was her turn. She had it all planned. They all got up late for breakfast. Byron had already gone down to his office.

Mam looked taken aback. 'But you've chosen the subjects for your higher . . . It's all arranged. You said you'd go on.'

'You said I should. You knew I wasn't keen.'

'Only two more years.'

'I'm sixteen,' Queenie said defiantly. 'I've had enough of school. Girls get married at my age.'

She saw her mother flinch. Any mention of marriage was guaranteed to do that.

'I was hoping you'd have a career. Teaching, I thought . . .'

'Mother, I've been telling you for years. I want to learn typewriting. Isn't that enough of a career?'

She could see that Mam was at a loss. 'Well – it has to be something you want to do.'

'Exactly.'

There was no mistaking Mam's reluctant sigh. 'Then we'll have to look for a commercial college for you.'

'Don't you ever listen to what I say?'

Queenie didn't know what drove her on to be so hateful to her mother. Across the table, Bobby had stopped eating. He'd told her he didn't know how she dared, and if he was Mam, he'd slap her face.

'No need to look far. I want to go to the Boardroom Commercial College. Down on the third floor. What could be easier?'

Mam's lips were pursing. 'We'll have to see, dear.'

Queenie knew that that meant she wanted to discuss it with Byron first. Queenie knew how to make him say yes. She'd bring it up at suppertime, before Mam got her oar in. She'd tell him what she wanted, flutter her eyelashes at him and smile. Byron wasn't the sort to refuse her anything.

Later that night, in bed, Byron said to Evie: 'Queenie's a determined little miss. If she's set her mind on leaving school we'd have a hard time changing it.

'I don't think the training at the Boardroom College is the best, but it's not the worst either. Why don't you go in tomorrow? See if they'll take her next term?'

Queenie was delighted when September came round and she found herself one of the Boardroom girls.

Long ago, she'd told the two middle-aged sisters who ran the school that one day she'd be one of their students. The Misses Ermintrude and Edith Worstenholm rented what had once been the boardroom of J. S. Connaught and Company and used it as their main classroom. They also rented two smaller adjoining rooms. One was their office and the other was the room with a typewriter set out on every desk where Bobby and Queenie had played as children.

The sisters called it the Boardroom Commercial College and charged higher-than-average fees. The prospectus claimed to train secretaries in the Boardroom, for the Boardroom; and to give them the extra polish and sophistication needed to handle management affairs.

For Queenie it was familiar ground. She'd been hanging round the place and the girls who attended it for years, in the way Bobby had hung around the Bulwark Insurance Company. She'd learned a lot from past pupils. They'd moulded her thinking on men, on working for a living, on clothes and hairstyles, on the need to colour her lips and her nails. She'd held them up as experts to her friends at school.

As she looked round the class on her first day, the present crop of pupils seemed younger and more callow than in previous years. Some were only fourteen, though most were at least sixteen. Queenie had been looking forward to the extra polish promised in the prospectus. She had only to look in a mirror to know she was very good-looking, but even a good-looking girl could look cheap and trashy, or intelligent, or cool and classy, depending on her clothes and make-up.

Queenie wanted to look fashionable and attractive to men – the sort who had money. She wanted to make sure she was always perfectly turned out. The 'extra polish' was provided by a Miss Dauber, who came on Thursday afternoons to teach grooming and deportment.

Queenie was disappointed to find that deportment consisted of walking in a line round the boardroom with a book on her head, and of sitting up straight at her typewriter. The grooming was keeping her fingernails clean and her skirts pressed. The girls thought Miss Dauber a bit of a laugh and said nobody needed grooming lessons more than she did. She wore skirts that were shapeless tweed tubes.

Queenie had also looked forward to learning to type. But every typewriter had its keys covered so that they couldn't see what letter it would type. She was given a chart of the keyboard.

'So you don't develop bad habits, girls,' Miss Ermintrude's voice brayed. 'No point in looking at your fingers. Keep your eyes on what you are copying.'

Within a day or two, the gramophone was being wound up and playing 'Alexander's Ragtime Band'.

'Listen to the beat, girls. Press one key to each beat. Return the carriage to one beat. Nothing like it for getting your speed up,' she told them heartily.

Queenie felt all thumbs, and the tune raced along far too fast. Miss Ermintrude seemed always to be behind her, shouting above the clatter.

'Keep in time to the music, Miss Collins. Strive for accuracy. Speed is no use without accuracy.'

And she kept winding up the gramophone and playing the tune over and over until Queenie was heartily sick of it.

She found it harder to master the skills of Pitman's shorthand than she'd expected, and Miss Edith's voice dictated at faster and faster speeds. It was just like being back at school and none of it was as much fun as she'd expected.

Both the Misses Worstenholm told them they must behave like ladies. It was very unladylike to ogle at the clerks employed in the Connaught Building, and it was absolutely forbidden to hang about the lifts and stairways in the hope of talking to them.

Years ago, Queenie had heard Wilf Hutchins laughing with Bobby, telling him that the lads in the buildings called the school the Passion Pick-up Point, and that they hung around the stairs and the corridors hoping to get themselves a girlfriend.

The girls thought that an even greater laugh. Each whispered to the other that they considered the clerks beneath their notice. They were seeking husbands who would be able to keep them in comfort. A clerk wouldn't do at all.

But as men of the right calibre were not competing for their attention at the moment, most girls thought they might as well meet the clerks halfway, just for practice and a bit of fun, so it went on all the time.

Queenie was having a late Sunday breakfast in the living room with Bobby when she heard Byron talking to her mother in the kitchen.

'Norman's going to start tomorrow.'

'You'll be pleased to have him. He'll be able to take some of the work off your shoulders.'

'I suppose so.'

'Of course it's so, Byron.' Queenie thought she heard her mother kiss him. 'It's what you planned. If you're ever to give up the office desk, he has to come.'

'Veronica will probably come with him and I'm not looking forward to that. She'll be trying to negotiate privileges. She'll call them his rights, but privileges are what they'll be.

'She'll want him to have a fat salary for a start. She'll expect the business to pay his fares and his lunches. It's nit-picking and it annoys me.'

'Perhaps accountants are all like that,' Mam laughed. 'Why don't you tell him he can have the whole business just as soon as he can manage it?'

'And give her the satisfaction?'

'This has more to do with fighting Veronica than anything else.'

'It's all she ever thinks about, making sure I don't do Norman down.'

'As if you would.'

'No, but I'll let her sweat on it a bit longer.'

When Queenie finished her morning class the next day, instead of going straight up to the flat for lunch, she took the lift down to the ground floor and peeped inside the office of Henry Ball and Sons. She'd never seen Norman and was curious about him. Besides, she wanted to give a full report to the girls in her class. Particularly Louisa Fanshaw, who boasted that she had a boyfriend who came from a wealthy family. Queenie was disappointed. He wasn't there and there were no signs that the spare desk had been taken over.

'Veronica rang,' she heard Byron telling Mam over the meal. 'She had to go to the dentist this morning and she wants to bring Norman in herself. She thinks nobody else could introduce him to our accounts. Talk about mother's boy!'

Mam asked: 'When will they come?'

'They'll be in this afternoon.' Byron was hacking irritably at the pot roast Mam had spent all morning cooking.

Queenie ate silently, thinking about wives and kept women. Byron's wife had upset him by delaying Norman's start. Mam's efforts to please had not soothed his irritation. It was easy to see which women held power in this world. Queenie had already decided she would become a wife as soon as she possibly could.

When she went again to peep into Byron's office late that afternoon, Norman was there with his mother. Both were seated at the spare desk, with documents spread out before them.

Queenie thought Norman looked a cut above the average clerk in the Connaught Building. At twenty-two, his shoulders had broadened out; he was already a man. He wore a good suit that had been made for him, not a hand-me-down. There was no look of the mother's boy about him.

He wasn't handsome like Bobby, but he wasn't bad either. Lots of straight brown hair that he kept tossing off his forehead. Nice clear skin, past the acne age, unlike many of the young clerks here. Queenie was sure the girls would vote him a winner. And he wasn't just a clerk. Soon he'd own that business. He'd be able to keep a wife in comfort.

His mother looked formidable and really sour. Her nose and mouth twisted as though she had smelled a bad smell. She was tall and angular, with eyes like organ stops, and grey waves set with mathematical precision.

Queenie could see why Byron preferred Mam. Anybody else in the world would too. Yet Veronica was dressed with more style, in a velvet dress of soft green, and she'd thrown back a handsome coat with a fox-fur collar.

★ ★ ★

Byron was in a worse temper when he came up at teatime.

'You'd think it was Veronica who was teaching him to run the business. She said she'd come every day for a month. So she could explain our accounting system.'

'He is a qualified accountant,' Evie murmured.

'I'm afraid I was rather rude. I said learning to make a profit was more important than counting every last penny.

'It's my business but she treats it as though it's hers. And then you wonder why I don't just say take it.'

'Could she run it?' Queenie wanted to know, her mouth full of sponge cake.

'No. He won't be able to either, unless I show him.' Byron crashed his cup down on his saucer.

'Veronica wasn't satisfied until she found out exactly what it earns now. She hasn't been near for eighteen months and just as I expected, she wanted to jump his salary up. And a car, she wanted me to buy him a car. To come to work in, she said.

'I told her he'd do the journey in half the time if he used the boat or the train. No one in their right mind is going to drive a car on and off the luggage boat just to cover half a mile or so on this side. And it's not so easy to park these days, not round here. Veronica had the neck to say he deserved one. Not from me he doesn't.'

Evie cut a slice of the sponge cake she'd made for him. He was too angry even to try it, though the whole flat smelled wonderful from its baking.

'Norman hasn't been near me in years. Even now, he wouldn't come without her. He'll have to learn to leave go of her hand or he'll never be able to run anything.'

'Don't let Veronica upset you,' Evie was saying.

'She put me in such a bad mood I refused to budge on anything. I said he's here to learn the business and that means others have to give time to him. I said he'd be more of a hindrance than a help for the first six months. I told him I'd think about a rise then, if he proved to be useful.'

Queenie lay back on the settee and let her gaze linger on the darkening skyline. The crystal set was on a stool beside her, but she held the headset an inch from her ear so she could hardly hear Henry Hall's orchestra. That was the way she wanted it. She was doing some serious thinking.

Norman Ball interested her. Mam's embarrassing position had made her decide long ago that she wouldn't get caught that way. She was going to be married. A legal wife, and she wasn't going to marry a poor man and have to work either.

It occurred to her now that Norman Ball was a likely candidate. Anyway, she knew of no other, so she might as well find out if she liked him enough. Mam wouldn't like her taking up with him, but she'd never known which way her bread was buttered, and besides, there was no need to tell her just yet.

Norman Ball chewed the end of his pen and looked round his father's office. He didn't feel at ease here. The only sound was the clack of Miss Parker's typewriter. The three clerks scribbled away in files and ledgers on their desks.

For as long as he could remember, his mother had been going on about his birthright. About how she'd fought to get him this chance to claim it. About how his father had reneged on all his other obligations, but he mustn't be allowed to renege on this. She was absolutely determined that Father shouldn't cheat him out of his share of this business.

'You'll have to go and work with him,' Veronica had

said. 'Learn all about it. I'm afraid he's built up other family commitments. He may want to keep the business for them. It'll be up to you to make sure he doesn't.'

Norman felt he hardly knew his father. He hadn't seen very much of him since he was eleven years old, and nothing at all in recent years. His mother spoke of Byron often, but never with affection. She told Norman that his father was a hard man, selfish, cruel and particularly mean with his money.

Norman had put off coming here for as long as he could. He thought now that it was a mistake, even though the profit generated by this small office was much greater than he'd expected. Greater than Mother had expected too. He'd seen her glow of interest when she finally got at the books.

'It's worth having,' she'd told him. 'You must stand up for yourself. Not let your father browbeat you.'

Then yesterday, on his first day, the staff here had spoken warmly of Father. They seemed to think he was a fair man. 'Generous and easy-going,' his secretary had said.

'I hope you'll settle down and enjoy doing the work, Norman.' Byron had shaken his hand when they'd met. 'The men of our family have been doing something like this for over two hundred years. I hope you'll want to carry on the tradition.'

Then Byron had taken them to his little office for privacy, and Mother had put forward her demands on Norman's behalf. She hadn't told him what she intended doing, or what her demands were. If she had, he'd have said she was expecting too much. Norman had been embarrassed to hear them arguing over what he should or should not be given. What he remembered most about the time when Father had lived with them was the way his parents were always at each other's throats.

Father had dug his heels in and both had ended up angry and frustrated. Mother had come with Norman again this morning. There had been more of the same argument. He'd tried to keep out of it this time. Then she'd opened the accounts for Henry Ball and Sons but was too angry to concentrate. He'd have learned more about them if he'd been left to examine them in peace. He was glad when she'd given up and gone.

All this made him wonder whether he'd done the right thing by coming at all. He hadn't been convinced it was what he'd wanted in the first place.

Accountancy hadn't been his thing either. He'd completed his articles and passed his exams because Mother was forever telling him it was a means to an end, and that he'd manage to run this business more efficiently if he had a background in accountancy.

He hadn't yet found his niche, and he didn't think he would here. At the back of his mind was the thought that he'd like to work with dogs. He had a Labrador and his mother kept a Pekinese. Yes, something to do with dogs would be more his sort of thing.

Norman pulled himself to his feet with a heavy sigh. First days in a first job could never be easy. He hadn't expected they would be. His father had disappeared, no doubt to his flat at the top of the building. Norman wished it was time for him to go home. He'd go along to the gents to get away for a few minutes, stretch his legs.

He was no sooner in the corridor when he saw a girl coming towards him with a swinging stride. An absolutely stunning girl. She was looking him confidently in the eye and smiling. He felt bowled over in those first few seconds.

'Hello, Norman.' She planted herself squarely in front of him. 'I'm Queenie Collins. Have you heard of me?'

His first thought was that she must be some star of stage or screen. She was wearing lipstick and nail varnish, but it was discreet and enhanced her beauty. Her dress was eye-catching too. Was this some publicity stunt?

He felt at a loss. 'No, should I have done?'

'I just wondered.' There was something almost intimate in her manner. 'I live in the flat on top of this building – with Byron.'

That took his breath away. Was she telling him . . . ? No, she must be too young . . .

'My mother and him.' Her smile was dazzling. 'I belong to the other half of the family.'

# CHAPTER SIXTEEN

Queenie smiled seductively. 'How about having a cup of tea with me?'

Norman's face lit up. She had him outside in South Castle Street in moments.

'I don't know whether I should be leaving the building now,' he protested half-heartedly. 'Got to keep my slate clean, new job and all that.'

Queenie laughed and steered him towards Macey's Café. 'You'll be safe for half an hour. Your dad's having his tea. He always takes his time.'

Macey's was only a hundred yards away and was much patronised by the Boardroom girls at lunchtime. It was open all day and specialised in light savoury snacks and cakes. The décor and the crockery were designed to appeal to office workers, of which there were many in the district. At four thirty in the afternoon, it was almost deserted. Queenie settled at a table near the window. Service was swift.

'I thought we should know each other. We're sort of related.'

'We are not,' Norman said firmly. 'Not related at all. I don't think my mother would approve of this.'

Queenie giggled. 'Your father won't mind. It's sort of bringing both sides of his family together.'

Norman's eyes were searching her face. 'I don't see it as a bad thing. We're adults, aren't we? Tell me about your family.'

He was listening avidly to all she told him about Mam

and Bobby. She found he knew nothing about them. He was even more interested to hear about Daisy.

'She's your half-sister,' Queenie assured him. 'Fancy you not knowing about her.'

He looked quite shocked. 'I didn't know she existed. My father has an illegitimate child! Mother will be shocked!'

Queenie laughed. 'She knows. She just isn't telling you.'

'Really?'

'I'm sure.'

Norman said slowly: 'Perhaps you're right. Once she did say something like: "He has other commitments. He may want to leave his business to . . ." '

'She feels Byron's rejected her. She doesn't want to talk about that and she doesn't like us,' Queenie said, never taking her eyes from Norman's face. 'No wonder she's got it in for him.'

'Has she?'

'Very definitely.'

Norman would have been willing to linger, now that Queenie had primed his curiosity. He wanted to know more about Evie, more about Queenie herself. When the bill came for their tea and scones, she made a show of picking it up, but he insisted on paying.

'When can I see you again?' he wanted to know as they were crossing the dignified foyer of the Connaught Building.

'Tomorrow?' Queenie turned her eyes full of eager anticipation on him.

'Lunch? The same place? We won't have to waste time getting there.'

'Lovely.' Queenie gave a little squeal of delight and surreptitiously planted a kiss on his cheek. That was to tell him they could be more than friends.

* * *

Queenie's first impressions of Norman were favourable. She liked the way his gaze explored her face; she liked the smile that played about his lips and the masterful way he'd taken that bill from her.

She spent most of the evening trying to work out the best way to manage this affair. All her instincts were to play it fast; she wasn't one to drag her feet anyway. A whirlwind romance might be the best way, not allowing him time to catch his breath.

The lunch was a great success. Norman seemed as eager as she was. He invited her to the theatre that evening.

'Shall I try to get tickets for the Playhouse? I've heard the new play there is very good.'

'Yes, please,' Queenie breathed. 'I'd love that.'

'What if there aren't any seats?' He couldn't get in touch with her once she was in class again.

'We'll go to the pictures instead, and you can try for tickets on another night.'

Some of the girls from her class had been eating in Macey's too. They wanted to know all about Norman. Even Louisa Fanshaw seemed impressed when Queenie mentioned that he was Byron's only son.

To meet Norman, Queenie had to miss family meals. She'd had to say: 'I won't come up for lunch today, Mam.' Now she had to add: 'I'll be missing supper tonight. I want to go out.'

'Where are you going?' Mam wanted to know.

'Lots of the girls eat at Macey's. It's fun, all of us together.'

'But tonight as well?'

'They're all going to the theatre. The Playhouse. I'd like to go with them.'

'All right.' Mam seemed reluctant.

'Let her go,' Byron had urged. 'Let her have her fling with her new friends.'

He'd taken out his wallet and given her a pound. 'To ease the financial strain,' he'd said.

Queenie had kissed him; Byron could be very generous.

In the following days Queenie flaunted Norman in front of the Boardroom girls like a prize she'd won.

Louisa Fanshaw tried to belittle him. 'He's not all that handsome,' she said.

'But he's going to be rich one day.' Queenie rushed to point out his advantages. She almost told them more than she should.

'And he knows how to treat a girl,' she added instead. 'Dinner at the Adelphi last night. Always the best theatre seats. Taxis to the door. He's fun to be with.'

It wouldn't do to start any gossip. Not about Byron's intention of handing over his business to his son. Byron wouldn't be pleased if it got to Norman's ears before he told him himself. He'd know it had come from Queenie.

Norman was showing an increasing interest in her company even though she'd told him every fact she could think of about her family. He asked a lot of questions about Byron; he said his father was going out of his way to be kind to him. That he thought after all that the job might suit him. He'd met Queenie through it after all.

Norman spent the first hour of every day with his father in his little office. He found these sessions very helpful. He was picking up the knowledge he needed to work here. He tried to be as attentive as possible and show enthusiasm for the job. He wanted Byron's approval.

Now, as he went back to his own desk, he wished he could get to know his father better. Byron never spoke of his new family, nor invited Norman upstairs to meet them.

He was affable, even friendly during working hours, but he kept his distance. Norman was careful not to mention that he was getting to know Queenie very well.

Last night, he'd taken her to dinner at a new nightclub that had just opened in Lord Street. He'd had a wonderful time, holding Queenie in his arms as they shuffled round the tiny dance floor. She felt soft and yielding and had put her head down on his shoulder. He hadn't meant to stay more than a few hours, but time had flown.

Norman stifled a yawn. He'd managed to get a taxi to bring Queenie back here. He'd seen her in, then climbed back in the taxi and asked to be taken to the underground station in James Street.

'Last train goes at half eleven, gaffer.'

Of course it did. Norman had sat back on the seat for a moment, trying to collect his wits.

'The Pier Head? You might just catch the midnight ferry if I put me foot down.'

He knew the boats only ran every hour during the night, and he'd have to find a taxi on the other side. It hardly seemed worth the trouble when he had to be back here by nine in the morning.

'The Stork Hotel,' he said. He'd stay overnight. No doubt his mother was waiting up for him. He'd have to ring her when he got there.

Norman sat at his desk, expecting his mother to come through the door at any moment. She was usually here by mid-morning. She'd agreed with Byron that she'd come in daily for a month until Norman had got the hang of the accounting system. After being articled for all those years to Lampton and Fiske, there had never been a need for her to come. He'd worked it out for himself within the first few days. He wished she'd give up coming.

The trouble was, if she hadn't gone by lunchtime, it made it difficult to meet Queenie. His mother would hate the very idea of his being friendly with her. Queenie was Byron's mistress's daughter. One day, he'd had to scribble a note at the last moment, and ask Miss Parker to run up to the Boardroom College with it when Queenie's class was being dismissed. He'd had a boring heavy lunch with Mother instead, and longed for Queenie's company.

Last night, on the telephone, Veronica had asked if he had a girlfriend who was keeping him out late. He'd had to say yes. What else would keep him out so many evenings on the run? At least, at that moment, he didn't have to introduce Queenie, and he hadn't explained who she was. Mother was none too pleased as it was.

Lunchtime came, and he was thankful there'd been no sign of his mother.

Queenie was all giggles. 'Wonderful night last night, wasn't it? The girls are green with jealousy. Not many have been to a nightclub.'

'A quiet night tonight, eh?' Norman wasn't used to so many late nights.

Queenie beamed at him. 'What about the pictures then? I'm dying to see *Sadie Thompson*, and it's showing at the City Picture House. Gloria Swanson's in it.'

Norman had been about to suggest that they have a night in to recover, but he didn't want to disappoint her. She was always brimming with energy and enthusiasm. At the back of his mind was the fear that if he didn't take her, she'd find somebody else who would. He'd seen the clerks ogling her and knew she'd have no difficulty. Queenie was a prize. He felt incredibly lucky that she seemed to like him.

There was also the problem that he was running out of money. The hotel bed had taken the last of what he'd had.

If his mother had come in this morning, he'd have been able to ask her for more. She was always generous if she had it. That was one thing he could say for her. A free spender herself, she expected it of him.

Since his father had left them, his mother had found her pleasure spending the money he allowed her. Everything she bought was of the very best. She liked getting out and about. Every few months, she went down to London for a week. She liked theatres and restaurants and expensive hotels. If she was going out, she telephoned for a car to come to her door.

Norman had always thought her attitude to money at odds with her training in accountancy. He'd told her so.

She'd laughed: 'It's fun spending it, but work adding it up.'

He thought she might still turn up this afternoon. When she'd missed the odd morning previously, she'd always come in later. He watched the clock, but by four he'd decided she wasn't coming. It was hardly worth her while.

Norman wondered if he dared ask his father for money. There was no other way he could take Queenie to the cinema, and she'd want something to eat afterwards. He quailed at the thought, but Queenie had said Byron was easy-going.

He made up his mind to do it before he disappeared upstairs for his tea. He had to get money from somewhere. He tapped on the glass door of his father's office. Byron was frowning when he lifted his head.

'Father,' he said slowly. 'Could I have a sub against my salary?' He was conscious of the searching look Byron was giving him, and tried to explain. 'Working for a whole month before I'm paid. It isn't easy to manage.'

'You weren't paid by Lampton and Fiske?'

'A small honorarium. Mother gave me an allowance.'

'And that's no longer forthcoming?' Byron opened his wallet and gave him five pounds. 'This once only,' he said.

Norman pocketed it quickly. Byron's eyes locked on to his.

'To be successful, a businessman must have a firm control on his spending. Whether his own or that of his business.'

'Yes, Father.'

Norman's cheeks were burning when he returned to his desk. It seemed that Byron's attitude to money was different to his mother's. He mustn't do that again, if he wanted Byron's approval.

Queenie sat beside Norman in the warm semi-darkness of the Palais de Luxe in Lime Street. His hand came over the plush armrest to hold hers. He squeezed it gently now. She turned to smile at him and he leaned across to kiss her. His arm went round her shoulders, pulling her closer.

'I'm falling in love with you, Queenie,' he murmured against her cheek. 'You're very beautiful.' She felt a spurt of triumph as she nuzzled against him.

It was a shame he wouldn't let her concentrate on Janet Gaynor. Queenie had been enjoying *Seventh Heaven*, but it was more important to bring Norman to the point of proposing, and this was a big step forward. She'd definitely made up her mind to marry him. Where would she find anyone more suitable?

She'd had to fight a battle with Mam at breakfast-time this morning to keep pursuing him.

'You're overdoing things, Queenie,' Evie had told her. 'Burning the candle at both ends. I don't mind you having the odd late night if you're out with the girls, but this is too much.'

'I'm sorry, Mam.'

'You'll stay in tonight?'

'I've said I'll go to the pictures.'

'Well, I think you should stay home.'

'Just this once, Mam. Please,' she wheedled.

'And you're missing too many meals. You aren't eating properly.'

'I'm too fat anyway.'

'Nonsense,' Mam said. 'You'll make yourself ill.'

'No, Mam, I won't.' Queenie had a healthy appetite and Norman was tempting her with wonderful food.

'You haven't got the money to pay for decent meals out.'

'I have a boyfriend now. He buys some meals for me.'

Queenie thought Norman paranoid about wanting to keep from his mother the fact that they were going out. She knew he was also worried about how his father would take the news. For her own part, Queenie couldn't see any special reason why Byron and Mam should object. But she didn't want to tell anybody of her plan. It wouldn't do at all for people to know about that. She'd thought it better to keep silent about Norman for the time being. Until she knew whether it was going to work out.

Telling Mam she had a boyfriend brought ten thousand questions about him, and a demand to bring him up to the flat. Mam wanted to meet him.

Choosing a moment when her mother had gone to the kitchen, Queenie had walked out at five o'clock to meet Norman. She knew there'd be more trouble when she got home. But it was worth it because she was having some success with her plans. Really, it hadn't taken all that long, not quite a month. Norman hadn't taken the final step and asked her to marry him, but she was fairly confident now that he would. He was like putty in her hands.

It was a fine evening, and for once they walked back to the Connaught Building.

Norman sighed. 'I do love you, Queenie, but it would be so much easier if you had no connection with Father.'

'It does make things difficult.'

'I'm worried that my mother won't like this.' Norman had an arm round her waist. 'I'm afraid she'll be upset. Because of your mother. I mean, living with . . .'

'It'll probably upset my mother too,' Queenie said. 'She'll blame herself, she's that sort. But I love you too much to let that put me off. We won't let them come between us, will we?'

When Norman reached home late that night, he found a note from his mother, telling him she'd gone to London for a few days and would be staying at the Savoy.

His first feeling was one of relief, but then he knew he'd have to be careful with his cash. It had to cover daily fares over to Liverpool, and lunches, and he'd already made a good hole in the five pounds Father had advanced. There was another week to go to pay day. Somehow he'd have to make it last out.

Queenie was in his thoughts as he snuggled down in his bed. He could see her smiling face before him, feel her lips against his and the touch of her fingers on the back of his neck when he took her into his arms. He wanted her beside him in the flesh, for always.

Towards the end of the following week, Norman felt he'd made a big step forward in his career. His father empowered him to sign cheques on behalf of Henry Ball and Sons. Only up to a limit of twenty pounds, but he felt he was taking on some responsibility.

Byron said: 'Veronica hasn't been in these last few days.'

'She's down in London.'

'Oh! I hoped she was backing off. Is there anything else she can teach you about the accounting system?'

'No, it's all straightforward. Easier for me to cope with than your import licences.'

'Discourage her from coming in again, Norman.'

That alarmed him. 'She'll probably want to. It makes her feel useful.'

His father said more forcefully: 'I don't like her sitting around my office, poking her nose into my affairs. She's come in from time to time over the years to make sure I didn't forget about you. You're here now, so there's no further need for her to come.'

'I'll tell her,' he said.

It wasn't something he felt he needed to worry about for the moment. Mother was away. Lack of cash was more pressing. His five pounds was dwindling fast. Queenie wanted to go out and about, and he was keen to take her.

Over lunch with her at Macey's, he'd admitted that he was a bit strapped for cash. 'Just until pay day on Friday. With Mother away, I can't borrow any.'

Queenie sighed. 'We'll still be able to go out tomorrow night? You said something about taking me to the Empire.'

Norman was tempted, but he knew he should say no.

'I can pay for myself, Norman. I want to go.'

He sighed. He was broke.

Queenie said brightly, 'I know what I'll do, I'll ask Byron. He'll give me at least a pound. I'll be able to treat you for once.'

That made Norman nervous. 'Won't he ask who you're going with?'

Queenie smiled. 'I won't tell him.'

Queenie was disconcerted. She hadn't expected Norman to say he was short of money. He always seemed to spend freely and have plenty. He'd never let her pay for anything, and pressed frequent gifts of chocolates and perfume on her. She thought of him as being rich. That was the whole point: she wanted to share his life of plenty.

She reminded herself it was only temporary because his mother had gone away. He'd be paid on Friday. He'd be wealthy in his own right once Byron had made over the business to him. Everything would be fine then.

Queenie knew that she and Byron would be eating lunch alone today. Bobby took sandwiches to the Liverpool Savings Bank, Daisy stayed at school, and Mam was going over to Birkenhead to see Gertie and collect her rent from Ida Pringle. She'd left a casserole and baked potatoes in the oven for them. The table was set for two.

It gave her just the chance she needed to talk to Byron on her own. She wasn't on good terms with Mam at the moment and she didn't want to ask him for money in front of her. Mam might tell him not to give her any.

Queenie had the meal on the table and had rehearsed her request for extra pocket money when Byron came through the door.

'Ah, Queenie.' He was rubbing his hands. 'It seems we're lunching alone for once.'

'Yes.'

'I'm glad, it gives me a chance to talk to you. Haven't seen much of you recently.'

'I'm here now.' She started dishing up the casserole.

'Yes, I want you to tell your mother what you're up to.'

Queenie let the ladle crash back in the dish. 'What?'

'You tell her you're going out with the girls from the school, but you're not, are you?'

He took over from her, heaping their plates. 'All these lies . . .'

She said defensively: 'I've told her I have a boyfriend.'

'But you haven't told her who it is.'

She knew her mouth had dropped open. She was shocked. He seemed to know . . . This wasn't going to be the right moment to ask him for money.

'Norman sits a few yards in front of my desk. I can hardly miss what's going on.'

Queenie heard her fork clatter down on to her plate. She'd been careful to stay well away from Byron's office. With those glass doors, she'd known he could see what was going on.

'I heard you laugh, Queenie, out in the corridor. Then Norman came in. I've even heard your voice. And then there's the gossip. It's difficult to keep secrets in this building. Anyway, what's the point?'

Queenie felt disconcerted. 'I didn't want to upset Mam.'

Byron hooted in derision. 'That's exactly what you are doing. You're a manipulative little minx. You're up to something and you don't want to tell us what it is.'

Queenie drew herself up to her full five foot five. 'Why should I tell you? You're not my father . . .'

'I feel as though I am. Do you know that? I feel as though I am.'

Queenie couldn't look at him. He looked hurt.

'Anyway, that's no reason to tell your mother lies. She's worried stiff about you. You're staying out late at night, missing meals, and you're rude and rebellious to us both.'

He was sitting back in his chair, glaring at her. She could see he was angry.

'It's got to stop, Queenie. I'm not putting up with any more. And you'll tell your mother that Norman is your boyfriend.'

Queenie managed to choke out: 'All right. I will.'

'I could tell her myself but it would be better coming

from you. If you don't want to drive an even wider rift between you.'

What was there she could say to that? Queenie moistened her lips.

'She loves you very much, Queenie. She's always thinking of your welfare. Yours and Bobby's. She's always put your needs above her own. Did you know that? Above mine too. It's time you started thinking of her.'

Norman was having a difficult day. His father seemed in an unusually abrupt mood, not only with him but with everybody in the office. He thought Queenie would be lucky to get anything out of him.

At lunchtime, he stayed at his desk, eating the sandwiches he'd brought and longing for Queenie's company. Harry Penn was eating at the next desk.

'Not going to Macey's today? he asked.

'Can't. I'm broke.'

'Never mind. Pay day tomorrow.'

Norman found himself thinking of Queenie all the time. He could see her face smiling up at him from every file he opened. He was desperate to know if he'd be able to see her tonight.

With his mother away, he'd toyed with the idea of taking Queenie home with him. He'd love to do that, and it wouldn't take much cash. He'd even told the maid to take the night off, but she lived in. She was middle-aged and not one for the pictures, and he was afraid she'd stay in and see Queenie. If she told his mother there'd be an inquisition. Mother might even come home herself. She rarely stayed away more than six or seven days.

She'd been very put out to hear he had a girlfriend. There'd been just the two of them for so long, it wasn't surprising she wanted to keep him close. She wanted him to spend time with her, not be out on the town with a girl, and definitely not married. And if she found out who Queenie was . . .

Norman sighed. It was too dangerous to take Queenie home with him. He'd have to think of some other way to see her.

Byron came back after lunch angrier than ever. He disappeared again without staying long. It was mid-afternoon when something of a crisis developed. Miss Parker, Byron's secretary, discovered she didn't have enough stamps to put on the day's heavier than usual output of mail. Then Harry Penn, who kept the petty cash, found he didn't have enough to buy more, and the banks were due to close in fifteen minutes.

'I can make out cheques on the firm's account,' Norman told them, and felt his credibility rise. He knew from the records that the usual amount withdrawn for petty cash was five pounds. His pen was poised over the chequebook when the idea came to him. Immediately his heart began to pound. Did he dare?

There was no time to think it through. He made out the cheque on the spur of the moment, tore it out and handed it to Harry. His writing looked shakier than usual.

Harry stared down at it. 'Eight pounds, eh?'

'It seems five isn't enough,' Norman said. Even his voice sounded shaky. 'Off you go, or the bank will be closed.'

Norman couldn't concentrate on work for the rest of the day. He was shocked at what he was doing, but he had found a way to have his night out with Queenie.

He spent the rest of the afternoon dreading that Byron would return. It would be so much more difficult if he were sitting the other side of that glass door. He had to wait until everybody else went home. When he was the only person left, he took the extra three pounds from the petty cash box and put them in his pocket.

He kept telling himself it was perfectly safe. Tomorrow was pay day and he'd put the money straight back. There'd be no paperwork to show what he'd done. He'd tell Byron later that he'd increased the amount, and it would never be missed overnight.

Queenie felt really churned up after Byron's ticking-off and had been too upset to keep her mind on shorthand dictation. Miss Edith picked on her and asked her to read it back. She made a hopeless mess of it in front of the whole class, and that made her feel an inadequate fool.

When school was over for the day, she went out and window-shopped up Lord Street. Norman had to work on until five o'clock and she didn't want to come face to face with Byron again just yet. When she got back to the Connaught Building, Norman was waiting for her in the foyer. She was delighted when he took her arm and said there was no longer any problem about money.

He took her to have a drink first. She always asked for a dry martini, although she didn't like the taste. It sounded sophisticated and very grown-up, and she didn't want to appear too young to Norman. She asked him twice where he'd managed to get the money, but he wouldn't tell her.

Then they went to the first house at the Empire to see a very slick variety show. The sand dancers cheered them both up. It did her good to hear Norman laugh out loud. Queenie began to feel better too.

When they came out, Norman suggested supper in a little place in Church Street that they'd tried before and liked.

'You've really solved your cash problem then?' Queenie was hungry. She'd hardly eaten anything at lunchtime.

'No. Haven't really,' Norman sighed, and then began

to open up and tell her what was on his mind.

'I wish I'd come to work for Father straight from school. I kept putting it off and I've wasted four years. I didn't need to train as an accountant to run his business. I'd be settled and earning a decent salary if I'd come straight away.'

Queenie was glad he hadn't. She'd have been only twelve when he was leaving school.

'It's so hard to think of the future without thinking of money. It makes such a difference to what one can do.'

'Norman, you've managed to get money from somewhere. Don't worry, we're having a nice time.'

'I don't just mean for a night out.' He was frowning.

'You'll be paid tomorrow.'

'A month's salary won't go far. It's real financial security I'm hankering for.'

Queenie felt hope spiral through her. If he was thinking of the future, and of money, could he be thinking of marriage?

'Why?'

'Oh, Queenie! I love you. I want to marry you, but how can I ask a girl like you when I've no money?'

Queenie was bursting with triumph. Her troubles were over. She was smiling. 'I love you.'

'I shouldn't really have mentioned it yet. We'd need a house and a hundred other things. Then living expenses . . . It'll be years before I can afford it.'

'It won't,' Queenie said. 'No, it won't. Your father's planning to give you his business.'

'Yes, I'm hoping to inherit . . .'

'No, you won't have to wait for him to die. He means to give it to you soon. Within a year or two. I know he does. I've heard him tell Mam he's had enough of working nine till five. He's rich, Norman. He owns the Connaught Building – and other things.'

Norman was staring at her, wide-eyed.

'I shouldn't have told you. I mean, it's something he wants to do himself. Don't let on I have.'

'Of course not! But are you sure?'

'Certain. He talks to Mam about it all the time. Perhaps he'll give it as a wedding present, if you marry me. We'll have a wonderful life, Norman.'

'If you're right,' he said cautiously.

'I know I'm right.' Queenie leaned across the table to kiss him. 'I know I'm right.'

# CHAPTER SEVENTEEN

Norman knew before he reached the gate that his mother had returned home. The lights were on all over the house. He let himself in the front door and locked it behind him. Veronica was on the stairs, wearing a white satin dressing gown trimmed with angora, and matching high-heeled satin mules.

'Hello, Mum.'

'Where've you been? I've been worried about you.'

A heavy pink sleep-net protected her permanent wave and cut across her forehead, at odds with the elegance of her clothes.

'There's no need to worry.'

'Darling.' She came and hugged him against her hard, angular body. 'I've been home since four o'clock. Waiting for you.'

'If only you'd let me know.'

He kissed her cheek. It had received its quota of night cream and felt sticky to his lips. Her face was grim and haggard. Norman knew he'd disappointed her again.

'I expected you to be here. Where've you been?'

'To see a show at the Empire. It was good.'

'But who did you go with, darling? Not the new girlfriend again?'

Norman was tired and wanted to get to bed. He'd been dreading a cross-examination about this since he'd admitted on the phone that he had a girlfriend.

'Yes.' He took a deep breath. 'What have you been doing in London?'

His mother wasn't easily deflected. 'You must tell me all about her. What's her name?'

He hated to upset her, and this was going to. He didn't feel up to it tonight. He knew he was everything to Veronica. She made all his decisions and fought all his battles. She provided him with everything he needed: a home, meals, holidays and entertainment. She chose and paid for his clothes. All she asked in return was his devotion.

He knew that without him, her life would be empty. She'd always resented his friends, even his schoolfriends. She'd managed to see off two girlfriends already. Veronica wanted to be all in all to him. Until now, he'd relied on her and basked in the close relationship. His only ambition had been to have an easy life.

Veronica had pushed him to train as an accountant and selected the firm to which he'd been articled. She'd always been paranoid about the need for him to work for Henry Ball and Sons. She was going to see that he inherited it as his father had done before him. She was going to make sure Byron didn't do him down.

Norman had gone along with it because his mother wanted it. He wanted to please her, though recently he'd begun to resent her very heavy hand. Now there was something else he wanted. He wanted Queenie Collins, and his mother was not going to let him have her without a fight.

'Queenie,' he said, though he knew it was going to change everything. 'Queenie Collins. She's Evie Collins's daughter. She lives with Father in the Connaught Building.'

'Queenie Collins? Don't be silly, darling. She won't do at all.' The colour was draining from her face.

'Your father introduced you?' Suddenly she was stiff with rage. 'He's done it to spite me. It's all a plot. You must have nothing more to do with that girl.'

'Mother, I'm very fond of her . . .'

'No! This was why he agreed to let you start. He wanted to get at me through you.'

'You're wrong. We didn't tell anybody.'

'Norman, they're using you. You just don't realise it. What's Byron been saying about me?'

Norman felt ready to collapse. But there was something he had to tell her and he might as well get it over with now.

'He doesn't want you to come to the office again. He says I know all I need to about the accounts.'

She clutched at his arm, her fingers biting into his flesh.

'I knew it. He wants me out of the way. He knows he can twist you round his fingers.'

'No, I'm sure it's all right.'

Well, he was almost sure. Perhaps he should tell her that Byron meant to give him the whole business. But Queenie had sworn him to secrecy on that. Norman found it hard to believe Byron would be so generous in the face of Mum's suspicion and hate, and it wouldn't do for Mum to go blasting off about it to Father's face.

'Ohhhhhh!' Veronica screamed with frustration. 'Silly boy, it's not all right. Ohhhhh!'

'Let's talk about this some other time,' he said. 'I'm very tired. I want to go to bed.'

'I'll never sleep. Not after this.' Norman could feel her shaking as he helped her upstairs. 'What am I going to do?'

He said: 'Don't do anything, Mum. Please don't do anything.'

It was close on midday. Norman felt agitated as he stretched his legs under his desk. His mother sat beside him. The day-to-day account books which catalogued the business of Henry Ball and Sons were spread between them.

He'd spent the first hour of the morning in his father's office. They'd read the mail. Father had been discussing the orders, and explaining how he'd handle them, when Norman heard the office door slam and saw Veronica come in. It made him catch his breath. He thought he'd said enough to stop her coming.

Beside him, Byron growled, 'Didn't you tell her not to come?'

They were both watching her. She slipped off her coat and sat down at Norman's desk.

Norman dropped his head in his hands. 'I did.'

'Tell her again,' he'd ordered brusquely. 'I don't want her in my office.'

Norman had been working himself up to that for the last two hours. He wished Byron would do his own dirty work. Veronica's eyes were red this morning, and Norman felt sorry for her. He didn't want to hurt her any more, and he didn't want her to start screaming as she had done last night.

But her presence was embarrassing all round. Harry Penn had nothing to do because Veronica had taken over his work. She was sorting small bills due for payment. Entering the cheques that came in in the mail.

Although Harry was twiddling his fingers at the next desk, she didn't say a word to him. Norman was afraid this would infuriate Byron. She was making no pretence of instructing him. Instead, she'd taken over the day-to-day book keeping.

Norman swallowed hard. This was interfering with the running of the office. It wasn't even his work she was doing.

'It's kind of you to take all this trouble for me, Mum, but I can manage now. Really I can. Father doesn't want you here any more.'

'So you said last night. But he agreed that I should.'

'For a month. To make me conversant with the accounting system. The month is almost up and you've done that very well. I can manage now.'

Harry Penn was picking his teeth. He got up noisily from his desk and stamped out of the office.

Mother's head came closer to his, and she whispered: 'I know you can, Norman. I have my own reasons for being here. I'm seeing to things now.'

'There's nothing that needs seeing to. I'm afraid Father will be rude to you. Order you out.'

Norman had his own reasons for wanting her gone. It was almost lunchtime and he wanted to meet Queenie. He was afraid Veronica would want to join them. That she'd be rude to Queenie, create a scene.

But his mother was getting to her feet and pushing her arms into her coat. Her face was like thunder but she was going. He felt awash with relief.

Queenie had been asking for a sewing machine for a long time. Evie had bought her one for her sixteenth birthday and thought it a very sensible thing for her to have.

'I'll be able to make all my own clothes now, Mam.' Queenie had been delighted. 'Magazines are giving away lovely patterns. The very latest fashions, and they say they're easy to make up. Just think of the saving.'

The living room had been awash with tissue paper and pink satin since then. The pink satin had become underwear of a sort Evie had never seen before. Queenie had even made French knickers.

'Artificial silk,' Evie had said. 'There's no warmth in that.'

'You're old-fashioned,' Queenie had laughed at her. 'Nobody wears flannelette underskirts any more.'

'Even I don't,' Evie had retorted indignantly.

Daisy had been painting. Colouring pictures in a book. Her eyes were going from one to the other.

'But I do,' she piped up. 'Why can't I have silk ones?'

'I expect you will when you're older,' Evie had told her. 'Children need warm underclothes.'

Black taffeta had covered the living-room table every day during Queenie's half-term holiday. Evie didn't think that very suitable either.

'You're too young to wear black,' she'd said several times, and suggested that Queenie add collar and cuffs in pale pink or blue to relieve the drab colour.

'Oh, Mam, it won't need it,' Queenie had said irritably. It was Saturday, and the machine had whirred all morning. Evie hadn't foreseen that the sewing machine could lead to further trouble between them.

She'd set the table for lunch, and was picking up off-cuts and bits of thread from the floor, when Queenie came back from her bedroom. She was wearing the dress she'd made.

'Do you like it?'

It was sleeveless and cut low round the neck. The long, straight bodice skimmed her hips, and it had a skirt of three narrow frills. She gave a theatrical twirl on the living-room lino.

Daisy stood up, clapping her hands. 'It's wonderful. Will you make one for me?'

Evie felt shocked. 'It's too short,' she protested. 'You can't be seen in public like that.'

'It's the latest fashion, Mam. Everyone's been wearing their dresses this length for years.'

'I haven't!'

'But you're old. The young and fashionable have.'

Evie gasped. She was thirty-seven; that wasn't old. She was wearing her dresses shorter, just covering her knees. She'd thought herself fashionably dressed. Byron had said she was.

'Come on, Mam, you must have seen them.'

Evie was afraid she wasn't coping with the roaring twenties. Or coping quite so well with her children, now they were grown-up. Queenie considered herself to be of the new generation that called themselves flappers, or Bright Young Things.

'That skirt's really very short. It shows all of your knees. And really, your hair too. It was a shame to cut off all those lovely curls.'

'Mam!' Queenie swung round on her mother, making her frills flare out. 'You can turn off your Edwardian propriety. Fancy you thinking short hair and exposed knees such terrible sins!'

Evie took a deep breath. The innuendo was there but she wasn't sure whether it was intended or accidental.

Queenie was twisting her face, making it ugly. 'You've got some very funny ideas, Mam. You're a kept woman, the mistress of a married man, yet you go on at me about short skirts.'

Evie felt the strength drain from her knees. It was the same problem over and over. Her children couldn't forgive her for that.

Queenie was angry. 'I'd be ashamed to do what you're doing.'

'You don't understand, love,' Evie said softly. 'Things were hard when your father died. Byron has always been very kind. I couldn't have managed without him.'

'Daisy's his illegitimate child. How could you bring such shame on us?'

'What's illeg . . .' Daisy's head came over the back of the sofa. 'What's that?'

Queenie gave a mirthless laugh. 'Everybody knows about you and Byron, and you just turn a blind eye. The girls in the college call you a scarlet woman. It makes me curl up.'

Evie felt cut in two. 'A husband and father couldn't have done more for us, Queenie. I owe him more than anyone else in the world. You've never gone hungry.'

'I'm hardly likely to have gone hungry.'

'Without him, you . . .'

'Well, I shall have more sense than to be caught like you. I won't spend my life living in sin. I shall be a wife and be taken out to dances and theatres, not kept on top of an office building and be called a caretaker.'

Evie felt tears sting her eyes. Byron had tried very hard. She loved him.

'I can't bring my friends here. I'd be ashamed to.'

Evie felt a spurt of anger. 'You've had too much of your own way. You're growing up half wild. What you need is a stronger hand.'

'Don't worry, Mam, I'm getting all that. Byron's been throwing his weight around on your behalf. He's ordered me to tell you . . .' Queenie paused and started backing out of the room.

'What?'

'That I'm going out with Norman. We're in love. He wants to marry me. There, so now you know.'

Evie felt transfixed. She could only stare at her angry daughter.

'I'm shocked at what you dare to do. You needn't worry about Norman or my bare knees. You've done much worse yourself.'

\* \* \*

Evie went back to the kitchen, feeling numb. She was making boiled beef and carrots for lunch. Bobby and Byron would be here at any moment now. A white-faced Daisy came in and slid an arm round her waist.

Evie pulled her closer, Daisy laid her head against her apron. 'I've put Queenie's machine away. What else can I do to help?'

That upset Evie more. This was the effect a row with one daughter had on the other. She gave Daisy the mustard to put on the table.

Byron came in, looking tired. 'A busy morning?' she asked.

'Veronica,' he murmured over Daisy's head. Then he smiled. 'What shall we do this afternoon, Evie? It's such a sunny day, a shame to stay in.'

She gave him the joint to carve.

The front door slammed behind Bobby. He came straight to the kitchen door, grinning all over his face, his coat on his arm. Evie made an effort to appear normal.

'Guess what, Mam?'

'Hello, Bobby.'

'Bob, I'm not a little boy any more.'

'Robert, then?'

'Bob will do. Guess what? I've been offered a transfer to the Birkenhead branch.' His eyes danced with satisfaction. 'I'm to be a fully fledged cashier from now on. Got a rise too.'

'Congratulations.' Byron thumped him on the back. 'That didn't take you long.'

Evie kissed him. 'I am pleased for you. Really pleased.'

'Is that good?' Daisy was pulling at his sleeve. 'Will you be rich too, Bobby?'

'Rich enough. I've brought you some chocolate.' He pulled it from his pocket.

'Not until after your lunch.' It was Evie's habitual caution. She was delighted for Bobby, and it went some way to make up for her brush with Queenie.

'We'd better eat. It's all ready. Get Queenie, love,' she said to Daisy.

Evie could feel Queenie's reluctance to come to the table. She looked white and drained, and took no part in the general chatter about Bobby's promotion.

'I'm proud of you, Bobby.'

'You've done well.'

Evie said: 'You'll have to get up a bit earlier in the mornings. Where exactly is the Birkenhead branch?'

Bobby didn't answer for a moment. He put down his knife and fork.

'I thought I might get lodgings, Mam. Over the water.'

Evie felt as though she'd been doused in cold water. This was Bobby's way. He didn't want anything to do with Byron. No help of any sort. But she hadn't expected him to move out of the family home so soon. She felt he was deserting her. It was hurtful.

'Easier,' he said, 'than travelling back and forth all the time.'

'It isn't difficult,' Byron told him. 'Harry Penn does it. Lots of people working here do. We're convenient for James Street station.'

'I know.' Bobby was looking down at his plate. Evie had to stop herself screaming out at him to stay. It would be the end of an era if he left home.

Byron went on evenly: 'It would be cheaper for you to live here and travel over daily. More comfortable too. It's only a few minutes on the train to Hamilton Square.'

'Birkenhead Central would be nearer,' Bobby started to eat again, 'and it's a fair walk up to Grange Road West from there. But it's not just that . . .'

'Stay with us a bit longer, Bobby. Your mother would like you to, wouldn't you, Evie? Seventeen is very young to go it alone.'

Evie felt sufficiently in control to add: 'Please stay. Lodgings can be lonely, you know.'

'You're a fool,' Queenie burst out. 'You don't know which side your bread is buttered.'

Bobby's face was pink with discomfort. He said quietly but firmly: 'I'd rather go, Mam. You know how I feel about things.'

'Don't go,' Daisy pleaded. 'I don't know why you want to.'

Bobby turned to her. 'It's like this, Daisy. I'm out of step with your father. I'm pulling in the opposite direction and it isn't good for Mam. Better if I go and leave you all in peace.'

Evie had to get out her handkerchief and blow her nose. She was proud of Bobby. He'd always done things his own way. There'd be no changing his mind. He felt Byron wasn't treating her properly, but he was wrong. There were tears in her eyes, her throat and her voice.

'You can always come back. You know we'll always be glad to have you.'

He nodded, pushing his hair off his face with an embarrassed gesture.

'Yes,' Byron added. 'Come back if you don't like it. You know we'd both want that. Welcome you back.'

Evie got to her feet hurriedly, glad of the excuse to fetch the treacle pudding from the kitchen. She wiped her eyes on the tea towel before going back. She hated to think Bobby would be leaving.

She lifted the pudding and the plates and opened the door with her foot.

'What a day this is for news,' she said, knowing she

sounded falsely bright. 'Queenie's been telling me about her boyfriend.'

'You mean Norman?' Bobby put in. Evie could see him watching Byron. 'That's last month's news.'

'They're talking of marriage,' Evie said in Byron's direction. 'Did you know?'

'Heard it on the grapevine.' Bobby was tucking into his pudding.

'It's serious then, is it?' Byron asked Queenie.

Evie's family started to clear away the meal and wash up. She had to leave them to it. She went to her bedroom and collapsed on the bed, letting her tears come. Byron found her there a few minutes later.

'I knew you'd be upset.' The bedsprings sank under his weight. He pulled her up to sit beside him, and put an arm round her shoulders.

'I used to find my children so rewarding. How could they have turned into such difficult creatures?'

'They've grown up, Evie. They're going to go their own way now. You'll have to let them.'

'Only sixteen and seventeen.'

'Bobby will be all right. He knows what he wants and he's got his feet on the ground. And Queenie . . .'

'I'm worried about her.'

'She told you she was going to marry Norman? I didn't realise it had gone that far.'

'Yes.' Evie sniffed into her handkerchief.

'Then nothing we say will change her mind.'

'Doesn't it bother you, Norman and her?'

'It doesn't make life any easier. I'd rather they'd both picked on total strangers. But we have to accept it, Evie, if that's what they want. Veronica won't. She's going to be furious.'

Evie was thinking of her own father. The fact that he hadn't accepted Ned had made her run away. She didn't want Queenie to do that.

Byron was going on: 'I don't know what Norman's planning to live on. He won't keep Queenie on the two fifty a year I pay him.'

Evie sighed. 'But you're going to give him the business. Queenie's heard you say that, even if he hasn't.'

He groaned. 'I should have been more careful, shouldn't I? I might have brought this on us.'

'You'll still make it over to him?'

'Yes, it's time I thought of you. I want to take you right away from this place. It's the only way we'll get away from the gossip. From now on, we're going to think of ourselves. Daisy too, of course.'

'Daisy's easy.'

'At the moment.'

'She always will be.'

'Because she belongs to us both? She doesn't have divided loyalties?'

'Because she's like you, Byron, easy-going. Takes everything in her stride.'

He smiled. 'I know what we're going to do this afternoon. We're going to start looking for a house. When I give the business to Norman, he won't want me here, breathing down his neck. Better all round if we get right away.'

Evie felt warmed by the thought of a new house. 'Something to suit just the three of us.'

'In a place where nobody knows us. We'll move in as a family. You, me and Daisy. We won't have the blessing of Church and state, but we'll be a family in every other way. Come on, wash your face while I get Daisy organised. We'll start looking today. Over the water, I thought.'

Evie was comforted. She liked going over the water, and was glad he wanted to live that side too. They took the car across on the luggage boat.

'Not Oxton,' Byron said. 'We don't want to be anywhere near Veronica. And it's got to be what you want. A comfortable house. Not too big.'

'A garden?' Daisy wanted to know. 'Can we have a garden?'

'Yes.'

Evie enjoyed the afternoon out. They came back with particulars of several very nice houses, but not exactly what they wanted. They hadn't even decided which district they wanted to move to. It was enough that the plan was under way.

Norman was not happy. His mother was becoming more difficult. She was on at him all the time about Queenie.

'Drop her, Norman. You've got to drop her before it's too late.'

Veronica's prominent eyes seemed to burn with a terrible intensity. 'Can't you see that Byron's tying you up with his mistress? You're going over to her side. Where do you think that leaves me? Out on my own. Have you no shame?'

Norman tried to explain that it wasn't like that, she'd got it all wrong. He'd been bowled over by Queenie the moment he set eyes on her. She was beautiful, outgoing and enthusiastic about his job with Byron. He thought about her constantly. He'd never felt like this about a girl before.

'Byron's getting his revenge on me. He wanted a divorce, wanted to throw me on the scrapheap. Now he's taking you from me. He's coming between us.'

'No, Mother!

'Stuffing this girl down my throat.'

For Norman, the only good times were those he spent in Queenie's company. She was so wonderfully loving towards him. Queenie's warmth went some way to make up for the terrible change in his mother.

Norman had never wanted anything more than a comfortable life. Suddenly nothing was easy any more, and he never had enough money to last the month.

'I'm not giving you money to spend on that girl,' Veronica stormed when he asked her. 'Come to your senses. Promise not to see her again and I might.'

He knew now how to sub himself, but it was dangerous. He couldn't hide the fact from Harry Penn, and now Nosy Parker had found out too.

His mother waited up for him every night. As soon as she heard his key turn in the lock she was out on the stairs. He oiled the lock but she still heard him and came down to nag about Queenie. She started getting up early in the morning to have another go at him while he ate the egg and bacon her housekeeper cooked for him. Norman always felt rushed at breakfast, but her presence guaranteed that he'd be out in good time for his tram.

She was still coming over to the office, though he told her repeatedly he didn't want it; that Byron didn't like it. She didn't travel over with him, but while he was in with his father, he'd suddenly see her sitting at his desk, pushing documents about. Not every day, but two or three times a week.

'What's the point of it?' he'd asked her. 'What are you doing?'

'Looking after your interests,' she'd hissed.

It was Harry Penn who told him that she was removing cheques. Taking them away. That he'd seen them come in the morning mail but then they disappeared.

Norman went cold inside. 'You must be making a mistake,' he'd told Harry.

One morning, Byron suddenly broke off in the middle of explaining something to Norman. He leapt to his feet and went bounding out. Veronica was shrugging off her coat. He pulled it back on her shoulders and tried to steer her towards the door.

'I don't want you to stay, Veronica,' he told her. 'I don't want you to come here again.'

She turned on him with the ferocity of a big cat. Norman crawled with embarrassment as he heard her say things to his father that she'd previously said only to him, while Harry Penn sniggered into his handkerchief. She called Daisy his bastard, and that transfixed Miss Parker and the older clerks. Soon the Connaught Building was buzzing with the latest turn of events.

Even that didn't stop her. She came again the following day, and Byron immediately walked her outside. Nobody heard what he said to her, but later he told Norman that he thought she'd taken leave of her senses.

# CHAPTER EIGHTEEN

Looking at houses became a regular weekend outing. Evie liked Byron to take his car across the river. One of the main routes through town took them past the pharmacy in Argyle Street.

'Surely your father should have retired by now?' Byron said as he drove past. 'He's still got his name over the shop.'

'Gertie says he's still working.'

'But how old is he?'

'Sixty-seven, I think.'

'Good Lord! Why doesn't he give up? I can't wait to retire. Just as soon as we can find somewhere to live.'

'You're not old enough, Dad,' Daisy said from the back seat.

'I am, I'll be fifty this year, and that's old enough for me.'

'Fifty's nothing.'

'Your dad's tired of spending every day in the office, and it brings nothing but problems.'

'What's the point of me working on? If Norman is going to have the business, he can do the work. I can afford to retire, Daisy, and I'm going to.'

It didn't take them long to decide that they'd prefer to live outside the town of Birkenhead. Evie thought that the Wirral countryside was very beautiful, and that West Kirby or Heswall would suit them. Byron had very definite ideas about the sort of house he wanted.

'It'll be our home for many years, perhaps for the rest

of our lives. I want you to be pleased with it, Evie.'

Evie thought she was more easily pleased than he was. The houses they looked at were at the top end of the market. She would have been delighted with many of them, but not one pleased Byron. Too close to its neighbours, or on a main road, or the rooms were too small. He toyed with the idea of buying a plot and building exactly what he wanted, but really he preferred houses of the older type.

Evie was disappointed that they weren't making better progress, and she missed having Bobby about the flat.

'I won't lose touch, Mam,' he'd told her when he was packing his belongings.

He came over to see her and have a meal at least once a week. He said he was pleased with his lodgings.

'Come and see them,' he invited. 'If you're over there motoring around looking at houses, come and see where I live.'

They did so the following weekend, and Evie felt that her worst fears were justified. It was in a terrace of small houses behind the gasworks.

'Very central,' Bobby had said. She'd known before seeing it that the neighbourhood was run-down. It looked terrible now that her eyes were used to the wide leafy roads of Heswall. The house itself was in need of a good scrub and a coat of paint. Bobby rented one room and shared the kitchen. The furniture provided for his use was battered and broken. There was no bathroom.

Daisy looked round and screwed up her nose. 'This isn't very nice,' she told him. 'Not like your room at home.'

Evie knew Byron would pass no comment. He'd already offered to pay for rooms in a better part of town. She said:

'Why not look for an unfurnished place? Then you can do it up. Make it more homely.'

'This is all right for me.' Bobby smiled. 'And it's near

Gran's. I go round there quite a bit.'

Evie thought Bobby was looking more like Ned as he grew older. She was glad Gertie had taken him under her wing, that he had somewhere to go to get away from these depressing rooms.

The following Saturday, after a trip to West Kirby, Evie wanted to call on Gertie while they were over. They found Bobby there, about to have tea with her. He seemed very much at home. Gertie was pleased to see them.

'Come and sit down. Bobby's brought cakes from Darty's for me. We haven't started on them yet, you're just in time. He's a real chip off the old block, always brings plenty.'

It brought the past flooding back to Evie. 'I suppose you still see Polly Darty?'

'All the time.'

'Does she ever say anything about my father?'

'Just that he's grumpier than ever.'

Bobby said: 'I went in to buy some aspirin the other night when my ankle was paining me. I told him who I was.'

Evie felt uneasy. 'What did he say?'

Bobby laughed. 'He said: "You needn't think you'll get them any cheaper by claiming to be related." '

She sighed. It was what she'd have expected from Father. It niggled that Bobby didn't have a higher standard of living. He had a better job than Ned, but his lifestyle seemed very similar.

'Cut off his nose to spite his face,' Byron said as he drove to Woodside that evening.

When Miss Parker brought his mid-morning cup of tea to his desk on the following Saturday, Byron said: 'What about a biscuit?'

'Sorry, they've all gone.'

'You've run out?' That surprised him. It had never happened before. Not since he'd told her to provide tea and biscuits twice a day for all his staff, and to buy what was needed with petty cash.

'Send Harry out,' he said. 'Ginger nuts.'

He sat back and sipped his tea. Through the glass he saw her go to Harry Penn's desk. Harry didn't leap up immediately to do what he was told. Instead he was protesting, waving his hands about. Byron watched him take out the petty cash box and show her what was inside.

They both appealed to Norman. It was the way his son turned round to look at him that first told Byron that something was wrong. Norman's face was running with guilt as he put his hand in his pocket. Harry went then.

Byron asked himself why there wasn't at least sixpence in the petty cash box. Usually it was replenished when it was getting low. All sorts of queer things were happening. Everybody seemed to spend more and more time looking for things.

A little while later, Miss Parker came in holding a tea plate with three ginger biscuits sliding about on it.

'Bring me the petty cash book and box,' he told her. 'I'd like to check them.'

He'd never, ever done that before. The whiskers in her mole twitched with alarm as she bustled out.

When the petty cash ran down, Harry Penn used to bring the book and cash box to him and ask for more, but once Norman had started, he'd told him to take care of it. Byron could see without moving from his desk that his request was causing consternation. When Miss Parker came back, he could see why.

The book showed a credit balance of four pounds two

shillings and threepence, but the cash box contained only three pennies.

Byron was angry. He bounded to the door, snatched it open and bellowed: 'Norman, come in here.'

There was no mistaking his son's guilt. His cheeks were scarlet, his step reluctant, his shoulders bowed. Byron threw himself back on his chair. For once he didn't invite Norman to sit.

'Explain this to me.' He spat the words out, jabbing his finger at the box.

'I borrowed it. I'm sorry, Father. But I always pay it back.'

'You mean you've done it before?' Byron was outraged.

'Yes, I'm sorry. I was short . . .'

'I don't care how short you are, Norman. Company money and private income are two different things. Never must they become mixed.'

'No, sir.' Norman wouldn't look at him.

'You are here as an employee. Helping yourself to the petty cash is dishonest. Akin to stealing. And you're a rotten example to everyone else. You wouldn't dare do it if you weren't my son. I ought to throw you out. I'm disappointed . . .'

'I'm sorry . . .'

'Disappointed that you'd stoop to this, and disappointed in what it shows. You've no grip on money, Norman. And that's vital in business if you are to succeed.'

Byron took a long, shuddering breath. 'I won't ask why you took it.' He guessed it had gone on entertaining Queenie. 'I'll give you until tomorrow morning to put it back, and don't you ever dare help yourself to company cash again. Now get out and let me forget about it.'

But Byron couldn't forget. The thought rankled. He was afraid that Norman took after his mother. Money ran through her fingers like water. Up to now, he'd not been displeased with his son's progress. Norman had been here just over three months now, and was managing to cope with the documents needed to move goods from one country to another. He'd assumed he would have no trouble with the accounts; after all, he was a qualified accountant.

Byron couldn't settle back to work. He felt uneasy. On the spur of the moment, he went to the door again and shouted for all the other account books to be brought to him.

He didn't really expect to find anything wrong. He just wanted to reassure himself that all was well. He'd trusted Norman; for the first time he wondered if that had been wise.

One o'clock came and the office emptied. Byron sat over the account books, his shoulders hunched in shock. He tried to tell himself he wasn't really suspicious, just upset and disappointed. The petty cash shortage had soured him.

The figures showed a big drop over the last few weeks. He hadn't expected that. In fact, he'd had the impression that turn-over was continuing to rise. He'd thought there were more orders than ever coming in, yet they didn't seem to be down in the book.

He was afraid Norman was taking more than just the petty cash. Up until three months ago the business had been thriving. The dates tied in. He compared this year's takings with the same period last year, and they were well down. Byron had a sinking feeling in his gut and was glad Norman had gone. He was angry and knew he'd have called him in and raved at him if he'd been here. He had to be quite sure before he accused him of fraud.

Some of the business they'd handled hadn't been entered in the books. He shivered when he pinpointed one item. John Robinson was one of their best customers. They regularly arranged for raw cotton to be shipped from Alabama to Liverpool on his behalf. Byron had handled last month's order himself. Demonstrated to Norman what exactly it entailed and how it must be shown in the books. Yet it wasn't here. No order, no sign of a bill being sent and no payment. Robinson's settled on the last day of the month. Always.

He looked through the freight book. Henry Ball had paid for shipping space for Robinson's. Byron felt sick. Could it be anything other than fraud? Norman had taken over the accounts, but Harry Penn dealt largely with routine bills, and old Simms kept the order book. Byron couldn't see how he could hide what he was doing from them. They'd always been very reliable. It couldn't be incompetence.

Until today, Byron had prided himself that he would be handing a growing business over to Norman. He wanted him to have a good living from it.

He himself had inherited a dying business. Nurturing it back to profitability had been the hardest thing he'd ever had to do. For him, the early years had been a fight for survival. He'd had to feel his way and change the nature of the business. He didn't think Norman would be capable of that.

Byron felt agitated, put upon. He knew that Norman went out with Queenie almost every night and must be spending more than he could afford.

He slammed the ledgers shut and made up his mind that if Norman was stealing, he'd sack him for theft as he would any other employee. There'd be no question of making the firm over to him. He'd put in a manager and cope with it himself. Norman could please himself how he made a living and Byron would do his best to see that Queenie didn't marry him. What chance of happiness would she have, married to a thief?

When he went upstairs, he found that Queenie had gone out with Norman again. After he'd had lunch and Daisy had gone to her dancing lesson, he sat on the yellow sofa with Evie and held forth at great length about Norman's failings.

At five o'clock he went down to his office to get the ledgers. He wanted to go through them again. He couldn't believe the mess they were in. Evie tried to help him tie bank statements to the entries in the book. It was impossible.

'He's a qualified accountant! What's he playing at? He must know he can't get away with this.'

'Are you sure it's his fault?' Evie asked.

'I gave him the responsibility of seeing to the books. I thought it would be in his line.'

'What can he hope to gain by this?'

'He's more likely to lose,' Byron thundered. 'Wait till I see him on Monday morning.'

'That's what I mean.'

Norman enjoyed his Sundays. It was a rare delight to turn over in bed and have another hour or so to snooze. He had a leisurely bath in the late morning and pottered about the house until it was time for a Sunday lunch of roast beef.

Today, the Yorkshire pudding was crisp and perfect, and there was his favourite apple pie to follow. He tried to close his ears to his mother's nagging voice. She was trying to persuade him to go out with her, but only because she knew he intended to go over to Liverpool to see Queenie.

'I'll ring for a car to take us to Parkgate,' she said with a great show of enthusiasm. 'A lovely run. We'll walk along the front to give ourselves an appetite, and then have tea and cakes at the Boathouse Café. You used to love doing that.'

Perhaps he had done once, Norman mused, but it didn't compare with what was on offer from Queenie. On Sunday afternoons they had the flat to themselves, because Byron took her mother and Daisy house-hunting. Norman would be spending it lying on the yellow sofa with Queenie in his arms. She was free with her kisses and didn't stop him going further. Last week, he'd fondled her breasts and thought himself very daring. This week he was hoping she'd allow more. The fact that he was doing it in his father's house made it all the more exciting.

He was in his bedroom, getting ready to go out, when his mother came running upstairs, her cheeks red with temper.

'Darling, I'd like you to light the boiler before you go. Bessie hasn't lit it today, would you believe? And now she's gone out on her half-day.'

'It's quite warm.' Norman looked out of the window. The sun was shining. 'You won't need central heating today.' He'd just put on one of the new sleeveless pullovers in Prince of Wales check. Queenie had chosen it for him and he didn't want to take it anywhere near the boiler.

'I can't stay in all evening without it,' his mother complained.

'The fire's set in the sitting room, you could just put a match to that.' It was May, for heaven's sake.

'It's still chilly in the evenings. Do light it for me, there's a dear.'

Norman was afraid it was a ruse to delay his going.

'You just can't rely on servants these days.'

Reluctantly he took his new pullover off. He didn't want to dirty his shirt either. In a bad temper himself now, he pulled that off too and rushed down to the kitchen to do the job as quickly as possible.

He didn't think the boiler had been lit for days. He found some paper and sticks and opened it up. On a bed of cold ash were a lot of documents that were browned and charred. He put in the poker and started to rake out the ash. A half-burned cheque fell out at his feet.

Norman straightened up in horror. It was a moment before he could bring himself to pick it up. The cheque was for three hundred and twenty pounds, and it was made out to Henry Ball and Sons.

He carefully lifted out the other papers. There were orders and letters and more cheques. Charred bits of paper disintegrated and showered down on the floor. He couldn't get his breath. His heart was thumping madly.

Norman was very late going over to see Queenie. He'd wrapped up the half-charred documents in a clean piece of newspaper and hidden them in his wardrobe. His head was reeling.

He knew his mother must have taken them from the office. He knew she must have stuffed them in the boiler and the fire must have been almost out when she did it.

He was still crawling with the horror of it. He couldn't bring himself to face her with what she'd done. He was too shocked. It must have had a terrible effect on his father's business. And perhaps she'd done it before. Perhaps several times.

He wished he knew why. For years she'd spoken of the business as a prize that one day he'd inherit. She'd worked hard on Byron to give Norman this chance of learning to run it. To get him involved in it. Now she was trying to ruin it. How could anybody keep track of what was happening if letters were being destroyed wholesale? And cheques weren't being paid into the bank?

Norman felt sick. It must be Mother's way of getting revenge. But revenge on Byron or revenge on Norman because he preferred Queenie's company to hers? He hadn't thought his mother capable of revenge like this.

He felt desperate. He was hoping for a lot from his father. Byron had treated him well so far, but what would he say when he found out about this? It would bring the business to its knees, ruin it.

He was also worried about how Queenie would take it. He couldn't tell her what his mother had done. She'd be distraught because it was going to upset her plans. How could they get married without the business to support them? This could ruin their future, and he didn't know what to do about it. For her sake, he had to think this out carefully.

By Monday morning, Byron felt even more bitter. He'd had two bad nights. He was down in his office waiting for Norman to come in.

'In here,' he said, the moment he saw him. He closed the door carefully, so the other staff wouldn't hear.

Norman was sweating and very pale. Byron could see a slight tremor in his fingers. He looked the picture of guilt. He hadn't meant to jump on his son; he just couldn't stop his own anxiety spilling out.

'You've got the books in a terrible mess. I trusted you to oversee them. What have you been doing?'

'Not my doing,' Norman stuttered, his chin quivering. 'Not at all.'

'What about this?' Byron's finger stabbed at an entry on the bank statement. A twenty-pound cheque had been cashed. He'd given Norman the power to sign cheques up to that amount. That had convinced him that Norman was at the bottom of it.

'No,' he wailed in agony. 'No.'

'I haven't signed it, Norman, so you must have.'

'Well . . . Yes, I've signed cheques. But . . . you think I've drawn money out for my own use, and I haven't. No, I haven't.'

'It wasn't so long ago that you helped yourself to the petty cash.'

'Yes, but not since. Honestly, not since. And never a cheque, not for me.'

'This cheque was made out for cash and it isn't shown in the accounts. There's another for petty cash on the same day, so it wasn't that. You can't have forgotten, it's only three weeks ago.'

'I don't know, I feel terrible about this.'

Byron sighed. 'I'll get the cheque back from the bank, it might tell us something.'

'I think I might have signed it. Probably did. I've been worried stiff. Out of my mind.'

Byron thought the lad was going to burst into tears. 'If it isn't you, it must be your mother. Did you sign that cheque for her?'

The tale came out then of how Norman had discovered cheques and letters stuffed in the boiler at home. Byron covered his face with his hands. That explained a good deal. He should have known Veronica would be up to something. She'd come so regularly; it wasn't like her to stick at things.

'Have you asked her about these burned cheques? Why she took them?'

Norman was shaking his head in misery.

'Why not?'

'Well, it couldn't have been anyone else.'

'Where are they? Have you brought them back?'

Again he shook his head. 'I didn't know what to do.'

Byron lost his temper. 'Didn't you think I'd want them? You can't run a business without records. Isn't that the first thing you learned as an accountant? You could have made a start at straightening things out. I put you in charge of the books. Surely you noticed that things were missing?'

'Harry Penn did. He said Mother was taking cheques.'

'For God's sake! When was this?'

'A couple of weeks ago.'

'Why didn't you say so then? You let your mother go on? Goodness knows what's missing, we're in a right mess. We've lost orders, we've shipped freight on behalf of unknown clients and cheques have gone missing before they've been paid in. And you do nothing!'

'I'm sorry, Father.'

'This was a profitable business. You'd have earned a good living from it. You've got to speak up, for goodness' sake! Why didn't you tell me?'

'She's my mother . . .'

'She's out of her mind. She knows this firm is going to be yours. She's always been on at me to hand it on to you. Why would she want to destroy it? It doesn't make sense.'

Norman gulped. 'She thinks you deliberately set me up with Queenie. That I'm going to turn my back on her and come over to your new family. That having me work here is part of some plan of yours to get even with her. That you're twisting both of us round your finger.'

'And that's what you believe too?'

'No,' he groaned.

Byron tried to think. 'No, you wouldn't. You're close to Queenie. She knew what I intended to do.' He paused.

'Queenie told you, didn't she? That I meant to make

the business over to you quite soon? And you told your mother?'

Norman nodded, too full of emotion to speak. Byron wondered how he'd managed to father someone so lacking in drive and common sense. 'And she didn't believe you?'

'No, she said it was all a trick. That you'd never part with it while you lived. You were too mean.'

Byron was appalled. 'She was bent on destroying me. Bent on destroying a profitable business. What a senseless waste.'

Norman blew his nose hard and then pushed his hair off his forehead. Byron recognised that gesture. It was the only thing Norman had inherited from him.

'Go home and get those papers you found. Don't let your mother take them from you. I've got to have them.' He sighed and asked himself if Norman were capable of that. 'Shall I come with you?'

'I'll get them,' he gulped. 'I'll see to it.'

'Make sure you bring them here.'

Byron closed his eyes and lay back in his chair. Norman was never going to run any business. He needed help even to wipe his nose.

When he could summon the strength, he got up and went to speak to Miss Parker. He made sure the rest of the staff heard him.

'Mrs Ball is not to be allowed into this office again. She's not to have access to any of our ledgers or records. If she comes when I'm not here and you can't get her to leave, ring security for help.'

Then he went upstairs to Evie and poured out his problems.

Byron felt he'd been sitting on the yellow sofa for hours, staring out over the rooftops of Liverpool. Evie had listened to his diatribe, made tea for him and held his hand. He wasn't feeling any better.

'What a mess I've made of everything,' he said sadly.

'Not you,' Evie said.

'I should have been more careful. I certainly will be in future. I said too much in front of Queenie. She stirred things up.'

'It was Veronica.'

Byron sighed. 'Yes.' It didn't stop him blaming himself. He remembered the vindictive hate he'd seen on Veronica's face. 'I made her hate me.'

'You've been very fair to her.' Evie was indignant.

That made him feel worse. Evie was trying to support him but her quick retort and indignation showed only too clearly that she felt he'd been too generous to Veronica. Perhaps he had. Evie's life would have been easier if he'd made a clean break in the first place. Not only Evie, her children and he himself would have been much better off. But the law saw Veronica as the innocent party and held Byron responsible for her and Norman.

He sighed. 'It'll be a miracle if Norman ever learns to manage anything. He hasn't got it in him.'

'You had to trust him.'

'He knew his mother was trying to ruin the business. He said he was worried sick about what he should do. I believe him. He was torn in two, Evie. Divided loyalties. He's a ditherer and he did nothing. Can't stand on his own feet. I've always known that. I hoped he'd grown out of it.

'I knew myself that Norman was borrowing from petty cash, I'd even searched the files for documents and failed to find them. That should have made me check through everything sooner.'

'Will you be able to sort it out?'

'I hope so. I hope they're working now on what Norman

brought back. They'll all have to work their fingers to the bone. I'll go down and see soon.

'I'll ring round our main clients, they should be able to give me details of our transactions. Certainly Robinson's will. Bedwell's too, and the salt manufacturers. We'll have to piece together the records for the last few months.'

'You'll have to tell them you've had your own records stolen.'

'Yes. This changes everything, Evie. I won't be able to give this business to Norman, not in the foreseeable future. He couldn't cope with it. After all the effort I've put into building it up, I can't just walk out. It would be like pouring money down the drain.'

He could see the disappointment on Evie's face. 'Does that mean no house for us? We stay here?'

'No.' He had to get Evie away from the Connaught Building and the gossip. She'd gone through enough, and so had he.

'I'll put a manager in. Travel over myself once or twice a week to keep an eye on it.'

'I was looking forward to having you at home with me.' Evie's smile was resigned. 'I suppose it's as well you found out about Norman now.'

Byron felt low all week. He'd been looking forward to having more leisure but instead he was working overtime trying to piece his records together. And worse, he'd have to go on working. By the weekend he had copies of most of the orders that had been given to his firm. He'd chased up many of the cheques that hadn't been paid in, and his main clients were going to issue replacements.

On Sunday, Byron suggested they go house-hunting again. It was a fine day and they all needed to get away from the Connaught Building for a while.

An estate agent had sent them details of a house in Heswall that looked interesting. This had happened before, but when they saw the house they'd been disappointed.

The moment Byron saw this one, he felt his spirits rise. It was square and sturdy under a blue slate roof. Ivy grew in profusion up walls of old brick. The sun gleamed on the small panes in its windows. It was built in the Georgian style, with a portico porch. It surprised him to find it was only forty years old.

'The garden's beautiful.' Evie's eyes sparkled with interest as she looked round. 'And the views . . .'

Byron turned to look. The house faced south over the River Dee. They could see the hills of Wales beyond.

'It's got a tennis court.' Daisy was pulling at his sleeve.

Once inside, Byron was sure. The whole ambience seemed inviting. Lots of space downstairs, and panelling in the drawing room.

'I love it,' Evie said, when they were out in their car again. 'But it's big for just us three. Four bedrooms on the first floor and three more in the attic.'

'Do let's have it,' Daisy pleaded. 'I'd love to learn to play tennis.'

'Shall I put an offer in?' Byron asked Evie. 'You do like it?'

'Living there would be fabulous,' she breathed.

'Let's go back to the estate agent and do it now.' It was just what he'd been searching for all these months. Sod's law that he should find it the week he discovered Norman wasn't capable of running the company. But at least he'd found the house he wanted for Evie.

# CHAPTER NINETEEN

Queenie had thought that everything she'd planned was falling into place. Norman had proposed and she'd told her family. She'd had to keep talking about him to Mam and Byron. To let them know that her mind was made up and there'd be no changing it.

'It's a bit sudden, isn't it?' Mam had said over dinner a few days after she'd told her. 'You've only known each other a few weeks.'

'I knew the moment I saw him. We want to get married, Mam. Soon.'

'All right, but you must finish your commercial course first.'

She'd flared up. 'What's the point in waiting until we're old?'

Byron had put down his knife and picked up his drumstick to nibble. 'You'll be finishing that next July and you'll only be seventeen. That's not asking you to wait too long. You won't be over the hill by then, Queenie.'

She'd had to agree. She had to keep on the right side of Byron because she wanted him to give his business to Norman. That was an important part of her plan.

'Anyway,' Byron went on, 'you were keen to do the course only a few weeks ago. You wanted an office career. You'll have to finish before anyone will employ you.'

'I'm not expecting to have to work, not when I'm married.'

Mam had pursed her lips at that. 'You never know what'll happen, Queenie. I'd have been very glad to have the sort of training you're getting. It might have made all the difference.'

Queenie had sniffed, but she knew there was no point in arguing; it wouldn't get her what she wanted.

She'd known Norman was apprehensive about how his mother would take it.

'We aren't going to worry about what our families think,' she'd said to him. 'The problems are of their making, not ours.'

Mam and Byron were expecting trouble from Veronica, but not trouble like this. Everything had been going so well until she'd wreaked havoc on the business. Queenie felt a hot flush of anger every time she thought about it. What on earth did Veronica think she was doing? Deliberately ruining the business so that Norman wouldn't be able to marry her. She'd never heard of anything more selfish.

Poor Norman had been very upset. He'd wanted to walk out and find himself a job somewhere else, where he wasn't related to the boss. It had taken a lot of persuasion to make him see that his prospects were better where he was. She'd spent all her time kissing him and trying to rebuild his confidence.

'After all,' she told him, 'it's not as though you've done anything wrong. It was your mother. You've had to work very hard to piece the records together again. Byron will appreciate all the help you're giving him.'

Byron had been in a foul temper. Mam said it was because he was worried and was working too hard. He kept going into a huddle with Mam, telling her all about it, but he was keeping the details from Queenie. He had never been like this before. Queenie knew he was watching his tongue.

But she'd got enough out of him. He said he was sorting

things out, that the business would survive. She heard him telling Mam that he'd still make a profit this year, though perhaps not as much as he'd hoped. She was glad then that Norman had seen sense and stayed with his father. Everything could still work out as she wanted, provided the business survived in a profitable state.

The girls in the college heard all about it and laughed at Norman's mother. Louisa Fanshaw crowed with delight: 'Who'd want to be saddled with a mother-in-law like that?'

That needled Queenie, but she thought she'd be able to sort Veronica out. She still thought Norman would make a good husband. He couldn't take his eyes off her; they were full of devotion. Couldn't keep his hands off her either. It gave her a lovely warm feeling to know he adored her; that as far as he was concerned she was the centre of the universe.

She could get him to do anything she wanted, and it made her feel strong and powerful. He was keen to marry her but thought he couldn't afford it. She kept telling him that Byron meant to give him the business.

'It'll happen, I know it will. I've heard him talking to Mam. All we have to do is to go ahead with our plans.'

Norman didn't seem convinced, but she was.

The house-hunting had dragged on so long, Queenie had thought they'd never make up their minds, but now suddenly they had, and the offer Byron had put in had been accepted. Mam said they mustn't count their chickens until the contract was signed, and anyway it would take about three months to complete.

Queenie counted up the months. She'd been pressing for an August wedding, and finally it was agreed. She wanted to go to Torquay for her honeymoon, and Mam's gift was to be two weeks at the Palace Hotel there. She was really looking forward to that. By the time they came back it would be September. The family would move to their new house and Byron would give the business to Norman. Everything she wanted was falling into place.

Evie was worried about Queenie. She was afraid that the way she lived with Byron had influenced Queenie in all the wrong ways and that she was determined to be a wife at any cost.

She wasn't acting like a girl in love. She was very determined and seemed to be ruled by her head rather than her heart. Evie tried to warn her.

'If you don't love him, you mustn't marry him. You won't be happy.'

'I'll be happy, Mam. Don't you worry about me. I can look after myself. I certainly won't end up like you. I'm going to get myself a husband who'll look after me. Keep me in comfort for the rest of my life.'

'What makes you think Norman will be able to do that?'

'He's got a job, hasn't he?'

Evie knew that Queenie expected the business to be made over to Norman. She'd heard her questioning Byron about what had transpired in the office, and knew he regretted letting her know so much. Nobody had told Queenie he'd had a change of heart.

Evie said very carefully: 'If that was all he had, would it be enough?'

Queenie's lovely eyes looked innocently into her mother's. 'Of course.'

Evie knew that she herself had married with less security than that. Perhaps, after all, she was wrong and Queenie did care for Norman. Perhaps she was worrying unnecessarily. She'd asked Byron to be careful not to belittle Norman in Queenie's hearing, not to let her hear how disappointed he was with him.

'A gutless, lily-livered fool,' he'd called him. 'He'll be putty in Queenie's hands, I'm sure. She might be good for him.'

'But will he be good for her?' Evie asked.

'I don't know, love. But we'll have to accept that the marriage is going ahead. They're both set on it.'

'But what are they going to live on?'

'Did you ask that when you ran off with Ned?'

'No.'

'Don't worry, I'll see they don't starve.'

Now that they were no longer house-hunting, Evie wasn't over in Birkenhead so often. They used to call in to see Ida Pringle and Gertie Collins from time to time before returning home. Now, Ida owed her rent. On Monday, Evie decided to go over while Byron was working. She meant to call in and see Gertie too, to tell her about the house.

Gertie's place looked more untidy than ever, but Gertie had had her hair cut and permed.

'D'you like it, love?' Gertie stood in front of her cracked mirror, fluffing it out with her fingers.

'All those waves, it's the very latest style. I've never seen you looking better.'

'Much less trouble, having it short. Bought myself a new frock too. I'll put the kettle on for tea, then you can tell me about your new house.'

But Gertie came back from the kitchen saying: 'Did you know your Bobby's got a girlfriend?'

It was only then that Evie realised she hadn't seen him for two weeks. He'd hadn't been over for his weekly meal. It made her feel empty inside. Somehow a gulf seemed to be opening up between them. She'd been afraid of this since he'd left home.

'Got better ways of spending his time now.' Gertie gave a hoarse, throaty chuckle. 'I met them. He was taking her to the pictures. *All Quiet on the Western Front*. Have you seen it? No? Don't miss it, it's wonderful, all about . . .'

'Tell me about the girlfriend,' Evie interrupted. Everything seemed to be happening at once.

'Her name's Sylvia,' Gertie reported. 'She works in the bank with him. A typist, I think he said. Lovely girl.'

'Is it serious, do you think?'

Gertie guffawed. 'How would I know? You'll have to ask him.'

Before she went home, Evie went round to Bobby's room, though she knew he'd be at work. She pushed a note under his door asking him to come over for his dinner the next evening.

She knew he'd ring if he wasn't coming. She made dumplings because he always liked them. Bobby came but seemed prickly about his girlfriend. He didn't want to talk about her.

'When are we going to meet her?' Evie wanted to know. Bobby wouldn't be like this if the girl wasn't important to him, and she was curious about her. 'What about next Sunday? Either lunch or tea.'

He asked: 'Will you be here, Queenie?'

'If you want me.'

'Of course I want you. Sylvia might as well meet the whole family if she's coming.'

'Ask Norman too,' Evie suggested. 'We'll make it a big family meal.'

'I told you, Norman doesn't like coming here,' Queenie said irritably. 'It embarrasses him, and his mother doesn't like it.'

'Queenie, you don't care whether his mother likes it or not.'

Bobby asked: 'Will Byron be here?'

Evie thought that Bobby was almost as embarrassed as Queenie about bringing his friends to the flat, but for a different reason.

She said gently: 'Yes, he's part of the family, isn't he?'

'I suppose.'

She kissed his cheek. 'You know he is.'

Evie had made up her mind that even if she didn't take to Sylvia, she'd do her best to hide the fact. This was up to Bobby. He was the sort who knew his own mind. She'd never forget her own father's attitude to Ned, nor that he'd been wrong about him. Ned had been a wonderful husband and father.

As soon as Sylvia came through the door, Evie felt reassured. She felt she could grow fond of this shy girl, with her big anxious brown eyes and fluffy brown hair.

It turned out to be a rather stiff lunch party. The young people had little to say and left as soon as they decently could. Bobby rang up and invited himself over to the flat the following week.

Evie was alone with him for the first half-hour. He said: 'I hear Queenie wants me dressed up like a dog's dinner for her wedding.'

'You men are all to be in morning suits.'

'I'll hire it. I won't be wanting a show like that when I get married.'

'You're thinking of it too? Already?'

'Must be catching, Mam. Yes, I'm thinking of it, but it won't be for a long time, we'll need to save up.'

'Byron and I . . . We've always tried to treat you and Queenie the same. If you don't want a big wedding . . .'

'Definitely not.'

'A honeymoon in a good hotel?'

'No.'

'Perhaps Sylvia would like that.'

'We'd rather spend the money on setting up house. More important to us.'

'Then I shall give you something towards that.'

'No, Mum, I'll do it on my own. I don't want Byron's money.'

'My money, not his.'

'Where does yours come from, Mam? Only from him.' He bent to kiss her cheek.

'You're too proud.'

'Yes – well.'

'He's a good man, Bobby. A generous man. We'd all have had a much harder time if it hadn't been for him.'

'I know, Mum. But I don't want to be beholden to him. This is the way I want it.'

Evie told herself she ought to feel proud of Bobby. He had strong ideals and wouldn't have them compromised. He was even more handsome than his father had been, and strong and wiry. A pity about his ankle, it had left him with a slight limp which became more marked when he was tired.

Evie was making a cottage pie for their Saturday dinner and felt rushed because she was late with her preparations.

Queenie came in, slid a hat box on to the kitchen table and flopped on to a chair. She'd been out all morning, going round the big shops with her friends.

'I've bought a lovely hat, Mam. The very latest. Just the thing for my going-away outfit. What d'you think?'

Evie turned to look. 'Very nice.' It was one of the new small caps covered with veiling. 'It suits you, dear. I thought you were going to look for a costume?'

'I didn't see anything I liked.'

Evie mashed the potatoes. They were a little hard and could have done with more cooking.

'Nothing smart enough. I want a stylish wedding.'

'Yes, dear.'

'It's my big day, Mam, surely I'm entitled to a bit of a splash? I know so many people, all the girls from the college. I can't invite some and not the others.'

'Why not? Surely you'll just invite your friends?'

'I don't want to make it a hole-in-the-corner affair. I want everybody to know I'm married.'

Not tarred with the same brush as her mother, Evie thought as she spread mashed potato on top of the savoury mince. 'How many guests do you think you'll want to ask?'

'More than a hundred. Norman's got a lot of friends.'

'But that's far too many for this flat,' Evie said, aghast. She'd thought of clearing out Bobby's bedroom and moving the dining table in there for a buffet.

'Mother! I'm not having my wedding reception in this place. I want it to be a smart affair.'

'We won't have moved to the new house. If you put it off for a month or two, let us get in and sort . . .'

'We were thinking of a hotel. Norman likes the Adelphi.'

'Good Lord! The Adelphi? That's the most expensive . . .'

Evie thought of her own wedding all those years ago. There had been no possibility of a hotel reception for her.

'Byron will be happy to pay. He's a rich man.'

'You can't expect him to foot endless bills for you, Queenie.'

'Why not? He'll be doubly connected soon. Father-in-law and acting father.' Queenie's smile was dazzling. 'I'm going to look in the shops up Bold Street to see if I can get a really elegant wedding dress. Norman will be in morning dress, of course.

'As the bride's mother, you'll have to get yourself something smart too.'

Evie was intent on putting her pie in the oven.

'You will, won't you?' Queenie asked anxiously.

'Of course.'

'Thanks, Mam. You're good with clothes. Always did dress nicely. Dressed me nicely too.'

Evie sighed. She knew Queenie would expect them to pay for her wedding finery. Queenie had inherited something of her grandfather's personality. Like Joseph Hobson, she was a person who took rather than gave.

'I made most of your clothes, Queenie.'

'Yes, but not this time.' Again the dazzling smile. 'Not for my wedding.'


Two weeks later, when Evie saw the wedding dress Queenie had chosen, she didn't like it. Not for Queenie.

It came in a huge box, packed in layers of tissue paper. Queenie lifted it out and held it against herself.

'Isn't it unbelievably gorgeous? What do you think?'

It was of stiff white silk, cut straight to skim the hips, with an uneven hem. There was a fringe which dipped from above the knee on the left side to mid-calf on the right.

'It's the height of fashion,' Queenie boasted. 'The very latest twenties design.'

Evie fingered it and thought it would be very easy to make. 'I could have run something like this up for you. There's nothing to it.'

'It wouldn't look like this. You'd never get the cut right.'

'It's not formal. The men are to be in morning suits. I would have thought a traditional floor-length gown . . .'

'That's all out now. Old hat.'

Evie found the price unbelievable too.

'Perhaps you could make a bridesmaid's dress for Daisy?'

Byron said: 'If it pleases her, Evie, why worry?'

'I've indulged her too much. She expects everything now.'

'Norman needs somebody like Queenie. Somebody who knows what she wants. She always looks beautiful, she'll make a splendid bride.'

'You've got a soft spot for Queenie.'

Byron smiled. 'Since she was four years old, and I saw her in a red wool dress with a lace apron over it. I thought she was absolutely charming, just like her mother.'

Queenie was feeling very pleased with herself. Her college course had finished and she'd come top of the class in the final exams.

'I'm proud of you.' Mam had been as excited as she was. She kissed her. 'Clever girl.'

'I'm delighted you've done so well,' Byron told her. 'We must have a special celebration supper. What about it, Evie? Tomorrow?'

'Bobby doesn't like me ringing him at work, and tomorrow doesn't allow much time to write.'

'We won't ask Bobby this time,' Byron said, giving Queenie a wink. 'Ask Norman up. There are things we need to discuss and get sorted.'

'The wedding,' Queenie said, because she didn't want to appear pushy, but it wasn't the first thing she thought of. She'd asked Norman several times if his father had said anything about giving him the business. It was high time Byron showed his hand on that. He'd signed the contract for his new house. They were to move early in

September so Daisy could start her new school at the beginning of the term. He would have made plans for his business. Byron always planned everything to the nth degree.

'The wedding, yes,' Byron said. 'Amongst other things.'

Queenie felt even more pleased with herself. She was certain he meant to hand over his business to Norman. He wouldn't want Bobby here while he was doing that.

Queenie visualised Byron opening a bottle of wine. The five of them sitting round the table, raising their glasses to her exam results. Then Byron would say he was moving out and was handing over the business. It made sense, that if he'd planned to give it to Norman, he'd be even more keen now they were getting married. He'd want to be generous to her too. Then they'd toast the future.

There was a ball of excitement in Queenie's stomach as she set the table with their best tablecloth and silver cutlery. Byron came up half an hour earlier than she'd expected. He went straight to the kitchen and opened a bottle of wine.

'Come and sit down, Queenie. I want a word with you before Norman gets here.'

Her heart leapt with pleasure as he put a glass of wine in her hand. This was working out just as she'd have wished. She wanted to know his exact plan and he was going to tell her now, before Norman came.

She went to the yellow sofa in front of the window and found Daisy curled up in the corner.

'Why don't you go somewhere else?' she suggested. 'Your father and I need this for a serious talk.'

'I will if you let me taste your wine.'

Queenie held out her glass for her to take a sip.

'Yuck.' Daisy pulled a face. 'Don't like it.'

'You will when you're older. Go away now.'

Queenie started talking about their wedding to give Byron a lead-in.

'You've been very generous. I should start by thanking you for that. I'm very grateful.'

Byron had agreed that they could have the reception at the Adelphi but insisted they must keep the number of guests below a hundred.

Fortunately, she had foreseen that. She'd kept mentioning a vastly inflated number of guests. Now she and Norman had sent invitations to everybody they could think of and the list totalled eighty-four. She was able to tell Byron that she'd kept his wishes in mind and had thought of his purse.

Byron began: 'We're all facing a lot of big changes in our lives, and there are many things to consider.'

Queenie felt a swirl of triumph. It was all going to happen just as she'd meant it to.

'Your mother and I need to know more about your plans.' Mam was leaning against the window, sipping her wine. 'Are you going to work, find yourself a job?'

Queenie was stunned. Everybody knew she wasn't. She'd made no secret of that. This wasn't what she'd expected at all.

They were all watching her, even Daisy, who was snuggling against Mam. Byron said slowly, 'You don't expect to be carried for the rest of your life?'

That infuriated her. 'Of course not! I shall have the house to take care of. My own duties.'

'But you've done very well on your commercial course. The whole point of that was to fit you for work. Wouldn't you prefer to come and work for Henry Ball and Sons? Help to run it?'

It was the last thing Queenie wanted. The whole point of marriage was to avoid that.

'One of my clerks is due to retire. Why don't you come down and see what he does? Come and use the training you've had.'

'Help Miss Parker, you mean?'

'No, not exactly. I think you could manage more than she does.'

'I thought Norman was going to manage the business.'

'He's going to need help, Queenie. He won't be able to do it by himself.'

'Can't you hire somebody to help him?'

'Yes, that's the other alternative. I've considered putting a manager in. To run it for me from now on.'

This wasn't what she'd been led to believe. It sounded as though Byron had changed his mind about parting with the business.

'But then I thought, Queenie's the bossy sort. She's got her wits about her. It wouldn't take her too long to learn what's what. I'll come in every day to teach you, until you do.'

Queenie put her glass down. There was a cold feeling in the pit of her stomach. 'But why can't Norman run it? I don't understand.'

'Not everybody is capable, Queenie. Norman is not a leader. I don't think he wants to be left in charge.'

'But he does, he tells me he does.' Tears of disappointment were stinging her eyes.

'I think Norman knows it's beyond him, he just isn't admitting it.'

'How d'you know I'd be any better at it?'

'You're very good at getting what you want from others. You're stronger, a more demanding personality. I hope you'll prove to have more money sense. A better grip on finances.'

Queenie didn't doubt that. 'You said you were going to

give him your business; that you were tired of coping with it; that you were going to retire.' It was a wail of distress.

This was death to her plan. Everything had hinged on that. Queenie was fuming. Norman was hardly earning anything – a clerk's wage. The wedding was almost on her, and it wouldn't give her the life of luxury she'd expected.

Byron sighed. 'I had hoped to do that, but I shall have to carry on.'

Mam refilled Byron's glass. Queenie had hardly touched hers.

'It's like this, Queenie. I've spent years of my life struggling to keep this firm afloat. It was touch and go whether it would survive at one time, but it has and it's thriving again. I don't want to see my work wasted.'

She took a deep breath. 'Norman will be very careful to . . .'

'What I'm trying to tell you is that giving it to Norman is no longer an option. It's going to be one of two things.

'Either I put a manager in now to run it for me. I would then leave it to Norman in my will.

'Or you can come and see if you can do it. I'll make it over to you both jointly if you prove you can.'

'That seems very fair,' Mam told her. 'There's no easy ride in this life, Queenie. You'll have to pull your weight.'

'Probably pull more than your weight, when you're married to Norman.' Byron was smiling at her as he refilled his glass again.

'You'll probably enjoy it.' Mam was trying to reassure her. 'Better to be in the thick of the things than just keeping house.'

Queenie couldn't help herself. 'How would you know?' she demanded. 'That's all you do.'

'It hasn't always been like this for your mother,' Byron

was saying gently as the doorbell rang.

Daisy was letting Norman in. Queenie felt numb. She had an unexpected disaster on her hands but she was too proud to let them see she'd made a mistake. She stood up and kissed Norman in front of them all, just to show that she did love him. Perhaps she'd been in too much of a hurry to tie herself down. Particularly since Byron seemed to think Norman was stupid. What was she going to do?

But Norman did look nice in the pearl-grey suit she'd persuaded him to buy. He'd brought flowers for Mam, just as she'd suggested, though he looked a bit self-conscious now as he presented them.

Queenie listened to Byron telling Norman what they'd been talking about. He cut out much of what he'd said about Norman being incapable, but Norman got the message. Queenie could see the colour running up his cheeks. His eyes wouldn't meet hers. She wanted to scream.

Once the roast chicken had been carved and they were all eating, Byron was off again. Queenie wished he'd give it a rest.

'We've all been so busy these last few weeks, we've left some important decisions to the last moment. You two will need a home of your own once you're married.'

Queenie tried to pull herself together. She'd already thought about that and taken Norman to see several houses. She'd have settled for one in Aigburth, which they'd both loved, but Norman had said: 'We'd better leave if for the time being. Until Father offers me the business. Can't think of buying until . . .'

She'd agreed they might have to rent for a while. They'd had a look at several for rent too.

Byron went on: 'As you know, this flat will shortly be empty. It seems a good place for you two to start married life. If you both come and work in the business, you can have it rent-free.'

Norman beamed round the table. 'Thank you, that's very kind. Very kind, isn't it, Queenie?'

Queenie almost choked on a roast potato. 'I'd like to get away from this place. We're looking for a small house.'

Byron turned his gaze on her. 'How are you going to pay for that? Then there'll be the fares backwards and forwards. You'll find it very convenient to live over the job.'

'This flat's very nice, Queenie.' Norman was diffident.

'It is not.' She could feel her temper rising. Byron knew she didn't like this place. Mam knew she hated bringing anybody here. It was a caretaker's flat.

'Don't be silly, Queenie,' Mam was telling her. 'It's a generous offer and you can't afford to turn it down.'

'Her business sense will tell her that.' Byron was leering at her. He knew he had her over a barrel.

'It's nice here,' Daisy said. 'Looking out over the roofs. Being on top of everything.'

Queenie didn't agree. They expected her to work for a living and live here in this awful flat?

'Think about it, Queenie, there's a good girl. I'll need to know very soon. If you don't want the job and you don't want the flat, I'll need time to find a manager.'

'And a proper caretaker,' Mam added.

Queenie was in a state of agitation for the next three days. She spent a lot of time alone in her bedroom. Evie could hear her jazz records being played very loudly on the gramophone. If she came to the living room she rarely spoke. She'd lean up against the window, staring down at the traffic in the street. As they waited for her decision, Evie felt worried.

'You've put her under pressure,' she said to Byron as they were getting ready for bed.

'She was trying to take us all for a ride.' They were keeping their voices low so that Queenie wouldn't hear them in the next room.

'Is she going to call off the wedding?'

'Norman asked me if she was ill. She hasn't been out with him since.'

'If she does, it's for the best.'

'You think she doesn't love him?'

'I think she was aiming to share his rosy future, and that wouldn't have worked out.'

'That's how Veronica saw me, and I wouldn't want the same thing to happen to Norman. I had to make Queenie take a more realistic look at him. Little minx! Seventeen and looking for a meal ticket for the rest of her life.'

Evie climbed into bed. 'Queenie's one who takes.'

'There's a limit to what she can expect others to give. Why shouldn't she work for a living like the rest of us?'

'She knows now she'll have to, whether she marries Norman or not.'

'She can run rings round him. She's more capable than he is anyway.' Byron opened his book and began to read.

Queenie announced on the fourth day that she'd take both the job and the flat.

'We won't be living here for ever, though, just until we see what we can afford.'

'That's fair enough. When you want to move out, you can offer it to a caretaker.' Byron took her down to the office before she changed her mind.

For him the next few weeks flew past. He'd never been so busy. He had to sort out the mess Veronica had made. As he'd expected, Queenie was picking up the work more quickly than Norman had. He told her so.

Her big brown eyes looked into his. 'I'm going to do my best. If I have to work, I want to learn to run the company, get the best out of it. I don't want to spend my time just typing letters.'

That pleased him. There was a quiet confidence about Queenie. Once he'd moved house, he'd travel over two or three days a week. He'd keep his eye on things for a year or so, but he'd make the business over to them once he was sure they could manage it. It wasn't fair to keep them waiting indefinitely when he didn't need the income from it. He had more than enough for his and Evie's needs, and to ensure Daisy's future. He was looking forward to having a more restful life.

The day of the wedding dawned. Veronica had been invited, of course, and he was a little nervous that she might make a scene and spoil the day. But she stood aloof and alone, staring at Byron but saying little to anyone except Norman.

Byron enjoyed himself. He looked fondly at Evie, who was wearing a very smart blue costume and little hat. She was beautiful still, a little tense on this very special day, but everything was going without a hitch. Evie meant everything to him.

He felt full of love for the rest of his family, particularly Daisy. She was Queenie's only bridesmaid, in a dress of mauve taffeta that Evie had made for her. He recognised himself in Daisy. She had his square figure and the russet-brown hair he used to have. Her eyes reminded him of Grace.

Daisy would never have Queenie's striking good looks, but she had her mother's dimple and wide, gentle smile. She had a quick mind too, and the same level-headedness that he had. As a daughter she was a delight, and he knew Evie found her so too.

'So much easier than Queenie,' Evie had said only that morning. 'She never pits her wits against mine. She goes out of her way to please me. Just like you do.'

Today, Queenie was dazzlingly beautiful beneath her white veiling. She'd made her choices and Byron hoped she'd be happy with them.

Her handsome brother was acting as best man. He'd have been proud to accept Bobby as a son, if only he would unbend and cease looking on him as the enemy.

Norman stood up straight and made his vows in a strong voice. Byron hoped fervently that Queenie would love him and be kind to him.

# Book Four

## 1930–1942

# CHAPTER TWENTY

Evie thought the move to the new house was near to being chaotic. They had to move in before it was redecorated so that Queenie and Norman could have the flat to themselves at the start of their married life, and so Daisy could start her new school at the beginning of the term.

'It'll seem funny, just the three of us. Without Queenie and Bobby,' Daisy had said when they sat down to a makeshift supper on the first night.

Evie knew Byron wouldn't be sorry. He said that it would make life a lot easier. She knew she'd miss her children, but they'd grown up and this was their choice.

'I want everything to be easier,' Byron had said when Daisy went to bed. He wanted Evie to be known as Mrs Ball.

'We'll change your name by deed poll to make it legal,' he said. 'Here in Heswall, where nobody knows us, it's the obvious thing to do. There won't be any more gossip. We'll seem too ordinary. After all, we have a daughter of eleven. It'll be a fresh start for the three of us.'

The painters and decorators came in. Evie's mind reeled with colour schemes. She was busy choosing furniture and carpets. She thought it a very grand house and knew it would take time to get it straight.

'It's too big for you to manage without help,' Byron said firmly. 'We'll have a cook and a maid. We don't have to worry about them gossiping about us now. We'll start as we mean to go on. We'll have a bit of comfort.'

Byron helped Evie hire Mrs Minto, a lady of mature

age who'd worked as a cook-general for the last twenty years. She would live in. She was plump and cheerful and came with excellent references. Evie picked out Kitty Hunt as their maid, chiefly because she liked her shy smile. She'd just got married and chose to live out. Her home was in the village.

They'd been in the new house a matter of ten days. It was beginning to smell of fresh paint and new carpet, and Evie was beginning to feel at home in it.

It was a Monday and a stormy autumn night. The wind was howling up the estuary and there were frequent heavy showers. She'd drawn the new heavy velvet curtains to shut the storm out, and Byron had asked Kitty to build up the fires.

'Come and sit down.' He put a glass of sherry in Evie's hand and drew her to the fire. She couldn't get used to waiting for Mrs Minto to serve meals. The habits of a lifetime made her feel she should be in the kitchen doing it herself.

Evie sipped her sherry and let her eyes linger on the handsome furnishings in her new sitting room. She was pleased with the way it had come together. Daisy had just started piano lessons and was practising at the other end of the room. Evie tried to ignore the occasional discord. She could see across the hall and through the open door to the dining table set for supper. The dining room hadn't yet been papered, but there was a bright fire in there too. Cook was just carrying in a steaming casserole dish when the front doorbell rang.

'Who can that be?' Byron frowned. Kitty went to see. They all listened. Even Daisy stilled her fingers on the keyboard.

There was a gasp of nervous astonishment. 'Oh, I'm looking for Evie . . . Is this where she lives?'

'This is the residence of Mr and Mrs Ball.'

Evie had recognised the voice. She sprang up and went to the door. The maid was eyeing Gertie Collins doubtfully.

'Come on in, Gertie,' Evie said. She was surprised to see her. She'd invited her to lunch and to see over the new house in two days' time, when Byron would be at the office and Daisy at school.

'Evie, I'm sorry to disturb you. I couldn't wait till Wednesday.'

Gertie looked old and anxious. Her nose was red and her face wet. Against the new and luxurious furnishings, she looked very shabby.

'Come to the fire,' Evie said. 'You're frozen.'

Byron pulled himself to his feet and put out his hand.

'I couldn't find the place and it's a terrible night. Been walking round for ages.'

'Let me take your coat,' Byron said, helping her with it. 'It's very wet. I'll get Kitty to shake it well and try to dry it off.'

'Sorry to come when you're just about to eat.' They could all see more dishes being taken to the dining room.

'As good a time as any,' Byron assured her. 'I'm hungry. Come and have something with us. There'll be enough, Mrs Minto, will there? Come along, Daisy.'

Gertie paused to look round. 'How posh,' she said, as Kitty, newly kitted out in full maid's uniform, set another place at the table for her.

'My, Evie, you've landed on your feet. You wouldn't have had anything like this with our Ned.'

'What brings you out on a night like this?' Evie wanted to know. 'Is something wrong?'

'It's your dad. Polly Darty says he hasn't opened the shop today. Miss Lister couldn't get in. She couldn't rouse him. Nobody's seen sight nor sound of him since he closed the shop on Saturday night.'

Evie felt a wave of guilt wash through her. She hadn't given her father a thought for ages. She'd turned her back on him. It was the only way she could deal with his vindictiveness.

'Polly reckons he's ill. He's an old man now, hasn't looked well for ages. Getting slow too. Anybody else would have given the shop up years ago.'

Byron's sympathetic eyes met Evie's. 'If he's not looking after the shop, Evie, you'd better do something.'

'That's what me and Polly thought.' Gertie nodded.

Evie was worried. 'What about Matilda?'

'No sign. Polly hasn't seen her for ages. The shop girls call round for the bread, but not today, of course.'

'But Matilda's still there?'

'Polly thinks so. Nobody's said otherwise. He doesn't let the shop girls upstairs and he hasn't taken apprentices for a long time.'

Evie shivered. Byron said: 'We'd better go and see if they're all right.'

'I had to come and tell you right away. I was scared to let it wait, in case something's happened.'

Evie's neck crawled with dread.

'We've got the telephone in,' Byron said, helping himself to mashed potato. 'Evie should have given you the number.'

'She did, but I don't know how to use them new-fangled things. I thought it would be easier to come.'

'I'll run you down in the car, Evie, as soon as we've eaten. You'll be anxious.'

'Can I come?' Daisy wanted to know.

'No,' her father said. 'Better if you go to bed, young lady. You've got school tomorrow.'

Gertie was tucking in. 'I'd be glad of a lift back.'

'Of course, Gertie. It was kind of you to come.'

'I don't know how we'll get inside,' Evie worried. 'Father was always security-conscious. He used to bolt the shop doors on the inside every night, top and bottom, and lock them as well.'

They set out as soon as they'd eaten. Byron drove to Gertie Collins's home first.

'I wish it was broad daylight,' she told him. 'So that the whole street could see me getting out of this posh car.'

'We'll have to do it again,' he said cheerfully.

As he pulled up outside the pharmacy, Evie said: 'The lights are on in the shop. He's got electricity now.'

'They have all along this parade.' The shop windows were all lit up. 'Had it for years now. But there's no light upstairs in the flat.'

'Father's bedroom is at the back. Matilda's too.'

'It's only half past eight.'

'But if they're ill . . .'

Evie tried the shop door. It was firmly locked, as she'd expected. She rang the bell but there was no response. 'I'll go next door to Darty's.'

The years had made Polly Darty rounder and heavier, but her pudding face shone with welcome.

'Evie, I'm right glad you've come. Your dad's been depressed for a long time and getting worse, everybody says so. Miss Lister says his temper's terrible. Can't help worrying about him, even if he is awful to everybody.'

'The lights . . .'

'They've been on all day, though there's been no sign of him. I think he switched them on when he closed up on Saturday and hasn't touched them since.'

Evie sighed. 'How am I going to get in?'

'We've been thinking about that. Our Herbie thinks he

359

could get in through the bathroom window. It's open a little at the top. We didn't like to do it off our own bat. You know what your dad's like. Herbie was afraid he'd bawl him out. We thought we'd wait until you came.'

'We'd be very grateful if he would,' Byron answered for her. 'We were thinking we might have to break in.'

'No, no, I'll shout for Herbie.'

'Does Herbie work in the business with you?' Evie put her mind back to the little roly-poly toddler she used to take for walks.

'No, we told him he'd have to find work elsewhere. He's got a job with a builder, so he's well used to climbing ladders.'

Evie wouldn't have recognised Herbie. He was now a young man in his prime, tall and slim and looking very fit.

'What do you want me to do when I get in?' he asked.

'Just let Evie in,' Byron said.

She said: 'There's a keyboard on the first landing at the top of the stairs. The keys are all labelled. You'll find the ones for the back door and the yard door there. They'll all be bolted too, top and bottom.'

She and Byron were ushered through the cake shop to the back yard. The first thing she did was to look up at the windows over the pharmacy. In Matilda's bedroom, the curtains were drawn, but she could see the glow of light shining through them. Her father's room was in darkness. She could see the others looking up too, but nobody made the obvious comment. It seemed an ominous sign.

They watched Herbie get out an extending ladder and climb up the dividing wall with lithe ease. Then Byron helped him lift the ladder over into the pharmacy's yard, and a few moments later he had it up against the building.

'Good job it's stopped raining,' Byron said. Evie shivered in the cold night air. Herbie was reduced to a darker shadow against the black building. She pulled her macintosh more tightly round her and wished the gale would blow itself out.

'There,' Polly said proudly as Herbie edged the bathroom window down and disappeared inside. The light went on inside, and then on the stairs. Moments later they could hear him struggling with the bolts on the yard door and went to the other side.

'If there's anything else we can do to help . . .' Polly was hanging back.

'We'll let you know what's happened,' Evie said. 'Thank you for what you've done so far.'

The strong medicinal aroma in the shop caught at her throat. It seemed stronger than she remembered. The shop seemed no different from other pharmacies now that it had been modernised. There was a new door at the bottom of the stairs. She went up feeling stiff and tense. Here, the atmosphere seemed to close round her, heavy and threatening and redolent with her adolescent misery. She was glad of Byron's supporting footfall behind her. She passed the living room, found the light switch and headed up the next flight.

'Father?' she called. The only sound was the creak of the stairs as they took their weight. All was in darkness on this landing. She knocked on her father's bedroom door and opened it.

'Father?' She felt for the light and put it on. She didn't know what she was expecting to find. She hadn't dared think about it. Gertie had said he could be dead in his bed.

For two awful seconds she thought Gertie was right. He was just a hump under the bedclothes. Then he turned over with a speed she wouldn't have thought possible, and his dark, malevolent eyes peered up at her.

'Oh, it's you! What do you want?' He was struggling to pull himself up the bed, but hardly seemed to have the strength. She went to help him.

'Walking in here in the middle of the night! You frightened me.' His hand brushed her away.

'I'm sorry. I came to see if you were all right.'

His face was grey and drawn. He looked ill and disorientated.

'I don't want you here. You left me.'

'I'm back now,' Evie tried to soothe.

'It's too late, I'm done for.' He was wearing a flannel nightshirt that badly needed a wash.

'Father, you need somebody to look after you.' Evie looked round the room. There was a thick layer of dust on his bedside table.

'I was fast asleep,' he complained. 'It's the middle of the night, isn't it?'

'It's evening, not nine yet. How are you?'

'What do you care?' His dark eyes glared up belligerently from the pillow. His chin was covered with half an inch of black stubble.

'You didn't open the shop. Everybody's worried.'

'Of course I opened the shop.' With a burst of irritable energy he sat up. 'What are you talking about? I wouldn't not open it.'

'Father, Mrs Darty says you didn't open today. Miss Lister knocked and knocked this morning and couldn't make you hear. That's why I've come.'

He stared at her as though he didn't believe her. Then dropped back against his grubby pillows with a long sigh.

'I'm sick. Flu or something. You could make me a cup of tea now you're here.'

'Where's Matilda? Is she all right?'

'Yes.'

362

'Is she making meals for you?'

'I don't feel like meals, damn you. I want a cup of tea.'

'I'll put the kettle on,' she said, and turned on her heel.

Byron shifted his weight to the other foot and marvelled at Evie's patience. He met Joseph's hostile gaze.

'I haven't seen you before. Married again, has she?'

'Yes,' he said shortly. This wasn't the time to go into that. 'I'm Byron. You'd better come to our house until you're better. Evie will look after you. I've got my car outside. The best thing is to take you now. We'll get a doctor out to see you in the morning.'

'Doctors,' Joseph snorted. 'They won't do anything for me. Don't know as much about prescribing as I do.'

Byron went over to a large cupboard and opened the door.

'What do you think you're doing?' Joseph was heaving himself higher in the bed.

'Looking for a suitcase. Evie will put a few things together for you.'

'I don't want to go anywhere. A cup of tea is what I want.'

'Yes, well . . . What do you want Evie to do about the shop?'

'Do about the shop? What can she do about the shop?'

'Get somebody in to run it for you. Another chemist.'

'I hired another chemist, and do you know what he did? He called me a miserable old sod and walked out without so much as a day's notice.'

Byron wasn't surprised. 'We could try and find somebody else.'

'Impossible to get decent staff these days.'

'You don't want the pharmacy to close, do you? You'll lose the trade.'

'What do I care?' Joseph asked with another spurt of antagonism. 'I've no further use for it. It'll have to be closed. I'm finished. Everybody's left me. Deserted me. I've nothing to live for.'

'The pharmacy could be sold.' Byron was determined not to lose his temper. 'Much the best thing.'

'Who are you to tell me what's the best thing?'

'You aren't well, and it's too much for you now. It's time you relaxed a little. Everybody's entitled to a year or two of retirement. We could find you a more comfortable place near to us.'

'I'm not going anywhere.'

'Well, come to our house for a week or two, until you feel better. Then we'll see.'

'Don't you understand what I'm saying?' Joseph's voice cracked with anger. 'I'm not leaving here. This is my home and here is where I'm going to stay.'

Byron looked round the unkempt clutter of the room and shuddered. This old man and his room were giving him the creeps. Joseph was so unlike Evie it was impossible to imagine them being father and daughter. He went in search of her.

Evie climbed the stairs to the attic, where Matilda had her bedroom. She could hear the rasp of Matty's breathing before she was halfway up. Her bedroom door stood ajar. Evie pushed it open. The sight shocked her.

Matty's eyes were closed and her mouth was wide open, showing a furred tongue. Her cheeks were sucking in and out as she breathed. Her false teeth were on her bedside table, one set on top of the other, with a thin layer of dust collected on top. Long grey hair, matted and wispy, was spread across her pillows.

Evie took the withered hand on the soiled counterpane

between her own. It felt deathly cold. It was going through her to see Matilda like this: a sick and wizened old woman who looked as though she hadn't washed or combed her hair in days. She'd been the one person Evie had been able to turn to for comfort as a child.

'Matty? How are you?'

She thought for one moment that the old woman was beyond hearing her. 'Matty?'

The breathing stopped, then after a second started again more softly. Matty closed her mouth and tried to open her eyes. They were sticky with exudate.

Evie ran down to the bathroom for a bowl of water to wipe them. There was no hot water to be had. No fire had been lit in this house for several days. She used the water from the kettle and put more on to boil for tea. She was shocked when she tried to wash Matty. The old woman was very weak and in a pitiful state.

'Evie?' she croaked, and the rheumy eyes searched her face. 'Little Evie?'

'Not so little now. How long has it been?' she wanted to know. 'How long since you were up and about?' Matty wasn't sure.

Evie looked for a clean nightdress in her drawers but failed to find one. She'd have to lend her one of her own. She eased Matilda's arms into a dressing gown she found hanging behind the door, which she recognised as once belonging to Aunt Agatha. Found a pair of bed socks to put on her poor deformed and swollen feet, and then put her feet into the men's carpet slippers that she usually wore. It was cold, so she tucked a coat round her too, then put her to sit in an old basket chair.

'I'm taking you home with me. I'll see you're looked after better than this. You're poorly, Matty.'

'It's my chest,' she wheezed.

There'd be plenty of room in the new house. 'I'll get you a cup of tea first.'

She went down to the kitchen and tried to stop the cold tap dripping over a sink full of dirty pots. It proved impossible. Byron came in and was more successful.

She said: 'I should have done something long before now.'

'Nonsense, Evie. He wouldn't have let you.' Byron came and put his arms round her. 'Still won't. He refuses point blank to come to our place. You'll never get him out of here. Goodness only knows why he wants to stay.'

'He's been working all these years. Why did I never stop to think? He's getting too old. He can't even look after himself.'

'He didn't exactly invite your concern. Doesn't invite anybody's.'

'Who else does he have?'

'Nobody would expect you to watch over him, not when he's treated you the way he has. Not many would want to help now.'

'I thought when we left the flat I was getting rid of my problems. Suddenly I've got a whole new set.' It scared her.

'We'll have to re-open the pharmacy as soon as possible. It'll need to be sold as a going concern.'

Evie liked the way he said 'we' to show he meant to help her. She half smiled. 'Trust you to think of the business first.'

'After all, it will come to you eventually.'

'Perhaps.'

'Who else does he have to leave it to?'

'He's the sort who'd leave it to the dogs' home.'

'Is he interested in dogs?'

'He used to treat all animals. Sometimes he was called

out to sick horses. Yes, he likes dogs well enough. He might want to do that to make sure I don't benefit.'

'I told him the best thing to do was to sell the business straight away. That it was too much for him.'

'I'll bet he told you it was none of your business?'

'Yes, we'll just have to do the best we can for him. Do you know any other chemists, Evie?'

'Once I did. I was quite friendly with Bertie Pugh. He was apprenticed to Father years ago. He's got a pharmacy of his own now in Conway Street.'

'Telephone him, Evie. He may know of somebody willing to come here at a moment's notice. I saw a phone down in the shop. I'll look his number up for you.'

Just like Father, Evie thought, to put a phone in the shop but not one up here. She found it in what used to be the dentist's room. It seemed he was doing his prescribing in there these days. She dialled the number Byron gave her.

'Bertie?' She recognised his voice the moment he spoke. 'It's Evie. Evie Hobson that was. Remember me?'

'Ye-es. Yes, of course. It's a long time.'

'About twenty years.' She explained about her father, and that she needed a trained chemist to run his pharmacy.

'Thought old Joseph would go on for ever,' he said. 'I'll find somebody for you, Evie. Maybe not for tomorrow morning, but as soon as I can.' They chatted briefly, and she learnt that he was married with three children now, then she gave him her home phone number and rang off.

Back upstairs in the kitchen, Evie found that Byron had already made the tea. She opened the cupboard where they kept their food. There was a small square of cheese covered with green mould, and a jar of jam crystallising into sugar. In the bread bin she found a heel of mildewed bread.

'There's nothing to eat in the house, and Matty's really ill.'

'They're both too old to cope, Evie. And that's not your fault. It happens to everybody.'

'I'll have to get some milk. I'll see if I can borrow some from Polly Darty.'

She ran next door and told Polly what she intended to do about the two invalids. As well as a pint of milk, Polly found two teacakes that hadn't sold and buttered them for her father.

'They'll do him for tonight, since he refuses to come to our house. I need somebody to clean the place up for him and make his meals. Can you think of somebody? You know everybody round here.'

'I'll have a think. There's always women looking for work.'

Evie took the tea and cake to her father on a tray.

'You've taken long enough,' he complained, reaching for the cup.

'Polly sent you the teacake.'

'Is there any jam to go with it?'

Evie called down to Byron to bring up the jar they'd seen. Then she said:

'Father, I need a bag to pack some things for Matilda. We're taking her home with us.'

'Sooner her than me.' He took a noisy sip of tea.

'A bag? Do you have one?'

'No.'

Evie knew he had. She opened his walk-in cupboard. His suits hung on one side, and there were shelves crowded with hats, shoes and bric-à-brac on the other.

'There's one here. Can I borrow it?'

She was pulling it out from below the bottom shelf when she saw some books bundled together and tied with string. One had a lockable gilt catch across its pages. Another had the name Helen Bryant inked across its closed leaves. She knew immediately that they must be her mother's diaries.

Feeling on fire, she glanced surreptitiously behind her. Byron had brought the jam and was standing between her and her father. She eased the bundle of books into the open carpet bag.

'What are you doing in there, Evie? I don't want you messing with my private things.'

She heard the tremor of fear in his voice. Was it just the diaries he didn't want her to see, or was there something else here?

'Just getting this bag out, it's exactly what I need.'

She stood back for a moment and looked more carefully. Under the carpet bag was another much smaller one. It looked vaguely familiar, and yet . . . She pulled it out. It came to her then and made her go weak at the knees. It was the bag her mother had been carrying when she'd come back to the shop the day she'd died.

'Leave my things alone. I don't want you touching anything.'

Father was more nervous, no doubt about that. Evie rammed the smaller bag into the carpet bag too. Joseph was throwing back his bedclothes as though bent on stopping her, but Byron was tucking them back like a mother hen.

She said: 'I'll bring this bag back tomorrow,' and made a breathless exit, flushed with excitement.

She ran upstairs to Matilda's room and surveyed her prize, unable to believe she'd had the luck to find her mother's things. Perhaps now the questions that had puzzled her for so long would be answered.

When she'd calmed down a little, she started putting

together a few things that Matilda would need, packing them round the books. She found less than she'd expected. Matilda seemed to have no clean clothes left. Getting her down to the car was no easy matter and took all Byron's strength as well as her own.

'Perhaps it's as well your father's refused to budge,' Byron panted as he half lifted Matilda on to the back seat.

Evie could think of nothing but locking up this oppressive house, getting back home and settling down to look through her trophies. But she knocked next door first and left a spare key with Polly Darty.

'So Miss Lister can get in in the morning.'

The sales of proprietary medicines and cosmetics provided an important part of her father's turnover.

# CHAPTER TWENTY-ONE

Back home in Heswall, Kitty had long since gone home. Mrs Minto had gone to bed, but she heard them and came in her dressing gown to help Evie make up a bed for Matilda.

'In the room next to mine,' she suggested. 'Then she can call in the night if she wants anything.'

Then she went down to the kitchen and warmed up some soup. Evie stayed with Matilda until she'd eaten and was settled for the night, but her mind was on her mother's diaries. She was thrilled to have found them.

When she went to her own room she found that Byron was reading in bed. She showed him her mother's grey canvas bag and the diaries. Explained what they were.

'Your father was all on edge when you opened that cupboard. He was worried you might find them. There's something he doesn't want you to know.'

Evie looked in the bag. 'He'd be furious if he knew I'd taken this. He wouldn't tell me anything about Mother. Wouldn't even talk about her.'

Evie undressed quickly, poured herself a cup of tea from the tray Byron had brought up for her and climbed in beside him. At last it seemed she might find out what had happened all those years ago.

She looked through the diaries and put them in date order, feeling a niggle of guilt. 'Was it wrong for me to take them, do you think?'

'Evie! You need to know and understand what happened.'

'Need? I'm certainly curious.'

Byron's dark eyes were full of affection. 'It *is* a need. Losing your mother suddenly like that when you were small; being brought up by your father, a despot; finding out your mother was still alive when you'd believed her to be dead: it's left you with a permanent wound.'

He moved across the bed and put his arms round her. 'That sort of upbringing is bound to have an effect. It would on anybody. You had a childhood deprived of love, and ended up full of insecurities.' He kissed her cheek.

'You haven't been able to grow out of them, Evie. You're full of worries and can't shake them off. You're too sensitive to other people's worries and take them on board as your own. You're tormented by ghosts of the past and you need to lay them if you are to be truly happy. You need the answers, love.'

'Yes.' Evie knew he was right. He understood more about her than she did herself. 'I'm going to start reading.'

'And I'm going to sleep.' He kissed her again and put out his bedside light, leaving the room in semi-darkness.

Filled with nervous anticipation, Evie opened the first diary, which was for 1887. The frontispiece was inscribed: 'The Diary of Helen Kathleen Bryant, Bryant's Pharmacy, Argyle Street, Birkenhead.'

Her mother would have been only eighteen when she started writing her diaries. It seemed another age. There had been no cars or aeroplanes then. Evie started to read.

*January 2nd, 1887* Today, my father Harold Bryant took on a new apprentice, who is much more to my liking than Joseph Hobson. He's called Bill Smith and he has a belly laugh that echoes through the whole building. I can hear him from upstairs when he's down in the shop. He seems very jolly.

Dadda isn't well again. Mama says he needs more help in the shop and this is the best way to get it. Bill Smith will be able to make himself useful after a few months' training.

Evie skimmed a few pages until her eye was caught again.

*May 2nd, 1887* Today, Joseph Hobson proposed to me and I giggled when I turned him down. That led to a lot of embarrassment. I apologised for showing amusement but it made things worse. It was so unexpected. He'd never given any indication that he even liked me and he's always so stiff and pompous.

Dadda was cross with me. He was expecting it because Mr Hobson had already asked his permission. Furthermore, he'd received it. Dadda said it was a great honour that Mr Hobson wanted me to share his life with him, and that he'd soon be in a position to support a wife.

He went on and on about him being a serious young man who'd make a good husband. I told Dad he was *too* serious for me. I don't like him. He looks so aloof, his hawk-nose is always in the air. Bill doesn't like him either, he thinks he's a cold fish.

I think Joseph might have been wiser to pay me a little attention first. I could have told him then, quietly and without fuss, not to bother proposing. He went to a lot of unnecessary trouble. The embarrassment is of his making. Anyway, Bill Smith is more my sort.

*May 3rd, 1887* Dadda came into the dining room and caught me and Bill laughing together. He accused us of laughing about Joseph Hobson, which we were. I'd just told Bill that yesterday Joseph had proposed and I'd turned him down. If Dad had come a moment or two sooner he'd have caught us kissing, and goodness knows what he'd have said then. He told us both off, and later that night, when Dad and I were alone by the living-room fire, he urged me to reconsider Mr Hobson's offer. He said he was much to be preferred to Bill Smith.

'Not by me he isn't,' I told him. 'Bill's the one I really want to marry.'

'He's not in a position to think of it,' Dadda snorted. It made him cross with me again. 'He's apprenticed to me for five years.'

As if we didn't already know that. It was the first thing me and Bill worked out. We can't marry all the time he's an apprentice and he's still got more than four and a half years to go.

He says he loves me and he'll never change his mind. He asked me to wait for him. I told him I couldn't even think of marrying anyone else. Bill makes me feel wonderful. Lifts me away from all that is humdrum, away from all the soft soap and worming powders I have to sell. Just hearing his voice from the drug run gives me a warm feeling. I'd wait for ever for him. Dadda doesn't like him half so much as he does Joseph, who he says will make much the better apothecary.

*July 8th, 1887* Bill very upset tonight. He confessed that he doesn't care much for the life of a chemist after all. He's thinking of giving up his apprenticeship. He hasn't completed one year of the five yet, and feels that after all it isn't the calling for him. His father and grandfather were in the army and he has a mind to follow in their footsteps. He says we could be married so much sooner. If that's the case, I'm all for it.

Bill has spent days working himself up to tell Dadda. Usually he and Joseph go to their rooms after supper to study, but tonight he came back down. He said he wanted me there when he did it, to lend support. Dadda flared up at Bill.

'What a waste of my time! A waste of your own too. A young man like you, not knowing your own mind for ten minutes at a time.'

Father is in an exceedingly bad temper as a result. Bill is packing his bags to leave and I don't like this a bit. It will be horrible not to have him here in the house with me. He kissed me and tried to cheer me up, but really it didn't.

*August 13th, 1887* The furore hasn't died down yet. Dadda is upset too. He told me he always knew Bill was a wastrel, and what a good job we found out sooner rather than later.

The days drag now. I'm lost without Bill. He writes every day to tell me his news. He's hoping for a commission. His father isn't pleased because he paid to have him apprenticed to my father, but his grandfather is willing to pay for a commission for him. It's just that it all takes time and I can't be with him.

*August 21st, 1887* Bill came to take me out today (Sunday). It was heaven to see him again and take his arm when we walked in the park. Dadda wasn't pleased. I thought he was going to forbid it. He only allowed it because Mother came too. Well, she walked ten yards behind us, so we could talk together. I know he'd have kissed me if she hadn't been there. I do love Bill. My tummy turns right over just to look at him.

*October 1st, 1887* Bill is now officially in the army and seems mightily pleased to have it so. He reckons it will be a good life. I'm just dying to see him in his uniform, I'm sure he looks exceedingly handsome. Dadda said it would be wiser if I put him out of my mind. He thinks he's not a man who will stick at anything. I'd find it easier to fly than do that. I think of nothing else.

*October 19th, 1887* Bill came today, looking even more handsome than I'd expected. Second Lieutenant William Smith. He asked my father if he could marry me. I pleaded and pleaded to have it so. Dadda rather unbending on this. He says he's given me too much of my own way in the past. I told him if I could have just this one thing more, I'd be forever grateful.

Mamma is not against Bill. She says she likes him, but she won't take my part against Dadda. He is trying to talk me out of it, but nothing will make me change my mind. I keep telling him that I love Bill and always will and nobody else will suit me so well. He said I must be exceedingly popular to have two proposals in so many months.

Bill came again to plead with Father. He gave his consent at last and insists it's to be a long engagement to give me time to change my mind, but I never will. I'm so happy, over the moon. Joseph Hobson is looking very dour at the news.

*November 10th, 1887* Bill has given me an engagement ring. An opal with a tiny diamond each side. Mother doesn't approve, she says opals are unlucky, but I love it and wear it all the time. I've started collecting for my bottom drawer. I have a pair of pillowcases and I'm embroidering them with hearts and flowers. To think of them side by side on our bed with our heads making dents in them makes me ready to swoon with happiness. Mother is tatting some cushion covers for me.

*December 1st, 1887* Such a crisis! I don't know whether to be pleased or horrified. Bill's regiment is going out to India, where they will serve for seven years. Probably before the new year. He came to tell us the news and asked as a great favour that we might be married before he goes.

He has thrown my whole family into a great tizz. Father stamped downstairs to the shop and refused to listen to any more.

Bill implored Mama to stay. She sat down again while he explained that if I am his wife, the army will provide me with a passage to India when he's served there for six months. He'll be allotted a married quarter and I will be able to share his life.

I am almost overcome with the anxiety and excitement of it all. If Father refuses to give his consent then we must wait until Bill returns, as he thinks it will be too difficult for me to go out as a single girl and marry him there. I would perhaps need to pay my own passage out too.

Mother sent Bill home but we talked late into the night. I pleaded and wept. I've never wanted anything so badly. Mama told Dad I'll be impossible to live with if I don't have my way with this. I told them I didn't think I would live at all. There can be no more wait-and-see, Father has to say one way or the other straight out.

He said he'd sleep on it, but I could hear them still arguing it out long after we'd all gone to bed. Mama has taken my part at last, thank goodness.

Father has said yes! I can't believe my good fortune and could hardly get the words out to thank him. Bill was over the moon when I told him. His belly laugh was ringing through our house every five minutes. The thing now is to fix up the wedding as soon as possible. Bill will sail on January the fourth.

Everything is such a flurry and an excitement and a joy. Christmas coming in the middle of it too, it's almost too much to bear. It has been decided and fixed, we are to be married on Boxing Day. The vicar has agreed, and after the service we'll all walk home for the wedding breakfast. Mama complains now about the lack of time to get things ready, but she is as thrilled and excited as I am.

Mrs Jackson, our dressmaker, is making me a dress of white satin. Mama suggested white velvet but the cost was very high and Bill says I will be able to wear satin for regimental occasions in India. I'll not want the warmth of velvet there.

Dadda is still shaking his head and hoping he's done the right thing, though I keep telling him he has. Boxing Day is very convenient because the shop would be closed anyway. For most of our guests too, because they will not be at work. Then Bill and I will go to Chester for a honeymoon. It will last until the day his leave finishes which is the day before he sails.

The last few pages of the diary were left blank. Her mother had been having too exciting a time to write in it. Evie hurriedly turned to the one for the following year. It was bound in Moroccan leather.

*January 6th, 1888* Our wedding and our honeymoon were absolutely wonderful. I've never been so blissfully happy in all my life as I was with Bill. Now he has gone everything seems very flat.

I've come back home. I'm working in the shop again. My wedding seems like a distant dream. I need my lovely, lovely dress hanging in my clothes cupboard and my wedding band on my finger to remind me that it all really did happen.

The thought of a new life in India fills me with anticipation. I have that to look forward to. I'm crossing the days off my calendar but only two have gone so far. Bill has given me a book on Indian history and its people. I shall read it from cover to cover and I shall keep myself busy helping Father in the shop.

He says he needs all the help he can get. He isn't feeling too well and has dropsy in his legs. I've started making myself a trousseau for India, and have bought ten yards of fine white cambric and some lace for this. I'm also still collecting for my bottom drawer and have a tablecloth to embroider.

I am not to bear his child just yet, though might so easily have found I was. I'm relieved, because it might have delayed my departure for India and Bill. There will be plenty of time for that when we are together. He says he wants a family.

A lovely, lovely letter came from Bill today, reams

long and written on the boat. He says he's eating huge meals and sitting in the sun, but that he misses me most awfully. I wrote back immediately. I told him it's a thousand times worse to be left at home trying to imagine all the delights he describes.

*April 4th, 1888* Another letter from Bill today, letting me know he's reached Bombay. He tells me he saw a line of thirty elephants roped together walking through the main streets of that teeming city with their young behind, the last of which was just a baby. He's horrified by the poverty and the beggars and I am not to be upset to see such things when I get there.

Evie paused and looked in the grey canvas bag. The letters her mother had received from Bill Smith were all here, neatly tied up in bundles and dated. Each was in its envelope, addressed to Mrs Helen Smith. Each had been read many times, as evidenced by the well-thumbed paper. It brought a lump to Evie's throat to see them so carefully preserved. She went back to the diary.

*June 6th, 1888* I have finished embroidering a fine cambric nightdress, which I stitched all myself. Mama says my needlework is improving fast. I need bodices now, and shall make them of fine cotton for the heat.

Father is much worse and has taken to his bed. The shop is very busy without him. Joseph Hobson is doing all the prescribing. Mama is worried about that, as he has three more months of his apprenticeship still to run and isn't qualified. Father says he's good enough but we should find another chemist.

There is too much work for one person. Mama advertised the vacancy today.

She sent for the doctor again today too. Dadda said it was a waste of money because his prescription is for foxglove tea, which he started taking last year without much effect. Poor Dadda has no energy and can hardly dress himself. There is no question of him working in the shop.

Mama is very worried. She wanted me and Hobson with her when she chose the chemist from the three who applied. It was Joseph who picked out Albert Vance. He's quite old. Joseph says that gives the customers confidence.

Poor Dadda hardly seems to care. Today he asked me to take care of Mama if anything should happen to him. He says he's sorry I shall soon be going to India, as he's afraid Mama will need me here.

*July 8th, 1888* Two letters came from Bill this morning. He and his battalion have taken up duty in a fort at Razmak on the North-West Frontier, and that is where he expects I'll join him. He tells me to bring warm clothes with me. He thought all India was hot, but finds it's freezing cold up there.

He has to go out on expeditions for a week or ten days at a time. It's meant to show the British strength and frighten the warring local tribes into submission. They march in a column through narrow gorges between huge high peaks very bare and raw. He hopes I won't be afraid of being left but there are other wives there, and always two battalions are left to guard the fort. I don't think I would be.

The post from India takes so long he won't yet know how poorly Dadda is. I sit with him in the evenings and write my letters or embroider my trousseau, but he hardly notices I'm there. I worry whether I could leave if permission came now.

Poor Mama is worried to distraction. Dadda doesn't rally at all. The dropsy is filling his limbs. Joseph recommended a purge. We try it, of course, but not with much hope.

There was another gap of several weeks, then, with another, larger lump in her throat, Evie read:

*August 2nd, 1888* Father died last night. He was only forty-three. His funeral is on Wednesday. Mama is prostrated with grief.

Poor Mama, she's found it very hard over the last few months. We gave up expecting him to recover some time ago.

*September 7th, 1888* Joseph Hobson is a great comfort to Mama. He brings up camomile tea and lavender oil to soothe her. Mama took to her bed last week. All the worry she's had with Father and trying to manage the business on her own has made her ill now.

Another letter from Bill, who says there have been more attacks recently by marauding Pathan tribes-men. The Pathans live high in the mountains and attack the villages of the lowland tribes on both sides of the mountain range. Bill says they have to because there isn't enough for them to survive on in the bare uplands. The army tries to keep order but last week the Pathan tribesmen attacked a column out on expedition.

He urges me not to worry and promises to take

good care of himself. He fears that the army won't want to bring out another wife to the fort until things settle down again.

He hasn't yet had my letter telling him that poor Dadda has passed away and the other troubles I have here. I don't think Mama wants to get better. She says she can't live without him. I've told her she must. I couldn't bear it if I were to lose her too. I couldn't possibly leave her just now, even if my boat tickets were to come.

The shop continues busy. Joseph is very helpful.

There were more blank pages in the diary. Evie turned them over with a heavy heart. Reliving the troubles her mother had gone through and expecting to read that her grandmother had passed away too was agonising.

To gain a moment's respite, she turned to her mother's grey canvas bag again, and noticed an official-looking envelope addressed to Mrs Helen Smith. Long ago, it had been torn open in a great hurry. Now she carefully slid out the single sheet of paper.

Evie's head reeled with the horror of it. She couldn't believe the run of trouble her mother had had at that time. The letter was from the War Office, and it reminded her of the one she'd received when Ned had been lost at sea. It offered condolences on the death of Second Lieutenant William Smith in a native skirmish on the North-West Frontier. It told Helen that her husband had died bravely, together with all the senior officers of his regiment.

This was a loss Evie understood only too well. Hadn't she gone through it too? She wiped away a tear and took up the diary again.

*November 15th, 1888* I haven't been able to do anything for the past month, not even write in my diary, which has always been a comfort to me.

I feel numb with grief. First Father and now Bill, all in the same year. The only good thing is that Mama is a little better.

Evie slid that book on to the floor beside her bed and reached for the next. She had to turn to June before she found anything written in it.

*June 15th, 1889* I ought to feel better about things. Mama is better and now gets up every afternoon. She says that next week she'll get dressed straight after breakfast. The shop is functioning well and is profitable, which is a great relief to us.

Joseph has taken on a Miss Lister to run the front counter. He's had to because I've needed to spend so much time upstairs with Mother. But even upstairs we are better organised than we were.

He heard of Matilda Best, who was working for some church acquaintance being sent abroad to do missionary work and has thus been released from service. Matilda is certainly a find. I virtually leave all the housekeeping to her.

If only Bill were still alive. I feel half dead without him. I'm desperately disappointed that I won't after all see India with him. I feel I was given a glimpse of Utopia only to have it snatched from me. What remains seems empty. If only I had been having his child, it would be something left of him.

I'm down helping in the shop again and feel better for it. Mama continues frail. She says she can't get over losing Dadda, that she feels useless without him.

I told her I feel the same about losing Bill. I don't even have a grave on which to put flowers each Sunday. It would be some solace to do that for him as well as for Father. It haunts me that Bill lies in such alien soil, and that I can never see the place. I can't really imagine what it's like either.

The other pages in that diary were all blank. Clearly her mother hadn't had the heart to write more during that year.

Evie knew that Byron was asleep. His breathing was deep and even. The house was silent, but for her, sleep was a thousand miles away. Her mind raced with the agonies her mother had suffered all those years ago.

Once she'd feared that it would be her lot to follow her mother's downward path. Joseph had predicted it, and the thought had given her nightmares. But she'd been fortunate. Her life had been good and would continue to be so. Byron was a kind and understanding man. Evie reached down for the next volume and went on reading.

*January 1st, 1890* Mama thinks that now that more than a year has passed I should be getting over Bill, though she puts it more delicately than that. She thinks it's easier for me because I was married for so short a time. I lived as a wife for a mere eight days; what could be more cruel than that?

She says that I'm young enough to marry again if only I would cheer up and smile a little. She said today that she'd like to see me settled before she goes. I told her she wasn't going anywhere, but it frightens me to hear her talk of death like this. She's very down. A ghost of herself really. She's lost so much weight. She praises Joseph Hobson. Father liked him and thought him most suitable for me. She says that he offered for me once and she's sure he would again. With the business being in her gift, what could be more suitable for me than a husband who could run it?

Joseph has been very good to us since our troubles, I have to admit that, and I know from the way he looks at me that Mama is right. But he falls so short of Bill.

I don't know if I'll ever get over him and the thought of another does not please.

There followed a good deal about working in the shop, but it wasn't answering the questions that thronged Evie's mind. She began to flick over the pages, and then turned to the next volume.

*January 1st, 1891* It's now over two years since I heard of Bill's death. Mother is no better. She eats little and does little. I fear she'll never pick up. Matilda waits on her hand and foot.

Today, Joseph Hobson proposed again. He said he has always loved me and has wanted to tell me for a long time but he saw that I grieved for Bill. This morning he heard me laugh with Miss Lister over the antics of a dog that was brought into the shop. He said I sounded as though I was over Bill, and would perhaps be able to consider him now.

He runs the shop, does all the ordering and prescribing, keeps the accounts and presents me with the results at the end of each month.

I asked for time to think about it, but I know of no other. Perhaps I'd be happier as Joseph's wife than as an old maid. I'd be more sure about that if he'd show more affection.

He's made no attempt to kiss me, though he did hold my hand. I don't feel for him one whit of what I felt for Bill. There's no warmth about Joseph, he's such a stiff, strait-laced sort of person. So earnest and wrapped up in his work, but he is a good apothecary. Everybody reports his medicines as effective, and he is kind to us.

Mama has hardly been to church since Dadda died. She hasn't been well enough. So every Sunday, Joseph and I walk there together. He talks of the weather on the way there and the sermon on the way back. Despite living under the same roof all these years, I don't feel I know him well.

*February 2nd, 1891* Mama is not at all well and has taken to her bed again. She pleads with me to accept Joseph. She thinks he'll make an excellent husband.

Mama doesn't come to the table for meals any more. Matilda eats with us but gets up quickly to clear away. After dinner, Joseph put his hand across the table to touch mine and asked me gently if I'd had enough time to make up my mind. He looked so hopeful and there was love in his eyes.

I said that yes, I would marry him. It made him lean across and kiss my cheek and take both my hands in his. He said I'd made him very happy and promised to do his best to make me happy too.

Mama was overjoyed when we went together to her bedroom to tell her. I haven't seen her so animated in years. She insisted I fetch the Sunday sherry bottle and some glasses. It's a Sunday ritual that we all take a glass of sherry before dinner.

'To warm us up when we come in from church,' Dadda used to say, though we did it even on hot Sundays in summer.

Joseph fetched Matilda from the kitchen and she raised her glass to us too. I feel better now I've made up my mind. Joseph seems quite different, all smiles. I don't suppose it's been much fun for him living here with Mama and me. Things will be different now.

Joseph wants us to be married soon and so does Mama. She says I already have a wedding dress. I took it out of my wardrobe for the first time in years and tried it on. It still fits. I went in to show myself to Mam and she said excellent, silly to think of getting another. I went back to my own bedroom and cried for Bill and for what might have been. It reminds me too much.

I haven't exactly told Joseph he'll be second best, but I said I still think of Bill, so I'm not marrying him under false pretences. He says love will come and he'll be happy with what I can give him. He really is very patient with me and very kind to Mama. Perhaps I could do worse.

*March 1st, 1891* The deed is done, I am now Mrs Hobson. I wore the same white dress and felt as cold as ice in it. I couldn't stop shivering all through the ceremony. Joseph hired two separate carriages, so that Mama could ride to church and not get tired out. Mr Vance, the assistant, gave me away in lieu of Father. I helped Matilda make a special lunch. It was a very quiet wedding this time. Only the shop staff and the Harveys from the butcher's.

Joseph is certainly kind and thoughtful but there

A LIVERPOOL LULLABY

is no passion in him. He is not such a good lover as Bill and doesn't show much affection. He's very self-contained. He says he would like children and I pray for them to come. I would like that very much myself.

Mama seems to be fading away. She says she's happy to know I'm settled and I've done the right thing. I can see her getting weaker, and though Joseph continues to prescribe for her and she says his medicines do her good, I fear they won't keep her in this world.

*June 3rd, 1891* Today I discovered I'm with child. Joseph is thrilled and even Mama whispered that she was delighted, though she hardly had the strength.

She said: 'I can go now with an easy mind. You're settled and will be content with your children.'

*June 4th, 1891* I sat up with poor Mama most of the night. Joseph persuaded me to bed at two in the morning. When Matilda went to her at six with a cup of tea, she'd gone.

I wept because I wasn't there at the end, but Joseph said it was his fault, that I must have my rest. Matilda said she'd gone peacefully in her sleep and that she'd been ill for so long I must look on it as a release.

Everybody is being kind. I'm hanging on to the thought of the baby and that keeps me going. I feel quite fatalistic. I'm afraid those I love are doomed to die young. Mother is only forty-three. Exactly the same age as Father was at his death.

# CHAPTER TWENTY-TWO

Evie looked at the diaries that remained. From this point on, Helen was not making regular entries. One book seemed to cover several years. She had a lump in her throat as she started reading again.

*February 2nd, 1892* My baby is born, a lovely little girl. Joseph wanted a boy but he says he's not unhappy as this is the first. He wants to call her Evelina and I think that's pretty. She has a dimple in her cheek and such dark, silky hair, not like Joseph's. We are both besotted with her.

I feel content at last. At peace with my circumstances. Joseph says there is no need for me to work on the front counter now I have the baby to look after, but I like to go down for an hour when Evie takes her rest. After all, Matilda is here in the house with her all the time and she likes to play with her too.

Working in the shop keeps me in touch with everything. I really enjoy the change. The customers seem to like Joseph and are prepared to wait for him rather than talk to Mr Vance.

He says he would like to start taking apprentices now that he's had some experience. He thinks the business would be more profitable because apprentices would pay us for the privilege of learning and we can utilise their labour and thus avoid paying Mr Vance, who is a trained pharmacist and expects a due wage.

Joseph is very wrapped up in all aspects of the business and I count myself lucky he's prepared to do so much. We had the old accounts out last night and find we have increased our turnover and are making more profit than did my parents. That pleased Joseph very much.

*May 8th, 1892* Evie has cut her first tooth. She is a delightful baby, always gurgling and smiling up at us all. Joseph brought up a little rattle from the shop and tied it over her cot. She tries to knock it, first with her hands, and then with her feet. She laughs and giggles when it makes a noise.

The rattle was by way of being a peace offering from Joseph. I realised I had not seen any figures for the shop for over two months. I asked him if he'd made up the books, and of course he had. He said he didn't want to bother me with figures but he didn't even mention them, and it is my business. My father started it, he willed it to my mother and she willed it to me. He was cold and cross all day, but tonight he brought up the rattle and Evie loves it. I'm glad we can melt his bad moods between us.

*June 9th, 1892* Something has upset Joseph and I don't know what it is. I've asked him several times but he says he's perfectly all right. The business is still thriving. I had to see the figures to settle my mind, I thought it must be that.

We have Monty Baines, an apprentice, living with us now. He seems to please Joseph. Miss Lister says there's been no trouble downstairs while I've not been there. Matilda says he's not found any fault with her. But Joseph seems so changed, everybody agrees with me about that.

I can't make up my mind whether he's frightened or angry. Perhaps it's both. He's very short with everybody, and cold even with little Evie. He's bottling something inside him and it's making him very intense. I do wish he'd confide in me. I can't think what's troubling him. If it isn't the business, or the family, or the staff, I don't know what else there is to upset him.

We all tiptoe round trying not to give Joseph any aggravation, but he gets no better. He blows up at us all without warning. He can be boiling with anger when five minutes earlier he'd seemed in a mild mood.

I chose my moment, and asked when he came to the tea table if he were ill, as it seemed the only possible explanation. He erupted like Mount Vesuvius. I'm sure they could hear him shouting in the shop. I fear his temper will never be what it was, he's been like this for so long now.

He's changing in other ways too. He doesn't like me to work on the front counter any more. Doesn't like me to be in the shop at all. It's useless telling him I enjoy it, that I want to help. He says nowadays for a man in his position it isn't seemly to have a wife working as a counter assistant.

I had to remind him that I was the owner, and he said I should act more like it then. In order to keep him calm I don't go down any more.

Old Mrs Cartwright, at the newsagent's, says she wishes her husband was more that way inclined. She'd like less to do in the shop. She's exhausted by the time bedtime comes. She thinks I'm making a fuss about nothing.

Sometimes I think Joseph's mind has turned. He says it's nothing I've done. He even said he loves me, but he does nothing to show it.

*February 3rd, 1894* I asked Joseph, now that Evie's two years old, if we should be trying for another baby. He said yes, he'd like a son, but he gets into bed and turns away from me. There's no possibility of having another child this way.

I don't understand him at all. Despite what he says, he seems to have gone off me. Sometimes I wonder if he married me for my business. Truly he takes more interest in that than he does in me.

Since the Married Woman's Property Act he cannot take it from me, but I fear he would like to. He doesn't consult me at all now. He runs it without any reference to my wishes, nor does he show me the accounts unless I ask.

When I faced him about this, he says he wishes to shield me from business worries as any good husband would, but I am so horribly suspicious of his motives. I feel so distanced from him. The profits are being banked in an account which is in our joint names. He doesn't question what I draw from it and since he works so hard I do not question what he takes out either. In truth, it seems little. I wish I did not have this suspicious streak.

*September 10th, 1896* Evie is very sweet. She started school today. I'm pleased because it gets both of us out of the house. Joseph doesn't like me leaving it, but I have a good excuse now, I have to take Evie backwards and forwards to school and once I'm out, I can go round the shops or the market before returning. I feel much better for the freedom.

*April 7th, 1897* Joseph was in one of his better moods at breakfast today. He sprinkled extra sugar on Evie's porridge for her and started telling her the story of the three bears. We had to rush all the way to school after that, but I was pleased that he seemed to be improving.

When I got back he was raving at Miss Lister because she'd gone to get more shaving soap from the store and left the front counter unattended for a few moments. We've always done that, sometimes several times each day, and he's been happy to have it so until now. In future, he said she must check the stock each evening and replace what's been sold before she goes home.

The apprentice whispered that it was something Joseph received in the morning post that put him in such a black mood. The mail was still on the back counter and Joseph caught me looking through it when he turned round. He blew up again at me, demanding to know what I was looking for.

I'd seen nothing but a few bills. It was just routine business mail. I thought the apprentice must be mistaken, but he said Joseph put one letter in the pocket of his white coat.

I'd swear Joseph is frightened. He had a nightmare last night and was talking in his sleep.

The apprentice tells me Joseph is often at the door when the post is due. That he seems uneasy and that he's told the postman to bring the mail to the drug run and not toss it on the front counter as he used to.

We have easier times that last sometimes a few

weeks and sometimes a few months, but according to the apprentice, it's always the post that sends him into one of his rages.

*June 6th, 1897* I'm the one who caused the trouble today. I came home from seeing Evie to school and found the sign-writers changing the name above the shop windows from Arthur Bryant to Joseph Hobson. I screamed at them to stop and caused a commotion in the shop that brought business to a standstill.

Joseph took my arm and led me upstairs away from them all. In our bedroom, he insisted I swallow some pills and lie on the bed. He said I was hysterical. He sat with me then and explained that it was bad for business to keep Father's name over the shop. Everybody knew Joseph now as the pharmacist practising here and it was only right his name should be outside. He said I was being unreasonable and that after a little sleep I'd see it his way.

I told him it was equally unreasonable not to give me some inkling that he was about to do it. Why could he not have discussed it first?

Whatever he gave me made me sleep all day. Matilda went to collect Evie from school in my stead, and next time I went outside it was Joseph's name that was up. I wept because all my suspicions seem confirmed by this.

I'll go to see Myerscough and Rudge and get them to draw up a will leaving the business to Evie. They know me there, they handled Father's will and know the business is mine. I want to guarantee Evie's future. Perhaps after all I am being silly about this. Joseph loves her too, she's the only one who can make him smile. He'd want to ensure a good future for her too, I'm sure.

If anything Joseph's temper is getting worse. He took on a new apprentice who left after two weeks saying he couldn't cope with such moods. Unfortunately, the rest of us have to.

Evie fell back against her pillows in a rush of anger. Her mother's suspicions had been well founded. Father had taken over the pharmacy as his own though he knew he had no legal right. He'd wrested it from his own wife. Deprived his own child of her legal right.

Evie let out a long, juddering sigh. If only she'd known this when she was eighteen! She could have had so much more of Ned's company. They could have lived together in comfort. There would have been no need for him to go away to sea; no need for the long, lonely months without him.

She felt hot tears roll down her cheek. She'd have given anything to have kept Ned at home with her. He could have worked on the front counter and helped where he could. The business would have paid him more than his seafaring wage. They could have made the most of the few years they'd had.

But even after Ned's death, when she'd been afraid they'd all go hungry, a job on the front counter and care for Queenie was all she'd dared ask him for. Even then, he hadn't told her that the pharmacy was legally hers. He'd refused any help, keeping all it earned for himself.

True, he'd given her the letter about Aunt Agatha's legacy, and that had cushioned her. He must have known what that was. No doubt it had salved his conscience.

Evie had read late into the night, totally absorbed in her mother's life, growing more and more astounded at her revelations. She flicked through the remaining pages for further entries, but there were none. The last date was 15 June 1898, the date her mother had disappeared. The date Father had said she'd been killed in an accident.

There was a lot more she hadn't yet looked at in her mother's bag, but her eyes were so tired she could hardly focus.

Evie had learned a lot about her mother and about her own early life. She was shocked at Father's deceit and the lengths he'd gone to to get his own ends, but there was still something she didn't understand. What had made her mother leave home without her? She mustn't think about it now. She yawned and switched off her light.

Byron was sleeping deeply beside her, but for Evie sleep was far away, even though she ached for it. She tossed and turned while her mind swirled with questions. She couldn't see to read any more tonight but she still craved the answers.

It came to her then that Matilda had been living with her mother through all those times. She must know what had happened. Once it was in her mind, she had to get up and see if Matilda was awake.

As Evie went quietly up to the top storey, she heard a little cough. She pushed open the bedroom door and said softly: 'Matty?'

The figure on the bed turned. 'Is that you, Helen?'

That made her shiver. 'It's Evie.'

She'd left the landing light on and the door open. In the half-light she pulled a chair close to the bed and sat down.

'Evie, yes.' Matilda's eyes shone feverishly. 'I'm thirsty.'

'A drink of water?' Evie raised her a little and held the glass to her lips.

'Matty,' she said. 'I want you to tell me about my mother. What happened to make her run away? You know, don't you? She must have confided in you. She had no one else.'

Matty's anxious eyes were searching her face. 'There's nothing to worry about now,' Evie soothed. 'Father forbade you to tell me, didn't he? He used to get angry if he saw us talking together, but this is my house. He isn't here. He has no power over either of us now.'

Evie was desperate to know what had happened to her mother. 'I want you to think back, Matilda. To the time Helen left home.'

'Yes.'

'Helen would want you to tell me. Why was my father so angry with everybody?'

Evie felt work-worn fingers close tightly on her own. 'Afraid,' the dry lips croaked.

'No need to be afraid. You're safe here with me.'

'Your father – was afraid.'

'What of?'

'Helen's first husband.'

'But he was dead long before this.'

'No, no, he wasn't,' she whispered.

Evie was afraid Matilda's mind was wandering. 'He was killed. In India.'

'All a mistake,' she wheezed. 'A terrible mistake.'

Evie had seen the War Office telegram and the letter of condolence that followed it. A further letter from an officer serving in India, telling Helen about the Pathan ambush in which so many had died.

At the back of her mind, doubt niggled. Years ago, somebody had whispered the word 'bigamy'. She thought it had been Bertie Pugh.

Matilda's eyes were flashing fear so tangible that Evie

felt the skin crawl at the back of her neck.

'What happened, Matty? Why did Helen go away? Try to think back. It was June 1898. I was six.'

Evie had to wait. She could see Matty's face creasing with concentration. When she started to speak, her voice was a hoarse whisper.

'There was always trouble. Joseph was always finding fault. The house was being turned upside-down. Painters and decorators were in.'

She coughed and cleared her throat.

'That morning there was more trouble at breakfast. Joseph said his bacon was overcooked but it wasn't my fault. He was late coming down.

'Helen tried to cut up your bacon for you. It was so crisp it snapped and shot right across the table. You laughed, and that upset him more. When Helen was getting ready to take you to school, Joseph was out on the landing, arguing with her.

' "That child's old enough to go on her own now. It's time she learned to stand on her own feet."

' "She's only six," Helen protested.

'He hated to see her leave the house. Hated to see her walk through the shop. He wanted her safely upstairs in the house all the time.

'Your mother felt like a prisoner. She wanted to go out. She told me she was going round the market to buy some cloth to make another dress for you, instead of coming directly home.'

Matilda's knotted fingers twitched at the sheet. 'It was an ordinary day, sunny and bright. I cleared the breakfast pots and washed up in my new sink.'

'And then?'

There was no hurrying Matilda. She'd been forbidden to speak of these facts for so long that now she wanted to tell her everything. Her voice was stronger now. Evie told herself she must be patient.

'There was a commotion in the shop. So loud I crept down the stairs to see what it was all about.

'A soldier was shouting at Mr Hobson: "Helen stopped writing to me. I was left out there in limbo, not knowing what had gone wrong. I thought at first it was the post, but others were getting mail."

'He was an officer in full uniform with a polished Sam Browne belt. A captain now, with three pips on his shoulders.

' "Where's Helen? I've written countless letters to her. I wrote to her mother, I wrote to you pleading for news, but nobody answered."

' "We thought you were dead," Joseph said. He was in a real state, all worked up. Absolutely terrified. "Killed in action. That's why." '

Evie felt the soles of her feet crawl with horror. Matilda was more animated now. She went on:

'Everything had stopped in the shop. All the customers were watching them. It came to me then, and fair took my breath away. I couldn't believe my eyes. It was Bill Smith all right. Knew him right away, though he'd filled out and held himself more upright. More of a man. My legs went weak, I can tell you. I had to hold on to the stair rail.

' "You knew I wasn't dead. You returned some of my letters marked 'Not known at this address'."

'Bill was sort of menacing him, moving closer.

' "Get out of my shop," Joseph shouted, staggering back. "I don't want you here." His face was the colour of putty.

'Bill moved even closer. They were in the drug run by now. I went up a couple of stairs, so that I could see over the ointment jars.

' "I know it was you, I know your writing, no one else writes so small and neat.

' "Didn't you understand what you were doing to me? You knew I was serving out on the North-West Frontier. I couldn't just come home to sort things out. I asked for leave on compassionate grounds but it wasn't granted. I'd volunteered to serve out there, and I was made to do it."

'It did me good to see Joseph so scared for once.' Matty's rheumy eyes smiled into Evie's in the half-light.

'Bill kept shouting at him: "I was given permission to bring Helen out, but she didn't reply to official letters either. I was out of my mind with worry. I asked my friend Walter Caine to call on you. To find out what had happened to her. He wrote that you now owned this business and you didn't know Helen's whereabouts. You told him you thought she was with another man. I couldn't believe it. Helen would never do such a thing. I asked my uncle to come down from Glasgow to see you, but he wrote much the same thing. He asked you to write to me direct but you never did.

' "I only found out this year that I'd been wrongly listed as killed in action. Then I understood why Helen had stopped writing to me. I could guess what you'd been up to then. You intercepted my letters to her, didn't you? You didn't want her to know it was all a terrible mistake".'

Evie felt overwhelmed. 'I don't understand,' she said slowly. 'How was it possible for him to be wrongly listed as killed?'

'I asked Helen about that later. There were two Lieutenant William Smiths in the same battalion. It was the other who lost his life, along with the senior officers who knew him.'

'In some sort of native uprising?' Evie had read of them in the diaries.

'Helen did tell me . . .' Matilda was frowning, trying to remember. The facts as she told them were disjointed. Evie had to piece them together in her mind. It was horrible, far worse than she'd supposed.

'The death roll had to be sorted out at headquarters, hundreds of miles away. It was a terrible mix-up.'

Evie understood now. Helen had married Joseph bigamously because the War Office had wrongly reported Bill as dead.

She said: 'Joseph knew Bill was still alive. He was intercepting his letters. He wanted to keep my mother in ignorance . . . I think that's horrible.'

'He was afraid she'd leave him. Bill was her rightful husband, not him.'

'What happened after that?'

Matilda went on: 'A punch-up. Bill had Joseph by the collar. The apprentice was trying to pull him off. We all thought he was going to kill him.

'I didn't notice your mother come into the shop until she dropped her shopping with a thud and the oranges she'd bought rolled all over the floor.

' "Bill?" Her voice was all squeaky.

'I thought she'd faint, she went so white, then the next minute they were clinging together, sounding hysterical. Laughing and crying at the same time. Everyone was excited and pleased to see Bill, and clapping him on the back.

' "What's this then?" they were saying. "A ghost back from the dead?" The news spread up the shopping parade and old Mrs Cartwright from the paper shop came in, and Florrie from the barber's.

'Everybody was pleased except Joseph. He had a face blacker than Satan. If anybody looked as though he'd seen a ghost, it was him.

'He was shouting at the apprentice: "Get everybody out who isn't buying. This isn't a peep show. We're going upstairs where we can talk."

'I went back up to the kitchen but Mr Hobson came to the door. "Away with you, Matilda," he said. "This is family business and not for your ears." He tried to shoo me up to my bedroom but I ran out to Gladys at the bakery with the excuse that I needed to get bread.

'Gladys could talk of nothing else. All along the parade they couldn't. They were all out on the pavement.

' "The child," they were saying. "She'll be the stumbling block. Little Evie." There was more talking than selling done that morning.

'Joseph was in the wrong, you see, Evie. He'd known for a long time that Bill Smith was alive. That's what turned his mind. He knew his marriage was bigamous and that Helen, if she knew, would leave him.

'He hid it from her and he tried to keep her out of sight in case Bill sent somebody else round and they saw her. The trouble was, both of them loved Helen. They both wanted her.'

Evie let out a long, agonised sigh. 'And that was it? She went off with her first husband and left me?'

'No! I went back after an hour, but nothing had been settled one way or the other. Helen's face was wet with tears. Bill Smith kept shouting that the law was on his side and that Helen was his wife.

'She had the letters out to show him. Those she'd received telling her he'd been killed. I made some tea. Helen asked me to. Then I went upstairs to make the beds and thought what a terrible mess it was.

' "If you go, you go without the child," Joseph was shouting. "She's my daughter and I'll not allow it." I could see Helen was torn in two.'

'But she left me.'

'She asked me to pack her clothes, and yours too. She was pleading with Joseph to allow her to take you. Helen planned to meet you from school and not come back.

'But Joseph foresaw that might happen and went to meet you too. There was no thought for the shop that day. The apprentice had to manage on his own.'

Evie felt wrung out. 'My father kept me against her will?'

'She tried to escape with you again the next day, but Joseph caught you on the stairs and sent you to your room. He sent her away without you. That was when she gave me that photograph to give you when you were old enough to understand. She guessed Joseph would get rid of everything that reminded him of her. Sort of banish her from memory.

'At suppertime the following night, Bill Smith came back to plead for you. He said Helen was heartbroken without you. He threatened to go to court to get custody.'

'But he didn't, did he?'

'Joseph remembered I was there and I was sent off to bed before I'd cleared the dishes. So was the apprentice. I don't know what happened after that. Joseph never let anyone know his business if he could help it. He liked to play his cards close to his chest.

'But there was a lot of noise and argument. Always about you. It went on for hours, well into the night. I don't think Bill Smith meant to give up. I was expecting to be called down to get you out of bed and dressed.'

'But you weren't?'

'No, I know there was a fight in the living room that night because one of the chairs was broken. He hid it in the attic. I heard him bring it up. Yes, definitely a fight.'

'Father won, you mean?'

'It wasn't what I'd have expected. Bill Smith seemed the stronger man, but you stayed where Joseph wanted you, so he must have won.'

Evie sighed again. 'Remember the photos on the landing. Father was a boxer. He had the greater skill.'

'I felt so sorry for Helen. Such a pretty, kind-hearted girl. She tried to stand between me and Joseph when his ire turned on me, which was more often than I liked. She deserved better of life than she got, poor girl. My heart goes out to her still.

'If it weren't for you, your mother would have gone away with Bill and that would have been the end of it. Having you gave Joseph the means to prevent her going. Poor Helen, there was no easy way out for her. She was in a cleft stick.'

Evie tiptoed downstairs to make a cup of tea for them both. It was almost five o'clock. She ached with fatigue but she'd never felt more awake. Her mind was on fire. She knew now how difficult her mother had found it to leave her. And years later, she'd come back to make her peace.

When she went back with the tea, she asked:

'What was my mother like, Matilda?'

'To look at? Smaller and daintier than you. Her hair was not so dark as yours, but there was the same look about the eyes, and the same dimple. She was more inclined to do what Joseph told her than you ever were.'

'Why didn't you leave, Matty? You knew what he'd done. How cruel he was.'

'You were still here and only six years old. I promised Helen I'd stay and keep an eye on you. She was afraid he'd turn on you once she'd gone. But you were his own flesh and blood, and in his way, he loved you.'

'He has a strange way of showing it,' Evie said.

'Then when you went I was too old to start afresh in another house. Soon too old to work at all. No one else would have wanted me. I decided it was better to stay where I was than go to the workhouse.'

'Poor Matty. You can stay here with me. This will be your home from now on.'

'Not for very long.'

'Yes, for always. You'll be no trouble to us.'

'Thank you.' Matilda's voice was low and lacking in energy. Evie could hardly hear her. 'I don't think I'll be troubling you for long. I'll be for the next world soon.'

Evie understood then. 'Not too soon, I hope.'

# CHAPTER TWENTY-THREE

The night was virtually over when Evie eventually went back to bed. Even then sleep wouldn't come. Her mind raced with the thought that some people gave and some people took, and those who took never knew when to stop. They could bleed others dry.

Those who gave often did so when they could ill afford to do it. And often to those less in need. Byron was one who gave. Bobby gave, and Gertie.

The takers, even when so much was given to them, never did seem happy. Father never had been. She didn't think there was a more unhappy man in the whole world. He'd trampled on others to gain personal possessions and money, and he'd antagonised everybody.

Evie slept at last, but it seemed no time at all before she heard Kitty come in with their morning tea. Byron was asking the maid in a low voice not to draw the curtains as she usually did.

Evie yawned and turned over.

'I didn't want to disturb you.'

'I was awake.'

Byron was solicitous. 'Have your tea, then try and go back to sleep. You were reading half the night.'

'More than half.' Already she could feel her indignation stirring again at what Father had done.

Byron said: 'I'll call out doctors for the invalids and then go down to make sure your father's all right. Mrs Minto can put some food together for him. Something that can be easily warmed up.'

'You're far too concerned about his welfare.'

Evie had hardened her heart. She told him what she'd found out from her mother's diaries and from Matilda. It brought another rush of anger.

'I'm getting up. I'll come down with you, I'm going to let him know what I think of him.'

'He's an old man and he's sick.'

'You're too soft. He had no thought for anybody else. What he did to my mother was despicable. He walked all over me when I was young. I'm going to let him know I've got his measure now.'

Evie climbed out of bed. 'But I'm not going to rush. We'll have breakfast as we usually do, and I'll see to Matilda.'

Matilda was drowsy. She drank the tea but took little interest in the porridge. Evie tried to feed her, but couldn't get her to take much. She ordered a fire to be lit in the old woman's bedroom and asked Mrs Minto to make her some soup for lunch.

When she went downstairs, Byron was on the phone, asking the local doctor to call and see Matilda. Then he rang Dr McDonald, whose surgery was round the corner from the pharmacy, and asked him to call on Joseph Hobson.

Evie collected the carpet bag she'd promised to return and the basket of food Mrs Minto had packed. Byron drove into town. When he pulled up outside the pharmacy, everything seemed as it should be. It was open for business, and Miss Lister and her assistant were behind the counter that sold toiletries. There were plenty of customers.

Evie was inside the shop before she heard the coughing and realised that her father was in what had once been the dentist's room. The door had been removed and dispensing was now done in there.

'He had the shop open before I got here,' Miss Lister whispered.

Evie was astounded. There was a customer waiting to consult him.

She went to his counter. 'Father, you aren't well enough to work.'

'So you're qualified to decide that?' He looked and sounded sour. He'd cut himself shaving, his face was grey and his chin had a bluish tinge.

'You were ill last night.' Byron was beside her. 'So ill you didn't open the shop yesterday.'

'All the more reason for me to work today. I've got customers to attend to.'

'I've asked the doctor to call and see you.'

'You've no business to do any such thing! I'm seeing no doctor. Don't believe in them. I've got all the medicines here and I know more about them than they do.' He lifted his mortar and pestle and started to pound. 'You can tell him not to bother coming here.'

'Come upstairs, Father,' Evie said firmly. 'I want to talk to you.'

'I've a shop to run. Say what you've got to say and get out. I can't be doing with you in here now.'

She said in a deliberately loud and clear voice:

'I came to tell you that I read my mother's diaries last night. The diaries you hid from me. I know now what you did . . .'

He abandoned any pretence of work and clutched at her arm. 'Be quiet!'

His fingers were biting into her flesh as he led her towards the stairs. Evie climbed up so quickly she left him behind. He didn't have much strength. She was glad to see Byron following. Once in the living room, he closed the door.

'I know what a cheat and a liar you are. I took her diaries . . .'

'I knew you were taking more than that bag from my cupboard,' Joseph blustered. 'You've no business to take anything. That's theft.'

'Don't accuse me of theft. I took what I believed I had a right to. My mother's diaries and the bag she tried to give me the day she died. You didn't want me to read those diaries, did you? They explained too much. Much more than you wanted me to know.'

'Of my personal concerns, not yours. I didn't want you involved. I didn't want you to worry about your mother's madness or be afraid that you might go mad too.'

Evie swallowed hard. That almost deflected her. She didn't know anything about any madness.

She said: 'The pharmacy belonged to my mother, not to you. You stole it from her. But she willed it to me. It's my inheritance.'

Byron put in: 'When she died, the will was never produced. Probate was never applied for. That's how you've managed to keep it.'

'She was not in sound mind when she had that will drawn up,' Joseph retorted. 'It was null and void.'

At that moment there was a tap on the door. Miss Lister called:

'Dr McDonald's here to see you, Mr Hobson.'

He snatched open the door. 'Get rid of him. I don't want the likes of him here.'

'I asked him to come,' Byron said. 'I'm going to bring him up. You aren't well enough to work yet.'

Evie went to the window, her heart pounding. She was afraid this wasn't going to settle anything. Her father was as hard as nails.

Byron brought the doctor in.

'Good morning, Mr Hobson.' He put his bag on a chair and opened it. 'How are you?'

'Get out,' Joseph said. 'I didn't ask you to come. I don't need a doctor.'

'Do be reasonable,' Byron put in. 'He's here now, you might as well let him check you over. You know you were ill over the weekend.'

'I noticed you didn't open your shop yesterday.'

'Then it would have been more appropriate to call then. I'm better now.'

'I'm glad to hear you're feeling better, but you don't look well. Was it flu? There's a lot of it about just now. Perhaps if I could listen to your chest . . .'

'No! Go, can't you?'

Dr McDonald was closing his bag. 'I'm sorry you don't think I can help. I'd advise rest in bed for another day or two. You might find your temperature goes up again tonight . . .'

'Get out.' Joseph's face was going purple. Evie saw the doctor turn without another word. Byron followed him downstairs to see him out.

'I don't think that was very wise,' Evie said. 'We won't be able to get him to come back, not after that.'

Joseph had sunk on to a chair. He looked depressed and ill.

She went on quietly: 'I'm not surprised you're a lonely old man. You rave and kick at everybody. You cheated my mother, but I'm not going to let you cheat me. Not any longer. I'm going to apply for probate on my mother's will.'

Byron came back.

'Did that scoundrel ask for his fee?' Joseph turned on him. 'I bet he did.'

'I thought he was entitled to it,' Byron said stiffly.

'Let's go.' Evie was impatient.

'This is getting us nowhere,' she told him grimly as she headed for Polly Darty's shop. They had to wait for Polly to finish serving a customer, then she turned to them with a smile.

'I hear your father's down in the shop this morning. From what you said, I thought he was at death's door last night.'

'So did we,' Byron said. 'Wouldn't let the doctor near him. But he thought he'd probably had flu and was now on the mend.'

'And Matilda?'

'Not on the mend yet,' Evie said sadly. 'She won't be coming back to work.'

'Well, she must be eighty, poor old thing.' Polly was wrapping up a cream cake for Evie to take to her. Evie hadn't the heart to tell her she didn't think Matty would eat it.

'I think I've found someone to take her place. I told you I'd have a think, didn't I? Do you know Eliza Cryer from Parkfield Avenue? About fifty? She kept house for John Martin, the tripe dealer in Lowe Street. He died last month.'

Evie shook her head: she didn't.

'I haven't spoken to her yet, but her husband was in for bread earlier on. He said she was looking for another job, and he'd tell her to come round.

'Speak of the devil, here she is. Good, you can talk to her now.'

Evie thought the woman looked very capable. Grey-haired and angular, she hoped she'd be strong enough to stand up to her father. She'd brought excellent references with her. Evie studied them in the cake shop.

'Just the person,' Byron said. 'Let's take her next door and settle this.'

Joseph was still sitting in the living room when they

went back. Even he had to accept that he needed help in the house. He agreed to Mrs Cryer and seemed pleased that she didn't intend to live in.

Satisfied that they'd done all they could, Evie and Byron went home after that. As the car turned into the drive, the doctor Byron had called for Matilda was just going up the front steps.

Evie showed him up to her bedroom and told him her symptoms. Matilda was hot and feverish and still drowsy. He looked down her throat.

'Another case of influenza,' he said. 'There's a lot of it about. It can be nasty.'

He listened to her chest. 'She's very chesty, I'm afraid. I fear for the very old. There's not a lot that can be done to stop it running its course.

'Keep her warm and give her plenty to drink. Light meals if she'll take them. She'll need an expectorant for her chest and aspirin for the aching limbs.'

Evie went to lie down on her bed after lunch. Her eyes were heavy and she was sure she'd sleep in the chair if she stayed downstairs, but once upstairs she was overcome with curiosity. Her mother's bag was by her bed where she'd left it. It looked shabby and smelled faintly of mildew. Her heart went out to Helen. She couldn't stop herself delving into the bag. She had to know more.

She drew out several envelopes. Her fingers shook as she untucked the flap of the largest and took out her mother's will. It cut her to the quick, took her back to that awful day when Helen had come to the shop. Making her relive all she'd felt then.

'I bequeath to my daughter Evelina . . .'

Tears clouded her eyes so she could read no more. If only she'd known. If only she'd received this when her mother had first brought it. She might have had a very different life.

She drew out another envelope. She saw it was addressed to Miss Evelina Hobson, and her heart seemed to turn over. It had been ripped open already. That could only mean that Father had read it. And, having read it, decided he didn't want her to do so. With a lump in her throat, she started to read.

My darling daughter,

I'm sure you must think I turned my back on you; that I went away without a second thought, abandoning you when you were a tot of six. Nothing could be further from the truth. Please don't think ill of me. I loved you dearly.

The truth is, I tried hard to take you with me. I pleaded with your father to allow it over several days. I stated the case for it over and over.

Bill wanted me to go away with him. I loved him and wanted that too, but I didn't want to go without you. Bill knew I wouldn't be happy without you, that I was being torn in two. We both pleaded for custody of you. Where is the sense in separating mother and child?

I was in a terrible state by this time, and hardly knew what I was doing. Twice I tried to escape with you but both times your father caught me and eventually he threw me out of the house.

I was in an overemotional state by this time, unable to get the words out or stop my tears. The next night Bill went alone to plead on my behalf. I was waiting outside because I couldn't face your father again. I was so sure Bill would do it better that I let him go in alone.

Evie, he never did come out again! Of that I am certain now. I waited outside, growing more and more desperate. I did hear voices raised in anger at one stage but only for a few moments. Mostly it was quiet.

I never saw Bill Smith again after that. I had been so uplifted, so overjoyed to have him return to me that to have him gone again so quickly seemed viciously cruel.

I knocked and rang the bell to get in then. Joseph ignored me for a long time but eventually came down and told me to make less noise. He accused me of being hysterical and said I'd disturb the neighbours.

He swore, first of all, that Bill had never gone in. I told him I'd seen him enter with my own eyes. Then he said he must have made off the back way in order to avoid me. I knew he wouldn't do that.

I've always been a little afraid of your father, but at that moment I was terrified. Of what he'd done to Bill and what he might do to you.

I ran to the police station in Brandon Street. I needed help and thought that the best place to seek it. I was hysterical with terror.

When I started to tell my story, they were sympathetic, but I couldn't tell it clearly. I told them about Bill, my first husband, being wrongly reported as killed in action. Of how he'd come back to look for me and found I had a child from a subsequent marriage. I told them how strangely your father had behaved. That he'd kept me a virtual prisoner for years and that I feared for the child he refused to give up.

I told them of how I'd been pleading for your custody until I could stand it no more. That Bill had gone in alone to plead one last time and had not come out.

I told them I thought Joseph had killed him. I think that stretched their credence too far. They didn't believe me then. I heard one mutter something about it being a far-fetched story. But I made such a fuss, demanding that a policeman should return with me to face Joseph and search the premises, that one eventually came.

The living room had been newly cleaned and tidied. Joseph was well in command of himself and put on a good performance. He told them I had strange obsessions that had upset our family life for years. He'd had to keep me at home for my own safety. He was always worried when I went out alone. He told them I wasn't capable of caring for my child. He'd had to employ help for some time. He said that I had delusions and was touched with madness.

At that moment perhaps I was. I raved at him that it was all untrue. With hindsight I don't know how I expected anyone to believe me. Joseph's story sounded so much nearer the truth.

A doctor was sent for and Joseph went through his version again. I heard him say so many times that he'd let Bill out the back way because he'd specially asked him to that I came to believe it must have happened. Joseph tied me up in knots. I was confused and didn't know what to believe.

The doctor gave me some pills and told me he'd arrange for me to have a good rest in hospital. That it would do me good and I'd soon feel better. The next day, Joseph gave me more pills and ordered a fly to take us to the station. My memory is blurred about what happened next, but I know we went by train. When we arrived, they put me to bed and gave me something to help me sleep.

I don't know how long they kept me asleep. I know, as soon as I stirred, that I was given something to eat and drink and then more pills. It was a long time before I discovered I'd been admitted to the Frensham Lunatic Asylum. They told me it was for my own safety and for that of my child. Once there, I found it impossible to convince anybody I was sane. I spent ten years there.

It was only when I needed treatment for physical illness that I was transferred to another hospital. They told me I had consumption, and I was sent then to a sanatorium, where they tried to restore me to health. I now know I cannot live much longer. I have no strength left.

I don't think I was ever mentally ill. I spent some of the years in that institution helping those who were, and I don't believe I was like them. Do not fear that it could be your inheritance from me. I think it suited Joseph to pay them to keep me there. I think he knew I would never live with him again from choice.

I have grieved endlessly for Bill. I've had many years to think about what happened on that dreadful night. He would not have walked out on me after waiting for ten years to be reunited. Had he been still alive, I'm sure he'd have found me in that asylum and rescued me. The only logical explanation I can give is that Joseph killed him and hid his body somewhere on the premises.

Evie dropped the letter and felt an icy shiver go down her spine. This was terrible, worse than anything she could have imagined, but she'd reached the stage when she could believe any ill of her father. She now knew he was an evil man. She picked up the letter to read the last page.

> Dearest Evie, for me, the worst effect of all this is that it deprived me of seeing you grow up. You will be a young woman now and I long to see you again before I die, even though I will have to brave seeing Joseph too. I want you to understand how things were for me and to make my peace with you.
>
> I want you to know that not one day has passed that I haven't thought of you and longed to be near you.
>
> Your loving mother,
> Helen Kathleen Hobson.

When she'd finished reading, Evie felt as though her heart would break. She curled up on her bed and cried for her mother. She understood now the agonies she must have suffered.

She was so tired, she fell into an uneasy doze, and the next thing she knew was that Byron was sitting beside her on the bed.

'It's four thirty and Daisy's home,' he told her. 'I didn't want you to sleep too long, or you won't sleep tonight.' He put a cup of tea in her hand.

Evie's mind was still on her mother. She poured out the awful details she'd read and saw the horror on Byron's face. Then she pressed the letter on Byron so he could read it for himself.

'I know the full story now,' Evie said slowly.

'Not quite.' Byron had a perplexed frown on his face. 'Even Helen didn't know what had happened to Bill Smith.'

Evie shivered. 'I can't bear the thought . . . Do you think my father killed him?'

'Perhaps Helen was mistaken about that,' Byron said. 'Don't worry about it.'

Later that night, Byron and Evie were getting ready for bed. Byron had found time to read Helen's story. He was shocked.

'What she must have gone through. Locked away from the world, unable to get out, parted from her child. It shows your father in a terrible light.'

'He's evil.' Evie shuddered. 'I'm not going to help him, not now I know what he did.'

'You've already done all that's needed. He's up and working again.'

'Bertie Pugh's even found a newly trained chemist to help him in the shop. A Mr Almond. He's going to start on Monday. I don't know how long he'll stay. He was told he'd be in sole charge.'

'You've done your best. Your father's going to do things his way. The best thing is to forget him.'

'I can't forget what he did to my mother. He isn't going to get away with that.'

'Don't fight him, love. I don't want you to be bitter. He's not worth it.'

Evie had already made up her mind. 'He took the pharmacy from my mother. She wanted me to have it. I'm going to take it from him.'

Byron said, 'Of course do that. Why shouldn't you? I've looked at the will. She owned the property as well as the business. She left everything to you. There was a note with it that she had a savings account at the bank in her own name. She also had a joint current account with Joseph. I expect he'll not give up anything from that without a fight.'

He took the will from the envelope again and spread it out. Her eyes caught the words:

'I Helen Kathleen Hobson, being of sound mind . . .'

'Was she of sound mind? Father says she wasn't.'

'At the time it was drawn up, yes. The solicitor – what what was his name?'

'Myerscough.'

'He must have believed she was. She appointed her bank as executors. Joseph didn't tell them she'd died, so they didn't apply for probate.'

'So I can do that now?'

'I don't see why not. It'll take a little longer than it would have done at the time.'

Evie smiled. 'I'm looking forward to telling Father that the pharmacy is mine. He won't like that. He must have wanted it very badly to do what he did.'

'What will you do with it?'

'Sell it.'

'He's refusing to move out. He was very determined about that.'

'If he wants to go on running it and living there, he'll have to pay me rent. Can I claim for all those years he's had it, when it was legally mine?'

'You'll have to ask the solicitor about that.'

Matilda didn't improve. The doctor came to see her again. He said her chest was worse. Evie had already noticed that she was having difficulty in breathing. That night she looked in on the old woman when she was going to bed at eleven o'clock. Matty seemed a little better, more animated. She thanked Evie for taking her in.

The next morning, Kitty came bursting into their bedroom. She'd found Matilda dead when she'd taken in her morning tea.

\* \* \*

It took the best part of two years to prove the will and for the solicitor to negotiate a settlement with Joseph Hobson. Evie didn't go near him in all that time, but she knew from Gertie Collins that Mrs Cryer was still keeping house for him and Mr Almond was still helping in the pharmacy.

When it came to the settlement, Joseph agreed, rather than moving out, to pay rent to Evie and to hand over a substantial sum to compensate her for loss of rent for the years since her mother had died.

'It's ridiculous,' she fumed to Byron. 'He's sixty-nine, well over retirement age. How much longer does he think he can go on?'

'You won't change him. Let him be,' Byron advised. 'You've got what you wanted.'

Evie found that less rewarding than she'd expected.

'It's come too late for me, hasn't it? It would have meant the world at the time of Mother's death, but now . . . I don't need more money.'

'There must be something you want to do with it.'

'Yes.' She'd been thinking it over for the past two years and had already made up her mind.

Bobby still came every week to have a meal with them. Often now it was Sunday lunch, and usually he brought Sylvia with him. They were engaged and still saving to get married.

This Sunday, when the meal was over and Byron suggested a walk down to the river, Evie asked Bobby to stay behind.

She took him into the room they used as a study and laid out all the documents she'd received from Mr Myerscough about the pharmacy.

'What's all this, Mam?'

'You know all about my mother leaving me the

pharmacy in her will, and how Joseph hung on to it. Well, this is the money he's finally had to pay to compensate me.'

Bobby whistled through his teeth. 'As much as that?'

'Do you know what I'm going to do with it?' She could see him trying to puzzle that out. 'I want you to have it and to take over ownership of the pharmacy.'

'Me?' His eyes opened in wonderment. 'Why?'

'Byron and I are very comfortable. We can afford to give Daisy a good start. Queenie and Norman are making a success of that business, but you're still struggling.'

'You offered . . .'

'And you were proud and you refused. You didn't want money that had come from Byron. Well, this hasn't. It's come from my side of the family, so there's no reason why it should offend you. I want you to have it.'

She could see he was tempted, but he was still cogitating.

'I don't know anything about running a pharmacy. I'm not trained to do it.'

'Your grandfather's going to carry on doing that.'

'But he won't be able to for much longer.'

'Then it can be sold.' Evie paused. 'I could look for a buyer now, but I can't just put him out. I want you to take this money, and have the rent in the meantime. I know what it's like to be poor. To want things you can't afford. There's no need for you to do that, Bobby.'

He grinned at her then. 'I'm daft, aren't I? Queenie thinks I am.'

'Byron and I . . . we admire people who stick to their principles, but this doesn't go against them. There's no reason to refuse.'

'No,' he said. 'Thanks, Mam.'

She hesitated. 'What will you do with it?'

'You know already. I want to get married. Set up home.'

★ ★ ★

Evie took Bobby to her solicitor and had the pharmacy legally made over to him. On Byron's advice, Bobby appointed an agent to act as an intermediary between him and his grandfather. He saw the business accounts regularly. Byron checked them through for him and confirmed that Joseph was managing well.

When Evie knew her father had turned seventy, she began to worry.

'I can't let him stay there for ever,' she said to Byron. 'He's too old to be working. I'm going to tell him so.'

'It won't get you anywhere,' Byron told her. 'Leave him be.'

'Surely he'll want to retire? Take things easier?'

'He's determined not to move out of that place.'

'I can't sell it until he does. I'll put it to him. Get him to move, if I can. Better all round.'

'I'll come with you,' Byron said. 'I don't want you going there alone.'

'You're not afraid I'll disappear like Bill Smith?'

He smiled, but said: 'I'm not going to risk it.'

They went when the shop was open. Now it had been modernised, there wasn't much to remind Evie of her early days there. Only the medicinal smell, and the four onion-shaped glass carboys filled with coloured water that remained in the side window.

Her father looked older than his years, bent and wizened. When he saw her, he said straight away:

'You'd better come upstairs. No point in letting every-body know our business.' He was much slower getting up than he'd once been.

Nothing had changed upstairs. The living room hadn't even been given a coat of paint. It was neat and clean, and there was a fire in the grate.

Father hadn't changed either. The first thing he did was to send Mrs Cryer out to do some shopping. Then he invited them to sit at the dining table covered with the shabby chenille cloth she remembered so well.

'Now then, what d'you want?' he said to Evie. She told him that Bobby was now his landlord, that she had handed over the business and property to him some time ago.

Joseph's lips tightened. She knew he'd hated having to relinquish that. 'I know. Agent told me.'

'You look tired, Father.' He looked pathetic. She felt a stirring of sympathy, though she'd told Byron she didn't mean to be kind.

'Yes, I'm tired. The shop's busier than ever and it's a long day for one of my years.'

'That's what I've come to talk about.' Evie was grateful Joseph had brought it up himself. 'Bobby would like to sell this place. Wouldn't you like to retire? It's really too much for you now. We'd help you move to a small cottage. You could take things easier.'

'No.' She watched him feel for a chair and lower himself on to it. 'This has been my home and my business all my life. I'm not moving now.'

'But why not? You say you're tired . . .'

'I'm not moving and that's the end of the matter. He's getting his rent. He's nothing to complain about. I'm keeping my side of the bargain.'

'I thought if you retired . . .'

'I decide when I'll retire. That's not up to you.'

Evie stood up. She could see she was never going to budge him.

Byron smiled as he opened the car door for her to get in.

'Told you so. Something's keeping him here. Bobby will have to let him get on with it.'

# CHAPTER TWENTY-FOUR

*February 1939*

Evie was sitting at her dressing table, dusting her cheeks with face powder. It was her forty-seventh birthday, a fact that was making her take stock of herself.

There were lines fanning out from the corners of her eyes now, but they were only noticeable when she smiled. Her hair had lost some of its colour but she wore it fashionably short and waved close to her head, and it suited her.

Her new red wool dress suited her too, with its long, swirling skirt. She wasn't as slim as she used to be, but she hadn't put on too much weight. She wasn't displeased with her reflection. She was wearing well. She pinned the cameo brooch, Byron's birthday gift, to her dress.

'You look more beautiful than ever,' he told her when she went down to the sitting room. It was a Sunday, and the scent of roasting beef was coming from the kitchen. The table was set for nine in the dining room. The children would be arriving any minute now.

Byron put a glass of sherry in her hand and raised his own to her. Evie was taking stock of her circumstances as she sipped it. She was very happy with Byron. They were rarely apart. She loved him dearly and couldn't imagine life without him.

Here, only the immediate family knew she wasn't his wife, and that made things easier. But it was the one thing she still wanted. She still wore Ned's wedding ring, but above everything else she wanted to wear one from Byron.

Apart from that, and the threat of war that was hanging over everyone, she thought that the thirties had been good to her.

Finding her mother's diaries had been traumatic. It had taken her some time to recover from the shock of learning the truth about her parents.

'I'm glad you haven't let it fill you with hate,' Byron said. 'Your father's an evil man, selfish beyond belief, depraved even. He wanted power over others but he's getting old, he no longer has his strength.'

'He fears others now. He even fears me. As if I'd harm him.'

'Ned helped you escape his influence while you were young. It was the best thing that could have happened to you. Living with a man who made demands like that was bound to increase your anxieties, but you got away before he did any lasting damage.'

Evie felt better now she knew the truth; she felt she'd laid the ghosts. She smiled sadly. 'But we still don't know everything. Did Bill Smith walk out on my mother? Such a cruel thing to do just when she needed him most. Or did Father . . . ?'

'You'll probably never know that.'

While Byron browsed through the Sunday papers, Evie reached for the field guide on birds which had been Daisy's gift to her. The garden here was full of them and she'd wanted to put a name to the species she could see.

Dear Daisy, thought Evie fondly. She was enjoying her third child. She'd been so much easier to cope with than the older two. Daisy was always happy. When she was seventeen and still at school, she'd announced her intention of training to be a chemist.

'There's a turn-up for the books,' Byron had chuckled. He adored Daisy too. 'It must be in your blood. You take after your mother's family. You'll be wanting to take over the pharmacy when your grandfather retires?'

'Not necessarily.' Daisy had smiled. 'Pharmacy's just something I want to do.'

She'd been training at Boots for some time. She was outside now, washing the Austin Seven they'd given her for Christmas, so that she could drive herself to work.

Evie heard another car pull into the drive and knew Queenie and Norman had arrived. It was a few moments before the bell rang. She could see them talking to Daisy. Byron went to let them in.

'Hello, Mam, happy birthday.' Queenie's kiss was a formal peck. Evie didn't feel as close to her as she would have liked. Queenie was very elegant these days, as well as being beautiful. She said she was happy, that she didn't care for children and didn't want any of her own; that she much preferred to manage the business. But there was a brittleness in her manner, and Evie wasn't totally convinced that that was so.

Norman followed three steps behind like a consort, with a ledger and a file under his arm. It was quite evident that Queenie was the driving force in the marriage. They came over every month or so, usually bringing the accounts of Henry Ball and Sons to show Byron, though he'd made the business over to them several years ago. They consulted him on major decisions and showed him the books regularly, and that pleased him. He still wanted to feel involved. He said that Queenie was making an excellent job of managing the firm, and generating more profit than he ever had.

Evie was unwrapping chocolates and champagne from them when Queenie said:

'We told you we were looking for a house in Oxton? We've found one we like. We'll be moving out of the flat.'

'We knew you would sooner or later,' Byron said. 'You've made no secret of that.'

Evie could hear Daisy coming in through the back door with Bobby and Sylvia. Bobby had two small sons now, Roger who was three and Paul who had recently had his first birthday. Bobby had bought a house in Heswall only some fifteen minutes' walk away. They often walked over with the children. Evie adored the little boys.

Bobby's cheek felt cold as he bent to kiss her. Evie couldn't get over how like Ned he was. He seemed very happy and very settled now, and was still working for the bank in Birkenhead.

Kitty came to tell them that dinner was ready. Evie led the way to the table. She really enjoyed having all her family round her.

Byron was worried by the steady approach of war. He knew only too well what it would do to the business of Henry Ball and Sons.

He talked to Norman and Queenie about how he expected exports to dry up as Britain's industries geared up for war. There'd still be imports if British ports could be kept open, but all shipping would run the gauntlet of the German navy. Imports would be cut to the basic essentials needed for survival. The business would shrink but staff would melt away too. They must be ready to expand again when the war was over.

Norman was likely to be called up. Byron tried to impress on Queenie that it would be up to her to see that the business survived.

War was declared at the beginning of September, and men of Norman's age were being called up even before that.

Things happened just as Byron had predicted. Norman got his call-up papers. His training gave him a commission and a desk job in the Pay Corps.

'He's lucky,' Evie told Queenie. 'He won't be in danger there.'

Norman was sent to Aldershot for nine months and was then posted to Chester. He didn't like army life. He bought himself an MG Midget and was able to get home regularly. Queenie found she could cope with the business.

As Evie had expected, Bobby was found to be medically unfit to serve in the forces. The old injury to his ankle had left him with a limp.

She was profoundly grateful now that he'd had that accident with Wilf Hutchins' bike. She felt it might well save his life. She couldn't forget that Ned and all his brothers had lost their lives in the last war. Sylvia whispered that she was relieved too.

Bobby said he wasn't pleased, but Evie knew he was torn in two. He didn't want to go away and leave his wife and young sons, but on the other hand it troubled him that he wasn't able to go and fight for his country. When he saw his colleagues and friends in uniform, he said he was afraid he'd be sent the white feather.

'You're no coward,' Evie told him.

Bobby enrolled with the Civil Defence and said he'd do as much as he could on the home front. He was soon involved in training, in building up resources and in enforcing precautions. After hearing Bobby's account of what he was doing, Byron decided he'd enrol in the Civil Defence and do his bit too. Evie, not to be outdone, joined the WRVS.

When the air raids started in earnest in the autumn of 1940, Evie was glad Queenie had moved out of the flat at the top of the Connaught Building. It was said that the enemy were aiming for the docks on both sides of the water, trying to put them out of action. Evie thought that Heswall, being on the River Dee, was much safer, and even Oxton was a lot less dangerous than central Liverpool.

The Connaught Building received minor damage almost immediately. Its windows were blown in. During the Christmas raids, there was damage to the roof. That had only just been repaired when in March, bomb blast weakened one corner and offices at the rear of the building were no longer usable. Bulwark Insurance moved out.

Then, in the May raids of 1941, the Connaught Building received a direct hit and a land mine devastated most of the rest of South Castle Street.

That news left Evie shaking. It was a night raid, and if Queenie had been living in the flat she'd have been killed. As it happened, the caretaker they'd installed had been so frightened by its position, and the fact that there were so few other people around at night, that she spent most nights with her daughter in Bootle and had therefore managed to survive too.

Although Evie saw Queenie and Norman every few weeks, and knew that the house they'd bought was close to Veronica's and that she took them out for a meal in a restaurant every Saturday evening, they never mentioned her when they came over. Byron had let them know that he didn't want news of her.

It came as something of a shock to find them on the doorstep very late one night. Evie was putting away her knitting before going up to bed. Norman's face was ghostly pale.

'It's Mother,' he said with an agonised catch in his voice. 'I thought you'd want to know.'

'What's happened?' Byron brought them to the fire. It had burned low. He tried to poke it into a blaze.

'She went to London,' Queenie told them. 'She said she needed to get away.'

'To London?' Byron sounded incredulous. 'Now, when it's being bombed?'

'She said we're being bombed here so what's the difference?' Norman took out his handkerchief and mopped his face anxiously.

'Everybody else goes to the country. Peaceful nights are what we all crave.'

'She said she was bored. She wanted to go to the London theatres and shops.' He blew his nose.

'She's been hurt?' Evie asked.

'She missing.' Norman sniffed into his handkerchief. 'I'm afraid she's been killed.'

Evie felt a flush run up her cheeks. Byron had told her years ago that Veronica had sneered at him: 'Don't set your mind on marrying your fancy woman, because you'll have to wait until I'm dead.'

Evie couldn't feel sorry now that it seemed she was, but Norman was upset. He'd been close to his mother. Byron got to his feet and poured some brandy for him.

'Veronica stays at her club,' Queenie explained. 'It's really just a place for women on their own. She's given up the luxury hotels. She went out one evening and never returned.'

'Where did she go?' Byron asked. 'That night?'

'To a show, they think. With another woman who was staying there. They left before dark and neither has ever come back. The first alert came early that evening, and there were very heavy casualties during the night. A direct hit on an air-raid shelter near Leicester Square, and two theatres badly damaged.' Queenie did not appear to be upset. Evie thought there'd never been much love lost between her and Veronica.

'When they hadn't returned to their club by the next day, the manager rang the police. The beds hadn't been slept in, all her clothes, her luggage was there. It seemed she meant to return.'

'They've been combing through those injured that night and admitted to hospitals.' Norman's hand trembled slightly as he reached again for the brandy. 'Mother isn't amongst them. It seems that many were killed that night who couldn't be identified.'

'Norman thought of going down to London,' Queenie added. 'But I've persuaded him not to. They've packed her belongings up and are sending her cases back.'

Byron poured himself a brandy when they'd gone. 'Trust Veronica to make things difficult. We don't really know, but I think we can safely presume she's been killed.'

By September 1940, Bobby felt he had plenty to do. During the day, he was kept busy in the bank because so many of the staff had been called up. During the hours of darkness, he had his Civil Defence duties. Air raids were often coming on consecutive nights. After a bad night, the little sleep he managed to get was in his office chair with his head on his desk. He washed in the staff cloakroom until the water mains were damaged and there was no more water.

The night the Argyle Theatre went on fire was terrifying. The bombers had been coming over in waves ever since nightfall. An air-raid shelter had received a direct hit, and he'd been doing what he could to dig out those who had survived. He felt sick with shock from that, and when his fellow workers pointed out a huge and growing fire in the night sky, and told him that incendiary bombs had fallen on the famous Argyle Theatre, he was relieved to hear that it was thought everybody had managed to get out.

He stood for a moment watching the theatre going up like a tinder box, and couldn't help thinking of all the good shows he'd seen there. Then it came to him that his pharmacy was only a short distance down the street and might have been damaged too.

Bobby knew that his mother had tried to persuade Joseph to move out, to get right away from the town centre. Mam asked him often if he'd been to see if the shop was all right. He knew it wasn't the shop that bothered her. If that was damaged by enemy action, he'd be given compensation.

He felt he had to check that his grandfather was all right. Argyll Street was busier than he'd ever seen it, teeming with fire crews, and the leaping flames were lighting up the street like day.

When Bobby reached the pharmacy, he saw that both shop windows had been blown in, and some of the upper windows too. There was glass everywhere, but he could see no other damage. He hammered on the door and had to wait an age for his grandfather to come. At last Joseph opened the door six inches.

'It's not safe here,' Bobby shouted. The blood was coursing through his veins. The blaze was awesome and there was chaos all round.

'You should be in a shelter. Get some shoes on and a warm coat, and I'll take you.'

The door opened another few inches, Joseph was wearing an old dressing grown over striped pyjamas, and seemed sleep-fuddled and confused.

Bobby had to draw the old man out on to the pavement to see the blazing inferno before he understood.

'Come on,' he urged. 'Quickly.'

'I can't, not with the windows gone. The place will be looted if I leave it.'

'I'll see it's boarded up. Made safe.'

'I'm not leaving. If I'm going to die I might as well do it in my own bed.'

'I'm ordering you to a shelter,' Bobby told him firmly. 'You've got to go, it isn't safe here. The place is lit up like day. The next wave of enemy aircraft will . . .'

Joseph stepped back and slammed the door before Bobby could stop him. That took his breath away. He hammered on the door again and shouted. Then he heard the bolts being slid home, and gave up.

The theatre was gutted, and what remained had to be pulled down to make it safe. There was a great empty space there afterwards. The pharmacy survived, and Joseph opened for business the next day.

As the months went on, Bobby felt there was no let-up. Even when there were no raids he had to take his turn on duty and be ready if he should be called out. He slept at home in his own bed when he could.

Christmas 1940 was a terrible time. The bombers came over every night. The building where Bobby worked was damaged, and although the bank continued to open for business, the window of his office was boarded up and he sometimes had to work by the light of a candle.

He felt stretched almost beyond his strength, but he had to keep going, do what he could for the hundreds who were buried beneath buildings that had collapsed and who needed urgent rescue. For him, it became commonplace to see the dead and the terribly injured and those who stared in numbed shock at homes and belongings that were reduced to rubble.

Every morning, after the all clear sounded, he went home to take a bath before going to the bank. Evie and Sylvia said they were fearful for him, being in the centre of Birkenhead and close to Cammel Laird's, the ship builders.

But he was equally fearful for their safety. He needed to see them and know that his own world was still safe.

January and February were not too bad on his side of the water, though he saw fire raging along the Liverpool skyline several times. Sometimes the flames were still visible twenty-four hours later. A ferry boat was sunk at her moorings. Other ships in the river and in the docks were damaged. Work went on tirelessly to keep the port open.

In March, the enemy bombers were coming over every night again. After the fifth very busy night Bobby felt exhausted.

When he heard the air-raid warning yet again on the sixth night, followed by the throb of enemy engines above, he felt he could bear no more. His eyes ached as he watched the searchlights cut swaths through the night sky, trying to track the enemy planes.

For Bobby that was the worst night of the blitz. Henry Street received a whole stick of high-explosive bombs. He'd been given charge of a rescue party and they worked for hours digging out people trapped under the rubble of their houses. He couldn't remember ever seeing so much carnage. His hands were sore with dragging at fallen beams, his eyes were prickly with grit and his mouth caked with dust. When there were no further signs of life beneath the debris and the last ambulance had departed, Bobby reclaimed the old bicycle he was using to get about.

The all clear had sounded. He was cycling along Argyle Street on the way back to his office. The road was filled with great chunks of masonry, plaster, bricks and broken glass. Debris of all kinds. After a heavy raid, there was a lot of clearing up to do.

He had to dismount to push his bike round the worst of it, and glanced up. He went cold when he saw the pharmacy. Much of the building had gone. It looked like a doll's house with the front folded back. On the ground floor, half the shop remained. On the first floor, it was possible to see into the living room and the kitchen behind it. The stairs were there, going up the wall. Above, he could see inside two bedrooms. He froze with fear, wondering which one his grandfather had been sleeping in.

A rescue party similar to the one he led was working its way towards the pharmacy. It was not Grandfather's shop alone that was damaged, but all the buildings along the side street.

He saw the body immediately. Somebody had covered it. He gritted his teeth and turned back one corner of the blanket. It was what remained of his grandfather. Bobby felt sick. It was so unnecessary. Joseph could have moved somewhere safer.

Mam would be shocked and upset, he knew. He glanced up at the open rooms above him, and for a moment thought he saw another person up against the wall. He looked more carefully; once there'd been a cupboard there. A soldier? Could that be a soldier? He was dressed in khaki. But no . . . Bobby caught his breath. He thought he knew what he was looking at. He could feel the sweat breaking out on his face.

He did something then he wouldn't normally have done. He knew he was endangering his own life. Somebody shouted that it wasn't safe to climb the stairs. He felt them swing beneath his weight. He was so weary he felt light-headed, but he had to find out. Mam wouldn't be able to rest until she knew for certain. He dragged himself up, sliding his back against the wall. He passed a keyboard with only one key hanging on it; a framed photograph hanging askew, showing Grandpa at the height of his boxing skill. Up again to the second floor and into the front bedroom.

The furniture had all slid to the ground, and the bare floor sloped down at an angle. It was unsupported on one side and swayed beneath Bobby's weight. He had to cling to the door frame to keep himself from falling. The cupboards had been blown off the wall. What he'd thought was a body looked very different from here.

Bobby didn't know what to make of it. He could go no nearer. It looked like some parody of Guy Fawkes. A soldier, an officer, with three pips on his shoulder and a Sam Browne belt. A captain then, in the uniform of long ago. The Boer War? The flesh had long since rotted; much of the cloth too. The bones remained, a skeleton that still wore shoes, the soles of which were separating into curling layers of leather.

Bobby felt everything swimming round him. His mother had shown him the diaries, told him the story of his grandmother. He'd found it hard to believe. Now he knew he'd stumbled on evidence of that final act. Evie would have the truth at last. Grandfather had killed Bill Smith and hidden his body in the cupboard being constructed at that time in his bedroom. Bobby knew now why Joseph wouldn't move out of the building.

A fireman had to bring Bobby down by ladder. He couldn't crawl back down those swinging stairs; he was paralysed by shock. Yet it all seemed unreal against the horrors of the night. Once down he vomited amongst the rubble and received a dressing-down for endangering his own life and that of the man who had rescued him.

It was a Sunday morning very early, hardly yet light. He went to Heswall then, straight to his mother's house.

It was the summer of 1942. Byron had taken Evie to

Windermere for their honeymoon. The wedding had been a discreet registry office affair, quieter than quiet. Only their children and their families had been present. He had booked a lunch table at the Adelphi for a party of seven adults and two children afterwards, and then he and Evie had driven up here.

Mrs Minto, who still kept house for them and their new friends in Heswall, thought they were having an ordinary holiday.

Byron felt they'd had a wonderfully peaceful morning walking in the hills. Now, after a lunch that was good considering rationing and all the shortages, they were sitting on the terrace, looking out over the shimmering lake.

He smiled at Evie. He could see here and there a gleam of silver in her dark hair. She was his wife at last. Her eyes were closed against the sun. He saw her smile faintly to herself.

'What are you thinking about?'

He reflected that you had to be truly close to a person to ask that with any hope of getting the truth.

Evie opened her eyes and looked at him gravely. 'That we never truly understand a different generation. My parents acted in a way I find unbelievable. When I think of what my father did, I go cold inside even now. Poor Mother, she had to put up with so much.'

'And as for our children . . .' She shook her head. 'I love them dearly. I admire Bobby and feel close to Daisy. Queenie's a beautiful girl, but . . .'

He laughed. 'The children do things that are no easier to understand?'

Her smile widened. 'I understand you, Byron.' It spread till it lit up her eyes, and the dimple he always watched for was plain to see.

# Mersey Maids

# CHAPTER ONE

*New Year, 1913*

'I wish Pa would come home.' Harriet Knell looked at the clock for the tenth time. The hands showed a minute to midnight. 'He promised he'd be back.'

'It won't be the same without him.' As her younger sister Maggie spoke, the first of the ship's hooters began to sound.

'It's here!' Maggie jumped to her feet, all smiles. 'Happy New Year!'

'Happy?' Hattie laid aside her sewing. 'Thirteen's unlucky anyway.'

'Only for some.' Thirteen-year-old Frances, the third sister, planted a kiss on each of their cheeks. 'Happy New Year.'

'Can't be worse than the last,' Hattie sighed. 'We weren't asked to even one party.'

The Mersey was filled with a cacophony of sound that could be heard for miles around. Every ship moored in the river was now celebrating the start of another year by making as much noise as it could. Sailing ships used their whistles; those with steam let it blow.

'It'll be better, much better,' Maggie insisted when the sound had died away, but Harriet knew they all shared the same sinking feeling that it might not. The front door slammed.

'Who's that?' Fanny leapt to the door to see. 'We must

1

be careful about letting in the new year properly. Not leave it to chance.'

'Not leave it to Pa, you mean. That's what happened last year.'

According to ancient custom, to guarantee a good year, the darkest possible person must come first over the threshold with a piece of coal in his hand.

'Pa's quite the wrong person.' His hair had so little colour, it was only possible to see where silver encroached on platinum blond when he sat right under the gas lamp.

Harriet watched Maggie push her mass of tight creamy waves away from her face. Most of her sisters had inherited his pale colouring.

'And you're no better.' Fanny's hair was much the same, but reached halfway down her back.

'It's like sheep's fleece,' Hattie told them often, to stop them getting too big-headed. She was a little darker than the rest of them. Her hair was pale fawn rather than creamy white, and she wore it up, as became a young lady of eighteen.

'Not you either, Hattie. Your strange eyes would put a jinx on it.'

Hattie knew that her huge green eyes dominated her small face. 'At least I don't have pig's eyelashes, like yours,' she retaliated. 'Long and straight and white.'

Fanny burst back into the kitchen with a young man, her face all smiles.

'It's all right, it's Patrick O'Brien from upstairs. Just the person, positively swarthy.' She brought him in.

It had been Hattie's idea that Pa should rent the whole house and then sublet the rooms upstairs in order to cover the cost of their own. They had the O'Briens on the first floor and the Platts in the attic.

'Happy New Year to you, Patrick.' Hattie could smell beer on his breath.

'Will you bring us luck?' Maggie snatched a piece of coal from the hearth. 'Here, take this and come in again.'

2

'I'll do a good job for you, so I will.' He grabbed the poker and raked out the fire.

'Not too much,' Hattie protested as glowing coals rattled down into the ash can.

'You've got to let the old year out before the new can come in. I used to do this when I was a boy in Dublin. For the neighbours, like. Now then, what's the rhyme I have to say?'

'What rhyme?' Maggie asked.

'There's something we used to chant, about the old year and the ghosts. I don't remember . . .'

'We've never heard of that,' Hattie said. 'Forget it.'

He ran to the front door, flung it open, banged on it with the poker and ran out into the street. He was back in an instant, crashing up the hall, rattling the poker on the stair rails as he passed.

'Not so loud, you'll wake the young ones,' Hattie protested.

'Now the back door. Out into the yard,' Fanny sang out. 'We can't take any chances, not with this year. We need all the luck we can get.'

She followed him out to pick up the black cat curled up inside the wash-house door. It belonged to the family who lived in the attic.

'Black cats are lucky.' She brought it into their kitchen. 'Tibbles should bring us the best year ever.' But the cat fought to free itself and fled squawking upstairs. It made them all laugh.

'Can we close all these doors now?' Hattie wanted to know. 'It's perishing cold.'

'How about a little drink to celebrate?' Patrick O'Brien hiccoughed. 'Now I've let the new year in good and proper for you.'

Harriet went to the teapot in the hearth. 'It's been quite a time, I'm afraid, but it's still fairly hot.'

'Is that all you've got, tea?'

3

'Yes.' Hattie always remained aloof, could never relax when other people came into their rooms.

'In Dublin, as a boy, they used to tip me, so they did. Half a crown and a mince pie. That would be about right.'

Hattie watched Maggie look up in dismay. They hadn't thought of this.

'I can offer you a mince pie.' Maggie opened their cake tin and offered it to him. They'd been keeping the last seven pies as a treat for New Year's Day. One for each of them. Patrick took two.

'I thought, being landlords like, you'd have something nice to drink. Whisky?'

'We can't afford whisky,' Hattie said with disapproval.

Patrick sniggered: 'Your dad can. Bet he's having his fill tonight.'

Hattie felt both her sisters recoil. Papa was drinking more than he used to – hadn't they been talking about it not half an hour back? Not that he was ever drunk, not like Patrick, who was swaying on his feet now. Pa drank just enough to jolly himself up and be his old self for a while. Usually, then, he fell asleep.

'He's working,' Maggie said coldly. Pa worked shifts, so it was always believable, but Hattie knew he wasn't.

'Right, Happy New Year to you then. All the best.'

When the door closed behind him, Hattie felt deflated. Was this all there was to the New Year celebrations? She folded away the pieces of cloth on which they'd been working. To add to their income, she took outwork from a local factory making baby clothes. For four rows of hand-smocking across the bodice of a matinée gown, she was paid three shillings a dozen. She examined Fanny's carefully.

'You're improving,' she told her. Fanny's smocking wasn't always up to the standard required.

'Let's go to bed, I'm tired,' Fanny said. 'I'll fetch our nighties.'

4

Undressing in the kitchen was a routine they'd got into, partly to avoid waking their three younger sisters, and partly because it was warmer here and saved lighting either the gas or a candle.

'We must put the bad things behind us. Forget them. Look forward, not back.' For fifteen of Maggie's sixteen years, family life for the Knells had been ordered and comfortable. Suddenly, last year, everything had gone wrong. 'There's nothing we can do about what's happened.'

'We can't sink any lower.' Harriet looked round the cramped and shabby kitchen with an air of disbelief. In order to seat all the family they had a bench behind the kitchen table instead of chairs. 'We're touching bottom.'

Pa had moved them to this run-down three-storey terraced house in Elizabeth Place when his business collapsed. When he'd been looking for the cheapest possible place to rent.

Hattie hated the continual grind of household jobs she had to do. Hated the single cold tap over the brownstone sink that dripped continually, and was the only place they had to wash. An even greater bugbear to them all was the lavatory out in the yard.

'There's no way we can get away from here now,' she said slowly. 'Without money, we're trapped.'

'We'll all marry rich men,' Fanny giggled. 'Live happily ever after in lovely houses with as much as we want to eat.'

'And where do you think we'll find these rich men? Patrick O'Brien is the only sort we'll meet round here.'

'He's very friendly,' Maggie said. 'And he has big, rippling muscles.'

'He developed those labouring on the docks. He's never going to be rich. And I bet he drinks most of what he earns.'

Maggie lost her patience. 'If you dwell on what might have been instead of what you've got, you'll make things worse. Nothing good will happen to you. You'll always be thinking things could be better.'

'You're an optimist.'

'Yes, well, it would be better if you were too. If we all were. That can be our New Year's resolution. We'll be more optimistic.'

'Come to bed.' Fanny was creeping into the next room. Maggie followed. Hattie paused in the kitchen doorway. From the O'Briens' rooms above, she could hear a quavering voice singing 'Auld Lang Syne'. The sound of shattering glass followed.

Pa was letting himself in through the front door, his shoulders bowed and his face downcast in the half-light.

'Happy New Year, Pa.' She went to kiss his cheek. It felt icy. Her sisters were crowding behind her to do the same. They all adored Pa.

'Shall I make you a hot drink?' Hattie offered, wanting to please him.

'No, off to bed with you. It's very late, and I want to talk to Maggie.'

She felt a rush of disappointment that he wanted Maggie and not her.

Maggie followed Pa into his own room and watched him light the gas lamps. He'd said he wanted to talk, but usually he wanted her to play the piano for him.

Pa's was the bigger of the two rooms they had. Originally it had been the house's main sitting room and was packed tight with furniture: two large wardrobes of fine mahogany, a dressing table, a china cabinet, a bookcase full of books and several chairs. There were boxes and trunks full of belongings piled everywhere.

Hattie had lit a fire for him this morning but he'd gone out before lunch and it had long since died out. Henry Knell raked out some of the ash, and on the spur of the moment pushed the morning's newspaper into the cinders. He achieved a momentary blaze, but the fire didn't catch. Maggie saw him shiver.

6

'Ineffective, that's what I am,' he said. 'Hopelessly ineffective.'

'Nonsense, Pa.' She tried to smile. 'You're tired, that's all.' It hurt to see his self-confidence crumbling. He didn't hold his head up any more and was beginning to shamble round.

Maggie whisked back to the kitchen and collected on to a shovel the glowing embers that remained in the grate. As she bore them at arm's length to Pa's room, she could feel the glow against her face.

'How practical you are,' he said, as she lowered them carefully into his grate and placed a few new coals on top.

'We'll soon have a nice fire now.' Maggie turned towards the piano.

'Where are your slippers and your dressing gown? You'll catch cold like that.'

He fetched his own dressing gown from the foot of his bed and helped her into it. It was big enough to wrap round her twice and felt rough and hairy. His best suit was flung over the bedchair that served as a cot for her younger sisters when they were sick and unwilling to leave him. He pushed his slippers across the hearth rug to her.

'Put them on.'

'It's never cold to the feet here.' Maggie smiled. Rugs were piled on carpets three deep in all their rooms.

'We let the New Year in properly, Pa.'

She threaded her way over to the small upright piano and sat down. They'd been unable to bring the baby grand from the Rock Park house. This one had been in their playroom. Pa had had it retuned for her. She lit the candles in the sconces on each side of her sheet music. Pa said he liked that, it created an illusion. Helped him forget their present circumstances.

Maggie played a few scales to loosen her fingers, and then went straight into a Chopin polonaise, enjoying the ease with which she could create such beautiful music.

7

Pa said her playing soothed him, brought tranquillity and peace to this crowded room. Often, he told her it was the only enjoyment left to him. She was glad she could do this for him, it was her way of pleasing him.

She knew she had a lot more to learn, but lessons were out of the question now. She practised all the time, striving to acquire greater skill, and she lived in hope.

She wasn't given to fantasies, but she had one that kept recurring. She saw herself seated at a grand piano on a concert platform, giving a recital. She could hear herself playing her favourite pieces by Chopin and Liszt and Berlioz. As the last notes died away, the audience was cheering and applauding her, giving her a real ovation. With her music, she was lifting her whole family out of their poverty.

Even in her down-to-earth moments, she was sure she could accompany a singer or another instrument if only she were given half a chance. She'd adore doing anything like that, to earn a little for the family budget.

Maggie felt capable of teaching others. She'd decided to take paying pupils, but the people who lived nearby couldn't afford to feed their children, let alone provide piano lessons for them. And parents who could pay refused to send their children to Elizabeth Place. The streets behind the gasworks had a bad name. Maggie only ever had one paying pupil, and she didn't stay long.

She'd also written to all the private schools within travelling distance, asking if they had a vacancy for a teacher of pianoforte. She did get one interview, but they thought her too young for the job.

She played a piece by Beethoven and felt her spirits soar with the melody. When she came to the end, she realised that Pa was standing behind her. He looked bereft of hope. She knew that for once her playing had not reached him.

He took her hand. 'I really do want to talk to you, Maggie.'

8

She let him lead her back to the fire, and perched on the edge of the chair opposite his.

'What about?'

He was feeling for her other hand too. 'I've found a job for you.'

She felt her heart leap with anticipation. She was the one who ought to be working. 'Oh, good. What sort of a job?'

'I hope you'll be pleased. Mrs Moody is willing to take you on as a nurserymaid.'

It took her breath away. A nurserymaid!

'I think the position might suit you. You're good with children, Maggie. You like them.'

The blood was pounding in her head. She only just stopped herself shouting 'No!' at him. She met Papa's eyes. Eyes of blue like hers. She saw shame and guilt and dread there.

'Daniel Moody used to be a business associate of mine. Mrs Moody's father is Stanley Dransfield, I know him too.'

Maggie thought herself a cut above being a nursery-maid. That was domestic service! It wasn't all that long since they'd employed a nurserymaid themselves. She swallowed hard.

'There's plenty I can do for the children here.'

In the next room, she could hear Ruth, her youngest sister, whimper and Hattie's voice trying to soothe her.

'There's Harriet, you see.' She watched her father tighten his lips. 'We have her to take care of the family, and Fanny's old enough to give a hand now.'

It had always been Harriet's wish, and Pa's intention, that she should stay at home and help with the family. Even before he lost his money. Maggie wanted to refuse to go, but she knew she couldn't. Pa hadn't said so, but it would mean he'd have one mouth fewer to feed. Poor Pa was almost going under with all his troubles.

She and Harriet had been telling themselves they'd put

the worst one of all behind them. It was five years since their mother had died in childbirth with her eighth child. It had been so unexpected it had left them all reeling. Maggie had seen her father weep that night.

'How can I possibly manage without her? We'll all miss her dreadfully. And another child to care for – as if five were not enough.' Their two brothers had already died in infancy.

She and Harriet had clung together in their agony over Pa's tears. They chose the name Ruth for their new sister. They'd thought those first weeks without their mother desperately difficult, yet they'd had a nanny for the new baby, and Aggie, who'd been part housemaid and part nursemaid, as well as a cook. Pa still had his work, and she and her sisters had been settled and contented in Herman House School. It hadn't occurred to them then that things could ever be worse.

Her father went on gently: 'It's an opportunity that might not come again, Maggie. I know this family, you see. They know who you are. It'll make a difference.'

Maggie didn't want to be reminded of Papa's business associates either, because she'd had to watch her father struggle and fail to keep his glove-making business afloat. That had been another terrible disaster. It had happened barely six months ago, and the results were still painfully raw.

'Three generations of Knells have made gloves for a living,' he'd said bitterly. 'What's the matter with me? Why can't I do the same?' More than the rest of them, he felt their reduced circumstances.

When Pa's bankruptcy first threatened, Hattie had whispered that she thought Pa was unable to keep his mind on business matters because he was still grieving for Mama. Now they thought he was losing heart for everything.

Maggie went to her room and climbed into the double bed with her sisters, but she couldn't get to sleep. Fanny's

10

knee was sticking into her back, and all round her she could hear deep and heavy breathing. Despite all they'd done to ensure the new year would be happy, now it looked as though there would be another change for the worse. She felt very fearful.

When Henry Knell had kissed his daughter and sent her off to bed, he stayed leaning against his mantelpiece. It seemed a shame to go to bed now that the fire was blazing up, although he had an early shift in the morning. He was left with a feeling of guilt, that he'd failed Maggie yet again.

He caught sight of himself in the mirror over the grate. He looked an old man, much older than his forty-six years. He felt older, well past his prime.

That made him laugh mirthlessly to himself. His prime had come and gone so quickly, he'd barely noticed it. His father had been a widower, his only interest in life his glove-making business. He'd seemed to think Henry was blessed with eternal youth. His apprenticeship with the family firm had been stretched out to twice the length any other had to serve.

'What are you complaining about?' his father had barked at him. 'The business is paying you a generous salary, isn't it?'

It was, but he wasn't allowed any responsibility. He'd wanted to be more involved in the business.

'You don't understand, Henry. You're young yet. Impatient to be given your head. You need more experience. There's more to learn about making gloves than you realise.'

Knell's Gloves came in at the top of the trade, with the finest leather and the best workmanship. Henry learned all he could. His father had seemed to show, by his lack of trust, that he didn't think much of his ability.

Henry was not allowed even a small say in how the business was run. Worse, any suggestions he made were dismissed out of hand. Father was very conservative. He didn't like new ideas, or even new styles in gloves.

He'd been kept waiting, just as Victoria had kept her Prince of Wales waiting for his throne. He'd been stranded on the sidelines without any power. His prime had come and gone before he'd started.

Henry had found other things to interest him. Found consolation in his wife and family. His whole world had revolved round Edith, and now she'd gone too.

He'd been forty-two when his father had died suddenly, and control was thrust upon him. The business had been thriving when he'd taken it over. It had thrived all the years he could remember. That had been the wonderful thing about Knell's Gloves: it could be relied upon to produce a good profit, year in and year out.

He'd decided to put in hand some of the schemes he'd been mulling over for a decade. He wanted to expand the business. Where had he gone wrong? Henry had asked himself that countless times.

It was no good pretending he didn't know. He'd done what he'd been urging his father to do: he'd borrowed money to expand. That had given him a loan to service, and before he understood what was happening, he'd turned in a loss. The following year the loss had been greater.

After a few short years under his control, Knell's Gloves was gone. He'd had to file for bankruptcy, and because of that his home was gone too. All his money had been used to repay his creditors, and he was left with none at all and the feeling that his father had been right. He had no aptitude for business. He'd never been able to throw off the awful feeling of failure.

Henry sighed. He'd been reading recently about family businesses. Statistics said that thirty per cent were still being run by the second generation, but only thirteen per cent by the third. Clogs to clogs in three generations was the average fate of a small business.

Hospital porter! There were times when he couldn't believe he'd descended to this. He'd been bred to be an executive and had nothing in common with his fellow porters. They thought him very strange not to be interested in keeping pigeons and betting on the dogs. He should be glad he had a job at all, but he didn't care for lifting patients on stretchers the way he had to.

Henry felt he had more in common with the doctors. The anaesthetist was always ready to chat with him as he changed the cylinders on the anaesthetic machine. He even looked like a doctor. He'd kept his bowler hat and fine wool overcoat; a cloth cap and boots were not for him. He hadn't been able to change – still couldn't, though Harriet had kept scolding and telling him he must. Only yesterday she'd really gone for him again.

'You're still trying to live the way you used to. You pretend nothing has changed.'

'How can I pretend? I've only to look round this room. It's awful.'

'Better than we have. You've taken over the best room here and keep it all to yourself. This furniture all came from the old house. There are six of us sleeping in the dining room.'

'Hattie, it wouldn't be seemly to invite you to sleep in here with me. Not now you're a young lady.'

He'd been half teasing her. Trying to stop her saying more. Talk like this brought him awful, gnawing guilt.

Hattie had looked ready to stamp with rage. 'We have nowhere to sit in comfort.'

'You have the kitchen. It's always warm because of the range.'

'While you have this sitting room. I light the fire in your grate. You have the big comfortable chairs and your books all round you. You don't want to share any of that with us.'

'Hattie! That's not true. I've told you to come in and

13

use my desk. I want you to go on writing your little stories.'

'Little stories?'

He knew that had upset her. Hattie rarely spoke of her desire to write stories for children. As a schoolgirl she'd tried to hide the fact, but he knew she had ambitions in that direction. It made him press on.

'I know Ruth and Clara still ask you to tell them stories. I heard the one about Millie the monkey last night. Well, part of it. There's no need to stop writing them down, if you enjoy it. Why give up your own interests? Maggie hasn't given up playing. She comes in often. I like to hear her.'

'Yes, Maggie! She's still hanging on to the past too. Practising her accomplishments instead of doing something useful like making a stew for dinner.'

'Maggie isn't able . . .'

'You tell her that, cosset her, and then she doesn't try. Everything is left to me, and I'm tired of it, Pa.'

It had been a wail of anguish. 'How can I write? I don't have time any more. I don't have the energy.'

Henry knew he'd said the wrong thing. He'd never handled Hattie properly. Hers was a complicated personality.

'It's not just giving up the tennis parties and musi-cal evenings. I look back and think of all that leisure time I used to have. I never have a minute to myself here.'

Hattie was quiet in company and seemed shy, but she could lay the law down and rant at her own family. She had a brusque manner that seemed designed to rub everyone the wrong way, but underneath, Henry knew she was trying to do her best for them all.

He owed her a lot. Hattie had been only thirteen when Edith had died, but it was she who'd taken the greatest interest in the infant daughter he'd been left with. She'd mothered her, still did.

The girls worried him terribly, particularly Maggie. He'd

14

been arranging for her to go to a school of music in Manchester when the collapse had come.

If he'd had just a little money he could have had them trained to earn their livings in some way. With the typewriter, perhaps. As it was, none of them had had any training, and the younger ones had had to be removed from Herman House School and would be without the polish that Maggie and Harriet had. He'd dragged his girls down with him.

His daughters were his only source of comfort now, and very precious to him. He felt well loved in return. They clamoured for his attention, had done since their mother had died, particularly the two older ones. Ever since they were children, he'd felt this rivalry for his affection, and yet they were closer than most sisters.

Perhaps he did cosset Maggie more. Everybody seemed to. She was slim and slight; prettier and more responsive. He knew he'd made matters worse by letting her take some of the limelight off Hattie.

Since they'd moved here from their comfortable house in Rock Park, Maggie had developed pale-mauve shadows under her eyes. They only served to enhance her beauty. She was the one who looked most like Edith. The only one with a real interest in music.

'Come and play for me, Maggie,' he'd say, and her fingers would conjure up magical sounds. She had such assurance, he felt carried away very often by her music. It was the one thing that could make him forget his problems.

Harriet's green eyes were angry. 'You've kept in touch with some of your old friends, you still go out to meet them and have a nice meal. You expect good nourishing meals here at home. I'd be glad to put them on the table, Pa, if you provided the wherewithal to make it possible.'

He felt Harriet's words like the lash of a whip. He knew it was the truth.

'And you never lift a finger to help. You step out of

your clothes when you've finished with them. You expect us to run round after you, tidying up, and cleaning and cooking.'

He did. It was the way he'd been brought up and the way he'd lived for years. He couldn't help it. He'd even given her some of her own medicine.

'You're turning into a shrew, Harriet.'

'I have to. If I didn't nag and nag, nothing would ever get done.' He saw tears of desperation clouding her big green eyes. 'Six of us is too many in this small space. We're all cross and tired, looking after the little ones, trying to sew late into the night to earn extra money.'

Henry knew he was still being selfish. He kept enough from the small wage he earned to buy himself the odd drink in a decent pub. He bought newspapers and books too.

'I'm sorry, I expect too much of you. You're the capable one, Hattie. You look after us all and keep us clean and fed. Without you, the family would fall apart. I owe you a great deal.' She'd taken over her mother's role as best she could. 'You're the one making some semblance of civilised life for us now. I am grateful.'

'Then do something, Pa. We can't go on like this.'

'Yes, love,' he'd said. If he knew what to do, he'd have done it long ago. But he wasn't being fair to Harriet. He shouldn't expect his six girls to live in harmony when they were all cooped up in so little space.

'If only we could get by without renting the next floor.'

'We've been through that a dozen times. We can't manage without the O'Briens' rent. Better if you could persuade Maggie to get a job.'

'Maggie? What could she do?'

'Play the piano. They must pay people to do that in theatres and music halls. You go to these places, Pa. Don't you hear of anything?'

He didn't, and anyway, the music hall? He'd been a little shocked. 'Not suitable for a young girl like Maggie.'

'Oh, I know she's not cut out for anything but being a lady. She's full of airs and graces. But she's good with children and she likes babies. Why can't she be a nanny?'

Henry was even more shocked at Harriet's vehemence.

'If you can be a hospital porter, there's no reason why Maggie can't be a nanny. She could live in, we'd be one fewer here.'

Harriet's words had preyed on his mind, making him feel woefully sorry for himself. Making him wish he was no longer in this world. That would provide Harriet with more of the space she needed, but he didn't have the guts to leave it; he hadn't been able to screw himself up to try.

He'd gone to the Woodside Hotel for a drink at lunchtime because he didn't want to go on thinking of such things. Daniel Moody had been there, thin and stiff and upright. Henry had always got on well with him; he seemed a decent fellow, one he could trust. Moody had insisted on buying him lunch. They'd had a good steak and kidney pie and shared a bottle of burgundy.

Henry had wanted to forget his own problems, preferring to hear other people's. He listened to how Dransfield's was faring. They'd taken over the running of his business and had made another loss, though it was much reduced. Moody was their accountant, as well as being Dransfield's son-in-law, so he knew what he was talking about. He was hoping that next year the business would break even.

Moody's wife was expecting the birth of a third child shortly, and under the influence of whisky and wine Henry had asked if she needed more help with the family.

Moody's natural caution had been discounted by the same amount of alcohol and holiday goodwill. The details of Maggie's job had all been arranged in moments.

Now Henry wished he'd not listened to Harriet, and that he'd drunk less whisky.

# CHAPTER TWO

Maggie felt fluttery. It was the seventh of January, the day she was to start work. It was also the first day back at school for her younger sisters. Getting them up and out in the mornings was always a rush. This morning seemed particularly fraught.

Unless Pa was on early shift, he usually stayed out of their way until the younger ones had gone, because there was hardly room to move when they were all in the kitchen. This morning, he'd got up and put on his dressing gown to have breakfast with them. Maggie knew it was to say goodbye to her.

Fanny was making the breakfast tea, while the younger ones were having their morning wash at the kitchen sink. Because they'd lost two brothers, there was a gap between Fanny's thirteen years and Enid's eight that made the family fall into two halves.

Maggie busied herself doing up buttons and shoelaces for her sisters. She finished twisting Ruth's hair into thin plaits and sat her up to the table. At only five years of age, Ruth still needed a lot of help.

Hattie was frowning with concentration as she dished up the porridge. She'd laid down strict rules about the size of helpings. Pa's was always the largest. Then there were three equal servings for the three older girls, two slightly smaller for Enid and Clara and a tiny portion for Ruth, who didn't eat much.

Maggie called: 'Clara? Come and get your breakfast. What are you doing in the bedroom?'

Clara was seven and built more robustly than her sisters. She thumped herself down on the end of the bench next to Ruth, jolting her.

'Is this for me?' She pulled a bowl towards her, sounding dissatisfied.

Hattie glared at her. Everybody but Pa had started to eat.

'You know it is,' Enid said between mouthfuls.

Both Enid and Clara had the family sheep-fleece hair. Both had bright blue eyes, but Clara's had an aggressive glint. If there was ever any trouble, it was usually Clara who started it.

'It's not fair,' she retorted. 'You never give me enough, Hattie.'

'We could all eat more,' Fanny said shortly.

'It's all right for you. You get the same amount as Hattie. Look how much less she's given me.'

'You've got as much as Enid, and she's a year older.'

'Enid isn't as big as me.'

There was no answer to that. Enid was thin and wiry. Her eyes were owlish behind their spectacles.

'Are you going to eat all yours?' Clara turned to Ruth, who had already laid down her spoon and was sipping her tea.

'She is,' Maggie answered for her. They were all concerned by Ruth's fragility and lack of appetite.

Then six pairs of eyes were transfixed as Pa spooned porridge from his own plate to Clara's.

She was squealing with delight. 'Thank you, Pa.' As she lifted both arms in jubilation, she caught Ruth's elbow, sending a tide of milky tea swamping down the front of her starched white pinafore. Ruth choked and let out a cry of distress.

'Clara! For heaven's sake!' Hattie was on her feet, lifting Ruth away from the table, trying to comfort her with a hug. 'She's only had this pinafore on for ten minutes.'

20

'I couldn't help it,' Clara wailed. 'I'm sorry.'

Pa got up to help, running cold water on the pinafore. 'It's not going to stain.' He, too, seemed to see his three younger girls as a big responsibility.

'We all know what the washerwoman costs!' Hattie was exasperated.

Maggie ran to fetch another pinafore for Ruth. At least there were plenty that the others had outgrown. She tried to still the butterflies in her stomach. She ought to feel glad she was leaving all this behind. When they all settled down to eat again, the scraping of spoons on bowls went through her.

'Pa, I'm not sure where I'm supposed to go.' She'd been worrying about that in the night. 'I've never been up that end of Oxton before.'

His eyes searched hers sympathetically. 'Hattie can go with you.'

Hattie's sharp intake of breath was very audible.

Pa asked: 'You'll help her carry her bags and find the right house, won't you?'

'Shouldn't you do that?' Hattie was short with him. 'You already know where these people live. You could take her in and introduce her.'

Maggie saw Pa straighten his lips. They all knew he wouldn't want to do that. Not when she was to be a nurserymaid.

'I'm expected to take care of everything.' Harriet hadn't calmed down. 'That's the trouble with being the eldest.'

Maggie wanted Hattie's company even if it was grudgingly given. To set off on her own, turning her back on everything she knew, would be harder.

'Do come, Hattie. And what shall I wear? I mean, what will they expect a nursemaid to . . . ?'

'The best you have,' Pa told her. 'First impressions are important.'

Maggie had put on her best navy serge skirt. It was hardly

21

worn but a little on the short side, because she'd grown taller. It showed too much of her elastic-sided boots but they were still smart too.

Both she and Harriet had just retrimmed their winter hats with velvet violets they'd snipped from an eye-catching hat that had once been Mama's best. They'd both wanted the glossy bird that had nestled amongst the flowers and had argued over which of them should have it. The only possible compromise was to leave the bird where it was.

As they set off, Maggie felt her heel slip on some putrid vegetable matter outside the grocer's on the corner. There were dollops of smelly horse manure left in the road.

Harriet said: 'Look where you put your feet. I should have thought you'd be glad to get away from here.' Her strange eyes blazed with emerald light. 'I wish I could escape so easily.'

'You can go in my place,' Maggie assured her, but of course she couldn't. Pa had arranged this for her.

They got off the tram where it turned round in Shrewsbury Road, and started walking with the heavy bag between them. Maggie's hand was pinched because the handle wasn't big enough to allow both of them to hold it comfortably.

'I like it better up here.' Harriet was striding out as she looked round. 'The whole place looks so prosperous.'

Maggie was nervous of what lay ahead. The crowded rooms and her big family spelled security. She'd never had to do anything on her own before. Always there'd been Harriet or Papa to take care of her. Except with her music, she'd always followed where others led.

'This is it.' Harriet relaxed her grip on the bag so suddenly that Maggie let one corner drag along the pavement. 'Ottershaw House.'

It was a square three-storey house set well back in a

22

garden of lawns and flowers. A turret with a castellated roof line ran up one corner, providing magnificent windows.

'You are lucky! You'll be able to forget all the family troubles here. Look at the size of it.'

'Much grander even than our old house.' Maggie paused to look more closely. It was an imposing stone-faced house, built in the middle of Queen Victoria's reign. Harriet had set a brisk pace, and they'd had to walk a long way. She felt drained and poised on the brink of something she couldn't handle.

'I bet you won't have to sleep six to the room here. I'm quite envious.'

Maggie didn't believe that. Harriet was just trying to bolster her courage. Her heart was beginning to pound with dread.

'They've even got a motor car.' Harriet was peering through the gate. 'It's parked round the side. That side, where the Virginia creeper is. Isn't it grand?'

'They must be very rich.'

Pa had never owned a car, nor a carriage either. If they'd needed transport they sent their kitchen maid down to the livery stables.

Maggie shivered. 'You're sure this is the right place?'

Harriet took out the piece of paper on which Pa had written directions. 'Look, Ottershaw House, and here's the name on the gatepost. Definitely the right place. You're on your own now.'

'Won't you come to the door with me?' Maggie begged. She was fighting the urge to turn and run.

'What for? All you have to do is tell them who you are. They'll be expecting you. They'll think you need a nursemaid yourself if I say I've brought you.'

Maggie knew that although Harriet could lay the law down at home, with a bossy manner and a sharp tongue, she was quite different with strangers, she never spoke up in front of them.

'You'd hate to find yourself a nurserymaid in a strange house. And to think of them being friends of Pa's only makes it worse.'

'I'm sorry.' Hattie's arms came round her in a quick hug. 'Why am I such a witch to you? Go on,' she said more gently. 'You'll be all right once you've settled in. This is the worst moment.'

'Goodbye, then.' Maggie took a deep breath and reached for her bags. The newly painted front door shone in the winter sun. But should she be knocking on the front door? This was the problem of working for Pa's fine friends. Mama had expected their staff to use the back door. She changed direction. It would take her past the motor car. As she drew closer, she could see that the bonnet was propped open.

It was a very fine car, with great brass headlights, sparkling wire wheels and wooden running boards. Her feet were crunching on the white gravel. The sound brought a head round from under the bonnet as she approached.

'Hello.'

Maggie jumped and lowered her bags.

'Sorry.' The young man had a friendly smile and a smudge of oil on his cheek. 'Did I frighten you?'

Other things were frightening Maggie more. She managed: 'What a magnificent car.'

'Hispano-Suiza. A joy to drive. Goes like the wind.' He put his head on one side in puzzlement. 'I know you, don't I?'

Maggie didn't think so. 'Are you Mr . . . Moody?'

'No,' he laughed. 'He's my brother-in-law. I'm Tom Dransfield.'

It was silly of her, she decided, to mistake him for her employer. He didn't look old enough to have a family. No more than twenty or so at the most.

'I remember.' He grinned at her. 'You came to one of our Christmas parties. At the Woodside Hotel. Not this year, though. You've a lot of sisters.'

Maggie remembered the party, but she didn't remember him. His grey eyes were searching her face. She'd tied her hair back neatly with a navy ribbon this morning, but he was taking in the creamy rippling waves that showed below her hat. She thought he'd noticed her horrible eyelashes. Not everybody liked pig's eyelashes, but she thought from his expression that perhaps he didn't find them repulsive. He was frowning at her bags.

'Has Sophie invited you to stay?'

She managed to choke out: 'No! I'm the new nursery-maid.' She could feel the heat running up her cheeks. 'Can you tell me where should I go?'

'Oh!' He laughed, and his eyes travelled over her again. 'Nurserymaid? I didn't realise. Let me show you.' He wiped his hands on a rag before lifting her bags. 'This way.'

Maggie's heart was beating fast as she followed. She liked him, she liked the way his bright honey-brown hair curled into his neck at the back. He was friendly. He led her down steps to the back door. The windows were only half above ground here.

She said: 'Do you live here too?'

'Yes, my sister didn't leave home when she married. Our mother didn't want her to.'

Maggie felt her anxiety lessen. She needn't have worried about coming here. The Dransfields were friends and erst-while business associates of Pa's. As he'd said, it wasn't like going to strangers.

She said: 'Will you tell me about your family? I need to know . . .'

'There's a lot of us. My mother and father, then we are three sons and a daughter. Sophie is married to Daniel Moody – he works for my mother now – and they have two children, Adam and Jane. Oh, and my grandmother, Mrs Clark, lives with us too. My mother's mother.'

Maggie hoped she was going to remember all their names as she followed him up a stone-flagged passage.

'My mother is very family-orientated. She calls us her dynasty.'

She glanced into a large kitchen as she passed, and saw two pairs of eyes riveted on her.

'I didn't know Sophie wanted another nurserymaid,' he said over his shoulder.

'You mean, there already is one?'

'Well, the nanny, you know. But Sophie's expecting an addition to her family.' He turned to smile again. 'Perhaps we'd better leave your bags here for a moment.' Maggie was hovering beside them. 'Come on, we'll find Sophie and let her know you're here.'

On then across a parquet-floored hall smelling of beeswax. How long since she'd smelled that?

Suddenly a voice demanded from the top of a wide staircase: 'Tom, who is that you're bringing in?'

Maggie swung round to see a tall middle-aged woman scowling down at her. Tom murmured: 'This is my mother.'

Lenora Dransfield lifted her skirts just sufficiently to show neat boots skimming downstairs with surprising agility. Bangs of pepper-and-salt hair were arranged over a somewhat forbidding face, though it had handsome bone structure. Her tight grey dress covered an over-large bosom. Her skirts were dropped to her ankles the moment she reached the ground floor.

'It's, er . . . Sorry.' He smiled down at Maggie. 'You didn't tell me your name.'

She stammered: 'Margaret . . . Margaret Knell.'

His mother's strident voice boomed: 'Knell? Henry Knell's daughter?' She seemed outraged. Eyes like cold steel seemed to bore into Maggie. 'What are you doing here?'

Maggie was quaking. 'My father said that Mrs Moody needed a nurserymaid. That she would . . .'

Tom's eyes were wide as he breathed: 'Henry Knell's daughter? Of course, I remember now . . .'

26

Maggie moistened her lips. 'You know my father?'

He wouldn't meet her eyes. 'Yes, of course. My father's in business too . . . I'm sorry . . .'

Maggie felt the colour rush up her cheeks. It made Pa seem somehow notorious. She didn't like to think that everybody knew of his disaster. It embarrassed him to talk about it. This was making her feel terrible.

'I know nothing of this.' Lenora Dransfield's chest was heaving. The magnificent brooch she wore on it flashed diamond fire with every breath. 'I don't approve.'

Maggie made herself say: 'I understood that I was expected. Mr Moody arranged it with my father.'

She caught the look of approval in Tom's eyes. He backed her up. 'Hadn't we better see what Sophie says, Mother?'

'I don't know what Daniel's thinking of. It's none of his business. He'd do better to leave the finding of staff to me.' Mrs Dransfield's thin lips parted in a grimace, showing a number of gold fillings.

'But the nursery,' Tom put in, 'is his and Sophie's business, surely?'

Maggie warmed to him. He seemed to be supporting her. She was facing the stairs and now saw an older woman clinging with both hands to one rail, as inch by inch she edged her way down. Lenora turned to follow her gaze.

'Mother! What on earth are you doing?' She bounded back up the stairs. 'You might easily fall. I thought you were going to wait for Bridie to help you.'

'My grandmother,' Tom murmured before going up to help too.

With support on both sides, Mrs Clark edged each foot forward and then painfully down, her face screwed up with pain. She wore a lace-edged cap on her grey hair but was otherwise dressed all in black.

Lenora seemed exasperated at their slow progress, and when they reached the ground floor she said to Tom: 'You

27

see to your grandmother. And *you* come this way,' she ordered Maggie.

Maggie found it difficult to keep up with her swishing skirts. After what seemed a great distance, the older woman flung open the door of a pleasant sitting room and barked:

'Sophie, are you expecting a new nurserymaid to arrive today?'

Sophie had reached the stage of pregnancy when it was no longer possible to hide it. She stood up and came towards them. Her hair was brighter than Tom's, a rich bronze shade, and quick little smiles came and went.

'Yes, hello. Your father told my husband that . . .'

Her mother interrupted with a snort of impatience. 'Whatever made Daniel take her on like this? I like to vet the staff carefully, particularly for the children.'

Then she swung round on Maggie: 'How old are you? Where are you living now? Are your nails clean? Let me see.'

The door opened and Tom supported his grandmother to a chair.

Maggie was taken by surprise, and struggling to take off her gloves, she dropped one. She watched Tom pick it up and stroke the soft leather.

'How many sisters do you have? Are any of them in service?'

'No.' Maggie bristled with mortification. It seemed she could expect no privileges from Mrs Dransfield just because she knew her father. She decided the woman's manners were atrocious. No doubt this was her usual way of hiring domestic staff.

Lenora was taking in every detail of Maggie's appearance. 'Turn round,' she commanded.

Maggie didn't move. She'd taken trouble with her appearance; this woman was not going to find a better-turned-out maid. Her family would never have treated anyone like this.

28

'I'm very fond of children,' Maggie told her. 'I believe in occupying their minds and bodies. Getting them interested in as many things as I can.'

There was a moment's silence. She wondered if she'd gone too far. That sounded more like a governess's job.

'Have you any experience?' her inquisitor wanted to know. 'What about new babies?'

'I've helped look after my younger sisters.'

'But can you do it properly?'

Maggie drew herself up to her full five feet one inch. 'Certainly I can. My parents were very particular and took a great interest in childcare. They wouldn't have . . .' She was about to say 'entrusted them entirely to hired staff', but changed it hurriedly to '. . . allowed any but the highest standards in their nursery.'

Mrs Dransfield's tone was condescending. 'Your family was able to employ a nanny?'

'Yes, we had a nanny. My father ensured we were well cared for.'

'Yes, of course, your father.' There was a sneer in her voice. 'Your mother died when you were how old?'

'Ten.'

'I can't believe your father will have taught you what you need to know. All girls in your family – how many are you?'

'Six.'

The old lady had straightened up in her chair. Maggie noticed that she too seemed to flash with diamonds. She wore them at her ears and on her gnarled fingers. 'Who did you say she was?'

'It's Margaret Knell, Gran.' It was Tom who spoke. 'She's coming to help Sophie with the children.'

'One of Henry Knell's girls, Mother,' Lenora told her. 'You remember Henry Knell? It seems Daniel has taken it upon himself . . . Probably sorry for him, but all the same, I don't think it's a good thing to have one of them here.'

29

Sophie said: 'Mother, they're having a hard time. Daniel told Henry we'd be willing to take her if it would help.'

Maggie was horrified. Nothing could be worse than being discussed by her employers like this. And she'd tell Pa he was wrong: the fact that she was a Knell was not guaranteeing her a welcome here. Certainly not from Lenora.

The old lady had sharp, clear eyes. They came up to meet hers.

'Bridie told me you were coming.' Her voice was not unfriendly. 'Can you read? From books and newspapers?'

'Yes, I read well.'

'Then I'll let you read to me.'

Maggie felt heartened. Reading to an old lady didn't seem too menial.

The old lady went on: 'She speaks nicely, Lenora. Not a bad thing for the children. We don't want them picking up a nasty accent.'

Lenora's gaze moved abruptly to her son. 'You can go, Tom. Hiring a nurserymaid has never interested you before. I thought there was something you wanted to do to the car before we could go to the factory. I'll want to leave in five minutes.'

Maggie hated to see him to go; she needed his protection. She found it hard to believe such a friendly person could have such a ferocious mother.


'I hope you'll be happy with us here,' Sophie said, as she took her up to the nurseries on the top floor. 'I'm sure you'll find Nanny easy to work with.'

Sophie had a crimson spot on each cheek but she didn't apologise for her mother. Maggie was still shaking from the reception she'd been given.

'She's quite young and go-ahead. Her name's Bridie McNammee.'

The day nursery was bright and cosy, with a good fire

30

burning in a high grate behind a guard. Sophie stood with her back to it, swaying back and forward on her heels. Maggie watched as two children who had been crayoning at a table ran to her. The fireside chair creaked as she collapsed on it and pulled them both on her knee.

'I told you, Nanny, that I'd get you some help before the new baby came. Here she is, Margaret Knell.'

Nanny wore her cap folded in half and pinned high on top of her head. Only an edging of lace showed above her upswept red hair. On her it wasn't a cap of servitude, more a halo. The skirt of her uniform dress was short enough to show not only slim ankles but also a good deal of shapely calf. Pa said short skirts were flighty; he was always ordering Maggie and her sisters to let their hems down.

'And these are my children. Little Jane, who's nineteen months.' She gave her a hug. 'And Adam, who's three and a half.' Adam had dark eyes and strong features for one so young.

Maggie heard him say: 'She looks nice, Mummy, doesn't she?'

Sophie's eyes smiled at her over the child's shiny dark hair.

'Yes, love, she looks very nice. I think we'll like her, won't we?' Maggie warmed to them. 'What are you going to say to her, Jane?'

The little girl was shy. Maggie could see the effort it cost her to lift her brown eyes to hers. She was chubby, with a pretty round baby face and hair that had more curl in it than Adam's.

'Hello.' She wore a white pinafore over a dress of tartan wool.

'And what else?'

'Happy New Year.'

They all laughed. 'I meant what is her name? Say it properly.'

'Hello, Marg . . . Marg . . .'

Maggie bent down to greet the child. 'Margaret isn't an easy name to say. Why not call me Maggie?' She saw Sophie's nod of approval. 'We're going to be friends, aren't we?'

'Nanny will explain your duties to you, Maggie. Oh, and there's a uniform for you somewhere.' Sophie was on her feet again, flitting about the room, seemingly unable to stay still.

'In the cupboard beside the fire.' It was Nanny who threw open the doors, and Maggie lifted it out. A uniform drove home the fact that she was now in service. There were three shapeless blue dresses and a pile of aprons and caps.

'You'd better change into it,' Sophie said before she went back downstairs.

The uniform didn't fit well. It was uncomfortable and it made Maggie look a drudge. Bridie McNammee's sultry eyes were watching her.

Maggie asked: 'What will I be expected to do?'

'Light the fire in the mornings and bring up the coal. Clean up in here and the night nursery. Make the children's beds and do their washing and ironing. Look after them, play with them, that sort of thing.'

Maggie's heart sank. It was exactly what she'd been doing at home, but doing it there, for her own family, was quite different.

She asked Adam to show her his toys. There was a bookcase with plenty of books, and a huge toy box with more bricks and balls and teddy bears than she'd ever seen before.

Bridie had a tongue that never stopped wagging. Her soft Irish brogue went on and on, always behind her hand. Maggie presumed that was in the hope that the children wouldn't understand.

'Better stay out of the grandmother's way. She's a right tartar, that one. You don't want to get on the wrong side of her. Their mother's a bit scatty but all right, and their

32

father's lovely. They're always talking of getting a house of their own but they depend on Dransfield money. Couldn't live like this anywhere else. I think they're scared to cut themselves free.

'Don't think Mr Moody likes working in the business either, but like the rest of us, he has to butter his bread somehow.

'Wish they would get a house of their own. Wouldn't have to see so much of the old ogre if they did. Have you seen the Dransfield sons?'

Maggie shook her head.

'Three, so there are. Tom . . .'

'I've seen Tom. He was kind.'

'A lovely boy. Wait till you see Luke and Eric.'

'What do they do?'

'Work in the business. Luke's the eldest and the handsomest.' She rolled her eyes appreciatively. 'Quite a catch for somebody.'

'You?' Maggie suggested.

'Chance would be a fine thing.' Bridie giggled. 'He wouldn't marry me. Got the world at his feet, that one.'

The rest of the day passed in a blur of first impressions. A house so large it was difficult to find her way about it. The children were polite, obedient and easy to manage.

Maggie was reading to them that evening when Tom put his head round the nursery door. He smiled at Nanny but pulled a chair up next to Maggie's. 'How are you getting on?'

'Fine.' She was pleased he'd come back to see her.

He whispered: 'Don't let my mother frighten you. Her bark's worse than her bite.'

She couldn't keep her voice steady after that and was glad when she'd finished the story.

Adam sidled up. 'Will you be a pony, Uncle Tom? Let me ride on your back?'

Tom got down on his knees on the hearthrug. First one

child and then the other was allowed to sit on his back while he pranced round the nursery on his hands and knees. They screamed with delight, and his eyes laughed up into hers every time he turned.

Nanny stopped the game. 'We'll never get them to sleep after this. You're making them too excited.'

'It's time I went down to supper anyway,' he said. Maggie felt quite cheered as she ran the children's bath. Perhaps it wouldn't be too bad here after all.

Harriet was wrong about her being given a bedroom to herself. Maggie found she was to sleep in the night nursery in case the children woke in the night.

'I've slept there since I came.' Bridie tossed her red hair. 'It's your turn now. I'm moving to a room of my own across the landing.'

Maggie thought the night nursery light and airy and more comfortable than the room she'd left. It was much larger, and her bed was in an alcove that allowed some privacy.

She found, over the following nights, that Jane woke frequently, so her sleep was broken. She didn't mind too much, she was used to it. At home, her youngest sister Ruth had had nightmares since they'd moved to Elizabeth Place.

It was all so new, and there was so much for her to take in, that the days seemed twice the length they had at home.

Visitors came to the nursery from time to time. Sophie came several times a day but didn't stay long. Their grandmother came less often, but hers were the visits Bridie feared. Tom dropped in most evenings, and sometimes he romped on the floor with the children. If he came early, he'd tease them by pretending to eat their supper. If he was late, he'd read them a bedtime story.

Bridie said, with a very obvious wink, 'He's taking more interest in his niece and nephew now.'

Maggie felt the heat run up her cheeks. She found herself thinking about him and looking forward to his visits. It was better than wondering how they were all getting on at home without her.

One Sunday teatime, she was alone with the children in the nursery when the parlourmaid was sent up to say that Mrs Moody wanted the children brought down to her sitting room.

Maggie found the whole family assembled there round a tea trolley elaborately set with silver and china, lemon and milk and a cake stand full of fancy cakes. Stanley Dransfield stood with his legs apart on the hearthrug, a tall man, with the shoulders of an ox. He had receding mouse-brown hair and mutton-chop whiskers on his cheeks that were half a shade darker. His eyes followed every movement she made. Sophie was fidgeting on the settee, next to her husband; he seemed thin and austere and older than Maggie had expected.

Tom winked at her, and she saw his brothers for the first time, though she'd heard their deep voices ringing through the house. Both Eric and Luke had bright bronze hair like Sophie's. Both smiled at her. Lenora, who was spreading jam thickly on to her scone, dismissed her.

'We'll let you know when we want you to come and take them back,' she said.

A week or so later, Bridie came in after seeing Mrs Clark into bed. 'Are you finished here for the night?'

'Yes, the children are all tucked up. Their parents have been up to hear their prayers and say good night.'

Bridie had changed out of her uniform and was putting on her hat and coat.

'I'm going out,' she announced. 'Now you're here to listen for the children, it won't hurt if I disappear for an hour.'

In one of her whispered asides, she'd told Maggie that she had a boyfriend, who worked next door as a gardener. She was constantly peering out of the casement windows that had fancy iron grilles on them just like the windows in Maggie's old nursery.

'Can't see him. Must be working in the greenhouse this morning. I hate the winter. We used to be able to talk over the hedge when the weather was good and I could take the children out to the garden.'

Maggie had been somewhat surprised, because whenever the children's father came up, or even Tom, Bridie's eyes became flirty and her smile coquettish. She had a way of laughing up at men and walking with such a spring in her step that her full skirts flared out.

That evening, Tom came up and found her reading on her own by the nursery fire. 'Where's Bridie?'

'Gone to see her boyfriend next door.'

'What?'

'Charlie, their gardener.'

He chuckled. 'She'd better be careful. Mother doesn't approve of followers.'

He stayed with her until it was time for bed. He told her he was regarded as a sort of apprentice in the family business. His mother expected him to spend a lot of time with her. He drove her about from one factory to another, and was presently spending several days a week in a firm that belonged to somebody else. It was a retail business with five haberdashery shops scattered around Merseyside.

She gathered that he found making blouses and baby wear a very dull way of earning a living.

As the fire died down, she started to talk about her own family and the effect on them of Papa's business collapse.

'I didn't realise it was common knowledge. That you'd all know about it. I thought once we'd sold our house in Rock Park and left the district it would be forgotten.'

Tom's grey eyes were full of sympathy, and he took her hand in his. 'We're business people too, you see. We were closely connected. I knew your father. I worked in Knell's Gloves for a few months, under him. My mother arranged it. She thinks I need experience of other businesses before settling down in the family firm.'

36

It took him a little longer to get round to saying: 'You do know my mother bought your factory?'

'No!' Maggie felt the strength drain from her legs. 'No, Pa won't talk about it. Doesn't even like to think about it. All he told us was that his business went bankrupt. That the factory had to be closed.'

'My mother reopened it. Gloves are being made again, and my father's in charge now. I'm told I shall go there again. To widen my experience.'

'But . . .'

'Mother likes to look for bargains. She won't pay over the odds for a business. It's still called Knell's Gloves.'

Maggie felt sick.

'She says it fits in well with the blouses. Sales outlets much the same and all that. It'll be why Mother was against having you here. She thought you'd be upset. It isn't that she doesn't like you, or anything like that.'

Maggie spent a wakeful night thinking about what he'd said. It seemed strange to her that Dransfield's had taken over Pa's glove business, and yet Pa had wanted her to come here to work for them. He still trusted them.

The following day was Sunday, and during the afternoon Bridie went to read to Mrs Clark, while Maggie was left in charge of the nursery. Tom came up and was romping on the floor with the children when Lenora Dransfield walked in unexpectedly.

'Really, Tom! All this horseplay!' She was frowning and looked more forbidding than ever. 'I came to fetch the children down to tea, but they look hot and untidy.'

Maggie hadn't yet changed Jane's apron. 'I'll have them ready in five minutes, Mrs Dransfield,' she said, hurrying them to the bathroom to sponge their faces.

Tom and his mother went downstairs together. Maggie could hear them now at the bottom of the nursery stairs. Lenora's voice was raised.

'What are you doing up there all the time? I hope it isn't that girl.'

She could hear Tom's voice, but not all he said. With the water running and Adam's piping voice at her elbow, his words were being drowned out. She turned off the taps, opened the door further. She was afraid Tom would be forbidden to come near her. She could hear the resonance of his voice again.

As she took the children across the landing to the night nursery, she heard Lenora's voice say crossly: 'What do you mean, does Dad know? It's my business, Tom.'

Maggie left the door wide open and was straining her ears. She was sure she heard the words 'Knell's Gloves'. As she pushed Adam's arms into a clean shirt, she heard Tom ask angrily:

'Is that how you managed to get your hands on the glove factory? It's dishonest, Mother.'

Maggie's heart was beating like a drum. Was Tom accusing his mother of taking Knell's Gloves by fraudulent means? Had her father been cheated out of his business? Her mind swam at the thought.

'Has Uncle Tom been naughty?' Adam was tugging at her skirt.

'No, no, nothing like that.'

Holding the children's hands, she led them down to the drawing room. She could tell by the flush on Tom's cheeks that he hadn't yet recovered. He wouldn't look at her. She took back to the nursery the impression of a gracious lifestyle; a prosperous family playing with their children in a very comfortable home.

The contrast between that and what her family now had could not have been greater. She felt upset and angry. The glove factory was just one more source of income to them. To her family it had been everything. She couldn't wait to ask Tom about it.

'You heard that?' He seemed embarrassed.

38

'Sounds carry up the stairwell. I'd have heard more if the children hadn't been chattering. Is it true? Were you accusing your mother of defrauding my family out of their business?'

'Did I say that?' He looked aghast.

'Something to that effect. I couldn't sleep last night for thinking about it. You don't know what a difference losing the business made to us. What did your mother do?'

'To be honest, I'm not sure.' Tom covered his face with his hands. 'I don't know. It was just something Mother asked me about the retail business I'm with now. It struck a chord . . .'

'She denied it?'

'Yes.' His cheeks were scarlet. 'I could be wrong, Maggie. I've no proof. Better if you forget what you heard. I was just arguing with Mother.'

Maggie knew she'd never be able to forget it. She was burning to know more. She thought Pa was mistaken about the Dransfield family being his friends. It seemed more likely that he had an enemy amongst them.

# CHAPTER THREE

Late one evening, when the children were asleep in bed, and dinner had been served and cleared in the dining room, Bridie said:

'Some nights I go down to the kitchen for a natter. You can come too. The rest of the staff are asking what you're like. They haven't had much chance to speak to you.'

Maggie followed her down. The kitchens at Ottershaw House were semi-basement and rather dark, even at midday. The windows looked out on a low wall but grass and railings could be seen above it. Tonight the curtains had been drawn.

There was a warren of sculleries, larders, pantries, laundry rooms and storerooms, and even a housekeeper's sitting room, though that wasn't used much nowadays. Mrs Summers, the cook, was the most senior on the staff, and she preferred to sit in front of her own range when her duties were finished.

There was a fourteen-year-old between maid called May. Tonight she was upset; her cap was sliding off her straight mousy hair. Lenora Dransfield had scolded her because they'd run out of coal for the drawing-room fire.

'All she has to do is ring the bell and ask for more,' she wept. 'How can I see how much coal they've got from here?'

But May had dropped a trail of slack on the carpet when she'd taken it in, and five minutes later Mrs Dransfield had rung for her again to sweep up the mess.

'She said the carpet sweeper didn't do a good enough job, they were treading it round. She sent me back for a dustpan and handbrush. Made me get down on my hands and knees.'

'She's sour, that one, if everything isn't perfect for her family.' Ruby, the parlourmaid, was the wrong side of thirty and had thin brown plaits wound tightly round her head. She wore black dresses and frilly aprons in the afternoon, once her heavy work was done.

'But if it's any consolation, things aren't what she'd like them to be.'

'She's got a lot more than we can hope for,' Bridie said smartly. 'Three different businessess, all churning out money for her.'

'How does she come to own them?' Maggie wanted to know.

'Belonged to her father. Old Mrs Clark's husband. He started Clark's Blouses.'

'And something very funny happened to him,' May said.

'You don't know that's true,' Mrs Summers said severely. 'Not for sure.'

'I do then.'

'That's family folklore now,' Bridie scoffed.

May tried to clip her cap more securely to her hair. 'Percy knows all about it, and he told me. He'd just started as under-gardener here when it happened. Everybody thought it very strange.'

Maggie asked: 'What did happen?'

'Osbert Clark disappeared whilst on holiday in Ireland,' Bridie told her. 'Didn't come back to his business. Mrs Clark and Mrs Dransfield inherited it.'

'Lucky things, I'd say,' May put in.

'But her husband isn't all she hoped for.'

'Mr Dransfield seems pleasant enough,' Maggie said. She thought him quite kindly.

'Oh, he is, but he always has a bit on the side.' Bridie gave her an exaggerated wink.

'Go on, you don't know that either.' Mrs Summers poured herself a glass of her mistress's sherry and flopped back on the rocker beside the range. She wore a cross-over pinafore tied tightly round her plump figure, and every bit of her grey hair was tucked under her cap.

'They have separate bedrooms, don't they?' Ruby said. 'Can't keep that a secret. Me and May have to clean them and make two beds.'

'Posh people like having separate rooms, married or not. They all do it. It doesn't mean there's anything wrong.'

'But there is,' Ruby said. 'Remember that mammoth row they had last year.'

'More than a year now,' May put in. 'Missus found out he had a mistress.'

'We think he made a baby.' Bridie giggled. 'And that he paid for her to have it taken away. The rich know the doctors who'll do it. The missus found out because of the money and was really mad. There was no pleasing her for months.'

'For years,' May corrected. 'Still can't.'

Cook raised herself in her chair. 'If you want to stay out of trouble, May, bring a cloth and wipe the mantelshelf now. I can see the dust from here. You know what she's like. She'll run a finger along there when she comes down in the morning to set the menus.'

'And if you want to stay out of trouble you should drink less of her sherry,' Bridie told her pertly.

'Probably blames Stanley for getting through too much.' Ruby stifled a giggle.

'No, it's her sons who get blamed for that.' Bridie tossed her head. 'I've heard her at it.'

'Last time she asked me about it, I told her I used it in the cooking.' Cook twirled the glass in her fingers. 'I'll make a sherry trifle tomorrow. I've got to have a drop of something at the end of the day.'

The bell whirred from the dining room.

'I wish they'd go to bed.' Ruby yawned as she got to her feet. 'Whatever can they want now?'

Maggie learned a lot about the Dransfield family from the staff. Mostly, though, she ate her meals in the nursery with Bridie and the children and didn't see much of anybody else.

It was usually Bridie who took the children down to see their parents at teatime. She was always looking for more reasons to go downstairs, asking the children if they wanted to show Grandpa their drawings, or recite their poems for Mummy. Bridie even wanted to fetch the nursery meals from the kitchen and take the dishes back.

'I'm tired of being holed up in here, so I am,' she laughed. 'I like to go down once in a while. See what's happening down there. Have a chat with the others.'

Maggie didn't mind. This way she could avoid Mrs Dransfield. When she went down for coal – which was not a job Bridie wanted to take over – she looked over the banisters to make sure the floor below was clear before going further.

The following lunchtime, they were all eating cod in white sauce at the nursery table when they heard a commotion downstairs. Bridie opened the door so they could hear more.

'It's not a row,' she said after a few minutes. 'Something's happened.' She left her meal to find out.

Maggie started to clear the plates and set about serving the sponge pudding and custard, but the voices downstairs were growing more agitated, and Adam got down from the table. She lifted Jane down from her high chair and they all went to see what was going on.

She was in time to see Bridie and Ruby escorting old Mrs Clark back to her room. Sophie was wringing her hands. It seemed her grandmother had fallen on the stairs and the doctor had been sent for. It was a long time before the house settled back to its habitual calm.

44

That same afternoon, when Bridie brought the children back from the drawing room, she seemed overjoyed.

'I've been asked to spend more time with Mrs Clark. Help her wash and dress and that. I've always to help her on the stairs from now on. Now there's two of us, they think I can spare the time. Nobody's ever bothered much about her up to now,' she whispered from behind her hand.

'How is she?'

'All right. Didn't break anything when she fell. Just bruised.'

Maggie understood that the old lady spent a lot of time alone in her room. 'The fall must have shaken her up. Poor old thing.'

'She's not all that old. She had Lenora when she was still in her teens. It's some sort of rheumatism that twists up her bones and makes her so helpless. She's quite lively in her mind. Likes to talk about the old days. I'm all ears, so I am. There's no stopping her anyway. She's had a better time than we'll have.'

After that, Bridie was always hurrying away to do something for the old lady. Maggie thought she stayed away longer than she needed.

Tom was making a point of looking into the nursery every night to see if Maggie was alone. Often she was, because Bridie was making a habit of going out. It had been arranged that Maggie should have one full day off a month. She was counting the days as it came nearer, for she was longing to go home. To spend a night there and have the following day all to herself seemed an immense treat.

'A treat?' Tom asked. 'What will you do?'

'See my sisters.' She'd missed Harriet's abrasive manner. Underneath, they'd been close. Maggie knew she'd have received her first wages by then.

'I'd like to take Hattie over to Liverpool and go round the shops. Perhaps take her to Cooper's Café for tea. We used to do that in the old days.'

'Really?' was all Tom said.

After Maggie had supervised the children's supper and tucked them into bed, she was free to leave. She could smell the gasworks as soon as she got off the tram at Central Station. The place emitted the most noxious chemical smells, that dried and stung her nostrils. When the sky was heavily overcast and the clouds low, it brought a bitter taste to her tongue too.

The gasworks had been constructed in Argyle Street South in 1840 and had cast a blight over the whole area ever since. It was not just the smells. There was the constant noise and the lights that never went out.

Elizabeth Place was close behind the gasworks and Central Station, caught in the narrow triangle of streets between the railway lines that ran through the town. There were goods depots and engine sheds, and locomotives shunted back and forth at all hours of the day and night.

The streets seemed shabbier in the half-light than Maggie remembered. She quickened her step, feeling nervous about being alone here after dark. There were sounds of alcoholic jollity coming from the Railway Hotel in Cambridge Place. As soon as she let herself into the kitchen her sisters were all trying to hug her at once.

'We have missed you.'

Fanny put the kettle on for tea. She seemed to have grown in that short time and was already taller and more robust than Maggie herself. Pa was out, so they settled round the kitchen table.

'We want to hear about everything,' Hattie said. 'Start at the beginning.'

Maggie looked round at their rapt faces. 'You remember, Hattie, that car we saw parked down the side of the house? Tom Dransfield was working on it. He sort of took me under

46

his wing.' She told them how he came to sit by the nursery fire and talk to her every evening.

'The son of the house?' Fanny's eyes were round with surprise.

'Do you like him?'

'Oh, yes,' she breathed. Every time his grey eyes met hers she felt the tug of attraction. He heightened her senses. She thought she was falling in love with him, but she wasn't going to tell her sisters that. Not yet.

'Does he like you?'

He had a way of looking at her that left her in no doubt about that. 'He seems to.'

'You lucky thing,' Hattie burst out. Her huge eyes were shining. 'Throw you in a pig sty and you come out smelling of roses. You have all the luck.'

'Luck? That's just like you.' Maggie grinned. 'You weren't jealous of me when you left me on the doorstep.'

'Come on, we want to hear every detail,' Fanny urged. 'Is he handsome?'

She couldn't deny that. Nor the way her heart raced whenever he came near. She went on quickly to tell them that his mother was a dragon and had given her a hard time that first day.

'What about the rest of the family?'

'His father has mousy whiskers and eyes that look sideways at me. He'd look like a pirate if he weren't so smartly dressed.'

'Is he awful to you too?'

'No. He has a voice that booms through the house but he's only spoken to me once or twice. He's quite kindly. There are two more sons, Luke and Eric, older than Tom but just as handsome. Only Sophie is married, she's the eldest. She leaves everything to do with the children to the nanny, who isn't all that good.'

She told them about the awful uniform, and that she had

47

to get up to light the nursery fire. It wasn't all wonderful. It was just that Tom was there and made it seem so.

'There's something else, Hattie,' she said, when Fanny was seeing the three youngest into bed. 'It upset me at the time. Tom told me that his father had bought our old business. Knell's Gloves are being made again.'

She knew from the way Hattie's mouth opened that she was shocked too. And there was worse. Maggie told her what she'd overheard Tom say to his mother.

At the time, she'd felt angry and suspicious; even so, she was shocked at Hattie's reaction. She was furious, blaming the Dransfields as well as Pa for their present privations.

'We've got to get to the bottom of this, Maggie. We've got to find out exactly what happened. This puts everything in an entirely different light.'

'Tom says he doesn't really know if it's true.'

'I bet he does.'

'He's not sure, just suspicious. I think he'd tell me if he had proof.'

'Then it's up to you to find the proof,' Hattie blazed back. 'You're in the house with them. You must ask the right questions. We can't let them get away with it. Just look what it's doing to us.'

Maggie thought of the long days she spent shut away in the nursery, and didn't see what she could do.

'You and Pa are just the same,' her sister raved. 'You take everything lying down. You must do something.'

'But what exactly?'

'I don't know. Tell me everything you know about these Dransfields. What do they make? Not just blouses?'

'They make a lot of things.' Tom had told her they made baby clothes too. She'd enquired more closely about that and found that the factory for whom Hattie hand-smocked baby dresses was owned and run by Dransfield's.

48

'So I'm working for them too?' she asked, her eyes wide with outrage. 'An outworker, paid three shillings for embroidering a dozen garments? I won't any more. Not for them.'

'Tom says the market's good. That up to now women have always gone to the local dressmaker for clothes for themselves and their children. But Dransfield's are mass-producing them and can make them cheaper and to a higher standard.'

'Pa said they were a powerful family.' Harriet was really wound up. 'I wish I knew whether they'd been honest with him. No doubt they'll make a good profit from our gloves.'

Maggie had been looking forward to sleeping late the next morning, but she was thoroughly woken when Harriet got her four younger sisters up to go to school. She'd forgotten how chaotic it was as they all tried to dress at the same time in the confined space. She also realised, now that she'd grown used to having a bed to herself, how little comfort there was for three to sleep in one.

The problem was that two double beds took up all the floor space that could be spared. As it was, they had to move one of them to get inside the wardrobe, and even moving the bed was difficult because there were boxes and trunks stored underneath. They had so much surplus crockery and glassware, curtains, blankets and towels from their old home.

Maggie stayed where she was until they'd all gone into the kitchen for porridge and tea. She could hear Clara and Enid bickering, and Hattie's voice trying to restore order.

The next moment the bedroom door burst open and Hattie was pushing Clara in, in front of her. 'Where is it? What have you done with it?'

Sheepishly, Clara was looking under her bed. She fished out a black woollen stocking.

'You knew you had a hole in the heel.' Hattie was exasperated. 'You should have mended it last night.'

Clara shot back to the kitchen while Hattie sank down on the bottom of Maggie's bed.

'She took one of Enid's. Tried to tell me it was hers. What are we going to do with her? We've no more clean ones.'

Maggie pulled herself up the bed. 'I'll darn it now.'

'Would you? She can't go without stockings. I'll send her in with the sewing box.'

The hole was enormous. As she weaved with her needle, Maggie was reminded just how fraught early mornings could be here.

When the crush in the kitchen suddenly moved out, Maggie got up. Harriet had collapsed on the one decent chair.

'It's pandemonium, isn't it? All of us struggling here like this, cooped up in two rooms and a kitchen.'

'Leaving home isn't exactly a bowl of cherries, you know. I miss you all.'

'We're living like animals. I wish Pa could get a better job. A porter . . . I can't believe . . .'

'Better if he can keep this one,' Maggie said. He'd been working at the Borough Hospital for four months. Before that, he'd had jobs as a shop assistant and a labourer and never managed to keep any of them longer than a week.

'But if the glove factory's working again, there must be work he could do there. He managed it. Couldn't you ask Mr Dransfield to give him a job?' Harriet was overcome by her good idea. 'You said he was kindly.'

'No,' Maggie said firmly. 'Pa's the last person he'd want there. And Pa wasn't good at managing it. He went bankrupt, didn't he?'

50

'I just wish there was some way out,' Harriet said furiously. 'I feel trapped. There's so much work to do here. I never stop.'

'Today you will.' Maggie smiled. 'I'll help you this morning, and we'll go over to Liverpool this afternoon. It'll do you good to come out for once. We'll have a look at the shops in Bold Street, just like we used to.'

'We've no money to buy anything.' Hattie was still out of sorts.

'I've been paid. Let's dress ourselves up in our best clothes and have a cup of tea at Cooper's.'

'I'll have to make a stew or something for dinner tonight.'

'I'll buy something nice. Something that doesn't take so much cooking. We can bring it back with us.'

They were getting ready when Maggie discovered that Hattie had decorated her best winter hat with the bird they'd both admired on their mother's hat. It peeved her somewhat, but poor Hattie had a lot to put up with, so she pretended not to notice.

From Elizabeth Place it was easy to catch the underground train from Birkenhead Central and go right into the centre of Liverpool, where the big shops were. Maggie had meant it to be a window-shopping expedition only, but she bought them each a pair of fine wool stockings.

It was cold, although it was an afternoon bright with winter sun. They were both ready for a cup of tea by three o'clock, and Maggie steered her sister down to Cooper's Café.

'This is more like old times, isn't it?' she asked as they were making their way towards an empty table. They were sitting down and undoing their coats when Maggie looked up to see Tom weaving his way through the tables towards her. She felt her heart race with pleasure.

'What a surprise to meet you here, Maggie,' he said with a wide smile.

'Is it?' She felt fluttery. She remembered telling him that she intended bringing Hattie here.

'Won't you and your sister join us at our table?' He indicated one by the window. Maggie could see Luke Dransfield watching them. 'We'd be very pleased if you would.'

She felt shaken and surprised. 'Are you sure?'

'Of course, been waiting for you.'

'Well – thank you.'

'Join them? The Dransfields?' Hattie hissed, her eyes wide with trepidation. 'We really shouldn't! No lady would. We hardly know them.'

'I know Tom.' She could trust him, none better. 'You said you wanted to meet him. Come on, now's your chance.'

'But it's quite improper. Pa would say they were very presumptuous to ask us. Taking advantage. You don't know him that well.'

'He comes to talk to me almost every night.'

'But you work for his family.' She was grasping Maggie's arm as they crossed the café. 'Be sure to introduce me properly, Maggie.'

That reminded Maggie of how tongue-tied her sister could be in company. Both men were staring with stunned admiration at the sparrow-sized bird on her hat. A wing of glossy feathers curved becomingly up the crown.

'This is Tom Dransfield and his older brother,' Maggie said. She'd barely spoken to Luke. Would he consider it a liberty if she called him by his given name?

'Luke,' he said, smiling at Hattie. He had bronze-coloured eyes that matched his hair, and a fashionable pencil moustache. He'd filled out more than his brother, looked older, more of a man. 'I've heard so much about your sister from Tom.'

'I'm surprised to see Tom here,' Maggie said. 'I'd have thought he'd see enough of me in the nursery.'

Hattie was always telling her she had the gift of the gab and was very forward, but that wasn't true. The problem was really Hattie's: she was introverted and couldn't shine in any company except that of her family.

'I've seen nothing of her at all,' Luke said. 'Tom's kept her well away from me.'

A new pot of tea was ordered for them. Maggie had meant to offer Hattie a teacake as a special treat to cheer her up. Luke was pressing a whole plateful of fancy cakes and cream pastries on them. It would have been hard to refuse, even if they'd wanted to.

Luke sat back and began to talk of the baby clothes business. Maggie looked at her sister; neither mentioned that they were more than familiar with his product.

'You're taking a day off?' Maggie asked. 'You're a long way from your factory.'

'Do you know it?'

'Yes, in Birkenhead, not far from where we live,' Maggie said, and received a warning glance from her sister. She'd never have admitted that.

'You must come in and see me when you're passing,' Luke said to Harriet. Maggie knew she wouldn't dare, she'd be afraid the woman responsible for the outwork might recognise her and tell him.

Tom helped himself to another chocolate cake, and started telling them about the Hispano-Suiza car his father had recently bought, but which he allowed them to drive because he didn't care for driving himself. He even spoke of taking Maggie for a ride in it.

Maggie thought Hattie had looked peaky this morning, but now her cheeks glowed with colour and her big eyes were shining.

'Hattie reckons I'm lucky to have a job,' she bubbled. 'She'd like to do the same herself.'

'Really?' Tom asked. 'I understood you had to stay home to look after your own family?'

'Mm, yes.'

It was typical of Harriet to volunteer no details about

53

herself. Maggie had to tell them of Harriet's responsibilities at home. Hattie herself was making light of them.

'We have another sister, Frances, who'll be leaving school after Easter. She's very good at looking after the younger ones. Does a lot for them now. I'm sure she'd be only too pleased to have me out of the way.'

It was the first Maggie had heard of this. It was she who brought the tea party to an end.

'We've stayed too long. All our sisters will be home from school before us. Pa too, and he'll expect a meal on the table,' she told them. 'Thank you for the tea. I can't remember when I've enjoyed myself so much.'

'You enjoyed yourself too, didn't you, Hattie?' she asked when they were going home on the underground. 'What do you think of the Dransfields? It doesn't seem likely they'd cheat Pa, does it?'

Seeing Tom and Luke, so fresh-faced and open, it seemed unbelievable. Like her, Hattie was torn in two directions.

'Perhaps not those two,' she allowed. 'But it's their parents who run the business, not them. I'm going to ask Pa exactly what happened between them.'

Harriet continued to seethe. 'I bet Pa would be easy to crook. You know what he's like. Too much of a gentleman even to think anybody might cheat.'

When they got off the train, Hattie began to worry. 'What are we going to eat?' Maggie knew there was no meal prepared, and they'd spent so much time in the café, she hadn't bought anything as she'd promised.

The shop on the corner of Elizabeth Place that cooked faggots and pease pudding was beaming light and appetising scents into the street, quite covering the sulphurous smell from the gasworks.

'I'll come home and get a couple of dishes,' Maggie said. 'And while you build the fire and get the kettle on, I'll run back to that faggot shop. I'll buy one each for us and two for Pa, with lots of pease pudding.'

Maggie's heart was singing. She was captivated by Tom, and the wonderful, marvellous, totally unexpected delight was that he seemed to be very keen on her too.

'I don't think you even care that his family could have cheated us,' Hattie complained.

'I don't really believe they have. You do like him, Hattie?'

'Yes, I liked him. I liked Luke too. You're lucky, you'll be able to see more of Tom. How can I meet anyone when I'm at home all the time?'

'We've both had a lovely time.'

'But it won't happen again. I won't see Luke again,' Hattie lamented. 'Not unless you marry Tom.'

Maggie felt her heart turn over at the very thought. She'd hadn't allowed herself to think so far. Anyway, Lenora Dransfield would be very much against it. She'd make sure it didn't happen.

'He seems very much attached. Couldn't take his eyes off you.'

'Pigs might fly,' Maggie said lightly.

'If only Pa hadn't lost all his money and got us into this mess.'

Harriet seethed all evening. Pa seemed to sense that they wanted to talk to him, and shot out again almost as soon a supper was over. It was one of the things that really infuriated her, to see him going out for a drink when it would be cheaper for him to drink at home.

'You'd think,' she said to Maggie, 'he'd be glad to stay at home when he's been out all day.'

Maggie had to go back. She was supposed to be in by ten.

'Don't lose your temper with Pa, Hattie,' she said as she left. 'Poor Pa, he's as upset as we are by all this.'

Harriet saw all her younger sisters to bed and waited up alone. She worked at her smocking; she'd done three-quarters of this bundle and knew she had to finish it or she wouldn't be paid, but it was the last bundle she'd do. Her eyes were closing when at last Pa came home.

'You still up.' He put his head round the kitchen door because he could see the line of light under it when the gas was lit. 'You'll strain your eyes working on fine stitching like that. The light isn't good enough.'

'Enid needs new glasses, Pa. She's broken the frame again. I have to get money from somewhere.'

'She's very careless with them.'

'She's only eight. It's not easy for her.'

'I'm glad Enid's the only one to inherit your mother's eyesight.' He was taking coins from his pocket. 'Here's something towards them.'

Hattie counted up what he was giving her. 'I've enough for new frames now, but it's time she had her eyes tested again, and sensible to do that first. She might need to have them changed.'

'Very sensible.'

'But it could cost a lot.'

He patted her arm. 'You'll manage, Hattie. You always do.'

She sighed. 'There's something else, Pa. I . . .'

'I'm tired now.' His mild eyes were wary.

'I'm dropping, but it's important.'

'Come to my room.'

'No, it's cold in there.' Hattie poked the dying embers in the range to a blaze. 'Please sit down for a moment and listen.'

Obediently he lowered himself. He looked spent. 'What is it?'

'How well do you know this Dransfield family? Maggie seems suspicious. Thinks they may have cheated you.'

'I thought she seemed happy with them. I was pleased to find her settling down well.'

'That's as maybe. You do know they now own Knell's Gloves?'

He sighed. 'Yes,' he admitted, looking a little sheepish.

'You didn't tell us. Why keep it a secret?'

'Not a secret, I just don't like talking about what happened.'

'I wish you'd tell me exactly what your connection was. You called them business associates, yet Knell's Gloves was always yours. It came to you through your family.'

It took Pa a long time to reply. Hattie had to bite her tongue to stop herself prodding him further. At last his pale blue eyes looked into hers, and he said: 'I borrowed money from the bank to take a lease on more factory space. I bought more machines. I was aiming to double my output.'

Harriet nodded; she'd known that much. 'And you didn't?'

'No. And the business was harder to run on two separate sites. I was trying to expand into muffs and bags and that didn't work out either.' Pa got up to poke the fire again. It was going out.

'Then what happened?'

'I doubled the workforce, and then I had to pay for twice as much leather. I needed more thread and more stockinet for linings, and I couldn't sell the finished gloves quickly enough to pay my bills. Couldn't pay the interest on the loan when it was due, so the bank wanted to foreclose.'

'But where do the Dransfields come in? You did know them at this time?'

'Yes, I've known Daniel Moody for years. His father and mine were friends. I used to have lunch with him occasionally at the Woodside. Sometimes he brought Stanley Dransfield too.'

'They're your drinking partners?'

'Friends.'

'But I still don't see how . . .'

'I borrowed money from Lenora Dransfield to repay the bank. So I could carry on.'

Harriet closed her eyes and gulped for breath. 'You borrowed money from her?'

'I thought it was a way out, it would give me more time, but things didn't improve. In fact they went from bad to worse. A year later, I couldn't pay her and had to file for bankruptcy.'

'Pa! Oh my goodness!'

'It was all legally done, Hattie. Stanley Dransfield was supportive. Daniel Moody too. They tried to help me.'

'What about Tom Dransfield?'

'The boy? Stanley asked me to take him in to gain experience.'

'In a firm that was fighting to stay in business? Fighting for its life? What sort of experience was that? He should have been learning good business methods, surely?'

'I thought he was a nice lad.'

'He's the one who's suggesting there might have been fraud.'

Pa was shaking his silver head. 'Doesn't know what he's talking about.'

# CHAPTER FOUR

Henry got up abruptly and went to his own room. He couldn't bear Harriet's accusing eyes any longer. The February cold seemed to penetrate to his very bones. He got himself ready for bed as quickly as he could, though he was no warmer there, even with his dressing gown across his feet. They felt like blocks of ice and he couldn't get to sleep.

Now Hattie had awoken his memories he couldn't get Lenora Dransfield's handsome, heavy face and steel-sharp eyes out of his mind. Over the last few years, he'd felt haunted by her and the need to raise money to keep his business running, but he'd never thought her capable of fraud.

When Stanley had suggested her as a source of finance for his business, he'd invited her round to see his factory, and gone through his books with her. He'd thought her knowledgeable. More knowledgeable than Stanley. The money had been forthcoming without much fuss. Her perfume seemed to hang about his office for days.

He'd thought Stanley a fortunate fellow to have such a wife. To be so informed in matters of business was unusual in a well-bred woman. Stanley had told him wryly that he'd married into the business, that it had come down to Lenora through her family and that she was very firmly at the helm.

He'd said he was only seeing to the day-to-day running of her factories. At the time, Henry had even envied him that.

He could discuss any difficulties with her and not have to take full responsibility.

Henry welcomed visits from Lenora: they were partly social, and she was always friendly. She started to come regularly on Friday afternoons. He kept her up to date with what was happening in his business. It helped to talk his problems over with her. Two heads were always better than one. She was supportive, suggesting ways and means by which he might keep himself afloat. She talked to him of her own businesses. He thought of her as a friend.

He was seeing more of her family. Lenora was very involved with them, particularly her children. 'The coming generation,' she called them. She gave him to understand that her whole aim in building up her businesses was to provide for her family. She'd invited Henry to their house for dinner several times. The Dransfields were offering him friendship as well as money. That only made it more difficult for him.

He'd been somewhat embarrassed. His mind went back to that morning when he'd been into Birkenhead to see a supplier of thread. He was later than usual going over to Liverpool and he caught the ferry from Woodside instead of Rock Ferry.

On fine mornings, it was the habit of all office workers to walk the deck on the crossing to the Pier Head. He passed the time of day with many people he knew. Now it had gone ten o'clock and most office workers were at their desks. There were fewer passengers than he was used to. Only the captains of industry and some early shoppers were on this ferry.

He was very surprised to see Stanley Dransfield, because there was no need for him to cross. All the Dransfield businesses were on the south side of the river. It was a blowy morning and the breeze was parting the mutton-chop whiskers on his cheeks. Henry raised his arm in greeting but Stanley didn't notice him. He was too engrossed in what his companion was saying. He was smiling down at an attractive woman.

Henry stepped back out of Stanley's sight. Afraid he might embarrass him. The fire ran up his face as he asked himself if Stanley had a mistress. He sat down and opened his newspaper, holding it up to hide his face.

He watched as they strolled round again in the thin crowd. No, it wasn't Sophie, his daughter, although this girl wasn't much older. Neither was there much doubt in his mind about this relationship. The girl was laughing up into Stanley's face and had her arm twisted through his so that he could hold her hand. Even worse, when the breeze parted her coat, there was no doubt but that she was in the family way.

It shocked Henry that Stanley was cheating on Lenora. He felt full of sympathy for her. He'd never known Stanley to show her this amount of affection. Now he thought about it, they didn't seem close. In fact, they were usually a little prickly with each other. All morning he thought of Lenora, wondering if she knew her husband had a mistress, but by lunchtime his perennial worry about money had taken over.

For Henry, that worry was growing week by week. The shortfall between the money his business was bringing in and the money going out was growing. The date he was due to pay interest on the loan he'd had from Lenora was coming closer and closer, together with the awful knowledge that he wouldn't be able to pay her.

He tried to tell her this one Friday afternoon, while her steel-blue eyes surveyed him, and her diamonds flashed fire. She said rather sweetly that she was prepared to wait for her money. He felt terrible about it. A loan from somebody like her was much more personal than one from the bank. He knew he was getting more deeply into debt. He wished now that he'd sold up a year earlier and paid off the bank loan.

The following Friday afternoon, Lenora didn't turn up at the usual time. He was a little uneasy, thinking she wasn't coming because he couldn't pay her the interest that was due. She came two hours late, and he knew immediately that something must have happened. She looked pale and shaky and her eyes wouldn't meet his.

He had his account books on his desk. He opened them and started to talk to her about sales figures for his gloves. He knew she wasn't concentrating. He heard her gulp and looked up to find her eyes glazed with tears. He was on his feet and round to her side of the desk in an instant.

'What is it, Lenora?'

He'd meant to put a comforting arm round her shoulders, but she stood up and clung to him. He held her tight while she sobbed.

'Bit of a shock. Stanley . . .'

It came out slowly that she suspected Stanley of having a lady friend because he was spending money he couldn't account for.

'That hardly seems like proof,' was the best Henry could manage, since he knew her suspicions to be well founded. She was dabbing at her eyes with a lacy handkerchief and wearing the soft floral perfume he found so attractive.

'Could be he's gambling or something like that.' He smiled. 'You could be worrying yourself unnecessarily.' She was upset and he wanted to comfort, not confirm. 'Did you ask him?'

'Yes, he denied it.'

'There you are then.'

'He looked . . . quite shocked, as though I'd found him out. I think I'm right.'

She was angry with Stanley: Henry could see her eyes burning with fury, almost feel her seething with it.

'He never loved me, Henry. He married me for my business.'

'Nonsense,' he told her. 'I've envied Stanley, having a

62

handsome wife like you. I'm sure you could have had a dozen husbands when you were young. The business didn't enter into it.'

'You're very gallant,' she said quietly. 'But what I'm saying is true. I suppose I should have expected this of him.'

Henry had had a cup of tea made for her, and left her alone in his office for ten minutes to pull herself together. When he went back, he told her it was time they all went home. She usually came over on the ferry and then picked up a taxi at the Pier Head.

'A walk will do you good,' he said. 'I usually walk on fine days.'

He'd meant to put her on a ferry bound for Woodside and wait for one to come in to take him to Rock Ferry. On the spur of the moment, he went on board with her. She stood at the rail, staring down at the muddy water swirling below, while the seagulls swooped and called over their heads.

'I've suspected it before, and allowed myself to be convinced I was wrong. It's not easy to accept after twenty-six years of marriage.'

'Lenora, you have your children, your family, and you immerse yourself in your businesses. You have a full life of your own.' Henry stopped, wondering if that was the right thing to say.

'You're a real gentleman, Henry,' she told him as he put her into a taxi at Woodside. 'Please be good enough not to speak of my problems.'

'My dear, of course I won't,' he assured her.

The following day being Saturday, Henry closed his factory at midday. He no longer enjoyed his weekends. The girls always seemed in high spirits, wanting him to join in their fun. He couldn't face their bicycle rides and shopping trips, preferring to be alone to take a stroll along the promenade.

It was a rather bleak and chilly day: not raining exactly, but from time to time there was drizzle in the air. In fine weather it was a popular place to stroll. Today, there were few people about. Because he felt restless and could think of nothing better to do, Henry went as usual, keeping his eyes down on the packed earth of the promenade with its edging of neat sandstone slabs. He was trying to keep his own confidence up, telling himself that all might still come right with his business if he just kept going a little longer.

'Henry?'

Lenora Dransfield stood before him, her eyes anxiously searching into his. She wore a very smart hat of mauve feathers and a fur cape over the shoulders of her mauve coat. It was an outfit he hadn't seen before, and it made her look very prosperous.

'Fancy seeing you here.'

'Not a pleasant day for a walk.'

'I had to get out for a while. Get some air.'

'Me too.'

Henry was sympathetic. The confidences she'd entrusted him with yesterday made him feel closer to her. He could feel the moisture in the air again, heavier than before, and she was struggling to put up a purple umbrella. He took it from her to open it, holding it over them both.

'It's becoming quite nasty, I'm afraid.' He turned round to accompany her back. They needed to stay close together to benefit from the umbrella's meagre protection. He took her arm to hurry her along. The clouds were dark and heavy as though threatening worse. By the time the slipway and the ferry buildings were in sight, it was raining quite heavily.

'What about a cup of tea in the Royal Rock?' Henry suggested. The hotel was close now. 'We can shelter until this passes over.'

'What a good idea.' They went up the path almost at a run and through the front door.

Lenora was much more animated now as she shook the

moisture from her furs. There was a heightened colour in her cheeks. He sat with her near the fire while a three-tier cake stand was brought to their table, together with the tea.

He watched her pour out and thought how long it was since a woman had done this for him. Henry counted up the years he'd been a widower: five now. He'd thought of marrying again. It seemed the best thing, for both him and the girls, but he hadn't found the right woman. Deep down, he had the feeling that nobody could take Edith's place.

Lenora's mouth was lifting at the corners. She was no longer petulant as she spoke of her business. They spent so long talking over their teacups that when Henry looked round, the cake stands had disappeared from the other tables. Lenora agreed to take a glass of sherry with him. When it came, she took one sip and said:

'Henry, I think it would be rather nice if you took me out to dinner tonight. What d'you think?'

The suggestion took his breath away. He didn't know what to say.

'I've nothing to go home for, after all. I don't think Stanley will even be there, and I'm enjoying this so much. It seems a pity to part now.'

He tried to smile. It seemed churlish to refuse, and yet . . . He thought he was making sympathetic sounds without committing himself one way or the other.

'We need to think of your reputation, Lenora. You can't be seen with me. So many people know you.'

'You're very gallant, a real gentleman. You're right, of course, but it's easy to take the ferry over to Liverpool from here, where no one will recognise us. You and I, we'd make a good pair, you know. We get on well together.'

Henry swallowed back the desperation that was rising in his throat.

'We could even make a habit of it. You're a widower, after all, you have nothing to lose. You must be lonely sometimes, feel the need of feminine company?'

'Yes, of course, but I have my daughters . . .'

'Didn't you say your daughters were more of a responsibility than a pleasure?'

He shook his head.

'A different sort of pleasure then.' She sounded coy.

Henry didn't know what to say. Was it an affair Lenora was suggesting? Her hand rested on top of his in a gesture of affection. He eased it away. She was reading more into their friendship than he'd intended. He'd never make a play for a married woman, he wasn't that sort. And anyway, he counted Stanley as a friend. He had to stop her. 'Stanley . . .'

'I don't think either of us needs to consider Stanley's feelings in this. He's forfeited any consideration from me.

'Very silly of him, because I've kept everything in my name. He's got nothing, absolutely nothing, and he isn't going to get away with treating me like this.' Her eyes flashed steel as she spoke of her husband.

Henry rolled his sherry round his mouth and tried to think. 'I'm not sure . . .'

'You understand me, Henry. I don't want you to worry about paying me interest. I can waive that to help you get your business back on its feet, and you can have all the time in the world to repay the capital.'

Henry could feel the sweat breaking out on his forehead. How could he stop her? Every minute was making things worse. Lenora was getting in deeper and deeper. They were both going to feel very embarrassed about this. Even more than he was already.

'You don't have to tempt me, Lenora. You're very kind. Of course I shall be very pleased to have more time to repay you, but . . .'

She smiled, showing the numerous gold fillings in her teeth. 'Then it's settled.'

'Lenora, no.'

He could see her expression of affection fading. 'No what?'

He was wallowing in embarrassment. The woman was propositioning him. How did he tell her that he didn't want it? He couldn't come straight out and say so: he didn't want to upset their business relationship, that was important to him. He must not convey to her this toe-curling embarrassment.

Should he take her out to dinner? No harm in that, but it would get him in deeper, perhaps bring even greater embarrassment later.

It took him an age to get himself together and choke out: 'You're distressed by what's happened, Lenora. I value your friendship, believe me. But you'd find me exceedingly dull company if you saw more of me. Not nearly so clever as you and Stanley.

'Wait a few weeks until you're over this shock, and you'll thank me for not adding to your difficulties.'

Her sharp eyes were full on him. He saw her lips tighten. He hadn't meant her to see this as rejection. He was trying to cushion it. She was getting to her feet.

'Perhaps you're right, Henry. Good day to you. Thank you for the tea.'

He stood up too. 'It's raining harder than ever. I'll get you a taxi.'

'Don't bother. I'll get it myself.' She headed straight across the lobby and out in the rain.

The commissionaire snatched up the umbrella kept for such purposes and rushed after her.

'I could have summoned a taxi to the door for you, ma'am,' Henry heard him say.

Lenora led the way to the ferry, splashing through the puddles, while the commissionaire followed, holding the hotel umbrella deferentially over the mauve feathers of her hat.

Henry went back to his sherry and tossed back what

remained in two gulps. On his way out, he collected her purple umbrella from the stand where she'd left it. He'd send a messenger down to her factory with it tomorrow.

He'd seen very little of Lenora after that. Her Friday afternoon visits stopped. He worried about her and hoped he hadn't upset her too much. He couldn't get over the fact that she'd offered to waive all interest on his loan. In the weeks that followed, as he watched his debts mount, he wished that he'd considered that more carefully.

When he was due to pay her interest on the loan, he hadn't sufficient funds to do it. He had to pay the wages and the bills for leather and other materials, so that the business could carry on. He was afraid he'd taken advantage of her friendship and decided the only thing to do was to make an appointment to see her in her blouse factory. He meant to apologise and ask if she was still willing to allow him more time.

He'd been a bit nervous about being alone with her, but her office was just a corner partitioned off from the workroom, with barely enough privacy to discuss delicate matters. His lack of ease made him stiff and formal. He called her Mrs Dransfield, not Lenora.

'Of course you may have more time, Henry,' she said readily. Her heavy features had seemed more tightly controlled than usual. 'Didn't I tell you you could have all the time you needed?'

Her manner seemed little different – perhaps a touch more distant – and when he got up to go, he felt much better. She didn't appear to have taken offence. She was more worldly-wise than other women, and it seemed he'd smoothed over what might have been an embarrassing incident.

He'd thought it a kindness that she'd allowed him more time to pay. But it had had the effect of driving him deeper and deeper into debt, and of guaranteeing that eventually he'd go bankrupt. He might have been left with something if he'd sold up sooner: his house and a little money to educate the girls.

Now, having heard what Harriet had to say, he wondered if Lenora had taken his rejection to heart and deliberately led him on with the end result in mind. It could have been her way of taking revenge on him.

It might, of course, have been her intention to get control of his glove factory from the start. He might have been able to thwart that had he taken her to dinner and gone along with what she'd wanted. He didn't know.

Like the fool he was, he hadn't believed her capable of anything like that at the time. He'd thought of her as a friend, who in her own distress over Stanley's behaviour had taken his words to mean more than he'd intended.

Either way, Henry decided, this wasn't something he could explain to his young and innocent daughters.


Maggie was seeing less of Bridie. For most of the time she was left to manage the children on her own. They were used to her now and gave her little trouble. She decided she preferred it this way.

On the nights Bridie was out late, Maggie sometimes heard her creep up to her bedroom on the other side of the landing, long after the rest of the house had settled down to sleep.

'Don't they lock the doors when they go to bed?' Maggie asked her.

Bridie giggled behind her hand. 'I've got a key to the garden door. Luke had it copied for me.'

Maggie couldn't stop her gasp of astonishment.

'Don't they bolt the doors at night?'

'Mr Dransfield does. He bolted me out one night.'

'What did you do?'

'Had to knock Ruby up, her room's down in the basement. Now she makes sure the bolt's off before she goes to bed.'

'You'd get into the most awful trouble if . . .'

'The Ogre would do for me if she found out.' Bridie flashed her flirty eyes. 'But I have to have a bit of fun.'

Maggie thought she was having fun in other ways too. One night, after she'd gone to bed, she heard such a scuffling outside on the landing that she got up to see what was causing it.

Bridie was there and immediately dissolved into a fit of giggles, and Maggie saw Eric Dransfield's back as he ran downstairs. Bridie's face was scarlet, and she'd never seen her eyes so bright.

Maggie found herself thinking about Tom a good deal. She knew she listened for his voice at times when she thought he might be home. Although isolated in the nursery, she was always very conscious of the other people going about their business in the house. From time to time, she heard footsteps, slamming doors and raised voices downstairs. Sometimes it was even possible to hear what the Dransfields were saying. Sounds from below seemed to funnel up the stairwell.

Yesterday, at dinner time, Lenora thought the joint of beef overcooked, and Mrs Summers was summoned to the dining room to hear her complaint. She left the door open.

'It's done like Mr Wood likes it.' Cook's voice echoed upwards, justifying her cooking. Maggie knew she'd worked for Mr Wood, an undemanding widower for twenty years before coming here.

'You're not working for Mr Wood now,' Lenora retorted. 'You're working for me, and I don't like it cooked to a frazzle. Beef should be pink and succulent.'

Tonight, Maggie was coming out of the nursery bathroom and on her way to bed when she heard another commotion going on downstairs. Bridie had gone out and the children were already asleep. Tom had told her he wouldn't be coming upstairs tonight because they were expecting guests for dinner, but even the guests had gone now.

She could hear Lenora's strident tones and knew she was angry. Her first thought was that Bridie had been caught coming in. She crept down a flight of stairs to hear better.

The three sons all seemed to be down there. Their mother raged on. Stanley Dransfield was there too. She could hear his deep voice. The argument went on for some time.

She was sure it was about Bridie, though she didn't appear to be there with them. Then Stanley's voice boomed out: 'She's staying, and that's that. I don't want to hear any more.'

She asked Tom about it the next time he came up. He was surprised she'd heard so much. Yes, he said, his mother had wanted Bridie dismissed.

'What for?'

'Mother thinks she's leading Luke and Eric astray. Dad said they can look after themselves. He doesn't think it's a good time to get rid of Bridie when Sophie's about to produce another infant.'

Bridie was still around, so it seemed that Lenora Dransfield's word was not always law in this house.

Over the next ten days, preparations were being made for Sophie's confinement. Maggie was sent up to the attic to bring down the cot, the cradle and the perambulator. She dusted and polished them and put the mattresses in the airing cupboard. Bridie took out baby clothes for her to wash and iron, and she and May worked hard at stripping a spare bedroom of all soft furnishings. May was left to clean it thoroughly. Bridie set out sheets and towels in readiness and told them that a doctor and nurse were booked to attend the birth.

'Mr Moody wants me to take charge of the infant, so he does.' Bridie was proud of that. 'Right from birth. He'd rather trust me than some stranger. Also, I'm to look after Sophie's needs in the following days. That means you'll have to do more for Mrs Clark and the children.'

Maggie didn't mind about that. She was getting used to life in Ottershaw House. Seeing Tom almost every evening made her feel she was walking on air.

'Don't say anything to Bridie about us seeing each other,' he'd warned. 'She goes round the house shooting off her mouth to everybody. I don't want word to get back to Mother.'

Maggie smiled. 'I'm so happy, I'd like to shout it from the rooftops.'

'No, Maggie.' He put a hand on her arm. 'I'm afraid Mother will . . . She'll blame you. She'll try to end it by dismissing you. The last thing we want.'

'I haven't said a word,' Maggie told him, 'but I don't need to. I'm getting winks and knowing glances from Bridie. She says you're coming up to the nursery much more than you used to. She knows why.'

'I wish there was somewhere else I could see you.'

'You saw me in the café on my day off.'

He smiled. 'What about your next night off? We could go to the pictures.'

Maggie felt a little shiver of pleasure. 'It'll be nearly eight before I can get away.'

'The following night then, when you're off all day? Probably better, then I can bring you back here afterwards.'

Maggie hesitated. It seemed a daring thing to do. Pa wouldn't approve. He'd be shocked.

'Luke wants you to bring Harriet again. Says you need a chaperone. Better for all of us if we go as a foursome.'

Maggie smiled shyly. Tom was very thoughtful. 'Hattie would like that, I'm sure. Yes, then. Thank you.'

Harriet was pleased when she told her and was very keen to go, but by the time they were getting ready, she seemed nervous. Hattie wasn't sure that young ladies should make arrangements to meet men outside the Savoy Cinema, but neither did she want them calling at Elizabeth Place. And really it was very forward of them not to see Pa and ask his permission first.

Maggie noticed that she took longer than usual to get ready, and was quite edgy on the walk up. But Tom and Luke were waiting, so meeting them was much easier than Hattie had feared. Their only moment of embarrassment came because Harriet was wearing her hat with the bird again, and was asked by the lady seated behind her to remove it during the performance.

'I'm bowled over by the cinema,' Tom said, full of enthusiasm. 'It's the entertainment of the future.'

They saw a one-reel film with the newest American star, Mary Pickford, called *Her Darkest Hour*, and a live news documentary of the Scott Expedition to the South Pole. The main feature was a French film.

When the show was over, they were persuaded to go to the Woodside Hotel to have supper. Maggie could feel Hattie's agitation at that.

'Pa goes there sometimes,' she breathed aghast. 'He'd forbid us . . .'

'He's working,' Maggie whispered. 'Won't be there now.' She took her sister's arm.

'Come on, I'm hungry,' Luke urged. He had the use of his father's car and they were down there in moments. When they were seated at a table behind a large aspidistra that shielded them from other diners, Maggie could feel Hattie's relief.

For both of them, it was the first time they'd been taken out by men friends. With his pencil moustache and bronze hair, Maggie thought Luke handsome and very attentive to Hattie. She could see her sister making an effort to be sociable, though she said little enough. It always surprised her that Hattie could lay the law down to her family yet clam up completely when she was with other people.

73

Tom had plenty to say: 'I can foresee the end of the music hall and straight theatre. They're making better and better films. I can see a huge demand.'

After the meal, Harriet wanted to walk home.

'We can't let you walk home by yourself at this time of night,' Tom said, and Luke insisted she get in the car.

She then asked to be dropped outside Central Station so that she could walk behind the gasworks, and thus avoid them seeing where she lived. Luke insisted on driving down Hind Street.

Maggie could feel Harriet growing tense. 'Pa will be home by now. He'll ask all sorts of questions if he sees me getting out of a car.'

Luke turned into Elizabeth Place and stopped. Maggie sat where she was, knowing that Harriet was stiff with dread that Luke would insist on escorting her to the door. He did, and Maggie watched them walk the few yards side by side, Hattie holding herself aloof. At the end of the street were the railings and the back gate to the gasworks, closed and locked at this time of night. The smell had never been worse. Nor had the noise from the pub in Cambridge Place.

On one side of the road were small houses with their front doors opening straight off the pavement. On their side, the houses were much bigger and had railings in front of them. On the doorstep, Maggie saw Luke raise Hattie's hand to his lips, and knew just how shocked her sister would be to find him so forward. She shot inside like a rabbit into its burrow.

Luke came briskly back to drive them home then, but stopped the car twenty yards from the gates of Ottershaw House. Tom got out with Maggie to escort her to the back door. In the darkness he pulled her against him, his body firm and strong. Then his mouth was on hers and they swayed together. In that heady moment Maggie felt on top of the world and brimming with love for him. He seemed so caring, not only for her but for Harriet too.

He left her to go back to Luke. They were going to have a cigarette and wait five minutes before driving in. It wouldn't do for any of the household to realise that they'd taken the nursemaid to the pictures.

take his turn in the bread line. They were going to
...take you... that state of affairs... we would... the
...teams, too, for all the bread lines. And had... had the
...taken his rations in our future.

# CHAPTER FIVE

A few days later, Tom came to the nursery beaming with pleasure.

'I've fixed up an outing for us,' he laughed. 'On the day Sophie has her baby. We're to take the children out, perhaps for a picnic. Daniel thinks it a good idea to get them out of the way, and Father's agreed to let me use the car.'

'Lovely,' Maggie said.

'Just to make it official, I had a word with Bridie. I didn't even have to suggest you came with us. She did.'

Maggie was tingling. 'Let's hope Sophie doesn't give birth at night.'

'Then we'll go the next day. Sophie doesn't want the children to feel left out. She isn't spending as much time with them now because she needs to rest.'

The morning arrived when Bridie came up from the kitchen with the breakfast porridge and the news that the midwife had been sent for. Sophie had started to feel unwell in the night.

Maggie felt a little shiver of anticipation, not just for the imminent birth. It was April and a blowy spring day; she could hear the cuckoo calling in the distance.

'Today's the day for the outing.' Bridie laughed and winked theatrically. 'Tom was in the kitchen asking for the picnic basket to be filled. He wants you to have the children ready downstairs by ten o'clock.'

'Ten o'clock.' Maggie felt like singing. She packed rugs, and parasols to keep the sun off them, and a sponge bag with a damp flannel for sticky fingers. She put on a clean apron and cap.

Mr Moody saw them off. He was already looking agitated and seemed glad to have something to do. He kissed the children as though they were going to the end of the earth. Maggie sat with them on the back seat, because he would see that as the right place for her. She felt tense with excitement and wished her sisters could see her now.

Adam's piping voice began to sing 'Lavender's Blue' – Maggie had taught them several nursery songs. She sat Jane on her knee and tried to encourage her to sing too, and joined in herself because her spirits were soaring. Then Tom added his voice, leading loudly when the road stretched emptily ahead, fading away if he had to make a turn.

The journey along the New Chester Road was fantastic. They passed the trams, and the horses pulling traps and carts. Private cars were still a rarity, and everybody turned to watch them roar past. She saw nothing as fine as the Dransfields' car all the way there. It seemed a huge juggernaut.

He drove down to Eastham Ferry and parked the car. The children ran about squealing with delight at the river and the big ships coming in so close to the bank as they headed into the Manchester Ship Canal. They each had a glass of lemonade seated out in front of the hotel, before climbing back in the car to drive closer to the woods.

Many of the trees were just coming into full leaf. Underneath, dappled by the sun as it filtered through, there were bluebells as far as the eye could see. The ground seemed to have turned blue. They almost had the place to themselves: they saw only one man walking with a dog, and three ten-year-olds running. Maggie sighed with satisfaction.

They strolled along a woodland path, the children scampering ahead. Tom carried the picnic basket and kept calling them back to point out a frog he'd seen amongst the roots or a red squirrel high in the branches.

'This is heavenly,' she breathed when the cuckoo began to call close to them. They'd walked almost across the wood when Maggie found a mossy dell where it was possible to spread out the rug without crushing the bluebells. Tom unpacked the basket.

When they'd eaten hard-boiled eggs and ham pie, she put the children down for their afternoon rest.

Tom moved a little distance away and spread out the other rug. The ground was a little higher here, and there were fewer trees. He stretched out on it and found he was in the full sun. He adjusted the parasols to shield them from the children's eyes.

Maggie sat down beside him, feeling very daring. She trusted Tom, though she knew many would disapprove of behaviour like this, calling it wanton. It wasn't at all what young ladies were supposed to do; it was very dangerous to lead a young man on.

'Wait a moment,' she mouthed. Little Jane's eyes had been closing, but Adam was growing out of his need for an afternoon nap and was humming to himself. The humming died away, and within minutes she could see both children were breathing more deeply.

Tom put an arm round her shoulders and pulled her closer. Maggie felt she could ask no more of life than to be near him like this. He began to pull the pins out of her cap to remove it. His touch sent frissons of pleasure down her spine.

'You're very beautiful,' he whispered. 'Such lovely hair.'

She smiled. 'Harriet says it's like sheep's fleece.'

He stifled a laugh, pulling at the ribbon that held it tight. 'Maggie, it falls to your shoulders in tiny waves and it's a lovely colour. Like cream.'

The breeze was tossing it about her face. He caught it in both his hands and pushed it gently behind her ears. It seemed such an intimate and loving gesture that her heart turned over.

'Even your eyelashes are blonde.'

'White and straight. Hattie says they're pig's eyelashes.'

He was laughing down at her and shaking his head. 'Don't listen to your Harriet.' His eyes were searching into hers. 'You laugh with your eyes.'

He moved closer and bent towards her. His breath was warm against her cheek. She thought he was going to kiss her. She could hardly breathe.

'What I'm trying to say, Maggie, is that I love you. Really love you.'

Maggie thought she'd burst with happiness. She'd longed for this, but thought she was hoping for too much too soon.

'I love you too,' she whispered. 'I can't think of anything but you.'

'I know.' His finger traced the line of her chin.

'How?'

'I can feel your love. It pulls me if I come anywhere near you. I can't take my eyes off you.'

'That's how I feel about you.' She felt heady with pleasure.

Tom laughed out loud. Triumphant and with delight.

'Ssh. We don't want to wake the children.'

He put his arms round her and his lips came down on hers. Maggie felt ready to die with love for him.

He whispered: 'With you I feel I can reach for the sky.' His voice shook slightly. 'I want to marry you. Will you, Maggie? Will you marry me?'

He ran his fingers through her hair, round her neck, undid the button at her throat, explored further, taking liberties that only a lover's fingers should be allowed.

'If only we could.' Maggie sighed and rested her cheek against his rough tweed jacket. She felt there was nothing more she could ask of life. She was in love, and marriage to Tom would be wonderful. She closed her eyes. 'If only we could.'

'We will,' he vowed. He meant it, she knew that. She wanted to believe it could happen.

'But what will your family say? Your mother?'

He kissed her again more passionately. 'She won't like it. She'll think I'm too young. She'll not approve of you. But I know we're right for each other. I'll make it happen.'

'How?'

He was shaking his head. 'I don't know. Don't say anything yet. I love you, and come what may, we're going to be married.'

Maggie smiled. 'It'll be our secret.'

'Until I can work out some way.'


Maggie felt on cloud nine. With her hair tied back and her uniform cap firmly pinned on top of it again, she rode back to Ottershaw House with an arm round each of her charges. She could hardly drag her eyes from the back of Tom's head. It seemed almost a fairy tale that in just a few short months her life had changed so completely. She also felt full of fresh air and sunlight, and the sharp, fresh scent of bluebells. She'd had a wonderful day out.

As Tom drove through the gates she could see his father looking at the tulips, smoking a cigar. He came over to them as they pulled up.

'Is Bridie not with you?' His voice was sharp; anxious, even.

'No, she never intended to come.' Maggie was helping the children out.

'Grandpa, I picked some bluebells for you.' Adam was trying to present him with a bunch.

'I think you'd better keep them for your mother. Just the thing for her.'

Maggie knew they'd picked enough to present every adult in the family with a bunch. She could see Mr Dransfield's whiskers twitching with agitation.

He said to his grandchildren: 'You have a new baby brother.'

'It's all over then?' Tom was smiling. 'Sophie's all right?'

'She's fine, but your mother's demented. Bridie was supposed to be here to help, and we can't find her.'

Maggie saw him staring at her. He asked: 'Do you know where she's gone?'

'No, sir. I thought she was going to stay here and help with the new baby.'

'Over eight pounds, a fine healthy son. He's to be called Jonathon Stanley George.'

Maggie said to the children: 'Lovely, a new baby brother.' They seemed excited, wanting to know how soon they could play with him. Jane was disappointed it wouldn't be today.

'Come on, Adam, we'll go up and put the flowers in water. What do you say to your Uncle Tom?'

'Thank you, Uncle Tom.'

Her mind was buzzing with curiosity about Bridie. This morning, she'd never stopped talking about the imminent birth. She'd seemed more on edge than usual, but that had been understandable. Where could she have got to?

Maggie shepherded the children up to the nursery. They looked hot and tired. It had gone five o'clock, and she decided she'd bath them now before their supper, expecting that they'd be sent for to see their new brother.

By the time she'd tidied herself up, it was time to fetch their supper. She shot downstairs. For once, nursery supper wasn't ready on time. The kitchen seemed in a turmoil.

'Bridie'll get the sack for this,' Ruby said.

'Deserves it, I'd say,' grunted Cook.

'Here, did she tell you where she was going?'

'I didn't know she was going anywhere.'

'Missing on the day she was needed most. Mrs Dransfield's very displeased.'

'Bridie McNammee's a flighty bitch. Always out after some fellow or other. She's gone too far this time. Surely she didn't expect to get away with this?'

'Here,' Ruby asked. 'Have her clothes gone too?'

Maggie's heart lurched. Why hadn't she checked?

'Go and look now,' Cook said. 'I'll have your suppers dished up by the time you come back.'

Maggie ran up to Bridie's room at the top of the house. The new baby was supposed to be coming here. The big cot had been brought in and was already made up. The cradle had gone down to Sophie's room. Maggie pulled open the wardrobe and saw a row of empty hangers. A clean uniform dress remained, but nothing else.

She took a long, shuddering breath. Bridie had meant to go then. She opened a drawer in the chest. Nothing but a few black stockings. She picked them up. They all had holes in their heels. She was hurtling back downstairs when she met Ruby coming up.

'Mrs Moody's asking for the children. She wants them to see the new baby now.'

Maggie could hardly get the words out. 'Bridie's taken all her things. She's gone for good.'

She expected that the house next door would be missing their gardener too.


Olivia Clark felt out of sorts. She'd had a most uncomfortable day. She'd spent half the morning waiting for Bridie to come and help her dress. For hours on end there had been the tramping of footsteps in and out of Sophie's room just along the landing. Raised and noisy voices, and not a few screams of pain, whilst she was being totally ignored.

Finally, Ruby had been pressed into service. She'd come unwillingly to help Olivia get up, and Ruby had no finesse at all when it came to personal matters.

She'd been sitting in this chair by her granddaugher's bed for the last half-hour. She couldn't help but remember how different things had been for her when she'd given birth to Lenora. The sun was slanting across this large airy room. For her it had been in a mean two-up and two-down house shared by nine people; in a dingy back bedroom with brown circles on the ceiling where the rain leaked through. Rain had been hurtling against the window too at the time, and trickling through the crack.

For her, there had been no doctor, nor even a proper midwife. Her mother had asked the woman round the corner to help. She assisted at most of the births in the street, and laid out most of the dead too.

Today Olivia had suffered almost as much as Sophie, and Sophie certainly didn't appreciate how easy things were for her.

Stanley came bustling in with two bottles of champagne. Not much hair left on his head now; his pale scalp was showing through. Too much on his face, though, and his mutton-chop whiskers needed a trim. The bang as he drew a cork made her jump. He put a glass in her hand, and Olivia watched the bubbles rising through it. She'd been desperate for a cup of tea after Lenora's birth, but of course, Sophie had already had all the tea she wanted. This was a celebration.

For her there had been shame, not celebration. Her father had threatened to throw her out for bringing disgrace on his name. He'd threatened to beat her too. It was only her mother's pleading and continual presence that kept him at bay. She'd been Olive Smith then, and sixteen years of age.

She shouldn't be thinking of Lenora's father. It never made her feel any better. He'd been a sailor who'd been glad to get himself on another ship the moment she'd told him that a baby was on the way. He'd abandoned her with her unborn child. She'd vowed to herself then that she'd make a good life for her child if she had to claw her way up with her fingernails.

And here was Lenora, sparkling with jewellery, trying to look as though she'd been born to all this. Pretending it had always been part of the family ritual, to celebrate the birth of a new member with champagne. She watched Stanley pass Lenora a glass that was not quite full. With a burst of impatience she snatched up the bottle to top it up.

'A fine pick-me-up,' Stanley was saying to his daughter as he handed her a glass. 'Does us all good to see you sitting up again like this. Got it all behind you now. You've done well, Sophie. Damn pleased.'

'We all are.' Daniel Moody beamed at his wife. 'Another son.'

'Building another generation to carry on the family business.' Lenora was smiling at her, showing her gold fillings. 'Very important. What life is all about.'

'You said you were building the business up to support our growing numbers.' Olivia raised her glass. 'Pity his name won't be Clark.'

'Won't be Dransfield either,' Stanley guffawed. 'To the baby, Jonathon Stanley George Moody.' They all solemnly raised their glasses and drank.

'To the family.' Lenora was beaming round at them all. 'It's lovely to see another in the direct blood line, another heir. Providing for his future gives meaning to everything.'

But however satisfied Lenora was with her new grandson, Olivia knew this wasn't the family she'd hoped to have. They were not all pulling in the same direction; even she could see that. Lenora blustered and complained, and tried to make them all jump to her commands, while Stanley quietly went his own way. There were frequent clashes.

Lenora believed in the family. She centred all her ambitions on those in her blood line, but her children had inherited more from Stanley than they had from her. Lenora had overindulged them. They'd been spoiled from the day they were born, all of them. They were not desperate to make money in the way Olivia and Lenora had been. They were all enjoying themselves to the hilt now they'd grown up. Pleasure was their main aim in life.

Luke went thorough the motions of pleasing his mother, but mainly, Olivia suspected, to receive her largesse. Eric, too, was easily malleable, but Tom was more independent and inclined to cleave to his father. Sophie was the family's favourite. She'd been brought up to be a lady. She was like a flower, more ornament than use.

Daniel, her husband, had a mind of his own. Already settling into middle age at thirty-nine, he was a dry stick of a man. Too old for Sophie, but he was reliable. He looked honest through and through. Lenora would never get him to bend the rules if he didn't want to. Already there was a coolness between them.

The newborn infant started to snuffle and whimper. Daniel lifted him from the cradle and put him in Sophie's arms. The soft down on the baby's head was close against his mother's bright hair. They'd both inherited their colouring from Lenora, though hers was faded now.

Olivia sighed. Pity it wasn't a girl. They were more of a comfort to one in later life.

There was a soft tap on the door, but nobody took any notice. Another tap and it opened cautiously. Her great-grandchildren, Adam and Jane, came in, followed by Henry Knell's girl. Maggie? Yes, that was her name. A pretty girl who never tried to hurry her as Lenora and Bridie did. Sophie wanted to put her arms round all three of her children.

Lenora barked at the girl: 'Is Nanny not back yet?' She'd been angry all day because the nanny had taken time off, but Lenora hadn't been as inconvenienced as Olivia had been.

'I don't know what that girl's thinking of. Disappearing like this. Today of all days.'

'I'm afraid her wardrobe's empty,' the girl said. Olivia

happened to be looking at Stanley. That had a bombshell effect on him. His face seemed to crumble.

'What do you mean?' Lenora barked.

'She's taken everything she owns. It doesn't look as though she intends to come back.'

'She didn't ask to be paid . . .' Lenora said slowly. 'She wouldn't go without what she'd earned. Without a reference.'

'Bridie gone for good?' Luke asked.

'I'm afraid so,' Maggie told him.

Olivia roused herself. 'How are we going to manage now? It would be hard enough with a new baby in the house even with Bridie here.'

'We'll get someone else quickly.' Lenora had recovered. 'Perhaps the midwife will stay for a day or two. We can't manage with just . . .' Her eyes had gone back to Maggie Knell.

'I have an older sister, Mrs Dransfield. I think she'd come at a moment's notice.' Olivia saw the girl swallow. 'She'd like to read to Mrs Clark.' She smiled in her direction. 'And she's used to children.'

'What a good idea,' Olivia said quickly.

Lenora had made it clear to everybody that she hadn't wanted one Knell girl. She certainly wouldn't want another, but neither would she want to be left short-handed at a time like this.

'I think we should ask your sister to come,' Olivia told Maggie.

She knew already that if they were short-handed she'd be the one to suffer most. She'd be kept waiting for help to get into bed while the children were being bathed. If the sister was anything like this one, she'd be all right.

It was only then that she realised Stanley was staring at the wall, looking quite shocked. Eric had gone white and Luke looked nervous. Olivia realised that Bridie's

87

sudden departure was having a marked effect on others in the family.

Stanley was putting his glass down. 'Excuse me,' he said, and shot out of the room. She heard his footsteps hurrying downstairs.

Lenora got to her feet. 'Stanley,' she called after him, her voice full of suspicion. 'Where are you going?'

'Just something I've forgotten. Won't be a minute.'

Everybody heard the study door slam shut behind him downstairs. Lenora was hovering uncertainly. This was breaking up their little celebration. Eric was already on his feet.

'Help me out of this chair,' Olivia said to him. She didn't want to be left alone here with Sophie for hours on end. Not at a time like this.

'Where do you want to go, Gran? Downstairs or back to your room?'

She felt she couldn't face the stairs again tonight. She was exhausted. It had been a hard day for everyone, and they were all on edge. She was afraid tempers would flare.

'My room. I'll have my supper on a tray tonight.' Between them Luke and Eric lifted her to her feet. She felt like a rag doll swinging between them.

'What about another glass of champagne, Gran?'

'Thank you, a good idea.' Luke refilled her glass and carried it for her.

'I hope you two have nothing to do with Bridie's departure?' She was out of breath when they reached her room.

'No,' they were saying to each other. 'No, not us.'

But they looked and sounded guilty. Both of them.

Stanley felt cold. He reached his study and locked the door behind him. Stood with his back to it, listening. He didn't want anybody following him down.

If Bridie had gone without her wages . . . Bridie McNammee

88

was fond of her pennies. He was afraid . . . He poured himself a stiff brandy.

His study was a large room, and like the rest of the house, it was full of heavy Victorian furniture. Nothing much had changed at Ottershaw House since Osbert Clark had moved in with Olivia in 1872. This study had once been his. The décor was dark and masculine. Olivia had used it but had left nothing of her personality here. Stanley had taken over this room lock, stock and barrel when she'd given up working in the business.

He took a painting from the wall. It was a scene showing the charge of the Light Brigade. Behind it was a safe set into the brickwork. Osbert Clark had known what he was about. Stanley turned back to his desk to get the key, fumbling through pencils and other odds and ends in his drawer to find it. Frustrated with impatience, he dropped it on the carpet. When he finally got his safe open, he saw that the money had gone.

He stood in front of it, staring at the empty shelf. It was what he'd expected from the moment he'd heard that Bridie McNammee had gone without collecting her wages. What a thieving floozie she'd turned out to be! How was he going to explain this to Lenora? She already suspected more than the truth.

He threw himself into a chair to think. Got up to get himself another brandy. He kept a decanter on a side table to save having to leave the room. That was the one change he had made to this study.

Bridie! He'd thought her a bit of fun; now he was not so sure. She'd followed him in here one night with some long-winded opinions about which school Adam should attend. He personally had no interest in such matters, and absolutely no say. He doubted Bridie's interest. Anyway, the child had been no more than two at the time. It was just an excuse to come in here and talk to him. He'd asked her to sit down in the green velvet chair for a moment.

Bridie was not a beauty. Not a lady, either: her mass of red hair and flirty eyes tried too hard to attract male attention. She was generously built, not fat, but with plenty of soft and dimpled flesh. Lenora had wanted her gone because she thought the boys might become enamoured of her. Sophie had fought it: Bridie had known how to turn on the charm for her too.

He could see Bridie now, sitting before him on that chair. That night she'd shown more leg than was usual, her already shortish skirt hauled up to show her legs right up to the knees. He'd let his gaze linger. Well-shaped legs, slim and long, encased in black stockings. She'd got up abruptly to come and perch on the corner of his desk. She was higher than he was and temptingly close, her silken knees still visible. Deliberately she'd bent closer, encouraging him. The temptation to run his hand up those lovely legs was too great. She moved it up against her thigh.

'Mr Dransfield.' Her breath was hot against his cheek. 'I do think you're a lovely person.'

Somehow he found her in his arms. She'd been quite blatant, her generous mouth straining towards his. She'd made all the running to start with. That had made him very daring. The bare skin at the top of her stockings was smooth and silky. Her suspenders were new and strong. His hand was ever more daring, exploring further under her skirt, such warm, soft skin.

Suddenly he felt himself go hot all over. He could hardly breathe. He could feel the sensual satin of her corset, but she wore no undergarment. No drawers, combinations, pantalets, whatever women called them.

There could be only one reason why not. An open invitation to him. He'd sighed with enjoyment and pulled her closer. Bridie would be wasted on the boys.

He'd known then it was very unwise to do this sort of thing at home, but the invitation was so obvious, he couldn't hold himself in check.

Bridie was a laugh, he'd hardly taken her seriously. She let him know it wasn't an affair for her, just a bit of fun on the side. That had been one of the attractions. There was to be nothing long-term, no permanent entanglement.

Of course, he'd let her see too much. He'd opened his safe while she was in the room. Given her money more than once. She'd let him know that she liked to be paid for the service she gave. He knew now he should have been more cautious about how he'd done that.

Now he'd calmed down and thought it over, he told himself that Bridie had proved to be expensive. She'd certainly blotted her copybook by helping herself to their money. But would she do worse? He was well aware that the ultimate revenge any mistress could take was to let the wife know what had been going on.

He knew Bridie disliked Lenora; he had to hope that she'd been too fond of him to do that.

He was about to get up for another brandy when he heard footsteps outside. He saw the knob turn and fail to open the door. 'Are you in there, Stanley?'

It was Lenora. Reluctantly he got up to let her in.

'What are you doing? What have you locked yourself in for?' Her eyes flashed with suspicion. Stanley felt his stomach heave with guilt. Had Bridie opened her mouth or not?

'Just having a few minutes to myself. A quiet drink.'

'I want to see if . . .' She was already feeling in the drawer for the key to the safe. 'I've been thinking about Bridie. Going off without her wages. Not like her.'

Stanley said, as calmly as he could, 'I've already looked. You're right. She's taken your money.'

'What?'

'The money Eric collects for you.'

'The bitch!' Lenora turned to him, her face ugly with rage. 'How did she know we keep money there?'

Lenora never took his word for anything. She swung the door open to look for herself. There were a few envelopes on one shelf; the other was bare. Stanley could smell the dank, airless odour of the safe.

'You're sure it was her?' Lenora was beside herself.

'It wasn't me, if that's what you're suggesting.'

'It has been known!'

'Not this time.'

'The boys?'

'They might put their hands in but they wouldn't take it all.' Just like him, Stanley thought. 'Why don't you ask them?'

Lenora's mouth was open in disbelief. 'It'll be Bridie! How did she even know we had a safe?'

'I don't know,' he lied. 'Unless Eric let her see him put it in. He comes breezing in here, leaving the door open. I sometimes think the boys are a little careless.'

'Bridie was all over the house, poking her nose into our business, the little trollop. You and Sophie should not have stopped me giving her the sack. If I'd had my way she'd have been dismissed ages ago. It need never have come to this. Have you been on to the police about it?'

'No.'

'I'll do it.' Her face was flushed with rage again. She was rushing for the telephone in the hall.

'Wait a minute,' he said, pulling her up with her hand on the door. 'Do you really want the police? I'd think twice about it if I were you.'

Her bosom was heaving, her favourite sunburst brooch flashing diamond fire. Lenora hated to be cheated out of anything.

He went on: 'What money was in there? What exactly has Bridie taken?'

'I went to the bank yesterday. Lucky in a way. I cleared everything from the safe, except for . . .'

'Your illicit gains from Fevers and Jones?' He knew that

92

was the case: he'd helped himself to a few guineas from it last night. He wished now he'd taken more.

'Yes, what Eric brings home. And the reason I didn't bank that was that we decided it was safer not to.'

'Until we've written it through our books. To make it look as though it's been earned by our own business.'

Stanley knew that Lenora was trying to take cheaply a chain of five haberdashery shops in Liverpool and Birkenhead. They had sold Dransfield's blouses for decades; now they sold their gloves too, along with handkerchiefs, stockings, scarfs and ribbons from other manufacturers.

She'd managed to plant Eric in their accounts department to 'learn' the business. Eric was a qualified accountant, a friend of the owner's son. They trusted him to collect takings from the shops and do their books. Lenora's objective was to run the business down by sidelining some of the takings so that it appeared less profitable than it was.

She'd already given Burney's Baby Wear and Knell's Gloves the treatment and had managed to get control of both at bargain prices.

'How much was in here?'

'Over three hundred.' Lenora went scarlet with fury. 'That's a fortune to someone like Bridie McNammee.'

Stanley reflected sadly that it would be a useful sum to him.

'You're saying it would it be safer to let it go?' He could see her twitching with indecision.

'Yes, if Fevers and Jones have noticed what Eric's doing.'

'He doesn't think so. Says it's like taking sweets from babies.'

'I'd still let it go. No point in causing trouble for yourself,' Stanley said. 'I wouldn't complain to the police that cash of that sort's been stolen. It might invite questions you wouldn't like.'

'It lets the little harridan off scot-free.'

'Are the police likely to find her? Whatever you do, you're not going to get your money back.'

'Ruby says she's gone off with the gardener from next door. She'll know his name. Surely the police could trace them?'

'You do what you want. You always do in any case, but if you want my advice, don't.'

Lenora was shaking with anger again. 'You're a fool, Stanley. Not careful enough yourself. Are you sure this isn't your fault?'

He took a deep breath. 'How could it be my fault?'

'If there's a woman involved it usually is. You never know when to leave them alone. But you know I wouldn't put up with that, not being shamed in my own house. I'd boot you out.'

Stanley pretended a lazy sigh. 'For better or for worse, Lenora. We've been through all the reasons why you wouldn't boot me out.'

Her pepper-and-salt bangs tossed with impatience. 'Did you let her see the safe?'

'No. Servants get to know everything, and they talk. Ruby dusts in here, she could have seen it then.'

'She doesn't dust that well. And what about the key? How could she possibly get to know about that?'

'We should get a new safe. More up-to-date. One of those with combination locks.'

'I'll get one fixed in my room,' Lenora said through gritted teeth. 'Then I'll have more control over my money. You and Eric are always helping yourselves anyway.'

Stanley felt he could breathe again. Bridie had taken the money but she'd kept her mouth shut.

Olivia lay back on her chair. She was more comfortable here in her turret window than she was downstairs. Eric's smooth young voice was reading from the morning papers. Nearly seven in the evening and not yet finished with the papers. That showed what a day it had been.

He said loudly: 'You're dropping off, Gran. Is this boring you?'

'No, dear, I'm not asleep, just resting.' It amazed her that Lenora had been able to give her children such middle-class polish. Eric was an attractive young man who combed his hair straight back across his head.

'Do you want to hear more of this?'

'I think I'd like to get into bed now. Have my supper there. Could you ask Maggie to help me?' If only Eric had been a girl, he could have done it.

'Of course.' He was on his feet in an instant. Not quite hiding that he was glad to be released from the chore of reading to her.

'I hope she isn't busy with the children. I hate having to wait.'

She hated being dependent on anybody. Hated to be pushed out of the mainstream of life by her infirmity. These last few years she'd had to limit her activities to things of the mind, but Lenora no longer listened to what she had to say:

'Things are changing. You've been out of the business too long. Leave it to me.'

Olivia felt she was discounted all round. It was only when a family row broke out that Lenora came running to her for sympathy.

'Shall I get you another glass of champagne?' Eric was a kind and thoughtful lad.

'That would be nice. Help me up so I can go to the bathroom now.'

She was back in her chair; it was the most comfortable place to wait. She closed her eyes for a moment, then Eric was standing over her, holding out a brimming glass.

'Only white wine now, I'm afraid, Gran. And Maggie's

not here. She's put the children to bed and gone home to fetch her sister. That's what you wanted, isn't it?'

Olivia tried to pull herself up in the chair. 'Yes, but I can't manage by myself. I need help to undress.'

'Mother said she'd come and give you a hand.'

She felt a prickling of anger. 'What about Ruby? Can't she come and help me?' Ruby was clumsy and had to be told every single thing, but . . .

'She's setting the table and getting things ready for dinner. Mother said she'd come.'

'Well, I hope she isn't going to be long.'

It could be midnight before Lenora stirred herself. Olivia wished Lenora's magnanimity to those of her blood line extended to her mother. But Lenora was focused on the future, and what they shared was the past. A past that made them cleave together for protection. They were bound by fear, not love. It was a past they both wanted to forget.

'Here's Mother now.' They could hear her rapid footsteps coming from Sophie's room. 'Good night, Gran, I'll make myself scarce.'

'Good night, dear. Thank you.'

Lenora's face was even more forbidding than usual. 'You want to get into bed, Mother? You could have started undoing your buttons.'

'I'd be afraid to, Lenora. I could be left sitting here for hours with my clothes half off.'

Olivia struggled but couldn't get out of low armchairs without help any more. Lenora lifted her up like a sack of potatoes and set her on her feet.

'I always come as soon as I can. I know how impatient you get. Everything has to be done the instant you think of it. Come on, step out with your right foot.'

'Don't rush me.' Olivia forced her feet to move. She knew she was slow, knew she was awkward too, but it was Lenora's elbow that swept the framed photograph off her dressing table as they passed. The sound of shattering glass made her straighten up in alarm.

'Oh, dear! What a pity, that's a nice silver frame.'

'For goodness' sake!' Lenora picked it up impatiently. 'Now there's all this glass to sweep up too.' She was scattering more as she lifted it. The photograph fell out too. It was of Lenora's four children, taken nearly twenty years ago. 'What's this you're keeping behind it, Mother?'

Olivia was left to undo the buttons of her dress after all. 'What is it?'

'A picture of Osbert Clark. Why do you keep such a thing?'

'You know why. It would have looked odd if I hadn't kept a photograph of my late husband, wouldn't it?'

'It gives me the creeps to see him again. Reminds me what a pig he was.'

'I haven't seen it yet. It would be better if you spent less time mooning over his picture, and more time helping me.'

That caused Lenora to drag Olivia's dress and petticoats over her head, and release her corsets in a frenzy of activity. At last she had her nightdress and bedjacket on. Lenora snatched back the bedclothes and tipped her on to the bed, none too gently.

'Here,' she said, tossing the photograph on to her coverlet. 'Now you can feast your eyes on Osbert Clark to your heart's content.'

'Don't forget my supper,' Olivia called after Lenora's retreating footsteps, then she picked the picture up. Lenora was right: even an old picture of him could bring back that feeling of dread. The years she'd been married to him had been hell. Pure hell.

# CHAPTER SIX

Most of the houses in Elizabeth Place did not have bathrooms, and that was what Harriet missed most of all. Once a week, she took her younger sisters to the public slipper baths just across the road from Central Station.

All except Enid dreaded going into that dank, steamy place to start with. It was the one time she allowed Enid to leave her spectacles at home. To be compelled to go there advertised their poverty. But Hattie found that the staff were good with children, letting two go in together to keep the cost down, provided she was there to make sure they didn't get into mischief. Frances usually took Ruth in with her, while she went to scrub the other two.

Usually they went on Saturday mornings, but it was busy then. When Harriet realised there was a half-holiday from school on Thursday, she loaded a bag with towels, soap and clean clothes and decided to take them then.

At first she'd hated waiting her turn in the reception room because the other customers looked so rough. It took her some time to realise that those who wanted to keep themselves decently clean had more in common with her than most who lived in the streets behind the gasworks.

'Next, please,' the attendant called, and she ushered Enid and Clara into the empty cubicle. He was cleaning down the bath with a wire brush after its previous occupant. They took off their hats and coats while he turned on the hot tap with a special key to provide their measure of hot water. At last he left, and they were free to lock the door and throw off their clothes as fast as they could.

This was the part they did enjoy, lying back in the hot water. There was always an argument as to who would have the end with the taps. Harriet insisted it must be turn and turn about. Then she was kept busy lathering and rinsing their thick creamy curls, while all around she could hear the rush of water filling a nearby bath, or the gurgle as it drained away. Voices and footsteps reverberated off the tiled walls. All too soon the attendant was back, banging on the door and shouting, 'Time's up!'

It was an equal rush then to dry and dress them both, and fix hats on top of damp hair for the walk home. All left their hair loose, hanging down their backs, looking much darker and straighter until it dried.

Harriet had so disliked the public baths when she'd first seen them that she'd got into the habit of taking a bowl of hot water into their bedroom when the children were at school and having a wash-down, but it never made her feel as clean as a proper bath.

This afternoon there was nobody waiting, and on the spur of the moment, she decided to send her sisters home on their own and have a bath herself. It felt wonderful to lie back in the hot water. How she missed the comfortable bathroom they'd had in the house in Rock Park.

When she passed the baker's on the way home, she was reminded that she should have spent the fourpence on another loaf instead of a bath for herself, but it was six weeks since she'd had one. When she reached home, she found Fanny peeling potatoes in readiness for their dinner.

'There aren't very many, Hattie,' she told her.

There were fewer potatoes than she'd thought – hardly enough to go round – but she had no money left to buy more. Tomorrow was pay day for Pa.

They were having cold boiled mutton left over from the

day before. Harriet spread it out to make the helpings look bigger than they were. She felt guilty when she saw how quickly the plates were being cleared.

'Is there anything else to eat?' Clara asked. Although there was no filling her sisters, they were all growing fast, and they all had rounded limbs and a healthy colour in their faces. She kept telling herself they'd grow up strong and beautiful.

'I'm still hungry,' her father said. The guilt she felt made her turn on him fiercely.

'It's no good grumbling, Pa. You can't have three-course dinners. Not any more.'

'One course will do. Provided there's enough of it.' He looked hurt when he lifted his eyes to hers. 'Is there no cheese? I'll have some toast with that.'

'If there was cheese it would be on the table.' She couldn't stop, not now she'd opened the floodgates. 'We could all eat more.'

Her younger sisters kept their eyes on the plates they'd scraped clean. She knew they all hated to hear her shouting at Pa like this.

'Just toast then.'

'Pa, if you have toast now, there'll be nothing left for breakfast. You don't want the children to go to school on empty stomachs. A slice of bread and marge is little enough.' She knew she'd made Pa feel guilty too. He hated to hear her going at him like this.

'Surely you can manage the housekeeping better than this?' he exploded. 'When Maggie was here last week, you gave us best butter on our bread. We had eggs for breakfast and there were oranges for the children.'

'Maggie bought those with her own money,' she snapped back. Was he pretending he didn't know? 'As well as the piece of bacon I boiled for dinner the next day. She even bought you half a bottle of whisky. I told her to get us a sack of potatoes next time and not waste her money on you, because you don't let yourself go short of much. If you didn't keep so much of your wages as pocket money, you wouldn't be hungry now.'

Hattie knew she was overstepping the mark. She shouldn't lay the blame on Pa like this. She could see his face crumpling. Already he looked guilt-ridden. Next week he'd give her a little more housekeeping, but he wouldn't keep it up. If he couldn't buy himself a drink, he'd get more depressed.

She couldn't stop her tirade. 'I'm tired of telling you. Thirty shillings a week isn't enough to feed us all and pay for coal and gas and candles. Let alone the washerwoman. It can't be done.'

She took a deep, horrified breath. The silence went on and on. Nobody moved a muscle. Then the coals settled noisily in the range and the cinders brightened.

'I'll get some more coal.' Fanny stood up and took the hod out to the yard.

'Start washing up, please, Clara,' Hattie managed to say, though her voice sounded strained. Her other sisters took their plates to the sink then. Enid gathered the tablecloth and went out to the yard to shake the crumbs off. The movement and clatter broke the uncomfortable silence.

'I'm sorry, Pa. I've said too much.'

Hattie could feel tears burning her eyes. She felt for his hand, wanting his forgiveness. She loved Pa.

'Much too much.' He pulled his hand free. His face looked ravaged. He got up slowly, and his heavy steps went down the hall. His door shut firmly and finally.

Hattie felt a tear roll down her cheek and wished she'd kept her mouth shut. Why couldn't she be more like Maggie, who was always so even-tempered and reasonable? No wonder Pa loved Maggie more. She couldn't expect him to show her much affection. She was driving him lower, making things worse for them all. She scrubbed her eyes angrily with her handkerchief and stopped Fanny putting more coal on the fire.

'We can manage without now, it's not cold any more.'

Fanny stood back with her hands on her hips. 'I'll take them all outside for an hour or so. To give you a break.'

They both knew that even if she didn't, the younger ones would play out in the street until dark. When they'd first moved here, Harriet had been totally against such a thing. Her sisters playing hopscotch or skipping out in the street with all the local ragamuffins? Impossible to think of it. But there was no space indoors, they were on top of one another and she hadn't the energy to confine them to the back yard any more. Hattie knew her standards were slipping. The grinding routine was wearing them all down.

'I wish you wouldn't rub Pa up the wrong way,' Clara said, before she went too, leaving the back door open. 'It makes him cross with us.'

Hattie dropped her head in her hands. Poor Pa. What was she doing to him?

He was right to call her a shrew. She'd seen ages ago how guilty he felt about what had happened, yet it didn't stop her heaping more blame on his head. She'd been horrible to him. Wasn't she equally selfish? She'd purloined that bird for her own hat, knowing how much Maggie wanted it. She must take it off in the morning, and sew it on Maggie's when she next came home.

Out in the street, she heard a shrill child's voice say: 'Don't yer all talk posh? Real la-de-dah, you lot.'

She wished she could see some glimmer of hope for them. There was no way they could work their way out of this place. They'd all end up in domestic service like Maggie.

She felt on edge and anxious, hungry too. At least Maggie already had all the food she could eat. She'd said the nursery meals were chosen to suit the digestion of young children, but that there was all manner of leftovers from the family she could have if she wished. Cakes and pies never went back to the table again once they'd been cut into.

She heard footsteps and looked up to see Maggie coming up the yard. She hadn't expected to see her again until next month when she had her day off. Her first thought was that she must have been given the sack. There was a sinking feeling in her stomach. Did this mean there was another problem?

Maggie was all smiles as she came into the kitchen. 'Guess what?' She threw herself in the basket chair, kicked off her shoes and tucked her feet under her.

'What?' Harriet knew she sounded grumpy.

'What about a cup of tea?' Maggie bounced out of the chair to coax the cinders back to flames. She put a lump or two of coal on, and filled the kettle.

Maggie's aquamarine eyes were searching into hers. 'There's a job for you at Ottershaw House if you want it. You'll be helping me in the nursery and be a sort of lady's maid or companion to Mrs Clark. That's Tom's grandmother. Are you pleased?'

'Domestic service?' Harriet's mind was whirling. How could she possibly leave here? Ruth was only five, and she'd never left her, not even for one night. Pa wouldn't be able to manage. And if she went, she might not like it. Probably wouldn't.

'But as a companion. That's less menial than being a nurserymaid. I'm to be nanny from now on.'

Hattie ran her fingers through her fawn hair. It was all working loose from its bun, hanging in long tails about her face.

'If I go, Fanny will be saddled with all the work here. Will she be able to cope?'

'Why not? You had to.'

Fanny was tougher than Maggie. She had her feet more firmly on the ground, but she was barely fourteen. 'Anyway,

104

if I did take a job, I'd want something better than domestic service. I could get that any time.'

'But as a companion?'

That was more tempting. And Maggie would be there in the same house. She'd ease her in. Tell her what she needed to know.

Maggie said: 'You'll have to help me in the nursery as well.'

Hattie watched her get up to make the tea. Busy herself with cups and saucers. When she turned round to the table, she was indignant.

'I wouldn't have suggested you if I hadn't thought you wanted it. What's the matter with you, Hattie? Now's your chance. I rushed to put the children to bed and came haring down here to fetch you.'

Harriet could feel her heart pounding. What was the matter with her? She had wanted it. Now she felt full of doubt. She didn't have Maggie's outgoing nature.

'You'll have to come straight away. Bridie just upped and went. I can't manage on my own. I thought you'd jump at it.'

Harriet sipped her tea and said nothing.

'Mrs Clark's needing more help now. She's grown used to having it, since her fall. I can't do much for her, not with a new baby to look after as well as the other two.'

Hattie tried to think. The trouble was, she always wanted what Maggie had. She glanced at her, lying back on the old chair, small and dainty, yet with a curvaceous figure, while she was tall and lanky and thin as a piece of string.

Maggie had the talents and the good looks. She also had a way of making things go right for herself and being content with her lot. Maggie laughed her way through life.

'You're the clever one, Harriet,' Pa kept telling her. 'The serious one who can think her way round problems. You'll have to help the rest of us.' Dare she desert him?

'You aren't listening,' Maggie was saying. 'They need

somebody right away. That's why they'll take you. There's no time to advertise and have interviews. A month's trial on either side, see how you get on. That's what Mrs Dransfield said.'

'It's her fault we had to come to live in this dump. Her fault Pa lost all his money.'

The anger and resentment Hattie felt about that had been building up ever since Maggie had told her. Yet the only Dransfields she could put a face to were Tom and Luke, and she couldn't feel resentment for them. They were both charming.

She needed to get closer to them if she was ever to get to the bottom of it. And it was no good waiting for Maggie to do something like that.

'You'll be able to see more of Luke.' Maggie was still smiling.

Seeing more of Luke was the real temptation. And she wanted to get her own back on his mother.

'She's awful, you said?'

'You won't like her, but she's mostly out in the day-time. Seeing to the businesses. Tom drives her round in the car.'

'Well, perhaps . . .'

'Luke thinks you're coming. He seemed pleased.'

'Really?' That cheered her.

Everyone knew that for young ladies in their predicament, the way out was to marry money. Perhaps Maggie would. Harriet thought that was possible. Perhaps, if she were lucky, she could too. Luke seemed a very nice person.

'I thought you wanted to get out of here?' Maggie's eyes were searching her face again.

Hattie made up her mind. 'I'd like to. Yes, I would. I'll have to talk to Fanny first, though, see if she's willing . . .'

'Good. I'll call her in, then I'll help you pack.'

'I'll have to ask Pa too. I can't just go off without a word.'

'Has he gone to the pub?'

'He's in his room. He might be glad to see the back of me.'

Maggie grimaced. 'You've not been arguing with him again? Let's go and ask him.'

Hattie couldn't believe it was happening so quickly. One minute there seemed no possible way she could escape the drudgery of Elizabeth Place, and the next, her bag was packed and she was getting off the tram with Maggie.

It was dark now. She was growing more agitated with every step. How easy it had been to deliver Maggie to this door. How much at home she seemed now as she led the way in through the kitchen passage.

'Leave your case here, Hattie. I'll take you to see Mrs Dransfield first.'

Harriet looked round the hall with approval. She liked the grandfather clock and the Persian rug laid on a parquet floor. She heard Maggie draw a deep breath before tapping on the drawing-room door.

'I've brought my sister, Mrs Dransfield,' she was saying.

The room seemed vast. Seated in armchairs, one each side of the fire, were the people Harriet had grown to resent. She felt two pairs of eyes fasten on her. Mr Dransfield stood up, as though she was a lady. It was his wife who spoke first.

'Thank you, Maggie, you can leave us. Come closer,' she said to Harriet, 'so that we can see what we're getting.'

Hattie advanced to the middle of the room, feeling the woman's cold scrutiny. There was an empty chair but she wasn't invited to sit down.

'So you're Maggie's sister – what's your name?'

'Harriet Knell.'

'Harriet, then, how old are you?'

'Eighteen, Mrs Dransfield.' She wasn't going to address her as ma'am. 'I'm the elder.'

Lenora Dransfield was on her feet and circling round her to take in every detail of her appearance. She put her face within a foot of Harriet, and Harriet couldn't help but notice the forbidding expression and the discontented droop to her mouth. Other similar questions were being fired at her. Hattie felt dislike for the woman stirring within her.

Mr Dransfield remained on the hearthrug, rocking on his heels. His gaze felt more affable. He was eyeing the bird on her hat with what she thought was approval. She wanted to hate him. This was the man who'd done them so much harm. He looked pleasant, even smiled.

'Thank goodness you've come. Our family finds itself much in need of assistance. I'm sure you'll fit in, my dear. Your sister gives every satisfaction, doesn't she, Lenora?'

That made Hattie feel a little better. 'I'll do my best, sir.'

'Good, my mother-in-law's settled down for the night now,' he told her. 'And probably Sophie too. It's getting late. Better leave everything else until morning.' He reached for the bell pull, and Maggie came to escort her back to the kitchen.

'We've made a cup of tea,' she told her. 'Come and meet the staff.'

They were all sitting round a large scrubbed table. She was introduced to Ruby, the parlourmaid, and May, the tweeny. Cakes were set out, and Mrs Summers, the cook, was cutting large slices of apple pie, and covering them with cream such as Harriet hadn't tasted in months. She cleared her plate in moments.

'You're not much alike,' Cook said. 'Another slice of the pie?'

Hattie put out her plate. She'd been taught that a lady shouldn't accept second helpings, but being thought a lady was now less important than staving off hunger.

She followed Maggie up to the nursery, where she was introduced to Daniel Moody. He'd been reading by the fire, so that he'd hear the children if they woke. He shook her hand and thanked her for coming at a moment's notice. Hattie thought of him as Pa's friend, and felt she was now in a better position to find out what had happened.

The new baby started that instant to whimper for his feed, and he went to see if his wife was awake. Maggie seemed efficient and bustled round showing her where the nappies were kept and changing the baby in readiness.

He came back to say that Sophie was too tired to feed the baby. They must give him a bottle and she'd see to him in the morning. Hattie followed Maggie back to the kitchen in order to see where the milk was kept and prepare a bottle. Then she sat down to feed the infant while Maggie got herself ready for bed.

Hattie wasn't so pleased with her bedroom. The bed had been made up with clean linen but nobody had got round to cleaning the room as thoroughly as she thought was necessary. She found Bridie's uniform bundled up waiting to go to the wash. She unpacked her case as quickly as she could.

Maggie said, 'I'm ready to drop. We've all been kept on the go since Bridie went. Ruby's been looking after Mrs Clark, and with Sophie newly delivered, it's been hard for us all.'

As Hattie slid between the sheets, she thought she'd like living in this house. She liked the feeling of uncluttered space in the big, comfortable rooms.

Long before Hattie felt ready for it, Maggie was thumping on her door and telling her it was time to get up. She decided she wasn't going to wear a uniform, although in the cupboard she'd found a clean print dress that had belonged to Bridie. Instead she put on a plain grey morning dress of her own, and covered it with one of Bridie's aprons for working in the nursery.

'It's almost as hectic here in the mornings as it is at

home,' Maggie said. She'd already lit the nursery fire and was feeding the new baby again. The older children were running round in their night clothes.

'Get them washed and dressed,' Hattie was told. 'There's an early start here, but luckily the old lady sleeps late.'

Overseeing nursery breakfast was somewhat easier than breakfast at home, because the porridge and tea were made for them. Then Maggie took her down to the floor below to meet Mrs Clark.

She didn't answer Maggie's tap, but they went in anyway. Her room was large, being directly over the drawing room and about the same size. It had the same turret window on the corner of the house, giving views round seventy-five degrees. Every pane was closed but bright morning light flooded in, while a newly lighted fire was begining to draw like a furnace.

Harriet would have liked to throw open the windows. There was a stuffy fug of medicaments. A whole table was given over to an array of bottles and ointment jars. In particular there was a smell of wintergreen.

The bed was against the back wall. The old lady was propped up against snowy pillows, with her breakfast tray across her knees. At first sight she seemed to be dozing again. She wore a frilled nightgown with satin ribbons round the neck and a fluffy pink bedjacket round her shoulders. A frilled nightcap covered most of her white hair. Her face didn't look very old, but her hands did. They were folded in front of her, knotted and misshapen.

'Good morning, Mrs Clark,' Maggie said in her bright and breezy manner. 'How are you this morning?'

Sharp eyes of pale blue shot open. They went from Maggie to Hattie. 'Who's this?'

'My sister Harriet. She's stepped into the breach at a moment's notice to come and help you.'

'Oh, yes, Bridie upped and went.' Harriet felt her scrutiny. 'I hope you're going to stay?'

110

'I hope I'll give satisfaction and be asked to stay,' Hattie returned.

'You look as though you might. Yes, I like the look of you. Bridie, now, she seemed the sort that would take off like that. Flighty. Impatient, too.'

'Harriet's very patient,' her sister said. 'Have you finished with your breakfast tray?'

'There's nothing else on it I can eat,' the old lady said. 'Is there?' The egg shell had been scraped clean; only toast crumbs remained on the plate.

'I'll take it out of your way, then.' Maggie snatched it up. 'Harriet will help you wash and dress. You'll have to tell her what you want her to do.'

'I'm quite capable of that.' As soon as the door closed behind her the old lady said: 'Your sister never stops talking.'

Harriet half smiled. Maggie had said the same about Olivia.

'I do hope you have less to say.'

'Very much less.' Hattie smiled.

'The first thing you can do then is go down and find the newspapers. The *Mail* will be in the dining room where Stanley's left it. *The Times* too. Then you can read to me.'

Harriet went downstairs, with no idea where to find the dining room. She was just in time to see the parlourmaid coming out of a room with a tray of dirty dishes. She whispered: 'Is that the dining room?'

When Ruby nodded, she opened the door to find someone still sitting at the table. The newspaper was being lowered. It took Hattie's breath away to find it was Luke. His bronze hair was still damp from his morning bath and his shirt looked fresh from the iron.

'Hello.' His face lit up in a delighted smile. 'I was wondering if you'd come. Glad you decided to. Very pleased.'

His eyes were searching her face. She thought his manner very forward. He certainly looked as though he hoped for as much from her as she did from him. She felt his welcome, and her spirits rose. Remembering why she'd come, she started looking at the newspapers lying open on the table.

'Your grandmother sent me to find the *Mail*.'

'Here.' He was trying to fold it into its creases.

'Sorry. You were reading it.'

'Doesn't matter. Granny won't appreciate being kept waiting. I'd take them all if I were you. She'll want you to go through them.'

'Thank you.'

'See you tonight.' He gave a conspiratory wink. Hattie felt her heart racing like a mad thing. She'd come here hoping to see more of him, hadn't she?

Harriet thought Mrs Clark was very alert. As soon as she had the papers, she opened them on her bed and brought a gnarled finger down on an article. 'Read this,' she demanded.

By the time Harriet had done that, Olivia had her finger on the next piece she wanted read out. Some of the articles were long; not many were missed out.

'Read the obituaries. People younger than me are dying off, you know. I like to read about them. Tell myself I'm doing better.'

'Indeed you are, Mrs Clark.'

'What do you know about that? Is there anything on recent wills? I like to know how much people are leaving behind too.'

Mrs Clark went through all the newspapers. Harriet thought she'd read everything of interest in *The Times*, only to find her returning to it. She was folding it to the pages that gave the share prices.

'Now, Harriet, we'll just check . . . Open this drawer for me.'

Her bent finger pointed towards her bedside table. A small key was offered: the old lady brought it out from under her pillow.

'That book. Thank you, I'll have it here. Now, what price are White Star this morning? You'll find that listed under Shipping.'

The old lady was writing figures down in her book. 'What about Royal Insurance?'

Harriet thought it went on interminably.

'You read well,' she was told when the book had been locked away again. 'Better than Bridie. You've been well taught. Where did you go to school?'

'Herman House, in Rock Ferry.'

'Really? It was called the Misses' Ladies' School when it first opened. It has a good name. Of course, you're one of Henry Knell's girls, aren't you?'

'Yes, Mrs Clark.'

'Poor Henry.'

Hattie wanted to ask how well she knew him. Wanted to ask a thousand questions. She wished Maggie were here to do it, she was as tongue-tied as ever.

'I want to get up now,' the old lady said. Harriet was kept busy rubbing her swollen joints, some with wintergreen ointment and some with camphorated oil. She discovered that the old lady wore a jacket of pink thermogene wadding under her blouse and she liked to have pads of the same stuff strapped to her knees.

'I find it a great comfort. It keeps my poor joints warm and stops them growing any stiffer.' When at last she was dressed, she said: 'I'll sit in the turret for a while now.'

'This would be a lovely place to have your bed,' Hattie said. It was some eight feet across, and the view down into the garden was lovely. The tulips were a mass of red in the flowerbeds, and beyond, near the hedge, was a summerhouse.

'Not a good place in bad weather.' The old lady shuddered. 'Almost like being outside.'

'But when the sun shines it catches it all.'

'That's why I have this couch here.'

The sun seemed to make the smell of wintergreen even stronger. It was catching in Harriet's throat.

Harriet found it a mixed blessing to be working at Ottershaw House. She liked the space and the comfort and the ordered way of life. She was quite taken with poor old Mrs Clark, who always had something interesting to say. She found her workload easier than it had been at home.

But she felt full of guilt when she thought of how she'd abandoned Pa and saddled young Fanny with all that work and responsibility. And it wasn't as if she was finding out anything useful about the Dransfields' business dealings. It hardly seemed possible that she would, here in their home.

Maggie said she should forget all about that, but she couldn't. She found herself seething inside when she thought of how Lenora had ruined their lives.

She often heard Maggie laughing with the children, and knew she was happy to be here because she was seeing a good deal of Tom. She was making no secret of the fact that she loved him.

Hattie looked to the future and hoped things could be the same for her and Luke. As she went about her duties she kept thinking of him: the way he smiled, the way his bronze eyes sought hers out. She'd never have met anybody she liked half as well if she'd stayed at home. Both he and Tom came often to the nursery when they were home from work.

Luke's eyes smiled into hers. 'We come up to play with our niece and nephews.' Indeed they did, but at the same time, on another level, they were paying more attention to her and Maggie.

Their presence was not so easy to explain when the children were in bed, and there was more secrecy about their visits then. Mrs Dransfield mustn't know. Late in the evenings was when she and Maggie had time to sit down and enjoy their company. Hattie looked forward to their visits then.

Tom was a little wary about coming. 'With neither of us downstairs, we're more likely to be missed.'

'Eric's usually around. He'll cover for us. Anyway, you know Mother works in her study once supper is over. We don't see much of her if we stay downstairs.'

'With four of us here, we make more noise. We wouldn't hear anybody coming until it was too late. It's a good job Sophie's still lying in. When she's up and about again, we'll find it harder to get away with this.'

'She never comes up after she's kissed the children good night.'

'But Dad's bound to miss us, sooner or later.'

'He often goes out, and even if he stays in, he falls asleep behind his newspapers. You worry too much.'

'Having you here hasn't done me and Maggie any favours.' Tom said, laughing from Harriet to his brother. 'Once we had the nursery fire to ourselves. Now we have to share it with you two. We've lost our privacy.'

'We could go out,' Luke suggested. 'We could take it in turns.'

'Bridie did for months, almost every night, and she was never missed,' Maggie told Hattie.

Tom took Maggie to the pictures once in a while. She always came back in an exhilarated mood, ready to tell Hattie the plot of the big picture. She always enjoyed herself. Hattie had been working at Ottershaw House for three weeks when Luke suggested taking her out.

'The factory's been working overtime on a big order,' he said. 'Mother thinks I should go back to make sure everything's turned off and locked up properly. She's even offered me the car. We'll be in time to catch the last house at the Argyle afterwards.'

Hattie's heart turned over with pleasure. She very much wanted to.

'Go on,' Maggie urged. 'It doesn't take both of us to listen for the babies. Nobody's likely to ask for you. Not once Mrs Clark is tucked up for the night. And if they do, I shall say you've gone to bed early with a headache and offer my services instead.'

Harriet changed into her best dress and put on her coat and hat. Her green eyes looked back at her from the mirror, anxious now about being alone with Luke. He was acting like an accomplice. Going downstairs ahead of her, seeing her out through the garden door.

'Go and sit in the car,' he whispered. 'Be careful not to slam the door. I'm just going to get the keys and let Mother know I'm leaving. Won't be a minute.'

The car was a huge luxury to enjoy. It seemed to Hattie that at last she could see her way clear of the poverty she'd hated so much. Luke was fun to be with. It would be so easy to fall in love with him.

A few moments later he was getting in beside her. Laughing, as though they were setting out on a great adventure. Hattie felt excited. It seemed strange to be approaching the baby wear factory by car.

'It's a bit eerie at night,' he said, as he showed her round. She looked at the rows of silent sewing machines and agreed, careful not to mention that she'd been here before. He took her to the storerooms, where there were rolls of material in pinks and whites and blues. She could hardly bring herself to look at the finished product.

'This is what we've been making today.' Some had the rows of smocking along the front of the bodice that was painfully familiar. 'We'll pack these tomorrow.'

Harriet felt her cheeks burn.

Luke was locking up carefully after them when she saw

the name painted over the door, and asked: 'Why do you still call it Burney's Baby Wear? Why not Dransfield's?'

'We took it over as a going concern,' he said. 'Sometimes it's better to keep the original name. The suppliers recognise it.'

Hattie felt uneasy. 'Like Knell's Gloves?'

'Exactly.' He was smiling as he opened the car door for her, not in any way disconcerted. 'That way, we keep a good reputation as well.'

She didn't like that. It brought back visions of Pa being cheated. She wondered if the Burney family, whoever they might be, had been treated in the same way as the Knells. She had to force that out of her mind. She looked up to meet his frank, searching gaze and easy smile. There was no animosity there. She didn't want to cause any.

'Right, the Argyle now. This is better than hanging about the nursery, isn't it?'

The show was. She couldn't stop laughing. She enjoyed herself more than she had for years. Luke was very attentive. It was late when the show finished, but he pulled the car off the road at Thermopylae Pass on the way home.

'The view's magnificent from here,' she was saying when he took her in his arms.

She could feel his excitement; there was an urgency to his manner she didn't share and hardly understood.

'Don't rush me,' she whispered. 'Please don't spoil . . .'

He was smiling down at her. 'You're like an ice maiden, Harriet, a snow queen. But I'll melt you slowly. We've got all the time in the world.

'I'll not do anything you don't want. I'm a gentleman. I'll just hold you, comfort you.' She felt his arms go round her, draw her close against him. She put her head down against his chest and could hear his heart beating.

'No harm in this, is there? Nothing to frighten you. You know I wouldn't harm you.'

He nuzzled her face with his. She could feel his moustache like silk against her cheek. They stayed there holding each other for a long time. Hattie clung to him, reassured. She wanted to share his life. This way she could find love and escape from poverty for ever.

Ottershaw House was in darkness when he drew up on the drive. He let himself in through the front door with his key and came tiptoeing immediately to the garden door to let her in. He saw her safely and quietly up to the nursery landing. Hattie decided that she mustn't worry about going out with Luke; that they'd had a good time and were perhaps a little nearer to having a permanent understanding.

# CHAPTER SEVEN

Hattie found that Luke and Tom organised things so that they could take turns to go out in the evenings. This meant she was able to spend a lot of time alone with Luke. She was thrilled that he wanted this.

The next time he took her out, he stopped the car again on the way home and took her in his arms. After a little while, he whispered: 'May I kiss you?'

His lips came down so gently on hers. Like a butterfly settling on them for a moment. 'Did you like that, Harriet?'

To admit she enjoyed a man making love to her like this was not easy. 'I did,' she whispered at last.

She soon discovered they had more privacy in front of the nursery fire.

'I want you to kiss me,' he told her. And she put away the strict rules her parents and society had instilled in her and placed her lips against his.

'I enjoy our nights in, better than going out,' he whispered, and Harriet decided she did too. She couldn't believe she could be so intimate with a man. Not any man, of course, but Luke. She felt she was beginning to live at last.

As soon as the children were settled for the night, and Maggie had crept quietly away to meet Tom, she'd bank up the nursery fire, remove the big fireguard and turn down the lights.

She'd listen for his step on the stairs, but often he was inside the door before she heard him. The moment he came in he'd take her in his arms. Luke was becoming more eager, more pressing. He'd taught her new ways to kiss him.

'You're learning fast,' he smiled when she kissed him with all the pent-up longing that had built up during the day.

Harriet thought that what she was learning from Luke was the nature of love. Up to now, she'd thought only of herself.

'Stop me if I presume too much,' he whispered.

Harriet couldn't bring herself to stop him. Pleasing him was more important to her than pleasing herself. She knew no lady should allow such privileges to a man. He excited her, lifted her out of her humdrum existence.

'Does Tom kiss you, and you know . . . ?' she'd asked Maggie. Maggie had giggled and said Tom was wonderful. Harriet got the impression he could do no wrong.

'I'll let you into a secret,' Maggie whispered, and Harriet saw her face light up with love. 'He wants to marry me.'

Harriet closed her eyes, tried to shut out the barb of jealousy that went through her. More than anything in the world, she wanted Luke to offer marriage. That would solve all her problems. It would even allow her to help Pa and her younger sisters.

One night, a few weeks later, it was her turn to stay in and listen for the children. Adam had started kindergarten, but he hadn't been that day because he seemed to have a bad cold. Maggie had told her he'd been cross and out of sorts.

'A bit off colour,' Sophie had said when she'd been told he hadn't eaten much supper. Harriet had had a hard job to get him off to sleep. She wanted him asleep because she was looking forward to the hours she'd be able to spend alone with Luke.

They were lying on the hearthrug in front of the fire, clasped in each other's arms, when she heard Adam whimper in the night nursery.

Luke lifted his lips from hers. 'Leave him a moment,' he said when she tried to move away. 'He'll go off again.'

His arms tightened round her again, but she could still hear Adam. 'Maggie?' he was calling weakly. 'Maggie?'

'I'll have to see to him,' she whispered, getting to her feet. Before she reached him, Adam had thrown up all over himself and his bed.

'I'm poorly,' he sobbed as she lifted him out and carried him to the bathroom. He drank a whole glass of water and asked for more. He felt hot and feverish. His pyjamas would have to be changed. She took them off. He'd made such a mess, she decided the best way to clean him up was to bath him again.

It was Luke who noticed he had a rash on his forehead and behind his ears, when he brought in a pair of clean pyjamas.

'Poor little thing! He's caught something at school.'

'What is it, do you know?'

Harriet shook her head. 'It might be measles. Maggie said it was going round the school. I'll have to let his mother know he's ill.'

She wrapped him in a blanket and took him to the fire. He was clinging to her, sobbing that his throat was sore and his head hurt.

'Will you go down and tell her?' Harriet asked. 'She might want to get a doctor here tonight.'

Luke hesitated. 'Better if you do it. We don't want Sophie to know I've been here. I'll disappear. Just leave him there in the basket chair. He'll be all right for five minutes.'

There seemed nothing else for it. She dried Adam's tears and ran down to see Sophie. The Moodys had a sitting room of their own. Both of them came running up behind her.

While they tried to comfort Adam, Hattie went to the night nursery to strip his bed and make it up with clean sheets. When she returned, Sophie had Adam on her knee, and Lenora had come up and was staring at a thermometer.

'The child has a temperature of a hundred and two. We must get the doctor out to him. Tom can go down and fetch him in the car. It'll be quicker than waiting for the doctor to harness up his pony.'

Hattie caught her breath. Tom had gone out with Maggie an hour or more ago. Lenora let the door slam as she went out. She made a lot of noise running downstairs. The new baby started to cry. Harriet turned to attend to him. It was time for his ten o'clock feed.

'It may be catching,' Mr Moody said. 'Almost certainly is. Better if we keep them apart. Let Maggie see to the baby.'

Harriet stood rooted to the spot, willing the baby to be quiet. For a moment she thought he was settling again. She could scarcely believe her luck.

'Can we move Adam's bed into your room?' Mr Moody asked. 'That's probably the best.'

'You don't think it'll mean the fever hospital?' Sophie worried. 'I wouldn't have let him go to school if I'd known this was going to happen.'

Adam's bed was half-sized, little bigger than a cot. Harriet helped Mr Moody carry it to her room, but they'd disturbed baby Jonathon again. He was letting rip as they crossed the landing and Lenora was coming back upstairs. 'Luke's gone for the doctor.'

'Where's Maggie?' Sophie asked her. 'Is she down in the kitchen?'

It was gone midnight. Maggie felt exhausted and frightened. She and Tom had come home an hour ago to find the gas still lit in every room and the household in an uproar.

'You've done it this time,' Ruby hissed as she scurried past them in the kitchen corridor, carrying a tea tray for the drawing room. Tom had squeezed Maggie's hand as he drew her silently towards the stairs.

'So you're back?' Lenora's voice came booming across

122

the hall. She'd seen them through the open door. 'Come in here, Tom, and bring that girl with you.'

Tom kept hold of her hand, but Maggie could feel her heart pounding with dread. The drawing room seemed vast; she never felt at ease in here. She hardly dared look at Lenora, who remained seated in an armchair by the fire. Her steely eyes were flashing with anger. She looked truly forbidding tonight.

'You went out without permission,' she accused. 'What have you got to say for yourself?'

Tom said, 'Mother, we went . . .'

'I'm not talking to you, Tom. Be quiet. Maggie?'

'I'm sorry.' Maggie felt panic rising in her throat. She could hardly get the words out. She was seeing Lenora through a sort of fog.

Tom drew her towards a sofa and pulled her down beside him. She'd never sat down in Lenora's presence before, and she knew this would only make her more angry.

'Sorry? We took you in, in good faith. Gave you a comfortable home, a generous wage and time off in exchange for your services. You were here in a position of trust, to care for those little children.' Lenora took a deep and furious breath. Her diamonds were flashing angry fire with every movement she made.

'Adam's gone down with measles. He's ill and he needed you. You weren't here and I gather it isn't the first time you've done this.'

'For heaven's sake, Mother . . .'

'I'm dealing with Maggie, Tom. I'll talk to you later. Not the first time, is it, Maggie?'

'No.' She was aware of his warm hand round hers, and of him pulling her closer.

'The first time you're needed, you're missing. You've taken advantage of our kindness. You wouldn't be here at all if Daniel had had more sense. He should leave the hiring of servants to me. He knows nothing about such matters. Words fail me.'

Maggie wanted to put her hands over her ears. She couldn't deny any of this. She was shaking because she was almost certain she was going to be dismissed. Words did not appear to be failing Lenora. She went on in the same vein for some time.

'My daughter's very upset. We all are. You went out without permission.'

'She was with me,' Tom said.

'That makes it worse. Loose behaviour on the part of servants. That's one of the worst faults.'

'There was no loose behaviour,' Tom said quietly and firmly. 'We went to the pictures after the children had gone to bed. What's wrong with that?'

'Everything's wrong. You've no business to take Maggie anywhere.' Lenora's nostrils flared with distaste. 'You must know she's expected to stay here. We needed her tonight. Poor Adam's ill. Probably all the children will catch it now, and if they do, it's your fault, Maggie.'

'Hardly, Mother. She can't do anything about that.'

'You're as bad as she is. Grow up, Tom. You've no business taking her out. A nanny! You shouldn't be paying her this sort of attention. It'll go to her head. It's time you learned to treat servants properly.'

Maggie was gripped with horror. She was mortally afraid Tom would let her down. That he wouldn't be able to stand up to much more of this from his mother. She thought it likely she'd be sent back to Elizabeth Place and never see him again.

It was coming. 'You can pack your bags, Maggie. We can't trust you after this. First thing in the morning, and thank your lucky stars I don't show you the door now.'

Tom half turned towards Maggie. His eyes met hers. She saw strength there, determination, and love too. She was suddenly fluttery with hope.

'Stop this, Mother,' he said quietly. 'We've heard enough. Now you listen to me. I want to marry Maggie, and she's agreed.'

Maggie's heart leapt. She'd always believed Tom was sincere when he said he loved her. She knew now she was right. He wasn't going to change his mind.

'What? Don't be silly. Of course you can't marry her. She's a servant.'

'Maggie's no ordinary servant,' he retorted. 'You know that as well as I do. She doesn't lack education. In fact, she's more of a lady than you are.'

'Don't give me any more lip,' his mother retorted. 'I won't stand for it.'

'What's going on?' Stanley Dransfield shuffled in, in slippers and dressing gown. 'Why doesn't everybody go to bed? I'd not have thought measles . . .'

'Tom wants to get married,' Lenora spat out. 'Tell him he can't. Refuse to allow it. Make him see sense.'

Stanley's eyes went from his son to Maggie. 'Marry Maggie, you mean?' He felt the teapot. 'This has gone cold. I'll ask for more.' He pulled on the bell rope.

'Of course it's what I mean! You've got to stop it.'

Maggie met his gaze. She felt better now she knew Tom would not turn his back on her.

'She is Henry Knell's girl. I mean, it's not as though . . .'

'For God's sake, Stanley,' Lenora ground through clenched teeth. 'You've got to stop it.'

Stanley paused, then took a deep breath. 'You're not old enough, Tom.'

Ruby's head came round the door. Stanley handed her the teapot. 'Fresh tea, please,' he said. 'Then go to bed. It's late.'

Tom seemed to have gathered strength. He was holding his shoulders back and his head up now. 'I'm twenty-one next week. After that I can marry who I like.'

Both his parents glowered back at them.

'I love Maggie. She's agreed to marry me, and I'm very happy about that. I'd have liked your blessing, Dad, but I don't need your permission.'

'You will not,' Lenora said spitefully. 'You'll not marry her and live in this house.'

'If I'm married, I won't want to, Mother. I'd prefer a place of my own.'

'There won't be a job for you, either. Not in our business. Either you take my advice, or I'll cut you off.'

'I'll get a job somewhere else.'

Maggie was shivering with horror again. She knew what had happened to her father when he'd tried to get a job.

'Not one that will support a wife, Tom. For goodness' sake. You aren't old enough to get married yet. What is the hurry?'

Even his father said: 'You need to work your way up through the business, learn how to manage a factory, before you take such a step.'

'I could run one now.'

'Nonsense. You're just a hot-headed lad. You need more experience.'

When at last Lenora had finished with them, Maggie felt spent. She climbed up to the nurseries, aware that Tom was following her. He steered her towards the day nursery, where he coaxed the fire back to life.

'Adam sounds poorly.' She could hear him sniffling, and Harriet's voice trying to soothe him in the room across the landing.

'This has done for us.' She was sick with apprehension. 'What are we going to do now?'

He drew her down on the rug beside him, put his arms round her and pulled her close. 'Tomorrow you must pack your bag and I'll take you home. We must talk to your father.'

'I'd rather stay with you, but I don't suppose Pa will

126

mind. After all, there's only Fanny now to look after the family.'

'You won't be staying there, Maggie. I'm going to look for a house. You haven't changed your mind? You do want to marry me?'

'Of course I do.'

'Then you must persuade your father to give his permission.'

'He'll like you.' She let her lips brush across his cheek. 'Approve of you.'

'You're not seventeen yet, and I haven't a job. He might not approve of that.'

'I was proud of you, Tom. You were so firm and strong.'

'I must start looking for a job. And a house.' He was frowning, worried now. 'Will your father let you marry straight away?'

'If you manage those things . . . I hope so.'

'He's going to think I'm rushing you. Not giving you time to think.'

When the baby woke for his two o'clock feed, it was Maggie who attended to him. At three she could stay awake no longer and they went to bed.

The next morning, Maggie was woken by the baby at six thirty, as usual. He was crying for another feed. She got up quickly to do it before he woke little Jane too. Jane slept on, so Maggie opened her bags on her bed and started putting her belongings in them. Hattie came to the door, her big eyes growing bigger as they took in what she was doing.

'You've been told to go? Oh, Maggie! I'm sorry. I couldn't hide it from her . . . that you'd gone out.'

'Not your fault. Tom said she was bound to find out sooner or later. How's Adam?'

'Says he feels awful.' Maggie could see the anxiety on Hattie's face. 'Mrs Dransfield didn't say anything about me, did she? She's not planning to throw me out too?'

'I don't think so. We were both very careful not to tell her about you and Luke. Don't worry. Nobody will think of it happening like this. Two sisters with two brothers.'

Hattie managed a smile. 'Luke did his best not to be seen up here with me, but I'm your sister, another of the Knells. She doesn't like either of us much.'

'She needs you now. Without me, she'll have to keep you. Won't be able to manage otherwise.'

'I wish you didn't have to go. We've had a good time these last few months. You've been happy here, haven't you? Elizabeth Place seems dismal when I look back.'

'What's happened isn't all bad.' Maggie felt a little frisson of excitement. 'Tom's told them that he wants to marry me. It's all out in the open now. We're going to, if Pa will let me.'

Hattie was all smiles, and Maggie felt her arms go round her in a hug. 'I'm happy for you.' She laughed. 'You are lucky, things always turn out right for you. Here am I, thinking how terrible it is that Lenora's found out about you and Tom, but all it's done is bring things to a head.'

'She's dead against it. Tried to forbid it. Said if he marries me, there's no place for him in the business. They'll have nothing more to do with him.'

'But that's terrible.' Harriet's eyes widened in alarm. 'He's prepared to do that for you, Maggie? He must love you very much.'

That gave Maggie a warm feeling. Tom did love her very much.

'You'll be poor. If Tom's cut off from . . .'

'Trust you to think of money. He thinks he can stand on his own feet. Get himself a reasonable job.'

'So did Pa.' Hattie's face was anxious.

'I love him. That's all that matters to me. Better rake out the grate and get the fire set. You're going to be on

128

your own today, so you should get moving. I'll go down and fetch some coal and sticks for you.'

She met Mr Moody at the door. He'd brought her what was owed in wages.

'I'm sorry to see you go. We all like you, Maggie. You're good with the children. If you'd only asked to go out, we wouldn't have said no. But now it's happened like this . . .'

Maggie knew that now Tom had said he wanted to marry her, she'd have to leave. She picked up the coal bucket and ran downstairs.

After breakfast, Tom came up to collect her. He carried her bags down to the tram stop. Maggie was feeling better about it. Hattie had seemed quite envious – well, until she'd thought they might still be poor.

When she and Tom got off the tram at Central Station, the stench from the gasworks caught in her throat. On this warm summer morning, everything looked shabbier than she remembered. She was seeing the place through Tom's eyes. In Thomas Street, the knife sharpener was busy grinding away, and lines of washing hung still, collecting smuts from the shunting trains.

A street urchin pushed past them with an orange box on wheels overloaded with coke. Front doors stood wide open, women sat on their steps with babies in their arms, shouting across to each other. Wailing infants crawled beside them. Vendors shouted their wares; the oil man was doing good business with paraffin for lamps. A greengrocer's cart was creaking along behind its horse, while its owner was still being paid by a customer.

'There's a bit of life about these streets.' Tom was looking round with interest. 'Plenty going on.'

'Harriet and I were glad to get away.' Maggie suppressed a shudder. 'You wouldn't like it if you had to live here. The noise never stops.'

Maggie didn't know what shift her father would be

working, or whether he'd be at home. She knew she could get in because she still had her key. This morning she didn't need it, for the front door was open here too. She led Tom inside, hoping it wouldn't look too squalid.

Her father was lathering his face with shaving soap, leaning over the slopstone sink, peering into the little round mirror he'd hung on the pipes above it. He was half dressed under his dressing gown.

The kitchen table had been partly cleared after breakfast. A newspaper had been dismembered amongst the crumbs. Maggie was relieved to find the breakfast pots had been washed up, though they were still piled on the draining board. Pa swung round when he saw she wasn't alone.

'It's Tom Dransfield, sir. Do you remember me?'

Pa said heartily: 'Of course.' He wiped his hand before putting it out. 'How are you?'

Maggie had to explain why she'd brought him. She didn't find it easy. Pa took out his cut-throat razor and started to shave.

'Can we make some tea, Pa?'

The fire hadn't been lit in the range. She'd never been good with the primus they used when it wasn't.

Pa rinsed his face and his shaving brush, then started to comb his mass of silver hair. Maggie was a little embarrassed to have caught him doing this at the kitchen sink.

'Lost your job? Well, I won't be sorry to have you back here. With Harriet gone, there's such a lot . . .'

'I'm not going to stay, Pa. Tom and I want to get married.'

'You're too young,' he grunted. His eyes went to Tom, who was sitting at the table. 'And so are you.'

'I'm of age, sir.'

'Marriage is a big step.' Her father looked very serious. 'Not something you should rush into.'

She tried to tell him what had happened and what Lenora

Dransfield had decided. 'So you see, he's burnt his boats with his family.'

'That's no reason to burn yours.'

'It's what I want. I love him.'

'What we both want,' Tom assured him. 'I'll not give up until we get it.'

'I need time to think about this,' Henry said. 'Come back tomorrow.'

'Can he come for his supper and meet the rest of the family?' Maggie asked.

'Yes,' Henry sighed. 'If you're prepared to cook.'

Tom went. He meant to go over to Liverpool to see his father. He wanted to talk to him while his mother wasn't about, in the hope that he'd be on his side and would persuade Lenora to allow him to continue to work in the family business.

'What's all the hurry?' Pa asked Maggie when they were alone. 'If you waited a couple of years, you'd know each other better, be more sure.'

'I couldn't be more sure than I am now,' Maggie told him. 'And Tom doesn't know whether he'll be allowed to stay at home or continue in the firm.'

'Better if he settles all that first, and finds himself a job if he has to. Better if he has time to save . . .'

'Pa!'

'He seems a nice enough lad. Seems to think just as much of you as you do of him. I wish your mother were here to decide things like this. Not really in my line.'

At Ottershaw House, there was only one topic on everyone's lips: that Tom wanted to marry Maggie Knell. They all knew he'd had an almighty row with his parents about it. Harriet felt bombarded by questions on all sides.

'What's going on?' Olivia demanded as she was helping her to dress the next morning. 'Sophie says she's dismissed your sister. She said it was Lenora's idea.'

Hattie was reluctant to discuss it with Olivia. Afraid that anything she might say would be quoted back to Mrs Dransfield.

'Maggie was a lot better than Bridie. Could read a lot better too. Bold as brass and a nosy parker, was Bridie. Wanted to know all my business, particularly about money. Knew all Stanley's, too, and Lenora's, I've no doubt. And now your sister's gone too?'

'She's going to marry Tom.' Harriet tried to stifle her envy of that.

'So I hear, but really! I don't know what Tom's thinking of.'

Harriet was drawing herself up indignantly.

'But of course, she is Henry Knell's daughter.'

'Like me,' Harriet added, and then wondered whether it was wise to keep talking about the relationship. It wouldn't make her popular here.

She'd helped Mrs Clark to her couch in the turret and had begun reading to her when Tom came in. He gave her a wry smile and said:

'I'm leaving, Gran, I've come to say goodbye.'

Hattie laid down the book and stood up.

'Don't go,' the old lady said. 'He'll only stay five minutes and then I'll be waiting for you to come back.'

Hattie went to the back of the room and took up some sewing. She'd made a cotton tabard and was lining it with fresh thermogene wadding. Tom slid into the chair she'd vacated.

'Don't cut yourself off from your family,' Olivia was saying to him. 'A big mistake. You'll be sorry if you do.'

'If I'm to marry Maggie, I've no alternative. Mother's very firm on that.'

'If you want my advice . . .'

'No thanks, Gran. Everybody's giving me advice.'

'You're going to get it anyway.' The old lady lay back on her cushions. 'Let things ride for a while, surely there's no harm in that? Stay in the business. You're used to having the comfort money can buy. Life can be very hard when you're deprived of it.'

'I'll manage.'

The old lady snorted with contempt. 'You don't appreciate what you've got, but you will when it's gone. Then you'll feel the difference. Tell your mother you've thought it over, apologise. You want to stay in the family firm?'

'I'm not sure I do, after this.' Tom's serious grey eyes met Harriet's across the room. 'Anyway, the rag trade isn't all that exciting.'

'It earns money,' the old lady insisted. 'You'll find it painful to be poor. Not being able to live as you do here. Very painful.'

'I'll have Maggie. That's what I want.'

'I hate to see you cutting yourself off from your mother. Her children, and their children, mean everything to her. Her whole aim in life is to provide for her heirs. Make life more comfortable for you.'

'She's other heirs. Plenty of them. I'm going, Gran, whatever you say.'

'Don't say I didn't warn you.'

'You've warned me, but it's still goodbye.' He bent to kiss her cheek. 'Mother's banishing me from these premises as of now. I hope you're going to stay friends with me?'

'Of course. I wish you well, you know that. I hope you'll be happy and contented. But I'm afraid you'll regret doing this.'

'You must come and visit us, once we're settled. Harriet can bring you.'

'Perhaps. I'll miss you, Tom.'

Hattie had been holding her breath. She felt that Maggie should be proud of him. He was standing firmly by his word to her. She was still sitting with the sewing in her hands when he left. She heard Lenora's voice on the landing outside.

133

'You've not come to your senses then?'

'I'm all packed, Mother. I'm leaving now.'

'You're being very silly. Throwing everything away on that girl. After all I've done for you. I've spent my whole life building up a business that'll support you all in comfort.'

'I don't approve of the way you do it. I shall sleep better at night this way.'

'What d'you mean?'

'We've been through it all before. You're going for another company now, aren't you?'

'You ungrateful little . . . To think that a son of mine . . .' Lenora was choking with fury. 'Be on your way. Just don't forget that you've made your bed and you'll have to lie on it.'

Hattie froze in horror. Tom was being cut off by his mother with dreadful finality. But was she also hearing that he thought his mother was trying to defraud another company? If so, could it prove she'd defrauded Pa?

She heard Mrs Clark's voice. 'Harriet? Stop day-dreaming over there and come back and finish this chapter.'

When Tom went to Elizabeth Place for his supper the following evening, he told Henry that he'd been asked to leave both home and job unless he was prepared to give up the idea of marrying Maggie. He'd already found himself lodgings for a week in Hind Street.

'A week?' Henry said. 'You'll not manage to fix yourself up in that time. Though I'm told there's another porter needed at the hospital. I'll put your name forward for that, if you like.'

Maggie could see Tom was embarrassed. He said a little stiffly: 'I'm hoping for a position from which I can progress. Something that'll bring in a good wage.'

Pa laughed. 'I hoped for that too when I started looking. It isn't easy, lad. You'll find out when you try.'

Later, they went out, so he could point out his lodgings to Maggie.

'Lodgings are not what I want,' he said. 'If I can get a job I'll find a small house to rent.'

'Not round here,' Maggie said.

'In a respectable neighbourhood. One your father can't object to you living in.'

By the end of the week, Tom had been hired as a clerk by the Co-operative Society.

'We won't get rich on what I earn,' he told her. 'But I don't care, as long as we can be together.'

The following day, he came again and was bubbling with enthusiasm.

'Maggie, I've seen a house to rent in Lowther Street and I think it might do. Come and see if you like it.'

'You aren't wasting any time!'

'Can't afford to, can I?'

It was a good walk away from Elizabeth Place and the gasworks, and only a short distance from Birkenhead Park. On both sides of the street were sturdily built terraces of shiny red brick, erected just before the turn of the century. The houses were modest in size and all the same. Each had two large bay windows in front, with eighteen inches of earth between those and a low wall. Nothing but a privet hedge would grow there. Upstairs, there were three bedrooms and a proper bathroom.

'Yes.' Maggie was thrilled. Tom was making everything fall into place. 'I love it. I think we'll be happy here, don't you?'

'It's nothing grand,' Maggie told her father. 'But we can make it comfortable.' They took him to look round the empty rooms.

'It's a nice little house,' he said slowly. 'In good repair. Doesn't even need decorating.'

'We'll need furniture, of course,' Tom said. 'I've a bit

put by. If we start by furnishing one living room and one bedroom I think we'll manage.'

'Please, Pa,' Maggie implored. 'Do let us.'

'All right then,' he said. 'Get married if that's what you want. You have my blessing.'

Maggie threw her arms round him and kissed him. 'Thank you, thank you.'

'Just be happy, Maggie.'

'I am happy. There's nothing I want more.'

'Remember, there's no changing your mind about this.'

'I won't want to.'

From that moment on, Maggie felt that everything in life was going exactly the way she wanted it. She felt as though she was walking on air.

'You can take carpets and rugs from my place.' Pa smiled at them both. 'No point in buying more when I've got them three deep. Come on back now, and we'll open up the boxes. See if there's anything else you can use.'

'That's very kind of you,' Tom told him.

'Can't afford to buy you a present, but when we moved to Elizabeth Place I brought a lot of my household effects. I thought we'd be moving to a bigger house quite soon. There are things there you'll find useful.'

That evening, after supper, Maggie started dragging boxes out from under beds and opening them up. There were curtains and blankets and towels. China tea and dinner services, glassware and pots and pans.

'Almost ten of everything,' Fanny laughed. 'Pa, you'll be able to set us all up when we get married.'

Maggie was thrilled.

'Take what you want, you can have first pick. Which of these tea services do you like?'

'It's a real treasure trove,' Tom said. 'I'll get a couple of lads to help carry this stuff up to Lowther Street.'

Fanny and Maggie helped him organise things in the house.

'We must buy a bed, then I can move in.' Tom laughed. Maggie knew he was as excited and pleased as she was. 'Save paying for lodgings.'

They fixed the date of their wedding for her seventeenth birthday, which fell on the last day of July. It was to be a quiet church wedding. Maggie could feel excitement fizzing up inside her. This was truly what she wanted.

She told Harriet when she came home for a day off.

'Lovely for you, Maggie,' she said. 'You really do have all the luck.' Hattie kept asking about the arrangements for the wedding, but Maggie knew how envious she was and how much she wanted Luke to think of marriage too.

'I'm going to choose a new outfit, but it must be something I can wear in the future. Ruth's asked me if she can be bridesmaid, and I've said yes, just her. Can't have all my sisters, can I?

'And we'll have to have the reception in our new home. Will you help me do the food, Hattie?'

'Yes.' She seemed quite pleased to be asked. 'Yes, of course. I'll try and get an extra day off, just beforehand.'

Maggie sighed happily. 'We're going to be blissfully happy, I know. Though there'll be no honeymoon, because Tom's just starting a new job.'

'Maggie.' Her sister seemed suddenly serious. 'I want you to help me. You know what you said about Tom falling out with his mother? About him suspecting she was defrauding . . .'

'What about it?'

'I overheard him accuse her of something . . . Taking over another company by some method he didn't approve. I want you to ask him about it.'

'Tom doesn't see her any more.'

'I want to know what he meant. It sounded as though he had some other reason to leave the business, apart from wanting to marry you.'

'He doesn't want to talk about it.'

'He'll tell you more than he would me.'

'No, we've put all that behind us. I think you should too. Don't you go bothering him.'

'But what about Pa?'

'It's no good trying to do anything for Pa. He won't thank you for it.'

Hattie's lips were straightening again. 'I'm not giving up on this,' she said. 'It means too much to me.'

# CHAPTER EIGHT

There was a backlash following Maggie's dismissal. It scared Hattie. Everybody at Ottershaw House seemed thoroughly churned up. Downstairs, she heard doors bang and tempers flare. Suddenly she was seeing less of Luke. The whole point of her being here seemed to have gone.

'I have to lie low for a while. Until this blows over,' he'd whispered when she'd met him leaving his grandmother's room the following day.

With Maggie gone, and Adam sick, she was kept on the go from morning till night. It was ten days before another girl was hired and ready to start work in the nursery. Hattie was afraid Gladys had been chosen for her plain face and stumpy figure. Lenora was not going to risk losing Eric or Luke to another nanny.

From Olivia's comments, Harriet gathered that Sophie didn't agree with her mother's choice. For her own part, she found Gladys slow and unable to get down to the level of her charges. The children didn't seem to take to her as they had Maggie.

Hattie had the awful feeling that she was clinging to the edge of a precipice and might be swept over at any moment. She'd committed the same fault for which Maggie had been dismissed. She was equally guilty, but she was never questioned about that. She could only assume the possibility hadn't occurred to Mrs Dransfield. She hoped it never would.

She was still spending some of her evenings in the

nursery. She had to sit there or in the kitchen once Olivia was settled for the night, but Luke didn't come up any more.

'With that girl Gladys watching us, it wouldn't be any fun. And besides, we don't know whether she'll keep her mouth shut.'

There was no privacy for them anywhere. Although they were living under the same roof, they rarely met. If she did see him about the house, she must give no sign, say no words, because there were others of his family about. She was missing him dreadfully. She couldn't stop herself thinking about him. Yearning for him.

Family prayers were said in the dining room before breakfast on Sunday mornings. The dining table was extended to its full length and the family, including the children, gathered to eat together. Only Mrs Clark didn't come. She said she couldn't get up and dressed in time for a nine o'clock breakfast any more. All the staff were expected to be present.

Harriet stood against the wall, while Stanley's voice droned on. She only half closed her eyes, so that she could watch Luke. He was keeping his handsome bronze eyes well away from her. She knew why, but it made her feel that what they'd shared could easily end here.

Once again, it seemed to Hattie that what had at first seemed a disaster for Maggie had given her sister an advantage, while it had brought her own hopes and plans to a full stop.

After prayers, Lenora looked up to run a cold eye across her staff.

'In future,' she told them, 'except on your days off, no member of staff must leave this house without permission.'

Harriet kept her eyes on the carpet to avoid attracting attention to herself.

'Too often, staff go missing when their services are

needed. You are entitled to recreation when your duties for the day are finished, but I would ask that you take it here in the house or garden. You may serve breakfast now, Ruby.'

Harriet followed the others back to the kitchen. She and Gladys ate breakfast there on Sundays.

'We're like prisoners here,' May complained as soon as she was far enough down the kitchen passage.

'It's like this in most places.' Cook sniffed as she tossed bacon into the hot pan. She had to raise her voice to be heard above the furious sizzling. 'Anyway, we're miles out of town. Where can you go at night?'

'It's not fair,' Ruby complained. 'Rest and recreation when our duties for the day are finished? Mine never are. They hang around in the drawing room till all hours, ringing bells for this and that. I like to stroll along to Thermopylae Pass once in a while, just for a breath of fresh air.'

'I wouldn't any more,' Mrs Summers told her. 'If you're seen with that follower of yours, you'll be in trouble.'

'She's asking for more hot milk. You didn't warm enough of it,' Ruby retaliated.

When Hattie went home to Elizabeth Place on her day off, her family couldn't stop talking about Maggie's forthcoming wedding. They were all thrilled for her.

'She won't want for much.' Fanny put into words what they all thought. 'She's leaving this place behind for good. Marriage is the only way out for the likes of us.' She'd found out just how hard it was to run Pa's household. Hattie couldn't have agreed more.

Only Pa had his reservations: 'Pity he's a Dransfield,' he said.

Hattie asked Olivia: 'Could I be very forward and ask for two days off this month? So that I can help Maggie with her wedding preparations.'

141

'You can be as forward as you like, but the answer's no,' she retorted.

Hattie was somewhat taken aback. Then she saw the old lady's face soften.

'You can take a few hours off in the middle of the day to help. In the middle of several days, if need be. Will that do?'

'Yes. Thank you.'

'Then you have what you want, and I don't have to suffer too much.' Olivia's tone was dry. 'I can't manage without you, Harriet.'

She wanted to know every detail of Tom's wedding. When an invitation arrived in the post, she said she was looking forward to going.

Maggie had changed in the few weeks since she'd left. Now her eyes shone and her cheeks were pink. 'I'm so happy,' she said. 'Things are really working out for me now.'

'Well, they're not for me,' Harriet retorted, and told her how very little she was seeing of Luke.

'He's coming to our wedding; he's going to be Tom's best man. Eric and Sophie are coming too.'

Hattie went back to Ottershaw House, hugging the news to her, counting the days. She was hoping she'd have a chance to talk to him then.

Maggie had a perfect midsummer day for her wedding. The sun was up early in the morning and the sky was brilliant blue. If anything, Hattie thought, it was a little too hot to dress up in their best clothes. In church, her eyes kept straying to Luke's straight back. She wanted him.

It amused her to think how displeased Lenora would be if she knew that it was Eric and the Dransfield car that took the bride to church, and brought her and the groom home to Lowther Street for the reception.

Even more displeased if she knew that Stanley came to the church to see his son married and wish him well, even though Lenora had refused the invitation on behalf of them both.

Sophie was now looking after Olivia on Harriet's rare days off. She and Daniel brought her into church supported between them. The wedding was a very quiet affair. The guests totalled only fifteen, but it was all done with simplicity and taste, and no bride had ever looked more beautiful than Maggie, in her pale blue costume. She had a lovely hat, with clouds of blue veiling, and a feather boa round her shoulders.

Harriet found herself watching Luke from the other side of Maggie's little sitting room. It looked smart now that it had been furnished with some of Pa's pieces. Luke was taller and more broadly built than Tom, more like his father. As he talked to Pa, the sun glinted on his bronze hair, turning it to gold. With his confident eyes, he was certainly the most handsome man here. She longed for what Maggie had achieved. A husband and home of her own.

She wondered if Luke had missed her as much as she had him. She reasoned that if Tom was happy to marry Maggie, there was no reason why Luke should think it wrong to marry her. She'd be very proud to have him as her husband. He met her gaze, smiled in greeting and shortly afterwards came across to her.

'I've missed you, Hattie. We used to have some good times.'

'Very good times.' She smiled up at him and forced herself to add, 'Why don't we do it again sometime?'

Hattie knew she was too ready to keep herself at arm's length. She needed, if she was going to get what she wanted, to be more like Maggie, more outgoing and more fun.

'Why not?' He was enthusiastic. 'We'll just have to be a bit more careful, that's all.' He smiled at her over his glass of wine. 'Now? As soon as this party's over?'

She felt a frisson of triumph. She hadn't lost him after all. He did like her; perhaps he even loved her.

143

'I'll need an hour. It'll look strange if I don't help to clear up.'

It was mid afternoon when she walked up to Central Station. Everything shimmered in the sun; the town felt stifling, even though she'd changed into a thin cotton dress. She'd told him how much she appreciated not having to wait for him in public places, and once again he was there before her. She could see him scuffling his smart shoes against the dusty pavement.

'Father wanted the car,' he said. 'How about going to New Brighton on the ferry?'

He took her arm, seeming buoyed up and in a playful mood. The euphoria of the wedding was still with them.

Harriet took off her hat once she was on board and let the breeze blow through her hair. It felt cool and fresh out on the water. The tide was racing in, swirling past them as it flooded the estuary. The journey took ten minutes longer because the ferry had to battle against it on its way downriver. She enjoyed it, thrilled to be with Luke again.

They strolled along the promenade with the holiday crowds, watching the donkey rides and the children with their buckets and spades on the sands below. The Irish Sea looked calm and blue. There were even a few bathing huts in the water, and an occasional splash to be seen from a swimmer beyond.

Harriet saw the photographer getting them in his sights. She smiled for the camera. It was all part of the fun. He gave her a ticket.

'It'll be a lovely picture,' he told them. 'Ready tonight.'

As they walked back, Luke led her towards the funfair. There were swing boats and roundabouts blaring out music. Hattie didn't want to go on any of them. Luke tried his hand at the coconut shy.

'Come on, Harriet, see if you can do any better.' It was a giggle but neither managed to dislodge a coconut.

'I'm not giving up now.' Luke laughed, and bought

144

more balls, and this time he succeeded. 'Do I get a prize?'

'Yes, from this shelf.' The stallholder pointed.

'You choose,' he laughed at Hattie. 'Is there anything you'd like?' She looked eagerly at the collection of fluffy toys and ping pong bats.

'For the ladies.' The man in charge pointed further along. There were vases and ornaments and trinkets to wear.

She picked up a little cardboard box. Inside, a locket on a chain lay on a bed of cotton wool. She was pleased to have a keepsake from Luke. As they walked away, she took it out of the box for a closer look.

Luke began to laugh. 'You can't possibly wear that. It's gold-coloured metal, and the locket doesn't even open.'

'I thought it looked pretty on the shelf.'

'I'll get you a better one.'

'There's no need,' Hattie told him. 'I didn't expect anything wonderful.'

'It's the most awful junk. I'd be ashamed to hear you say I'd given it to you.'

They walked into town to look for a jeweller's, but they came to an antique shop first, with several black velvet pads in the window displaying Victorian trinkets.

Luke paused. 'Let's go in and take a closer look.' There was only one locket.

'Victorian,' the shopkeeper said. 'About eighteen-sixty. Eighteen carat.'

'Do you like it, Harriet?'

'It's lovely.' She opened it up. Two locks of hair, one dark, the other auburn, were intertwined behind the glass. 'But you mustn't, I can't accept . . .'

'Of course you can,' Luke said warmly. 'To make up for the awful time since Tom was caught with your sister.' He was already fastening it round her neck.

'Thank you, then. I'd like to put our hair inside. Yours and mine.'

145

Once out on the pavement, Luke dropped the fairground locket into the next rubbish bin he came to. They went back to the seafront and into the Grand Hotel for tea.

'Only one cake each,' he said. 'We'll have dinner before we go back.'

'I couldn't eat anything,' Harriet laughed. 'Not after all that food at Maggie's.'

The evening sun was pleasant out on the terrace. They sat on for a long time, talking about the wedding and the disruption Tom had caused them. By the time they were heading back to Liverpool on the ferry, the heat of the day had gone.

To Hattie it was an exciting escapade. They both enjoyed it.

'We must certainly do this again,' he whispered as he left her at the bottom of the nursery stairs, very late that night.

After that, every month on her day off, he always took her out. They went further afield, where they were unlikely to meet anyone who knew them. Over to Liverpool, to the theatres and cinemas and restaurants there.

She tried to take her days off on a Saturday or Sunday, when he wouldn't have to work. He'd hire a car for the day and take her driving round the Wirral. Perhaps to Raby Mere, where they'd hire a skiff and row round the mere. Always they had one meal out, sometimes two.

The only other time she saw anything of Luke was on the night Gladys went home to her family. Harriet was expected to babysit and cover for her in the nursery. Luke didn't come up until the household settled down for the night. He said it wouldn't do for them to be caught together. They must avoid that at all costs now.

Hattie lay in his arms in front of the nursery fire until very late on those nights. She always felt half asleep the next day, when she had more work than usual to cover for Gladys, but she deemed it well worthwhile.

But she wasn't content with seeing Luke on only two occasions in the month. The string of nights she had to spend without him seemed endless. She comforted herself by bringing out the photograph taken on New Brighton promenade on Maggie's wedding day. He was holding her close, his head slightly bent to hers, and they both looked so happy. Harriet kept it under the lining paper in her stocking drawer.

She wore the locket he'd given her all the time, under her dress so that his family wouldn't ask about it. It was the only jewellery she owned. All her mother's had had to go to help pay her father's creditors. That made her prize it even more highly. She'd asked if she might snip a lock of hair from his head to twine with hers in the locket. His was several shades brighter than her own.

Hattie was a little shocked when Pa asked if he'd done anything to offend her, because she was spending so much less of her free time in Elizabeth Place. It brought another rush of guilt. She went more often after that, and did as much as she could to help Fanny, though she seemed to be coping reasonably well.

The months were passing and she felt she was no nearer getting what she wanted. She hated to be alone upstairs and hear Luke's voice or his laugh down in the dining room. She craved more of his company. Loving Luke was becoming an obsession for her.

One night, she'd gone to bed and was reading when she heard a gentle tap on her bedroom door. Instantly she was wide awake and shaking with excitement. It couldn't be Gladys: her head usually came round the door a second after she'd tapped. Hattie shot out of bed and pulled on her dressing gown. Luke was leaning against the doorpost, smiling down at her.

He shut her door quietly but firmly behind him, and reached out for her. He'd never come to her bedroom before. His eyes went round her deal wardrobe and truckle bed.

147

'I was wondering if you'd like to see a play at the Royal Court? Shall I get tickets for your night off on Saturday?'

Harriet didn't care where he took her. All she wanted was to be with him. She'd invested all her hope for the future in him and had been unable to speak to him for the last fourteen nights. She was hungry for him. Luke was a passionate man; on this night, she felt swept along by his kisses, and only afterwards was she a little horrified by what she had allowed him to do.

She knew her father would be more than horrified. It went against the teaching of home, school and church. It even went against her own personality. She wasn't the demonstrative sort who gave her kisses freely; she was the sort who held herself aloof, stayed in her shell. It was some measure of what she felt for Luke that he'd persuaded her, but she was a little worried that she might find herself with child.

'No need to worry about that, Hattie. I wouldn't let that happen to you, not until the time is right. I've made a study of contraception. You'll be perfectly safe with me.'

They laughed together one night when their passion had spent itself. 'Did you know the Egyptians used camel dung for that? And in England in Beau Brummel's day, lemon juice was found to be effective? Then they made sheaths of pure fine silk. Nowadays, we have rubber, so nothing can possibly go wrong. I'll make sure it doesn't.'

Harriet wasn't entirely convinced, but as time went on, it seemed that Luke was right. She began to relax on that score. Nothing mattered but being with Luke. She told herself Maggie must have done the same to encourage Tom to propose, but she didn't know and she couldn't ask more plainly than she already had.

Luke was coming to her room often now. The more she had of him, the more she wanted. She just couldn't get enough. She could think of nothing else.

'What a good job you have a room up here on your own,' Luke said.

'We're not that far from Gladys,' she reminded him. 'And the baby wakes her, so we must be quiet.'

Luke began telling her he loved her. Harriet was ready to burst with happiness and started to hope that soon he'd propose.

All the same, she knew that the effort of keeping her feelings hidden from everybody else was exacting a toll.

She was in Liverpool with him a few days before his father's birthday.

'Come and help me choose a hip flask for him,' he said, leading her towards a jeweller's.

Harriet didn't think she helped much. Luke had a very clear idea of what he wanted. There was a display of wedding rings on a black velvet cushion drawing her attention further along the counter. While Luke was waiting to have his gift wrapped, she studied them. He noticed and came closer.

'One day,' he said quietly, 'I'll put one on your finger. We'll be married.'

It seemed like the proposal she'd been longing for. Her head was swimming with pleasure. Yet already, they had gone further . . .

'I'm your wife in everything but name now,' she whispered. Her throat felt tight. He stood staring down at her.

'You're right,' he said at last. 'Let's buy it now, then. Which one do you like?'

She was suddenly reeling with emotion. The long months of hoping and needing and praying for his love had come to an end. She felt triumphant, radiantly happy. It seemed a golden moment. She'd thought of it happening so many times, but never like this, in a shop. She could feel her eyes prickling with tears of joy.

'This one, Harriet?' He picked one off the velvet cushion. 'It isn't unlucky to try it on first?'

'No,' Harriet said firmly. 'It can't be.' They'd tried everything else first.

They walked out of the shop with a twenty-two carat wedding ring, with the names Harriet and Luke inscribed inside. Over lunch, Luke put it on her finger, but of course it couldn't stay there.

'We'll do it officially one day, have a really big do with all the trimmings,' Luke promised.

Occasionally, Maggie and Tom would invite them both to Lowther Street for supper. Luke would always take gifts for them: wine and sometimes brandy and cigarettes for Tom; always flowers or chocolates for Maggie.

Hattie thought the newly-weds seemed very happy together. Tom was always exchanging intimate smiles with Maggie, reaching out to touch her, or praising her cooking. After they'd eaten, Maggie would play for them, and the little house would resound to Chopin or Grieg.

'I'm glad it's working out for them,' Hattie said to Luke as they went back to Ottershaw House.

'Depends what you mean by working out.' He frowned. 'Tom's struggling to make ends meet. He says he'd like to take Maggie out more. His wage from the Co-op doesn't go as far as he'd hoped.'

Hattie knew that life hadn't taught Tom to manage without luxuries.

'Neither is he finding clerking at the Co-op very interesting. He thinks he could handle a bigger job, but promotion isn't coming.'

She realised then with a shiver that Luke would not want to find himself in Tom's position. He'd want to avoid being cut off from his family, go on working in their business and earning a generous salary.

For her own part, Harriet had reached the point when she wanted Luke on any terms. Even if, like Tom and Maggie, it meant they wouldn't have much money. She wanted to be with him all the time. She wanted him to acknowledge her openly, not take her to places where they weren't known.

She went about her daily work, saw to Mrs Clark and occasionally helped with the children, but her mind was always on Luke. He was five years older than Tom and was managing the baby clothes factory. His mother stood over him, of course, and made many of the decisions, but he was well paid and free with his money. Always the best seats when he took her out, and if he didn't have the family car, he used taxis freely.

'Luke is Lenora's favourite.' Maggie had laughed when she'd said that, but Hattie thought it was true. Lenora relied on Luke in a way she hadn't on Tom. That might mean that Luke was in a stronger position, but Lenora would be dead set against him marrying her, and she'd shown just how ruthless she could be if crossed.

She told herself she must be patient and not rush things. Luke was being more careful than Tom. He said he wanted everything to be right for them.

Harriet spent most of her time with Olivia, and was doing more for her. When she was tired and her mouth was dry with reading aloud for hours, the old lady would put a grateful hand on her arm and ask:

'What would I do without you, Harriet? Nobody else has any patience with me. Nobody else cares.'

'Of course they do,' Hattie would insist. She was growing fond of Olivia. 'It's just that they're so busy.'

To start with, Olivia had kept her portfolio of shares under lock and key and had not allowed her even one glimpse of it. Now she was asking her to do the monthly sums and work out how much it had gained or lost.

Because Olivia had complained that Bridie was nosy, especially on money matters, Harriet was careful to hide the fact that all the reading of financial advice and doing the additions had awakened her curiosity. Over the following months, Olivia's obvious satisfaction with her investments caused the grip on her tongue to loosen and Hattie's curiosity to burgeon.

'I always buy sound stock and keep it,' she explained. 'I rarely sell, only if the future prospects look hopeless.'

When Hattie finally understood what the total was, it took her breath away. One fraction of that would have supported her family in comfort through Pa's bankruptcy.

'Why don't you invest in the family businesses?' she asked her.

Olivia's creased old face had lit up with a smile. 'It's the other way round. I've built up my portfolio from the profits of Clark's Blouses. I can't work as I used to at the factory, but this way, I'm making my money work for me. I can still look upon it as turning over my pennies.'

'Very clever of you,' Hattie told her. 'But how did you learn to do it?'

'It only takes an interest in money matters. There's advice in most newspapers. Books written about it too.'

Hattie thought that in her case she didn't even need that first interest. It was her daily duty to read all the information on money markets that could be found.

Olivia's other great interest was gossip. She wanted to talk to her family every day. She wanted to know exactly what was going on both at home and in the business. Hattie kept a lock on her tongue about Luke and volunteered nothing. She heard Luke being equally guarded with his grandmother when he came to see her.

After her day off, she was always questioned about Maggie and Tom. She told Olivia all about Tom's house and his job, and how happy he was.

Lenora ignored Harriet and seemed constantly exasperated with everybody else. Hattie had thought of Stanley as a successful businessman but it seemed he was a disappointment to his wife. Rumours from the kitchen said he had a continually changing string of lady friends, and the staff didn't blame him.

Lenora wanted her four children to jump to her commands. Since Tom had gone his own way, Olivia thought she was coming down more heavily on Luke and Eric, in an attempt to keep them in line. Even Sophie wasn't in favour any more.

Olivia was the one member of the family Lenora couldn't control through her purse strings. Olivia complained that her daughter had little patience with her, and always expected her to do more for herself than she could. Neither did she think she was being kept fully in the picture about work at Clark's Blouses, though that was the one company she personally owned.

Olivia was inclined to swap one confidence for another, so nothing could stop the constant drip of personal stories about the family that Hattie was sure Lenora would have preferred to keep secret. She knew that Lenora tolerated her in the house only because she provided the old lady with the attention she had to have.

She'd been working at Ottershaw House for over a year when she realised the atmosphere was becoming charged again.

She was woken up one night by voices raised in argument. She'd been in bed for half an hour and was in a deep sleep. She recognised Lenora's voice as it reverberated up the stairwell, but wasn't sure of the others. The sitting-room door was slammed shut almost immediately and the voices were muffled after that, so she didn't know what the argument was about. The whole family seemed to be involved – certainly Sophie was – and there was a lot of activity: footsteps crossing the hall, bells ringing in the kitchen for Ruby to provide service. It took Harriet a long time to get back to sleep.

The next morning, she found that Ruby knew more.

'It's the old, old story,' she grinned at her. 'Mr Moody's

153

at odds with the missus again. The mother and father of a row last night. He says he's definitely moving his family out to a home of their own.'

Before lunch that day, Mrs Clark had two glasses of sherry, and Harriet knew that that meant she'd take a prolonged nap afterwards. She settled the old lady down on her bed as usual for her rest. Harriet could hear her snoring five minutes later and went quietly up to her own room so that she wouldn't disturb her.

An hour later, she made her a cup of tea and went to wake her up, because if Olivia slept too long in the afternoon she had difficulty sleeping at night. Harriet was surprised to hear agitated voices as she opened the door. She found Sophie and her husband with her.

'I'm not prepared to put my name to accounts that are not strictly honest and above board.' Daniel Moody was sitting stiff and upright on his chair, his dark eyes glittering with indignation. 'I've told Lenora I won't act as her accountant any longer. I want no more to do with her business.'

'Tell him, Gran, he's got it all wrong.' Sophie was grimacing with distress. Twitching at her grandmother's bedding. 'He must be wrong.'

'I've brought you a cup of tea, Mrs Clark,' Harriet said, wanting to make her presence known.

'Thank you, dear.'

Mrs Clark liked her to stay nearby, so Harriet went to her favourite place, the couch in the turret, where she wouldn't intrude on them. She picked up the sewing she kept to hand to fill her time when Olivia had visitors. She was tacking squares of thermogene wadding on to bandages, so they would stay more securely in place on knees and elbows.

Daniel was far too angry to worry about what she might hear.

'I drew up the accounts for this year, had them all finished. And when I showed them to her she disputed the figures for the amount of stock we've sold through Fevers

154

and Jones. By her reckoning, it's only half as much, and she wanted me to alter everything.'

Olivia said: 'Fevers and Jones? The haberdashery chain?'

Harriet stopped stitching. She felt the fire run up her cheeks. She knew what was upsetting Daniel Moody now.

'What Lenora's doing is blatantly dishonest. She's deliberately trying to drive the business down and make it appear less profitable than it is, so she can buy it cheaply. She wants control of those retail outlets. It'll make everything else more profitable.'

Daniel's angry voice went on, interspersed with clucks of horror from Sophie.

'Mother wouldn't do any such thing. Tell him, Gran, he's making a mistake. He's been going on about his horrible suspicions for years.'

'They're not suspicions now. This is proof enough . . . You don't know anything about the business, Sophie, you never go near it. You don't see what I see.'

'I think you're getting paranoid.'

Mrs Clark said: 'It must be legal. Lenora wouldn't do anything that wasn't.'

'Of course she wouldn't!'

Daniel was grim-faced. 'She gets the law on her side. Ties everything up with her solicitor so that it appears legal. Even her victims believe it's legal, they trust her. She makes friends of them, gives them big loans on very good terms. Then they follow her advice and lose half their business, because she's planted somebody with them who makes sure it doesn't go through their books.

'When she's got them in a corner, she forecloses and the business is hers.'

'Surely not!'

'I'm getting out. I've applied for a position as an auditor with Liverpool Council.'

Olivia sighed. 'If that's how you feel, then perhaps it's the best thing.'

Harriet pressed herself back into the cushions. She knew now, quite definitely, that Pa had been cheated by Lenora Dransfield. It had been fraud that had reduced them to two rooms and a kitchen in Elizabeth Place. Poor Pa! She hadn't been able to make up her mind until now. Pa was such a kindly, lovable, bumbling person, with no idea about money. He was quite the wrong sort of person to manage a business. Probably he'd been putty in Lenora's hands.

'But that isn't all.' Sophie was on her feet now; she was never still for long. 'Daniel doesn't want us to stay here.'

'Not with Lenora. She interferes in everything. Even with the children. She wants to dictate schools . . . She's inculcating them . . .'

'Nonsense, Dan.' Another grimace of disbelief flickered across her face. With her bright hair and continual movements, Sophie was like a flame on the hearth.

'We've got to get a place of our own.'

'You're always on about that too.'

'What's wrong with us having a place of our own? I don't feel master of my own household here.'

'But I don't want, I don't believe . . .'

Hattie felt some sympathy for Sophie. It couldn't be easy to believe this of one's own mother.

Olivia said: 'Lenora will be very upset if you move out. I do ask you, Daniel, to think again about that.'

'I've thought a hundred times already. I know Sophie's against it. But Lenora spoils the children. Indulges them to the hilt. Sophie too.'

'They are her life. Everything she does is for her children and her grandchildren. She'll provide them with wealth, she wants them brought up as though . . .'

'These are my children, not hers, and I don't approve of it. It's not good for them.'

'The family is her passion.'

'It's mine too, and I can't go on like this. Lenora's getting

156

me down. Sophie, I want you to come and see this house I've found.'

'I can't make up my mind. I don't want . . .'

'Let me make it up for you. It doesn't matter what you say. She's a bad influence on the children. We're going.'

'Poor Lenora,' Olivia said to Hattie when they were at last alone. 'She isn't going to like this, especially now Tom's no longer here.'

# CHAPTER NINE

Over the last few months, Maggie had begun to feel a prickling of disappointment. She did her best to stifle it.

Tom was taking his week's annual holiday. He'd organised it now because it was their first wedding anniversary, and also her eighteenth birthday.

'Can't afford to go away, I'm afraid.' He pulled a face.

'It doesn't matter,' she said quickly. 'Just having you with me all day is a treat.' She'd heard him speak with longing of sailing off Anglesey, where in previous years he'd had holidays with his family.

Tom's face brightened. 'We'll do something to celebrate. Can't let your birthday go past without making a bit of a splash.'

'How about taking a picnic to the beach at New Brighton?' Maggie suggested. 'We can sit in the sun. Walk along the prom.'

'All right. Then we'll come home, get dressed up and go out for a slap-up meal.'

Today was the big day, and they'd woken up to the sound of rain gurgling in the gutters. Although it was July, Tom was having bad weather for his one precious week of freedom.

She watched him feeling under his pillow. He brought out a small box and put it in her hand.

'Happy birthday.' It contained a brooch in the form of a spray of flowers.

'It's very pretty,' she said, leaning over to kiss him. 'It'll look good on my best frock.'

'It's crystal, sorry it's not . . .'

'It's lovely. I like it, Tom.'

Maggie knew he didn't like his job in the Co-op office. He felt pinned down during working hours, and he'd not been used to that. It was routine work that he found dull. The promotion he'd been half expecting had gone to someone else, and he'd been passed over for a pay rise.

She was afraid he was beginning to feel he'd paid too high a price to marry her. He was still happy with her – it wasn't that – but he had lost heavily in terms of material comfort. He grumbled about being short of money. Maggie felt she'd gained from their marriage, but Tom had lost out. She hoped he wasn't going to regret what he'd done.

To start with, he'd hired a general maid to live in. He'd really thought anything less would mean a life of drudgery for her. One thing that life at Ottershaw House had taught her was that with servants living in, there was no privacy. She knew she could manage without live-in help.

'It's such a small house,' Tom agreed. 'She did seem always underfoot.'

Now they had a woman who came to do the heavy cleaning three mornings a week, and Maggie did the cooking herself. She didn't feel that was a burden: with just the two of them there wasn't enough to fill her day. She seemed to spend most of it waiting for Tom to come home.

'I could go to work too,' she said, but the women who lived in the street, if they worked at all, were in domestic service or in a factory. Tom wouldn't hear of her doing that.

'You'll probably have a baby to look after before very long,' he'd told her.

Maggie would have welcomed that, but there was no sign of it happening as yet.

'It isn't for want of trying,' he'd grinned.

Over breakfast, he said: 'It's not a day for the beach; we'll have to change our plans. That new American film, *Birth of a Nation*, is showing in Liverpool. It's had wonderful reviews and I'd like to see it. We could go to the matinée, then I'll take you to the Adelphi for dinner. How's that?'

'Sounds lovely.' Maggie would have fallen in with any suggestion he made. All she wanted was for Tom to be content with his lot.

She enjoyed the film and thought Lilian Gish a spectacular heroine. Tom was enthralled with the technicalities of making it. They'd seen Abraham Lincoln shot, and it had appeared to be the real Abraham Lincoln.

'The make-up was perfect.' Tom loved everything to do with cinema.

They came out blinking in the late-afternoon sunshine. Maggie said: 'It cleared up after all.'

'Can't think of dinner yet.' Tom frowned. 'Too early.'

'We can look at the big shops.'

'They're on the point of closing now.'

'Look in the windows . . .'

Tom pushed his hands deep in his trouser pockets and rattled his change indecisively.

'I'd like to see Dad. If we get a tram down to the Pier Head we'll catch him before he goes home.'

Maggie shivered. He was suggesting they go to the factory Pa had once owned. His father had been managing it since Dransfield's had taken it over.

'If I get him on his own, talk to him, he might be willing to do something for me. If I could get a loan, I could start my own business.'

'Can't you go to the bank for that?'

Tom shook his head. 'They don't lend that sort of money to just anybody. They'd expect me to have cash of my own to put into a business, and I haven't.'

'But your mother . . .'

'Perhaps Gran would lend it to me.'

161

'What if your mother's there with him?'

'She won't be. The glove factory is the only one this side of the water. Mother spends most of her time between the blouses and the baby wear. She'd have to get the ferry over here, so she doesn't often come.'

A tram was coming and Tom was leading her out into the road to get on.

'After that we can have a walk round the Pier Head,' he said. 'More interesting than the shops.'

'When they're closed,' she allowed.

Maggie knew Tom hadn't seen his father since their wedding day. That Stanley Dransfield had come to that must mean he didn't want to cut him off completely, but she was afraid he'd refuse to help. She didn't want Tom to be upset.

She was apprehensive on her own account too. As soon as she saw the building, with the huge sign reading 'Knell's Gloves', she felt her stomach turn over. Pa had brought her and Harriet here a few times when they were children

Tom led the way confidently through the front door and up the stairs. She remembered the strong smell of new leather, but not much of the corridor. Tom paused before a door.

She asked: 'Is this his office?'

'His assistant, sort of secretary.'

They went in. 'I'd like a word with my father,' Tom was saying to the middle-aged man behind a desk. He sprang to his feet with hand outstretched.

'How are you, Tom? Very pleased to see you. You're looking well.'

Maggie's hand was shaken too. Through the window, she could see a freighter pushing against the Mersey tide, with black smoke streaming from its funnel.

'I'm afraid you've missed your father. I don't expect him back now. Not before tomorrow morning.'

He opened an adjoining door, perhaps to show them

that the room beyond was empty. Maggie stood in the doorway. This had once been Pa's office. It was a most handsome room.

'I was just passing and thought I'd pop in to say hello.' She knew by Tom's voice that he was disappointed. And the glove factory wasn't on the way to anywhere else. Outside, the dock road stretched on to Seaforth. Poor Tom, he'd had to swallow his pride to do this.

'Perhaps I'll come back,' he said.

'If you'd like to set a time,' the man was opening an appointment book, 'he'll be free first thing, or after three in the afternoon.'

'No.' Tom was backing towards the door. 'I'll just pop in again on the off-chance.'

They were going downstairs again. Maggie tugged at his arm.

'Could I just have a peep inside the workrooms? I'd love to see . . . My father . . .'

All the Dransfields had self-confidence, and Tom's had not been much dented. He led the way, ushering her through double doors. The noise here was an assault on her ears. She certainly remembered all these women bent over their machines, sewing tiny seams, twitching the gloves this way and that with practised fingers.

The smell of leather was overpowering now. Maggie had to fight the impulse to put her handkerchief to her nose. She noticed that some of the machinists were working on linings of stockinet. A foreman recognised Tom, and they shouted greetings above the noise. Moments later he was showing them to the cutting room and then on to see a new machine which imprinted marks on the soft sheep's leather that made it resemble more expensive pigskin.

Suddenly the power was cut off and the lights went out. The silence was broken by whoops of joy. All the workers were on their feet in an instant. Work was being tossed into piles. There was a race to the cloakroom for hats and coats.

'We'd better go.' Tom took her arm. They were caught up in the stream of workers rushing to leave.

'They seem glad to go home.' Many raced up to the overhead railway; others strode past them towards the Pier Head and the trams.

Maggie took in deep breaths of fresh air. To see inside that factory had been strangely upsetting. To think that Pa's family had started it up and run it for three generations. Yet it was Tom who the workers recognised, not her. She felt like crying for Pa. Understanding now just what he'd lost, and feeling the conflict between the two families more sharply. It took her a while to notice that Tom, too, had been moved by the experience.

'I will go back tomorrow,' he said grimly. 'You don't know how boring it is filling up those dockets at the Co-op. I wouldn't mind going back to work under Pa. He'd be all right.'

It made Maggie feel sick. After one year, he was ready to swallow his pride and go back to his family. He was sorry he'd cut himself off from their money. Perhaps even sorry that . . .

He squeezed her hand. 'I'm not sorry I married you, though, don't you be thinking that.'

At the Pier Head they watched the ferries come and go. They were full up at this time of the evening. Office workers tied to desks all day took turns round the top deck to get a little exercise. The Wirral was Liverpool's bedroom.

'It's very pleasant to have time to stand and stare,' Tom said. 'Come on, we'll catch a tram back into town. We'll have a drink before dinner.'

The city seemed empty. The shop doors were closed. They walked the last hundred yards to the Adelphi Hotel, Liverpool's finest. A liveried doorman held open the door for Maggie.

'This way.' Tom had been here before. He took her arm and led her towards the lounge bar. It was he who spotted the empty table. They were no sooner there than a barman came over. While Tom gave their order, Maggie was unfastening her jacket. A flurry in the far corner of the room caught her eye. She gasped with surprise.

'What is it?' Tom was giving her his full attention again.

'Is that Luke?'

The smart jacket straining across the broad shoulders, the bright hair curling into the nape of the neck: it certainly looked like him. He was taking care not to look in their direction as he hurried an attractive girl to the door.

'Who's that with him?'

He was holding on to the girl's arm in a way that left Maggie in no doubt about the relationship. Her stomach was suddenly heavy with foreboding. This girl went to a good hairdresser and wore fashionable clothes; she had the gloss that money bought.

'He didn't want us to see him.' Tom was frowning. 'Looked positively guilty.'

Maggie watched them go. Poor Hattie! The last time she'd seen her she'd been talking about Luke, and her face had lit up with love. She was going to be devastated. She'd never made any secret of what she felt for him, or what she hoped would happen.

Suddenly their celebration seemed flat.

'Poor Hattie! I'm sure she's no idea. How can I tell her? Should I?'

Tom shook his head.

Maggie felt a rush of anger. Luke had been monopolising Hattie's time for more than a year. Of course she had expectations. This was a case of like father, like son. Luke was one for the women.

'Nothing works out for Hattie,' she said sadly.

Maggie wanted her to be happy. Of all her sisters, Hattie was the most important to her.

\*     \*     \*

165

Lenora was very cross when she found that Daniel was determined to move Sophie and the children to a house of their own. She kept coming to Olivia's room to recount the arguments she'd put up against it.

Hattie had started to read the morning papers to Olivia when she came in early one morning.

'I never did take to Daniel. He's far too set in his ways. Turning on me like this! When all I was doing was trying to provide for Sophie's future.' She was quite agitated.

'Let it go,' Olivia said wearily. Hattie gave up her chair to Lenora and went to make up the fire. Olivia liked it to roar up the chimney unless the day was very hot.

'They're none of them grateful, though I'm doing my best for all four of them.'

Hattie made as little noise as she could with the coal, though she already knew exactly how Lenora had provided for her children's future.

She'd heard her say often enough that when she and Stanley retired, Luke was to have Knell's Gloves, Eric was to have the baby wear factory, and Sophie, Clark's Blouses. Lenora had wanted to acquire Fevers and Jones for Tom, and had found it particularly galling that he was the one who had objected to her efforts to get it.

'It was a mistake to take Daniel into the business. I wish I never had,' she fulminated.

'The mistake,' Olivia said slowly, 'was not bringing Sophie up in the way the others were. In the way you were. We were wrong to keep her out of it. It's all very well being a lady, but she can't look after her own interests.'

'It's not as though Daniel can provide that well for her. An auditor? He'll not earn as much as he could have done in our business. And here I am, struggling to find another man to do his work. It's not easy. I don't like giving responsibility to perfect strangers. The family was meant to run it.'

Olivia was refolding her newspaper, a hint that she'd

166

prefer to have it read to her than hear Lenora's complaints over again.

'First Tom and now Sophie deserting me. Turning their backs on what I've spent my life building up for them,' Lenora said crossly. 'What are they thinking of? Not their own interests, that's for sure.'

'Aren't you going to work this morning?' Olivia asked.

She no longer wore her diamonds – her fingers were too gnarled for the rings to go over her knuckles. Lenora's were flashing fire: on her chest, her fingers and in her ears. She was dressed for work. She got to her feet.

'Somebody has to, I suppose.'

'Poor Sophie,' Olivia said to Hattie when the door had closed behind her daughter. 'She's being torn between the two of them. Always been very fond of her mother. I shall miss her too.'

When the vans took away the Moodys' possessions and the family left, Hattie found Ottershaw House suddenly much quieter. Lenora continued coming to Olivia's room to complain. She seemed irritable, and so depressed that Olivia suggested she give a few little dinner parties to take her mind off things.

All the staff hated her having guests, because it made more work for them. All day, Mrs Summers was kept busy cooking and preparing the feast. It took Ruby longer to serve than any family meal, and it was very late indeed before May had finished washing up all the extra dishes.

It kept Harriet up later than usual too, because she had to see Mrs Clark into bed afterwards. She was in the kitchen, eating her share of the luxury foods coming back from the dining room. They'd had smoked salmon and roast pheasant.

Ruby had taken up the pudding, a huge confection of peaches in melba sauce with meringues. The aroma of coffee still hung about the kitchen, though she'd taken that to the drawing room. Now Ruby was picking at the

167

pheasant carcasses, and May was washing up the dishes from the first courses.

All except Cook were waiting for the dinner to be over. Nothing more would be required from Mrs Summers tonight, but instead of going to bed, she was lying back in the basket chair, with her swollen feet up on a stool and a glass of the mistress's sherry in her hand.

'So what's she like, Ruby?'

'Who?'

'The young lady, of course. The one Luke wanted invited.'

Harriet went rigid. 'What do you mean? He hasn't got a young lady.'

'His mother thinks it's time he had.' Ruby giggled behind her hand. 'He's twenty-seven, isn't he? Got a roving eye. Time he settled down.'

Harriet said stiffly: 'You mean there's somebody here tonight? Someone for him?' There'd been only a middle-aged couple in the drawing room when she'd taken Olivia to her chair.

'Heiress to a dog biscuit company. Here with her mother and father.'

She smiled to herself. 'He won't like her.' She felt sure of that.

'Ruby, will you fetch the pudding plates down?' May was letting the water run out of the sink. 'They must have finished eating by now.'

Ruby went. Harriet sat on at the table, feeling less confident. 'He won't like her,' she repeated. But what if he did?

Ruby came back with her tray loaded with dishes, scurried off again and returned with the remains of the pudding.

Harriet said: 'Come on then, tell us what she's like. You did see her?'

'Good-looking. She's got everything, that one. Her name's Claudia.'

'I'll have some of that meringue.' Mrs Summers got up to help herself. She pushed a clean plate in front of Harriet and offered her the serving spoon.

'Save some for me,' May said.

Ruby was collecting clean dishes to reset the dining table for breakfast.

'I've heard the missus going on at Luke, openly telling him to get married.' She laughed. 'Not tonight, of course. Not in front of anybody.'

'Except you,' May said. 'Is this the last of the pots?'

'There's still the coffee cups. You'll have to wait, they don't like me barging in to get them. Come on, Harriet, are you going to have some peaches?'

'No.' She pushed the huge glass plate away from her. Suddenly she felt a little sick.

'There's the bell.' Cook heaved her bulk off the chair to get herself another glass of sherry. Ruby went upstairs but was back again in moments.

'Party's breaking up at last. Mrs Clark wants you, Harriet.'

As Harriet reached the hall, she saw Luke holding out a wrap for a pretty girl of about her own age. She wore a gown of filmy peach crêpe. Until that moment Harriet hadn't believed Luke would take any other woman seriously. He was bending towards her with such a look of rapture on his face that Harriet felt her stomach muscles contract. She pulled up short, causing Ruby to cannon into her.

Harriet recognised that look of love: she'd thought it was for her and her alone. Luke had told her he loved her. He'd promised they'd be married one day.

'Such a lovely evening.' The girl was smiling up at Luke. 'I've enjoyed it.'

'I've enjoyed having you here,' Luke returned with more feeling than mere politeness required. Harriet felt the blood rush up her face. She wanted to turn on them, tell the girl he was spoken for. Remind him that they loved each other. He didn't need anybody else. She helped the old lady across the hall.

'Good night, Mrs Clark, I'm so pleased to have met you.' The girl kissed the lined cheek and totally ignored Harriet.

'I expect we'll be seeing more of you,' Mrs Clark told her. 'I do hope so.'

Harriet felt she was having a nightmare. Servants were invisible to the Dransfields, she knew that, but surely not to Luke? Luke had never treated her in this way before.

'Such a nice young lady,' the old lady puffed as she climbed the stairs.

'Who is she?' Harriet's voice sounded choked to her own ears.

'Miss Eliot, Claudia Eliot. Her parents are in dog biscuits. I think she'll suit Luke very well.'

That made Harriet's cheeks flame again. When she was free to go to her own room, she didn't try to sleep. She expected to hear Luke's tap on her door at any moment. He'd want to apologise, to assure her there was nothing he liked about that girl. That it was just an act to keep his mother quiet. He'd want to make love to her then, he always did. He was always just as eager as she was, but tonight she'd tell him no, to punish him.

It was two o'clock before she realised it, and it dawned on her that he didn't intend to come. She couldn't believe it, not when he must know she'd be upset.

Having decided she should go to sleep, Harriet found she could not. In her mind's eye, she could see the young lady in the peach gown standing at the foot of her bed. She wanted to tell her never to come near Luke again.

She fell into an uneasy doze at last, and when it was time to get up she felt fuddled with sleep. Once again, she had the feeling that she was overhanging a precipice and might be swept over at any instant.

She dragged herself through her duties all the next day,

and was glad when Mrs Clark decided she needed to retire early. Harriet went straight to bed herself. She woke from a heavy sleep to find Luke at her bedside.

'Couldn't wake you up,' he told her, snuggling in beside her.

'What time is it?'

'Only half ten. Everybody's gone to bed early.'

She didn't send him packing. She clung to him, craving all the love he could give. Luke was reassuring.

'Of course it's you I love,' he whispered. 'You look so distant and cool but you aren't. You're all flames inside. You're much more exciting than Claudia Eliot.'

Harriet didn't feel he'd set her mind at rest. She'd seen his face as he'd looked down at Claudia, but she wanted him so badly herself, she closed her mind to that. She knew he went out the following evening, and he was evasive when she asked where he'd been. She told herself she mustn't be jealous of Claudia. She could think of nothing else but that she might lose Luke.

She asked herself over and over, where had she gone wrong?

All summer, the likelihood of war was growing closer and closer. Harriet felt it gave her something else to worry about, apart from whether Luke still loved her. Every morning, as soon as Harriet took in Olivia's breakfast tray, the old lady asked for the newspapers, to have the latest news from Europe read out to her.

Everybody was growing concerned. There were countless rumours that Germany was mobilising. Olivia never stopped discussing the situation. Because everybody else wanted news, papers were sold out quickly. Some days they weren't delivered to Ottershaw House, and they had to rely on Stanley buying one in town and bringing it back for them in the evening.

Then came the dreaded news that Germany had declared

war on Russia, but had occupied Luxembourg and attacked France without declaring war on them. There were rumours that Germany was marching against Belgium. On August Bank Holiday Monday, Lenora went to work as usual. By the afternoon Olivia was the only member of the family still at home. Harriet was in the drawing room, reading to her from a Somerset Maugham novel, when the telephone rang.

'See who that is.' The old lady was screwing up her face with impatience at the interruption.

Harriet went out to the hall to answer it. 'Dransfield residence.'

'I want a word with Olivia.' She didn't need to ask who it was.

'It's Mr Dransfield for you.'

'Good Lord, what does he want?' Olivia made an abortive effort to get up from her chair. Harriet went to help her, but she was waved away.

'Can't be bothered. Don't like telephones anyway, new-fangled things. Find out what he wants.'

Harriet picked up the receiver again. 'Mr Dransfield, Mrs Clark would like me to take a message.'

'I thought she'd like to know,' he boomed. 'You too. England has officially declared war on Germany.'

Harriet gasped: 'It's come, then?'

'Tell her I'll bring the paper home with me. You can both read all about it.'

'Thank you.'

When she told Olivia the old lady didn't seem too upset. 'It shouldn't last long. The Empire's very strong. All the newspapers say so.'

'But what about your grandsons? Won't they get caught up . . . have to fight?' Harriet couldn't mention Luke by name, but it was of him she was thinking.

'No need. The army's at full strength. Better if the boys stay here and carry on with the business.'

A vigorous recruiting campaign began because there was no conscription into Britain's armed forces. Notices appeared in every newspaper urging men to sign up. On her day off, Harriet saw posters on the hoardings, on trams and trains and buses. All with the same message.

The news from France was of heavy fighting and lost battles. Luke took her to the music hall at the Victoria Gardens in New Brighton. Two of the artists sang ditties about King and country needing young men to fight:

'England needs you so. You really ought to go.'

A wave of patriotism was sweeping through the country. They were heady days, of brass bands playing in the parks, of military marches through city centres with mounted cavalry and flags flying. There was tremendous enthusiasm for war, everybody thought it would be over in a few months. Luke talked of missing the fun if he didn't get into the army soon. He told Harriet he and Eric had been to see one or two people about becoming officers. It filled her with dread.

She was seeing less of Luke. He was trying to pretend nothing had changed between them, but she didn't trust him as she once had. All the same, she hated the idea of him being under fire in the trenches. She knew his parents were against him going too. But he wanted very much to go, and wouldn't listen when she tried to dissuade him.

'I'll miss you,' she said, 'and I'll be worried stiff that something might . . .'

'I'll miss you too, Hattie. I'll be back when it's all over, you'll see. It's going to be great fun.'

It came as a shock to hear that Luke and Eric had received forms from the adjutant of the Cheshire Regiment, with instructions to fill them up and appear before a selection committee.

'It's all right,' he told her. 'Even if we are selected, the adjutant says we'll probably have to wait some time.'

Harriet knew just how horrified the family was. She heard that Lenora grew very angry with them both at supper and forbade them to go. She found it harrowing to listen to Olivia, who could talk of nothing else, and difficult to hide just how much she cared about Luke.

'They'll be selected,' Olivia surmised. 'They were both in the Officers' Training Corps at school. They're just what the War Office is looking for.'

Hattie tried to prepare herself. When both Luke and Eric heard they'd been nominated for commissions and were required to go immediately to Chester to start their training, Lenora declared herself devastated.

'All my children gone,' she mourned.

'Sophie isn't far,' Olivia had tried to comfort.

'How can I possibly run the business without the boys? Chasing off to the war. Wanting a bit of fun. Not the first thought for their own future. They'd be better off here, building up this business. And why, for heaven's sake? They could be killed!'

For once, Hattie understood and shared Lenora's feelings. She too was filled with dread that Luke might be killed. The only comfort was that officer training would keep him in the country for some time.

The news reaching them daily from France was horrific, and casualty lists of British dead and wounded began to appear in the newspapers.

Maggie knew from the very first that Tom would want to fight for his country. He saw it as an honourable way to escape the boredom of clerking for the Co-op.

'Don't go,' she pleaded. 'I couldn't bear it if anything happened to you.'

'Nothing will happen to me,' he told her. He stayed at his desk for a another month, but patriotic fervour was gathering pace. Soon she was begging him to stay. She wept at the thought of losing him. When his brothers volunteered, and men who didn't were branded as cowards, Maggie knew she'd lost the struggle.

There was no commission for Tom. He didn't even try to get one, but went in as a private. Within weeks he and his regiment were under orders to embark for France. Maggie felt half crazed as she went to see him off on the special train leaving from Woodside. The regimental flags and banners were all on show, and the band was playing. It brought a lump to her throat. The platforms were crowded with soldiers, weighed down with heavy packs on their backs. Countless wives and parents were seeing them off.

'Please write often,' she pleaded, as she clung to him during the last painful minutes. 'I want to know exactly what's happening to you.'

'Of course I'll write.' He smiled.

'I'm so afraid for you.'

'Don't you worry, I'll be back. You wait and see.'

Then the guard was blowing his whistle and she couldn't hold on to Tom any longer. He waved from an open window until she couldn't see him. Then, as the crowd moved slowly out of the station, there was no longer any need to hide the tears. People were sobbing all round her. For Maggie it was a relief to cry with them, and wonder, as they all did, whether they would ever see their loved ones again.

Tom's letters came often, as he'd promised, but they were of football matches between regiments, of his lodgings behind the lines during rest periods, and of amazement that the French opened their bars and cafés only a mile or two behind the front lines. While the newspapers carried ever-increasing lists of those killed in battle.

Maggie's life became a nightmare. She followed every scrap of news from the front. It was of heavy bombardments; of a mile or so gained and a mile or so lost; of wire and rain and puddles and mud, and of corpses everywhere.

# CHAPTER TEN

Hattie thought Luke looked magnificent in his uniform. He had leave several times and came home for the weekend. Even though he wasn't able to take her out, he spent a good deal of time with her in her room. He said he was enjoying the war; having a fine time with the boys.

At Christmas he had leave again, but Hattie wanted to see more of him. An hour or two in her bedroom wasn't what she wanted. She longed for his company, just to be with him to talk to him. Instead, Claudia Eliot and her family came to supper. Harriet felt excluded, unable to share the fun and little luxuries of Christmas with him.

'Forget him.' Maggie was overbracing with her advice. 'Luke's a real chip off the old block. You'll never know where you are with him. He knows how to charm the ladies.'

It wasn't advice that Harriet wanted to hear. She thought Maggie rather lacking in understanding, but made allowances because she knew her sister was worried stiff about Tom fighting in the trenches.

When the old year ran out and 1915 was welcomed in, Harriet knew it wouldn't be long before Luke was sent to France.

One March night, she'd seen Mrs Clark into bed and was undressing in her own room when the telephone rang up the stairwell. Afraid it might be news of Luke's embarkation, she opened her bedroom door, her heart racing.

Lenora answered it. 'Lovely to hear from you, but I hope it isn't . . .'

Harriet hung on to her door knob, listening for clues as to who might be on the other end.

There was resignation in Lenora's voice. 'Yes, of course, we knew it was bound to come. A week's leave first?'

Horrors, that must mean embarkation leave! Harriet swallowed hard and crept noiselessly to the bottom of the nursery stairs, straining to hear. Was Lenora talking to Luke or Eric? Would they both sail for France at the same time?

But now Mrs Dransfield was letting off hoots of joy. It seemed, after all, that she was pleased about something. Perhaps neither of them was about to embark?

'I'm delighted for you, darling, and your father will be too. Many congratulations.' There was another silence. Harriet's gut feeling was that she was talking to Luke. All the strength was ebbing from her legs. It almost sounded as if . . .

His mother was speaking again. 'It doesn't give anybody much time, but I'm sure they'll do their best. The Eliots will put on a good show for you, I'm sure.'

That left Harriet clinging to the banister for dear life. Surely Luke wasn't telling his mother he was going to marry Claudia Eliot?

'What news this is! Stanley, come and have a word with Luke. Come along, do hurry. I'm so pleased for you both.'

Harriet's head was spinning. She didn't need to hear any more. Stanley's voice was booming up the stairwell, confirming the terrible news.

She closed her door and groped her way over to her bed. As she fell on to it, her face was wet with tears. Rejection was very hard to stomach, especially when she'd given freely of her body and her love. There was nothing more she could have given him.

Hattie hardly slept, and when it was time to get up the next morning, she felt terrible. She was sick in the nursery bathroom and had to spend a long time holding a cold wet flannel against her eyes. They were red and puffy from crying, and her cheeks were drained of colour. She loved Luke and wanted him desperately; she couldn't believe this was happening.

The whole household was agog with the news at breakfast, pleased and happy. Harriet felt stirrings of resentment and anger at the way he'd treated her.

Luke's leave was to start in less than a week. He planned to spend one night at home and be married the following day by special licence. He and his bride would spend the remainder of his week's leave on honeymoon.

'He's a dark horse.' Mrs Clark seemed quite buoyed up by the news. 'Kept it very quiet. Give us all something to look forward to, a bit of excitement.'

'You'll be going to the wedding?' Harriet wondered if Mrs Clark was too frail to attend the church and the reception. 'It'll mean a long day out.'

'I don't want to miss it.' Her lined face lit up. 'I'll be all right. I feel safe if I have your arm to hang on to. If it gets too much for me, you'll be able to ask Mary Eliot for somewhere quiet where I can lie down.'

'Me? I won't be invited.' Harriet was shocked. She wanted nothing to do with this wedding. She hadn't expected to have to witness it. 'I mean, it's not my place . . .'

'I won't be able to go without you, Harriet. I need you. You're a great help and comfort to me. The Eliots know that. I'll ask if I can bring you. They'll expect it anyway.'

Harriet had to swallow back her objections. Like everyone else in the house, she was plunged into a frenzy of preparations. She called in Mrs Clark's dressmaker to make her a new outfit.

The dressmaker spread her samples of silk and chiffon and taffeta on the rug Olivia had over her. The old lady deliberated a long time over her choice.

'I've worn nothing but black for years, but for a wedding? I'll have this taffeta in gun-metal grey, I think. With a white jabot at the neck. Can you make a new dress for Harriet, too? You'll have enough time.'

'It isn't necessary, Mrs Clark.' Harriet couldn't bear the thought of going. Sackcloth and ashes suited her mood.

'You won't want to feel less smart than the rest of us, I daresay.'

'It's very kind, but . . .'

'Come now, which of these materials do you like? I want you to have a new dress.'

'I have brighter colours, ma'am.' The dressmaker was taking more samples from her bag. 'These may be more to your taste.'

Because she had to choose something, Harriet picked out a deep royal-blue chiffon. Then the sewing room was opened up and the dressmaker worked long hours over the next three days in order to complete the two outfits. Sophie and Lenora preferred to go over to Liverpool and buy their outfits ready-made from the shops in Bold Street, though with the war, the choice was limited.

'We should have a grand wedding.' Harriet heard Olivia holding forth. 'As befits a hero going to fight for his country.'

'There isn't time to prepare anything,' Lenora worried.

Mrs Summers was given the task of making the wedding cake. 'How can I do that in four days?' she grumbled. 'A rich cake needs weeks to mature, and there's hours of work in all that icing.'

'You'll have to do your best, Mrs Summers,' Harriet heard Lenora bark impatiently.

The reception was to be at the bride's home in nearby Noctorum Lane. When Harriet arranged for a hire car to take her and Mrs Clark into Birkenhead in order to buy new hats, they saw the marquee being erected on the Eliots' lawn. Tubs full of flowering plants were being unloaded from a cart at the gate.

At the milliner's, Harriet was persuaded to choose a hat in a shade of blue that matched her new dress. It cost the same sum as the hat Mrs Clark chose for herself.

'You're very generous,' Hattie told her.

'You won't want to look out of place amongst the ladies,' she retorted.

Harriet went to see Maggie on her day off. Tom had already been in France for several months and Maggie had not been invited to the wedding.

'Tom reckons Luke was playing the field all along,' she said. Hattie felt it like a knife through her heart. If only Tom had said that to her when he'd first introduced them, she wouldn't have been so generous with her love.

She listened to Maggie's worries. 'Did you read in the papers about the losses at Neuve Chapelle last Thursday and Friday? I'm sure Tom's not far from there. They say about twenty thousand.'

Harriet largely discounted Maggie's worries. Maggie already had what she'd wanted. She was Tom's wife, and there was nothing either of them could do about keeping him safe now.

When Luke and Eric arrived at Ottershaw House in a taxi, Harriet watched from Mrs Clark's window. The family made a great fuss of them. They both looked like gallant heroes in their officer's uniforms. Eric had been granted two days' leave, though he was not to go to France just yet.

Laughter and jollification carried up the stairwell long into the night. They didn't get up from the dining table until after eleven. Mrs Clark wanted to go up to bed straight afterwards. That was the first time Hattie had had reason to go close to Luke. She was careful to keep her face averted from him.

'Good evening, Harriet,' he said. It surprised her to be addressed in front of the whole family, and made her turn her head. His cheeks were flushed; no doubt he'd enjoyed the plentiful supply of wine. 'Glad to see you're still taking good care of Grandmama.'

'Good evening,' she said, as coldly as she dared.

'So many are deserting their posts in these difficult times.'

That rather rubbed her up the wrong way, though she knew he was referring to Ruby, who had given in her notice. She was going to collect the tickets down at the ferry. The Corporation had started taking women in men's jobs now, and she'd earn a better wage.

After that, Hattie expected him to come to her room later that night. For days, she'd been trying to make up her mind how to receive him. One part of her fulminated in rage against him; the other longed for his kisses. She didn't expect kisses now, but she thought he'd come to talk, to explain. He owed her some explanation, surely?

She lay on her bed waiting for him, growing steadily more bitter. At two o'clock she woke from a light doze to realise that he didn't intend to come. The house was silent now, and she was tempted to go to his room and face him with his double-dealing. Hurtful sentences had been forming in her mind all evening. She'd imagined herself saying some harsh things to him, but in the end, she decided she hadn't got what it took to confront anybody. She tried to sleep, but her mind raged on and on, not allowing her any peace.

Harriet put on her new finery for the wedding, feeling shaky with nerves. The sun was shining; it was unseasonably warm and spring-like for so early in the year. As she waited in church, sitting next to Mrs Clark, she was struggling to hold back her tears. It was an effort to drag her gaze away from the back of Luke's head as he waited at the front of the church.

There was a flurry behind her and she knew the bride had

arrived. She'd seen her only once before; she managed now to take in her radiant face and the lace wedding gown that was said to have been her mother's. She longed to change places with her.

She was churning in a sudden rush of jealous rage, feeling cheated because this girl had taken the man she'd so wanted. Claudia Eliot would have a prosperous life even if she didn't marry Luke, but Harriet had lost her chance of prosperity as well as of happiness. And lost her chance of helping Pa and her family out of their poverty.

She sat with downcast eyes throughout the ceremony and wished she could close her ears too. She tried hard to imagine it wasn't happening. But of course it was, and she was going to be brought face to face with the newly-wed couple. She stood in line with Mrs Clark, as Luke and Claudia received their guests.

'Congratulations, darling.' The old lady kissed both her grandson and his bride.

Harriet put out her hand without a word. She couldn't look either of them in the eye. Her venom was directed at Luke, handsome and upright in his newly pressed uniform and highly polished Sam Brown belt. He'd said he loved her; he'd led her to hope for this for herself.

Hattie found it a relief to have the wedding over, and now made up her mind that the sooner Luke was dispatched to France the better. He came back to Ottershaw House to collect some of his belongings, and brought his bride, but they stayed only for a meal.

She caught sight of her reflection as she tiptoed across the hall while they were eating. The mirror showed her grim-faced, with angry green eyes. She was so white as to look ill. In truth she didn't feel well. She'd been actually sick more than once.

Once he'd gone she tried to forget him, but it wasn't easy here in his home. Olivia kept her up to date with all his news. He was in France and finding his first days in the trenches exciting.

The family had shrunk, but staff were being lost too. May, the tweeny, had been promoted to housemaid when Ruby left. Now she gave in her notice too. There were other jobs for women outside domestic service, and May was going to a munitions factory where the pay was better.

'Eight to five is what I'm going to work. I'll be free to do what I like every evening. You must be mad to stay here,' she told Harriet.

Harriet had more to do now: she was having to act as housekeeper. Women came in daily for a few hours to do the heavy cleaning. Mrs Summers complained because she felt she had more to do too.

The weeks were passing, and Hattie continued to feel unwell. When she went back to Elizabeth Place on her day off, Pa was complaining about the shortages. Some foods had virtually disappeared off the market, and everything was becoming much more expensive.

'You're putting on a bit of weight, though, so you aren't going short at Ottershaw House.'

Harriet said nothing about the bad stomach she'd had for ages. She wasn't interested in food just now, and Mrs Summers was complaining about shortages just like everybody else.

It was only when she went to put on her new blue dress to go to church with Mrs Clark that she realised Pa was right: she was putting on weight. Her abdomen, usually so flat, was definitely more rounded. She took her calendar from the drawer of her dressing table. When had she last seen . . . ? The very thought, when it came to her, was so devastating that she had to lie down.

Could she be with child? If she were, then she was in desperate straits. Who could she possibly turn to? She lay rigid with fear for five minutes. Why had it not occurred to her until now? Only the fact that Mrs Clark was waiting for help with her dressing and would then expect her to accompany her to church made her move. She took in nothing of the sermon; she was panic-stricken.

Was it possible? Luke had said he knew how to safeguard against that. He'd told her he was making it absolutely safe, taking good care it wouldn't happen. But she knew enough of Luke now not to believe all he'd said. Hattie felt ignorant about such things, and it was impossible to ask. But even when she'd calmed down a little, she still couldn't believe it was happening to her.

On her next day off, she waited until she was alone in the rooms at Elizabeth Place, and then started looking through the boxes of books in Pa's room. Some of these had belonged to her mother. They used to consult the books on childhood fevers when one of her younger sisters fell ill, and she'd seen then . . . Yes, this was what she needed: a book on pregnancy and childbirth. She slipped it into her bag and took it back with her. In her own room on the nursery floor she had the privacy to study it fully.

She was more than sure; after reading the signs and symptoms she knew she'd have to accept it as fact. She was with child, and since it couldn't have happened after Christmas, she knew she was well on in her pregnancy. How much longer did she have before it became obvious to everybody? She had another panic attack, and for the next few days went about her duties like a zombie.

She felt desperate, for there was nobody she could confide in, and she couldn't make up her mind what she should do. She could hide herself away somewhere. She had a little money saved up from her wages but nothing like as much as she'd need.

She blamed Luke. If only he were here now he'd help her. He'd have to. It was his fault; he was the one who had sought those favours. What could she do?

Tell Pa? She felt the heat run up her cheeks at the very

thought. She was ashamed. Would he want her back at Elizabeth Place? If not, she'd be in big trouble.

Confide in Maggie? No, Maggie always managed everything very well for herself. She'd never get herself into a mess like this.

Hattie wanted to cry, but she'd done so much of it that she knew it wouldn't help. She wasn't sleeping well. She felt truly ill. She couldn't think of what was to become of her.

'You're the clever one,' Pa used to say to her. 'The competent one, the one who can stand on her own feet.'

She hadn't been clever with Luke. Reason told her that he should share this dreadful burden. She could write to him. Why should he not be worried about it too? She'd ask him to send her money so that she'd be able to go away somewhere to have his child.

She'd seen at least one letter come from him to his parents. She knew Lenora had written back. While all the Dransfields were out at work, and under the pretext of dusting Lenora's study, Harriet looked in the address book she kept on her desk.

It was an army address. Feeling like a thief, Harriet scribbled it down.

Harriet had no idea how long it would take for her letter to reach Luke and for him to reply from France. When she deemed that enough time might have passed, she made a point of being in the hall when the morning post came through the letter box. There was another delivery in the afternoon, but by then the Dransfields were out of the house and she needn't worry about them seeing it.

One afternoon she was crossing the hall when she saw the envelope on the mat. She recognised Luke's scrawl before she picked it up. Looking guiltily round to make sure nobody was watching, she snatched it up and raced upstairs to her room to read it. She was a fraction of an instant away from ripping it open when she noticed that it was addressed to his father, not to her.

She was damp with perspiration as she turned it over and over in her hand. Luke's return address was on the back. Perhaps she hadn't allowed enough time? Perhaps it was just a coincidence that Luke had written to his father now?

Hattie was very much on edge as she went about her afternoon duties, but she had to do her best to hide it. Mrs Clark was not feeling too well either, and went to bed early saying she'd have her supper on a tray. Hattie had settled her down for the night and was returning the tray to the kitchen just as the other members of the family were leaving the dining room.

'I want a word with you,' Stanley said quietly, as he crossed to his study. 'As soon as you've got rid of that tray.'

Hattie felt the strength drain from her legs. They felt like lead. Did he know? She felt all churned up and agitated as she went back to tap on his door.

'Come in, Harriet.' She felt his eyes studying her. 'Sit down. I've had a letter from Luke.' He waved it at her.

She tried to focus on his feet, but the room was beginning to spin.

'He tells me you're in trouble, and he's asked me to help. Is that right?'

Hattie swallowed. Her mouth was dry, she couldn't speak. It was all she could manage to lift her eyes to his. He was still watching her closely, and she sensed he had some sympathy for her.

'Come on,' he said. 'Yes or no?'

'Yes,' she whispered.

'Right. First you must go and see a doctor. We must make quite sure. You understand?'

Hattie nodded, her cheeks on fire, wanting to sink through the floor.

'I'll help you as Luke has asked, but only on one condition. You must not talk about this. Not ever. Nobody must know.'

'Talk? I don't want anybody to know!' She felt totally mortified.

'Luke's a married man, and no word of this must ever get to his wife's ears.'

'No.'

'You probably aren't aware . . . but I might as well tell you. She's expecting Luke's child too.'

'What?' Harriet felt her face flame anew. This was the final humiliation. She'd not been the only one he'd been making love to. She wanted to die.

'I have to protect Claudia. She is his wife.'

Harriet had nothing to say to that. She was staring at him aghast.

'Quite apart from that aspect, there's Luke's own reputation. I don't want that tarnished in any way. The family must never know, particularly his grandmother. It would upset her.'

Harriet was so engulfed with fury she couldn't stop the words coming: 'It upsets me. It's not of my choosing. I wish . . . how I wish it weren't so.'

Stanley was silent, fiddling with Luke's letter. He sighed heavily. 'But since it is . . . Harriet, I can only help you if you promise never to reveal the name of your child's father. Not to anybody. Not ever.'

'I promise,' she gasped. She had nothing to lose by that. It suited her too.

'Right. Then this is what I suggest. I'll make an appointment for you to see a doctor. Not near here, over in Liverpool. Then, if he finds it necessary, we'll do something about it.'

'I know it's necessary,' she choked.

'Luke thinks it may be too late – to have it taken away.'

Harriet felt sweat breaking out on her forehead.

'Don't worry, I'll find somewhere for you to go.' She raised her eyes to his again at that. She had to have his help. 'And I'll pay for what's needed. Arrange for the child afterwards. Everything.'

'Thank you.' Harriet counted herself lucky that he'd uttered no words of censure. She knew she'd have broken down with shame and humiliation if he had.

His eyes came sideways to her again. 'You don't look well.'

'I don't feel well.' She suppressed a sob. It sounded like a choking cough.

'Have you a cough?'

'No.'

He gave another long sigh; rubbed his fingers through his whiskers.

'It might be as well to pretend you have. Everybody will want to know where you're going and why. I shall tell them you have a touch of consumption; that the doctor suggests a sanatorium and complete rest for a few months. That's to be the story, all right?'

She nodded.

'Right. Go and cough all over everybody then. Make it sound authentic.'

Hattie stumbled up to her room. She couldn't face anybody yet, it was all too much. Perhaps if she'd announced she was with child before Claudia Eliot had, he might have married her? But she didn't want him as a husband now. She was seeing Luke in a new light. He'd been using her.

She'd known there were nights when he'd gone out. He must have been seeing Claudia then. She'd thought he'd married the heiress to a dog food fortune because he couldn't face being short of money. Now it seemed there was this other reason. It filled her with anger.

Things began to move quickly for Hattie after that. Mr

Dransfield gave her the address of the doctor she was to see. It was not far from their old glove factory, but she didn't know that district.

'Make your way there for three o'clock,' he told her. 'I've told Olivia you aren't well, that I'm sending you to a doctor. Don't forget the story now: you've got a cough, you've not felt well for months.'

Harriet had dithered for so long on her own, she was glad he'd taken charge. She did as she was told. The doctor was not impolite in words, but his manner told her that he regarded her as a fallen woman. He examined her and told her that her baby would be born towards the end of September. It was already May. She was counting up the number of weeks ahead when he said:

'Go back and wait in my waiting room. You'll find Mr Dransfield there now. You can ask him to step in and see me.'

Harriet hadn't realised he'd meant to come, and she was blushing again as she gave him the message. She hadn't long to wait. He came back to the waiting room door and said: 'Come along, Harriet. Our business is concluded here.'

He took her to a tea shop round the corner. It was close to the dock road and not the sort of place she'd have gone into on her own; nor, she thought, his either. It was full of dockers in their working clothes. Two mugs of tea were placed on the table before them.

'I'm afraid you're right. About being in trouble.'

She was uncomfortable sitting this close to him. She could see beads of tea that he'd dribbled on the whiskers on his chin.

'The doctor is arranging a place for you in a respectable nursing home in Market Drayton. You'll be given a room to yourself and you'll be able to come and go as you wish. You'll find it comfortable. Use it like a hotel. You might, if you're lucky, find another young lady in a similar condition

190

and have a companion. You'll give birth there when the time comes.'

She was sweating with relief. 'Thank you.'

'Do you want something to eat?'

She surveyed the brightly coloured cakes and thick doorsteps of bread and margarine and shook her head.

His eyes were raking her face. 'Who else knows about your – condition?'

'Nobody.' Her voice was strangled.

'Your sister? Maggie?'

'No, I couldn't . . . I've told nobody.'

'Good, the fewer people who know the better. We must keep it this way. You must tell everybody you've been spitting blood. That I insisted you saw a doctor and you're now awaiting tests to see if it really is consumption.'

'Yes, Mr Dransfield.'

'Next week you must tell everybody that the tests were positive, and that I and the doctor have arranged for you to have treatment in Market Drayton. There's a big sanatorium there.'

'But the address?'

'Don't leave one. You need to disappear for the next few months.'

'What about my family? They'll expect me to write to them and they'll want to write back. If I don't, Pa will know something's wrong.'

'Don't tell them the truth. You promised, didn't you? You can spin them some story about having treatment at the sanatorium but having to stay in a small private nursing home nearby. That it was easier to get you in quickly; it's more comfortable, whatever you like. But don't let your family visit you. The nursing home takes maternity cases, not consumptives.'

'My family don't have money to spare for travel,' Harriet said stiffly. She felt reasonably sure of that.

'Right. When the arrangements are made and I get a date

191

for you to go in, I'll arrange for a hire car to take you to Woodside station. You must buy a single ticket. When you get off the train, take a cab and give the driver the address of the nursing home. You'll be all right there.'

Stanley was being more helpful and more sympathetic than she'd expected. His eyes slid sideways every time a new customer came in. He looked out of place here, uncomfortable.

'But what about the baby?' Harriet asked. 'How am I going to manage when it's born?'

'Adoption,' he said, frowning. 'We agreed, didn't we? I understand the nursing home will arrange it for you. It can go to an orphanage until a new home can be found for it.'

Harriet didn't think that was sympathetic. 'I'm not sure . . .'

He was suddenly much more decisive. 'It's the only option open to you. The only way you can put this whole unhappy incident behind you.'

'If there was some way I could keep . . .'

'No, it's the only way we can all be sure that nobody ever finds out.'

Harriet hadn't given the coming infant much thought until now. What had occupied her mind was how to cope with the waiting time and the birth itself. She'd felt overwhelmed by the sheer practicalities and the awful shame.

Stanley Dransfield was looking more serious. 'Perhaps I should have spelled it out more carefully. There are two conditions for this help I'm giving you, Harriet. The second is that the baby must go for adoption. You couldn't keep your first promise if you took the child home and brought it up yourself. That's out of the question.'

Harriet felt anger rising up her throat. Luke had written to his father asking him to shut her up so she wouldn't ruin his reputation and marriage. The Dransfields didn't care about her feelings. About what she wanted, or what was best for the child.

'Do I have your promise on that? The baby will be adopted?'

Hattie was seething with frustration, but what else could she say? She had to have the nursing home arrangements. 'Yes.'

'You're sure?' She'd instilled the seeds of doubt in his mind.

'Yes.'

'I must insist. It's to your advantage too, Harriet. If you can put all this behind you, you'll have lost nothing.'

She felt her life would never be the same again.

'How can a young single girl like you bring up a child? Your reputation would be gone. No decent man would look at you.'

The way Harriet felt, she'd never look at any man again, decent or otherwise. She was going to stay single. She wasn't going to let another man within a mile of her.

He said, more kindly: 'You'll need cash in your pocket to meet expenses.' He handed over a drawstring purse of soft suede, and she felt the sovereigns move inside it. 'I'll meet all your bills at the nursing home as well, of course.'

Harriet nodded numbly.

'There'll be more for you when this is all over. A lump sum of a hundred pounds. Provided it's all kept secret and there's nothing to connect your baby to Luke. All right?'

'Yes.'

'Go back home now and try to continue with your duties. Remember what you must tell everybody.'

He got up and left her sitting at the table. She ordered another of the thick mugs of tea to help her recover.

Quietly, and under the table, so as not to be seen, she counted the number of sovereigns in the purse. There were twenty: as much as she earned in six months. And a hundred more when it was all over. She was in such a position that she had to accept Stanley Dransfield's help, and his money. Hattie wanted to pound her fists on the table with rage. It wasn't that she thought him ungenerous, but she was being bought off. She, Harriet Knell, was being bought off! That really rankled.

Harriet was still gripped with fury when she got back to Ottershaw House. Luke was being protected, she was the one having to face all the problems. She told Mrs Clark the story with which Stanley Dransfield had primed her. The old lady was very upset.

'You haven't looked well. I've thought that for a long time. All big green eyes in a white face. But I haven't noticed you coughing.'

'It's bad at night,' she lied. 'It's a good job nobody sleeps near me or I'd keep them awake.'

'The sanatorium is the best place for you, but I shall miss you, Harriet. I don't know how I'll manage without you. How long will all this take? I don't suppose you know?'

Harriet shook her head, feeling she was taking advantage of the old lady. She'd grown fond of her, despite her sharp tongue.

She went home to tell her family. She had ten minutes alone with Pa before her sisters returned from school.

'Consumption? My poor Harriet.' Pa pulled her to him in a big hug. She held in her stomach, hoping he wouldn't feel it bouncing against him.

'Such a terrible thing, consumption. Your mother had it, you know. She should never have had another baby, she wasn't strong enough. I've never forgiven myself for that. She might have been here with us now if it hadn't been for Ruth.

'And I've always been afraid for Maggie. She's so like your mother. Slighter build, frailer than the rest of you. Funny, I never thought it would happen to you. You never caught any illnesses as a child.'

For the first time Harriet realised how this would worry

her father. She was a cheat and a liar and she felt very guilty about the concern she was causing her family.

If only she could be more like Maggie.

# CHAPTER ELEVEN

Maggie was very frightened for Tom. He wrote often, but told her little about life in the trenches. Only that he'd heard distant gunfire, or they'd had a quiet night. If he mentioned anybody being wounded they were always from another battalion. Yet the newspapers spoke of fierce fighting and the casualty lists were terrible.

She knew he was trying to shield her by withholding the worst details, but not knowing only made her imagination run riot. She lived in daily dread that he'd be killed. She felt so lonely without him; the house seemed silent and empty. When she couldn't stand her solitary state any longer, Pa sent her sister Clara to stay with her, but Clara was at school during the day and the time seemed very long.

Women were taking over men's jobs as the men went to the front to fight. Maggie felt she'd be better if she had something to fill her day. She saw vacancies advertised for bus conductresses and applied. She was given the job and spent a day under instruction before she went down to tell her father.

Pa's eyes glazed over. 'No lady should ever work on the buses.'

'Don't be daft, Pa. In the old days you used to say no lady ever took paid employment. Things have changed with the war, and anyway, I had to work before I was married.'

'But riding round on an omnibus . . .'

'It's not the old two-horse bus with straw on the floor and smelly paraffin lamps. I shall be working on a modern motor bus. No metal rims to the wheels these days, they all have solid rubber tyres. And electric bells to signal to the driver.'

'You'll catch your death, out in all weathers,' Pa said slowly. 'It's not suitable for a woman.'

'The top's open to the weather, but it's all right downstairs. When it's raining, I'll stay down if I can. Bet most of the passengers will too. I'm going to like it, Pa. Better than staying at home by myself all day. I'll save up. When Tom comes home, we'll have a holiday.' Pa was staring at her silently.

Maggie thought: it's *if* Tom comes home, not when. She knew her father was thinking that too, but he wouldn't say it. It was there, a dread they couldn't speak about. Every day she combed the lists in the newspapers of those killed and injured.

'D'you know Patrick O'Brien's been killed on the Marne? Patrick from upstairs? His name was in yesterday's paper.'

Maggie suppressed a shudder. She'd seen it, and knew Tom was fighting in the same area. She couldn't bear to think about it.

'You might get on my bus sometimes. I'm starting on the route that goes past the hospital.'

'Does that mean free rides for me?' he joked.

'No free rides for anybody,' she laughed. 'I'll have an inspector checking up on me.'

Over the following months, Tom continued to write of being taken out in digging parties to deepen a trench, or of laying more duck boards. He said he was taking good care of himself by keeping his head below the parapet, because one man had been killed in this way by a sniper. Yet she knew he was near Compiègne, and the papers spoke of the British forces there being forced to retreat after fierce fighting, during which the Germans had used poisonous gas.

When she didn't hear from him she imagined the worst. Only when another letter came did she know he was safe. One day, she returned home to Lowther Street, tired after a shift of nine hours. As she opened her front door she saw a yellow envelope lying on the mat. It was a telegram.

She couldn't breathe, couldn't move. She knew what this meant. Something had happened to Tom. She'd thought him safe because she'd had a letter yesterday.

It was a long time before she could bring herself to open it. When she did, she let out a sigh of relief. Tom had been injured in battle. He was in a field hospital behind the lines.

There were no details about his injuries. Maggie knew that he could be badly hurt and that a great many soldiers died of their wounds. Even so, she felt a surge of hope. Whatever his injuries, Tom was now in hospital and not in the trenches. If he could survive his wounds – and he'd survived long enough to reach hospital – then she could be reasonably sure he'd be safe from enemy action over the next few weeks. She hoped and prayed he'd be brought home now.

She wanted to tell everybody the news. She didn't bother changing out of her uniform, though Pa wouldn't approve because the skirt didn't even reach to mid calf. She wore button gaiters of leather to keep her legs warm and respectable. Nobody could cope with long skirts if they were to get up and down the outside stairs of a bus. When she arrived at Elizabeth Place, she found Hattie sitting at the kitchen table, drinking tea. The rest of her family seemed in anything but high spirits.

'Our Hattie's got consumption,' Frances told her.

Maggie was shocked.

'You aren't going to die are you, Hattie?' Enid was blinking hard. 'I'm afraid . . .' She pushed up her spectacles to wipe her eyes.

'No, no.' But Hattie sounded as fearful and horrified as the rest of them.

'No, of course not,' Pa said confidently, but his eyes too looked anxious.

Maggie swallowed hard. Betty James, who lived next door in Lowther Street, had died of consumption six months after they'd moved there. She'd been only seventeen.

'That's dreadful! I've thought you looked a bit peaky recently. You poor thing.' Maggie hugged her, feeling selfish because she'd been thinking only of Tom over these last months.

'They tell me they've caught it early,' Hattie insisted.

'You're very brave.'

'You mustn't worry, they think I'll be all right with rest.'

'A sanatorium, though,' Maggie mused. 'You must have it quite bad to be going there. Looks like my nearest and dearest are all going to be in hospital.' She told them the news about Tom.

She was tired and set off home before Hattie. She walked up to Central Station and was waiting at the bus stop, thinking again of Tom, when a taxi drew up on the other side of the road and his mother got out. Maggie watched her pay it off. Lenora was frowning, looking more forbidding than ever.

Suddenly she looked up. Maggie met her gaze and saw recognition, then Lenora's mouth opened as she took in her uniform; her expression telling Maggie as clearly as words that she disapproved of such a job, that she disapproved of the short skirt and gaiters.

Maggie raised her hand, meaning to cross over to tell her the news of Tom. A bus drove between them, shutting her off from view. When it had passed, Mrs Dransfield was heading inside Central Station and the chance had gone.

It was Lenora's loss, Maggie decided. Serve her right. After all this time, she'd be bound to want news of her son. She was glad now she hadn't rushed to tell her.

Harriet began to pack her belongings. She tore up all the theatre programmes she'd kept as souvenirs. She wanted nothing now to remind her of Luke. The things he'd given her that were of value she locked in a little mahogany box Pa had given her. She'd be able to raise money on them later. She left it with most of her other belongings in Elizabeth Place.

She was nervous about going alone to Market Drayton, but everybody expected her to feel that way.

'I'll come with you,' Pa offered. 'See you safely in. Carry your bags.'

His kindness should have given her a warm glow; instead, it made her feel frantic. She had to say that she'd be perfectly all right on her own, that she didn't need him. He looked disheartened. She came very close to clinging to him and sobbing out the whole truth.

When the time came, she did what Stanley Dransfield had told her to do. She found her room at the West View Nursing Home very comfortable. The matron told her she'd be known here as Mrs Knell, and loaned her a wedding ring to put on her finger. It was a cheap rolled-gold affair; nevertheless, she preferred to wear that rather than the one Luke had given her. Both were merely a pretence.

There was a day room with a long refectory table on which she and perhaps another dozen took their meals. The food was nourishing and good. There were comfortable chairs and well-stocked bookcases, a garden with benches on which she could sit. The nurses were kindness itself.

She saw a brochure for the home. The terms were far more expensive than she'd expected. She'd never have been able to meet them herself. Many of the patients had already been delivered of their babies and were lying in. She could hear newborn babies crying on the floor above.

There were a few, like herself, with some time to wait for the birth. She was not immediately able to pick out those who were unmarried. Some mentioned husbands away fighting. Others spoke of having a medical problem that kept them here for the last weeks of their pregnancy. Every patient had a weekly visit from the doctor, and more often if it was required. It was, she thought, a very discreet place.

She was encouraged to walk in the park on fine afternoons, or take herself to the cinema on wet ones. The other ladies were friendly, inclined to stay in groups and spend a lot of time chatting. They were ladies in the social sense too, but Harriet preferred to go out alone and keep herself to herself. She never volunteered any personal details to them, and if asked directly, usually managed to avoid revealing anything about herself.

She went to the shops and bought herself two loose maternity dresses and some easy shoes. To start with, she enjoyed the freedom from work, and after a week felt better for the rest.

The nurses thought she was spending too much time by herself and took her along to the nursery, where they could talk to her while they fed and cared for the babies. Maggie was the one who'd been besotted with babies and children. Apart from her own sisters, Hattie had held herself apart from babies until now, but during the endless days of idleness, she began to take more interest. She began to think about her own child, and grew to hate the idea of turning her back on it. The last thing she wanted was to abandon it to strangers.

She was torn between feelings of anger against the Dransfields and despair at the position in which she found herself. She missed Pa and her family, and was saddened by the unnecessary worry she was giving them. She wrote letters to them, though it wasn't easy when she dared not mention babies. It was a highlight to receive a letter in return. If the truth was to be told, she missed Olivia too.

Maggie wrote to tell her how pleased she was that Tom had been sent back to England. He was in a hospital near Southampton, but was expecting to be sent nearer home any time now. He'd been gassed, and wrote of offensive clouds drifting over the trenches that had turned slowly from greenish-yellow to a white haze. It had left the men panic-stricken, coughing and spluttering. His chest was badly affected. He'd also had his left knee shattered by a bullet and would need an operation on it at some time in the future. They were waiting for his breathing to improve.

Maggie wrote:

I haven't seen him yet, so I don't know how he is really. He tries to stop me worrying by putting a good face on things, but he definitely won't be going back to the front. I'm so happy about that.

Tom says both Eric and Luke came to see him when he was first injured. Said Luke's been in heavy fighting but seems to have a charmed life. Apart from the dysentery most of them suffer from in the trenches, he was fine.

That set Hattie thinking of Luke again. It brought back the longing and the anger. She couldn't forgive him for marrying another. For rejecting her when he'd declared his love. He'd abused her trust. She thought of herself as a bitter person who had made a mess of her life.

She went into labour ten days earlier than she'd expected. The midwives seemed calm, but she was not. There was pain but she was given help to bear it. To Hattie, the indignities of birth seemed the worse part. When her seven-pound baby girl was put into her arms, she feasted her eyes on her, searching for some likeness to Luke. She failed to find any. Her baby was perfectly formed, with beautiful even features and pale crinkly down on her head. She had the Knell colouring.

Hattie had not allowed herself to think of a name for her baby – she knew a name would be chosen by the adoptive parents – but almost without conscious effort, she started thinking of her as Rebecca. When the infant pulled on her breast to feed, Hattie felt a burst of possessiveness. This tiny, perfect creature with rosebud lips was all hers.

Rebecca was one week old when a wasp came into Hattie's room through the open window and hovered over the cot. The baby was restless. Hattie had wrapped her up tight in her swaddling cloth, but she'd worked her fists out and was waving them in the air.

Hattie leapt out of bed in a panic, afraid that Rebecca would be stung. She wafted the wasp out of the way and clasped her child to her. It was the searing pain on her knuckle that made her realise the wasp had stung her instead.

It didn't stop the flood of relief that she'd prevented it from hurting her daughter. It came as a surprise to find she'd put the child before herself. She knew at that moment that she could die for her. She hadn't expected to feel such mother love; it was overwhelming her, changing the way she thought of everything. From that day on, she could hardly bear to let her child out of her sight.

All babies were taken to the nursery at night to allow their mothers to have a good night's rest. Hattie could lie in her bed and distinguish her baby's cry from all the others. She felt ready to burst with pride.

Now that the birth was behind her, she felt better. She knew she had a six-week lying-in period ahead in the nursing home, to get her strength back and to enjoy her baby.

She wrote to both Pa and Maggie that she was getting better and hoped she'd be discharged with a clean bill of health in another six weeks. She wouldn't let herself think of going home and leaving the baby behind.

Maggie had been so looking forward to having Tom back home, but when finally he did come, she was shocked at the change in him. He'd gone away little more than a boy; he came back eight months later gaunt and ill and looking at least a decade older.

He was on crutches and hadn't learned to use them properly. He couldn't get about and couldn't get up the stairs in Lowther Street. A neighbour helped her to carry down the mattress from their bed, and she slept on the front-room floor with him.

He coughed all night, and tossed and turned. At times he was fighting for breath. In the darkness he told her of the terrible carnage, the corpses left unburied in no man's land, the mud and the countryside laid waste, the rats and the body lice and the fearsome bombardments. The war that had opened on such a high note was proving an appalling waste of life.

Then, every morning, there was the difficulty of getting him back up off the mattress and on his feet. He was too weak to do it without her help. He was low in spirits.

'I'm a cripple,' he told her. 'What good will I be to you now? What good am I to anyone?'

Maggie felt full of love for him. She was glad to have him back whatever state he was in, and told him so. She didn't want to leave him alone for long hours in the day, so she gave up her job to nurse him. He still had a German bullet in his knee. They both hoped he'd be able to use his leg more when he'd had it out. The date for its removal was arranged. He was to have it done at the Borough Hospital, which was just round the corner.

The atmosphere in Lowther Street was already emotionally charged, even before Tom found Luke's name printed within a black border in the newspaper. Lieutenant Luke Stratford Dransfield. Killed in action at Loos, 20 September 1915.

Tom clung to her that day. 'Sometimes I wish they'd finished me off,' he said. 'Better than leaving me like this.'

Maggie tried to be strong. 'You'll not always be like this. You're better now than when you first came home.'

'Not much.'

'I can see the difference. You'll feel better once you've had that bullet out.'

It was several days more before she dared bring it up. 'Shouldn't we let your mother know you're back?' she asked. 'With Luke being killed, she must be worried stiff about you.'

'Why should she? She cut me out of the family. Said she wanted no more to do with me.'

Maggie sighed. 'The war's changing everything. When something as bad as this happens, quarrels are forgotten.'

'Mother doesn't forget.'

'She'll want to help you. She'll be glad to have you back.'

Tom looked depressed. 'There's nothing I can do now. I'm done for, Maggie.'

'No, you're not. Your mother may need you, Tom. In the business.'

'I don't want to work in her business.' Tom's mouth was straightening with obstinacy. 'I've no stomach for the way she goes about things. She isn't honest in her dealings.'

Maggie's heart turned over. Tom had never admitted it, never put it in so many words before.

'Did she cheat my father? Did she deliberately make him bankrupt?'

'You know she did,' he said.

'You said you had no proof when I asked you.' She could hardly get the words out. 'That you weren't sure.' How she and Hattie had once mulled over this, and all the time Tom had been keeping it back.

'It's not easy to say things like that about your own mother.' Tom wouldn't look her in the eye now. 'And besides, I didn't want to put you off. I didn't want to put your father off either. If you'd known then, you wouldn't have married me.'

'I would, Tom.'

'Your father wouldn't have let you. And who could blame him? My mother turned you all into paupers.'

'You're sure?'

'Of course I'm sure,' he flared at her. 'I couldn't help but notice what was going on. She asked me to do things . . . That's why I was so keen to cut myself off.'

So Hattie had been right. She'd said she was sure as time had gone on. She'd said Daniel Moody was of the same opinion, but Maggie had never really been convinced. She looked up to find Tom's grey eyes watching her.

'But you don't want to go back to the Co-op?'

He shook his head, looking demoralised. 'I don't feel I could work. I'm to have an army pension.'

'You might not want to work now, but you will when you're over this. I still think you should let your family know you're home.'

The Knell family had been rallying round. Pa and her younger sisters had been in and out of the house almost daily.

'Your Hattie will have kept them in the know. They'll be right up to date with our news.'

'She isn't working for them any more. I told you in a letter, she's in Market Drayton with consumption.'

'So you did! Poor Hattie. You should go and see her. It's not nice being ill in hospital a long way from home.'

Maggie felt a niggle of guilt that she'd not done more for Hattie.

'I'll go the day you have your operation.' It was now imminent. 'It'll take my mind off that.'

'You might have to tell her about Luke.' Tom's lip

trembled. He'd been very fond of his brother. 'His being killed drives it home how close I came to it. How close Eric still is.'

'She'll know, she'll have seen it in the newspapers,' Maggie said.

The following week, Maggie took Tom into hospital for his operation, which was scheduled for the next morning. She went home to spend a lonely evening thinking about him, hoping he'd feel better when it was over.

The day of the operation was autumnal but pleasant. She was glad to have somewhere to go. She sat back in the train with the sun on her face. She would not be allowed to see Tom today, but she'd be able to phone and find out if things had gone well.

She had to change trains at Crewe. It was a lovely peaceful journey, and she wished she'd made the effort to come before now. At Market Drayton she looked around and decided that the only way to find the West View Nursing Home was to take one of the cabs drawn up outside the station. She could see the place as she approached. A pleasant building with a wide veranda.

As she went inside, she heard the crying of newborn babies and turned back to the door, afraid she'd come to the wrong place. But the cab had driven off. A nurse was crossing the hall.

'Have I come to the wrong place? I'm looking for the West View Nursing Home.'

'That's us. Who did you want to see?'

'Harriet Knell.'

'Third door on the right, down there. She's in her room.'

Maggie was smiling as she gave one tap and went in. Hattie was sitting up against her pillows, cuddling a baby, with such a look of love on her face. Then, as she saw her sister, her face registered alarm. A crimson tide flooded up her neck into her cheeks.

Maggie swallowed, unable to go back or come forward. Shock, surprise, horror and disbelief whirled in her mind. After what seemed an age, she stammered: 'You've had a baby?'

Harriet's face was deathly white again, and tears were glistening in her enormous green eyes.

'Is it Luke's?'

Harriet emitted an agonised sob. Maggie felt so overwhelmed with sympathy that she rushed to the bed to gather mother and babe in her arms. She felt their tears mingle.

'Why didn't you tell me? You could have stayed with me. I'd have loved to have you. I was lonely and empty and not used to being alone.'

Hattie couldn't say anything at first.

'She's a lovely baby.' Maggie scooped her up in her arms and took her to the window to see her better. 'What's her name?'

'Rebecca.'

'How wonderful! Oh, Hattie, I've longed for a baby! Wanted one for such a long time. For me, it doesn't happen. Sod's law, isn't it?'

'Happened to me when I'd much have preferred it not to.' Harriet was drying her eyes, trying to smile. 'She'll have to go for adoption.'

Maggie straightened up. Her arms tightened round the child. She knew straight away that she'd never wanted anything as much as she wanted to keep this baby. She felt alight with excitement.

'Let me have her, Hattie. Tom and I will bring her up. Much better than letting her go to strangers.'

'I promised I'd have her adopted.' Harriet's eyes seemed to be growing even bigger. 'I had to. He demanded that in exchange for helping me.'

'Who did?'

'Stanley Dransfield.'

209

'We can adopt her. Tom and I.'

'He wants her to go to strangers.'

'We're her aunt and uncle. Better for the baby, much better. And you'll be able to see her grow up. Better for you too.'

She could see her sister turning it over in her mind. Could see that she wanted that too.

Maggie heard then how Stanley Dransfield had arranged for her sister to come here, and about the conditions he'd laid down. Total secrecy as to the child's father, and that she must be formally adopted.

'Oh, Maggie, he'd be furious if he knew that you were here. He didn't want me to give the address to anybody, but I had to tell Pa.'

'He cut you off from us?'

'Cut me off from everyone I knew. That's why I'm so far from home. But I wanted to get away. I felt awful . . .'

Maggie was rocking the baby. 'Bridie told me Stanley had a mistress. Probably didn't think there was anything wrong in Luke having one.' She caught sight of her sister's shocked face. 'Oh, Hattie, I didn't mean . . .'

'That's what I was,' she said, keeping her eyes averted. 'His mistress, though I was aiming to be his wife. Oh, yes, Stanley thinks it quite acceptable for a man to have a mistress, but it has to be kept secret, and if one's about to give birth, that makes it very difficult and . . .'

'Totally harrowing,' Maggie sympathised, hugging the child more tightly.

The infant opened her bright blue eyes and looked up into Maggie's face, then widened her tiny mouth in a yawn. Maggie was captivated.

'We'll just go ahead. We won't tell Stanley we're adopting her.'

'I'd much rather you had her, Maggie. I feel guilty enough without handing her over to complete strangers. If I can't have her, then much better that you do, but

. . . he made me promise to have the baby formally adopted.'

'We'll do that.'

Hattie felt torn with indecision. 'I'm afraid he'll ask me where she's going. Or that doctor will.'

'Bet they won't. They just want to get her out of the way.'

'Stanley wanted everything kept absolutely secret,' Harriet agonised.

'I know now. Nothing can change that.' Maggie felt on fire with the idea. 'Tom will have to know, but nobody else, I promise you. We'll keep it a secret from his father.'

Tom had no job to return to; he was afraid he'd never work again. But he'd been promoted to sergeant while he'd been at the front. They had his army pay for the time being, and when he was discharged he'd have a small pension. She'd saved most of what she'd earned while she'd been working. They'd manage somehow. She didn't care how. Nothing mattered but keeping this baby.

'I think I know how you could manage it,' Harriet said slowly. 'Matron left me some forms from the adoption society. "To read and think about," she said. "And then sign."'

'Where are they?'

'In the top drawer, over there.' Maggie found them and snatched them up to read.

Hattie said slowly: 'The adoption society has an address in Liverpool. I did notice that. If you really mean it, if you really want . . .'

'I do. I won't change my mind.'

'Think hard first, Maggie.'

'I don't need to.'

'Talk it over with Tom. Perhaps he won't want to.'

'We've been trying for a baby of our own.'

'Having my baby won't be the same.' Hattie's big green eyes wouldn't leave her face. 'And you haven't been married . . . all that long.'

'Tom will let me do it, I'm sure. He tries to give me what I want.'

'Well, if you do decide . . . I'll sign the adoption papers for you now. You fill in your own names and then hand them in personally to their Liverpool office. You're both close relatives. I'm sure they'll think it's best for the baby to stay with her family. Best that you formally adopt her too. They won't think strangers are preferable.'

'But what about the matron here? She'll be expecting you to give the papers back to her when you've signed them, and to hand the baby over to go to the orphanage.'

'I'll put off telling her anything for as long as possible. Then just that I've arranged it privately. You'd better start adoption proceedings straight away, and have papers to show that you have.'

'How much longer before you leave?'

'Another month. You'd better come to fetch us.'

'I certainly will, if you let me know the day. We must take Rebecca with us.'

'Bring some baby clothes with you.' Hattie was blinking hard again. 'You are sure?'

'Very sure. It's the best thing for everybody.'

Maggie stayed much longer than she'd intended. The baby's existence and the plans they were making for her had driven everything else out of her mind. When she reached the door, she remembered.

'Have you heard?' she asked awkwardly. 'About Luke?'

Harriet's face was expressionless as she replied: 'I read in the newspaper that he'd been killed at Loos.'

'Terrible news,' Maggie sympathised. 'Especially at a time like this.'

'I've had to face that I can't have him. Now nobody else can. He died the day Rebecca was born. Very fitting.'

'Hattie!'

'He deserved it, if anybody did.'

\*     \*     \*

Hattie had a little cry when Maggie went. She cuddled her baby closer and bent her head over the tiny form. She didn't feel nearly as tough about Luke as she'd pretended to Maggie.

She felt a heart-stopping pain every time she thought of him lying in a grave in foreign soil. He'd been so handsome and full of life. There was nobody in the world she knew as well. She'd felt his arms round her; she'd loved him, and she couldn't stop loving him despite what he'd done.

The baby was wakening, struggling against the pressure of her arms. During the months she'd been here in the nursing home she'd been in an emotional turmoil. Her mind had seethed with frustration. She hadn't known what she wanted or what she should do. Only now was she beginning to see things clearly.

Once she'd believed that marriage was what she'd wanted. She'd wanted Luke and she'd wanted to be lifted out of the rut of poverty. Now she thought marriage too close and intimate a relationship for her. She doubted she'd really have suited it. Perhaps, just perhaps, with Luke, if he'd been of like mind; if he'd remained true for the rest of his life. She wouldn't seek it with any other man. She'd be better off without a husband.

It was time for Rebecca's feed, and Harriet knew she'd need to change her first. She climbed out of bed, took a clean napkin from the cupboard and began to unfasten the baby's pins.

Since Luke had betrayed her, she'd been asking herself who her nearest and dearest were. Pa, of course, and Maggie, and yet like the fool she was, she'd neglected them. When she'd found out just what Lenora had done to Pa, she'd decided she'd force her to right that wrong. Instead she'd given herself up to enjoying Luke's company and forgotten all about what she'd wanted to do for Pa.

Her baby was beginning to fret with hunger. She climbed back into bed, adjusted her pillows, undid the buttons on the front of her nightdress and put the infant to her breast. She felt the pull, heard the rhythmic slurp and felt exquisite pleasure in the moment.

Maggie had been so keen to take her baby and bring her up as her own. That pleased Hattie, made her feel closer to Maggie than she had for a long time. If Maggie brought Rebecca up it would be another bond between them, tying them closer still. That was what she wanted.

Since she'd held her baby in her arms, Hattie had come to realise how powerful mother love was. She had another little weep. She was feeling desperately emotional about everything at the moment.

Maggie's mind whirled with plans. The following Sunday afternoon was visiting day at the hospital, and she went to see Tom. He seemed more cheerful in himself now the operation was over. She told him about Hattie's baby.

'Good God! Hattie and Luke?' His face told her he found it hard to believe.

'You'd believe it if you'd seen them.' Maggie went into a long description of the baby. 'I want us to adopt her, Tom. Please . . .'

'It'll be another mouth to feed!' He was aghast. 'I'm a crock. I've been telling myself it's as well we don't have children yet. We can't afford it.'

'I'm good at managing, you know that. I told you how little we managed on at Elizabeth Place.'

'But what if I can't get a job when I'm discharged?'

'You will. There's a war on now. There's plenty of work about.'

'I'm not really against you having the baby,' he said awkwardly. 'I know how much you want one.'

She started to tell him what had happened to Harriet. The harrowing time she'd had when Luke had abandoned her. Tom was silent for a long time.

'He was always one for the girls. He told me his

214

wife was expecting a child about now. Has she had it yet?'

Maggie shook her head. 'We've heard nothing. But it's for her sake the affair with Hattie has to be kept quiet. Only your father knows about it.

'You ought to get in touch with him, Tom. You always got on well with him. It might solve all your worries if you were back on good terms. He might want to have you working for him.'

'No chance of that if you have Harriet's baby here. It'll be a black mark against us. And Luke's secret will be out.'

Maggie went to visit Hattie again; held the baby in her arms once more. Poured out her own problems to her sister.

'Why not tell the Dransfields it's your baby?' Hattie suggested. 'How would they know it wasn't? They've had no contact with you and Tom since you were married. I haven't been there for the last five months. They won't have had any news of you.'

'But Hattie, Stanley knows you've had a baby. Won't he make the connection?'

'Luke's wife has had one too, or we must assume she has. Why shouldn't you and Tom?'

'No reason.' Maggie went home and thought about it some more.

She remembered then, with sinking spirits, that Lenora Dransfield had seen her on the day she'd received the telegram about Tom. If the baby were hers, she would have been in the last stages of pregnancy then. Instead, Lenora had seen her looking reed-slim in her bus conductress's uniform, with a skirt only a few inches below her knees. She would know the baby couldn't be hers.

Maggie hadn't told anybody she'd seen Lenora that day. She'd gone straight home to her empty house. She wanted the baby so badly, she told herself that perhaps she hadn't been recognised. Even if she had, Lenora wouldn't remember exactly when she'd seen her. And it could be years before they met again. She couldn't give up this chance for so small a reason. She wouldn't tell Hattie. Wouldn't tell anybody. Nobody need know that Lenora might not believe the story.

By the next visiting day, Tom was up and walking about the ward on his crutches.

'If you really want that baby,' he whispered, 'perhaps we should go ahead. I'm sure Luke would want me to be a father to her, rather than send her to an orphanage.'

Maggie was thrilled. She kissed him there and then and couldn't keep a smile from her face all afternoon.

'Harriet thinks we should tell your family that she's our own baby. Then her identity is kept secret for ever.'

Tom's face showed the doubt he felt about that. 'Hang on a minute, Maggie. All your family will know she's not. What are you going to tell them?'

'I was going to say we'd adopted her, but I think Hattie wants to tell Pa the truth. Easier now, she thinks, than a few years on.'

'And what about the baby? Will she grow up thinking she's our child?'

'I hope so.' Maggie smiled. 'She looks more like me than she does Harriet.'

Tom sighed. 'It takes a lot of thinking about. Your sisters might tell her, without meaning to.'

'If we have to, we'll tell her she's adopted. Not about Hattie and Luke. But I'd rather she was accepted as ours.'

'We could have children of our own, Maggie.'

'That won't stop me loving Rebecca. It won't stop you either, once you see her.'

'I suppose it will be all right.' Tom pushed his hair off his forehead. 'How's Harriet taking all this? She must be upset.'

'She flares up if I mention Luke, but you know Hattie, she doesn't say much about how she feels.'

'Keeps it all bottled up?'

'Exactly. She's like a bottle of the ginger beer we used to make. All fizz, but under control when the stopper's screwed down tight. She'll talk about other people's problems but never her own. She used to say: "I'd rather forget my problems, put them out of my mind." But she doesn't forget them for a minute, they seethe away inside her.'

'Poor Hattie,' he said.

'She wants us to have her baby. She thinks it's the best thing for her, and you'll love Rebecca the minute you set eyes on her, Tom. She's gorgeous.'

The next day, Maggie went to the adoption society with Rebecca's forms. Because of the close relationship, there seemed to be no problem.

Tom was kept in hospital for two weeks. When he came home, he was stronger in himself, and his chesty cough was better. He'd learned to use his crutches properly and was crawling up and down the stairs. His knee was less painful, but it would never be completely right. He was ready to accept that it would always be stiff.

Maggie felt much happier about everything. She played the piano for Tom most days, and he said her music soothed him.

When Harriet wrote to tell her when she'd be discharged, Maggie prepared her spare room for the baby, and told Pa she'd be fetching her sister home.

# CHAPTER TWELVE

Hattie went back to Elizabeth Place alone. She didn't want Maggie and the baby with her. She knew she'd have to tell her family the truth about where she'd been, because they'd all know the baby Maggie had was not her own. Maggie had said nothing as yet, leaving it for Hattie to explain. They'd be asking questions and talking about it if they didn't know the truth.

'Fanny?' she called as she went up the shabby hall. She could hear voices upstairs, but the downstairs rooms were all silent. She looked in each in turn. They seemed more cramped and untidy than she remembered. She thought Fanny must be out shopping. Her younger sisters would be at school and Pa must be at work.

She poked the fire into a blaze and swept the hearth. Then she started tidying up. She felt lost without her baby to attend to. She'd done nothing else over the last six weeks. When the time had come to part with her, she hadn't wanted to give her to Maggie.

'I think I'll call her Becky.' Maggie had been all smiles, and looked supremely happy as she'd bottle-fed her on the train coming home. 'Rebecca is such a big name for a tiny babe.'

Hattie wanted to say no, that she'd chosen the name Rebecca and liked it better. She knew any other adoptive mother would probably have changed her name completely. She didn't doubt that Maggie would love and care for her baby, but she wished that things were different, and she could keep the child herself. Giving her up to Maggie was the lesser of two evils. As things were, she couldn't possibly look after her herself.

Anger had been smouldering inside her for all the months she'd been in the nursing home. She'd had little else to think about but the way the Dransfields had used her and her family for their own ends.

She couldn't forgive Lenora for causing their poverty. Luke had brought her heartbreak. Stanley had helped her, but she didn't feel much gratitude, because what he'd done had been primarily for the benefit of the Dransfields.

Hattie had had plenty of time to make her plans. She was going to use Stanley as he'd used her. She felt justified in cheating him. She was going to trick him into thinking Rebecca was Maggie and Tom's baby.

She was also going to persuade Tom to get in touch with his family again. She'd already sown seeds about this in Maggie's mind. She didn't want to see Tom struggling to make ends meet as a clerk; she wanted his family to help him. She wanted him to be able to support her child in comfort.

Nobody could come through what she'd experienced unscathed. She'd had her fingers burned, and it had changed the way she looked at everything. She'd intended to use the money Stanley had promised her to train as a shorthand typist. Every newspaper she picked up advertised vacancies for lady typewriters. She'd meant to take Maggie's advice: forget about revenge and start afresh.

She wasn't normally a cheat or a liar; she had her faults, but they were different. Her problems were jealousy and selfishness, and she thought too much about her need for money. Once she'd done what she wanted to the Dransfields, she made up her mind to strive to be a better person.

Frances pushed open the kitchen door and lowered two heavy shopping bags to the floor.

'Hattie!' She rushed at her sister to sweep her into a hug. 'Lovely to see you well again.'

Hattie thought her sister had grown. She'd changed from a child to a young woman. She had Maggie's platinum-blonde curls, but they fell to her waist. Today, she had them tied back with ribbon. She was taller and more robustly built than Maggie, and her eyes were of deep cobalt blue. She was tougher, better able to hold her own.

'I've been out to buy some ham. For a special meal tonight. Wonderful to see you. Welcome home.'

Hattie no longer felt at home here. She was on edge.

'You're feeling better?'

'I'm fine, Fanny.'

She could hear Pa's heavy step coming up the hall, and braced herself to tell them now. Better to get it over before the young ones came in at four. But all her family would have to know, and be sworn to secrecy.

Pa looked tired and older. Again Hattie was swept into a bear hug of welcome. The Knells had always stuck together, supported each other, tightened their ties in time of need. Hattie hoped they would for her now.

'Can we go into your room, Pa? There's something I have to tell you.' Fanny was putting the kettle on to make tea. 'Both of you.' They both looked suddenly serious, expecting dire news about her health.

She'd tried to tell herself that the worst part was over, that she'd managed to survive giving birth to her baby without anybody knowing. This was worse. She was dreading it, dreading seeing their smiles turn to censure. She'd known from the start that if she wanted to see Rebecca grow up, she'd have to do this. It was part of the price she had to pay. They sat her down, Pa holding one of her hands, Fanny the other. Hattie had rehearsed this time and time again, but her throat was tight with nerves.

'I've been telling you terrible lies,' she said softly,

221

watching their faces. 'I haven't had consumption. I've worried you about that when there was no need. I hope you can forgive me.'

'Hattie! What then?'

'I've been away because I've had a baby. Luke Dransfield was the father.' She saw disbelief, bewilderment and shock, but their hands were tightening on hers in sympathy. 'Maggie has her now. She's going to bring her up.'

'You should have let me help you, Hattie.' Even Pa was close to tears. 'You should have known you could rely on me. Whatever you did.'

They all cried a little, and only dried their eyes and washed their faces when the younger girls were due home from school.

Hattie found their support very moving, and felt wrapped in the love of her family.

The next morning, Hattie walked down to the general post office to telephone Stanley Dransfield at the glove factory. The way her family had accepted her back amongst them gave her renewed strength and confidence to carry out her plan.

'I'm home, Mr Dransfield,' she said. 'I've done what you asked. You promised me a hundred pounds.'

'Home already? I didn't expect you out for another week or so.'

'I stayed my full time. Everybody believes I've recovered from consumption.'

'What about the baby?'

She'd toyed with the idea of telling him she'd had a boy, to make it harder for him to connect Maggie's baby with her. But she decided it was too dangerous. If he'd had any contact with the nursing home, he'd know she'd had a girl.

'Up for adoption, as you wanted,' she choked, and heard something like a grunt from Stanley.

222

'She was very small, weighed barely five pounds at birth,' she lied. He mustn't recognise Becky as hers. 'Not a very strong baby, I'm afraid. I called her Beryl.'

'Gone for adoption, you say?'

'Yes.'

'All right, Harriet. If you've kept your side of the bargain, I'll keep mine. Give me a week. Then you'd better come here to the factory to get your money.'

'Thank you, Mr Dransfield,' she said. Her hand was shaking as she put the phone down. She was worried, of course. What did he need a week for? Was he planning to talk to the matron first, to get confirmation? If so, her plan would backfire. Hattie felt on edge all week. She wished she knew what was going on.

On the appointed day she dressed herself up in her best to visit the factory. She was very nervous by the time she reached the front door. The smell of leather filled her nostrils, taking her back to the times when the business had belonged to her family. As a child, she remembered her grandfather lifting her up at the end of a long row of sewing machines so she might see them better.

It served to remind her how she felt about the Dransfields. Not Olivia, she was fond of her. Tom, too, and she had no quarrel with Eric, but the others . . .

'Come in, Harriet.' She knew from Stanley's manner that he was not suspicious about anything she'd told him. As she'd hoped, he must have left all the arrangements with the West View Nursing Home to that doctor. It was never so easy to check up on details through a third person. Or perhaps he'd spoken to the adoption society. Maggie said they wouldn't divulge the name of the adoptive parents. She relaxed a little.

'You're well? Over it now?' His pale eyes searched into hers.

'Yes, thank you.'

223

'You've heard – about Luke?' She saw the look of pain in his face.

It made her say primly: 'A terrible loss.'

'We're all devastated. Lenora's been quite depressed, and as for Claudia . . .' She saw the effort it cost him to carry on. 'Olivia's been worried about you. She keeps asking how you are.'

'I hope her rheumatism is no worse?'

'It's no better. It's been giving us all a bad time. She didn't take to any of the girls we had in your place. To tell the truth, it's very hard to get anyone to stay with this war on. She was talking about you only the other night. She'd like you to come back.'

Hattie was somewhat taken aback. She hadn't expected to be offered her old job back. Wasn't sure whether she wanted it again.

'Would you want me there? After all this?'

'Nobody else knows about your baby. Luke's gone. So there'll be no embarrassment that way. Things have changed now, for us all. We have no live-in help at all, only women who come in to clean in the mornings. It's very difficult with Olivia in the house. She needs a lot of attention: more and more, in fact.'

Hattie tried to think. She'd made her own plans. Pa had said how pleased he was to have her back with him in Elizabeth Place, but it looked more squalid than ever after an absence of five months. Clara had been sharing the bed with Fanny, but now Hattie was back, the three younger ones had to sleep in the same bed, and were complaining about it.

Maggie had offered her a room at Lowther Street, but Hattie couldn't believe she really wanted her there, with Tom only recently home from the front. Besides, they were getting to know Rebecca, and it would be painful to watch them take her over.

'I didn't think you'd want me back.'

'Harriet, Olivia's very fond of you. She was upset when you left. We were all pleased with you . . . with your work. You've handled your trouble well, and provided you never speak of it, all will be well. I'm not bothered about that part now.'

Hattie closed her eyes to hide the triumph she felt. She would succeed in keeping Rebecca close to her.

'Then yes, Mr Dransfield, I would like to come back. Thank you.'

This time she meant to have her revenge on Lenora. She'd get back what she'd fleeced from Pa if it was the last thing she did.

He smiled then, and there was complicity in his eyes when she looked up.

'I'm glad,' he said. 'We can hardly cope at home and there's extra work here. We're all stretched to capacity. And without the boys . . .'

. He got the money from his desk. It was in a paper bag, the sort that came from the bank. It had the amount printed on it.

'About the baby,' he said. 'It's gone to the orphanage in Market Drayton and it's up for adoption?'

Hattie nodded, rigid with nerves. 'They had prospective parents in view, but it takes time to finalise such things. They told me she'd be going to a very good home.'

'Right.' He pushed the money nearer, but kept his hand on it. 'You must never breathe a word about this. Claudia's in a terrible state as it is. She's had a child too. A boy. There must be no mention of Luke's name. No breath of scandal. He died for his country.'

'No, I promise.'

'Well, let's put it all behind us now, shall we?' The money came to rest in front of her.

'When do you want me to come to Ottershaw House?' The bag was heavy and packed tight with sovereigns. She moved it to her handbag. It weighed it down.

'The sooner the better, I suppose.'

'The first of next month?' It was three days off.

Stanley agreed, and Hattie stood up. She had no reason to stay longer, though there was something else she wanted to get across to him. She was forming a careful sentence in her mind when he said: 'Do you hear anything of Tom? How is he?' He looked saddened.

She'd been hoping for this. It was her cue. She knew she must be careful. He mustn't get the impression that she and Maggie were colluding to deceive him.

'He's been injured, did you know?'

'Yes, Olivia saw his name amongst the injured. In a newspaper list. I rang the War Office, and they said he was in a hospital near Southampton.'

'He was gassed and had a German bullet in his leg.'

'Yes, I rang the hospital several times.'

'He's back here now in the Borough Hospital, having the bullet taken out.'

'Really?'

'He might even be home by now. Maggie's very pleased that he won't be going back to the front.'

'He's better then?' Stanley was all smiles.

'I haven't seen him yet, but I believe so.' Hattie paused. She'd reached the door and the moment had come. 'Did you know they had a baby?'

'No!'

'A girl. A strong, healthy child.'

'Good Lord! Young Tom?'

Hattie turned on her heel and hurried away. She'd got it in without saying too much.

On the underground going home Harriet had plenty of time to think. Now that she knew Olivia wanted her to go back, and Stanley seemed happy that she should, she changed all her plans. She saw this as a second chance to get her own back on Lenora. She was seething with a need for revenge again, after seeing with fresh eyes how her family had to live. She decided she could train on the typewriter later.

She went straight to Lowther Street to see Maggie and Tom. Maggie was giving Rebecca a bottle, and the baby's eyes were fixed on her face as she sucked. Hattie had to move a baby's hairbrush from the chair before she could sit down. She couldn't take her eyes from her daughter.

'How she's growing, Maggie!'

She wouldn't hold her in her arms. That would only make it harder to walk away. The living room was much changed: there was a little cradle in the corner, and a maiden laden with nappies airing at the fire. Tom moved it awkwardly out of the way.

'I'm managing without my crutches now.' He smiled. There was an air of exhilaration about him, though he looked haggard, much changed by the few months he'd spent at the front. He had a marked limp.

Hattie said: 'I'm going back to work at Ottershaw House. Your father's asked me.' She told them what had transpired. 'He'd welcome you back too, Tom.'

'I don't want to go back,' he said. 'Not to work in their business.'

She guessed from their air of collusion that they'd been talking about it. Maggie bent to kiss the baby. Her cheeks were flushed and her eyes shining like aquamarines. 'Tom's a real cinema buff. Always has been.'

'I'd like a cinema of my own,' he said slowly, savouring his words.

It took Harriet's breath away. 'A cinema? You certainly think big.'

'It doesn't have to be big. We've seen just the place, haven't we, Maggie?'

'Where?'

'The Gem. It's up for sale. We saw it the other night, when we were walking back from Pa's place.'

'The Gem? But that's . . .'

227

'In Hind Street, yes.'

'Have we ever been there? We usually walk into town. To the Queens, or the Savoy.'

'Picture houses are going up all over the place, not just the town centres. In the suburbs and even the back streets. It's the business of the future. People go week in and week out. Twice a week even.' There was no doubting Tom's enthusiasm.

'It's finding the money for it.' Maggie put the empty feeding bottle down and hugged Rebecca closer. 'It would be wonderful if Tom could persuade his mother to help.'

'Ask,' Hattie urged. 'You never know your luck till you try. Your father asked about you. I told him you'd had a daughter. I hope I said enough to stop him thinking Rebecca could be mine.'

'You're a close one, Hattie.'

'Let them know you're home, Tom. Let them see your injuries. You've done your bit, fought for your country, now you need their help. With Eric away fighting, and Luke losing his life, they'll both feel different about you.'

Hattie allowed herself another glance at Rebecca. She'd dropped off to sleep, and looked so utterly beautiful that Hattie's heart turned over with love for her child. It made her offer Tom and Maggie the money she'd received from Stanley, to help meet the expense of keeping her.

'Thank you, Hattie,' Tom told her seriously. 'But if I'm adopting her, that includes paying for her keep.'

'We'll manage without it.' Maggie smiled. 'Why don't you pay for our Fanny to train for an office job?'

By then Harriet had decided to keep it as a nest egg for herself. It pointed out to her just how much more generous Maggie was. When she went home to Elizabeth Place, she forced herself to offer it to her younger sister.

'You've been very good, Fanny, looking after the family as you have, but Enid's leaving school now. Let her take

228

a turn. If you can learn to type, you won't have to accept menial work.'

Fanny was over the moon and wrapped her arms round Hattie in a hug of gratitude. Pa thanked her too.

Maggie was nervous about getting in touch with Tom's family, but the next day, when she took the baby out in the pram to get some shopping, she telephoned the glove factory from a phone box and spoke to Stanley Dransfield.

She told him that Harriet had called round to see her and that Tom was now home. Stanley was on the doorstep at Lowther Street that same afternoon. Before he'd even been back to Ottershaw House.

'You did the right thing,' he told Maggie when she let him in. 'Thank you for letting me know.'

As it happened, Tom had the baby in his arms and was playing with her when his father came in. Becky had just reached the stage when anybody could make her smile. Stanley made a fuss of her too, chucking her under the chin and pressing a gold guinea into each of her tiny palms.

'The spitting image of you, Maggie,' he told her. And the most fantastic thing was that it was true. Maggie tucked her into her cradle and went to the kitchen to make a cup of tea.

She could hear them talking. Tom sounded awkward. They seemed to have so little in common, but both were trying hard. Maggie decided that Hattie was growing more devious. She'd put them both up to this, and it wasn't easy. As he was leaving, she heard Stanley say:

'We'll make sure you have some means of earning a living, Tom. We won't let you starve. Not now you've a family to support.'

Trust Hattie to have worked it out properly.

Hattie went back to work at Ottershaw House, feeling

insecure and less at ease. She was half afraid the truth about Tom's child might come out.

Nothing much had changed. She was still the only live-in servant, and as such, had to act as housekeeper as well as companion to Mrs Clark. She didn't do much cleaning or cooking, but she had the responsibility for arranging daily women to come in and do it.

There were just three members of the family living there now, and Stanley and Lenora were often out. There was no pretence of them being a close-knit family. Each seemed to have less to do with the others.

She'd hoped to find that Lenora had mellowed, now that help in the house was so much harder to get. These days, few would be prepared to put up with her when they could get jobs easily elsewhere.

Instead, Hattie found her even more overbearing, as though she had new grounds for disliking her.

'So you've come back?' Her eyes flashed with aggression, letting Hattie know it hadn't been her choice. She was glad Stanley had assured her that Lenora didn't know. However, she saw little of her, Lenora was spending less time and energy in the house. Hattie put it down to the fact that she had more to do in the business. The blouse factory had turned over to war work and was making shirts, mostly for the navy. The machines were running flat out. Gloves, too, were now being made for the forces. Hattie thought it could be a good time for Tom to ask for a loan.

Olivia seemed quietly triumphant, as though she'd got what she wanted. Hattie guessed she'd had to press for her to return. The smell of wintergreen ointment and camphorated oil seemed stronger than ever.

'I'm so glad you decided to come back,' she told her. 'Lenora failed to find anybody reasonable to look after me. Three of them, one after the other, and they were all hopeless. I do hope you're cured and won't have to leave me again?'

'Thank you, yes, I'm very well now.'

'You look much better. Plump and robust.'

Then her eyes slid sideways with what seemed like suspicion. 'You did go to the sanatorium at Market Drayton?'

The question made Hattie shiver. She wondered if Olivia had reason to doubt that she had. It sounded rather like it.

'Yes, that's right.' She hated telling lies, but she couldn't change her story now. The old lady seemed about to say something else and then changed her mind.

'I'm very glad you're back.'

Yet Hattie felt she was watching her more closely than she had in the past. It added to her unease.

When Lenora and Stanley were not at home, Hattie enjoyed the space and fine surroundings of Ottershaw House. She felt closer to Olivia. The old lady had a sharp tongue occasionally, but Hattie understood that discomfort and pain could make her irritable. Olivia was always telling her how grateful she was for what she did, and showed affection for her.

Her days were spent as before, rubbing the old lady's painful joints with camphorated oil and reading aloud from the newspapers. She penned letters for her and added up the value of her portfolio. Olivia was interested in all businesses and was less careful now to hide things from her. She received copies of accounts from the companies she invested in.

'I can't get my mind round figures when you read them out,' she told Hattie. 'I prefer to study these for myself.'

When she was in the mood, Olivia would explain them to her. She had a sharp mind. Hattie found her company stimulating and was learning a lot from her.

Occasionally, when the weather was good, Olivia wanted to go out. She felt she could manage outings now she had Hattie with her. Mostly, they went to church, but occasionally to a cinema or a theatre matinée. Usually she was exhausted when they returned home.

Because there were no other living-in servants, the rules were more relaxed. Hattie was allowed more time off. It was accepted that she might go out after lunch when Olivia took her nap. She could go out any evening after Olivia had been helped into bed, and unless there were guests for supper this could be quite early.

As the weeks began to pass, Lenora often came up to see her mother.

'Nobody but me to talk over her business dealings with now,' Olivia told Hattie wryly. 'Nobody at work she can trust. She's finding it a great deal harder. She has to do more herself.'

Hattie heard details of all their businesses. She discovered that Mr Fevers of the retail business Fevers and Jones had gone bankrupt during the months she'd been away, and that Lenora had bought the business from the receiver.

'When Tom's well enough to work, she's going to persuade him to come back and manage Fevers and Jones for her.'

A day or two later, Olivia was quite indignant. 'Tom won't hear of Fevers and Jones. He has some wild idea about wanting a cinema. Stanley must have put him up to this. He's no sense when it comes to business. I don't know why Lenora puts up with that man.'

She said a good deal more about Lenora being so overworked that she'd had to ask Sophie to help her.

'Big mistake, bringing Sophie up as a lady. What good have her nice manners done her? All that money on singing and piano lessons. We thought she'd never need to work, not with three brothers.'

'But now?'

'Lenora has asked her more than once, but her husband is set against it. Very set against it.'

Hattie had noticed that Sophie and the children were visiting quite often, but Daniel didn't come with them.

'Old school tie, expects his wife to be subservient to him.'

Hattie reflected that her mother had been subservient to Pa. That even Maggie was to Tom.

'Don't all men expect that?'

'They do, but not all get it. It's the last thing Lenora is. In this world, those who hold the purse strings call the tune.'

Hattie thought ruefully that she was very unlikely to forget that.

Lenora was inviting guests to supper less frequently nowadays. The hospitality she offered was simpler too. Hattie had let her know that without a parlourmaid, she would be unable to provide service at the table. She would bring in the meal and they must help themselves. Sophie came regularly, and so did Claudia Dransfield and her family.

Sometimes Claudia brought her son, Edward, to tea on Sunday afternoons. The first time she saw him, Hattie found herself searching his face, looking for a resemblance to Rebecca. She could see none. He was much darker, more like Claudia. She asked his age. He was just six weeks older than her own child. That made her toes curl up in agony. Luke had been bedding them both at the same time. Would it have made any difference, she wondered, if she'd become pregnant first?

Lenora made a great fuss of Edward, and so did Stanley. Hattie found it hard to contain her anger that he should accept this child of Luke's while expecting her to hand Rebecca over to an orphanage.

As she wheeled the tea trolley into the drawing room, she wondered what he would say if he knew Tom was caring for Luke's other child. It helped that she was getting the better of the Dransfields in some small way, but it wasn't enough, Hattie knew her need for revenge was growing. She wanted to make Lenora suffer.

Hattie thought Stanley's manner had changed towards her. She thought he was now over-friendly, and his hands came out more often to touch her. She didn't like it. She was only too aware of his reputation with women but couldn't believe he was thinking of her in that way, though his manner suggested he was. She tried to avoid being alone with him.

A week or two after her return, on an evening when Lenora had gone out and Hattie had seen Olivia into bed, she was crossing the hall when he came to his study door with an empty whisky bottle.

'Is there any more in the storeroom, Harriet?'

'You brought a whole case home the other day,' she reminded him. 'I'll bring you another bottle.'

She took it to his study. He was at the window, looking out at the garden, rocking backwards and forwards. She noticed he'd developed a beer gut. She put the whisky in the cupboard where he kept his drinks, and when she turned round he was close behind her. He pulled her to him and pressed his prickling mutton-chop whiskers into her face as he tried to kiss her lips.

'No!' She fought against it, pushing him away with all her might, then brought her palm up against his face with all the force she could muster.

'Don't you dare touch me,' she screamed, pressing herself back against the cupboard. Her heart was thudding. She was horrified to see him stagger back, breathing heavily.

His pale eyes were staring at her, and he looked as shocked as she was. 'I'm sorry,' he said.

Angry tears prickled her eyes, and she felt engulfed with rage. 'I suppose I've given you every reason to think I'm a loose woman,' she gasped from between clenched teeth.

'Oh, come on, Harriet . . .'

'I'm not! Do you hear, I'm not. I won't have this.'

'I'm sorry,' he repeated, nursing his cheek. 'My mistake.'

'Luke was the only one, and I loved him. Fool that I was, I loved him.'

'Look, Harriet, I've said I'm sorry.'

'He used me, and you want to use me too. I'm not having it. I'll tell Mrs Dransfield.'

'Listen to me. There's no need to tell Lenora, or Olivia, for that matter. I won't touch you again.'

She stood staring at him, transfixed by his abject eyes and bald dome.

He laughed self-consciously. 'They know what I'm like anyway. Won't be news to them.'

'We all know what you're like. Pleasuring women is what you call it, isn't it? Well, Mr Dransfield, I get no pleasure from it, and I'm never going to let any man near me again.'

She'd recovered enough to move towards the door. She wanted to put as much distance as possible between them.

'No hard feelings, Harriet,' he said. 'I won't try it again.'

She felt mortally embarrassed. Her cheeks burned for half an hour. She had to go to her room to recover. Stanley Dransfield considered her to be a fallen woman. She supposed most people would if they knew she'd had a baby out of wedlock.

# CHAPTER THIRTEEN

Hattie had been back at Ottershaw House for about three months when the news came that Eric had been killed in action. She saw Lenora weep then. 'I can't believe he won't come back.'

Hattie was full of sympathy. 'He gave his life for his country. He died a hero.'

'What do I care about that?' Her voice was harsh. 'Two of my sons gone, and after all I did to secure their future. They would have had very good lives in the business. I feel as though part of me has died. If I'm not expanding the business for my sons, why am I bothering?'

Olivia's grief she could understand better. 'I hate to see my grandsons cut down in their prime. What life have they had?'

Hattie mourned as much for Eric as she had for Luke. Eric had never done her any harm.

Now she was used to the much quieter household, Hattie felt it suited her better, but old Mrs Clark missed the company of other members of her family. She'd always liked to talk of the old days. Now there was rarely anyone but Hattie to listen.

One very cold day, when the rain was hurtling against the windows, Hattie settled the old lady down as usual for a nap on her bed after lunch. She covered her with her eiderdown and retreated to the turret, but ten minutes later Olivia called her to her bedside, saying she was unable to sleep.

She talked for an hour about Sophie, who was her

favourite grandchild. Hattie heard how well she'd done at school, and how she'd met and married Daniel Moody, but now there were signs that the marriage was no longer happy.

'Sometimes I worry that her mother's come between them. It's very difficult for Lenora, with two sons being killed, and Tom not wanting anything to do with the business. It's all for Sophie and her family now. It's bound to upset Daniel.'

Hattie's mind was still on Sophie when Olivia said: 'It's always me talking my head off. I never hear any little confidences from you.'

Sometimes, Hattie felt she was being needled for information. Olivia was always asking questions, encouraging her to talk of her own affairs. She smiled, but said nothing.

It made the old lady cross. 'The best I can get out of you is "Mm, yes" or "Oh, right." You never volunteer any details about yourself. You're very kind and you're gentle and thoughtful. You can't do enough for me in many ways, but you don't show your feelings and you certainly don't talk about them.'

'Perhaps I don't feel things as . . .'

'Of course you do. You don't look at me. You don't even make eye contact, Harriet. You keep yourself aloof. You're introverted, that's your trouble.'

'Perhaps a little shy.'

'Extremely introverted. You're withdrawing more and more into yourself. You always did erect a front. You'd be better company for me if you'd let yourself relax.'

Hattie felt there were a lot of things she dared not talk about. Mrs Clark was pulling herself up her bed.

'There's something I want to show you. Open the drawer there, in my bedside table. You'll find two letters under those books.'

Hattie did as she was told. The letters were still in their

238

envelopes. They were addressed to her at the sanatorium in Market Drayton. 'Not known at this address' was pencilled on both. She felt the strength draining from her legs.

'Let me have them.'

Her hand was shaking as she lifted them out. She knew Olivia was watching her like a cat watches a mouse. How much did she know?

'When you went away, I missed you. I thought you were ill,' she accused. 'I was worried about you and wanted news, but Stanley said you'd not be allowed to write letters. It might spread the infection.

'I thought you might be comforted by a letter from me. I dictated these to the women Lenora found to stand in for you.' The old lady laid the two envelopes out on the counterpane in front of her. 'When the first was returned, I thought it was a mistake and tried again.

'I asked Stanley where you were, several times. He was evasive but I'm sure he knew, he just wouldn't tell me.'

Hattie could hardly breathe. She was panic-stricken. This was worse than anything she'd imagined. Olivia's lined face took on a wily look.

'You never were at the sanatorium, were you?'

Hattie could feel her heart pounding against her ribs. She covered her face in desperation. She'd thought Stanley's arrangements had hidden her shame, that they'd got away with it. Now it was all rebounding on her.

'You didn't have TB, did you, Hattie?' Olivia was going on remorselessly. What could she possibly say? The old voice dropped an octave.

'Do you want to know what I think?'

Hattie stared into her knowing eyes. She couldn't get any words out.

'I think you had a child.'

Hattie felt the rush of blood to her cheeks and knew words would not be needed. Guilt and shame were running through her. She was clinging to the side of that precipice again, and this time her handhold was pulling free, and she was about to fall. She felt sick with shock and fear. Her disgrace would be public knowledge. She'd be asked to leave her post. She closed her eyes, wanting to escape from this excruciating embarrassment.

'It's all right, Harriet.' The knotted old hand was patting hers. 'This needn't go any further. I understand only too well what you must feel. I've been through it myself, that's why it wasn't difficult to guess.'

'But you've said nothing till now.' Hattie was choking. 'You knew all the time? I thought . . .'

'Didn't want to frighten you off.' Olivia's tone was dry. 'Had to wait until you settled down. Couldn't face being left again at the mercy of a lot of ham-handed women.'

Hattie whispered. 'I don't want to leave.'

'It takes a lot to get you to talk. I'll say that. So who was the father?'

Hattie swallowed hard. She'd promised above everything else not to reveal Luke's name. His widow must be spared that. She'd been paid to keep her mouth shut.

The clawlike fingers were biting into her wrist. 'Was it Stanley?' Hattie was horrified. She couldn't speak.

'Of course it was. You don't have to tell me,' Olivia went on knowingly. 'Stanley can't keep his hands off the girls. You weren't the first and he knows how to cope with the little problems when they come. I hope the arrangements he made for you were comfortable?'

Hattie felt she was sliding into an abyss. She covered her face with her hands again.

'You'll have to excuse me,' she choked, before fleeing to her own room.

She spent an hour on her bed. She couldn't stop shaking. It had come so unexpectedly. After all these months she'd thought it was safely behind her. And worst of all, she'd let Olivia believe that Stanley was the father of her child.

\*　　　\*　　　\*

Hattie dreaded going back to Olivia's room, afraid that she'd carry on her inquisition, but she had to go. There was nobody else in the house and Olivia would want to get up and have her afternoon tea. No doubt she was already impatient at being kept waiting.

She washed her face and went back to find the old lady just waking from a snooze. She went to the kitchen to make some tea and took it up on a tray. Olivia was yawning as she helped her to the couch in the turret. The rain was still hurtling against the windows.

'You don't realise what Stanley's like. Sometimes I think he's possessed by the devil. His appetite for women . . . Prodigious. No other word for it.'

Hattie knew she ought to say, straight out, that Stanley was not the father of her child, but that would invite more pressure to divulge Luke's name. She couldn't bring herself to do it. She felt a nervous wreck.

'He's been the cause of a great deal of unhappiness in this house. A grave disappointment to Lenora. I warned her at the time, but she wouldn't listen. There was always that look in his eye. I knew women would be his weakness.'

Mrs Clark's dislike of him was obvious. 'Goodness knows what Lenora saw in him, those face whiskers and thinning hair.'

Hattie thought that when he'd been younger, most women would have found him a charmer.

Olivia's voice dropped another octave. 'He's been associating with one woman for years, has two sons and a daughter by her. Another complete family on the wrong side of the blanket. Disgraceful, I call it.'

'Must be very upsetting,' Harriet murmured. 'For your daughter.'

'Of course, when she found out, it was the end of normal married life for her. She wouldn't allow him near her after that.'

Harriet was not sorry to know definitely that Lenora was

241

unhappy in her marriage. That not everything was going her way. Ruby and May had been right.

'And even that isn't enough for Stanley, he's always seeking new conquests. A stupendous appetite for women.' Olivia leaned closer. 'I'm telling you this so you won't let him do it again.'

Hattie couldn't answer.

'I'm sure he would, given half a chance. You must take care. Poor Lenora, after all she's done for him. He brought nothing to the marriage, you know. Sometimes I think it's only our money and this house that keeps him with us.'

Hattie was shocked at what she was being told. Surprised, too, that Lenora hadn't shown the same ruthlessness to Stanley that she had to Pa. Surely she must hate him more? He must have hurt her more, as husband and father of her children.

'Does she not . . . think of divorce?'

That brought Olivia's eyes to meet hers. She was wary now. 'Oh, no,' she said. 'Not for Lenora. She doesn't believe in divorce.'

Hattie kept her eyes down on her sewing, unable to believe what she was hearing. Lenora was driven by love of money and greed for more, and perhaps the power money gave her. She'd be the last person to take a moral stand against divorce. So why was she allowing Stanley to stay? It didn't make sense to her.

One day, Olivia asked her to hire a car to take them down to Clark's Blouse Factory. Harriet knew the district. She'd been brought up in Rock Ferry and was looking forward to seeing where the family business had started. Olivia, she thought, seemed quite reluctant, when it came to the point.

'I don't like the place,' she admitted in the car. 'Don't like coming here.'

It was reached by an outside flight of stone steps. It took

Olivia a long time to climb them. They were narrow, and this made helping her more difficult. Hattie thought it was these she disliked.

At last they reached the top, and Hattie surveyed the small workroom heated by an open fire. On one side of it, Lenora's cubbyhole of an office had been partitioned off. Some of the older workers knew Mrs Clark and greeted her warmly.

Lenora then took her into the office to discuss something. There was no room for a third person there.

Harriet was surprised to see how small the place was. The cutting-out tables and machines were cramped together. Far smaller than the baby wear factory that Luke had taken her to see, and minute compared with Knell's Gloves. She thought the blouses attractive and couldn't help wondering why they'd never tried to expand this side of their business. Surely that was the obvious thing to have done, instead of taking over other businesses and trying to run them together?

In the car on the way home she said to Olivia: 'I imagined Clark's Blouses to be a much larger business. It's just a workroom.'

'It's very old. My husband set himself up in business there twenty years before we were married, about the middle of the last century. Garments were mostly hand-sewn in those days, of course, and that was done by outworkers at home. He needed room only for cutting-out and pressing and packing. It was a disused sail loft when he took it over.

'Have you heard of Mrs Amelia Bloomer? She was a campaigner for women's rights and designed a knee-length skirt combined with loose trousers gathered at the ankles. My husband made up the outfit for her, and had her permission to make it up for sale to ladies of like mind. Turnover was never large but it was steady, and then when the cycling craze came in the 1880s the demand for it increased. We always did blouses as well.'

243

'Would it not be possible to find larger premises?'

'No.'

'If only there was more space, more blouses could be made. I'm sure they'd sell very well.'

'No,' Olivia repeated, and shivered. There was finality in her voice. 'We've no plans to move the factory.'

It didn't make any sense to Harriet. It would take men time and energy to carry the bales of cloth up to that old sail loft, and more time to carry the finished blouses down. And the steps rose up in a narrow passage, and would be awkward for a cart to get close. It seemed that Lenora was turning one factory into a museum, yet at the same time managing to take over bigger and more prosperous concerns.

The weather had turned chilly again. Summer this year seemed slow to start. Mrs Clark sat on the couch in her turret and shivered.

'Would you get me a shawl, Harriet? The blue one, dear. That's my warmest and it will suit this dress.'

'You haven't used that for some time.' Harriet thought she remembered putting it in the bottom drawer of the chest. As she drew out the shawl, she saw a photograph frame without any glass in it.

'It's solid silver,' she said, lifting it out. 'Beautiful. Shall I have new glass cut for it? A shame not to use it.' She was looking at two photographs underneath it.

'I remember it now, it used to be on your dressing table. This picture was in it.' She was looking at Luke as a child, surrounded by his siblings. Then she turned to the other picture. 'Who is this?'

'Let me have it,' Olivia snapped.

Harriet was staring at her. She knew from the sudden change in her manner that the man had been important in her life.

'That's my husband, Osbert Clark.'

Harriet was beginning to get over her embarrassment that Olivia knew about her baby. Her confidence was returning. She said: 'You must have been proud to have such a handsome husband.'

'Yes.' Agreement was grudgingly given, but the old face was screwing up with dislike.

Harriet wanted to keep her talking. She wanted to learn more about Olivia's background and the family businesses. She'd come back with the intention of exacting revenge. Yet the months were passing and she was no further forward. All her energies had gone on blotting out the agony of the West View Nursing Home and easing herself back into Ottershaw House. The fire had gone out of her and she'd lost impetus, but what Lenora had done rankled as much as ever.

She went to stand behind Olivia so she could study the sepia photograph. Osbert Clark had dressed with smart formality. He was wearing a frock coat and striped trousers and carried a silk top hat. He looked a bit of a dandy, with fairish hair and a large, luxuriant moustache.

Olivia croaked: 'He was proud of his moustache. He made it shine with brilliantine and was always curling the ends up with his fingers. Now I think back, when he got into bed and doused his candle, he used to put hot wax on the ends to keep the the twirl tight and set it overnight. He used a moustache cup to protect its beauty too. Didn't want to darken it to the colour of tea.'

Hattie said: 'We all have our little vanities.'

Mrs Clark hated to be without her cap. It hid her thin and wispy hair and the pink scalp that showed through.

'Yes, when I first saw him, Osbert seemed the answer to all my difficulties. He was a successful businessman. The Clark factory was one of the first to have sewing machines, and he trained women to use them.'

Hattie was touched by envy. She'd desperately wanted Luke as a husband but had failed to get him, while Olivia had apparently had no difficulty. The young Osbert Clark sounded ideal.

She said: 'A very suitable husband for a young lady such as you'd have been.'

'He was not the eligible bachelor I'd thought he was.' The old lady's voice dropped. 'His first wife committed suicide, but I didn't find that out until after I'd married him. He told me her mind had turned, but if he treated her the way he treated me, I'd swear he caused it. He'd have driven anyone out of their mind.'

Hattie's sympathies were aroused. She felt taken aback by such a frank confession, but wanted to hear more.

'What a frightening situation in which to find yourself.' She sank down on a chair beside the bed. 'Especially for a gently brought-up young lady.'

Mrs Clark was staring up at her with a wry smile. 'Things were not as you suppose, Harriet. I told you, Lenora was born before I was married.'

Harriet gasped. 'Did you?' If she had, she hadn't taken it in.

'When we were talking about you, the other day.'

'Lenora born before you were married?' That changed all the ideas she'd had about Olivia. About Lenora, too.

'I was the eldest in a family of ten children. We all had a hard and hungry upbringing. Not like yours, my dear.' The misshapen hand patted hers. 'It does me good to dwell on how far I've come since those days. By my own efforts too.'

The wily eyes were staring into hers again. Harriet realised that these secrets were being divulged in exchange for hers. Secrets it had been impossible to talk about until now.

'I was only sixteen when I made the same mistake you did. I was plain Olive Smith in those days and I thought I was in love with a sailor. He'd seen the other side of the world and was full of stories about the good life in

Australia. He was going to take me there, but as soon as I told him about the coming baby, he went looking for a ship. The first he found was going to Russia. He signed on as a deckhand, and I never saw him again.'

Hattie couldn't believe what she was hearing. She could see from the faraway look in Olivia's eyes that her mind was already in another world.

'My father was furious when he found out. He belted me until I was black and blue. Threatened to throw me out on to the streets.

'"Shaming us all! Bringing a bastard here to my house." I was terrified of him, we all were. He was violent when he'd had too much ale, and knocked my mother about. He was a navvy when he could find work. Drank most of what he earned too.

'Mam had said: 'What does one more child matter?' In the chaos and poverty in which they lived, it probably didn't. Mam had gone on to give her two more brothers younger than Lenora, before he'd knocked her senseless one night and she'd never recovered.'

Olive had forced herself to blot out these bitter memories. She'd made herself think of what was to come, not of what had been. She'd put them behind her. It was years since she'd last thought of them.

'I worked as a chambermaid at the Royal Rock Hotel once I'd turned thirteen. It was a lovely hotel, lovely.' Her eyes closed, she went on talking.

She'd spent most of her daylight hours in the hotel and disliked having to go home to sleep. The job had seemed a lifeline. The scraps from the kitchen meant she was never hungry again, and she took all she could home to her mother to help feed the family. She was in a position to see how differently the middle classes lived.

The standard of comfort provided by the hotel took her breath away when she first she saw it. Royalty had stayed here – not the present good Queen but the Georges. They came because the Mersey air was so good.

The elegance amazed her. The money that was spent in the bar and the restaurant seemed phenomenal in amount. Olive talked to the personal maids that the ladies brought with them to help them dress. She was sometimes asked to help those who had not brought their own maids, and was then rewarded with generous tips. She'd often fingered the fine fabric of the gowns she cared for and envied their owners the ease of their lives.

She named her baby Lenora, after one such lady. A pretty young wife, said to be enjoying a prolonged honeymoon. She used to watch the couple stroll about the gardens and along the promenade. Sometimes they went for a sail on the ferry to Liverpool or New Brighton, just for the pleasure of the trip. Hansom cabs were summoned to the door if that Lenora wanted to go shopping, and she always took her maid to carry the parcels.

Olive longed to have what they had for herself and her daughter. She wanted to live as they did, not in the crowded hovel that was home to her.

'Not just wanted. I dreamed of it, I was obsessed by the idea of money, and how it could change my life.'

She was nineteen years old and Lenora three when her mother's sister was widowed. Her Aunt Sarah had been married to a hard-working teetotaller who'd been employed on the corporation ferries sailing between Liverpool Pier Head and Woodside. He'd worked himself up from deckhand to captain, and the old *Claughton* had been his boat for the last thirty years of his life. He'd thought of himself as being decent working class. Sarah had had aspirations to climb a little higher. She'd been delighted when he was promoted to captain.

They'd lived in a small two-up and two-down house in River Street, which Olive had often visited. Her mother had envied Sarah's comfortable life and was delighted to receive her hand-me-downs. Mam had not been in a position to see how much better life was for the ladies who stayed at the Royal Rock.

Newly widowed and without children, her aunt wanted somebody to keep her company. She was getting old, and her biggest fear was that she'd die alone.

She shivered. 'I could lie dead on my bed for a week before anyone came looking for me.'

'I'll come and live with you.' Olive had jumped at the chance. She wanted a better home for herself and her baby, and this gave them a room to themselves. 'Then if you die in the night, I'll find you straight away the next morning,' she'd teased. She'd promised to stay with her for the rest of her life.

Olive got on well with Aunt Sarah, who was also happy to look after Lenora while she went out to earn their living. She enjoyed sewing for the child, making pretty dresses with lacy frills. She told her neighbours that Olive's husband had been drowned.

'Fell overboard. He was working with our Ernie. Two widows together, that's what we are.'

That was the way it had to be, to explain Lenora's existence. Because she'd moved from the dock area of Birkenhead into Rock Ferry, where nobody had known her before, Olive thought she'd turned over a new leaf and gone up in the world.

One of her aunt's neighbours was an outworker for a small factory. Her aunt helped regularly with the simple embroidery that was required. Olive first saw Osbert Clark when she helped the neighbour carry back the finished garments to his premises. While a forewoman dealt with the woman, Olive had time to look round.

Mr Clark sat at a table near the fire, writing in a ledger, while his other hand idly twisted his glossy moustache. All round him sewing machines whirred. She thought him a real toff. She saw him again in the Rock Hotel shortly afterwards, drinking in the bar. She watched him from a distance.

'Handsome, ain't he?' Ida Parsons, one of the kitchen maids, was tucking her red hair under her cap. She counted Ida as a friend. 'Don't yer fancy him?'

Olive had heard he was unmarried, and thought how wonderful it would be if she could become his wife. It was just a daydream; she didn't really believe it was possible. Aunt Sarah laughed at her when she spoke of it, but said he was handsome and a real catch for some girl.

Olive thought of asking for work in his factory, but soon abandoned that idea. He'd think the girls who stitched for him beneath his interest. He'd choose a wife from a different class. He wouldn't want to know any woman who had to do work like that for her living.

Many of the guests staying in the hotel made a habit of taking evening strolls along the esplanade on fine summer evenings. It was a popular pastime for the middle-class residents of Rock Ferry. Olive was leaving the hotel one evening when she saw Osbert Clark setting off for a walk with another man, and it occurred to her then that the esplanade was one place where she could meet him as an equal.

She persuaded her aunt to walk there too, and on many evenings she dressed herself and Lenora up in their best clothes in the hope that they would meet him. Her aunt enjoyed the walks: they gave her an opportunity to get out and see people. Often, Olive felt more like resting after working all day, and Lenora wanted to play on the sand rather than walk sedately along the prom. Olive had to hold her firmly by the hand all the time, because there was no rail to protect her from the twelve-foot drop on to the sands below.

One Sunday evening, Olive and her aunt had walked the mile along the promenade to New Ferry. They'd rested on the sand at the Gap for an hour and Lenora had had a paddle. The wind had got up, it was high tide and the waves were rolling in to thunder against the sandstone wall of the esplanade. They were more than halfway back and were all getting tired.

Lenora was swinging on Olive's arm, dragging her feet and getting tetchy. Aunt Sarah usually held her hand, but tonight she'd lost patience with her. Lenora wanted to walk along the edge so she could look down. The esplanade was twelve to fifteen yards wide and Olive was walking as far away from the edge as she could get. Not only did an occasional wave splash right up to spray the unwary, but she was determined to keep Lenora safe.

She was about to raise her hand to Lenora to wallop some sense into her when she saw Osbert Clark coming towards them. Her heart began to hammer: this was the chance she'd been hoping for. She waited until he was only a few yards away and then pretended to lose her grip on Lenora's hand. She shot predictably across his path towards the edge.

He automatically stepped forward and grabbed at her to keep her out of danger. At that moment an extra large wave hurled itself against the wall with such force that foam and river water sprayed five feet above it to splatter down on them both. Lenora's best leghorn hat was swept off and over the edge and could be seen below, tossing on the dark waves. Olive didn't have to pretend to be nervous. She was shaking.

'Lenora! Look what you've done. I'm so sorry, sir.'

'We must blame the spring tide for this.' He'd taken out a large handkerchief and was trying to mop himself dry.

'Lenora might have been swept over with her hat.' Aunt Sarah was aghast.

'I'm afraid you're very wet. I can't thank you enough for your kindness.'

Osbert was smiling down at her. There were still splashes of river water on his face. He raised his bowler.

'Osbert Clark,' he said. 'Glad to be of service.'

She told him her name was Olivia because that sounded more middle class, and anyway, she liked it better. She introduced Aunt Sarah to him, giving the impression that they were two respectable widows. Having been doused with cold water, Lenora was crying bitterly. Osbert turned to mop her down.

'Hush, now, you've come to no harm. Just lost your smart hat. You must pay more attention to your mother, young lady.'

'Please see to yourself,' Olivia told him. 'I'm afraid you had more of a soaking than she did. Lenora, that was a very dangerous and naughty thing to do.'

Because he was wet, he turned round to walk back with them. He also kept a restraining hand on Lenora for her.

Olivia hadn't noticed until then just how invigorating an evening it was. In the last of the evening sunshine, the stiff breeze was buffeting them all. They had to raise their voices to be heard above the thunder of the waves and the suck of the undertow.

As she walked beside Osbert Clark, her body moved easily and gracefully. She held her head high. Her hair was long and heavy and golden-blonde, her face firm and young. She felt on top of the world.

# CHAPTER FOURTEEN

Olivia set out to charm Osbert Clark. Her aunt aided and abetted her. Now that she'd seen him close to, he looked older than she'd first thought, about forty. She added five years to her own age and told him she was twenty-five. She didn't want him to be put off by too great an age difference and she must allow a year or two for her first marriage. To admit she'd given birth at sixteen didn't make her sound like a respectable widow.

Aunt Sarah insisted on taking him home to dry him off. Her house wasn't grand, but she had nice furniture and she kept it clean and tidy. She gave him the last of her husband's brandy, which he'd bought cheap from some dockers after they'd unloaded a cargo from France. Ernie had bought it to ease his colic, and used it only for medicinal purposes. She'd set the table for supper before going out, now she insisted he take some refreshment with them and shared out the ham and pork pie Olivia had brought home from the Royal Rock.

By the time he went home that night, Osbert had been made to feel on good terms with them. And, of course, he had to return their hospitality. Olivia gave up her job – she couldn't afford to let him recognise her about the hotel now. That would ruin all her plans. He'd have thought a chambermaid beneath him. They'd led him to believe they were respectable widows in reduced circumstances. Down on their luck, but not so far down as to need a job like that.

She didn't love Osbert Clark, but he could provide her with the comfort she craved. Lenora was an attractive and energetic child of four. Olivia encouraged her to throw her arms round Osbert and show him affection. It didn't take her long to lead him to the altar. For a moment, she let herself savour again the triumph she'd felt on their wedding day.

Olivia had discovered from her marriage lines that Osbert had had a previous wife, but she'd been careful to hide any facts she didn't want him to know.

They'd been married at the church Sarah had attended all her married life. Sarah had gone with her to see the vicar when she'd arranged for the banns to be called. He already knew Olivia as a widow, and she declared her age to be older than it was. She'd thought she'd made her fortune, and that of Lenora and Aunt Sarah too.

Osbert had his home in Bedford Road. It was a narrow four-storey terraced house, but it was roomy and comfortable and a big step up from River Street. Aunt Sarah had not wanted to stay on alone there. He asked them all to move in with him. It was a matter of great pride that Lenora was entered at Herman House School. She was going to be brought up as a lady.

Osbert had more of a social life than Olivia had ever had. He taught her to play bridge and took her to bridge and supper parties given by his married friends. They made much of her. She knew he also had a circle of bachelor friends whom she wasn't invited to join.

To Olivia, it had come as an added bonus to find that Osbert was ambitious. He was eager to earn more from his business and hoped eventually to move his new family to a much better house. These were ambitions she shared wholeheartedly, and she was quite prepared to work hard and do all she could to further them.

She was disappointed by the size of his business when she looked more carefully at it. The old sail loft was over a boat-building business, and all day long she could hear men talking and working below. They sawed and hammered and sawdust flew everywhere, inside and out.

It fascinated her all the same. Olivia was quick to learn all she could about it, even teaching herself to use the sewing machines. Osbert had the newest ones that sewed with a running stitch, and a machine to make button holes. She mastered the skills of cutting out and sewing up.

Apart from the bloomer outfits, his trade was largely in blouses, and she was particularly interested in making these. She discovered she had a flair for fashion. She designed new styles for each season, and learned how to get the best effect from styles that were not labour-intensive to make. Which meant they had a good profit margin. Demand for their blouses was growing. She insisted on going with him to the factory every day. He'd laughed at her.

'I thought you wanted to be a lady. Ladies don't work in factories.'

'I can't be a lady until you're rich enough.'

'When we have our new house, you can stay at home and do the flowers.'

'If we can afford a proper staff of servants, and not just a cook-general.'

Actually Olivia was very proud of having a cook-general to do her housework. She thought of herself and Osbert as a team: they both worked hard and they prospered. It was the team spirit that kept them in harmony.

On the debit side, she discovered that Osbert was obsessed with power as well as money. He lorded it over the women who worked for him, and told Olivia that he could make women do anything he wanted. He would bark at his seamstresses if they so much as looked up from their sewing. They were paid on piece rates, so there was no inclination to waste time with gossip. They feared him. She found he had a quick temper, and as a husband, he could be very demanding.

It took three years of hard work to enable them to move

to Ottershaw House. She'd never been inside such a grand house before and felt she was achieving the near-impossible. But she wasn't finding life all roses by then. Aunt Sarah's health was failing fast. They moved her to Ottershaw House just four months before she died.

Olivia felt that three years of marriage had exacted a toll. She'd had to keep her origins hidden from Osbert and a front in place. Lenora was a bright little girl and Olivia had had to make her understand that there were things that must not be said in front of Osbert. Always at the back of her mind was the nagging anxiety that the child might let something drop.

She was glad they'd be leaving Rock Ferry, because Osbert had continued to visit the Royal Rock Hotel and sometimes tried to persuade her to go with him. She dared not set foot in the place because the staff knew her too well. The last thing she wanted was for him to find out she'd worked there as a chambermaid from the age of thirteen. He was a self-made man but he'd come from middle-class stock.

Osbert was giving a lot of thought to their new house. He bought a plot in the most favoured part of Oxton and hired an architect to plan it for their personal needs. Olivia watched it being built, and it was turning out to be far grander than she'd ever expected. She was thrilled with it.

Osbert had strong opinions about décor and furniture, and mostly insisted on having his way. Only the best would satisfy him now. Olivia was allowed some choice for her own boudoir and the rooms for Aunt Sarah and Lenora, and Osbert consulted her about hiring staff to keep it in apple-pie order. Olivia felt she was arriving at the pinnacle of her ambitions.

Once they'd moved into their new house, she spent more time at home, because there were many details needing her attention, but she still went to the factory. She felt involved with it and she enjoyed it, and Osbert relied on her now to see to many aspects of the work.

Olivia had designed another blouse and they were working together on the pattern it would need when she looked up and saw, through the window, a red-headed girl climbing the outside steps on her way in.

Olivia felt paralysed. She couldn't get her breath. She recognised Ida Parsons immediately. Perspiration was breaking out on her brow. There was nowhere she could hide.

Ida paused in the doorway. She'd been the friendly kitchen maid at the Royal Rock who had kept special titbits for Olivia, food that was returned from the dining room. Her face broke into smiles of delight as she crossed the room.

'If it isn't my old mate Olive Smith! Bit of luck seeing you here. I got the sack from the Royal Rock. Any chance of a job?'

Olivia's heart was pounding. She knew her cover had been destroyed. Ida had said too much before she could stop her. Osbert's mouth had opened in surprise, but now he was stiff with outrage. He kept the girl talking, finding out every last detail, while all the seamstresses watched through their lashes and tried to look as though they weren't listening too. She'd been mightily embarrassed.

Osbert's face was twisting with ill-temper as he dismissed Ida. He sent glowering looks in Olivia's direction, but he said nothing. Halfway through the afternoon, he flared up in fury and dismissed one of his best seamstresses for poor workmanship.

On their way back to Ottershaw House, he said icily to Olivia: 'So you were put to work as a chambermaid at thirteen. Why did you try to keep that from me?' She'd told him she'd been a full-time housewife and never worked. 'Why did you think it would make any difference?'

Olivia did her best. 'That night on the prom I thought

257

you were . . . I fell in love with you.' She tried to smile and be her normal self. 'I wanted you to think well of me. To like me.'

Osbert's eyes were hard. She was afraid he didn't believe her. He spent a long time alone with Aunt Sarah that evening, sending Olivia off on some errand when she tried to join them. She knew that Sarah was no longer in a fit state to watch her tongue, and that Osbert would get the truth from her.

By the time they were getting ready for bed, he knew that she'd lied about being a widow, and about her age too.

'You married me for my money, didn't you?' His face was cold, his eyes like steel. 'You were a little slut and you wanted a leg-up in life.'

She'd denied it, of course, protested her love, but Osbert changed towards her after that. From then on, he allowed her no privileges. He gave the orders both at home and at work. He began to treat her as he treated his employees.

He insisted she work a full day in his factory. She acted now as forewoman, handing out work to the seamstresses. He designed the blouses himself, telling her he could do it better, but she knew he was adapting her ideas. If anything went wrong he always blamed her, and was abusive in front of the others. She soon found it hard to hide her dislike of him.

From that day, she was kept well away from the accounts, and he maintained a particularly tight hold on his money. He paid all the bills himself, both for the business and for the house. Every week, he gave her housekeeping money, but she had to account for every penny she spent and he always scrutinised her figures. She was allowed pin money, just enough to clothe herself reasonably. She was not allowed to run up bills of any sort.

He was very much stricter with Lenora. They'd found a new school for her, another seminary for young ladies, near to Ottershaw House. Osbert now changed his mind about sending her there. Olivia thought he'd only agreed on school at all because she was working all day and the only alternative was to pay somebody else to look after the girl.

'You thought I was an easy meal ticket, didn't you? Well, you're not going to sponge off me,' he said when she protested. In vain did she remind him that she'd worked as hard as he had, and helped him earn money for the house.

He often went out to see his friends, but from then on he didn't ask her to go with him. Even on the nights he stayed at home, Olivia went to bed before him, tired after her day's work. He often woke her up when he came to bed, demanding his marital rights. She soon found it didn't pay to refuse. The first time she excused herself with a headache he brought his fist against her jaw with such shattering force that it made her head sing.

Harriet was appalled at what she'd heard. Olivia seemed to have dozed off and looked at peace again. Even after all this time it was easy to see that she found reliving her marriage to Osbert a harrowing experience.

She took up the frame and his photograph. He'd been an attractive man to look at. It was hard to believe he'd given Olivia such a hard time. She decided she'd take the frame to be repaired.

Not wanting the poor old lady to be troubled any further, she shut the pictures out of sight in a drawer, but her curiosity had been whetted. She wanted to know what had happened after that.

She'd disturbed Olivia by moving; the old lady opened her eyes and went on, her voice at some times strong, and at others faltering and fading.

'Those were the most terrible months for me. Aunt Sarah was ill. I poured it all out to her but there was nothing she could do to help. The reverse, in fact: she needed help from

259

me. I did my best. I went into the chemist shop near the factory and asked for something to ease her. You saw the shop, with the great glass jars filled with red and green liquid in the window?

'The apothecary there recommended laudanum to me. He said he sold a good deal of it for invalids and babies, and for the first time in weeks, poor Sarah had a good night's rest. She asked for it every night after that and it always gave her a good sleep.

'All the same, she seemed to fail before my eyes. Within months she was dead and I was alone. Except for Lenora, and I was always afraid he'd use his fists against her as well. I was glad I'd brought her up to be careful. I didn't want her to give him reason to lose his temper.

'Osbert craved power as well as money. He enjoyed the power he had over me. He would thump me in the ribs and the stomach so my bruises wouldn't show. He held his hand over my mouth if I made any noise. He didn't want the servants to hear.

'I had visions of turning on him. Kicking and hurting him in the way he hurt me, but I knew they were delusions. I could feel myself growing more frightened, more timid. I knew he was wearing me down, and that soon I wouldn't be able to stand up to him over anything.

'The long days at work made me tired and I hated having my sleep broken by Osbert at night. He thought of himself as a virile man who needed a woman almost every night. I was too weary to be a plaything for him. It was the very last thing I wanted.

'I had half a bottle of laudanum left over from Aunt Sarah's use. My first intention was to take a dose myself, though I knew I'd sleep all right if I were left in peace. It occurred to me that if instead I gave it to Osbert, perhaps he'd prefer to sleep too.

'He was in the habit of taking a nightcap. A glass of hot milk well laced with whisky. It had always been my duty to prepare the tray and measure the whisky into the tumbler because he didn't trust servants with his spirits. He thought they were all inclined to help themselves, so he kept it locked away. He knew I didn't care for whisky and wouldn't drink it.

'Every night, he kept one maid up late in case he should need anything after his dinner. At eleven o'clock, it was her duty to lock up the house and heat the milk for Osbert's nightcap.

'I found it easy to deliver a dose of laudanum to the glass when I poured in his whisky. It had exactly the effect I wanted. He came up to bed and within minutes was snoring. He slept all night and seemed in no worse a humour the next morning. Thereafter, Osbert regularly had his tranquilliser and I had my rest.

'I was worried about the nights when he went out, because then he didn't have a nightcap. Well, not the usual one at home.

'He was going out on three or four nights a week, and I dreaded them. He didn't sleep at all well, tossing and turning half the night after having his way with me. His temper was terrible the next day: he'd blow up in an instant over nothing. He also raised his fists more.

'"I must be missing my nightcap," he said in the middle of one such night. I lay there rigid, thinking he must have found out about the laudanum, waiting for his fist to crash into my ribs.

'"Get up," he ordered. "Go and heat me some milk, and don't forget the whisky." I almost wept with relief, I can tell you. Laudanum was a saviour to me.

'I don't think it did much for Osbert, not in the long term. He felt it raised his spirits, but his memory suffered. So did his appetite, and most of all his temper.

'It dragged on and on. It wasn't at all the sort of life I'd planned for myself and Lenora. I began thinking of how we could escape. We lived in a wonderful house

261

with staff to take care of every need. I had no ladies' maid, of course, but the parlourmaid pressed my clothes and she could thread new ribbons and mend small defects in Lenora's things. This was what I'd set my mind on when I was sixteen.

'The only way we could escape Osbert was to pack our bags and leave. He knew I'd find it difficult to turn my back on wealth that I'd helped earn and felt was partly mine. He was most careful with his money, and left nothing where I could put my hands on it. I'm sure he kept me short to make it more difficult.

'The fact that he slept heavily now allowed me to take a few coins from his pockets, but I dared not take much in case he missed it. I took enough to buy more laudanum.

'I knew he kept money in the safe in his study, but he always kept the key with him. It hung on his watch-chain, together with his watch, a handsome half-albert. He was very careful with that key.

'When he undressed at night, his watch and chain were laid on his bed table, within reach of his hand. For months I looked at it from my side of the bed and wondered if I'd ever pluck up courage to take it. I knew I'd have to, or accept things as they were.

'Then, one night, I put a double dose of laudanum in his whisky and took the key. There was only forty guineas in the safe that night and I decided it wasn't enough. I'd hoped for much more. I took two of them and hoped he'd think he'd miscounted, though he was careful about that too. I decided I'd try again another time, and in the mean time, start to save up.

'I thought of pawning some of his things to raise money, but it wasn't easy to get away from him. Even if he went out in the evening, Ottershaw House was a long way from town, and I'd need money for a cab. He left his gold cuff links in his shirt one day, and I hid them. I thought I could easily carry so small an item and I'd be able to raise cash on them when I needed it.

'I shouldn't have done it. It caused a terrible row and he accused the maid of stealing them. She was put out that day without notice. I didn't dare admit I'd taken them; he'd have thrashed me. I salved my conscience by writing a good reference for the poor girl.

'Then, one day, Osbert told me to move out of his bedroom to a room of my own. My first feeling was one of relief. He berated me, told me I was useless as a wife and that he'd found another woman who suited him better. She was prettier, better company than I, and knew how to satisfy a man.

'"Does this mean divorce?" I was hopeful it might and that I need never see him again.

'"Certainly not. Not good for my reputation. I wouldn't want my business to suffer. Only you and I will know that you are no longer my wife."

'I hated him now. And I was terrified of him, but I could see no way to change things. I'd managed to save only twenty guineas from the safe, and never found a large amount there. Even the laudanum didn't seem so effective as time went on. I had to keep increasing the amount I gave him.

'When Lenora reached the age of twelve, he insisted she came into the business. "She can learn to use a sewing machine and work for her bread now. I've kept your bastard long enough."

'I wept with fury, I can tell you. Getting my hands on enough money was becoming an obsession. And I wanted to hurt Osbert. He gloried in the power he had over us, and it goaded me to take revenge.'

For days, Hattie was left to wonder what revenge Olivia had managed to take, if any, and she was very curious to know what had happened to Osbert Clark.

She thought of him as she went about the house he'd built and furnished. The dark wood panelling and the heavy furniture had been to his taste. Yet apart from that one photograph, there was no sign that he'd ever existed. She wondered, since Olivia seemed to hate him so much, why she'd kept even that.

Hattie had the glass replaced in the silver frame, and set it up on Olivia's dressing table to show the photograph of her four grandchildren. She turned round to find the old lady watching her, so she said: 'I've put Osbert Clark back in his place. You won't be disturbed by him again.'

Olivia said wearily: 'He's never stopped disturbing me. I shouldn't let myself dwell on the past. That's all dead and gone, and yet my mind goes over and over . . .'

'You didn't tell me what happened to him,' Hattie dared. The old lady was silent, and Hattie didn't think she was going to.

'I'd like to sit in the summerhouse. It's a sunny afternoon and I need a breath of air.'

'All right.' Hattie busied herself collecting the rugs and cushions she knew would be needed. She carried them down and then came back to help Olivia. As she sat beside her, the sun was hot on her face, and a bee buzzed amongst the delphiniums in the border.

'Osbert loved this house,' Olivia said drowsily. 'It was the one thing he was passionate about.'

Harriet looked up at the handsome building. She admired the gracious proportions and the turret – she'd not seen one like this anywhere else. She too could get passionate about the comfort within.

Olivia sighed. 'He wanted it to be the finest of houses. He was always trying to improve it. This summerhouse was the last thing he added.'

'You use it a good deal.'

'He didn't have it built for me.'

'All the same, it's lovely to sit here out of the wind.'

They often used to in the summers, though recently, as Olivia found the stairs harder, perhaps not so much.

'He tried to improve his business premises too,' she went on in a voice so measured, so changed, it made Hattie shiver. Olivia sat back and closed her eyes, it was almost as though she was afraid of what she was about to tell her companion. There was a tremor in her voice, Hattie had to strain to hear.

In those long-gone days, it had been usual to close the business for a week's holiday in high summer.

Osbert had drawn up plans to partition off a corner of the workroom to make a small office for himself. He'd hired a carpenter to make some drawers and cupboards to fit under the window. Over them, he planned to have a tabletop on which he could cut out patterns. There was to be a large knee-hole between the drawers, so he could also use it as a desk. And he planned to have new shelves on the other wall.

He said to Olivia: 'I'm going away. For a holiday in Ireland with my lady friend. I want you to come in every day to keep an eye on this carpenter. Don't let him slack. Make sure everything's finished and the place cleaned up by the time I come back.'

She was looking forward to his absence. It meant a rare week of freedom for her and Lenora. She planned to sell some of his belongings. That he had another woman no longer bothered her.

In order to get the most out of his holiday, he'd bought tickets for the Saturday-night sailing to Dublin. The workroom was to close at four o'clock in the afternoon instead of five, as a special favour before the holiday.

Osbert made his own arrangements. He packed his bag, a new one of good cowhide, and brought it to the workroom with him that morning. He meant to cross directly on the ferry to Liverpool to catch the Irish boat.

All the workers were excited that day. There was a lot of hilarity and less work than usual was done. At four o'clock the seamstresses were paid and allowed to go home.

Osbert had told the carpenter to start work at four that afternoon. He and his mate carried up the cupboards and drawers they'd made and fixed them in position under the window. Osbert didn't trust Olivia to do much that he thought important.

She worked hard that afternoon, and so did Lenora. It was necessary to move and reposition the sewing machines. Then Osbert wanted all the finished garments packed up ready for dispatch, and all other materials covered, so that they would not get marked by dirt during the refit. There was dust and sawdust flying everywhere because the carpenter was honing his furniture to fit the space exactly.

'Oil the machines and cover them too,' Osbert ordered. Olivia was hungry and knew Lenora must be too, because they'd had nothing but the piece of pie and the apples they'd brought with them. Osbert had been out to lunch and seemed to have superhuman energy. But he no longer looked well. His moustache had lost its shine and his cheeks their ruddy colour. He looked older than his years now, and his temper could blow up in seconds.

The carpenter left about six, saying he'd return on Monday morning to erect the partitions. Osbert kept Olivia and Lenora working on, finding jobs for them that could quite well have waited until Monday. Olivia could see that Lenora was tired; she looked white with exhaustion.

'I want to go home,' she whispered when Osbert wasn't near. 'How much longer before he has to leave?' Olivia could feel her daughter seething with resentment at being treated like this.

'Get a brush and sweep this floor,' he barked at her. It was usually Lenora's last job on a Saturday afternoon. 'Get these wood shavings up.'

'What's the point?' she dared to ask. 'They'll only make more on Monday when they fit the partitions.'

His face flushed crimson, and his temper turned suddenly savage. 'Do as I tell you,' he thundered.

Lenora's sullen and mutinous eyes stared up at him. Then his arm swiped viciously at her, and Olivia closed her eyes in dread. The crack as his palm slashed against her daughter's face filled the room. The girl gave a strangled scream and fell back against one of the machines.

Olivia felt sick. He'd often done that to her, and she'd always been scared that he'd turn on Lenora. 'Don't do anything to upset him,' she was always telling her. 'Just do as he tells you and stay out of trouble.'

Lenora was straightening up, glaring up at him, struggling for breath. The marks of his fingers showed fiery red on one cheek; the other was the colour of paste. She was fourteen by this time, strong and almost as tall as Osbert.

Olivia was rigid with fear. She was afraid Lenora was making matters worse for herself. She knew just how nasty Osbert could be when he was roused.

She heard Osbert's gasp of exasperation, saw his arm lift to have another go, when suddenly Lenora lunged, throwing all her weight at him. Together they crashed to the floor. Osbert's head caught the corner of the cutting-out table as he went over.

Olivia screamed, knowing that they could expect terrible repercussions from this. Her heart was hammering in her chest. Lenora let out a crow of triumph as she struggled to her feet.

Osbert remained still, spread-eagled on the floor. That he didn't move seemed to encourage a greater effort to hurt him. They both leapt on him, kicking and punching. Years of ill-treatment had given them a fierce hunger for revenge. For the first time, it seemed Osbert was in their power instead of they in his.

The carpenter had left two canvas bags of tools open, ready to use. Olivia snatched up a big screwdriver and laid into him with the wooden handle. Lenora was reaching for the hammer when Olivia screamed.

'Stop!' She felt they must have taken leave of their senses.

Osbert's head was battered and covered with blood. More blood was leaking out into the wood shavings.

'Oh, my God. What have we done?'

'He deserves it. All of it.' Lenora was breathing hard.

'He isn't breathing. I'd swear he isn't breathing. He's dead! What are we going to do?'

'He deserves . . .'

'We'll hang for this.' Olivia couldn't think. 'He's dead. We've killed him.'

'We'll drop him in the river.' Lenora was full of bravado. 'The tide will take him out. We're not hanging for the likes of him.'

Olivia covered her face with her hands and moaned. 'How will we get him to the river? We'll be seen. We'll be caught.'

'After dark,' Lenora panted.

'But will we be able to move him?' Her mouth felt dry. They tried. There was no question of moving him far. Certainly not to the river. Across the room would be their limit. They were spent anyway.

'Let's get him out of sight. There – into the knee-hole between the drawers.'

Osbert was a large man, and they had no strength left. Olivia was choking with desperation. They had to drag him across the floor. It was easy to see the track through the wood shavings and sawdust. There was blood splattered everywhere, some on the wooden floor.

'Wipe it up quick, before it dries,' Olivia sobbed, as she snatched at a duster.

'At least the sawdust has soaked up most of it.' Lenora

was kicking at the clean sawdust that remained, spreading it out to cover the tracks.

It was even harder to push him into the knee-hole space between the drawers, and it took them a long time. They had to sit him up and bend his knees to get him in. Lenora, being smaller and more supple, crawled in after him, pushing him back as far as he could go. They swept in the bloodstained wood shavings and threw the duster in after him. Olivia was panting with exhaustion, and sweat was pouring off her. She knew their troubles had multiplied a thousand times.

'We've rid ourselves of him,' Lenora kept crowing. 'We've rid ourselves of him.'

But Lenora was only a child. She didn't see that the consequences could be terrible. Far worse than living in Osbert's power.

'We'll never get away with this.'

'We will, Mam. We'll be all right. Don't you see?' Her face was hot and shiny, and she was shaking sawdust off her skirts.

'Osbert's told everybody he's going to Ireland. The maids packed his bag for him. He told them he'll be away for a week. He's sent most of them off for their own week's holiday.' Only Vera, the kitchen maid, was left to take care of them and the house.

'And he's told everybody here. He even got one of the seamstresses to make him a new dressing gown for his holiday. Everybody saw his bag.'

'His bag!' Olivia stared at it with horror. 'What will we do with it? We'll have to get rid of it.'

'We'll have plenty of time . . .' Lenora broke off suddenly, her eyes widening with dread. 'Mam, what about his lady friend? She'll be waiting for him, expecting him to come to the boat.' Her tongue slowly moistened her lips. 'What if she goes to the police?'

Olivia clutched the edge of the table as a wave of panic

washed over her. She needed to pull herself together, keep her wits about her.

'She won't. No decent woman would dare. A clandestine relationship like that would ruin her reputation. She'll think he's changed his mind, that he's thought better of taking her. Thrown her over . . .'

She saw Lenora relax. 'Found somebody he liked better, you mean? Yes, I'm sure you're right. We'll come back tomorrow. Nobody else will come in on Sunday. We can clean the place up, make sure we've left no traces.'

'What d'you mean, traces?' Olivia took a shuddering breath. 'I can see him from here. Anybody who comes to this part of the room will see him. The carpenters are going to put up partitions on Monday. There's no way they can avoid seeing him. We can't leave him there.'

Olivia felt desperate. This was the most awful disaster. 'What are we going to do?'

'How many bricks would it take to fill in the knee-hole?' Lenora asked. 'We'll brick him in. Nobody'll see him then.'

'Oh, my God!' Olivia made herself look again. With the four-foot-wide table on top, could they brick him in?

'There'll still be room to sit at the desk,' Lenora said. 'And there's bricks at home. Isn't Osbert having a summerhouse built? We'll bring them from there.'

'The carpenter . . . He'll know bricks were never intended. Not under there.'

'He'll not think anything of it. Why should he? He's working to Osbert's design. If he asks, we'll tell him Osbert wanted it, had arranged for the bricklayer to come tonight. Tell him it's to support the table, that men sometimes stand on it in our work, tell him anything.'

'Lime.' Olivia's mouth was dry. She felt ready to drop. 'We must have lime. It'll speed the time it takes to turn him to dust. The brick wall must be airtight. We'll need cement.'

'We can bring that from home. There's cement for the summerhouse. Sand too. Tomorrow, Mam. We'll feel better then. Let's go, I'm ready to drop. Can't even think . . .'

'Wash. You must wash your hands and face. There's blood on your chin,' Olivia said faintly.

'You too. And on your dress.'

Very carefully, they sponged off every mark. Then Lenora went to find a cab, and Olivia, feeling unsteady, locked up. They sat close together, holding hands, on the way home.

'We must pretend nothing is the matter,' Olivia whispered beneath the noise of the horse's hoofs.

'Mam, you're a nervous wreck.'

'Vera mustn't notice. Thank goodness it's only Vera, and she'll hardly leave the kitchen.'

'And she isn't very bright.'

'We'll pretend we're pleased and happy because Osbert's gone away. She knows how things are for us.'

As she went into the kitchen, Olivia clasped her hands firmly together to stop them shaking. She found some soup left over from the night before, and the remains of a joint of mutton.

'That'll be more than enough for us,' she said. 'Put the soup on to heat up, Vera.'

She was no longer hungry, and when the meal came to the table she had to force herself to eat. Lenora seemed to manage better. She was humming a jolly tune as they went out for a turn round the garden in the last of the evening sun.

'What would be more normal than for us to take a look at the summerhouse?' Lenora asked. The first few rows of bricks had been laid that day.

'Everything we'll need is here.'

'But how many bricks will it take? And how are we to get them down to the workroom without being seen?'

Olivia measured them up with her eyes and made an

271

estimate. There were two of Osbert's carpet bags that he'd thought too shabby to take on holiday. She'd use them.

She felt she had to lie down then; she ached all over. They went to bed early, but Olivia couldn't sleep. When it was really dark she got up and dressed again. In the garden shed behind the house, the gardener had lime as well as some sacks. She put together what she thought they'd need, and hid the sack and the bags in the bushes near the front gate.

It was too much for them to carry. The next morning, Lenora would have to fetch a hansom cab. It could wait at the gate. Vera would notice nothing out of the ordinary. Nobody must.

# CHAPTER FIFTEEN

Once the Great War came to an end, Harriet found the years passing more quickly than ever. On her days off, she was in the habit of going to see Maggie and the baby. Rebecca was thriving and seemed to have grown every time she saw her. She had turned into a pretty little girl.

Hattie wanted to hug and kiss her, but the child would grow tired of it after a few moments and push her away. It pulled at Hattie's heartstrings to see her lift her arms to Maggie and call her Mummy.

If Hattie went out to the shops with them, it seemed that every other person they met marvelled at how closely the child resembled Maggie. She had the same creamy-white curly hair and delicate features, and was like her in personality too, friendly and outgoing and wanting to chat to everyone.

So far as Harriet could see, the only thing her daughter had inherited from her were her green eyes, but they were more beautiful than her own had ever been. Maggie told her wryly that another thing Becky had in common with her mother was her stubborn streak and her determination to make things go her way.

Hattie knew she took the child too many gifts of pretty dresses and warm coats. When she rarely saw Rebecca wearing them, she began to sense Maggie's resentment. She was no longer encouraging her to drop in whenever she felt like it.

Tom was often out when she did go – he had his cinema

now, but Maggie told her little about it. Most of Hattie's information about that came from Pa. When she could get a night off, Pa or her sisters would take her there. 'Our cinema', they called it, and thought Tom was doing very well for himself.

Tom's knee remained stiff, causing him to swing it as he walked. Now he had the cinema, though, Pa thought he had everything he could ask of life and he shouldn't let a gammy knee stop him having a good time.

'His chest bothers him more than his knee,' Maggie confided. She said that there were days when he struggled to get his breath. That she dreaded heavy days of fog, because of the effect they had on him. Tom was always chesty. The doctor said he had chronic bronchitis, and that when he was gassed, it had permanently damaged his lungs.

Hattie thought the three of them were happy. Maggie and Tom always seemed to have their arms round each other. Maggie was, as usual, getting more from life than her sister was. On Rebecca's third birthday, Maggie invited the whole family to Sunday dinner, followed by a birthday tea.

'Pork is really too rich for young children,' Hattie told Tom as she cut it up on her daughter's plate.

'A little won't hurt her,' he smiled.

When the meal was over, Hattie suggested that Becky should be put down for a nap.

'She won't sleep, not with everybody here,' Maggie told her. 'She's excited with all the fuss and the presents.'

Hattie couldn't stop herself from saying: 'I think you should try. Even a rest on her bed . . .'

'She's all right,' Maggie snapped. 'Stop trying to interfere. Pa likes to play with her when he's here. She can go to bed early tonight.'

Hattie shut up then, but she couldn't help feeling hurt. She said so to Pa as they walked to the bus stop afterwards.

'You put your oar in too often,' he told her. 'Don't

keep offering Maggie advice and telling her what she should do.'

'I try not . . .'

'I know you're the big sister and you kept them all in order when they were small, but Maggie's bound to resent it now. You know she's good with children. You're both good with children. Brought young Ruth up between you when your mother died.'

Hattie reflected sadly that they hadn't felt like rivals over Ruth.

'And she's doing fine with Becky. If you want some advice from me, I think you'd be wiser not to see them so often,' Pa told her.

Hattie found it very hard to keep away. She hated to give up. What she had hoped would draw her and Maggie closer was actually pushing them apart. By the time Rebecca was seven, Hattie felt she'd been squeezed out, and she saw her daughter only on family occasions after that.

Maggie did invite her to a special high tea to celebrate Pa's fifty-fifth birthday, and afterwards they were all to go down to the Picturedrome, Tom's cinema, to see Charlie Chaplin in *The Idle Class*. Hattie knew that the place fascinated Becky. She was always chattering on about it.

'Daddy's picture house is the best in the world,' she told Hattie, who loved to take her daughter's small hand in hers as they walked.

'Why did he choose this one, Mummy?'

Maggie was holding firmly on to Becky on the other side.

'We saw it one night when we were walking home from Grandpa's. There was a "For Sale" sign outside.'

'It used to be a mission hall,' Pa said. 'The Salvation Army used to show magic lantern slides here when I was young.'

'What are those?' Becky wanted to know.

'Still photographs. It was a free show, so we all used to go.'

'If the pictures didn't move, it couldn't have been much fun.' Becky was frowning.

'We loved going. They told a story, though it always had a moral to it. The Salvation Army asked us all to sign the pledge before we left.'

'What's that?'

'A promise never to touch strong drink. We all signed. It was a small price to pay for the privilege of seeing the slides. Bet it didn't stop the big lads enjoying their beer, though.' Pa chuckled.

'Hasn't stopped you with your whisky, either,' Maggie laughed. Becky swung on Hattie's arm. 'Fancy turning a mission hall into a cinema.'

Pa was often a mine of information. 'It was built in the eighteen-eighties as a roller-skating rink. Then it was a billiards hall for a while. It was turned into a cinema in nineteen ten by Hyman Cohen. Tom bought it from him in nineteen fifteen.'

'The year I was born! It must have been one of the first.'

'No,' her grandfather laughed. 'The first picture house opened in Paris before the turn of the century. It showed a train coming right at the audience and nearly caused a panic.'

'But here in Birkenhead. Was it the first?'

'No,' Maggie said. 'There were several when we were young. The Argyle Music Hall had that screen that came down so they could show films too. Long before our cinema. The Queen's Hall showed animated pictures too.'

'*One* of the first then,' Becky persisted.

Pa smiled at Hattie. 'The first film I saw shocked everybody. A man kissing a woman, we'd never seen such intimate detail. The screen brought it so close, not like in the theatre. Quite shocking. Soon picture palaces were opening all over the place, and audiences were flocking to them.'

As they turned into Hind Street, Hattie could see in the glow of the cinema lights the line of people waiting to buy their tickets. A large notice advertised that there were seats at 3d, 6d and 9d, and that no vulgar scenes would be shown.

Hattie knew that nothing pleased seven-year-old Becky more than to be brought here. She'd seen almost every film they'd ever shown and they changed the programme twice a week. She spoke of famous film stars like Mary Pickford and Douglas Fairbanks and Fatty Arbuckle as though she knew them better than the neighbours in Lowther Street. If Hattie were honest, she didn't approve of her spending so much time here, but she didn't say so. Maggie had to bring her, if she was to be involved in the running of it.

All the same, she didn't like hearing Rebecca saying that once she was ten, she'd be able to earn pocket money by helping the cleaners sweep it through in the mornings. And when she left school, she was going to ask Daddy to let her be an usherette.

Harriet still saw a good deal of her younger sisters. They'd grown up now and Pa no longer saw them as a responsibility. Ruth was fourteen and as strong and healthy as the rest of the family. She'd left school and was keeping house for her father. Between them, they were looking after him.

Fanny was twenty-two and being courted by a master butcher. When she'd completed her course in shorthand and typing, she'd taken a job in an insurance office.

'I love it,' she'd told Hattie. 'I feel very grateful to you. I shudder when I think I might have had to do factory work or go into domestic service. Now I'm working, I could pay you back out of my wages.'

Hattie had shaken her head.

277

'Then I shall pay for Enid to do the course. I know she'd jump at the chance.'

'We'll do it between us,' Hattie had said. So now Enid was working in a solicitor's office.

'We'll pay for Clara and Ruth in their turn,' Hattie had said. 'It's only fair that they should have the chance too.'

But Clara had had other ideas. Now that she was sixteen she'd started training as a children's nurse. Ruth said that when she was old enough, she wanted to do the same.

On her days off, Hattie usually went to see Pa. He was working mostly in the operating theatres now, and had responsibility for autoclaving all the instruments and dressings. He still had to help lift patients on and off the operating tables, and that was heavy work but he was happier now he had more responsibility.

He told her he'd lost touch with most of his old friends, but he still went to the Woodside Hotel for a meal or to the Railway Hotel for a drink. He often went to Tom's picture palace, where the staff knew him and, on Tom's instructions, let him in to the best seats for nothing.

She always asked how Becky was. He always reported her to be in top form, but never seemed to think things were going well for Maggie. It worried him that Tom always seemed generally dissatisfied with life.

Hattie tried to centre her life on her job. The years were mellowing Stanley. His hair was white and his mutton-chop whiskers often long and wispy. There was nothing about his manner to frighten her now. He'd kept his distance, as he'd promised. He was not unfriendly, and seemed to regard her as an ally.

Lenora more or less ignored her, speaking to her only in relation to her duties. Her interests now seemed vested in her grandchildren. Claudia and her son were frequent visitors. Edward was growing up, but he was destined to enter the dog food business.

Hattie spent most of her time with Olivia, and was content to have it so.

Maggie Dransfield told herself she'd had some happy years in the little house in Lowther Street with her husband and daughter.

'We did the right thing by adopting Becky,' she'd said many times to him, when they were counting their blessings.

'Certainly did,' Tom would agree. There'd never been the slightest sign of them having a child of their own. Becky had bound them together, made them the complete family. Maggie had tried to teach her to play the piano.

'Becky doesn't have your talent for music,' Tom had smiled. But Becky really tried very hard.

'I want to do what you do when I grow up,' she told Maggie. 'I want to play in the picture house.'

Eventually, she learned to strum along well enough. Once or twice Maggie had let her try accompanying the short supporting films in the programme, but she couldn't keep up with the changing tempo it needed, and she never gained enough confidence to play throughout a whole performance.

But recently, things had begun to turn sour for Maggie. She was worried about Tom. Tonight, as she'd seen Becky into bed, she'd felt like crying. Tom had been silent and withdrawn on the walk home from the cinema. He didn't even look at her now when she went to their bedroom and started to undress.

She'd made out to Pa that it was Tom's health that concerned her, but it was more than that. Things between them had been a bit flat for some time.

Maggie thought they were taking each other for granted and supposed that most couples were like this after some years of marriage. Happiness and contentment seemed to elude Tom. He was never satisfied with what he had.

He even said that the cinema was never going to make them rich.

'I wasn't ambitious enough,' he told her. 'I should have asked for more money when I had the chance and gone for a bigger and better place. Like Hyman Cohen did.' Cohen had built a bigger cinema, in the centre of Liverpool. 'He knew what he was doing, and look at the cinemas they've built since. Grand places with chandeliers and carpets.'

'We aren't starving,' Maggie had pointed out.

She did her best to tell him that she needed nothing more. Once Becky was old enough to be taken to the cinema with them, she'd started playing the piano accompaniment. She enjoyed doing it and it kept the wages bill down. She didn't play for every performance. They had another part-time pianist and they shared the work between them. The bigger, more up-to-date cinemas had started to employ bands these days, but Tom thought the Picturedrome couldn't run to that.

Really, everything had been all right until Tom took on a new cashier, an attractive brunette called Stella Lee. Maggie's first intimation of trouble had been that it took him much longer to count the takings with her than it had with their previous cashier. When she joined them in the ticket office, the atmosphere seemed charged, and Tom usually shot off somewhere else. Stella never seemed relaxed with her.

On Thursdays, when the other pianist was on duty and there was a matinée, Tom had given up coming home for a meal before the evening performances.

'There isn't much time,' he said. 'Too much of a rush. I'll get a snack at the Copper Kettle Café instead.' They usually had a light supper when he came home after closing for the night.

Things had come to a head tonight. They were showing Rin-Tin-Tin in *The Man from Hell's River*, and it was the first time Maggie had accompanied a film about an animal.

This afternoon at home, she'd gone through all her sheet music, looking for tunes with canine connections. She thought she'd made a good choice, and the evening had gone well for her. Becky was ten years old now and happy to sit through both performances.

'Rin-Tin-Tin's wonderful,' she told her parents as she walked home between them. 'I loved every minute of his picture.'

Maggie had enjoyed the novelty and asked: 'How did they get a dog to act so well? What did you think of him, Tom?'

Before he could answer, Becky said: 'Daddy hardly saw any of it. He stayed in the ticket office with Stella.'

Maggie's heart missed a beat.

'We couldn't get the cash to balance against the number of tickets sold,' he said lightly. 'Then I went up to the office to answer some letters.'

Maggie felt her world was coming to an end. She'd been telling herself for some time that it was silly to be suspicious of him; that Tom would never do such a thing, that he loved her. Now, it seemed, she could be wrong about that.

'I did see some of the film,' he added. 'Thought the dog was good.'

'It was nearly the end when you and Stella came in,' Becky giggled. 'You missed a good film, Daddy.'

Maggie was horrified, but Becky was chattering on.

'D'you know what Stella told me? Rin-Tin-Tin's a German shepherd dog who was found in the trenches during the war. An American soldier took him home and trained him to work in films.'

Maggie could think only of the way Stella's melting brown eyes followed Tom, and wanted to cry. She'd waited for this moment, when they would be alone in their bedroom.

'I'm thinking something terrible, Tom.'

She had to whisper so that Becky wouldn't hear in

the next room. Tom was sitting on the bed. He seemed engrossed in taking off his socks.

'I'm your wife. I thought you loved me.'

Tom rolled under the blankets, pulling them high around his ears.

Maggie shivered and made haste to get under the covers too. There was a great gap between them. After a moment she turned her back on him and started to cry. She couldn't help herself. After five minutes she had to feel for a hanky to blow her nose.

'Oh, come on, Maggie,' Tom said softly. He came closer, put an arm round her waist. It felt like a log resting across her stomach.

'What's happening to us, Tom?'

'Nothing's happening.'

'You're in love with Stella Lee, aren't you?'

He withdrew his arm. She had to wait an age for his answer.

'Perhaps I am,' he sighed. 'I didn't ask to be. It just happened.'

Maggie lay stiff and tense, unable to breathe. 'Why?'

'I don't know. I'm a man, I suppose.'

'You're a Dransfield,' she spat angrily. There was nothing he could say to that. She couldn't stand his silence. 'What about me?'

'I don't know. I'm sorry.'

There was another terrible silence. She couldn't stand this. She jerked herself off the bed and went downstairs. She made a cup of tea, but she let it grow cold in the cup.

The next morning, Tom said nothing directly to her. Maggie was in agony, and tried to pretend in front of Becky that nothing was wrong. As soon as she could, she went home and poured out all her troubles on Pa's shoulder. She never had been able to keep anything to herself.

'I don't know what I can do to help you, Maggie.' He

didn't seem surprised. He didn't say, 'What do you expect from a Dransfield?' But she sensed it was in his mind.

Maggie knew she'd have to handle this herself. That evening, she and Becky walked to the Picturedrome a few yards behind Tom. They were always the first to arrive, because Tom had to open up. As soon as he had, he went to his office.

Maggie waited in the pay box for Stella Lee as the staff began to arrive. She watched the projectionist come in, and heard Becky talking to him about Mary Pickford as she followed him upstairs to his room. Stella was on time. She came up the entrance hall with Dolly, one of the usherettes, and stood talking to her for a few moments. Then she flung back the door, expecting to have the cubbyhole of a pay box to herself. Maggie stood up and faced her.

'There's something I want to say to you, Stella.' The girl's eyes were glazing over with shock.

'Leave my husband alone. I know what's been going on and I'll not have it. Do you understand? Stay away from him.'

Dolly was still outside, her face screwing with shock. So was Albert Jones, the commissionaire, all dressed up in his red and gold uniform. Maggie swept past them and ran upstairs to the cloakroom to tidy her hair and get herself ready to play. She came down to start the performance five minutes early, thumping out a march by Souza as loudly as she could.

After that, when she passed the ticket office, she put her nose in the air. Stella wouldn't meet her gaze. Tom's affair became very public. Both the usherettes sided with Maggie and said Stella was a real baggage. Maggie's younger sisters rallied round with sympathy.

At Pa's house, she came face to face with Hattie, whose green eyes seemed very strange as she said: 'He's a Dransfield, I suppose you should have expected it.'

Maggie knew her face fell. It was the last thing she'd expected. She loved Tom.

'Maggie, I'm sorry.' Hattie's arms came round her in a hug. 'I wish I could help you. What are you going to do?'

'Pa says I can come back home. Take Becky if I want.'

'Back here? I can't believe . . .'

'I'm seriously thinking of it,' she said. She'd thought of nothing else for days.

The first thing Maggie did was to stop going to the cinema. She told Tom she couldn't bear to be pegged to the piano, rolling out tune after tune, knowing that he had Stella Lee up in his office from the moment the pay box closed.

'I'll have to look for another pianist then,' was all he said.

Staying at home gave Maggie more time to think. Tom hardly spoke to her. He went out in the mornings and didn't return until the cinema closed. He slept in the marital bed but stayed as far away from her as he could. Maggie packed her bags and went home to Pa without telling him that she was going to do it.

'There'll be plenty of space for us,' she told Becky. 'Not like it was when we were all young.'

Fanny was married now and Clara and Ruth only came home for their nights off from the hospital. Enid still lived at home but that still allowed a double bed to themselves.

But Elizabeth Place seemed worse than it ever had, and Becky couldn't hide how much she disliked it. She spoke of Lowther Street as though it was luxurious. Maggie felt more miserable then ever, especially as she had to walk past the Picturedrome whenever she went out. Pa took her and Becky out when he had an evening off. They went to different picture houses now. Hattie came home and tried to cheer Maggie up.

'What you need is something to take your mind off Tom. Another job.'

'He sends me money. He says I don't need to work if I don't want to.'

'He's not that bad, then?'

'Pa says it's only right he should support us.'

'Yes, but you need something to fill your day.'

'I wish I had my piano here.' She'd walked out and left it in Lowther Street.

Pa said: 'We'll get a carrier to bring it down. You need your music, Maggie. I've always been sorry I wasn't able to send you to music school. You might have had a brilliant future.'

'You could take lessons now,' Hattie told her. Maggie knew they were both trying to get her to do more.

'It's a question of finding the right teacher,' Pa said.

'And the question of how to pay for them hasn't gone away.' Actually it had – Tom was quite generous – but Maggie felt out of sorts and didn't want to be helped.

Hattie's green eyes were shining. 'If you still want those lessons, I'll pay for them.'

'Would you, Hattie?' Pa was delighted. 'I've always blamed myself that Maggie never had her chance.'

'I'll pay for them myself,' Maggie retorted before she could stop herself.

'Let's see if we can find you a teacher.'

'Not just any teacher. It'll have to be . . .'

'Somebody good.' Pa was nodding his agreement.

A few days later, Maggie had a note from Hattie, giving her a name and address in Bebington. She said Sophie had heard that this man taught at an advanced level. Pa urged her to find out if she thought he could help and if he'd take her on. So that she could practise, he asked the new tenants on the first floor if she could use their piano. They hadn't got round to bringing her own down here.

*     *     *

285

Maggie had owned the leather music case since she was a child. She went up to Lowther Street to get it at a time when she knew Tom would be out. She put in the certificates she'd earned for her music all those years ago. They were creased and yellowing now. Would this teacher think it a little silly of her to be taking it up again after all this time? She put in some sheet music, some of her favourite pieces.

She'd looked forward to her first appointment for days, and played for half an hour before she left home so that her fingers would be supple. She wanted to do herself justice, play as well as she possibly could.

It seemed a long journey into Bebington on the bus, but she found the address without any difficulty. The house was solidly built and mid Victorian, with four bay windows, two on each side of the front door. Curtains of white net covered each of them, so it was impossible to see in. It was in a terrace of similar houses and opened straight on to the street. On a brass plate set into the wall, she read: 'Justin James, Mus. Doc. Teacher of Pianoforte.'

She'd half expected to hear piano music tinkling out, but all was quiet. She rang the bell and stood back until a maid came to show her into a sitting room. The piano was a concert grand. It took up most of the floor space. The walls were covered with bookshelves, there were two easy chairs and not much else. She went over to look at the instrument, it was a fine Bechstein in a rosewood case. She tried a note or two.

'Hello.'

It made her jump; she hadn't heard him come in.

'Does it meet with your approval?'

'Oh, yes, Mr James! It's a beautiful piano.' She was embarrassed to be found tinkling on it.

'Tell me about yourself.' He was slim and upright, dark, and balding a little.

286

Maggie was afraid her words were disjointed. 'I didn't keep my music up, though I loved it at school. And now I'd like to work at it again, improve.'

His eyes were kindly and seemed half hooded. It gave him a sleepy appearance, but every so often his eyelids would shoot up and she'd see alert brown eyes studying her minutely.

'I've played in a cinema, accompanying the films. I'm afraid I picked up some bad habits there. Trying to keep up and . . .' Her voice trailed away. For some reason, she'd expected an older man. Justin James was about her own age.

'Come and play for me. One of your favourite pieces. Have you brought something?' He smiled, and his eyes crinkled at the corners.

'I've brought Chopin. I love his polonaises.'

She found number six, in A flat major. This was a favourite of Pa's too. She'd played it many times for him and knew it by heart.

'It's a long time since I've played a piano as fine as this,' she said as she settled herself on the stool.

She told herself she mustn't be nervous of playing in front of a teacher. She'd pretend she was playing for Pa. She relaxed once her fingers touched the keys and the music began to fill the room. She was carried away with the familiar melody.

As the notes died away, he said slowly: 'You love music.' He chose another piece from the music she'd brought. 'Let me hear you play one of his preludes. Do you like number thirteen?'

'Quite his most beautiful,' she said. She knew this very well too.

When she came to the end, he was pensive and said nothing for a long time. 'I hardly know what to say. You play exceedingly well, with great feeling.'

They discussed Chopin at length. Then Justin James said:

287

'I'd like to find an obscure piece that you don't know. To see how well you read music.'

'I can.' She smiled.

He had trouble finding a piece that was truly unknown to her, but at last he produced a modern piece that she'd never heard of. Maggie didn't care for it, but she managed it well enough.

'I'm a little worried about how much I can teach you.' His smile was lopsided. 'You're as good as I am, you know. Do you intend to teach?'

Maggie shook her head. 'I thought at one time . . . But I'm more a player than a teacher.'

'Then what do you have in mind? What do you intend to use this skill for? What do you hope to get from more lessons?'

Once started, Maggie poured out details about her life. It was almost as though he'd opened floodgates. About why she'd been unable to carry on with her music when she'd been young; about her sisters, about Becky.

He was the first person she'd met who truly shared her interest in music. She learned that he'd been teaching for nine years and been a widower for the last three. He laughed and told her that he was very interested in the cinema organ too, and that he was taking lessons on that at the moment.

She told him then about Tom's cinema. It seemed something else they had in common.

'You're a happy family then?' He sounded almost disappointed.

She hadn't meant to tell him about Tom – she hated admitting that things had gone wrong between them – but somehow all that came flooding out too. His dark eyes watched her sympathetically. She told herself on the way home that he was very nice. Not perhaps measuring up to Tom, but at least she'd found a friend. Justin was balm to her shattered emotions.

\*      \*      \*

Maggie had had four lessons and enjoyed them. She felt she was improving. It was a month since she'd moved back to Elizabeth Place. Having just seen Becky off to school and Pa off to work, she was washing up the breakfast pots in the old slopstone sink. Suddenly, the kitchen door opened without warning, making her jump. Tom was standing there, looking ill and shamefaced.

'Come home, Maggie, please. I've found a new cashier and I've given Stella the sack.'

Maggie had been telling herself she enjoyed Justin's company, but she hadn't stopped hankering after Tom. He looked pale and haggard.

'It's over, I promise.'

She felt fluttery with pleasure. He wanted her back.

'I'm sorry, I hate being without you and Becky. Please come home.'

She packed her bags straight away and left a note for Pa on the table. Tom tried to help her carry her things, but he had to keep stopping to get his breath. He said he hadn't been feeling well, he'd spent the last few days in bed, his chest was tight. Maggie insisted he went straight up to bed as soon as they got home.

'It's good of you to look after me like this,' he whispered, as she ran up and downstairs attending to his needs. 'I don't deserve to have you.'

Maggie knew she wanted to be here with him. To do what she could.

He was racked by a fit of coughing. 'After what I did, I was afraid you'd hate me,' he gasped.

She tried to smile. 'How can I hate you?'

All the same, it took her a long time to get over it. She found it hard to trust him again until Hattie, at another chance meeting, said: 'He didn't love her as much as he loved you. He threw her over, didn't he? Chose you again. You ought to feel more sure of him, not less.'

'But he betrayed . . .'

'Maggie, you don't know what it is to be betrayed by a man. Tom's stood by you, hasn't he? Better if you forgive him and forget all about this. You'll have to, if you want things to get back the way they were.'

Maggie thought it over and decided her sister was right. Hattie knew what she was talking about. Tom insisted she keep up her music lessons, because she was enjoying them.

As the winter weather closed in, Tom was brought low with another bad attack of bronchitis, and had to stay in bed for several weeks. Becky ran backwards and forwards to the cinema with notes of instruction to the staff. Maggie asked the other pianist if she'd like to work full time so that she could stay at home to look after him. She had to cancel some of her lessons.

'You're more important to me,' she told Tom.

One day, when he could scarcely get his breath, and Maggie had done all she could to make him comfortable, he panted: 'You do so much for me. More than I should expect after the way I treated you.'

'I love you,' she said. 'And you need me now. Need Becky too.'

Tom lost weight, and after that winter never managed to put it back on. Each winter brought him more illness and a further loss of weight. The doctor talked of emphysema now, rather than chronic bronchitis. But when he was well enough, they all went back to their normal routine.

# CHAPTER SIXTEEN

Maggie had known Justin James for several years. The lessons he'd given her had never been regular because Tom's illness always interrupted them. Justin laughed and said he didn't feel he could teach her much more anyway. He'd talked to her a lot about technique, and she felt he'd helped her refine hers.

She looked upon him as a friend; she knew no one else who shared her love of music. She'd invited him to her home at Christmas when others of her family were coming. He'd wanted to take her to a concert at the Philharmonic Hall in Liverpool, but though she'd have loved to go, she knew Tom didn't want her to. In fact, he'd been dead against it.

When she explained this to Justin, he bought three tickets and took Pa too. Maggie had an utterly blissful time.

'Concerts were something else you missed because we were so poor,' Pa told her. After that, they went regularly as a threesome. Even if Tom was ill, Pa insisted on her going. He said she needed a break. Maggie always enjoyed both the concerts and Justin's company.

One morning, she went into Rushworth and Draper's shop in Grange Road to buy some more sheet music. Justin was there, bent on the same errand.

His dark hooded eyes smiled down at her. 'Help me choose some cinema music,' he said. 'I've started giving organ recitals at one of the new cinemas in Liverpool.'

She knew that Justin was also an organist and had taken

up the new electric cinema organ with great enthusiasm. She hadn't seen him for some weeks.

'It's quite a long way to go just to play for fifteen minutes in each performance, but I've got to start somewhere. And a little experience will make it easier to get into a cinema in Birkenhead.

'Theatre music, something cheerful. You know better than I do what I need. What do you advise?'

'Don't know much about the organ,' she smiled, but that didn't stop her choosing some pieces for him.

When they'd made their purchases, he said: 'Do you have time for a cup of coffee? So I can catch up with your news.'

They went to a nearby café. He took out all the new music he'd bought and together they arranged it in the best order to play it. Maggie felt the pull of his personality. She knew he found her attractive, that was why Tom resented him. They talked about Tom, who was well enough to work again. They always talked so much that the time flew past.

Suddenly he jumped to his feet. 'I'll have to go. I'm so sorry, I got carried away. I'm meeting a pupil at the Regal.'

'That new cinema in Bebington?'

'Yes, near where I live.' He told her that he'd started teaching the cinema organ too. 'I'll have to hurry or I'll be late.'

'You give lessons at the cinema?' Maggie had seen it being built when she'd gone to his house. Now it was the sort of cinema Tom would have given his eye-teeth to own. 'They let you teach your pupils on their organ?'

'For a fee.' He smiled. 'In the daytime, when there's no matinée. It's too expensive to get one of my own. Would you like to come in and see it?'

Maggie wanted to. She sat alone in the stalls where she wouldn't distract the young man who'd come for a lesson. The sound enthralled her, so rich and heavy and with such resonance that it seemed to vibrate through the auditorium.

The splendour of the cinema came as a shock. It made the Picturedrome look like something that had survived from the Middle Ages. There were plush seats and thick carpets and such a marvellously ornate ceiling. The organ could come up out of the floor with the organist already playing. When his pupil left, Justin waved Maggie to come forward.

'What fun,' Maggie enthused. 'I've never seen anything quite like this.'

'The Wurlitzer electric organ.' It sparkled in the dim light.

'I'd love to play it. I want to learn. Will you teach me?'

'Of course, I'd like to. For you, it would just be a question of adapting to using several keyboards at once. You'll not find it hard.'

'When can I come?'

He took his appointments book from his pocket, and she decided to try two lessons a week to start with.

'I want to get the feel of it, and I can't practise at home.'

'Once you get started, I can arrange practice sessions here for you.' He smiled.

'And when I've learned, I'll try to get a job playing it,' Maggie breathed.

His eyes twinkled. 'I'm hoping to play this one.'

She laughed. 'Really? I'd love to do that. Play my own music in my own time.'

'If there's a silent picture showing, I sometimes accompany that as well.'

'I'm well practised at that.'

He sat at the instrument and started to play. He showed Maggie how the organ could sink into the floor while it was being played. The strains of 'Little Grey Home in the West' grew fainter as he disappeared. She was very impressed.

Maggie was thrilled with her organ lessons, and knew she was learning fast. She was getting used to the luxury of a modern cinema. The following year, Justin told her he'd got what he'd wanted. The job of playing in the Regal.

Now he was nearer, Becky kept asking to be taken to hear him play. Eventually Maggie persuaded Tom to come too. Instead of watching the short supporting films, she took them downstairs to see Justin. He was sorting through his music.

'Isn't it huge!' Becky couldn't take her eyes off the instrument. 'I can't believe . . .'

'Wouldn't you like to learn to play it too?' He was half teasing, Maggie knew.

'No, but I'm dying to see you come up out of the floor playing it.'

Maggie said: 'I've never yet heard you play in public.'

His half-hooded eyes looked at her dreamily. 'Won't be much different from what you've heard in private. You could do it yourself, Maggie. You're near enough ready for it. With your experience, you'd have no difficulty. Would you like to take a few nights here?'

'Take your job from you? I can't do that.'

He laughed. 'You wouldn't be. I can't come every night. They play records when I don't.'

Tom shook his head. He was frowning. 'Can't spare her from my place,' he said brusquely. Maggie had gone back to playing on three nights each week.

'I've heard such a lot about your cinema.' Justin turned to him. 'Quite something to have your own.'

'You wouldn't like it.' Tom sounded ungracious. 'I'm afraid it compares badly with this one.'

The first half of the programme was coming to an end.

Maggie hurried them back to their seats. The lights came up and they could hear the strains of 'I Do Like To Be Beside the Seaside' as the instrument came rising out of the floor. Justin had his back to them. At the end of the introduction, he got up to bow to the audience and announce his programme.

'Doesn't it sparkle,' Becky breathed. The lighting changed colour. A brilliant green spotlight focused on the instrument. The notes of the organ began to fill the cinema.

'Not exactly a recital.' Tom pulled a face as several in the audience got to their feet to buy ice cream from the two usherettes who had appeared in the aisles.

Maggie thought Justin's performance very polished, and was thrilled that he'd said she'd reached a standard when she could do the same.

They didn't stay to see the film through. Tom was restless and depressed. She knew he'd been comparing this much finer cinema with the Picturedrome, and that he didn't feel the same warmth for Justin James that she did.

'I thought he played absolutely beautifully,' Becky said, as they took the bus back.

When Becky reached the age of fourteen and was about to leave school, Tom insisted that she take a commercial course.

'It'll give her a skill,' he said to Maggie. 'She'll be able to earn a living with that.'

Maggie was dead against it. 'Becky wants to work in the Picturedrome with you. She's really keen.'

'What if it can't support us all?' he'd asked gently.

'You could give her a job. It would save paying wages to someone else. Cashier, say, or usherette. She's stood in many times as usherette, you know she can do it.'

'Better if we give her something different to fall back on.' Tom frowned. 'She might need it.'

Becky resisted when they told her. 'That's the last thing

295

I want to do.' She felt very involved with the cinema and wanted to help him run it.

'I'm thinking of what's best for you,' Tom told her. 'Do this typing course first, and then we'll see.'

These days Tom had hollows in his cheeks and looked really gaunt.

'You're working too hard,' Maggie told him. 'You're out late every night. It's too much for you.'

'I can't stop working, can I? I'll be better when the warm weather comes.' But he wasn't. His cough grew worse. He seemed to croak half the night, and he had less energy.

Maggie had to watch him become more and more breathless. There were evenings when he came home before he finished his work. As time went on, there were other evenings when he couldn't find the strength to go. He had to send Becky in his place to drop the takings in the night safe at the bank.

Maggie knew that the picture house had never fulfilled Tom's expectations. He always seemed to be telling her of some reason why the profits were down. She left the running of it to him and was content that it provided enough for their day-to-day needs.

She knew Tom couldn't rest for worrying. She heard him say to Becky: 'You'll have to help Mam keep the Picturedrome going, Becky. You'll need the money to live on.'

Hattie was feeling soporific. She'd spent most of the afternoon reading to Olivia in the turret, and the sun had been hot through the glass. The old lady seemed to need more and more heat, and refused to have a window open even in warm weather. She was about to take the tea tray back to the kitchen when Stanley came in with an armful of documents.

'What's all this?' Olivia wanted to know.

He dropped his voice. 'I want to talk to you, Olivia.'

He sat down on the chair Hattie had vacated. As he offered the documents to Olivia, Hattie could see that they were the accounts for Knell's Gloves, not only for the present year, but going back all the years that Dransfield's had been running it. Instantly she was alert. She wanted very much to have a look at those accounts.

She knew Stanley was waiting for her to go. She picked up the tray and went to see if the preparations for dinner were on schedule. She'd find out later what he wanted from Olivia. The old lady wouldn't be able to keep her tongue still. When she returned Olivia was alone, and the documents were spread round her.

'Stanley wants money,' she said, looking at Harriet over her glasses. 'He wants us to put more capital in.'

'Into Knell's Gloves?'

'He wants to expand, get larger premises. Wants me to support him, but I've told him this isn't the time. This depression is affecting everything and Knell's is already the biggest of Lenora's enterprises.'

Hattie could see the old lady watching her. 'It must be hard for you to see Stanley managing your father's factory. Does it make you feel bitter?'

It did, but it was second nature for Hattie to hide her feelings. She couldn't show the hurt festering inside her. It was an ugly side of her nature and she didn't want to turn Olivia against her. On the other hand, she wanted her to know what a disaster it had been for the Knells.

'Impossible not to be.' She tried to keep her tone mild. 'Very sad for Pa. It wasn't just the factory he lost, it was all purpose to his life. We've been terribly poor ever since. Penniless.'

Talking about it brought the memories rushing back. She'd intended to get her own back on Lenora all those years ago and yet she'd done nothing. She felt the need for revenge again, and was curious to know what the

297

Dransfields had made from the business. She counted up the years they'd been running it, and found it hard to believe it was sixteen.

The old lady wouldn't look at her after that. It rankled between them.

'Help me down to the drawing room,' she said. 'I'll have a glass of sherry before dinner.' She didn't go down very often these days: she was finding the stairs more difficult.

Stanley was already there. All three would be dining at home tonight. As soon as Hattie had settled Olivia on a chair, she shot back upstairs to the old lady's room on tiptoe.

She left the door ajar so that she'd hear if Lenora were to come. The documents were strewn over the couch. Where to begin? She was shaking with anticipation.

The glove factory had made good profits during the war years and had never looked back. If only Pa had had that advantage. She was heaving with frustration and not sure she understood what she was looking for.

She turned to the accounts for the year Lenora had bought the business. Now she could see exactly how much she'd paid for the lease of the factory, the materials, stock, all the new machines and the goodwill. It left her gasping. It was almost nothing in view of the current profits, but at that time, Hattie told herself, nobody had known there was a war coming.

She knew that money had gone to pay Pa's creditors – of whom Lenora had been the largest – but he'd owed money for leather and thread and packaging, and on the newest machines. Hattie could see little that she hadn't known before. She could feel her stomach churning with rage that Lenora had had such a bargain.

'Harriet?' Lenora was calling up the stairs. 'We're all waiting for dinner. Isn't it ready yet?'

She jumped up. Lenora expected dinner to be on the table

at seven, and already it was ten past. She'd not noticed time passing. Hattie hired the women who came in to cook and set the table, but it was her job to dish the meal up and take it to the dining room.

Because she was the only live-in help, she'd been eating her meals with the family since she'd returned. In the kitchen, she tipped the soup into the warmed tureen, added the hot soup plates to the tray and rushed to the dining room. The family were seated in readiness. She knew they'd been having an argument; the atmosphere bristled with irritation.

'What's the matter with you tonight?' Lenora asked testily. 'We're tired of waiting.'

'Sorry.' Harriet felt rushed as well as angry as she filled the plates. Soup splashed on the white tablecloth.

'Look how careless you are. No wonder the laundry bills are high.'

'Sorry,' Harriet said again, and took a mouthful of soup.

'I know it means more work if we expand the gloves,' Stanley was saying earnestly. 'But work for me, not for you, Lenora.'

She turned on him in fury. 'Haven't I said no? I'm not prepared to do anything more for you.'

'But it's your own business you'll be investing in.'

'No! Absolutely not,' Lenora thundered. 'I've had enough. It's over, Stanley.'

'What?'

'I've put up with a lot from you, but after this . . . Shaming me in my own house. I won't have it.'

'What are you talking about?' Stanley's spoon went down on his unfinished plate.

'You've been telling me lies. You told me Harriet was ill, all those years ago. I should have had more sense than to believe that. Consumption indeed!'

Hattie felt the blood coursing to her face. Her throat was

299

suddenly tight. She'd put all this behind her long ago, and thought the time had gone when it might surface here.

Stanley wouldn't look at her now. 'What's brought this up? It's ancient history.'

'You've had her here in my house. All these years. A mistress, under my roof.'

'No,' Harriet denied hotly. 'No, nothing like that.' She felt outraged at the suggestion.

'Certainly not,' Stanley confirmed. 'Don't be silly.'

Olivia was the only one still spooning up soup. She was trying to look as though this had nothing to do with her. Hattie froze. After all these years of silence, something had made her tell Lenora about the baby. Hattie knew it had stayed in her mind; she spoke of it from time to time. She'd always known Olivia's tongue could run away with her. Why hadn't it occurred to her that this might happen?

Lenora's face was scarlet with rage. 'I know you've sent your fancy women away to give birth before now. You've an heir of your own for the glove factory, haven't you, Stanley? Now you're going to try to swindle me out of it.'

'Of course not.'

'Then why so many lies? Tom's child indeed! It certainly isn't Maggie's, so I don't believe it can be Tom's. I saw Maggie in some bus conductor's uniform just about the time it was born. Disgracefully short skirt, only a few inches below her knees, and she was certainly not expecting a baby.' Lenora was breathing fire. She looked at Hattie. 'It's yours and Harriet's, isn't it, Stanley?'

'Nonsense.' He laughed, and his eyes sought Hattie's then. She felt the blood rush up her cheeks again. It made her cringe to hear Lenora going on like this.

'You're always feathering your own nest. Taking more than the salary we agreed. Defrauding the business to support your mistress and your fancy women. I've had enough. You can get out of this house and out of my glove factory.

'Peverell, the undermanager, can cope as well as you can. Probably does most of the work anyway.'

Hattie could understand why Stanley wanted to stay. Lenora held the purse strings. He might have another family on the wrong side of the blanket, but he'd never be able to support himself and them at this standard without Lenora's money.

But what she'd never been able to fathom was why Lenora hadn't sent him packing long ago.

'I'm not budging,' he said now.

'You will this time. You won't be able to stop me. I know exactly what you're going to say: that you'll go to the police, you'll tell them I've fraudulently acquired companies. That's blackmail, isn't it?'

Hattie could hardly breathe. She couldn't listen to this, it went right to her heart. She jumped to her feet, collected the soup plates and rushed to the kitchen with her tray. Lenora's voice followed her.

'But there's no proof I did anything wrong. I've been very careful about that. It'll be my word against yours, Stanley.'

In the kitchen, the woman pushed another tray into Hattie's hands. It was set with vegetable dishes and a casserole. There was an ominous silence when she returned to the dining room. Three angry faces glared at each other.

'And I've come to the end of my patience with you, Harriet,' Lenora said, as she set the dishes on the table.

Hattie could see her steel-grey eyes radiating venomous hate. 'You can go too. Pack your bags and leave tonight.'

Hattie gasped, almost unable to take it in. The last thing she wanted was to leave now. The lace-trimmed cap on Olivia's head jerked up angrily. The strength of her voice surprised Hattie.

'No, Lenora! Don't be ridiculous. I pay Harriet's wages, she works for me. I won't have her sent packing.'

Hattie started dishing up the casserole with automatic movements. Inside, she could feel her own anger building up against Lenora.

Olivia went on: 'What would I do? Here by myself all day. Don't be silly. You can't sack her.'

'Mother!'

'Of course you can't sack her, Lenora. I won't have it. You want to stay, don't you, Harriet?'

Hattie swallowed hard, put a few vegetables on Olivia's plate and slid it in front of her. She wasn't at all sure what the outcome of this was going to be. 'I don't like all this argument. I don't know . . .'

'There you are, she doesn't want to stay,' Lenora cried. 'We give her a good home and a very generous wage, and she doesn't know whether she wants to stay or not.'

'She's been here for fifteen years,' Olivia pointed out.

Lenora's heaving chest flashed with diamond fire. 'You're an ungrateful little baggage, Harriet. I'll certainly be glad to see the back of you.'

'Ungrateful? Me ungrateful?' Hattie crashed the serving spoon down in the dish. Fury overtook her. She was so livid, that for once she lost all her inhibitions and spoke out.

'You cheated my father out of his business. Am I supposed to be grateful for that? It's no secret in this family. Your husband says so.'

Everybody but Stanley had long since given up eating. 'Your son says so . . .'

'Tom? He wouldn't say any such thing.'

'He is, believe me. He's apologising to Maggie for what you did. Your family all know what you're like. You became rich on what you took from my father.'

'You have no proof of that.'

'There's proof enough for me. And I know you bent the circumstances to make Burney's fall into your lap, and Fevers and Jones. I want recompense for my father, and I'll not let this rest until I get it. I'll let everybody know how you operate. Trumpet it from the rooftops if I have to.'

She stopped, out of breath. She'd thought Lenora held the position of power in this family – she'd seen her trying to manipulate others over the years – but Olivia had not pleaded for her to stay; she'd countermanded Lenora's order.

Hattie was paid to wait on Olivia, pick up their dirty clothes, answer the door, serve their meals, and write and post their letters. Yet if she could make Lenora pay Pa back, she'd have achieved power in her own right.

Lenora was staring up at her. 'You've grown too big for your boots. Pack your bags and get out.'

Hattie stood her ground. She took a deep breath. 'I'm staying. And you're going to give Knell's Gloves back to its rightful owner. I'm going to make you.'

She couldn't believe it of herself. She'd never, ever demanded anything. It wasn't her way. She was the sort who grumbled behind peoples' backs but hadn't the courage to face a confrontation. It was only Lenora's thunderstruck face that made her realise what she'd done now. She could feel the blood coursing through her, she was excited that she'd taken this huge step towards getting what she wanted.

'More carrots, please, Harriet.' Stanley held out his hand for the dish. 'That's settled then. Like it or lump it, Lenora. I think we're both here to stay.'

'Do your damnedest,' Lenora spat out. 'Both of you do your damnedest. You haven't an atom of proof. I'm not giving an inch.'

Stanley went to his study and slammed the door, then poured himself a stiff brandy and sat down in his armchair to think. Lenora had accused him of being the father of

303

Harriet's child, and for once he was innocent. He'd got the message, though: the child that Maggie and Tom were bringing up was not their own.

There was a tap on his door and Harriet came in with his coffee.

'Is it true?' he asked. 'That baby at Tom's house? If it isn't Maggie's, it must be yours.'

Harriet usually looked as though butter wouldn't melt in her mouth. He wouldn't have believed she'd be able to deceive him, but she had. She was looking as guilty as hell now.

'You cheated on me.'

He'd never seen her so put out. She didn't know where to look now, didn't know how to take him. She was jumpy. Keeping a low profile suited her better.

'I just had to. I couldn't bear to walk away from Rebecca. Give her up to strangers. Never see or hear of her again.'

Her green eyes were anguished, almost tearful. He'd been about to put the boot in, but her expression made him soften his approach.

'You've caused a bit of trouble, Harriet. Almost got us both thrown out of here.'

'I'm sorry. Olivia got it wrong. But you could have told them Luke was the father. That's all you had to do. Lenora was upset because she thought you were.'

'It was supposed to be a secret.'

'Does it matter after all this time? If Lenora knew the truth, she'd have no reason to want you to leave. You might even have persuaded her to invest more money.'

Stanley was running his fingers through his whiskers. His smile was wry. 'Too late for that now.'

'Luke was her favourite. She'd not think ill of him for what he did.'

'No.'

'She might think more highly of Rebecca if she knew she was Luke's child. Perhaps even more highly of me.'

Stanley sipped his coffee. 'We've played our cards wrong, Harriet. Tom gave me to understand that Rebecca was his child, and while I believed him, Lenora had reason not to.'

'You can tell her the truth now.'

'After she's told me to get out? I wouldn't give her the satisfaction. She idolises Luke. And you know what she's like when it comes to the blood line. It would be giving her another heir. A prize beyond pearls.

'So we'll keep her in ignorance. And don't you tell Olivia. That's like putting a loudspeaker on the roof.'

He chuckled. 'You delivered quite a kick. Off your own bat too.' It had surprised him. The girl was more devious than he'd thought.

She said: 'I'm no nearer getting what I asked for. I haven't achieved anything, have I?'

'What you've achieved is to break down Lenora's state of armed neutrality. It's open warfare from now on.'

Her big green eyes shot to meet his nervously, then equally quickly darted away again. 'Will she make us leave?'

'I can handle her, Harriet. I know too much.'

'But what about me?'

'You'll be all right. Olivia will make sure you weather this.'

She was backing towards the door, wanting to get away from him now. He watched her go, the girl had more guts than he'd thought.

A row with Lenora always churned him up. Especially one so public as this had been. Theirs had not been a marriage made in heaven. Lenora thought she'd bought him lock, stock and barrel, but he'd proved to be no bargain.

'I should have known better,' she'd said to him more than once. 'I thought you were just a cutter.'

'A good tradesman,' he said. He'd been one of her

employees in the blouse factory when she'd picked him out. He'd been working long enough to know that the wages paid to a tradesman would never provide comfort, however good he was, whoever he worked for.

He didn't like being at the beck and call of two women either, and it hadn't taken him long to start looking round other workshops, hoping to better himself. Of the two, he found Olivia easier to get on with. Lenora was only four years older than he was, and at twenty-nine was tough and brash and inclined to throw her weight about. She had somewhat gingery hair and a big bosom, and she drove all their employees hard.

He thought Lenora had the world at her feet, because her mother owned and ran a prosperous business. What he hadn't realised was that Lenora wanted a husband and a family. She'd kept him working late one evening and faced him across the cutting table.

'Queen Victoria had to propose to Prince Albert, so there's no reason why I can't ask you,' she'd said. 'I want a big family like she had so I can hand this business on.'

Never had Stanley been taken more by surprise. Nothing in the way she treated him had led him to expect this, but he didn't think twice about it. Opportunities such as this only came once in a lifetime.

He'd been living at home, sharing a poky room with four brothers and not getting on with them. It hadn't been too crowded because two of them worked on permanent night shift. It just meant that the bed never had a chance to cool down.

The Clarks had brought him here to this most comfortable house. He still thought it a grand place with all these rooms; he felt he'd fallen on his feet. He had wonderful meals cooked for him, and the garden was kept neat and tidy for his pleasure.

He understood very soon that he was here for Lenora's pleasure. She dictated every facet of his life. She told him exactly what he must do, both at work and at home. She chose his clothes for him. He felt bought, but happy with his side of the bargain – at least to start with.

He soon discovered why she'd had to turn to an employee when she wanted a husband. She'd had no social life at all. She and her mother did nothing but work. The whole point of their lives was to work hard and save as much money as they could. They were not free spenders, either of them. More the hoarding type. They treated themselves to gold bracelets and diamond rings just so they could show everybody else how much richer they were.

The first problem that surfaced after the early months was that he was allowed only limited access to Lenora's bed. There had been an obvious answer, and he'd gone ahead and found himself a lady friend. Alice had worked for them too at the beginning; she was a seamstress and a whole lot more fun than Lenora. He'd always had to watch his manners with her.

Alice had told him that there was something of a mystery about Osbert Clark, the founder of their business. That he'd disappeared whilst on a holiday in Ireland. Nobody knew why he didn't come back to his family and his thriving business. It didn't make sense to anybody that he should turn his back on a nice little earner.

Stanley had become very curious indeed about Osbert's disappearance. Olivia, who was given to verbal diarrhoea on most subjects, wouldn't let a word about Osbert come from her lips.

Then he found that Lenora wasn't always strictly honest in her business methods. She was expanding fast. As far as he was concerned, the faster the better. There was nothing he could have done to persuade her otherwise, and he had no intention of cutting himself off from her money.

It hadn't all been bad, of course. They'd had four children. They both dearly loved Sophie, their first-born and the only girl. Lenora's greatest delight had been to bring her up as a lady. The boys? He'd felt very close to them too, especially Tom. Lenora's whole life was aimed at bringing them all into the business.

'It's a family business in the true sense of the word,' she'd said. 'We can expand it to support us all.' Support them all in luxury was what she meant.

It hadn't worked out that way. The war had wrought havoc on those plans. Her sons had been Lenora's pride and joy; he didn't think she'd ever get over the double loss.

He still felt raw himself that Luke and Eric were no more. War was such a terrible and pointless waste. He was well aware that though they'd died like heroes, they certainly hadn't lived like them. Luke and Eric had picked up the worst traits from both sides. Both would do anything for money, and women were not safe near them. Tom was always more idealistic, but Lenora had discounted him ever since he married against her wishes and turned his back on her business.

Stanley got to his feet to pour himself some more brandy, and decided to go in search of the newspaper he'd been reading before dinner. Lenora was striding up and down the drawing room, fulminating.

'Aren't you packing, Stanley? I meant what I said. Get yourself out of here and don't ever come near me again.'

'Don't start that again.'

'You've had a good innings. You'll get nothing more from me. I'm calling your bluff. Do whatever you want, you can't harm me. There's no law against buying bankrupt businesses.'

'I won't let you cut me off without a penny.'

'You can't stop me.'

'I think I can make you change your mind,' he said angrily, tossing the newspaper aside. But he'd need to rethink his position after this. Decide what he really wanted before he made his next move. He'd have to go out.

Harriet's head was spinning as she helped Olivia to undress. She couldn't believe she'd stood up to Lenora and demanded that she should hand Knell's Gloves back to Pa.

'She won't do that,' Olivia said as she helped her into bed. 'Stanley's turned it round, it's very profitable. She's far too fond of it now. So is Stanley. They won't let it go.'

Hattie was already having second thoughts, even if Lenora did give the business back. She was worried that Pa wouldn't be able to cope with it after all these years. He'd been out of the trade, and no doubt there'd been many changes. She didn't know how good a businessman he'd been in the first place, and it wouldn't do his confidence any good if he let a profitable business go bankrupt a second time.

'Would she give my father cash in lieu?'

Olivia laughed. 'You'll be lucky to get Lenora to part with anything.'

'I will.' Hattie felt very determined about that. She hadn't come this far to give up now. 'It's for my father. Losing his business ruined his life, and it wasn't his fault. I've got to do what I can for him.'

'Well, I do see that,' Olivia said slowly. 'Right is on your side, but Lenora won't look at it that way.'

Hattie was in the kitchen, warming some milk for Olivia's nightcap, when she heard Stanley let himself in through the front door and go to the drawing room.

A moment or two later, she heard the most awful scream. It went on and on, sounding like an animal caught in a trap. It took a few seconds before she realised it was Lenora who was making the noise. She went rushing to the drawing room, expecting to find she'd had some terrible accident.

She was cowering back in an armchair, hiding her face

309

in its velvet cushions. Stanley was standing triumphantly over something wrapped up in a cloth. He was swinging a handsome half-hunter pocket watch on a gold chain. There was menace in his voice.

'You didn't believe me, did you, Lenora? You called my bluff. All right, so I'm showing my hand. You recognise Osbert's watch, don't you?'

She lifted her head to glower at him.

'I've all the proof needed. A word or two in the right place and I could start an investigation that would have you hanged.'

Harriet was transfixed by the bundle on the carpet. She recognised the pale cambric cotton; it was typical of that used to make Clark's blouses.

'What's in it?' she asked, coming forward to lift one corner.

'Don't touch,' Lenora screamed. 'Leave it alone.'

'Come on,' Stanley said. 'Let's all have another look, shall we? Not only his watch, but Osbert himself.'

Lenora looked distraught. 'How did you find . . .'

'You thought you'd hidden him safely. Out of sight and out of mind. How many years since, Lenora?'

Her tongue moistened her lips.

Stanley went on: 'I was trying to work at that desk built into the corner of your workroom. I found it uncomfortable. There wasn't enough room for my legs, because the knee-hole didn't go far enough back.

'When I complained about it, you said it was big enough for you and your mother, but you'd already told me that Osbert had designed that space for himself.

'I rested my feet against the bricks, Lenora. Didn't you see me do that often? I got into the habit of leaning back when I had something to think about, balancing the chair on its back legs with my feet against the brick wall. It used to annoy you no end when you saw me do it.

'"Stop that," you'd say fiercely, and jerk my chair forward.

'One afternoon, when you'd gone down to Burney's, I felt a brick move. I'd loosened it, and I got to thinking, what is the wall there for? Clearly a space had been bricked off, so I pushed the loose brick in and had a look.'

Lenora looked horror-struck. 'Did any of the girls see you?'

'Yes, they saw me on my hands and knees loosening more of the bricks and taking them out. They asked: "What's under your desk, Mr Dransfield?"

'"I can see bones here," I told them.'

Harriet was spellbound. Stanley's pale eyes met hers.

'My first thought was how disgusting that somebody should brick a dog up in that space.

'The girls thought I was joking and had a good laugh. One said she'd lost a terrier called Fido. And another that she'd heard the poor thing trying to burrow its way out under the floor.

'Then I realised it wasn't a dog at all. Much worse . . . I got up and slid back on to the chair, Lenora, feeling sick, because the penny was beginning to drop. Poor old Osbert never did get to Ireland for his holiday, did he? I knew I'd have to wait until they'd all gone home and I had the place to myself.'

Hattie could feel the hairs on the back of her neck lifting. She shivered and risked a glance at the pieces of bone showing through the cloth. She felt sick.

Stanley went on: 'Then I exhumed him. Poor old Osbert, he had a fractured skull. Nobody will mistake the cause of death. My first thought was to take the bones on the late-night ferry when there was an ebb tide and drop them in the river.

'But then I thought again. If this is what you Clarks do to your husbands when you get tired of them, I

311

thought, I'd better be careful. I didn't want to end up the same way.

'I decided I'd keep Osbert, Lenora. I thought, if you ever turned really nasty, he might give me some bargaining power.'

Her teeth were showing in a desperate grimace, the light catching her gold fillings.

'I reckon that moment has come. So here's my proposition. You want me out of this house, so yes, I'll go. I couldn't very well stay after this, could I? I'll go to my fancy woman, as you suggest, but I'm not going empty-handed. I want Knell's Gloves made over to me.'

Harriet gasped: 'But I want . . .'

'Me first, Harriet. I've been running Knell's for years and I've got attached to it. I want the cash to expand too, Lenora, as we discussed earlier.'

Hattie felt light-headed, but she knew she'd have to speak up quickly or she'd come out of this with nothing.

'If my father is not to have his business, then I must insist on money. A sum equal to what you paid for it.'

'Don't be ridiculous. I can't.' Lenora was shocked. 'I don't have that sort of money. Not to pay both of you.'

Hattie straightened her lips. 'That's little enough for what you did to my father.'

Stanley chortled. 'Right, Lenora, now you know what we want. See your solicitor tomorrow. In fact, I'll come with you to make sure he understands my terms.' Lenora was staring at him, white-faced. 'And when I get what I want . . .'

'What about me?' Harriet put in angrily.

'When we both get what we want, I'll let you have Osbert here, to dispose of as you think fit. In the meantime, I'll look after him, to make sure you don't change your mind.

'Look on the bright side, Lenora. You'll be able to sell the old sail loft now and find more suitable premises.'

By the time Harriet took Olivia's hot milk up to her, Lenora was sitting on her bed, pouring out the story. Her face twisting with rage and wet with tears, she looked beaten. Hattie thought she'd never be in awe of her again, and felt a wave of satisfaction. She'd finally achieved what she'd set out to do all those years ago.

# CHAPTER SEVENTEEN

Harriet felt things began to change rapidly at Ottershaw House after that. The next morning, she helped Olivia to dress and put her to sit in a chair while she made her bed.

She knew the old lady was upset; she was silent and there was a forlorn look about her. When she did speak she was quite aggressive.

'I hope you realise what you've done? Lenora's really taken against you now.'

Hattie tucked in the bottom sheet. 'It's what you did! What made you tell her about . . . my trouble? After all this time. I thought that was behind me, that you'd forgotten . . .'

Olivia looked contrite. 'I didn't mean to, it just came out.'

'You're a gossip and you don't watch your tongue. You said you wouldn't tell anybody.'

For her own part, Hattie felt she'd had enough. If she could get Lenora to repay Pa, she'd want to go. It wouldn't be comfortable for either of them after that.

'She's been on at me again to sack you. Says she wants you out of the house.'

'I'm not surprised.'

'Don't worry, I told her she'll have to put up with you because I can't manage otherwise. You won't let her freeze you out, will you, Harriet?'

The old lady looked so pathetic that Hattie said: 'I suppose . . . If you want me to stay . . .'

'I do, you know I do.'

She sighed. 'All right.'

'I don't have to worry? You won't abandon me? Promise you won't?'

Hattie hugged the pillow to her with the clean pillow slip only half on. She knew that Olivia needed her help and appreciated what she did. She felt too involved with her after all this time to turn her back on her.

'I shouldn't have told Lenora. I'm sorry . . .'

'I'll stay as long as you need me.'

'You promise? It might mean staying a long time.'

'Yes, I promise.'

'Good, good.'

When Hattie had finished making her bed, Olivia said slowly: 'I want you to arrange a little outing for us. Phone my solicitor and make an appointment. If he asks, I want him to draw up a new will for me. Tomorrow, if possible, in the afternoon, when Lenora's out. Don't say anything to her about this.'

'Of course I won't.'

Hattie always enjoyed Olivia's little trips out. She ordered a car to collect them.

Mr Maxwell was watching from his office window and came to the front door himself to take Mrs Clark's other arm to help her to his office. As soon as she was settled on a chair, she turned to Hattie:

'I want you to take yourself to the waiting room while I give Mr Maxwell my instructions. Drawing up a will is a private matter.'

Hattie smiled. It was very rare for the old lady to send her away. Clearly, Olivia didn't want her to know who she was leaving her money to. She guessed that sooner or later she'd tell her.

'Not all to Lenora,' she said in the car on the way home. 'She can more than look after herself. There are others more in need.'

316

'Of course. You have grandchildren and great-grandchildren to think of.'

She hoped Tom would benefit – it would make a big difference to Maggie and Becky if he did – but she couldn't ask about that.

A week later, they went to see Mr Maxwell again so that Olivia might sign her new will. When she came out of his office she said to Harriet: 'Lenora and Stanley have been in to see him. He's preparing the documents, so it looks as though you'll both get what you want.'

They took a drive out to Parkgate and had tea at the Boathouse Café before going back home. Hattie saw Stanley as something of an ally now. She knew he was systematically packing up his belongings. Crates and boxes were building up in his study.

'Give it another ten days or so,' he told her. 'It's coming.'

Two weeks later, Stanley took her to see his own solicitor, who, he said, was acting for them both. They both signed documents for the property and money that Lenora was making over to them.

As they came out into Hamilton Square in the afternoon sunshine, he was chortling. 'I've beaten Lenora this time.'

Hattie shivered. 'It was horrible, what you did. It gave me nightmares, thinking about Osbert's bones.'

He laughed. 'Sheep's bones, picked clean by the crows in a field. That's all that I had in my bundle, Harriet. Bet the sheep died of natural causes, too.'

Hattie tried to equate that with the menace she'd felt that night. 'Lenora was terrified.'

'I frightened her into it. It's surprising how guilt can colour the imagination. Lenora couldn't bear to take a proper look. Didn't question what I said. That's a guilty conscience for you.'

'Those bones really weren't – Osbert's?'

He shook his head. 'Just bleached bones from an old ewe. When I saw them in a field, I thought I might just be able to trick her. By then I'd discovered how badly I might need the upper hand.'

Harriet dabbed at her nose with her handkerchief. She felt queasy. She could smell camphorated oil on her hands. 'What happened to Osbert's remains?'

He laughed. 'I found him all right, poor devil. He gave me the creeps, I can tell you. I dumped him in the middle of the Mersey as fast as I could. Couldn't stop shaking until I'd got rid of him. I wanted to protect Lenora and my new lifestyle then. I didn't stop to think, and I should have done. He was my strongest card and I didn't have the stomach to hang on to him.'

'But you didn't tell her at the time? That you'd dealt with Osbert? After all, you were making things safer for her.'

'She'd never confided in me. Never mentioned Osbert.'

'Even so, I'd have thought you'd have wanted to tell her. It would have pleased her, wouldn't it?'

'No, I almost bungled it. A sailor on watch on the bridge saw Osbert pitch into the river and thought he saw a man go overboard. The ferry stopped and circled back to try and pick him up. I was in a terrible state, I can tell you. There was moonlight and I could see him bobbing on the tide.

'There were hardly any passengers on the boat – it was the last of the night from the Pierhead – but they were all crowding the rail, keeping their eyes skinned for him.

'I knew I should have weighted him down with bricks but I felt quite conspicuous carrying him. He was surprisingly bulky. Lucky for me the tide was on the ebb and there was a sixteen-knot current running. I'd expected that to sweep him out to sea. They didn't manage to retrieve him but it was reported in the newspapers as a possible drowning. I couldn't say anything to Lenora after that.

'I was panic-stricken for weeks. Worried he'd be washed up on a beach somewhere. Afraid he'd be identified from his clothes. His skull was obviously fractured: his death could be seen as nothing less than murder. I'd kept his watch, thought it a waste to throw that in the Mersey too, but then I had to hide it. I was terrified somebody would recognise it. I thought it wiser to say nothing. Didn't want to panic her too.'

As she went into town to open a bank account in her father's name, Hattie couldn't get Stanley's audacity out of her mind. Or the dreadful picture of Osbert's bones being thrown into the river at midnight.

It took away some of the triumph she wanted to feel, that she'd succeeded at last in getting back what Lenora owed Pa. When she arrived back at Ottershaw House, she told Olivia that she'd received the money for her father, but was very careful to say nothing about Osbert or sheep bones. She was afraid that if she did, sooner or later Olivia would tell Lenora, and it would give her another reason to hate her and Stanley.

That evening, Olivia was working out the current value of her investments.

'I was very lucky,' she chortled in self-congratulation to Hattie. 'I weathered the nineteen twenty-nine stock market crash very well.'

Hattie knew that in the weeks before it, Olivia had been tidying up her portfolio. Selling off several holdings that she thought had reached their full potential, and getting rid of holdings she considered too small. So she was liquid when the crash came, and had been able to reinvest her money at the very bottom of the market.

Hattie was looking up the share prices in the newspaper for her when Olivia stopped to think for a moment.

'Do you want any help? To invest the money sensibly for your father? He'll want to live on the interest, won't he?'

'Invest in shares, you mean?'

'Of course in shares. Nothing else will do so well

319

for him in the long term. I'll help you pick out some good ones.'

Hattie smiled. 'I was going to ask you if you would. Pa's going to need help, but I thought I'd have a word with him first. He isn't the sort to be sensible with money.'

'Prices are still down on what they were in the late twenties. Bargains to be had. I'll put my mind to it right away.'

The next day, Hattie rushed home to see Pa as soon as she had Olivia settled for her nap after lunch.

The front door of his house was wide open, even though the day had turned chilly. Two people Hattie didn't know were coming through the lobby door with its stained glass in vivid reds and blues. She'd known the hall and stairs to seem as busy as Hamilton Square station, with people coming and going.

The kitchen at Elizabeth Place was chaotic. The sink had started to leak, and Pa was mopping water from the floor and looking for a bucket small enough to fit under the trap to stop more water dripping out.

'Hello, Hattie.' Her youngest sister, Ruth, was struggling with the ancient Primus they used when the range wasn't lit. She was making scrambled eggs for their lunch. She lived in at the hospital but was home for two weeks' holiday.

Hattie had managed to put Osbert's fate behind her and was excited now that at last Pa had the means to get away from all this.

'I've got some wonderful news for you,' she said when he kissed her.

Neither of them would believe it until she showed them Pa's bank book. Then they were fizzing with excitement too.

'You were always the competent one.' Pa couldn't stop smiling. 'You never give up. Always the strong one, you kept the family together when your mother died.'

'Brought me up, too.' Ruth was starry-eyed as she hugged

her sister. She was the only other Knell with pale fawn hair and green eyes like Hattie's.

'You gave up your own interests for our benefit,' Pa went on, still full of joy. 'I've never told you how much I appreciated that.'

Ruth straightened up from the range, her cheeks scarlet. 'You wanted to be a writer of children's stories, didn't you? I thought they were smashing when I was tiny. Do you remember the one about the hippopotamus?'

'You kept asking for that one. I must have told it fifty times,' Hattie laughed.

'It was better than anything in the storybooks I had. Did you ever write it down?'

'No. Didn't have the energy after we came here.'

'You should have,' Ruth insisted.

Hattie had told herself that many times. She'd even decided she should start now. She had a quiet room to herself at Ottershaw House, but she didn't have much time, and never the energy.

'I should have made sure you had time to yourself,' Pa told her.

'Don't start a guilt trip, Pa. The bad times are over.' Hattie was exhilarated. 'We'll find you a more comfortable house to rent. And somebody to come in to keep the place clean, and cook a meal by the time you get home from work.'

She felt she had her reward in the look of utter relief on her father's face.

'Work? He won't have to work any more,' Ruth chortled. 'You can give up portering, Pa.'

'I don't know – what would I do all day?'

'You and Hattie can enjoy yourselves. You'll both find lots to do. You've always wanted a garden; now you can grow all the flowers you want.'

Hattie found her father's gaze on her. 'And you'll be able to get down to writing your stories at last.'

'Pa, I won't be coming. Not to live with you. Not just yet.'

Her father's beaming smile faded. 'You can't mean to stay on at Ottershaw House after this? With Lenora? She'll go for your throat.'

'I promised Olivia I would.'

'What on earth for? I want you with me. That's half the pleasure.'

Hattie felt a glow that he did, and wished she hadn't committed herself to staying. 'I felt sorry for her, I suppose.'

'You do things for everybody else, Hattie. Never for yourself. It's time you did.'

'I do think of myself.' Hattie's smile was a little wan. Didn't she?

Ruth was dishing up the scrambled eggs. 'I've overcooked them. They'll be rubbery, I'm afraid. All this good news took my mind off them. I'm glad I'm home now. I'll be able to help look for a new house. What sort of place do you want?'

'One with plenty of space.' Hattie had already eaten, and now she busied herself making tea for them all. 'It's what's lacking here.'

Henry said: 'Space? I know Enid is still living here, but she's planning to get married soon. Then there'll only be me.'

'You need a big house,' Ruth told him. 'What about me and Clara? We come and go from the hospital, and we think of this as home.'

'So do I,' Hattie said. 'You need at least four bedrooms so we can all stay in comfort.'

'Well, let's start looking straight away.'

'I can come with you to the estate agent,' Hattie said, 'to see what they've got on their books. But then I'll have to get back to Olivia.'

'Oh, you!' Ruth was exasperated.

Hattie wasn't able to get away for the next two days, and by the time she went back to Elizabeth Place, Ruth and Pa had found the house they wanted and couldn't wait to take her up on the bus to see it.

'We've taken Maggie and Clara, and Fanny's coming tonight. They all think it's ideal.'

'It's in Oxton,' Pa told her. 'Fairview Road, a very nice part. Sort of cottage proportions, quite old. Four big bedrooms and a boxroom. Too big, really, just for me.'

'It isn't,' Ruth said quickly. 'You can afford it and you said you liked it. You'll be able to spread out the furniture you have here. Oh, and it's got a lovely garden, Hattie.'

Hattie felt exultant when she saw it. 'I love it.' The rooms were light and bright, the very opposite to Elizabeth Place. It was quite high up, with a view over the roofs of the houses and gardens below, and the air was fresh and clean.

They went from room to room trying to decide which of Pa's possessions would suit it best. He began to measure up the windows for curtains.

'You must see the garden,' Ruth said, unlocking the French doors and leading the way outside. 'It'll be Pa's pride and joy.'

Hattie followed her down the path. It had lots of tall trees and mature shrubs, but the hedge had been well trimmed on one side, and she could see a man working over an easel he'd set up on his lawn.

'The next-door neighbour,' Ruth said softly. 'He introduced himself when we came with Clara yesterday. He's an artist and lives there alone. Just the sort to appeal to Pa. With a bit of luck, he'll make a friend of him.'

'Hello again,' Ruth called over the hedge. 'We've definitely decided to take the lease on this house. My big sister here likes it too.'

The man got to his feet and came over. Hattie knew

323

Pa would think his dark hair rather too long. It was on his collar, and it made him look artistic. His gentle eyes smiled at her. 'Another sister to introduce?'

'This is Harriet, our eldest.'

'Jim Temple,' he said, clasping Hattie's hand firmly. 'Your father's a lucky fellow. How many daughters does this make?'

'There's six of us.' Hattie smiled. 'But we won't all be moving in here with him.'

'What a pity. I've never seen so many handsome young ladies.'

'Jim does pen-and-ink drawings for magazines,' Ruth told her. 'Are you working on one now?'

'Yes, for the *Bystander*. I'd better get back to it. They're in a hurry for it.'

'He's nice, isn't he?' Ruth asked as they went back indoors.

'Yes, but he's a good bit younger than Pa. Do you really think he'll want to be friends with him?'

The more she saw of Pa's new house, the more sorry Hattie felt that she wouldn't be moving in with him the following week.

Harriet found there were big changes at Ottershaw House too. Sophie had been visiting her mother much more in recent months, and as soon as Stanley moved out, she left her husband and brought her three children to live there permanently.

'Lenora's been begging her to come,' Olivia confided. 'And poor Sophie hasn't been getting on well with her husband.'

Hattie feared it would mean much more work for her, but Sophie brought a full-time cook-general with her – although she didn't live in.

'Sophie needs something to fill her day now,' Olivia said dryly. 'A chip off the old block really, was never that interested in tennis and bridge. For the first time, she's going to work with her mother.

'Lenora's over the moon. She's got what she's always wanted. Not only does she have Sophie to help her, but she's taking her grandchildren into the business. She's got her heirs again.'

Ottershaw seemed more of a family house again, but Lenora didn't soften towards her. Hattie could feel her radiating resentment every time she went near her. She found fault with everything she did.

Olivia complained that the youngsters were noisy, but she liked them to come to her room. Especially Adam, the eldest. He had his father's dark colouring but had inherited the broader Dransfield build.

'He's a lovely boy,' she told Harriet. He came every afternoon as soon as he arrived home, to tell her about his day and eat titbits from her tea tray.

Olivia was becoming increasingly frail. She was now almost seventy and needing more help. She was still interested in everything going on around her and gossiped all she could, but she rarely went out. It surprised Hattie, when she thought about it, to find that it was months since they'd even been to church.

Olivia was having more of her meals in her room, virtually spending her time between her bed and the couch in the turret. The stairs were becoming too much for her.

Harriet, too, gave up eating her meals in the dining room and relinquished many of her housekeeping duties to Sophie's cook-general. The only way she could cope with Lenora's hate was to stay out of her way. She couldn't say she was content to be at Ottershaw House, but she meant to stay for Olivia's sake.

The years seemed to rush by, punctuated by family occasions. Pa was pleased he could afford to give Enid a big wedding when she married a member of the borough council. They had the reception in the new house. Three years before, Fanny had married a butcher with six shops to his name. She had a little boy called Harry and, last month, had given birth to a daughter whom she called Edith, after her mother.

'She seems happily settled,' Pa said contentedly to Hattie. 'I hope Enid will be too.'

Both Clara and Ruth had trained as children's nurses in Alder Hey Hospital in Liverpool, then come back to Birkenhead to the General Hospital for their training. Clara never did what the family expected her to. She'd emigrated to Canada as soon as she was fully qualified. Ruth, in her turn, had decided to stay on as a staff nurse.

Rebecca was growing up, but Hattie saw little of her. Occasionally, when she went to Pa's new house, Maggie and Becky would be there, but otherwise she saw her only at Christmas and birthdays, when the whole family came together.

This wasn't what Harriet had expected when she'd wanted Maggie to adopt Becky, but what had seemed a good idea in theory was not so in practice. Maggie didn't want any input from her; she seemed almost afraid of it. Harriet supposed it was self-defence that made her stay away.

She thought of her daughter a good deal. In her dreams, she saw herself and Becky moving into Pa's house to live with him, but she knew that was pure fantasy.

It was seeing Sophie's children on a daily basis that made her think of her own daughter's future.

Adam was twenty-one and just qualified as an accountant. Lenora took him into the family firm straight away.

Jonathon was presently articled to a firm of accountants but she hoped in due course that he would do the same. Jane was now nineteen and had been at home with her mother since she'd left school. Lenora persuaded her to do a typing course, with a view to joining them in the family business.

'Best thing for her,' Olivia said. 'Bring her up to earn her own living. Better than being dependent on others. We made a mistake bringing Sophie up that way.'

Harriet believed they were right about that. It was what she'd have chosen for Rebecca. She wanted her to have a proper career; one that would give her satisfaction and a salary on which she could live in comfort. She didn't want Becky to find, as she and her sisters had, that marriage was the only possible way out of poverty.

She often went to see Pa. His new house was closer to Ottershaw than Elizabeth Place had been. She could spend an hour or so there any afternoon after she'd settled Olivia down for her nap. If she knew it suited his shift, she sometimes went in time to have her lunch with him.

His house seemed peaceful. It was kept neat and tidy, and she found herself looking forward more and more to the time when she could go and live there too. Pa never stopped trying to persuade her to join him.

Every so often, he would open up the *Radio Times* and show her a pen-and-ink drawing that was signed with the name Jim Temple. Pa was friendly with his next-door neighbour and said he enjoyed his company. Hattie had found them having a drink together once or twice when she'd come round in the evening.

Pa was thrilled with his new house. All his daughters came and went regularly – even Clara had been back from Canada for a holiday. About Maggie, he seemed less happy. He'd always worried more about her than the others, and, of course, Tom was becoming an invalid.

Hattie grilled him about Rebecca because he saw a good deal of her. She heard she'd left school and was taking a typing course, but he didn't know what her plans were for the future. He said she was doing more at the cinema because of Tom's failing health. She knew Pa was growing more concerned about the three of them.

\* \* \*

327

On her day off Harriet sometimes took a trip into town. She had money now to buy clothes when she needed them, but she'd taken less interest in fashion as the years rolled on. She went out so rarely that it hardly seemed worthwhile. She usually took afternoon tea in a tea shop.

After one of these expeditions, she was heading for the underground to go back across the river when she saw Stanley buying a paper from a news vendor outside Central Station.

'Hello, Harriet. How are you?'

It was a few years since she'd seen him, and his hair had turned white. Even his mutton-chop whiskers had grown thin and wispy.

He asked after Sophie and her children, and she told him that Adam had started in the blouse factory, which Lenora had moved to more suitable premises.

On the spur of the moment she asked him if he'd take Rebecca into his glove factory, then wondered if she'd asked too much.

'But perhaps you have sons of your own that you want . . .'

He smiled. 'The eldest has decided against gloves. He's in the navy. I think the other's going to follow him.'

'Then would you be prepared to take Rebecca?'

'How old is she?'

'Fifteen – almost sixteen now.'

'Perhaps a typing course first?'

'She's doing one this year, but I don't want her just to be a typist. I want her to progress up the ladder.'

'I know what you want, Harriet. And she's Luke's daughter. I'll give her every chance if she wants to come.'

Hattie felt warm with satisfaction as she caught the train back to Birkenhead Park and went straight round to see Maggie. She felt she'd opened up a good opportunity for her daughter, and surely, after having so little contact over the last decade, Maggie wouldn't feel she was interfering.

328

Maggie put a finger to her lips as she opened the front door to her. 'Tom's in bed,' she whispered. 'He's not very well.'

It was several months since she'd seen Maggie, and now she looked pale and drawn and a little unkempt. For the first time, Hattie could see fine lines round her sister's eyes. Harriet followed her into the kitchen, where Maggie put the kettle on for tea. She was telling her about Stanley's offer before she'd even taken off her hat.

Maggie swung round from the stove belligerently. 'Becky won't want to work for him! Whatever made you think she would?' Her brows were tight with anger.

'It's a good opportunity.'

'She wants to run the Picturedrome.'

Hattie tried to explain about the career Becky could have. That it was a chance that shouldn't be turned down, at least not without a good deal of thought; that Stanley seemed only too pleased to help Luke's child.

'Luke's child! She's ours.'

'I meant he sees her as family.' Harriet tried to placate her. 'Pa said Tom didn't want to take her into his cinema.'

'He wanted her to learn to type.'

'Stanley thought that was the best thing, before she went into . . .'

'You've no business to go asking him. You know nothing about her.'

Hattie was appalled. 'Maggie! I just want the best for her. I want to help.'

'I wish you wouldn't. You agreed to give her up. We adopted her, it's no good wanting her back now.'

Harriet felt that like a stab through the heart, and opened her mouth to deny it, but it came to her that really, it was true. 'I'm sorry,' she said lamely.

It wasn't like Maggie to get het-up like this. She was slopping tea into the saucers.

329

'Is something the matter? Something else?'

'Becky's the only one I can count on now.'

Hattie didn't understand that. 'She's at typing school?'

'No, at the cinema, there's a matinée. She'll be back soon.' The yard door slammed. 'Here she is now.'

Harriet was turning to the back door in anticipation.

'Don't say anything to her about this,' Maggie hissed crossly.

When Becky came in, Harriet couldn't take her eyes from her. She found it hard to believe that this beautiful girl was of her flesh and blood.

She had two plaits that hung to her waist, each as thick as a man's fist. It was typical Knell hair, creamy-white and crinkly, but she'd grown it long, and the weight had straightened it out.

'How you've grown, Rebecca.' She seemed to have reached her full height.

'Hello, Aunt Hattie.' She came and planted a cool kiss on her cheek. The Knells always kissed when they met, it was routine. Hattie had to fight the urge to throw her arms round her.

She was saddened as she went back to Ottershaw House, and asked herself if she'd have been happier if she'd let her daughter go to that orphanage. If she'd shut her out of her life completely. She didn't know. Only that having a child in those circumstances had never ceased being hurtful.

It made her think more about Maggie. She'd always been the sister she felt closest to, the one whose company she enjoyed most, even if it had been a love-hate relationship. She tried to tell herself she was pleased that life had given Maggie everything she needed to be happy. But Hattie felt offended because she'd turned down her offer of help, and aflame with jealousy because Maggie had Becky.

She knew that was driving them further and further apart.

*    *    *

330

When Hattie left, Maggie took a cup of tea upstairs for Tom. She felt very low. His illness was overshadowing everything else. She could no longer pretend to herself that he'd ever be really well again, and found it very painful to see him going steadily downhill.

He still had his good days, but they were getting fewer.

Becky had finished her secretarial course, but there could be no question of her getting a job. Hattie had really been jumping the gun there. Tom needed her to run to the picture house for him. These days, Maggie stayed at home with him. She couldn't bear the thought of playing the piano through two performances and leaving him at home by himself. He kept her awake a good deal during that night. His cough was worse and he'd run out of cough mixture.

'I'll go round to the doctor's and get another bottle,' she said the next morning. The doctor made it up himself and charged sixpence. There was a penny discount if you took the empty bottle back.

'Ask him for the green sort,' Tom gasped. 'I'm sure it does more good than the red.'

The doctor was showing out a patient as she went in. 'Come and sit down, Mrs Dransfield,' he said, taking her into his consulting room. 'About his X-ray . . .' Tom had been to the hospital the week before to have one done. 'I've had the report.'

Maggie's heart jerked with apprehension. Something in his manner warned her of bad news.

'How is he this morning?'

'Struggling for breath. He looks blue.'

'You do realise your husband is very ill?'

She nodded, feeling numb.

'I'm afraid the X-ray shows degenerative changes in his lungs, and his heart is enlarged.'

Maggie didn't know what to say. His face was very serious.

'It's my duty to warn you that he won't be able to go on much longer.'

She felt the room begin to spin. 'What do you mean, go on? That he's . . .'

'I'm afraid so, Mrs Dransfield. When he was gassed in the war, it did irreparable damage to his lungs. Now his heart's affected too.'

'There must be something you can do?'

'I'm afraid not.'

For a moment, Maggie thought she was going to be sick. She was rocking herself backwards and forwards in the chair, appalled that she hadn't seen this coming. It had taken her by surprise. She'd grown so used to Tom being ill.

'How long? Before . . . ?' She was tense with horror.

'Another month or two.'

There was to be no treatment. The doctor offered only sympathy. Maggie walked home, feeling shocked and dazed, clutching the bottle of green cough mixture.

# CHAPTER EIGHTEEN

Becky Dransfield was coming home from Grandpa's house with a big bag of marrow bones. Her Auntie Ruth, who was a nurse, had recommended them to build up Dad's strength, and had given her a recipe for Mam to follow. Aunt Fanny, who was married to a butcher, had provided them. She hurried up the entry behind her home and pushed hard against the door to the back yard. It scraped open.

'Mam! What are you doing out here?'

Maggie was sitting on an upturned bucket behind the door of the shed. Her eyes were red and swollen.

'Can't go in. Can't face your dad.'

'What's happened?'

Mam had clung to her then, letting it all come out. Sobbing that the doctor had told her that Dad would only live for another month or two.

'It could be ages,' Mam wept in rage and grief. 'Who can say it'll only be two months? How can any doctor know exactly how long?'

Becky turned cold with horror.

'He's got to get better,' Mam was insisting. 'We need him, don't we? We love him. We want him here with us.'

It was an age before they felt able to go in and face him. Becky made a pot of tea while her mother bathed her eyes. They told him only half the story, that his heart was enlarged, but neither of them said anything about how much longer he had. Only that he must be strong and fight it.

Becky's comfort came from the help she was able to give him. Recently he'd begun dictating his business letters to her, and she was helping him choose and order the films to be shown. He handwrote little notes of instruction to the staff, which Becky delivered. She brought their replies to his sick bed. There was always one from Hilda, the cashier, giving the number of tickets she'd sold and the amount of takings for every performance. Often there were brochures describing new films which were for hire, and gossip about the projectionist's bad back, and Dolly the senior usherette's husband, who was out of work.

He talked over all his worries with her. 'Look after your mother, Becky,' he said one day. 'She'll need you when I'm no longer here.'

'Dad! You're not going anywhere!'

He was overtaken by a fit of coughing and couldn't get his breath. 'Hate the thought of leaving you and Mam.'

'You've got to fight it, Dad. You're strong.' But Becky knew he was no longer as strong as he had been.

'He's been a good husband, and a good father to you,' Mam told her.

'A very good father.'

Becky loved Tom wholeheartedly. But sometimes she had to swallow back a niggling doubt about whether he'd been a good and faithful husband.

She knew that Gloria Golding, the pianist at the cinema, had written frequent notes to him, and unlike Hilda, she had no business reason to do so. Dad always read them and then immediately tore them to shreds, so nobody else could. Occasionally, he wrote back to her.

If Becky went to the cinema at a time when Gloria wasn't playing, she'd always make a point of quizzing her about him. Had he slept well? Eaten his meals? Was he feeling a little better today?

The cinema staff considered Gloria a bit of a joke. So

Becky had thought little of it until Dad had pulled himself painfully up the bed to clutch her hand.

'Don't tell your mother,' he'd pleaded. 'It'll upset her. Don't ever let her know. Promise, Becky, please.'

Mam was the sort of person everybody tried to protect from the harsher things in life. She seemed less able to take knocks than the rest of them.

'You know what Gloria's like.'

'Overflowing with affection?' Becky always received a rib-crushing hug from her when they met, and usually a kiss on each cheek too.

'Can be a bit of a nuisance.' But Becky had seen her follow her father round with sheep's eyes. She didn't do that to everybody.

'She's a good cinema pianist or I'd ask her to go. That's all there is to it as far as I'm concerned.'

Becky had promised, because the last thing she wanted was to give her mother more hurt. She couldn't breathe a word about it. It would upset Mam even more.

It was Thursday afternoon, and Becky had spent most of it in the Picturedrome, working through the list of jobs her father had given her.

She felt as much at home here as she did in Lowther Street. As a baby, she'd been brought here in her cradle every night. She'd been put down to sleep in the projection room while her mother played the piano throughout the performance. George, the projectionist, had children of his own and had offered to keep an eye on her.

It was part of family folklore that one night she'd had colic and George had had trouble rewinding a film. Mam had heard her cries from the front of the auditorium, so after that, she'd been left in Dad's office. If Dad was busy elsewhere, the usherettes kept an eye on her.

It was only when she outgrew her cradle and could not be guaranteed to sleep that Mam had given up playing and

335

stayed home with her for a time. As soon as she was old enough to sit quietly through the show, Mam brought her regularly so that she could play the accompaniment again. This picture house was her life.

Becky went to see George in the projection room, where the fug of cigarette smoke was at its thickest. Dad had found it affected his breathing and had rarely come in recent years. Becky liked coming. She found the buzz of the projector soothing; it reassured her to look down the beam to the changing images on the screen and see everything functioning smoothly.

George was middle-aged, with a greyish tone to his skin that made him look as though he never left the semi-darkness of the cinema. He'd worked here so long, he almost seemed like one of the family.

She brought with her a catalogue of films for hire that had come in the post.

'I'll need to order more.'

She was leafing through it. Greta Garbo's *Anna Christie* headed the list, but it was one of the first talkies, and they didn't have the equipment yet to show it at the Picturedrome. The same went for Marlene Dietrich in *Blue Angel* and Eddie Cantor in *Whoopee*.

George said: 'Let's show Charlie Chaplin in *The Circus*. I hear it's smashing. And Buster Keaton, he's dead funny. There's his new one there, *In College*.'

'It's not all that new. Made a couple of years ago.'

Dad had let her choose many of the films they'd shown recently. Mam seemed barely interested, but she'd take this catalogue home and try to involve her.

'Norma Talmadge in *Secrets* and Rudolph Valentino in *Cobra*.' She ticked those two.

'We'll need another serial soon,' George said. 'I think I've three more episodes to run.'

Becky turned over the page. 'There's Tom Tyler in *Phantom of the West* in ten parts. No, no good. That's a talkie too. There was a Pearl White in last month's catalogue, I'd better look it out.'

She found George staring at her. 'Will you be able to keep this place running? Now your dad's so ill – and everything.'

'Yes, of course. Me and Mam will manage all right.'

She left before the end of the matinée, knowing she'd have to come back later in the evening. The rain had been coming down in sheets all day. As she stood on the steps, buttoning up her mackintosh, she wished her father was well enough to do more. She needed his expertise to decide on and install the new sound equipment. She wished she was older and had had more experience.

When she got off the bus and turned into Lowther Street, she pulled up with surprise to find a car parked in front of her home.

Since Tom had been so ill, his own father had been to see him once or twice, but this wasn't his car. As she ran up the back entry and let herself in through the kitchen, she wondered if he'd bought a new one.

Her mother was there, setting a tea tray. She looked harassed as she pushed a cluster of white curls off her forehead.

'Have we got visitors?' Becky shook the raindrops off her hat at the back door.

'Grandpa's brought some people to see your dad.'

A young man came down the hall. He was tall and stripling thin, with dark hair and penetrating eyes. Becky thought him handsome.

'I hope I'm not a nuisance to you, Maggie.'

'Of course not. Tom's feeling better today, he'll enjoy your father's company. He hardly sees anybody these days except us.'

'I'm Adam Moody.' His dark eyes met Becky's. 'I suppose we're cousins?'

'Are we?'

'Yes.' Maggie nodded. 'Adam and his father were having lunch at the Woodside. They met Pa there.'

'I've been up to say hello, but Uncle Tom hasn't seen me since I was a sprog. I don't want to tire him, too many visitors at once. He's more interested in my father.'

Maggie clattered four cups and saucers on to her tray.

'I don't think your mother recognised me.' He smiled at Becky.

'I did. Though you've grown a bit. Grown a lot.' She turned to Becky. 'I used to look after Adam. I was his nanny.'

'Taught me all sorts of nursery rhymes. I missed you when you went.'

'Becky, make another pot of tea for yourself and Adam. There's scones here.'

Maggie lifted the tray and shot off upstairs. Becky felt she was being left to entertain a stranger, though a least she knew who he was now. She started to set another tea tray.

'Mam said you were a lovely little boy. Polite and very good.'

'Oh dear!'

She could see a faint flush running up his cheeks. 'Sorry, not the right thing to say.'

He laughed. 'A bit like seeing photographs of a naked baby being passed round and then finding it's yourself.'

She didn't know what to say next. His face was all angular planes. He stood with his shoulders back, looking confident, as though he had the world at his feet.

He cleared his throat. 'Your mother says you run a cinema? That sounds exciting.'

'It is. I love arranging the programmes.'

'If I came down one evening, would you show me round?'

That made her look at him with fresh eyes. 'Yes, if you'd like to.'

'It sounds much more fun than our blouses and baby

338

clothes. I'm learning to manage those, but I'm not allowed to do much on my own. I do admire you, being able to run a cinema.'

'I've only done that since my father became ill. And he's always here, reminding me what I have to do.'

'This must be awful for you. I know I'd feel dreadful if anything like this happened to my dad.' His voice was soft with sympathy.

What could she say but, 'It is dreadful.'

In a rush of emotion Becky remembered skipping along the pavement, holding tightly on to Dad with one hand and Mam with the other. They used to meet her coming out of school. Between them, they'd given her a secure and happy childhood.

When she was very young, they used to spend many hours together because Tom worked mostly in the evenings. He'd loved her, she had no doubt about that, and he'd been an indulgent father, often bringing home toys or sweets for her, flowers or chocolates for Mam.

There had been regular outings too. For birthday treats, he'd hire a car and drive them into the country for picnics. Becky felt full of love for him.

'It's very hard, seeing him as ill as this. You don't know how lucky you are having a healthy family.'

She was lifting the tray. Adam took it from her and followed her into the living room.

'We're healthy enough, but it doesn't mean we don't have problems.'

Becky poured the tea, wondering if he'd think her nosy if she asked what problems they had. She couldn't do it. 'You're working in the family business, you said?'

He nodded. 'My grandmother's.'

'You don't like it?'

He pulled a wry face. 'She's not an easy person to work for. And baby clothes and women's blouses – not really a man's thing.'

339

'I seem to remember . . . Weren't you articled to a firm of accountants?' She offered him the plate of scones. 'Grandpa told me, I think.'

'Yes, I'm an accountant. It's considered the best training for running a business.'

'But couldn't you do what your father does? Work as an auditor?'

She saw him wince. 'You've touched a raw nerve. My father keeps trying to persuade me to do that. My mother, on the other hand, is convinced I'll be throwing away a wonderful opportunity if I don't set out to run the family business. It's splitting our family in two. There are days when I feel like running away to sea.'

Becky could hear footsteps coming downstairs. His finger came up to rest against his lips for a second. Then Grandpa and Mam were back, and she was being introduced to her Uncle Daniel.

Three nights later, Becky turned into Hind Street to see the arc of bright light spilling out of the Picturedrome on to the pavement. The billboards advertised Douglas Fairbanks in *The Black Pirate*. It had been going the rounds for a year or two but they hadn't shown it here before.

She was thinking about her cousin Adam, and wondering if he really would come round, when a car drove past. In the fleeting second it took, and in the semi-darkness, she thought it could be Adam. She told herself she was letting her imagination run wild. In these streets behind the gasworks, cars were not often seen, but it wasn't the one that had been parked outside on the day he'd come to her home.

The cinema doors were open. Customers were going in. Hilda gave her a wave from behind the pay-box window. Becky ran up to the staff cloakroom to take off her hat and coat. She looked with dissatisfaction at her reflection in the mirror. Her thick plaits looked childish, made her look twelve years of age. She bent one up. She'd like to cut it off at shoulder length, or perhaps shorter still. Loose wisps across her forehead clustered in tight curls. She tried to comb them in and keep them flat.

One of the usherettes came running up. 'There's someone asking for you in the foyer,' she said. 'Looks a bit of all right, too.'

Had she really seen Adam? Her green eyes looked nervous now, and she wished she had a lipstick with her. She went slowly down to see. Under the bright lights Adam looked more attractive than she remembered. More confident too, with his head high and shoulders back.

'Hello, Rebecca.' Only Aunt Hattie and the Dransfields called her that. 'You said if I came you'd show me round. I'm dying to see it all.'

'I'm called Becky,' she said. She liked him, but the Knells thought of this as their cinema, and she was afraid they wouldn't approve of her allowing Adam here. She told herself this was nothing more than the friendly visit he'd asked if he could make.

'This is the entrance hall.'

It was the best thing about the Picturedrome, but that said, it was too small to be called anything as grand as a foyer. Tiles in black and white covered both the floor and the walls to shoulder height. Above the tiles were a series of posters, portraits of famous film stars. She pointed out some of them: Charlie Chaplin, Greta Garbo, Pola Negri, Rudolph Valentino.

Adam had the sort of face that ought to be up there amongst them, all strong planes and angles, yet his eyes were gentle. Becky found it hard not to stare openly at him.

'I can't wait to see it all.' He smiled enthusiastically.

'Have you never been here before?'

He could have come in any time and paid his sixpence. No, he'd have paid ninepence for one of the best seats

341

at the back. She was surprised he hadn't. If her relatives owned a cinema, she'd have been so curious she wouldn't have been able to stay away.

She introduced him to Gloria Golding, who was wearing her dress with the sparkling bugle beads on the bodice. A considerable amount of plump bare bosom showed at the front.

Adam shook her hand. 'What an exotic name. No excuse to forget you.'

Gloria smouldered with sensuality, lifting her face to his. 'My . . . aren't you handsome? I certainly won't forget you either.'

'Now, now, Gloria! Leave the young man alone.' Big Billy, the commissionaire, came over. He wore a maroon uniform with lots of gold braid, and had the shoulders of an ox. 'You're old enough to be his mother.'

'Take no notice, darlin'.' She chucked Adam under his chin. Before gliding off, she swung to Billy. 'Age has nothing to do with it, you big bully.'

'Thinks she's Mae West.' Billy guffawed. Becky had meant to bring a needle and cotton to repair his epaulette. The gold braid was tearing away from one shoulder, and he really needed a new cap. 'Bit over the top for most people.'

'Is she really like that with everybody?' Adam wanted to know as Billy shook his hand.

'Certainly is. We're all terrified of her, but it's just her way, isn't it, Becky?'

'Yes,' she said, but Gloria had been different with Dad. More sincere. She thought it was an act that Gloria put on, pretending to fall for every man she knew, to hide what she felt for Tom. Becky led Adam into the auditorium.

'Not very big,' he said, looking round. The walls had once had windows but they'd been bricked up and the walls distempered all over in cream. Six plain lights swung from the ceiling, that was turning yellow from all the cigarettes that were smoked. There was no ornamentation, no balcony, no boxes, no organ to come out of the floor. Not even any carpet in the sixpennies and threepennies, just plain brown linoleum.

The seats were set out on a flat floor. Once they'd had wooden forms at the front, but Dad had had to put better seats in a few years ago. They were beginning to fill up. Gloria, the pianist, came to take her place at the upright piano, sorting through her sheets of music, seeming to shimmer in the spotlight.

Adam shivered. 'It seems quite cold. How do you heat it?'

Becky shook her head. 'Everybody keeps their coats on.'

He paused. 'Needs quite a lot doing to it, doesn't it? Have you seen the Plaza, just opened in Borough Road?'

Becky hadn't, but she could imagine how much better it was. 'Come upstairs and I'll show you the projection room.'

The staircase was narrow, of bare stone and very steep. They were halfway up when Gloria broke into a vigorous march. The programme was about to begin.

For two more to get into the tiny room was a bit of a squeeze. There was a fug of tobacco smoke, the lights were already dimmed and the projector was buzzing noisily. Becky looked down at the screen advertising Rinso washing powder. She introduced George, only half listening to the conversation.

'Talkies? Haven't seen one yet. Have to spend every night in here. If I had a night off, I wouldn't want to see another picture, not even a talkie.'

'They're wonderful, so true to life.'

For her own part, Becky wished they hadn't been invented. They were causing terrible complications, but she read every word about them that came her way.

Adam said: 'They say all pictures will be talkies in a few years.'

'I don't know,' Becky said. 'Charlie Chaplin doesn't think so.'

'He started shooting *City Lights* as a silent but he's changed his mind,' George said. 'I read all about it.'

'They say talkies are a shot in the arm to the cinema industry.'

George laughed and lit another cigarette. 'Couldn't run them here. Not till we get the right equipment. It's not all that long since we got our second projector. Before that, the audience had to wait while I rewound the film and changed the reel.'

'Are you going to get the new equipment?' Adam asked.

'Sooner or later, yes, I expect so.'

'I think you'll be forced to,' Adam said slowly. 'Talkies are all the rage, and once all the other cinemas can show them . . .'

Becky knew he was right. Her dad was saying much the same thing. She was seeing the Picturedrome through Adam's eyes, taking his criticisms to heart. He didn't realise how hard it would be.

She took him to the office. He was very interested in how she booked the films, the way they were delivered, and how much it all cost. Even here, she could hear Gloria tinkling away; piano and pianist seemed to pervade the whole building.

'I didn't realise how much went on behind the scenes,' he said as he drank tea with Gloria and George in the interval between first and second house. Once the second house got under way, he followed Becky to the pay box and watched her count the takings for both performances with Hilda. While she was entering the figures in the books, he wandered to the door to the auditorium.

'The big picture's just about to start. Have you seen it?'

She hadn't. She joined him inside the door. 'The place smells nice, doesn't it?'

He wrinkled his nose. 'Not very. In fact, no, I don't like it. It's sort of fusty and airless. Catches in my throat.'

She loved it. The warm fug of scent and Woodbine smoke danced visibly in the projector beam.

He said: 'Will you stay and see the film through with me?'

The thought of sitting next to him in the darkness made shivers run up her spine. His dark eyes were telling her how much he liked her and wanted to be friends. He told her he enjoyed Douglas Fairbanks. For her own part she found Adam a distraction. For once she couldn't concentrate on the film. Her mind was running riot. After Gloria had played 'God Save the King', and the cinema was emptying, she showed him the leather pouches she used to take the money to the bank.

'I drop it in the night safe on the way home.'

'I'll run you home in my car,' he told her. He carried the takings for her. With all the copper the bags were always heavy.

'Is it safe for you to carry it through the streets like this?'

'I always do.'

It had been raining, and the wind was sharp. He led her towards an Austin Seven parked round the corner.

'This isn't the car you came to our house in.'

'That was my father's.'

'This is your own? You are lucky!'

To have a car was everybody's dream and out of the reach of most. Even Dad hadn't achieved that.

'It was a birthday present from my grandmother.'

'Lenora?'

He looked uncomfortable. 'Well, you know what she's like.'

'No.' She got in beside him, pushed her thick ropes of

hair over her shoulders and watched him start the engine. 'What is she like?'

'Obsessed.'

'Really?'

'With the family. She shapes her whole life round us. Refers to us as her blood line. Everything she does is for us. I think she sees us as an extension of herself.'

Becky watched him as he drove. 'Dad did mention something like that once.'

'Uncle Tom blotted his copybook by getting his own cinema. By refusing to work in her business. And Luke and Eric were killed in the war, and Stanley left her. She's lost so many of her heirs, it makes her cling more tightly to us.

'She dotes on Edward, that's Luke's son. She's trying to lure him into blouses too, but he'll go into the dog food business. That's from his mother's side.

'Gran works terribly hard. Her one aim in life is to build up her business so that it'll provide for all our needs. She wants to make each of us rich.'

Becky smiled in the darkness. 'Then you're more than lucky.'

He sighed. 'That's what my mother thinks. She tells us we should be grateful and learn to run Lenora's business. There's only Mum and us three left. Mum isn't happy but feels she can't leave her.

'Dad's trying to persuade us all to go back to live with him. Whatever benefits Lenora is offering us, she's certainly split our family.

'Dad says she's buying us, that's why she's given me this car. He thinks we should learn to stand on our own feet. I'm coming round to the idea that he may be right.'

He stopped outside the bank so that Becky could push the takings into the night safe. She thought this the most exciting part of the evening, and didn't want to leave him now. But she was worried about what her mother was going to say. When he turned into Lowther Street, she stopped him before they'd reached their house.

'Don't want you to wake Dad,' she said. 'He doesn't sleep well, and he keeps Mam awake with his cough.'

She was about to get out when he put a hand on her arm.

'Will you let me take you to the Plaza? It only opened last year, and it's said to be the last word.'

'I'm needed at our own place,' Becky began, but she wanted to see more of him. Wanted to see a really up-to-date cinema too. There had been lots about it in the press when it had opened.

'First house, you could manage that? I'll run you back to the Picturedrome in time to see to anything that's needed. You really ought to see what a modern cinema's like.'

She smiled. 'Mam took me to one, years ago. I don't remember much except there was a lovely organ that came up out of the floor.'

'They all do that now, it's old hat. You come and see the very latest.'

All the next day, Becky couldn't stop thinking of Adam. It was as though he'd lit a fire inside her.


Without saying anything to anybody, the next day Becky went to the best hairdresser in Grange Road.

'You've had your plaits cut off,' was the first thing Adam said when she met him that evening. She could see admiration in his eyes. 'It makes a big difference.'

Instead of being pulled straight by the weight, her hair was now a mass of tight shiny curls.

'My head feels light without them.' She smiled. 'A lovely feeling of freedom. Mam wasn't very pleased, though.'

'I liked them. They made you look like a little girl doing a man's job. Running that cinema and looking about twelve years old. That really impressed me.'

'But you didn't like our cinema?'

347

'It's a bit old-fashioned. Wait till you see the Plaza,' he said. 'You'll see what I mean. I'm told it seats two thousand five hundred.'

That made her gasp. 'Surely they'll never fill all those seats?' But when they'd parked the car and walked back to the entrance, a bus was disgorging passengers to join the crowd thronging the pavement.

Adam had to wait in the line at the pay desk. It gave Becky time to take in the fine walnut panelling in the vestibule. There was a magnificent foyer beyond: over a hundred feet long, with a ceiling that was twenty feet high. She couldn't believe her eyes when she saw the fountain gushing water and the marble staircase at the far end.

'There's another crush hall on the ground floor,' Adam said, 'but we have tickets for the balcony.' On the way he took her to peep into the tea lounge and soda fountain.

'A café inside a cinema? I did read about it when it opened, but seeing it . . .'

'Not just any café.' It was very smart. A high-class place.

Her feet sank into the carpets, and the seats felt like armchairs. The lighting was all concealed.

'They call it golden sunshine lighting,' Adam murmured. 'To prevent the dark cellar feeling.'

The ceiling in the auditorium was of silver leaf and blue paint to simulate the outdoors.

'And it's all heated by hot-water pipes.'

Becky thought it opulent. Beyond anything she'd imagined.

The programme started with an organ recital.

'It's said to be the biggest on Merseyside, and it's been installed with acoustics in mind.'

She knew her mother would love this, knew she'd love to play in a place like this. The show was made up of five short films, a silent Charlie Chaplin film, the Pathé news and a Mickey Mouse cartoon. There were two of the new talkies, the first she'd ever seen. She found them unbelievably realistic. Becky felt it was an entirely new experience.

Afterwards, Adam drove her down to the Picturedrome to count the takings and take them to the night safe. George was in a chatty mood. He said he knew the projectionist at the Plaza and was full of information about the things they hadn't seen.

'They've installed a Western Electric sound system, and they've two talkie and three silent film projectors. And you should see their projection rooms – yes, in the plural – and they have a smoke loft and a special rewinding room.'

'Makes me see the poor old Picturedrome in a different light,' she sighed. She'd known it was shabby and old-fashioned, but seeing the new Plaza drove home how strong the competition was. It surprised her that so many of their clients continued to come.

In Lowther Street, Adam kissed her before she got out of his car. Becky's heart turned over.

'Didn't dare do that before,' he said. 'With those plaits you didn't look old enough.'

'I'm old enough,' she laughed.

'You seem very grown-up for your years. More adult than my sister, though she's older.'

She met him again the following night, and several times the next week. Becky began to think she was a little in love with him.

# CHAPTER NINETEEN

Maggie heard the doorbell ring and watched Becky, with her mouth full of egg, leap up from the table to answer it.

It was Pa's voice she could hear; he sounded upset.

'I've come to fetch your mother. Sister sent me.' His voice dropped. 'Bad news about your father, I'm afraid. You'll have to be brave and help her, Becky. She is in?'

Becky was leading him in. Her face was deathly pale and had lost all its recently acquired maturity. She looked a child again, not a young lady of sixteen.

Maggie put down her knife and fork and pulled herself to her feet. She felt overwhelmed by what was happening to Tom.

'Hello, Pa. It's visiting this afternoon, we were just having something to eat before setting off. Do you want a cup of tea?'

He bent to peck her cheek. 'You heard me then? No, we'd better go straight away.'

'Sister promised she'd let us know in plenty of time if . . .' Butterflies were fluttering in her stomach. 'If there was any change. She wouldn't let me stay with him. Said he'd rest better if I didn't.'

'Yes, well, the time is now. Maggie love, Tom's failing fast.' Pa gathered them both into his arms in a gesture of agonised sympathy. Maggie could smell the hospital on him. She fought to free herself.

'Let's go then. He'll want me there.'

She'd been dreading this moment since that awful day

when the doctor had told her what she must expect. Since then, the whole point of her life had been to help him. She'd cooked meals he could digest, done her best to conceal her own pain, and played Mozart and Chopin to soothe him.

On Tom's good days, they'd all had hope. Even Pa had said: 'Tom seems stronger this morning. Perhaps he's taken a turn for the better.'

They'd brought a bed down to the front room, when he could no longer get upstairs. There was the anguish of watching him fighting for breath, the strain of having to keep a cheerful face. He grew thinner and weaker, wasting away before her eyes. The time had come when he needed oxygen and they'd taken him into hospital.

Becky fetched their coats and hats. They set off down the street with Becky holding Maggie's arm on one side and Pa on the other. She was shivering, although it wasn't all that cold.

It was a short walk to the hospital, but a tram was coming. They rode on the platform to the next stop. Maggie dabbed at her eyes with her handkerchief.

'He's been a good husband to me,' she told Pa. The woman in front of her was laughing with her companion. Life was going on normally for everybody else. For her and Becky, it would never be the same again.

She felt scared as she followed him up the hospital stairs to ward five. Everybody knew Pa, but people looked twice before greeting him because he wasn't wearing his porter's coat. Then they looked sideways at her and Becky, and the sympathy in their eyes was hard to bear.

Maggie peeped through the open door and up the ward. Her stomach turned over to see screens round Tom's bed.

'I'm terribly sorry.' Sister's face was solemn as she came to her office door. 'Come in. Nurse, bring three more cups of tea.'

Maggie could feel a wall of dread building up inside her.

352

It came like a stab in the ribs to see the woman already sitting in Sister's office. Maggie hadn't seen her mother-in-law in years, but she'd have known her anywhere. She tightened her grip on Becky's arm.

'Hello, Margaret,' Lenora said through tight lips. She'd grown stouter and looked old now. 'All my sons gone before me. None left now.'

Sister's muslin headdress crackled with starch. 'I'm very sorry, Mrs Dransfield. I'm afraid your husband passed away ten minutes ago.'

Maggie thought her heart would burst. She'd been looking death in the face over the last few weeks, but she still felt unprepared.

'No! I wanted to be with him.'

Sister was practised at offering comfort. 'He's been suffering, Mrs Dransfield. You wouldn't want to prolong that. He was very peaceful at the end. In no pain.'

'I'm too late? You said you'd let me know in plenty of time.' Maggie covered her face with her hands. 'I didn't want him to be alone when . . . He was afraid, you see.'

'He wasn't alone.' Sister's tone was full of bland reassurance. 'Fortunately, his mother came in time.'

Maggie drew back, shocked.

Lenora said: 'Don't worry, Margaret. Tom knew I was with him at the end. I'm glad I was able to comfort him.'

Nothing could have added more to Maggie's distress. She clung tightly to Becky. It made Pa put an arm round her shoulders from the other side. She was shaking with grief and rage.

'I'd like to see him,' she choked.

'Of course.' Sister stood up. They all did.

'Let me know when the funeral is to be, Margaret,' Tom's mother bade her stiffly, before heading for the stairs. 'We'll all want to pay our last respects.'

Maggie couldn't speak for the tears stinging her eyes.

*    *    *

353

Maggie didn't want to go home with Pa. She didn't think Becky did either.

'Not a good time to be alone,' he'd said gently, and they hadn't the strength to resist when he pressed them. They'd let her sit for a little while with Tom, but Pa hadn't thought that a good thing for her either. Then there'd been the awful business of signing for his belongings.

Pa felt he had to do something for them in their hour of need, but she could see he was ill at ease with their grief. He couldn't fully share it because he'd never been that close to Tom. Maggie had always felt she'd been her father's favourite, but he didn't know how to comfort her now.

'At least you won't be short of money,' he said. 'You've got the cinema.'

She hadn't given any thought to money, not for ages. Her mind had been wholly on keeping Tom alive.

'This isn't the time to worry about money.'

Everything in Pa's new house seemed clean and fresh. They followed him to the kitchen and watched him fill the kettle at the new porcelain sink, and light the latest gas stove, mottled in blue and white on four neat legs. Maggie sank down on a chair and rested her elbows on the table. She felt full of pain, unable to believe that Tom had really gone.

'Let's go to the sitting room.' Pa was ushering them towards it. 'More comfortable.'

He put a match to the fire that had been laid in readiness in the grate. She still found it strange to see Pa's familiar furniture set out in the smaller rooms. The red Turkey carpet was a little large for the floor and went up over the skirting boards at one end, but there was room to spread out his books and his pictures. There was a dining room too, where they could all eat in comfort.

When Pa went to make the tea, Maggie collapsed on his

red velvet armchair. Becky came to perch on its cushioned arm, and she felt her arm go round her shoulders in a comforting hug. They'd spent the last few weeks with their arms round each other.

'It's profitable, is it?' Pa came back with the tea tray. Maggie hardly recognised his silver teapot; she was used to seeing it so tarnished it looked brassy. He took three Royal Albert cups and saucers from his china cabinet. It was almost unknown for him to wait on them. He'd always expected his daughters to see to his needs.

'Is what profitable?'

'The picture house, of course.'

Maggie's mind had been elsewhere. 'I've never had much to do with it. Tom saw to all that.'

'He was worried about it,' Becky began.

Pa said gravely, 'Tom isn't here to look after you now, Maggie. You'll have to face up to that.'

She flinched. 'I'll have to run it myself, won't I?'

'My dear child, you're lucky he's left you with a means of support.' Pa was at his most gentle.

'I'll help you, Mam,' Becky assured her. Maggie pulled her closer, down on to the chair beside her.

'What would I have done without you, Becky? You've kept me sane these last few weeks.'

'Oh, Mam!'

Maggie sighed. 'You know more about the picture house than I do, love. You were a great help to your dad, going there and seeing to things when he couldn't. He really appreciated all you did for him.'

'We should go tonight,' Becky worried. 'There's nowhere safe on the premises to keep the takings.'

'Oughtn't we to close it? As a mark of respect for your father?'

'It's Thursday,' Becky reminded her. 'It's been open all afternoon. Hilda will have started selling seats for this evening by now. It's too late. Perhaps tomorrow?'

355

The back door slammed. 'I expect that'll be Hattie,' her father said. 'She often pops round for an hour.'

Maggie stood up with a jerk. 'It's time we went home.'

'Stay and have something to eat first, Maggie. You'd like to, wouldn't you, Becky?

'Yes, of course you will. Hattie'll fix something for us all, it's not a problem any more. In fact there's no reason for you to go at all. Why don't you both stay here for a few days?'

Maggie shook her head. She wanted to be alone. She followed him to the hall, feeling restless and on edge. Hattie was removing her hat in front of the mirror, and anchoring stray wisps of pale hair into her bun. Maggie thought her sister was beginning to look spinsterish.

'How's Tom?' Hattie turned round. 'Olivia's always asking after him.'

Maggie felt numb. 'Hasn't Lenora told you? She was with him.'

'No.' Hattie's fingers went to her throat.

'This afternoon. He died.'

'Oh, Maggie! I'm sorry. How awful for you. I haven't seen Lenora since breakfast.'

Maggie was fighting tears again. She could see that Hattie wanted to come and put her arms round her, but wasn't sure whether she'd give her the sharp edge of her tongue again. They'd never made up that quarrel.

If Hattie couldn't forget it, neither could she. She burst out petulantly: 'I suppose you told Lenora that Tom was in hospital?'

'I told Olivia, she passes most things on.'

'His mother went to see him in hospital. Had the nerve to tell me she comforted Tom on his deathbed. Tom wouldn't have wanted that. She didn't come anywhere near us when he was alive. Why start nosing round now?'

'Don't think about her, Mam.'

356

'It's all your fault, Hattie. I don't know why you can't keep your nose out of our business.'

Becky said: 'Why is there such a rift? Between us and the rest of the Dransfields?'

'And she wants to come to his funeral.'

'She just wants to pay her last respects, Maggie. That's all.'

'Why did you have to tell them?' Maggie couldn't stop herself. She felt overcome with rage that this had happened to Tom. 'I suppose you've kept them posted all these weeks? Letting them have regular bulletins on his illness?'

'I suppose I have.'

'You'd lose face if they only found out after Tom was buried, wouldn't you?'

'Yes, I'm close to his grandmother. I couldn't keep things like that from her.'

'You should have.' Maggie felt ready to burst with resentment. Hattie was always putting her oar in where it wasn't wanted.

Suddenly, she felt herself being hugged against her sister's hard, thin body.

'I'm sorry, Maggie. Olivia kept asking about him. She was fond of him. I saw no reason not to tell her what was happening.'

Maggie didn't know what made her struggle to free herself. 'Why Tom? Why did he have to die?'

'He was gassed in the war and never got over it. He was in agony, Maggie, the last time I saw him. Struggling for breath. Perhaps it's for the best.'

'It's not the best for me.'

Pa came back and said: 'Poor Tom, he was only thirty-nine, too young to die.'

Maggie could see Hattie trying not to lose patience with her. 'You're even younger, Maggie. Young enough to make a new life for yourself.' She was thirty-five.

'How am I going to manage without him?'

'Becky will help you,' her sister said, her voice shaking with emotion.

Maggie said: 'I can't go to the picture house now. I don't want to talk about . . .'

Becky put her arm through her mother's as they walked down to the bus stop.

'Dad would want us to. He didn't like leaving everything to Hilda. He always sent me to bank the takings.'

'Yes,' Mam sighed. 'He did.'

'I could go by myself. You could go straight home.'

'I could walk to Lowther Street from here, it's a lovely night.'

'Here's my bus now. This one goes past Central Station.' Becky could feel her mother's indecision. She knew how anguished she was feeling, and wished she could take her mind off their awful loss.

'Come with me, you might as well.' She kept hold of her arm. There was only a moment to make the decision: her mother got on the bus with her.

It was already dark when they reached Central Station, and the smell from the gasworks hung heavily in the air.

'It's all so familiar round here,' Maggie said. 'I'm glad Pa no longer lives here.'

They were heading down the straight stretch of Hind Street. Ahead of them, Becky could see the blaze of light that was the Picturedrome. She could feel her mother's steps slowing.

'I don't want to come in.'

'Just for a minute. You don't want to wait outside. Come and watch the picture, then you won't have to talk to anybody. We're showing *Breakfast at Sunrise* with Constance Talmadge. They say it's good.' Her mother made a sound that sounded like agreement.

It's a good time to come, Becky thought. The show will

have started. Gloria will be playing the accompaniment. She and Mam needn't come face to face.

'Your father,' Maggie's voice shook, 'thought it would be more profitable than any other business.' She pulled Becky to a halt as they drew near.

'I remember it as it used to be. Tom's left his mark on this building. Changed it out of all recognition.'

Becky had heard this many times. 'He had a false front built on.'

'Look, it goes up six feet higher than the roof. Doesn't it make the place look grand?'

'It's very ornate.'

Her mother sighed. 'But only on the outside. Just a decorative façade. He didn't put that on until well after the war. Other cinemas were being opened by then, purpose-built and much grander.'

'Dad said he had to try to compete.'

'This was called the Electric Picturedrome when he bought it.'

'Doesn't that sound old-fashioned now?'

'Well, he dropped the Electric. Everybody was calling it just the Picturedrome anyway.'

'In daylight, it's possible to see the old name through the paint. Just faintly.'

As they went into the entrance hall the cashier said from behind the pay-box window: 'The last show started half an hour ago.' She was counting the takings and didn't lift her eyes.

'It's me, Hilda.'

'Oh, hello, I started without you, Becky.' She was a brisk young woman with thin brown plaits wound round her head. 'Not many in tonight, I'm afraid. How's your father?' She looked up and saw Maggie. 'Oh, Mrs Dransfield!'

'He died this afternoon,' Becky said quietly.

'Oh, my goodness! Oh, my dear! I am sorry. We'll all miss him very much.'

Becky could see the tears start to her mother's eyes. 'I'll just see Mam inside,' she said. 'I'll be back to do the books in a minute.'

Becky felt steadied by that task. It was what she'd be doing if life was normal. She checked the takings against the ticket sales just as Dad had shown her; entered the totals in the books and then went back to sit next to her mother. Even in the semi-darkness, Maggie's eyes looked puffy. The piano was tinkling along prettily at the front of the auditorium.

She could remember Mam playing here regularly during performances. She'd said it was quite hard work with two shows every evening and three on Thursdays and Saturdays. Over the last few years, she'd shared the job with Gloria. Since Dad had been ill, she hadn't come at all.

'Does she mind playing for every performance?' Mam whispered.

'No, she prefers full-time.'

The Picturedrome smelled like nowhere else on earth. Although it was behind the gasworks, the sulphuric smells from outside couldn't compete with the heavy scent inside. It always heightened Becky's anticipation; she loved the smell.

Her father had told her that all cinemas used a disinfectant spray to get rid of the fug and the cigarette smoke, because there were no windows they could open. That in the old days he used to go round spraying the audience. Now they waited until morning, when the place was empty.

She remembered that she'd never be able to speak to him again and felt the sting of tears. Next to her, Maggie blew her nose. Becky loved Constance Talmadge, and *Breakfast at Sunrise* looked good, but for once she couldn't lose herself in the show.

The piano was crashing out a crescendo, drawing her attention. Gloria held her head at an angle so she could peer up at the screen; her plump shoulders worked like pumps and her fingers lifted theatrically a foot above the keyboard.

A light shone down on her music, making the bugle beads sewn on her bodice flash, and putting highlights in her dark hair. Becky remembered the last time she'd spoken to her.

'How's your father?' She had a breathy voice and a big bust. She always wanted to know everything. What Mam was giving him to eat and personal things like that.

'We're all so worried about him. Is there anything we can do?'

Becky had shaken her head. What could anybody do?

'Just a little note to cheer him up,' and she'd pushed a tightly sealed envelope into Becky's hand. 'Will you give it to him? We do miss him here.'

If Becky didn't arrive before the show started, Gloria left her envelopes with Hilda. There had been one in the pay box for the last three nights. She recognised the mauve envelope at twenty yards. She'd left it where it was. She didn't want to take it to him in hospital in case Mam saw it.

She didn't think he'd deceived Mam. He'd said there was nothing in it, but Becky wasn't absolutely certain. It had made her cling more tightly to Mam.

Maggie had tossed and turned all night, unable to sleep, not knowing whether it was shock or pain or sadness she felt.

She knew she'd disturbed Becky in the night; it was hard to avoid when they shared a bed. But Becky was up, throwing back the curtains. In the bright, crisp morning light, Maggie caught sight of Tom's best suit hanging in the open wardrobe.

'Everything here reminds me . . .'

She couldn't bear to see his things about the bedroom. They served as a reminder that he wouldn't be coming back. She wanted them gone.

361

Tom had taken care of everything. He'd always paid the bills and ordered the coal, and made all family decisions. He'd prided himself on taking good care of her. She was filled with a searing sense of loss.

She threw on her clothes and started turning out the drawers in his chest. She made one heap of personal letters and old household bills to burn. Another of papers relating to the business. She'd bundle them up and keep them out of sight. She knew it would upset her if she was reaching for a handkerchief or a pair of stockings and unexpectedly came across something of Tom's.

She could feel her head throbbing when she came across a copy of the will he'd made. That had been only weeks ago, but already it seemed like another life. He'd said it would make things easier when . . .

Tears were prickling her eyes again. He was wrong. This was the hardest thing she'd ever done. She opened it up and found a copy of another document inside it. Suddenly she was shaking with fear. She couldn't cope with anything else, not now.

Below, the front doorbell rang. She felt like a zombie as she went to the window to see who was there. She was looking down on Pa's trilby. She ran down to let him in.

'Thought I'd pop in on the way home from the hospital.' Pa kissed her. 'I've brought you each a new pair of black leather gloves. You'll need them for the funeral.' Maggie knew they'd come from his big steamer trunk still half full of gloves made decades ago when he'd been in business. 'Fortunately, fine leather gloves never date.'

Neither of them told him that gloves were the last thing they needed. He'd always kept them well supplied. She felt a little better when she found that Becky had lit the living-room fire and tidied up.

'I'll make a pot of tea, Mam,' she said now. 'And I'll make you some toast.'

Maggie sat down with Pa. 'I'm worried about something.

I've just come across a legal agreement Tom made with his mother. I need your opinion.'

Her father was pulling a face. 'Legal agreement? Hattie's better at that sort of thing. Why don't you ask her?'

Maggie sucked at her lip. 'You know what Hattie's like. We've had a bit of a tiff. Not on speaking terms.'

'She'll be glad to help you at a time like this, love. She won't bear any grudge.'

Becky came in with a tea tray. 'We ought to sort things out in the front room. Collapse the bed.'

Pa was smiling at her. 'I could help with something like that.'

Maggie had to steel herself to go into the front room. There were so many things here to remind her of Tom's sad end. She dragged the sheets off the bed, trying not to remember how she'd made it up clean for him to use when he came home from hospital.

Becky was right: she wouldn't feel better until it was back upstairs and Becky was sleeping in it again. It used to be Becky's bed. She'd been sleeping on Tom's side of the double bed over the last few weeks.

'We'll get everything back the way it used to be,' she said, fired with the urge to be busy. Pa helped them move the furniture and take the sickroom equipment out to the shed in the yard, where they wouldn't see it.

'Do you want any of Tom's things?' Maggie asked him, carefully keeping her face a blank mask. 'I'd like you to take them now if you do.'

She had to banish everything he'd owned from this house. Perhaps then she'd be able to rid herself of this awful feeling of loss.

'You'll want some keepsakes,' Pa said.

'I have the wedding ring he gave me. What better keepsake could there be?' She had a lot of photographs of him, his fountain pen and his watch. Becky was to have the camera he'd treasured, and his books. They wouldn't need anything else.

She led them up to the bedroom she'd shared with Tom. Pa and Becky sat on the bed while she emptied Tom's wardrobe. Pa was taller and broader than Tom had ever been, so few of his clothes fitted.

She was lining up all Tom's shoes along the floor. Pa picked up a pair of brown Oxfords. 'I remember Tom buying these,' he said. 'And they're hardly worn. Good quality too.'

'He paid a lot for them, Pa.' His pale eyes looked hopelessly into hers. She remembered, then, his change of circumstances.

'But you won't want Tom's shoes. I was forgetting . . .'

'They don't fit anyway, not wide enough.'

'What about his hats?' Becky suggested. It hurt to see Pa's face, old and lined, under Tom's best trilby.

'This is fine, thank you.'

Maggie tried to press scarves and pullovers on him too, and then thought of Tom's dressing gown and slippers.

'I really don't need . . .' Pa said.

'Of course you don't. What am I thinking of? I'll pack his best suit and overcoat. Becky, you can take them to the picture house tonight. George might like them. And that usherette can have the rest of his things. What's her name?'

'Dolly.'

'Yes, the one whose husband's out of work.'

'You could sell them,' Pa said. 'Tom had a lot of good stuff.'

She shook her head, feeling desperate. 'I want all this to go. As soon as possible.'

Becky's green eyes were overbright and glistening, too, as she helped parcel up her father's clothes.

The doorbell was ringing again. 'I let all your sisters know,'

364

Pa said. 'That'll be Enid. She said she'd be round early. We thought you might be worried about the funeral. She's going to go with you to make the arrangements.'

Enid hugged her on the doorstep. 'You poor thing.'

'Thanks for coming. I don't know what I'd do if you didn't all come flocking round.'

'I haven't got anything in black. Shall we go to the shops together?'

In front of the hall mirror, Enid eased off last year's blue cloche. It had flattened her tight creamy curls, and she shook her head to loosen them. The light reflected off the lenses of her spectacles, and the mirror doubled the effect.

'Why don't you show Enid that document you're worried about?' Pa suggested.

'It's Dransfield business.' Maggie frowned. She didn't like being reminded of it. 'I suppose they'll all come to his funeral? I don't want to talk to them. I don't want them here. I won't have to ask them, will I?'

'Why not let them see where their son lived?' Pa asked gently. 'You haven't been kept in luxury all these years. They thought that was why you wanted to marry him, didn't they? They didn't think it would last.'

Maggie ran a worried hand across her brow. 'I'm scared of them.'

'No need to be now. After the funeral, you need have no further contact.'

'I'm afraid they won't leave us alone.'

'Why not? You said Tom had made a will. That's all right?'

'Yes, but there's something else. I came across it. When I was sorting . . .' Maggie shivered. 'It's really bothering me. I'll fetch it.'

Her bedroom was a shambles. Every drawer was open, there were piles of paper everywhere. For a moment, she couldn't find what she was looking for. She'd left the envelope on the windowsill.

'Let's see.' Enid put out her hand for the documents and opened them up.

'He's left everything to you, Maggie. The will's quite straightforward.'

'He hadn't much to leave.'

'There's the Picturedrome. You'll have income from that. Enough to make life comfortable,' her sister said. 'You don't know when you're well off.'

Maggie hoped she was right. 'There's this too. I'd forgotten about it until now.'

'What is it?'

Becky was peering over Enid's shoulder. 'It's a legal agreement,' she said. 'Between Dad and his mother. Taken out in nineteen fifteen.'

Maggie blew her nose. 'Tom borrowed the money to buy the Picturedrome. From his mother.'

'It's a fifteen-year loan.' Pa's voice was heavy with dread.

'Interest-free for the first five years, thereafter he was to pay two per cent.' Enid looked up. 'Has he been doing that?'

Maggie shook her head. 'I don't know. Tom saw to everything like that.'

'He also agreed to repay it in instalments. Do you know if . . . ?'

Maggie had to shake her head again. She watched her sister's questioning eyes swing to Becky. She shook her head too.

Maggie said, in a voice that cracked with fear, 'It says it all has to be repaid. Half within ten years and the whole within fifteen. The time's up, it's all due.'

'Surely,' Becky whispered, aghast, 'she won't keep you to that? Not now.'

'I'm afraid . . .' Maggie felt sick.

'She can't rob you of everything. Only ask for the loan to be repaid,' Enid said. 'Don't be silly.'

366

She could see Enid was thinking. 'Perhaps she's forgotten about it. It was drawn up sixteen years ago.'

'She isn't the sort to forget things like this,' Maggie said. 'Lenora can be ruthless. What can I do? To stop her taking the cinema?'

Pa said briskly, 'Wait and see what she does. There's nothing else you can do.'

'There is,' Enid said slowly. 'Let me take this copy of the agreement. I've a friend whose husband is a solicitor. I'll try and get his opinion. His legal opinion as to where this leaves you. That would help, wouldn't it?'

Maggie nodded, feeling numb.

# CHAPTER TWENTY

In the days that followed, Becky felt in limbo. Time seemed to stand still. Mam had decided that the picture house should be closed for the night of Tom's funeral as a mark of respect, but in the meantime she continued to run it. She thought Lenora meant to take it; Mam was convinced she would. They talked endlessly of that possibility. She'd told her mother some time ago that Adam had come to see round it.

Now Maggie said angrily: 'He was spying out the ground for Lenora. She can't wait to see what it's worth. You shouldn't have shown him anything.'

That made her feel dreadful, and it raised doubts about Adam. She hadn't told her mother she was seeing quite a lot of him.

She was glad to escape from the house and go to the Picturedrome, but things were getting on top of her there. Adam came almost every night. He was gentle and sympathetic, and tried to help by doing routine jobs for her. At any other time it would have amused her to see him dealing with the mail by using two fingers to pick out the letters on the typewriter. But now, if he so much as asked how the ticket machine worked, or how she paid the staff, it made her heart thud with fear that he was planning to take the place from her.

She would have liked to discuss Lenora's intentions with him, but he was from the Dransfield side of the family and was living in her house. He'd explained very clearly where

369

Lenora's ambitions lay and seemed not to approve, but he was still working in her baby wear factory. He seemed happy to be one of her heirs. Becky waited for him to bring the subject up, and when he didn't, she couldn't bring herself to broach it either. It lay between them instead, a hurdle she couldn't get over.

The funeral was like a black curtain. Becky felt she had to get that over before she could cope with anything beyond it. The Knell family gathered round, offering support. All her aunts were in and out of the house several times a day. Almost as though they didn't expect Maggie to manage without their help.

'We'll give you a hand with the catering,' Fanny said. 'You'll want to put on a good spread for the funeral.'

They took her mother shopping and came back with a large piece of ham and the ingredients to make two big fruit cakes and several batches of scones.

The following day, Frances and Ruth took over their kitchen. The ham was put in to bake. Soon, lovely scents filled the house. Becky was relieved that Mam seemed to accept that life would go on, and that her family was taking charge of her.

Aunt Harriet came round that afternoon. Becky had never seen as much of her as she had of her other aunts, and she had the impression that Harriet and her mother had avoided each other for years. There was an uneasy coolness between them.

'Hello, Rebecca.'

Aunt Hattie was the only person who ever called her that, and her voice always sounded charged when she spoke to her. Her small oval face was dominated by enormous green eyes. Becky could feel them on her now, shining with a frightening intensity. She'd asked her mother once why Aunt Hattie seemed to single her out like this.

'It's just her manner, love,' she replied. 'She can be a bit strange at times.'

'What can I do to help, Maggie?'

Her mother was shaking her head. 'What can anyone do?' It surprised Becky to find how kind Harriet was trying to be now. She felt a wave of sympathy for her. Poor Aunt Hattie, always thinking of others, never of herself. She looked old-maidish, older than her years, because she'd worn her skirts almost to her boot tops when everyone else, including Mam, was wearing them to their knees. Mam had always dressed fashionably, and though her skirts were longer now, they were not like Hattie's. That was the way Dad had wanted it, her clothes up-to-the-minute. Harriet always looked as though time had passed her by.

She put an arm round her sister's shoulders and said: 'You had him for quite a few years, Maggie. You must be thankful for that.'

On the day the funeral was to be held, Ruth and Fanny came round early with starched white cloths, and Pa's best china and sherry glasses. Becky and her mother were pressed into use slicing and buttering bread and scones. A feast of ham and pickles was laid out on their living-room table. The clock ticked on, filling Becky with dread for what was to follow.

As she changed into her new grey hat and coat, she knew that Mam was putting on her widow's weeds in the next bedroom. The rest of the Knell family was collecting downstairs. The chink of china came drifting up as they made and drank their everlasting cups of tea.

From her window, Becky watched the hearse pull up outside their front door with two other highly polished limousines behind it. The coffin, all polished wood and brass handles, was visible through the glass of the hearse. She couldn't let herself think of her father being inside. She concentrated instead on the single red rose that lay on top. She could see the card attached to it. She'd helped Mam compose the message. 'For a much-loved husband

and father.' Mam had wanted that. Just a single flower from both of them, as a symbol of their love.

There were more wreaths laid around the coffin than she'd expected. She knew the Knells had provided the big bunch of chrysanthemums because she'd been with Grandpa when he'd ordered it.

The staff at the Picturedrome had provided a simple wreath. Becky had seen the projectionist collecting for it. But there were many more. Expensive and ornate wreaths and sheaves of lilies. From the Dransfield side of the family, she supposed.

Becky sat in the rear of one of the cars, where she was grateful to find her family talking of everyday affairs. Grandpa was bemoaning that he had to go on duty at two this afternoon. Ruth was regretting that she'd forgotten to ask him to open the pickles. She'd been unable to get the lids off the jars that Fanny had made, and they all hoped the onions were still crisp.

They bustled her into church, where she sat between Mam and Aunt Hattie, with the rest of the Knells in a close group. Mam was twisting a very damp handkerchief between her fingers and then scrubbing her eyes with it. Aunt Harriet kept bringing her dry and lacy handkerchief to her nose with dainty, ladylike movements.

They were all watching the Dransfield relatives collect. She'd already seen Tom's mother at the hospital. The large black hat was held at a haughty angle, and beneath it could be seen bangs of grey hair and cold eyes. She strutted up the aisle with her pouter-pigeon bosom held well out in front.

Becky was looking out for Adam. He came now with his mother hanging on his arm, a youngish matron with bright brown hair. Hattie called her Sophie. Three steps behind them came Adam's brother and sister, just a few years older than she was herself.

'Daniel Moody hasn't come,' Harriet whispered across her to Mam.

'He's behind us, on his own,' Becky whispered. She knew him well enough. He'd kept in touch with Dad.

Then came a man who was as big as Grandpa, but broader across the shoulders and more heavily built. He wore a formal morning suit and swung his top hat from huge fingers. The hair on his head was sparse and grey. Far more of it grew on his cheeks and chin, where it was two shades darker.

'Your other grandfather,' Aunt Hattie whispered.

Becky thought how strange it was that she knew the Knells so intimately yet would not have recognised some of these Dransfields. She took a deep breath as it dawned on her that she was the only one who had both Knell and Dransfield blood running in her veins. She saw herself as the bridge between them.

She spent the funeral service fighting to control her tears. Mam was in floods throughout. Becky wanted it over, but there was still the ceremony at the graveside to get through. Mam was leaning heavily on her arm as they followed the coffin out into the cool morning air.

'In the midst of life we are in death.'

Becky closed her eyes to shut out the scene. Somebody coughed behind her.

'Earth to earth, ashes to ashes, dust to dust.'

She bit her lip. How could she stop such words reaching her? Self-control was almost impossible.

At last it was over. Becky lifted her face to the cool breeze. People were standing about chatting. Neither she nor Mam were in any condition for small talk. Dad's wreaths had been set out close to the grave.

With Mam still holding on to her arm, she went over to look at them, trying to blot out the agony from her mind with the beauty of the flowers. She read the cards attached to them.

'From Sophie, to a much-loved brother.' 'From a grieving mother.' She found another from his father. The most ornate

373

of them all said: 'For darling Tom. Forever in my thoughts. Rest in peace. From your own Gloria.'

Becky felt the strength drain from her legs. She mustn't let Mam see that. It would really upset her. She looked round the gathering of mourners. Everybody from the Picturedrome was here. Gloria was wearing a black two-piece that was a size too small and strained on its buttons. Becky tried to walk Mam back towards the church.

'Can't we go home now?'

All her doubts about Dad were flooding back. Had Gloria been his mistress? She hated to think she might have been. Becky was only too familiar with the heartache mistresses brought, the problem was featured in many of the films she watched.

Mam had her handkerchief to her eyes, and didn't seem interested in anything until her aunts started reading the messages on the flowers too. Becky watched them, appalled. Ruth jerked back with such surprise that Enid bent to read with greater interest. The look of shock she exchanged with her sister took Harriet's eyes down too.

She knew her mother had noticed. Maggie freed herself from her grasp in order to read the gold card nestling between the exotic white blooms. Becky heard her gasp and saw her face screw up with shock.

Anger was washing through her that Gloria could do this. She must know how Mam would feel. Maggie's face was hardening with horror and disbelief, her puffy eyes searching the faces of those gathered round.

Gloria's eyes were red from crying too, and her tears had blotched the heavy make-up on her podgy face. It was hard to believe Dad could have preferred her to Mam. Mam was much prettier and younger.

Becky felt cold with agony. Mam had enough to be upset about without adding this. Her ordeal was not yet over. Harriet was marching her forward to invite the Dransfield relatives for some refreshment. Aunt Hattie was good at making sure everybody else did their social duty while avoiding it herself. Becky hoped most wouldn't come. It was a vain hope.

They went back to Lowther Street, the cars lining up against the kerb and the mourners crowding out on to the pavement.

'Is this where Tom lived?' Lenora's voice told everybody that she thought the place hardly suitable for a son of hers.

'She's only come to have a good look at the place,' she heard Hattie whisper to Grandpa. He was ushering everybody inside. Soon every seat in the front room was in use, though Becky had brought chairs down from the bedrooms. The younger ones perched on the windowsill and on chair arms. The rest had to stand. The Knells and the Picturedrome staff filled the living room and overflowed into the hall.

Becky saw her mother rush straight upstairs, heard her bedroom door click firmly shut.

'Your poor mother.' Grandpa accepted a glass of sherry and stood in the corner, looking very sad. 'We all want to cosset her.'

'Why is that?'

He was shaking his head. Becky thought the last few months had taken a toll on her mother. Her complexion was dull and showed fine lines of strain and worry. Even her creamy hair had lost its shine. She'd had it bobbed when that style was the height of fashion, but now it had grown to shoulder length again and needed a trim.

'Proud of my girls, all of them. Maggie might have gone a long way.'

Becky was looking round for Gloria.

'I stopped her coming,' Big Billy told her. 'I was afraid she'd upset your mam.'

'She already has. Couldn't you have stopped her sending that wreath?'

'I thought we had,' Hilda said. 'There was to be the one from us all. That's what we agreed.'

Becky plucked at George's sleeve. 'Tell Mam what she's like. You've got to tell her it's not just Dad.'

She ran upstairs to find her mother. Maggie had bathed her eyes and was looking a bit better.

'Come on down,' she urged. 'Gloria isn't here.'

Mam's eyes were glistening with unshed tears. 'Did you know about her?'

Becky tried to explain. 'All I know is that I brought mauve envelopes home with the cinema mail. I knew they were notes from Gloria.'

'Why didn't you tell me what was going on?'

'Dad tore them up. He thought it better if you didn't know. You know what he was like, he didn't want you to be hurt. It was his way of protecting you.'

'Or did he need me to look after him? I don't suppose she'd have wanted to do that.' Mam's voice was tight with agony.

'No!'

'How long had it been going on?'

'Nothing's been going on. It was all in Gloria's mind.' Becky choked. 'He said he'd get rid of her if she wasn't such a good pianist. He did nothing wrong, Mam, believe me.'

Her mother stared at her helplessly. 'Silly to believe ill of him now.'

Once down in the hall, she edged her mother towards Big Billy, who was surrounded by the cinema staff. They were all giving her hugs of sympathy.

'We'll all miss Tom.'

'One of the best.'

'A good boss.'

Hilda said: 'We all thought him wonderful. Not just Gloria. Take no notice of that wreath. She lets things run away with her.'

Big Billy was close behind her. 'Gloria's got a thing

about men. Frightened the life out of me, it did, the first time she launched herself at me.'

'All very well for you.' George gave a wry smile. 'But she's twice my size. Last year I used to keep my door locked until I heard her starting to play. That was after she came up and threw herself at me, had me pinned against the projection-room wall.'

'Lucky for him I went up,' Big Billy said.

'Couldn't get away from her. The show was five minutes late starting.'

'The girls thought it a great joke. Dolly was in tucks.'

Becky said: 'Mam didn't believe me when I told her Gloria was like that.'

Maggie's face was a picture.

'Like being mauled by a tiger.'

'Gloria goes overboard for anything in trousers.'

Adam was close behind Becky. 'That's right,' he agreed. 'Even went for me, didn't she, Becky?'

'I'm not surprised.' George smiled.

Becky thought her mother looked much happier as they went into the living room. Immediately, Harriet's big eyes fastened on her as though she were the only person in the room.

'Make sure the Dransfields are helped to food and drink,' Aunt Hattie hissed at her. They were too many to sit round the table, so plates had to be balanced on knees. Lenora refused ham and pickles, but everyone else was tucking in.

It seemed strange to see Adam mixing like this with her family, though his presence felt like a lifeline. He was trying to stay close by following her round with other plates of food.

'This is Jane,' he said, drawing her in front of his sister. 'I've told her about us.'

Jane's alert young face leaned forward to kiss her cheek. 'He thinks a lot of you,' she smiled.

377

Enid was pouring tea. Mam was busying herself passing round the cups. Becky was following her with a plate of cake when Lenora halted their progress.

'Tell me, Margaret, was Tom still running his business? His cinema? What is it called?'

'The Picturedrome. Yes.' Maggie sounded nervous. 'We've managed to keep it going. Becky had to help towards the end . . . had to help a lot.'

'Is this Rebecca?' Becky felt her grandmother's penetrating gaze fasten on her face.

'Yes,' she said. And then, because such brevity might appear rude, she added: 'Grandma.'

Lenora's lips pursed into a thin line. 'Do not presume to call me that.'

Becky felt a flutter of nerves. Why would she not like that? As she offered the last slices of currant cake further round the room, she heard Lenora ask Mam: 'It is profitable, I hope?'

Mam squeezed her arm as they escaped to the living room. 'She's taking too much interest in the picture house.' She knew Mam was fearful for it.

Aunt Harriet seemed to be taking cover in the kitchen. She came out from time to time to cut slices of cake at the living-room table and send Becky round with the plate again.

She heard her mother hiss at Harriet: 'Who's that?'

Becky followed her gaze and saw another well-dressed woman examining their carpet square with disdain. She had a boy of about Becky's own age in tow. She'd thought them of little importance until she'd heard Hattie's choking response.

'That's Claudia Dransfield, Luke's widow.' She could see that to Harriet, they were very important indeed.

'Who's Luke?' Becky asked, but they ignored her.

She watched the two families – the Knells small and very fair, the Dransfields tall and a little darker – not

378

mixing easily on Knell territory. Almost all of them were dressed in black. Lenora held herself apart. Like a crow, she thought, searching for carrion.

The chatter in the living room died away. Lenora had come to the door and was pulling on her gloves. Leather gloves, Knell gloves, of a pattern only too familiar.

'Thank you for your hospitality, Margaret.' Her voice was cool and distant. 'We're much obliged.'

'Not at all,' Mam said. 'Are you going now?' Behind her in the hall, Sophie was tucking strands of bright hair under her hat.

'You'll be hearing from our solicitor shortly.'

Maggie's white face went grey. She was clutching the black bow at the neck of her blouse. 'What about?'

'I'm sure you already know. Goodbye, Margaret.'

Becky saw Mam turn to stone. She knew she was having to take one knock after another; it seemed that their worst fears were justified, that they were about to lose the cinema. Why else would they be hearing from her solicitor?

The front room was emptying rapidly now. The cars outside were pulling away one by one. At last only the Knells remained. Grandpa left because he had to go home to change before going to work. Harriet had to get back to see to the old lady. There was a frenzy of washing-up going on in the kitchen. A fresh pot of tea was being brewed to assuage the Knell thirst.

Clara was up in arms about what Lenora had said to Maggie. 'What a mean bitch that woman is.'

'I can't believe it.' Ruth was blinking hard. 'I think she's going to take your cinema.'

Enid took off her glasses and polished them. 'And she has so much already . . .'

'I can quite see why Tom wanted to cut himself off from her,' Fanny said indignantly.

Becky was relieved to have the funeral behind her, but in

379

the days that followed, sitting in the stuffy little office that had been her father's, Tom seemed very close to her.

She knew he'd hardly mentioned his business worries to Mam. He'd seen it as his job to look after her, not burden her with his difficulties. Becky had been trying to explain them to her, but she wasn't managing to get them across. It was almost as though Mam couldn't take in any more problems. She looked exhausted.

All the family worried that Lenora meant to ask Mam to repay the loan she'd made to Tom. Becky was filled with dread. Even if that didn't happen, there were other problems ahead that Dad had thought insurmountable. She thought it very likely that they'd lose the cinema.

A week after the funeral Becky picked up an official-looking envelope from the doormat. It was addressed to her mother. Across the top corner were stamped the words 'Lister and James, Solicitors'. She took it to the living room where Mam was eating breakfast and propped it up against the milk jug. Mam stared at it, transfixed. 'They were your dad's solicitors.'

She had to ask: 'Shall I open it for you?'

It invited Mam to call in and see their Mr Lister regarding a business transaction of her late husband, Thomas Edward Dransfield. It seemed he'd received a letter from Lenora's solicitor. Becky felt her stomach heave. It looked as though their worst fears were going to be realised.

She could see her mother was shocked. 'What are we going to do?'

As it happened, Fanny and Hattie arrived on their doorstep together after lunch. By that time, her mother had really worked herself up. 'I shan't go,' she told them.

'That'll only delay matters,' Hattie said. 'Don't you want to know where you stand in all this?'

Becky knew Mam was as desperate to know what was involved as she was, but she raged at her sister.

'Whose side are you on? You've brought this on us. If

you hadn't gone running to Lenora with the news that Tom was ill, they wouldn't know anything had changed. If he was alive, they'd leave us alone.'

'Stop bickering,' Fanny said, but Hattie ignored her.

'They'd find out sooner or later. No point in putting your head in the sand. Do you want me to see the solicitor with you?'

'No,' her mother said stubbornly. 'Why would I want you?'

'Oh, come on, Maggie, I'm only trying to help.'

'I don't need your help. You poke your nose in too much.'

Becky could see her Aunt Hattie was angry too. Her green eyes glittered at both of them.

'If that's the way you want it, I'll go.' She was poking her hatpins viciously into her old grey cloche. 'And I'll not offer any help in future. I'll wait to be asked.'

'No, Hattie,' Fanny protested. 'For heaven's sake!'

But she swept up the hall, and for the first time ever, Becky heard Hattie slam the front door.

'You shouldn't have said that!' Fanny turned back to them. 'Hattie would be the best one . . .'

Maggie burst into tears. 'I don't know what's the matter with me. I keep flying into the most awful rages.' Becky put her arms round her.

'I suppose it's understandable,' Fanny said. 'At a time like this. Let's make some tea.'

'Tea won't help.' Maggie sniffed. 'I won't let Lenora take the picture house. Tom meant it for me and Becky.'

'It's just the loan, Maggie,' Fanny said. 'Did Tom repay any of it?'

Maggie shook her head.

'What about interest? Did he pay any, or not?'

'I don't know.'

'Anyway, the value of the Picturedrome could be far greater by now. He spent his whole life making it pay.

381

Perhaps they're only going to bring your attention to it.'

Maggie was shaking her head again. 'I've talked to Enid about it. She showed our copy of the agreement to a solicitor. He says it'll be a charge against his estate. A debt that has to be paid.'

'That doesn't mean you won't be left with enough to live on.'

Becky stood up. She couldn't stand it any longer. They were going round in circles.

'That's only half the problem.' She pushed her shortened curls off her face. 'Dad was worried, I know he was, he talked about it a lot towards the end.'

'Worried about Lenora taking the cinema?'

'Worried about the competition. There are all those big purpose-built cinemas opening up everywhere. They have carpets and chandeliers and can show talkies.

'There's not just the new Plaza, there's the Regal and the Savoy. Even the Queen's . . . They're very grand compared to ours, and it doesn't cost all that much more to get in.'

They were both staring at her now. 'Dad said that all films will be made with sound tracks soon, and it'll cost a lot to get new projectors and sound boxes so we can show them. The Picturedrome's old-fashioned. Out of date. It needs a fortune spending on it.

'You're thinking it'll be worth more than Dad borrowed. He was afraid it wouldn't be worth very much at all. He'd open his account books on his counterpane and mull over them for ages.'

'Where are they? The books?' Fanny's cobalt-blue eyes were blazing.

'Upstairs in his bedside cabinet.'

'Haven't you looked at them, Maggie?' Fanny was aghast. 'Surely we can find out what the business is worth?'

382

Becky ran up to fetch them and laid them out on the table. 'These go back for all the years the cinema's been running.'

She opened the accounts for the first year. 'Look, here's how much it cost to buy.'

'But what it cost isn't what it's worth?' Maggie was screwing her face in concentration.

Fanny shook her head. Having married into the meat trade, she'd had to learn about business matters.

'What it's worth depends on how much money it makes. Look, Tom did pay interest on the loan. It's here. So the agreement hasn't been forgotten.'

'If it had been forgotten, we wouldn't have been asked to see the solicitor.'

Fanny opened the book for the current year. 'Look at this! The amount of the loan hasn't gone down. So he never did pay any of it off. That's not good news.'

Becky's finger went down the page.

'Here's how much it costs to rent the films, and pay the staff. And here's what it earns. Dad didn't think it was enough.'

'We managed . . .' her mother said.

'It's nothing to do with what you need to live on, Maggie,' Fanny said impatiently. 'It's earning less than it used to. The Picturedrome isn't big enough.'

'It's got four hundred and fifty seats.' Her mother sounded indignant.

'It's getting shabby and it's cut off between the railway lines. I know it's only a few yards behind Central Station, but the crowds walk the other way to the shops. No buses pass it, so few people see it, just those who live in the streets nearby.'

Maggie moistened her lips. 'It's even worse than we thought, isn't it? I'm sorry, my mind's been on other things.'

Becky knew it had been on preparing beef tea and such

383

things for her father. She could see tears glistening in her mother's eyes. She gave her a reassuring hug.

Mam straightened up. 'You're right,' she said. 'I'll have to go and see what it's all about. It's no good worrying about it like this. You'll come with me, won't you, Becky?'

# CHAPTER TWENTY-ONE

On the appointed day, Becky walked round Hamilton Square with Maggie, looking at the brass plates to find Mr Lister's office.

It was Becky who rang the bell. She knew what it had cost her mother to get this far. A clerk showed them into an empty waiting room. It was bleak, with dark walls and hard chairs. She could see perspiration breaking out on her mother's forehead.

Within five minutes they could hear somebody else being shown out, and then an old and very bent man came to the door, announced that he was Mr Lister, and ushered them to another room. This overlooked the gardens of the square and was almost filled by a large partner's desk.

Becky watched him give Mam the client's chair. He addressed all his remarks to her mother. Then he was taking the originals of her father's will and his loan agreement out of their envelopes and spreading them on the desk in front of him.

'With regard to the will . . . I drew it up for your husband, by the way. Quite recently, yes. Quite straightforward. You've seen the copy?'

'Yes.'

'Then you'll know he appointed me as executor. I understand,' he twitched out the letter from Lenora's solicitor, 'that he died on the fourth?'

'Yes,' Mam's voice squeaked.

'Do you wish me to apply for probate?'

Enid had been explaining to both of them that Mam should ask for this.

She nodded. 'Yes. About the loan . . .'

'Yes, the loan. I drew this up too, let me see, sixteen years ago now. Your late husband's mother has asked through her solicitor to have this regarded as a debt against his estate.' It was what Auntie Enid had told them to expect. 'As the agreement was drawn up, she's entitled to do that.'

Maggie said hotly, 'Do many parents use the services of a solicitor when making a loan to their son?'

He looked Mam in the eye. 'Perhaps they should. Then everybody involved knows where they stand.'

'We can't afford to repay it,' Mam choked. 'We need to keep the business running, you see. And we need money for new equipment now the talkies are coming in.'

Becky tried to explain. 'Dad hasn't left much money. Not enough to repay the loan. It won't be possible.'

The old man swivelled his chair to see her better, then swung back to Mam.

'But your husband still owned the business? Yes, we still have the deeds of the property here. I'll need his bank books, and details of any other securities he had. Have you brought them?'

Mam looked mutinous. 'No.'

'Perhaps you'll let me have them? If he hasn't left enough money to pay his debts, then the cinema will have to be sold. His debts will be paid and the balance made over to you.'

'We can't part with the business,' Maggie said. 'His mother can't expect us to.'

'I'm afraid that under the terms of the agreement, the legal position is . . .'

'No,' Maggie said. 'Tom wouldn't want me to do that. He'd want us to have the cinema. We're his family, we need it to support ourselves.'

The old man sat back in his chair and said gravely, 'There

386

is no way to avoid paying the debts of a deceased person. What your husband owes has to be repaid. It reduces the amount he can leave you, but that is the law. If you went to another solicitor, he'd tell you the same thing.'

Becky saw her mother run her fingers through her hair. Her curls were tight and darkened with perspiration. Auntie Enid had already told them that.

'The only thing you could do would be to discuss this directly with the person to whom the debt is due. She is, after all, your husband's mother, a relation.'

Becky saw her mother shudder. 'By marriage.'

'You know each other. According to the terms set out here, half this money should have been repaid to her six years ago. She allowed your husband more time. If you appeal directly, tell her what you've told me, you may well be able to come to some agreement.'

'I can't face . . .' Mam was beginning. She looked on the point of dissolving in tears.

Mr Lister was on his feet, indicating that the interview was at an end.

'It's the best advice I can give you.' He was patting Mam's shoulder to show sympathy. She had that effect on men.

'She may want to help you. You talk to her, Mrs Dransfield. You are family, after all.'

Becky found herself out in Hamilton Square again. Mam's fingers were biting into her arm as they walked to the tram stop.

'I don't want to face Lenora. Ask favours from her.' Mam was mutinous.'

'He said it was the only way. We must.'

'Perhaps Hattie . . . Perhaps she'll negotiate for me. She knows her better than I do.'

Becky said: 'We could go up to Ottershaw House and talk to Aunt Hattie now.' She could see her mother drawing back. 'Everybody else is out at work all day, aren't they?'

'I can't face that either. Not yet,' her mother said. 'Let's go round to Pa's. He'll be at home now.'

When they got there, they found Pa in bed with a dose of flu, and Hattie in the kitchen giving detailed instructions to his cook-general about how he was to be looked after.

'I knew he wasn't well yesterday.' Hattie was rather harassed. 'I've rung the hospital to let them know he won't be going in this afternoon. It's a good job you've come. He needs cheering up and I've got to get back.'

'We've got troubles of our own,' Maggie told her. 'We've just been to see Tom's solicitor, about the loan. He thinks it best if I discuss the whole thing directly with Lenora. Appeal to her better nature.'

Aunt Hattie was skewering her hat on to her hair with huge pins. 'She hasn't got a better nature.'

'But he says it's our best course of action,' Becky pleaded. 'We have to try.'

Maggie said: 'Hattie, I'd like you to do this for me. You know her . . .'

'You'll have to leave me out of this.' Harriet looked aghast. 'Lenora hardly deigns to speak to me. She hasn't forgiven me for making her pay Pa back.'

Becky had never seen her mother so desperate. 'You've got to help me, Hattie.'

Harriet, prim and unbending, was buttoning her coat. 'You said you didn't want my help. That I wasn't to interfere.'

'I know, and I'm sorry. I do now. You know Lenora better than I do.'

'It's better if you do it, Maggie, honestly.' Hattie's tone was softer. 'It won't help your case. Lenora wants to get her own back on me as it is, don't you understand? If she thinks it's one in the eye for me too, she'll be even more determined to do you down.

'This is your business and Tom's, you must see to it

388

yourself. She'd refuse me anything she could, out of spite. She doesn't like me.'

'Doesn't like me either,' Maggie sniffed.

'All the same, you were Tom's wife for eighteen years. She's more likely to do you a favour. You'll stand a better chance if I have nothing to do with it.'

'I'd like you to be there when I talk to her,' Maggie implored. 'You can explain things better . . .'

'No, Maggie. For anything like this, it's better if you have Becky with you.' Harriet's lips were compressed. 'Better if I stay right out of it.'

Hattie left her father's house in a downpour of rain. She'd rushed round to see Pa because he'd phoned and asked her to; he'd told her he wasn't well. She'd done what she could for him, but now he had Maggie to keep him company.

She had to wait at the bus stop, sheltering under the umbrella she'd borrowed from Pa's hall stand, but her skirts were wet by the time the bus came. She wondered if Olivia was heading for a dose of the same flu that Pa had. She'd had a bad night, kept awake by a cough, and she hadn't been herself this morning.

Hattie felt vexed with Maggie, but sorry for her too. She knew only too well what it was to lose a loved one. She'd tried to help her and Becky, had felt very hurt when Maggie refused to let her. She wanted to be friends again; to be close to her as she had when they were young. Most of all, she wanted to be closer to Rebecca, but it seemed Maggie was unwilling to allow that.

She wiped some of the moisture off the window to stare out at the familiar leafy roads of Oxton. The trees dripped. She felt miserable.

For all the years Maggie had cared for her daughter, she'd kept Hattie at bay. Maggie had never wanted to talk to her about Tom's business affairs. What she knew

389

of them she'd been told by Pa or Fanny. Maggie had shut her out of her own tight family circle.

Now, suddenly, she'd made a complete turn-round and was asking Hattie to intervene between her and Lenora. She hadn't been able to make Maggie understand that she couldn't help in that way. She wasn't even sure it was necessary. She didn't know half the details about her present trouble and didn't want to. She thought her sister was worrying unnecessarily, perhaps fussing too much.

When she got off the bus the rain was gusting more than ever. When she reached the house, Harriet felt thoroughly damp and out of sorts. She wished she'd listened to Becky's plea for help. She should have spared a few more minutes and talked their problems through. She went straight to the kitchen to ask for a tea tray to be set, and then went up to Olivia's room.

She thought at first Olivia was asleep, but her eyes flickered open as she came close to her bed.

'A drink,' she croaked through dry, cracked lips. 'Water, please.'

Harriet had to lift her so she could take sips from the glass. She felt on fire.

'I feel terrible.' Her cough was dry.

'In what way?'

'Pain here, when I breathe.'

'I'd better get the doctor to you,' Hattie said. 'I'm going down to the phone. I'll bring some tea back. You'll like that better than water.'

Her heart was pounding as she ran downstairs. What had she been thinking of? She should have rung Enid and asked her to see to Pa, not leave Olivia. She'd never seen her so ill. The doctor came within the hour, and Lenora and Sophie arrived home before he left.

'I'm afraid it's pneumonia,' he told them. 'She'll need nursing day and night.'

Hattie was kept very busy over the next week, heating

poultices and offering drinks. A nurse was employed, but Olivia would get very distressed if Harriet wasn't there. She hardly left the sick room except to sleep. The doctor came every day and they all feared for Olivia's life.

Harriet forgot Maggie's problems and thought of little else but nursing Olivia. On the sixth day, her temperature suddenly returned to normal and her breathing became easier. From being in great distress, she seemed suddenly much more comfortable.

'The crisis is over,' the doctor told them.

'She'll get better now?' Harriet asked with relief.

'I hope so.'

She found it took many more weeks to nurse Olivia back to health. She never did regain all her strength and energy.

Becky had a sinking feeling as she rode up to Oxton on the clanking tram. Beside her, Mam was staring out of the window, white-faced. She'd not been able to eat any lunch. Her hands were clasped tightly together, and Becky could see them shaking slightly.

She'd phoned Lenora this morning and asked her if she'd see them.

There'd been a moment's pause. 'I suppose I ought to,' Lenora had replied coldly. 'This afternoon, then. Come to the house at four thirty; I'll leave work early.'

Becky knew her mother was afraid, she was finding her fear infectious. They'd spent an hour rehearsing what they were going to say. On the long walk up to Ottershaw House, their steps grew slower and slower.

She'd heard so much about this house she was curious. Her father had been brought up here, Mam had lived here once, and Aunt Hattie still did. She'd wanted to see it, but now she was shaking like Mam.

A plump woman in a print dress and white apron let them in. Becky felt Mam grope for her hand as they were

391

shown into a large study. There was a fire in the grate, but the afternoon sun was streaming in through the window. Lenora was sitting behind a wide desk; she didn't bother to get to her feet. Becky's heart sank.

'You wished to see me, Margaret?' Lenora was looking at them over half-moon spectacles.

'Yes, about the loan you gave Tom.'

Becky had tried to tell her mother to look Lenora straight in the eye and be confident; as though she was in a position to negotiate. Mam seemed to be projecting a wounded stare.

'I was wondering if you would be good enough to wait . . .'

'I'm afraid there's no question of waiting once Tom's will is proved.'

Becky saw her mother straighten up at that, but she went on with what they'd rehearsed. She was screwing her eyes up against the sun.

'The reason being that Tom had very little money to leave.'

From the forbidding look on her grandmother's face, Becky was afraid she didn't mean to give an inch. She said: 'We won't be able to repay you straight away.'

'What do you mean, won't be able to?' Lenora barked. 'I have a prior claim against his estate. Tom signed the agreement.'

'We'd like to carry on running the Picturedrome to see if we can . . .' Mam looked ready to weep.

Becky was afraid she'd give up. She tried: 'The business hasn't made very much profit over the years.' The sun was blinding her. 'Do you mind?' She pulled her chair out of the glare.

Lenora's eyes had switched to her face. She looked affronted. 'Are you saying Tom wasn't a good business-man?'

Becky supposed she was. She tried to rephrase it: 'I'm

392

saying the cinema hasn't earned enough to pay you back. Surely you know that? My father didn't repay the first instalment when it fell due. You were kind enough to allow him to pass that up.'

'Tom is no longer alive, and I see no reason why I should wait any longer. If he couldn't make it pay, it's unlikely you'll do better. More likely you'll lose what business there is. It could be worthless in another year or so.

'You know, Margaret, that I didn't approve of his marrying you, but Tom wouldn't listen. We couldn't dissuade him. He came crawling back to his father a little later wanting this loan. We listened with sympathy. Did our best to help.

'But now things have changed. I don't feel responsible for you. If the business can't repay its first costs after all this time, then it should be sold off. There's the freehold of that hall. That's worth something.'

'Please don't do that,' Maggie breathed.

'Margaret, I don't expect you to understand business, but the whole point is to make money. You're telling me the cinema doesn't make much. Then the best thing to do is to sell it and try to make money in some other way. Have you brought the accounts with you?'

'No . . .'

'Mr Maxwell's handling this for me. You can give your accounts to him, or to Tom's solicitor, if you don't want to bring them here.'

Becky could see her mother blinking in confusion.

'Has his man . . . Lister, is that his name? Have you asked him to apply for probate?'

'Yes,' Becky answered for her. 'What we're trying to say is that the cinema is worth less than your original loan.'

'Then both the cinema and what money Tom leaves will come to me. And if that doesn't equal the original loan, I must suffer a loss. Either way, it won't be yours.'

Becky felt a terrible weight in her stomach. She was sick with disappointment.

Mam slumped back in the chair, looking defeated.

'It is still a going concern?'

'Yes.' Becky was scared now.

Lenora seemed deep in thought. 'When I've looked at the accounts, I might decide to keep the cinema running. Perhaps Adam would like to see if he can do any better. He's of an age when he needs to cut his teeth on something. Tom would have learned to run it properly if he'd stayed longer with me.'

Becky felt a cold shiver run down her spine. She was astounded. Adam run the Picturedrome? She didn't want to believe what she was hearing. Suspicions were whirling in her mind. Was that why he'd come round to see it? Why he'd asked all those questions about how she ran it? He'd talked about its profitability, giving her his accountant's point of view.

She'd been grateful, thinking he was trying to help her. She'd thought he was interested in her, but had he known all the time that he'd be taking over the running of it? Becky could feel the strength ebbing from her legs, afraid that things were not what she'd supposed between her and Adam.

She'd lost the thread of what Lenora was saying. Mam looked ready to crumble. Anger stirred within her. If she didn't put their case soon, they'd lose everything.

'What about us?' she demanded. 'I know Dad meant us to have the Picturedrome. He talked to me about it. I spent a lot of time with him over his last months. He wanted to provide us with a means of support, Mam and me. I know he did. Surely we have a right.'

'What right? This is my money, I want to use it to help my family.'

Becky gathered her courage in both hands. 'But we are your family.'

394

'Come now, only by marriage. And as I've said, I didn't approve of that.'

'I'm a Dransfield by birth,' Becky said fiercely. 'As closely related to you as Adam. We're both your grandchildren. It belonged to my father; why take it from me in order to give it to him?'

Lenora was drawing herself up, and her glance was cutting. 'You're not Tom's daughter. He brought you up as though you were, but in truth you are not. So why should I concern myself with your welfare?'

To Becky, the world seemed to stop. Nothing was as she'd supposed. She looked at Mam for support.

'Not Tom's daughter? Of course I am.' Panic was fluttering in her throat.

Maggie suddenly sprang to her feet. 'You bitch!' she screamed. 'You bitch! Did you have to stoop to this? You are hateful.'

In the stunned silence that followed, she felt Becky steering her towards the door. It would do no good to stay, not after she'd called Lenora a bitch. Maggie had always known there was no real hope. She shouldn't have allowed herself to be persuaded to come.

She looked up at the vaulted ceiling as they crossed the hall. The ornate plasterwork, and the lights that had once been gas sconces but now had electric bulbs. It seemed only yesterday that she'd lived here too. The woman who'd let them in was hovering in the hall. As she opened the front door to see them out, Maggie snatched at Becky's arm and swept her down the front steps.

Becky was gasping: 'Mam, is it true?'

Then she was striding down the path in such high dudgeon she was leaving Becky behind. Beyond the gate, out on the pavement, she felt Becky catch at her arm and swing her round.

'Mam, is it true what she said? About Dad not being . . .

He was my father, wasn't he?' Maggie wanted to rush on, but Becky wouldn't let her. 'I've got to know.'

In a rush of panic she flared out: 'Of course he was. That woman's just trying to make trouble. Of course he was your father. He loved you very much.'

Becky said nothing. She walked beside her, staring straight ahead. Maggie knew she was desperately upset. At the terminus, they both stared at the conductor as he unhooked the pole and wheel from the overhead cable and ran it round in front to turn the tram round. As if they hadn't seen it a thousand times before.

They sat together on the hard wooden seat. Becky seemed withdrawn and distant. Maggie was jolted against her as the tram screeched and ground on its way. She wanted to reach out to her, tell her the truth, but she couldn't. She felt locked in anger at what Lenora was doing. She was afraid she was about to lose everything.

Hattie had been so confident, crowing about how she'd brow-beaten Lenora, made her pay that money back to Pa. But Hattie had misjudged the situation. Lenora was about to do it again. She was taking their picture house.

And even worse than that, Lenora had deliberately made mischief by telling Becky that Tom was not her father. Perhaps it shouldn't have come as a shock that Lenora knew, but all these years, she'd thought the Dransfields had accepted the story Harriet had told them.

Maggie didn't know what to do with herself when they reached home. Becky said she had to eat something before going to the cinema, and began frying egg and bacon for them both. She couldn't force hers down. She'd set Becky's mind at rest, but for how long?

When Becky had left, Maggie sat with her head in her hands over her half-eaten meal, unable to summon the energy to clear away. She shouldn't have lied to Becky, of course she shouldn't, but she was afraid she'd lose her if she knew the truth. Maggie felt bereft. The house was still and very empty. It was easy to imagine that she'd hear Tom call to her in a moment. Wanting his cup of tea.

She heard the doorbell ring faintly. Probably one or other of her sisters. She dragged herself reluctantly up the hall. It was not the company of her sisters she wanted.

The surprise of seeing Justin James on her doorstep jerked her out of her lethargy.

'I've just heard . . . I'm sorry, Maggie. It must be a terrible time for you.'

He was pushing a posy of violets into her hand. Soft and velvety, with drops of moisture sparkling on them. She buried her face in their fresh, woody scents.

'I knew he must be very ill. You cancelled your lesson so many times.'

Maggie tried to smile. 'Such a long time . . . since I saw you. Probably forgotten everything you've taught me by now.'

'You won't have forgotten, don't worry.'

She lifted the flowers to her face again. 'The flowers from his funeral are all dying. Nice to have fresh ones to put on his . . .'

'No, no, they're for you.'

'Oh! They're lovely.'

His dark eyes seemed full of sympathy. 'If there's anything I can do, you know where I am.'

Maggie was shaking her head numbly. She didn't know what to say to him. 'That's very kind . . .'

'I don't suppose I've chosen a good moment to call. Though at a time like this, I don't think there is a good moment.'

He was turning to leave, and she put out her hand to delay him. He took it between both of his, then suddenly raised it to his lips and kissed it.

It took her by surprise. When she looked into his dark eyes they were full of understanding, of affection for her. It brought an ache to her throat. She

397

couldn't say any more, not even to thank him for the flowers.

'I'll be in touch, Maggie.'

She stood on the doorstep clasping his posy, watching him stride away, and wanting to call him back. She felt refreshed by his violets, and warmed by the love she'd seen on his face. Why hadn't she asked him in?

Becky was uneasy. Her mother wouldn't give any reason why Lenora should say Tom wasn't her father. Mam was on edge and didn't want to talk about it. Becky felt unconvinced. She was even more uneasy with Adam.

She'd thought she'd come round to accepting that Lenora would take the cinema, but to find that she was proposing that Adam should run it in her stead was just too much to take.

During the difficult weeks since her father's death, she'd found Adam a comfort and a support. She'd been telling herself they were in love. His manner hadn't changed. He was coming to the cinema to see her just as often, offering to do the routine jobs just as before. He took her to a café for afternoon tea, suggested a trip to the cinema. But she sensed something in his manner: that he wanted to talk about the future, but was finding it as difficult as she was to bring it up. It was raising terrible doubts and suspicions in her mind.

He was driving her home in his car, kissing her too, but never once did he mention that he expected to be taking the cinema over from her. She was asking herself whether he'd still want to see her when she'd taught him what he needed to know about running it.

As Becky walked down to the picture house, she made up her mind that she'd have to have this out with him. He'd told her he wouldn't be able to come tonight, so she was surprised to find him waiting on the cinema steps amongst the crowd going in for the second house.

He looked very serious as he came towards her. 'I've got to talk to you,' he said urgently.

'Not here.' Late customers were pushing to the pay box. 'Come up to the office.'

He was blinking in the strong light when she switched it on. She closed the door and went towards her father's chair.

He caught her arm. 'Becky, I've just heard . . . My grandmother says that under the terms of a loan she made to Tom, this picture house will come to her.'

She said miserably: 'I wondered why you never mentioned it.'

'I didn't know. I wouldn't have had the nerve to hang about like this! You've known all along?' He seemed surprised.

'Since he died.'

'My grandmother wants me to run it.'

She nodded. 'Mam and I went to see her the other day. She told us straight out she wanted it for you.'

'Why didn't you say something? Yesterday, when I was here?'

'I couldn't,' she choked. 'Didn't know how . . . But I couldn't think of anything else.'

Becky had been trying to tell herself that she was glad she wouldn't have to make decisions about sound equipment. She and Mam would have had to ask for a loan at the bank, and she knew Mam would be dead against doing any such thing.

She felt his arms go round her. Felt herself being hugged against his tall, thin body. 'Becky, you must have hated seeing me here. Must have been hell for you.'

'No, I wanted you to come. But I was afraid . . . Afraid it was the cinema you wanted.'

'No, no.' His arms tightened round her. 'It's you. It's you I want. I love you, Becky. I've been trying to pluck up courage to tell you. To ask you . . .

399

'Goodness, I'm being so ham-fisted about this. It's been on the tip of my tongue for ages. I was afraid it was too soon after . . .' His smile was lopsided and tender. 'I'm trying to ask you if you'll marry me. What d'you say?'

Becky's heart jerked, but she couldn't stop a wide grin spreading across her face. 'Yes. Yes, please.'

'I do love you.' His arms tightened round her again.

# CHAPTER TWENTY-TWO

Maggie felt anxious, because Becky was out late. Now she thought about it, she'd been much later coming home these last few months. She'd seemed a changed person since she'd had her hair bobbed. As though she'd grown up overnight.

Maggie sighed. The day had been a bad one. She'd had another letter from Mr Lister reminding her that she'd not handed over the business account of the cinema, or Tom's bank books. She didn't know why she hadn't: nobody else could draw on the money there. They were getting by on the wage Becky drew from the cinema takings. Becky had taken them all in this afternoon. She'd said there was no point in delaying matters, there was nothing they could do about it.

It wasn't often cars came into Lowther Street. When Maggie heard it, she twitched up her curtain. It had stopped right under the streetlamp on the other side of the road. The couple inside were embracing, she wondered who they could be.

A moment later, the shock made her jaw drop as she realised that the girl was Becky. She recognised Adam Moody then, as he reached across to open the door for her. Becky sat there for another moment or two, her face animated as they talked. She was laughing!

Maggie could hardly get her breath. She dropped the curtain and stepped back. She felt betrayed. She knew now why Becky was coming home later and later, why she'd been so secretive about having her plaits cut off. She was with Adam Moody. Him, of all people.

Shaking with fury, she rushed downstairs to meet her daughter as she came in.

'I hope you know what you're doing, young lady! Riding round in a car with a man!' Becky looked taken aback. 'You're a bit young for that, aren't you?'

'It was Adam Moody.'

'I could see that! Kissing him in the street! You've been doing this for some time, I could see that too. Ever since your dad's . . . Why didn't you ask him in?'

'I wanted to, but the light was on in your bedroom. I didn't think . . . if you were in bed . . . you wouldn't want to come down in your dressing gown, would you?'

'But why keep it a secret?'

'I wasn't keeping it a secret. I did tell you he'd been to see over the Picturedrome. That he'd taken me to the Plaza.'

'That was weeks ago. Before your dad died.'

'I was afraid of upsetting you.'

'So you knew it would?' Maggie could feel herself bristling.

'You're upset anyway, Mam, I can understand that, and I didn't want to give you more to worry about.'

'You were laughing with him!'

'Yes . . .' Becky's green eyes searched her face. 'He's asked me to marry him.'

'What?' Maggie felt shocked. 'Throwing in your lot with the Dransfields? I don't know how you can.'

She could see Becky straightening up to her. Pushing back her shortened curls. 'You did.'

'What?'

'You did exactly the same. You took up with Dad when his mother had defrauded Grandpa out of his business. That was worse. It was out-and-out fraud.'

Maggie froze. The next moment she felt Becky's arms

go round her, and she managed to choke out: 'We were in love.'

'You don't understand, Mam, so are we.'

'But you're so young.'

'I'm sixteen! As old as you were. Grandpa had to give his consent for you. Adam wanted to come in and ask you for yours.'

'Well, I don't know . . .'

'You've always liked Adam. Ever since he was small.'

'He'll be running Tom's picture house instead of you.'

Becky's composure seemed to collapse. 'Yes, well . . . You all know him. Grandpa's been friends with his father for years. Stay up tomorrow night and I'll bring him in. He can talk to you. Explain.'

Becky was worried about her mother. She hardly seemed to leave the house and was doing very little except lie on her bed and mope. Her temper could flare up in an instant with anybody. She was complaining that Aunt Harriet had let her down, and said she wanted nothing more to do with her.

Maggie had always kept the house immaculate, but now she was letting the dust gather. Becky started doing more herself and found that was the answer. Mam couldn't sit and watch her: she'd take the duster or broom from her hands and carry on.

Mam had taken over from her a moment ago when she'd been mopping the kitchen floor. Becky moved on into the front sitting room. She was running a duster over the candle sconces on her mother's piano when it came to her that she'd not seen any music on it since Tom had died.

'Do you play when I'm not here?' she called down the passage.

She saw Maggie lean against the mop handle in the kitchen doorway and shake her head. 'Not any more. That belongs to another life.'

403

Becky ran her duster along the piano top. Mam's problem, as she saw it, was that she had precious little in the present life. Anything from the old one might help. She opened the stool where Mam kept her sheet music, chose a delicate piece by Schumann, opened the lid and sat down. It was a long time since she'd played, too, and she'd never been all that good.

It was anything but delicate the way she played it. She was ham-fisted, her timing was rotten and there was the occasional wrong note. She gave up and started on a Strauss waltz. This she knew by heart; once it had been her party piece. She sounded a bit rusty even on this.

'For heaven's sake, Becky.' Maggie had come in with her hands over her ears. It was the first time she'd seen Mam laugh for ages. Then she was edging her off the stool. She played the piece by Schumann, making it sound beautiful. Mam was able to put her soul into music, make the notes sound like liquid crystal.

Becky put polish on the tables and plumped up the cushions on the sofa. She kept her mother playing by asking for different pieces. She knew she was doing the right thing. Everything felt more normal when there was music in this house. Maggie seemed more relaxed by the time they were eating lunch, and it made Becky realise how much she needed her music.

Becky left the cinema early that night. She was taking Adam home with her to ask for consent to their marriage. They were both a little on edge because Mam had not been keen on it last night.

'She'll want us to wait,' Becky predicted.

'Not until you're twenty-one, I hope.'

As she led him in through the back door, she realised that tonight Mam wasn't alone. Grandpa looked up from the living-room fire where he'd been toasting a teacake. The scent was filling the room.

He said: 'I looked in on my way home. I'm on lates this week.'

Becky hoped he wouldn't stay long. Especially when she saw the astonishment on his face as Adam followed her in.

'Good evening, Mr Knell,' he said, and his formality froze them all. There was an uncomfortable silence.

Becky said defensively: 'Mam knew I'd be bringing Adam in to see her tonight.'

Her mother was clearly on edge, but as Becky went to make more tea, she heard her say: 'Hello, Adam. Haven't seen you since . . . How are you?'

Mam usually cut a sandwich for Becky and kept it between two plates. Tonight, double the amount of beef sandwiches was laid out on a doily in readiness, together with more teacakes.

'Has it been a good night?' her mother asked as Becky handed the food round. 'Did you get full houses?'

'About average.'

Grandpa cleared his throat grumpily. He was staring at Adam. 'What's this I hear? You're taking over the Picturedrome?'

'It's my grandmother who . . .' This was not the reception they'd been hoping for.

'I can't believe Lenora's doing this again. She's taking Maggie's livelihood. How are they supposed to live?'

'I'm looking for a job,' Becky said quickly. 'I've applied for every possible vacancy advertised in tonight's *Echo*.'

'I'm sorry,' Adam put in. 'My grandmother's put me in a terrible position. I hate taking over the cinema like this.'

'Then don't!' Grandpa turned to Becky. 'You can come to live with me. Both of you. I want you to, anyway. Much the best thing for us all. I've a comfortable house now. What do you say?'

'I don't know, Grandpa.' This was something her mother

405

would have to decide, but she thought it might be the best thing.

'Taking the picture house!' Grandpa grumbled on. 'It's history repeating itself.'

'History repeating itself in more ways than one, Pa.' Maggie's face was pale with anxiety again. 'Becky wants to get married.'

'To you?' Grandpa's pale eyes went back to Adam.

'Yes, sir.'

'Good gracious!'

'It turned out well for Mam, didn't it?' Becky put in eagerly. 'It'll be the best thing for me.'

'Do you want to keep the Picturedrome that badly?'

'It's not that . . .'

'I'm going home. Raking over all this does no good. Upsets me.' Grandpa was on his feet and out in the dark hall, fumbling for his hat and coat. Becky got up to switch the light on for him. It sparkled on his crinkly silver hair. She followed him to the front door.

'How do you find Mam tonight?'

'Low, what do you expect?'

'I thought she was better. Did she play for you?'

'No, we stayed by the fire. It's too cold in your front room. She doesn't seem interested in playing any more.'

'She is.'

'Give her time. She was very fond of your dad.' He patted her arm. 'Do what you can for her.'

He was out on the step when he turned back to her. 'Never really trusted the Dransfields. Not Lenora, not after what she did to me. But he's a Moody . . . If he's anything like his father, you'll be all right with him.'

He bent to kiss Becky's cheek, and she asked: 'Why didn't you say that to Mam? I'm afraid she needs persuading.'

'She'll come round to it.' He smiled. 'I had to.'

The best they could get out of Maggie was: 'We'll have to see.'

Adam stood up to leave.

'Will you help me move the piano into the living room?' Becky asked. 'If it's where Mam can see it, perhaps she'll be tempted to play again.'

Adam supplied most of the strength needed. He whispered to her, 'I feel dreadful about the Picturedrome. I can quite understand how your family feel.'

'She'll come round,' she whispered, as she showed him out. 'Don't worry.'

Mam was in the kitchen, washing up the cups, when she went back. She said, 'He's a nice boy. I was fond of him when he was little.'

Maggie began to feel better after that. She began to play more often: not only the classical pieces that had been her first love, but the popular tunes she'd played in the cinema. She no longer felt out of practice.

When Pa came round he'd say: 'Play the Scarlatti for me, Maggie. I love that.'

It soothed her to fill the house with music. It relaxed her, restored her to normality and brought back an inner peace that had been missing for far too long. She started to dress herself with more care. Paid an overdue visit to the hairdresser. She had more energy and found the colour was coming back to her cheeks. Her problems were by no means over, but now she felt she had the strength to face them.

The postman was knocking at her door. When she opened it, he put a package into her hands. Maggie recognised the writing. Justin James had been sending her a note almost every week. Just a few words saying that he was thinking about her. He'd sent her a book of poems last month. It had helped to know that he was there, urging her to get in touch when she felt well enough. Today, she unwrapped a biography of Gershwin.

407

She flicked through the pages. It made her decide that for far too long she'd stood back and left everything to Becky and Pa. She phoned Justin.

'Maggie! Hello, how are you?' The sound of his voice cheered her. 'A lesson on the Wurlitzer? Of course I'll fit you in. I'll be free from eleven thirty onwards this morning. Can you make that?'

He was waiting for her as arranged on the steps of the Regal cinema. As soon as he caught sight of her, he came striding towards her, his dark eyes seeking hers.

'Lovely to see you.' He kissed her cheek. 'You're looking more your old self.'

'I feel as though I've been in a black hole.'

'I've been through it too,' Justin said simply. 'I didn't know what I was doing for weeks. Nothing seems to help. You've got to work through the grief and the loss.'

'You helped,' she told him.

The cinema was closed, but he had his key to the side door. It was like stepping back in time to be in the scented semi-darkness of the auditorium, to hear again the throaty vibrations of the organ. She felt a little out of practice here.

He took her back to his house for a lunch of sandwiches and coffee, and then, when a pupil arrived at two for a lesson, Maggie went back for a private practice session on the organ. Justin had heard they were looking for an organist at the Plaza, and she wanted to feel confident about applying for the job.

By the time she got back to the house in Lowther Street, she was looking at it with fresh eyes. She and Tom had rented it for seventeen years, but she decided the time had come to move on. Pa had never stopped urging her and Becky to go and live with him. Becky thought it was the right thing to do, and so did her sisters. Pa had said he'd retire from the hospital if they did.

Maggie felt she was coming back to the real world.

408

She'd see Pa tonight and tell him she would accept his offer. They'd all be better off.

Becky knew the Picturedrome would officially belong to Lenora from today, but Adam had pleaded with her to keep on coming.

'I need a decent hand-over. There's so much I have to learn.'

She was beginning to feel desperate about finding a job, although Adam had said: 'Don't worry, you can be on the payroll here until you do.'

It was Thursday, and the matinée performance had just started. Becky was in the office with the *Liverpool Echo* open on the desk in front of her. She was running her finger down the Situations Vacant column when she heard Adam's footsteps coming upstairs.

Full of pleasure, she got up to meet him at the door, laughing as he took her in his arms to kiss her. 'I thought you said I wouldn't see you until tonight?'

'I can't stay. Just popped in to warn you.' His face told her that what she'd been dreading had taken place.

'My grandmother got a set of keys and the account books from her solicitor this morning. She's studying them now, and she wants me to bring her to look over the place this afternoon.'

Becky felt despair that it had come to this. 'I'll get out of the way before she comes.' She couldn't face Lenora. She'd be triumphant, glorying in it.

That she'd been expecting it didn't make it any easier. 'I wish I could find a job. If Mam can do it, why can't I?'

She knew from his face that he felt for her. His arms tightened round her. 'I feel terrible . . . taking your job like this . . .'

'Yes, well . . . It's hard to think of parting with it. No point in saying it isn't. It seems so unfair.'

Adam gave her another comforting hug. 'My grand-mother's a tough nut when it comes to business.'

'A tough nut whatever it comes to. She's my grandmother too, don't forget. She just doesn't want to recognise the fact.

'I could understand it better if my name were not Dransfield too. If she could lend my father money to start the cinema up, why does she demand it back now? I'd like to carry on running it. I'm family too. You're a Moody. I'm more a Dransfield than you are.'

'Not really.' He looked uneasy.

'She has other businesses you could run. What does she have against me? Tom was your uncle but he was my father.'

'He wasn't,' he said softly.

'Of course he was,' she said with a rush of irritation.

He was shaking his head. 'Grandmother told you, didn't she?'

She had. Becky pulled up short. Lenora had made that quite clear on the day they'd seen her at Ottershaw House.

'My mother says he was. I asked her.'

His dark eyes looked into hers, denying it. It increased the agitation she felt.

'Haven't I got the Dransfield nose? Dad used to tell me I had.'

'I don't know about that,' he said mildly.

She accused: 'You're nothing like the Dransfields to look at. You take after your father.'

'I know. That doesn't matter . . . doesn't bother me.'

'It shouldn't.' Becky had to laugh. It sounded a little wild. 'You Moodys are very good-looking.' He was pulling her closer again.

'Look, Tom adopted you. That's what my mother says.'

'Adopted?' Becky struggled free, her head whirling. 'Who is my mother then?'

410

'Not Maggie.'

'What nonsense! Dransfield nose or not, just look at my hair.' She took a handful and held it out as evidence.

'It's very pretty.'

'And exactly like my mother's. And Aunt Fanny's, and Enid's. I've inherited the Knell colouring. Anybody can see that.'

Adam was feeling for her again. He kissed her. 'You asked me why – it's the only way to explain Grandma's . . . You aren't of the blood line, that's all. And she's got a thing about the blood line.'

Becky found that hard to accept. She wanted Tom to be her father, not some stranger. He'd treated her as his daughter. No father could have shown more love, more interest in her.

'Who was my father?'

He was shaking his head. 'I don't want to say that it doesn't matter any more, because I can see it does. We'll be married as soon as we can. Once you've a husband you won't need parents in quite the same way.'

'But still . . . I want to know. I've got to know.'

'You'll have to ask your mother again.' His dark eyes were staring down into hers. Becky felt torn in two.

'Do you know?'

'No.'

Shock was seeping through her. What Lenora had told her that day had been the truth. Maggie had been as upset as she was. Maggie had lied because she knew how strongly she'd feel about it. Nothing could be worse than knowing Mam wasn't her natural mother and yet not knowing who was. This was worse than anything she'd had to face yet. Becky's mind seethed, she could think of nothing else.

She rushed to the cloakroom to get her hat and coat. She wanted to have it out with Mam.

Adam had followed her. 'Shall I give you a lift home?'

411

She shook her head. 'No, Mam will be at the Plaza. I can't talk to her there.'

'Where do you want to go, then?'

'I'll just get away from here for a bit. Walk.'

He was hesitating. 'Wouldn't you be better at home?'

'I'd rather walk,' she said.

He seemed reluctant to leave her. It made her set out briskly towards town. It didn't matter where she went, she needed to think.

It was almost a month before Hattie went further than the garden of Ottershaw House. She was glad she'd had the phone put into Pa's house. She was able to tell him why she couldn't come to see him. It helped to find out it wasn't flu he'd had, just a heavy cold and cough, and that he was back at work.

Olivia, on the other hand, was taking a long time to recover and was still very weak. Hattie thought she was losing the will to live.

'I'm weary of this world, Harriet,' she said, sounding so old. 'I've been dogged by ill health for years. I feel caged up here, waiting for the end.'

'You're not caged up,' Hattie contradicted. 'I could order a car to the door, we could go to Parkgate tomorrow.'

'I haven't the energy any more. Lenora's written me off. She doesn't need me any more now she's got Sophie.'

'I haven't written you off. And you mustn't write yourself off. There's a play just starting on the wireless. You used to like a good play. Shall I put it on for you?'

She did, but Olivia went to sleep instead of listening to it.

The following day, Hattie had persuaded Olivia to dress and sit in the turret for a change. They'd had their afternoon tea there together, looking down on the garden. They saw Adam drive Lenora's car into the drive, and Lenora,

Sophie and Jane get out. Jonathon was in London, gaining experience auditing another business.

'Home early today,' Olivia commented.

Adam came up to see his great-grandmother a few minutes later. Hattie thought he looked upset, and left them to take the tea tray down to the kitchen. On her return she busied herself making up the fire, taking little notice of what they were talking about until she caught Becky's name and then the word 'cinema'. She straightened up and went to join them in the turret.

'Adam! What's happened? What's this about Becky and the cinema?'

'Tom's solicitor has been granted probate, and he's sharing out his assets. Lenora's very excited about getting the cinema. She asked me to take her to see it this afternoon.'

Hattie couldn't get her breath. 'She's taken Maggie's cinema?' She was shocked.

Adam looked disconcerted. 'Tom never repaid the money he borrowed from her. Haven't you heard?'

She hadn't heard a word. Hadn't given the cinema a thought for weeks.

'Nobody tells us anything,' Olivia grumbled.

Hattie could feel fury building up inside her. Lenora had been coming to the sick room to see Olivia and had never so much as mentioned the cinema.

'She wants me to run it for her.' Adam looked aghast too. 'I feel awful about that. I know what it means to Becky.'

'Becky's being pushed out?'

Hattie couldn't believe this had been going on while she'd been nursing Lenora's mother back to health. And this time, it was Maggie and Becky who were being hurt. She'd been a fool, too confident that she'd brought Lenora to her knees by getting back some of what she owed to Pa.

'What's Maggie going to do? She needs the cinema to support herself and Becky.'

413

Choking with rage, Hattie strode downstairs. Lenora was not in her study. She threw open the drawing-room door, but the room was empty. She rushed towards the kitchen. Jane was coming up the passage with a tray of champagne glasses.

'Where's Lenora?'

'She went to her room.' Jane looked little more than a child, all innocence and smiles. 'We're going to have a celebration, Harriet. Up in Great Gran's room.'

Hattie could hardly speak. She turned to follow her. 'What for?'

'Gran's got the cinema at last. You know how she's been looking forward to this.'

'I didn't. This is the first I've heard.'

Lenora came bustling behind them with the bottle of champagne. 'What's the matter?'

Hattie turned on her. 'Adam's just told me. You've taken Maggie's picture house.'

'It was never Maggie's.'

Jane led them to Olivia's room. Hattie saw Olivia and Adam's faces jerk round as they came in.

'All right, Tom's, then. I haven't come to argue about that. He wanted his family to have it. It's their only means of support now.'

'It's nothing to do with you,' Lenora told her.

'No doubt you think you're clever. You cheated my father. Turned us Knells into paupers. Now you're doing the same to Maggie and Becky. You're foreclosing on a loan you made sixteen years ago.'

'Mother!' Sophie was aghast. 'You said that it was Tom's wish you should have it. That he thought the cinema too much of a responsibility for Maggie. That she wouldn't want to run it.'

'She's still got to live!'

'Mother? You said Tom had provided adequately for her and his daughter!'

'You can leave us, Harriet.' There was a flash of diamonds as Lenora's fingers twisted at the wire on the cork.

Hattie stood her ground.

Lenora ignored her. 'Here.' She pushed a brimming glass into her daughter's hand.

'Becky can run the cinema,' Adam put in, 'better than I could. There's no problem there.'

Jane's dark eyes went slowly to her brother. 'Adam, you can't push Becky out, not now.'

'Of course he can. That's what I wanted it for. Adam wants to run it, don't you? You said you did.'

'I might have said I'd prefer a cinema to your baby wear factory. But I can't possibly push Becky out.'

Sophie looked dazed. 'Dan's always said . . .'

'Have you come by it legally?' Olivia barked, her old eyes sparking. 'Adam can't take it over if you haven't.'

Lenora was tight-lipped. 'Of course, legally.'

Hattie took a deep breath. 'Legally, Lenora's on firmer ground with this than the other businesses she acquired. The money *was* originally hers. But morally . . .'

Adam turned on Lenora. 'Have you looked at the accounts? It's not making much profit. I'm surprised you even want it. It needs further investment to bring it up to date. As it stands, it isn't worth all that much.'

Lenora's heavy features puckered in a frown.

'It's a bit of a disappointment. Tom was so sure it would earn him a fortune. It's not much good to any of us.'

'It is to Becky,' Adam insisted.

'It's everything to Maggie,' Hattie added. 'She has nothing else.'

Sophie's face was flushed. 'You can't take it from Maggie, Mother! Not if it makes paupers of Tom's family.'

Hattie hardened her heart. 'You don't care what its value is, do you, Lenora? That's not the point. You did it to get your own back on me. To hurt me. It's your way of clawing

415

back what you had to pay out to my father. Your way of getting revenge.'

Sophie looked shocked. 'Why did you take it, Mother? Why do you want it?'

'You know why. For my family.'

Adam was mutinous. 'Not for me, I hope. I've told you, I don't want it.'

'Becky is your family,' Hattie said quietly. 'Of the direct blood line you think so important.'

'She isn't.'

Hattie looked into Lenora's cold eyes. 'You know she's my daughter, and you think Stanley's her father. Well, you're wrong on that count.'

Lenora's face had gone grey. Her voice was little more than a whisper. 'I know it was Stanley.'

Hattie shook her head. 'Olivia drew that conclusion too, didn't you? But you're both wrong.

'Your husband had the morals of a tomcat. You can't see beyond that, can you? He humiliated you by pawing every woman near him. Oh yes, you're quite right, he tried it on with me, I had to fight him off. He's older than my own father. Why would I let him put a hand on me?'

Adam looked stunned. Sophie was holding her breath. Lenora's mouth had opened with shock, she was pulling herself to her feet. 'Get out.'

'You're going to hear me out before I go. I've always known you had the wrong idea about me and Stanley. Do you know why I haven't enlightened you?'

Hattie glowered at Lenora, remembering all the indignities and insults she'd endured from her. She felt she had the upper hand at last.

'Because your husband asked me not to. Luke, your favourite son, was Rebecca's father.'

There was suspicion on Lenora's face. 'You're just saying that. You think it'll make me change my mind about the cinema.'

416

'No. Stanley wanted to protect Luke's wife and child – and Luke's good name.'

'I don't believe you.'

'Ask Stanley.'

'I wouldn't believe one word he says.'

Hattie wasn't going to let her get away with that. 'There's another reason. He didn't want to give you the satisfaction of another heir. We all know how you dote on Luke's son. How you wish his future wasn't to be in dog food.'

Lenora's brow was tightening. The others were all trying to speak at once. Sophie accidentally knocked over her glass. Champagne soaked into the carpet, unheeded.

'Is this true? Dan kept telling me you were devious, downright dishonest sometimes, but I didn't believe him . . .'

'I can't take over the cinema, Grandma, I don't want to,' Adam insisted. 'Not like this, not from Becky.'

Sophie was shaking her head. 'Dan didn't want to be involved in your business. Didn't want us to be involved. He said terrible things.'

'Is it true? About you and Luke?' Olivia's eyes were staring into Hattie's.

'Yes, Luke.'

'I don't believe it's possible.' Lenora's eyes were full of suspicion. 'Not Luke.'

It came to Hattie then. 'I do have things he gave me. Things to prove it.'

She shot up the nursery stairs to her room and looked round wildly. She'd put his gifts away many years ago. Where were they? She kept her room spick-and-span to the ninth degree. In a few moments she'd opened most of her drawers, tipped out the contents of several boxes. She came across what she was looking for at last, and ran back to Olivia's room again. They were still arguing.

Hattie held out a wedding ring on the palm of her hand, so that they might all see it.

417

'Luke bought me this. To con me into believing we'd be married.'

'One ring is much like another.' Lenora's voice was heavy with sarcasm.

'This one has our names engraved inside.'

'That means nothing: you could have had it done. What proof is there that Luke had anything to do with that?'

It made Hattie stiffen with determination. 'He bought me this locket too. You'll find a lock of his hair entwined with mine inside. You'll know his hair? Then there's this photograph.'

She couldn't bear to look at the picture of Luke and herself walking along the promenade at New Brighton. She'd been so happy that day. His head was bent close to hers.

Lenora's face was full of doubt now. Sophie was convinced. Jane was nursing the photograph.

'Luke inherited some of his father's traits,' Hattie said wryly. 'He made two of us pregnant at the same time.'

'Luke was my brother, so was Tom. I can't believe . . .'

'There's a great deal you wouldn't believe, Sophie. Shall I tell you how your mother came to defraud my father out of his business? And how she did the same to get Fevers and Jones and the baby wear factory? Shall I drop my souvenirs in Claudia's lap? Let her know that she was the lucky one?'

She stopped, breathless. It was all ancient history, what Luke had or hadn't done. Would Claudia even care? But she'd never remarried.

Lenora did care. 'Give those things to me.' She spat the words out. 'The ring and the photograph.'

'You can have my locket too. Just as soon as Maggie hears from your solicitor that you've returned all the cinema accounts to him and retracted your claim on Tom's estate.'

'She might have to gift it back to Maggie now,' Olivia said thoughtfully.

'Dad did say the whole thing was suspect.' Adam's face was flushed. 'He didn't want us to come here.'

Lenora's face was crumbling. 'All right. Maggie can keep the cinema. To invest in it would be throwing good money after bad anyway.'

Hattie smiled. Whatever the cinema was worth, she wanted Maggie and Rebecca to have it. She felt she'd won again.

Lenora's face was drawn as she looked round at Sophie and her children. 'I did it for you. For all of you. I didn't want my family to suffer as I did.'

'That's no reason to defraud others,' Harriet put in. 'Other people have families.'

'I did it so that you wouldn't know what it's like to be the dregs of society.'

'You don't know either.' Olivia was getting angry now. 'I was the one who came from nothing. You never knew just how bad things had been.'

Lenora was livid. 'We had to pull ourselves up by our bootstraps. We couldn't afford to have scruples about how we did it. We killed for it, didn't we, Mother?'

Olivia's face was grey. Sophie looked frightened, Adam incredulous.

'I wanted to spare my children and my grandchildren that. And what gratitude do I get?'

Sophie was moistening her lips. 'You wanted to found a dynasty. That's what Dan says.'

'What does he know about it? He's middle-class born and bred. I wanted you to have money and privilege. I was prepared to do anything to achieve that. You were all happy enough to go along with it, and nothing's changed.'

Adam said quietly, 'It has. You might as well know, I've asked Becky to marry me.'

'Good gracious!'

'She's said yes. I feel dreadful about going along with your plans at all.'

'Marry the girl? It's out of the question! Sophie? Did you know about this?'

'I've already told Mother and Jane.'

'You didn't tell me,' Olivia complained.

'I was on the point . . .'

'It's Tom all over again. It did him no good to marry into the Knells. Have more sense before it's too late.'

Harriet felt things were moving too fast. Adam to marry Becky? Wouldn't that mean they'd be running the cinema together?

Adam was on his feet. 'Come on, Mother, let's go and talk this over sensibly with Dad.'

'Don't leave me.' Lenora was on her feet too, sounding hysterical. 'I don't want to live here by myself.'

'You won't be alone. There's Gran and Harriet.'

'I'll be alone in the business. I can't manage it. Not without you, Sophie. Not by myself.'

Sophie's face hardened. 'You won't be by yourself. You've a staff of hundreds.'

'But they aren't family.' There was desperation in Lenora's eyes. Her plans for the future had come to naught. Her family didn't want what she wanted to give them.

Hattie was shaking as they left her alone with Olivia. She could make herself do things for Rebecca that she'd never do for her father or herself.

# CHAPTER TWENTY-THREE

Lenora had shut herself in her room and Sophie had swept her family out of the house. With her mind on fire, Hattie went to the kitchen to curtail the preparations for a big dinner. Only now did it occur to her that it was meant to be a special celebratory meal.

She went about her evening chores, helping Olivia into bed and taking her supper up on a tray. She had her settled down shortly after eight o'clock, and decided to go and see Maggie straight away.

She wanted to tell her that Adam had refused to take over the picture house from Becky. That after all, it would still be theirs. Maggie must surely be sick with worry about that.

She felt she couldn't put it off. Her conscience was troubling her and she still felt on edge. She should have listened to Maggie when she'd asked for help. If she'd understood what was going on, she might have been able to do something sooner.

Hattie had been out so rarely during the last weeks, she saw everything with fresh eyes. The park was lush now in midsummer. As she went past on the tram, two games of tennis were being played on the courts in the last of the evening light. She felt calmer by the time she reached Lowther Street.

Maggie opened the door, looking much better than when she'd last seen her. 'You look tired, Hattie.'

She felt exhausted. It had been an emotional onslaught to hear Lenora had taken the cinema. She'd been drained anyway by the weeks of wakeful nights and busy days nursing Olivia. She started telling Maggie what had happened before she had her hat off. She could see amazement on Maggie's face.

'You mean Lenora's agreed to let us keep it? That's marvellous! You've worked a miracle.'

'It was my fault she wanted it. Lenora's known for years that Becky is my daughter, and I let her go on thinking Stanley was her father. This is her way of taking revenge. I should have foreseen it.'

'I accepted it had gone. Had to,' Maggie said. 'So did Becky. I've got myself a job at the Plaza Cinema.' Hattie saw a smile of triumph cross her sister's face. 'Playing the organ.'

'That's wonderful! What you've always wanted. I am pleased for you.'

'Yes, and it's not playing for hours on end. Usually just a fifteen-minute slot in each performance. Do you know what's really been bothering me? That I refused, when you wanted to find a job for Becky.'

'Nothing's changed there. Stanley was in no special hurry. I could phone him and . . .'

'But she won't need a job now. She'll want to run the picture house.'

Hattie said slowly: 'I'm not sure how long it can go on. Whether it's a viable business. It'll need some thinking about.'

Maggie sighed. 'Becky's been saying much the same thing. It's not worth as much as I thought, but at least it's still ours. I wish I had your knack of managing things. Envy it, always have. We all relied on you. You didn't need to be looked after, not like me. You look after everybody else.'

'I haven't managed everything well.' Hattie pulled a face. 'D'you mean that? Envious of me?'

'Green with jealousy.'

Hattie smiled. She was not the only one to feel jealous, then.

'And you never give up on anything. Didn't give up on me.'

'I couldn't give up on you. I hate being at loggerheads . . .'

Maggie's eyes met hers tentatively. 'I used to feel closer to you than the others. We used to be best friends as well as sisters.'

'Couldn't we be again?' Hattie asked. 'Let's put these last years behind us.'

'We must! Of course we must. I'm sorry, I haven't been myself. I've had the most awful anger about . . . Well, you know, Tom and everything.'

Hattie noticed then that the living room was in chaos.

'We're packing up, ready to move in with Pa. Didn't he tell you?'

'I didn't realise you'd definitely made up your mind.'

'We didn't have much choice when we were losing the picture house, but I want to go anyway. Pa says he'll retire when we do. He's lonely there on his own, and was afraid having no job would make it worse.'

Hattie felt a little lonely too. This was another of those times when Maggie was going to get what she wanted for herself. Through the busy nights she'd had, she'd thought longingly of the peace of Pa's house.

Maggie's sea-green eyes were studying her again. 'You ought to come too. There's loads of room. Surely you won't be able to stay at Ottershaw House after this?'

Hattie sighed. 'Can't yet. There's still Olivia to think about.'

Becky walked and walked, agonising about what Adam had told her, hardly caring where she went. It was hard to believe she was adopted, and yet . . . She wanted Tom to be her father, and even more she wanted Maggie to be her mother. She couldn't accept that she wasn't.

When she could walk no more, she sat in a back street café for an hour over a cup of tea. Then she walked again, up the dock road and into the park. It was a lovely summer evening, and she sat on a bench watching the ducks on the lake.

Her heart went out to Maggie – everything had piled on top of her that day – but she'd lied to her. Now Becky didn't know where she fitted into the family. As the shadows lengthened, she began to feel cold. When she saw the streetlights come on, she started walking again.

She turned into Lowther Street and looked along the terrace to her home. By this time of night, Mam's bedroom window usually showed a greenish glow through the curtains. Tonight the upstairs bay was in darkness. She had to talk to Maggie, get to the bottom of this. She hoped she wasn't already asleep.

As she went up the back entry into the yard, Becky could see both the living room and kitchen lights still on. In the kitchen, she found Maggie pouring boiling water into the teapot. She looked up as if to tell her something. Becky could hold it back no longer.

'Mam, the other day, you swore Tom was my father. But he isn't, is he? It's not just Lenora saying it now. Adam is too.'

She saw the denial springing to Mam's lips again. 'He says I was adopted.'

Mam's hand flew to her mouth. That told her it was true.

'It's right then, I was?'

Mam looked shocked, her eyes were glistening with unshed tears. Becky was afraid it wouldn't be long before they were running down her cheeks. She steeled herself.

'I need to know, Mam. I need to know everything. I want Tom to have been my father as much as you do.

But if he wasn't, then I've got to know who was. I can't stand the Dransfields saying I'm not one of them, and not knowing why.'

Her mother was shrinking back against the stove. 'Adopted, yes.'

The colour had gone from her face. Becky felt nothing was real. Nothing was as she'd supposed.

'Then you aren't my mother! That's even worse. And why keep it so secret? Why?'

'I wanted a baby of my own, but it didn't come. Then I saw you. I wanted you very much.' Mam's voice was a whisper. 'I had to promise never to let anyone know who your parents were. I was only allowed to have you on that condition.'

'But that was when I was born. I'm old enough to understand now. I need to know.'

'Don't ask me,' Mam pleaded.

'I've got to know.'

Becky felt in turmoil. All afternoon and evening, she'd been trying to work out exactly what she did know. Her platinum-blonde colouring meant she definitely had Knell blood in her. If Maggie wasn't her mother, it must have been one of her sisters.

It wasn't hard to guess. It had to be Harriet. Becky had always felt she'd singled her out, looked at her strangely. Harriet was too ready with advice and help. Overgenerous. And anyway, the others were too young.

Becky sensed a movement behind her and turned. Harriet had come to the kitchen door, her face colourless and aghast. Becky knew she'd heard everything.

She said: 'You're my mother, aren't you? You've caused all this trouble?'

She saw Harriet's lips move. 'Didn't mean to cause you trouble.' Her eyes glittered like emeralds; she looked shocked.

She was breathing hard, leaning against the door jamb.

Becky could see her pulling herself together. Within moments she was in control again.

'Everybody else knows, Maggie. Becky will have to know now.'

Becky looked from Harriet on one side of the kitchen to Maggie on the other. She'd always been aware of the rift between them, and she knew now that she had been the cause. She felt she was widening it now, pushing the sisters apart.

Hattie said slowly: 'Yes, I'm your natural mother. Your father was Tom's brother, Luke. He was killed in the war.'

Becky took a deep, shuddering breath. She didn't want Harriet to be her mother. Harriet was spinsterish, didn't seem the sort of person . . . She'd never been married, and Becky had seen too many films not to know the heartache a baby would have brought her.

'Is that why you gave me to Maggie?'

Hattie's old-fashioned fawn bun nodded. 'I was ashamed of what I'd done. The lies I'd had to tell, the disgrace. I'd have had to saddle Pa with both of us. Two more mouths to feed, when already he had so many. I was afraid we'd be too much of a burden. I couldn't keep you.'

'He'd have done it if you'd asked,' Maggie whispered. 'But I wanted Becky.'

Hattie was blinking hard. 'I saw that as a lifeline. I wanted so much to see you grow up. Keep you in the family. I was being pressed to have you adopted by strangers, and I couldn't bear the thought of that. Even so, when it came to handing you over to Maggie, a bundle in a shawl, with tiny waving fists . . .' There was no mistaking the searing agony on Hattie's face.

'My father, Luke? I've hardly heard anybody speak of him.'

Harriet cleared her throat. 'It's come at a bad time for you, Tom dying, everything at once. Makes it harder.'

426

'Would it ever have been easy?'

Becky heard the facts over and over. Disjointed and jumbled, they weren't easy to follow. The only thing that hadn't altered was that she was part Dransfield and part Knell.

She'd always felt the rivalry, like a tug of war between the sisters, but never understood it. Becky felt she was being asked to choose between them now, and was agonised. She wanted to draw them together.

Maggie said quietly: 'You were supposed to think you were mine and Tom's.'

She swallowed the lump in her throat. 'I always have. I still do.' Becky was glad Maggie was so much better. Last week, she'd have been distraught. She went over to hug her. 'Nobody can take your place, Mam.'

When she looked up, she could see tears shining in Hattie's green eyes, and she wanted to comfort her too.

She tried to find the right words. 'I'm all mixed up, not on an even keel yet. But I know you have my welfare at heart.'

She saw Hattie flinch. It went through her, made her try again.

'When Adam said I was adopted, I thought the worst. It's not so bad. To find it's all in the family, after all.'

Hattie tossed the contents of the cold teapot down the sink, and put the kettle on to boil again.

'I was too proud of being the one person in the family everybody could rely on. The one who supported the others. I couldn't ask for Pa's help, though he'd have given it willingly. I've thought about it almost every day since, regretted that I didn't. I couldn't bear to see you in Maggie's arms.'

Maggie had collapsed on a chair. 'And I wanted Becky all to myself. I could share her with Tom, but not with you. You had a right to her.'

Hattie sighed. 'The truth is, Becky, we both wanted to mother you.' Why had it taken all this to make her realise where she was going wrong?

'I've prided myself on never giving up, never letting go.' But she'd been wrong not to let go of Becky. She should have had the sense to see that.

'Come on, Maggie, Becky's grown up without either of us realising it. All mothers have to slacken their hold on their children. They can't hang on to them for ever, however much they'd like to.'

Maggie was trying to smile at her. 'Becky's not really grown up yet.'

'She's had to grow up quicker than most of us. To help Tom run the cinema, support you through your worst moments.'

She saw Becky smile with relief that she understood. 'I feel grown up.'

'You are grown up,' Hattie told her. 'Hardly in need of one mother, never mind two. I'll not be pushing myself on you. But . . . if ever there is anything I can do for you, you'll know I want to do it.'

'Thank you.' Becky was smiling from one to the other. 'Two mothers? I should count myself lucky, shouldn't I?'

Hattie felt happier now it was all out in the open. 'Maggie and I mothered four little sisters. We should have been good at it, all the practice we had.'

'Didn't stop us sparring over you, though,' Maggie said.

'We were both more involved with you. You were more than a younger sister.'

'But we've put that all behind us. We're going to be good friends from now on, aren't we, Hattie?'

Hattie nodded. 'Yes, thank goodness.'

She could see that Becky had something else to say. 'Mam, you wanted to marry Tom when you were my age, didn't you?'

'She did.' Hattie spoke for her. 'Pa had to accept that.'

'Adam and me, well, we want to do the same.'

'And we'll all have to accept that too,' Hattie told her sister gently. 'I think the time has come when we'll both have to loosen our hold on Becky.'

It was a month later, and Hattie felt rushed. She was afraid she was going to be late for the special supper Maggie had arranged for Pa. Now that she and Becky were living with him, he'd decided to retire on his sixty-second birthday. The party was to be a double celebration.

Olivia had had a better day than usual: she'd been animated, more her old self, and in no hurry to go to bed. Sophie had dropped in to see her in the middle of the afternoon, when she knew Lenora would be at the factory. Sophie had told them both that she felt happier now she'd made the break, and Daniel was delighted to have his family back together again.

When Hattie had finally settled Olivia in bed, she rushed to change into her best crimson dress and catch the bus up to Fairview Road. She knew she'd be the last to arrive. It was another warm summer evening. Many of the windows were open. Hattie could hear Maggie playing her piano as she walked up the path.

Pa came to the front door with his thick silver hair brushed into place, and wearing the silk cravat which was her gift to him. He kissed her and drew her down to sit with him until Maggie had finished the piece. Hattie let the music flow through her. There was an air of tranquillity and contentment about Pa's house that she envied. Maggie had the old house looking its best now that she was living here. There were vases of fresh roses from the garden.

As soon as Maggie realised that Hattie had arrived, she ushered them all in to supper.

Becky came up shyly leading Adam. 'Aunt Hattie, I've something to show you.' She held out her left hand. A

429

small diamond sparkled on her finger. 'It's official now, Adam and I are engaged.'

'Just like her mother,' Pa said fondly. 'Can't wait till they're of age.'

Hattie found it wasn't hurting quite so much to have Maggie accepted as Becky's mother. She said: 'We've certainly got a lot to celebrate tonight.'

The table looked magnificent. It had been extended to its limit and was set for twelve. Fanny had made the cake: the blue lettering, which had run slightly, read: Happy Birthday and Happy Retirement, Pa.

Hattie found herself seated next to Jim Temple, the artist who lived next door. She found him very attentive, very charming. Over the meal everybody began to talk about the Picturedrome. The family had always referred to it as their cinema, and now Becky was keeping it running.

'I can't get over that you stopped Lenora taking it from us,' Becky said. She looked exactly as Maggie had at sixteen.

'It was Adam who did that. He refused to run it.' Hattie smiled at him. Adam had accepted a position in the same firm as his father; he'd decided he'd be an auditor like him. 'He told Lenora it was wrong to take it.'

'We want to keep it if we possibly can.' Becky's green eyes danced.

Maggie said: 'I suppose they're young enough to work at it. Overcome the problems.'

'I don't know whether that's possible.' Adam helped himself to more ham. 'It can't survive much longer without showing talkies.'

'He's been trying to work out exactly what it will cost to change.' Becky looked at him fondly.

'To be honest,' he said thoughtfully, 'its fate hangs in the balance. It's too small, the position isn't good. It might be better to sell it for what it's worth.'

'So Lenora was right about that?'

'Yes. I've asked my father to look at the figures. He'll have a more objective eye. If you decide to keep it, it will need more money. A big investment.'

'Couldn't I put mine in?' Pa looked eagerly round at his family. 'Now that . . .'

'No,' Hattie, Enid and Ruth replied simultaneously. 'That's for your retirement.'

Adam said: 'Tom didn't get a proper return on the money he invested. It may be that no one else would.'

Hattie looked down the table to where Maggie was sitting next to Justin James. From the way he was looking at her, Hattie knew he loved her. He'd helped her over a difficult patch, and now she was able to accept the big changes in her life: that the cinema might go and that Becky would marry. There was colour in her face again and her eyes sparkled. Maggie would need time, of course, but Hattie could see her sister getting married for a second time.

Hattie was late returning to Ottershaw House because Adam had offered to drop her off on his way back to his father's house. She didn't feel she could drag him away sooner, with Becky clinging to his arm, and anyway, they were all enjoying themselves.

Adam drove carefully. She found it hard to believe, looking at him now, that she'd known him since he was three. He'd been the reason Tom had spoken up about wanting to marry Maggie. It really was history repeating itself.

When Adam drew up at the gate, she could see the light in Olivia's room showing round her curtains.

'I thought she'd be asleep by now,' she said. 'Lenora is. I'd better look in on her.'

Olivia was propped up against her pillows and seemed to be wide awake.

'I've been listening to the wireless. Come and tell me about your party. Have you had a good time?'

431

Hattie told her that Adam was talking of a wedding date early next spring.

'What news!' Olivia pulled herself up the bed. 'I'll go to it, Harriet, if it's the last thing I do. I must think about a new outfit. I shall never sleep now.'

Hattie went down to the kitchen to heat some milk for her. She refilled the hot-water bottle that Olivia couldn't manage without, even in summer.

It was after one when Hattie was undressing in her own room. She was very tired and slept heavily. When her alarm sounded in the morning, she felt sleep-sodden and didn't get up straight away. After being awake so late last night, she didn't think Olivia would be in a hurry for her.

Her first job was to let in the daily woman who came in time to make breakfast. Hattie delayed so long she had to throw on her dressing gown and rush down to answer the doorbell. She still felt half asleep when she'd washed and dressed, and Olivia's morning tea tray was set with its embroidered tray cloth and matching tea cosy.

Olivia was an inert mound on her bed when Hattie went in. She put the tray down and swept back the curtains from both windows.

'Good morning,' she said, and was surprised to find that Olivia didn't move. It took her another moment to realise the old lady was no longer breathing.

Panic drove away the last vestiges of sleep. She ran to Lenora's room, banged her knuckles once against the door as she opened it. Lenora's mouth was opening at her temerity. She was dressed as far as her pink underslip.

'Your mother,' Hattie gasped. 'She's . . . she's dead.' Her hands were shaking. She ran back to Olivia's room.

Lenora was right behind her, barefooted and still in her underwear. 'When did she . . . ? I wouldn't have minded being woken in the night. Not for . . .'

'She didn't ring for me.' Hattie couldn't get over that. She'd had an electric bell fixed to ring in her room. The last thing she'd done last night was to make sure the bell push was within Olivia's reach. She used it quite often.

'She should have rung for me. She'd have wanted me with her. She always did.'

Lenora was swaying at the door, white with shock, hardly able to look at her mother. 'She must have died in her sleep.'

'It means she died peacefully,' Hattie choked. 'I can't believe it, she seemed so well last night, quite talkative. She seemed so pleased about Adam.'

'What about Adam?'

Hattie knew she wouldn't like it. 'He's set a date for his wedding.'

Lenora looked ill. She snapped: 'You'd better let the doctor know.'

Hattie felt sick all morning. She was lost without Olivia's needs to attend to, and upset that she'd not been with her at the end. Normal routine was shot to bits as the doctor came and Lenora wandered about the house in a daze.

Hattie said to her: 'Olivia has no further need of me now. You'll want me out of your way. I'll start packing. I'll go as soon as I can, perhaps by tonight.'

'There's no rush.' Lenora looked forlorn. 'Stay and help. Until after the funeral. There'll be plenty for you to do.'

'A week's notice, then,' Hattie said.

'There'll be no one left but me then. No one at all.'

Hattie went back to her room and started to pack. At last she could please herself. She'd been so looking forward to going home to live with Pa and Maggie. Strange how only last night she'd thought the time would never come.

Over the following days, Hattie found time hung heavily. The nights seemed long and the house enormous now there was only her and Lenora living in it. It felt empty and silent, and full of the ghosts of those now gone.

They both kept their distance. If they met on a landing,

433

they passed in silence. Lenora didn't speak unless it was to give some domestic instruction. When the daily women came in to cook and clean up, Hattie felt relief that there was somebody else in the kitchen. It was the only room in the house that seemed normal.

She missed Olivia's company; it used to fill her day. She told herself over and over that Olivia had not wanted more of the half-life she was living.

She went to see Pa. He gave her a hug and said: 'I'll be glad to have you back home with us. You know that. We'll be quite a family again. I'm delighted about that, didn't much like being on my own.'

Maggie was supportive too, and after some persuasion agreed to come to the funeral with her. Hattie didn't want to be the only Knell there.

Packing her things seemed an endless job. It was almost everything she possessed in this world. She hired a van to move her boxes to Pa's house. Lenora called for her help in sorting and moving Olivia's things to the attic. They covered her bed and her couch with dust sheets. It seemed the end of an era.

Not many people came to Olivia's funeral, apart from her family. Her long illness had isolated her from the business, and she'd had no friends of her own. Lenora ignored Hattie and Maggie, but Stanley was there, and so was all the Moody family. Mr Maxwell, Olivia's solicitor, came to speak to Hattie as they were walking away from the grave.

'You are Miss Harriet Mary Knell? Mrs Clark's companion?'

'Yes.'

'Will you be returning to the house for refreshment?'

'No.' She'd had enough of Lenora's icy manner over the last few days, and Maggie didn't want to set foot in the place again.

'Oh! I thought . . . Would you like to be present at the reading of the will? You're a beneficiary.'

'Am I? Goodness! I suppose I should come then.'

Maggie whispered as they moved away, 'She's left you a bequest.'

'It's very kind of her. I didn't expect anything.'

'You've done everything for her for years. Why shouldn't she show her gratitude?'

'You'll come with me, Maggie?'

'I suppose so.'

'We won't stay a minute longer than we have to.'

'I'm curious anyway. To know how much she's left you.'

To Hattie, the time they had to spend standing round seemed interminable. They sipped the sherry and nibbled on the bridge rolls and sandwiches that Lenora had asked her to organise. She would have preferred to busy herself passing round food and refilling glasses as she always had in this house.

Maggie stopped her. 'Nobody's paying your wages here any more.'

So she let the two daily women do it. At last, Mr Maxwell was summoning her and the family to the study.

As she went in, Lenora gave her a baleful glance from the armchair that had been Stanley's favourite. The Moodys were gathered in a tight group on the other side of the room. Hattie went to stand by the window.

Mr Maxwell came to sit at the desk. He looked round at them over his half-moon spectacles. There was instant silence as he opened Olivia's will.

'It's very brief and to the point. I'll read you what it says:

'This is the last will and testament of Olivia Clark. It revokes all previous wills and codicils.'

As he began reading the preamble, Hattie noticed Lenora's air of expectancy. She turned to watch a bee buzzing round the flower arrangement in the hearth. When he came to the

435

part everybody was waiting for, she felt the tension in the room tighten.

'To my daughter, Lenora, I bequeath my dwelling house known as Ottershaw House, together with all contents.'

The satisfaction on Lenora's face was fleeting.

'To my granddaughter, Sophie May, I bequeath my company, Clark's Blouses, the freehold premises it occupies, together with all fixtures and fittings.'

Lenora's gasp was audible.

'Also, all my personal jewellery. After paying my debts and taxes I leave to my companion, Miss Harriet Mary Knell, provided she is still in my employ at the time of my death, in gratitude for her unfailing help and kindness and to redress the injustice done to her family . . .'

Harriet straightened up in concentration. She was aware of Lenora's deepening frown.

'. . . the residue of my estate, comprising the monies held in my bank accounts and my holdings in stocks and shares.'

Harriet went rigid. She gasped too as she realised what that meant. 'The residue? All?' She could hear the blood pumping through her temples.

'Yes, all. A very substantial amount.'

It wasn't something Hattie had ever admitted, but Pa's bankruptcy had left her with a deep-rooted fear of poverty. She needed the security of knowing she had money behind her. Olivia had understood that. It was something they'd shared. She felt a wave of elation building inside her. She need never worry about being poor again. A smile of satisfaction pulled at her lips.

Mr Maxwell's voice was reading through the last details. Hattie was aware of the new restlessness in the room.

Lenora was interrupting indignantly: 'That's not the right will. She left her money to me. I've a copy of it in the desk drawer. Right there in front of you.' She was on her feet, bounding over to get it for him.

Hattie felt herself go hot with embarrassment.

Mr Maxwell said: 'Mrs Clark did make a previous will. Two, in fact.'

Lenora was pushing a document in front of him.

'Yes, this is one of them. It's dated, let me see, yes, March nineteen oh nine.'

'That's the right one.'

'Mrs Clark came to my office in . . .' he picked up the will he'd been reading from, 'January nineteen sixteen, and as I read out to you, it says, "It revokes all previous wills and codicils." That one is no longer valid.'

Lenora stared at him, shaking with rage. 'I'll contest it.'

'I'm afraid,' he was looking at her over his spectacles, 'there aren't any grounds on which you can. This is your mother's legal will.'

She swung on Harriet in fury. 'You devious little . . . I should have known you'd get at her. Persuade her to leave it to you. She wasn't of right mind when she changed . . .'

Hattie could feel herself shaking as she got up and walked out. She didn't so much as look in Lenora's direction; she never would again. She collected Maggie from the drawing room and went down the front steps of Ottershaw House, vowing never to return.

She felt better by the time she was on the tram going back to Pa's house, more hopeful. Things were going her way at last. Everything was out in the open, she knew where she stood with Becky, and she was so glad to be back on good terms with Maggie.

Maggie put a hand on her arm. 'You're rich.'

'Yes.' She could hardly believe the difference in her circumstances. It was all so sudden.

'All in stocks and shares? Do you know how much?'

She smiled. 'I've a good idea. And I've been helping Olivia look after her portfolio for the last sixteen years. I know how to manage it.'

'How are you going to spend it all?' Maggie breathed. 'You could go round the world, buy a mansion.'

'I shall do what I've always wanted. Move in with Pa and you. Have time for myself at last. I might even get down to writing those stories for children.'

She smiled to herself. Best of all, she could afford now to help Becky with the Picturedrome. She could set them up in a much better cinema if that was needed. She wouldn't lend her money, she'd give it. She'd have to think about it first, of course. Find out a lot more. Oh yes, she was rich.

'You don't ask for much, Hattie. I saw Jim Temple yesterday. You know, the artist who lives next door. I told him you were moving in. He asks after you a lot. You'll be pleased to see more of him?'

'Not specially.'

'But you like him?'

'He's good company, but he's Pa's friend. Maggie, I'm not like you. I don't need a man to look after me.'

'We'll see,' Maggie said.

# A Glimpse of the Mersey

## Anne Baker

Daisy Corkill has spent all her life living above Sampsons – the local fishmongers and greengrocers in Market Street. But she's never discovered who her parents were – nor why they left her to be brought up by the couple she now calls 'Uncle' Ern and 'Auntie' Glad. Daisy yearns for a family of her own, despite the close relationship she has with Brenda, her very beautiful, older 'sister'.

It's Brenda, however, who, in 1919, gets married first – to local businessman Gil Fox. But Gil is not quite the man he appears to be. While happiness continues to elude Brenda, Daisy hopes her dreams are about to come true. Ellis – Gil's upright, kind and dependable brother, a survivor of WWI – falls in love with her. Will marriage, and a family of her own, really give her true happiness? And are they enough to get her through some stormy times ahead?

Don't miss Anne Baker's previous Merseyside sagas, also published by Headline:

'A heartwarming saga' *Woman's Weekly*

'A stirring tale of romance and passion, poverty and ambition' *Liverpool Echo*

'Truly compelling . . . rich in language and descriptive prose' *Newcastle Upon Tyne Evening Chronicle*

0 7472 6777 4

**headline**

# Goodbye Liverpool

## Anne Baker

When Josie Lunt is widowed the day before her daughter's tenth birthday, she turns to her husband's colleague, Luke Palmer, for comfort. Luke is handsome and caring but, unbeknownst to Josie, he has many secrets.

Luke is keen to marry Josie – and with a growing daughter to feed and a single income to survive on, she decides it's the right thing to do. But Luke is not what he seems, and it's not long before Josie regrets her decision. In order to escape a man they now fear, Josie and Suzy must flee from Liverpool, leaving everything they love behind. Crossing the Mersey, they arrive at 'The Lawns', where Josie is taken on as a cook for the difficult Mrs Smallwood and her family. Despite the many tensions within the house, happiness at last seems within reach. But the past eventually catches up with Josie, bringing with it fresh terror and heartache . . .

Acclaim for Anne Baker's novels:

'A heartwarming saga' *Woman's Weekly*

'A stirring tale of romance and passion, poverty and ambition' *Liverpool Echo*

'Highly observant writing style . . . a compelling book that you just don't want to put down' *Southport Visiter*

'A gentle tale with all the right ingredients for a heartwarming novel' *Huddersfield Daily Examiner*

0 7472 6778 2

**headline**

# So Many Children

## Anne Baker

Beth Hubble has grown up in extreme poverty in Dock Cottages – a filthy slum teeming with scruffy, malnourished children. And, although she loves training to become a nurse, problems at home are never far from her mind.

Beth is shocked when doctors tell her mother that, although a fifteenth pregnancy would be fatal, they will do nothing to help prevent it. She resolves to learn more about birth control, but, in 1920, it's a taboo subject, and Beth's quest for knowledge is thwarted at every turn.

Meanwhile, romance blossoms with Andrew Langford, a hospital lab technician, who Beth hopes will take her away from the tenements for good. But will he want to marry a girl from Dock Cottages? And will Beth ever find the love and happiness that she deserves?

Don't miss Anne Baker's previous Merseyside sagas, also published by Headline:

'A heartwarming saga' *Woman's Weekly*

'Another nostalgic story oozing with atmosphere and charm' *Liverpool Echo*

'A compelling book that you just don't want to put down' *Southport Visiter*

0 7553 0134 X

## headline